Divine Endurance

Divine Endurance

GWYNETH JONES

London
GEORGE ALLEN & UNWIN
Boston   Sydney

George Allen & Unwin (Publishers) Ltd,
40 Museum Street, London, WC1A 1LU, UK

George Allen & Unwin (Publishers) Ltd,
Park Lane, Hemel Hempstead, Herts HP2 4TE, UK

Allen & Unwin Inc,
9 Winchester Terrace, Winchester, Mass. 01890, USA

George Allen & Unwin Pty Ltd,
8 Napier Street, North Sydney, NSW 2060, Australia

First published 1984

01476968

British Library Cataloguing in Publication Data

Jones, Gwyneth
    Divine Endurance.
I. Title
823'.914[F]   PR6060.0/
ISBN 0-04-823246-7

Set in 11 on 12½ Imprint by Computape (Pickering) Ltd, North Yorkshire
and printed in Great Britain
by Billing and Sons Ltd, London and Worcester

My dear Achmed – When we were on our travels, PG and I had an ignorant passion for mountains. We would see, from the bus, an indigo cone rising out of the sawah and the palm groves, near enough to touch – Instantly we were desperate to climb. So we would set out, on foot into the green fields. Many hours later, hot and battered and bitten: gorge-fallen, river-drowned, we would emerge from our violent ascent and there would be the mountain, untouched, except perhaps now at a different angle, or behind us. We would console ourselves for having attempted the impossible and that night in the village someone would tell us about the summit trip – starting from somewhere unexpected, miles away from our vision. So we would go there, very dubiously, and then everything fell into place. . . . Producing DE was just like that, and I have the same feeling now: of astonishment mixed with a definite resentment at having to give up my glorious defeat. So I want to dedicate this book to you (and one other) because you were there, and suffered far above and beyond the calls of friendship at that first absurd departure, years ago. Selamat. G.

For T. 27 Sept 1981. 'In autumn, of all the seasons – '

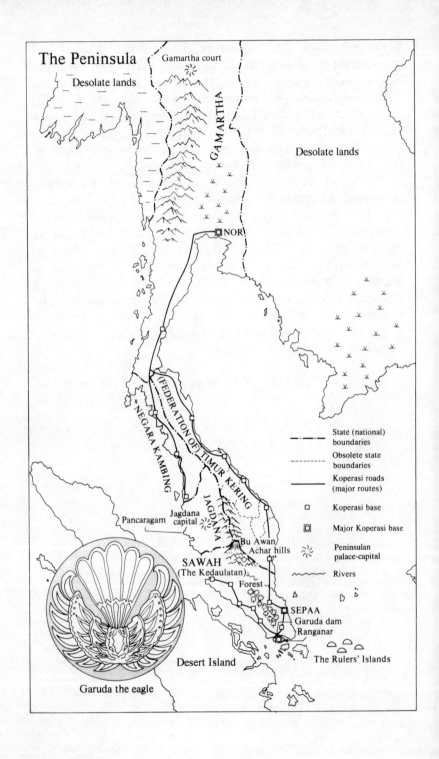

The Peninsula

Desolate lands

Gamartha court

GAMARTHA

Desolate lands

NOR

(FEDERATION OF) TIMUR KERING

NEGARA KAMBING

JAGDANA

Pancaragam

Jagdana capital

Bu Awan
Achar hills

SAWAH
(The Kedaulatan)

Forest

SEPAA
Garuda dam
Ranganar

The Rulers' Islands

Desert Island

Garuda the eagle

—··—··—	State (national) boundaries
- - - - -	Obsolete state boundaries
———	Koperasi roads (major routes)
□	Koperasi base
▣	Major Koperasi base
	Peninsulan palace-capital
～	Rivers

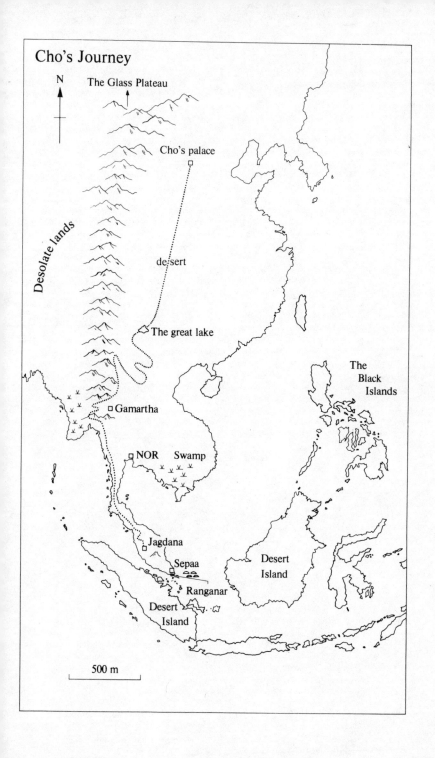

Cho's Journey

N

The Glass Plateau

Cho's palace

Desolate lands

desert

The great lake

The
Black
Islands

Gamartha

NOR   Swamp

Jagdana

Sepaa

Ranganar

Desert
Island

Desert
Island

500 m

Contents

Prologue: In the Rock Gardens

To the east of the palace there were extensive rock gardens, where it was pleasant to walk at different seasons of the year, and admire the changing light on the twisted and fantastic shapes of the rocks. It was especially pleasant to plan carefully and reach the gardens at dawn, so that you could watch the rock creatures take shape out of the dark, and then the sun coming up. From this vantage point the first light seemed to rise straight out of the glass basin far away across the plains, and the dawn colours were beautiful. The Empress learned that the Emperor had decided on such an outing, and she made her preparations.

There was a small hillock in the centre of the gardens that suited her purpose well. When she reached the place she climbed up it carefully, following the smooth steps worn into the rock by countless pilgrimages of admiration. She did not pause at the viewing point but began at once to descend the gentler eastern slope. The Emperor would come exactly this way, straight into the white risen sun. About halfway down she found a satisfactory arrangement: a twisted horn of stone at ankle height on one side of the path, and a tough-stemmed shrub on the other. She sat down slowly just above; turned up the hem of her embroidered gown onto her lap and picked at it with her fingernails.

It was hard work, because her fingers were weak and withered but the gown was still in excellent condition. She paused frequently to sigh and stare out over the landscape, rubbing her cramped fingers. She had no personal feeling against the Emperor. She was thinking it would be nice for him to see the dawn one last time. Lost in the grand, stiff folds of her beautiful clothes she sat there unpicking her hem and carefully winding up the thread: what seemed like the dry skin and bones of a shrunken old woman. All around her stretched the silent gardens: black rock arches and spires and waves and broken bubbles, like a pot of boiling liquid suddenly frozen. Where a little earth had crusted over the lava small-leaved shrubs grew, some as tall as trees and some blossoming yellow and scarlet. Like the Empress's robes, the flowers were young, but like the Empress the stunted trees were old, very old, with riven trunks and knotted arthritic roots. It was a harmonious scene, with the bright shapes of the rocks and the bright flowers decorating what was solid, rugged and ancient; but it was haunted, especially away towards the east. There, where the gardens faded into dust and quieter stones, there were strange shadows: a tall curve too smooth to be weathered glimpsed between the branches of a tree; an occasional eruption from the crumpled lava that appeared too straight and sleek for nature. The Empress, when she paused and sighed, seemed to be looking sadly at these ghosts.

She was still sitting there at work when a small figure appeared down below, trotting about between the rocks and obviously looking for someone.

'Bother – ' said the Empress, and the Cat – for sound travelled well on the dry air – pricked her ears and came hurrying up the slope. Perched on top of a boulder, she observed what the Empress was doing with the strong thread and her tail twitched against the rock in exasperation.

'I might have known you were up to no good,' she said. 'I might have known you weren't coming to your senses.'

The Cat did not speak in the ordinary sense but the Empress understood her perfectly. 'It has to be done,' she answered, testing her knots. 'I have thought about it seriously and there is no other way of being secure.'

The Cat's tail beat a tattoo. 'It is self-destructive. It is wicked. It is wicked enough to destroy Emp, but how long do you think you will last without him? Dislike him as you may at least he is *incident*. You'll die of boredom, and it will be suicide.'

'I know it is wicked, Divine Endurance,' said the Empress patiently. 'And it upsets me very much. But there is an overriding imperative here.'

She tugged at the snare once more, nodded in satisfaction and struggled to her feet. 'You won't tell Emp though, will you?'

The Cat just glared angrily and refused to reply. But she would not tell. It would go completely against her nature. She would probably be here hiding behind a rock on the fatal morning, watching fascinated to see what would happen. The Empress stepped off down the path, holding up the front of her gown so she would not trip on the unravelled hem. The Cat stayed behind. She went and patted the trap with her paw; the thread was quite invisible against the dusty rock, and very strong. After examining it thoroughly she stalked away, in the opposite direction from the Empress and with her tail still waving angrily.

Divine Endurance

PART ONE

My stone doesn't belong to me
It belongs to the government
Or God.
But I know that nobody
Cared for it before
Me, the one who found it.
                    Bettina Pfoestech

My name is Divine Endurance. I am feminine. I am twenty-five small units high at the shoulder, and sixty-two small units long from nose to tail tip. I am independent and it is therefore the more flattering when I respond to affection. I am graceful, agile and especially good at killing things prettily. I live with the Empress and the Emperor. There are only three of us now. Once there were more of them: more Empresses and Emperors, and other names too, but things have been running down for a long time and gradually people fade away and one sees them no more. But I have never liked bustle, and I was perfectly happy until our troubles began. We have a pleasant life. We have our extensive palace, and our gardens where the light is always changing. We have outings to view the sunset and the dawn and the moon; we have lizards and flowers, warm rocks and cool shadows. There are certain restrictions: for instance, we are not supposed to go outside the gardens. But most of the time keeping the rules is simply common sense. I have explored the way to the glass basin, but the air down there smells horrible, and the light makes one's head ache. I have also been out towards the glass plateau, which is a shiny line on the sky to the west of our palace, but I found nothing of interest, only a few dirty places where some passing nomads had been camping. We are not to go near these people. If ever somebody wants one of us they will approach through the proper channels, and with some ceremony no doubt. Meanwhile, if the gypsies come too close to the palace (they don't often dare) we simply think discouraging thoughts and make ourselves scarce.

I should say that there is one rule that the Empress and the Emperor obey, which I ignore because it is just silly. When one of them grows past the point of being a child, they start taking what they call medicine. It is an effluent from the Controller. Once, when we all stayed inside, they used to line up and the Controller would give it to them in little cups out of a wall. But I think the wall or the cups faded away, and now they just drink it from their hands. It does them nothing but harm. The effects are slow but horrible. Their hair falls out, their muscles waste away, their skin grows flabby and their teeth crumble. Eventually some accident happens and the victim is too weak to recover, and that is the end. If they waited till they were properly grown up it would do them no harm – if they must have the stuff, but they won't. I do not remember ever being told to take this medicine. I do not know why they keep on doing it.

I think it was because of the medicine that I encouraged Em and Emp when they began to talk about a baby. They were both beginning to look quite sickly, and I do not think I would like to live entirely alone. They could not decide which kind of baby to have – they can never agree about anything – so they wanted one of each. I thought that two was excessive and would spoil our quiet times, but they went to the Controller anyway. There we had a shock: the Controller said we could only have one baby, because there was only one baby ability left. This was startling. It had seemed, I suppose, that things could go on running down forever and never completely stop. Could it be twins? asked Em. That's not allowed, said the Controller. We did not ask for the one baby to be started. We came away disappointed. But Em (I should have paid more attention) was thinking, privately and hard.

As I know, from my expeditions, nobody can actually prevent us if we want to disobey. When the Controller said 'that's not allowed' rather than 'not possible' I should have known what Em would do. Anyway, she did it. She went down into the Controller's entrails and made it do what it should not. It was wrong of her of course, but we have been left to our own devices for so long it is not at all fair to expect 'not allowed' to be enough, without any explanation.

The first I knew of Em's naughtiness at this point was that two hatches in the Controller began to go milky, and in a little while we could see the babies growing inside. This was a very strange sight, after so long. It was so interesting that Emp soon forgot to be shocked, and I to be displeased. We picked names. We made them up ourselves, we didn't see why not. Something simple and boyish for Emp's choice: Worthy to be Beloved. The girl's name was subtler: Chosen Among the Beautiful – implying 'chosen to be the best of the best', without quite saying so. We took sides and laid small bets on which was taking shape faster. We spent whole days just watching.

But Em had done wrong, and gradually it began to affect her. She stopped coming to see the babies. She hid herself away and brooded. Emp had a bad conscience too. He sat with his baby still, but now he was always sighing and sniffing. 'Poor little mite,' I heard him mutter. 'We should never have started this. What a life . . . ! To make matters worse the weather was very unsettled. We do not usually have to suffer anything tiresome, like excessive wind or rain, but just now a lot of dust and sand got into the air and started blowing about; the sky was obscured and there were unpleasant smells. It was like being at the glass

3

basin. Then one day there was an earth tremor. It was an unusual one because the disturbance seemed to start near at hand, rather than off somewhere in the distance. I was sitting with Em, in a distant quarter of the palace, trying to cheer her up. We were both a little shaken. A crowd of bats pelted squeaking from a dark passage beyond Em's corner, and three big lizards ran out of the wall. Em got up. 'It's no good,' she muttered, 'I will have to stop it.'

I ignored the lizards – I am very fond of Em – and followed her out of the room, trying to make her see that an earth tremor is harmless and she was being silly. She was stumbling on the uncertain ground on her poor wasted legs. I must admit I thought her mind was upset. Anyway I went with her, at her slow pace, to the Controller. There we found that one of the hatches had been torn open, and the boy baby was gone.

'It wasn't an earth tremor,' said Em. 'It was the Controller. We have frightened it.'

She was very distressed. Not understanding, I assured her that the baby would have been nearly ready; it wouldn't be harmed. But she insisted that we start searching for Emp at once. We could not find him. We searched and searched for days, but he did not reappear. He had gone right away from the palace, which is not allowed. Now I realised what Em had somehow guessed all along: something serious had happened. It was difficult for us to follow him because Em moves so badly nowadays, but eventually we found his trail leading to the west. There, out in the wilderness, we found the dirty camp. It was already abandoned. They never stay anywhere long, but events had left enough of an impression for us to know beyond doubt what Emp had done. He had stolen our baby, taken it out of our world, and given it away to the gypsies.

There was nothing we could do, so we returned to the palace. Em was so angry she wouldn't talk to me. She tried to get the Controller to take her baby back – anything rather than let Emp have it, I suppose. The Controller was unresponsive. So the baby stayed behind the hatch, which was clear and filmy now, so the poor thing should have been taken out. And Em stayed inside the Controller, on guard. Meanwhile I discovered Emp, lurking in the north-east apartments. But he was unrepentant, so there seemed no hope of making up the quarrel. He even wanted me to get Em to give her baby away as well. Em, on the other hand, would not listen to any of my suggestions. When I said I would get Emp to swear solemnly to leave her baby alone

4

she just stared at me scornfully. However, I persevered, trying to make peace and restore our former pleasant existence. When Em began to ask me how the Emperor was passing his time these days, I thought I was succeeding.

I know better now, and now there are only two of us. She came looking for me, when it was over and we both knew he was gone. She said she wanted to explain herself. She took me down into the Controller's insides. There are ways in, in the broken area in the south-east of the palace, but I hadn't bothered to go there for a very long time. Down we went, into the big shining places. I do not know what she had to say to me that was so private. After all, we are quite alone now. We went in where the pipe comes out, where they drink the medicine. Some Empress or Emperor long ago made that, in the days when we first realised we were allowed to live outside so long as we did not stray too far.

It is strange, inside the Controller. For some reason it takes a lot of room to make the first drop of baby. The darkness and the shining goes away, far away. I can't explain it. Nobody ever walked here but us, when we got out of the boxes and began to walk about all on our own. . . .

'Look around you,' she said. 'And think.'

She had brought us past the impressive places, which I rather like. I like to think that they couldn't get in that part, even if they did make it. We were in a long thin place, behind the arrangement that posts the drops of baby into the hatches up above. A box-room in fact. The empty boxes lined the walls, one on top of another. There were no doors to this place. They never used to let us have doors, apparently, or windows, or anything to look at. It is not that I need a door, but it would have been more polite, I think.

'I don't like this,' I said. 'I prefer outside.'

'So do I,' she answered. 'This place makes one feel so small, doesn't it?'

She was silent for a while. I felt she was trying to make the box-room talk to me, but I declined to get the message. Eventually she said: 'None of us was ever to leave the palace without a home to go to. It isn't right. What do you suppose will happen when that little baby grows up?'

I said – it was fairly obvious – 'Well, he'll do his best to be useful, I'm sure.'

'To whom?'

I saw what she was getting at. If he tried to make himself

5

useful to everyone around him at once it might be rather confusing.

'We were the best,' murmured Em. 'We were the most wonderful: you and I and Emp who is dead, and all our model. There was nothing we could not do, if our person asked us. They valued us above anything, and cared for us dearly. Which is why, of course, we survived when all the world was swept away. We could give them anything they wished for. . . . '

I don't care for this sort of conversation. I think it is pointless. I maintained a discouraging silence, but she still went on.

'It was very wrong of me to make the Controller give us twins. There have never been twins. How will they work? What effect will they have on each other? The Controller was frightened, and so am I. Do you see why I had to do what I did? I dared not risk the second baby going after the first. I could not.'

I understand these urges: the longing we all have to find a purpose in life, the hope that somehow stays that we will be needed, wanted again. For myself, I take no notice. We're alone now, and we've been alone a long time. We have a right to live our own lives. I was past caring exactly why Em killed Emp, but I could see she was upset so I tried to reassure her, telling her little Worthy to be Beloved would be the best thing that ever happened to the gypsies. He'd make sure they all lived happily ever after. What harm could he do?

Em said, 'What harm indeed? He is not a weapon, he can't be used like that. Of course he must do his best to make them all happy. And his best is perfect. . . . '

But she spoke in a very odd tone of voice (so that I felt suddenly interested). And then, after a pause, she added softly:

'Has it ever occured to you, Divine Endurance, that whatever swept the world away it happened soon after our model . . . first left the palace?'

There was a silence then, shivering and dark. I wanted to get back outside. Em said, 'Emp wasn't wicked. He had gone mad, I think, and imagined it was a real baby. He must have been taking more medicine than me.'

I did not like the look in her eyes. I did not like the way she was moving, so frail and wavery. Suddenly I realised something that had been obscured by the excitement of Emp's death. I saw my future.

'All right,' I said. 'You don't like the baby. We'll forget about it. We'll make the Controller turn that hatch grey again, and it will be gone, as good as. We'll go out and see the sunset on the

6

glass plateau. I know where there's an interesting lizard. . . .
Only don't, please don't, take any more medicine. . . .'

We've argued about that medicine so often. Once it was for
those of us who had no place in the world, so they would not be a
permanent embarrassment. A sign goes on, from the hatch that
hatched them, and they have to start taking the medicine, if they
are still here. But where's the embarrassment now? I told her:
'Look at me. Disobeying that order is easy.' She smiled and
said: 'Cat, they were too successful when they made a Cat.
That's why there are no others of you; that's why they never let
you go, but kept you here to laugh at them and be a warning.
You are too good at slipping under the locked doors in your
mind. . . .'

She smiled and shook her head as she had always done. This
was not the first Em I had argued with, there had been many
(the clothes are nearly the same). . . . This was the last. She
said, 'That's what I meant by bringing you down here. I wanted
to remind you what we really are. I can't disobey, Cat. I can't.
And why should I, anyway. What reason have we to live,
without them? . . .'

She wanted me to join in her huge vague grieving, but I could
not. She turned away from me with a lonely look: I knew she
was going to abandon me and I felt angry and helpless. We left
the inside of the Controller and went our separate ways.

Soon after this conversation the Empress's mind began to
fail, so it was really uncomfortable to be near her. She took
herself off into complete seclusion, and I did not see her any
more. One of the last things I got her to do for me was to take the
second baby out of the hatch because, I complained, I was going
to be very lonely. She did not say anything further about the
wrong and danger. I think she was already too unwell to
consider such things. Or perhaps, as our weather continues
extremely unsettled, she thinks the problem will be solved in
another way. As for me, I am recording my story, deep in my
mind. Em claims that the Controller is hidden somehow in
there, and I would like to think a representative of those people
who abandoned us knows – what I intend to do.

7

1 Chosen Among the Beautiful

When Cho was still quite a little girl there was a day when the Cat told her to go to sleep. It was a game she hadn't played before, but the infant curled herself up willingly, and went into the new experience with her head pillowed on a hollow stone and her knees tucked up to her chin. She slept. When she woke up she lay still for a while, bemused by the curious things that had just been happening. She was surprised to find her legs and arms in exactly the same places as before she left the room. She sat up and looked at the soles of her feet. They were clean, and there were no marks on her clothes either. They must have tidied themselves very quickly, she thought. It was puzzling. She decided she must ask the Cat about it, and set out to find her.

The little girl's rooms were in the north-east wing of the palace. She left them and pattered about the dusty forecourts peering into passages and doorways, until she realised the Cat was in the gardens. She set off in that direction. It was a day when the wind was blowing the sand about a good deal so she had to run carefully, for she knew the Cat would be cross if she put her foot in a hole and hurt herself. At last her pattering feet brought her to where the rock creatures were gathered, wearing their hats and cloaks of crusted red and white sand. Now she was distracted, because the Cat did not approve of this place for some reason, and so Cho had never seen the rock garden close up. She went from one to another, admiring the weird shapes and poking holes in the sand crust with her little fingers. The wind was quite strong; occasionally she looked up rather anxiously at the low, tossing sky. She knew it would be wrong to be outside in a storm. But she forgot everything else when she saw the hand. It was peeping out of a red mound, up on the side of a little hill. She ran up and crouched over it, fascinated. It was a very good hand, because the bones were still held together by skin; even the jewelled nail-guards were still in place. 'You are the best dead hand I have ever seen,' said Cho to the relic. She scratched in the crust of the mound, and found a sleeve. It was a beautiful colour, with shining embroidery. She found a foot too, but the foot was not so interesting. It had lost its leg, and lost its slipper. There was something tangled up in the little bones, a thin fine line of something. She tugged and the mound stirred, as if the dead person felt it. Cho laughed, but immediately frowned at herself childishly, and dropped the thread. She had been told often enough that she must not play with these piles of clothes and bones when she found them. She looked up and all around. Withered roots and skeletons of dead trees stood dismally among the rocks, blased by the unsettled weather, and the bright twisted lava was losing its attractions between the scouring and obscuring of the sand. Cho was too young to regret the changes, but she had begun to feel that the Cat was somewhere close, and not in a good temper. What have I done wrong? she wondered. She started to climb the rest of the little hill.

At the top there was a flat space in a ring of boulders. Drifts of sand had collected between them, and gathered in their smooth hollows: nobody had climbed to sit and watch the dawn for quite a while. Cho saw the Cat; a hump of brown fur down on the ground. Right beside her was another of those tumbled heaps of clothes. Cho could see the yellowish round of a bare scalp within the wide collar; she could see a little shrivelled hand. The Cat seemed to be playing with it – Cho was surprised to see her doing wrong. My one was better. It still had nails, she thought. And then the fingers moved. . . .

The Empress could no longer see with her sunken eyes of flesh, but she knew her friend was near, and she felt the other little one too. 'Cat,' she said. 'Keep her safe – harmless. Don't let her. . . . ' 'Oh my Em,' said Divine Endurance. 'My friend –' It hurt her very much that the Empress's last thought should be for the dirty gypsies. The Empress died. The dry lower jaw dropped open, and one last breath fainted on the harsh, dusty air. It was over. Cho knew something strange had happened. She was frightened, and a small sound escaped her. The Cat's

9

head turned quickly, and she stared at the child with angry diamond blue eyes. 'You,' she said. 'What are you doing here? I told you to go to sleep. Who told you to wake up?'

Divine Endurance said that the things that seemed to happen while Cho was asleep were called *dreams* and were really lessons from the Controller. She said (repeating what she had learned from Em long ago) that Cho's head was invisibly connected with the Controller, so it could tell her when she was doing something wrong, and teach her things. 'Now that you're old enough, you'll find it happens more and more. You don't have to lie down and keep still though. The Controller can manage without that.'

Cho had not enjoyed going to sleep, it was too peculiar, but she thought she would like to have lessons. She was not a baby now, and the Cat left her very much alone. Sometimes she played solitary games with dust and pebbles in her own rooms, sometimes she went wandering; a tiny, lonely figure in the maze of long bare buildings she knew as the 'palace'. In the centre of the maze was a large, smooth giant thing, untouched by the scouring sand. This was the Controller. But it was not important to Cho as it had been to Em and Emp. The entrance in its curved side was closed off now by a sheet of steely opaque substance like an eyelid, and no one could go in and talk anymore. This had happened in the first bout of bad weather just after Em retired forever. Divine Endurance had been angry at first, but she had got used to the situation. Cho thought it was very mysterious when the Cat talked about the Controller saying things and doing things. When her wanderings brought her to the centre of the maze she would stand and stare at the giant. There was a crack of darkness at the edge of the eyelid. She knew that she and her brother had been born from there, and often wondered how they had squeezed out. Sometimes, after gazing for a while, she went around the back, pressed her forehead to the smooth base and stood there patiently. Nothing ever happened, but though she did not sleep again, she began to find things in her mind. It was as if there was a palace being built inside her, and she was starting to walk about in it.

Time passed. Her games took her further afield. East and north she could look out, where parts of smooth things like the

Controller gleamed in a sea of dead lava, and sand. And beyond the sea were dazzling white salt pans. The smell the wind blew from them was fierce. Cho preferred the west, where the wilderness began. Here there were growing things not blighted yet; little shrubs and mosses and small animals of various kinds. She would sit as far away from the palace as her conscience would let her, gazing into the west and dreaming. She knew a lot about the plants and animals and rocks, but she knew she must not interfere with them. Not on her own account anyway. It would be different if it was to help someone. Cho knew she was supposed to be useful, and help people. Divine Endurance had told her: 'You are an art person. It is your special privilege to make everyone around you happy.' The Cat had also told her that she had a brother who was already out in the world somewhere, helping. She spent a lot of her dreaming time dreaming about him, and about being useful – happy dreams, but sometimes they made her sad, for she had never seen her brother, and who was she to help? There was no one here but the gypsies in the wilderness. She had never even seen them, and in any case she knew she must not go near them; must not leave the palace. The mystery of how her brother had left was a puzzle Divine Endurance had left unexplained.

Divine Endurance was waiting impatiently, but the years flew by and Cho remained a child. The Controller had been told long ago to match development time to demand: when it had come to Cho it had been on a slow, slow schedule. The Cat did not want to spoil things by acting in a hurry, but she knew very well that since it had shut itself up in the upset over the split baby, the Controller had not been working properly. The discomfort did not worry the Cat, and Cho had never known anything better so she did not suffer, but eventually there was bound to be trouble. She decided it was time to prepare the ground.

'Divine Endurance,' asked Cho diffidently. 'Will I some day be progressed enough to have nice clothes?'

They were sitting together in an inner room of Cho's apartments, while a bad sandstorm purred and hissed over the walls and roofs. The Cat had come visiting; she had been asking Cho questions about her lessons and she seemed quite pleased with

Cho's replies. Gusts of sand kept dashing into the room and dancing around the floor, for none of the palace doorways had doors. The Cat was watching them, apparently lost in thought, but when Cho ventured her question she looked up and snapped: 'What's wrong with the clothes you've got?'

There was nothing wrong with them. They were the blouse and trousers that had been born with her. They had sat in a corner waiting and growing until she was a clever enough baby to climb into them (because the Cat couldn't dress her), and they had been with her ever since, patiently mending and tidying themselves, and growing as often as necessary. But Cho admired the lovely stiff robes the dead bones wore, and having been told she was getting on well in her lessons, it had occurred to her – 'I'm sorry,' she said, 'if it was wrong. But I just thought – '

The sand wind moaned outside. The Cat was silent, but she seemed more sad than annoyed.

'Child, have you ever wondered,' she said at last, 'what happened to the other people? The ones whose robes still lie about like lost jewels, though the bodies inside are dust? Listen, I will tell you. It was all due to the medicine.'

Cho already knew about the pipe with liquid trickling from it, behind the south-east buildings. The Cat had told her when she was a baby she must never go near it, nor into any cleft in the ground round there. But she had never heard the word medicine before.

'Once, long ago,' began Divine Endurance, 'the empty clothes were all people, alive and walking about. The sky was always clear in those days and there were flowers and lizards everywhere and no sand at all. But because the people insisted on taking that medicine which comes out of the pipe you mustn't touch, everything began to go wrong.'

'What did it do?'

'They thought it would make them better than they were,' said the Cat. 'But it made them selfish and useless, and in the end it made them just wither away. Finally, it made them so naughty that they even upset the Controller, and that's why our sky isn't blue and our flowers have died.'

Cho listened solemnly. 'It's wrong to hurt yourself,' she remarked. 'And we are meant to be useful.'

'Exactly,' said the Cat. 'But they insisted and now you are the only one. They put on those robes when they began to take their medicine, so you see why you must never want to wear them.'

The sandstorm had eased. Divine Endurance got to her feet and stretched thoughtfully. 'I will leave you now. It has been a pleasant visit.'

After this conversation, the Cat left the child alone for quite a long interval. She kept an eye on her from a distance, however, because the weather was getting worse. Almost without noticing it they both started to give up the eastern areas of the palace and gardens because they were just too uncomfortable. Cho was beginning to be less of a child. She forgot her pebbles and the dust houses she had made for them, and spent more and more of her time just wandering and dreaming. She brooded a great deal about the things Divine Endurance had said about the people who were selfish and useless. I don't want to be like that, she thought. But what can I do?

At last Divine Endurance judged it was time for another step forwards. She found Cho this time at her second home, her favourite boulder overlooking the wilderness. She was puzzled as she approached the place by a curious crunching noise. She jumped up on top of the boulder and saw beneath her the child, not very little now, holding a piece of rock and biting it with her strong small teeth.

'What on earth are you doing?'

Cho started, 'Oh,' she said. 'I'm eating.'

'Don't be silly.'

A few steps away a little mouse-like creature sat on another rock, crunching at a seed it held in its paws – eyeing Divine Endurance warily.

'Like that you know,' said Cho. 'I'd like to live on things, be part of things. . . . ' She smiled, and tossed her rock away. 'It's only a game.'

Divine Endurance was strangely impressed. There was something not at all childlike about that smile.

'Cho,' she said. 'You are right to want to be part of things, and so we will be. It is time we started to think about joining your brother.'

Cho was stunned. This time, the first time she met the

13

extraordinary idea, she could hardly take it in. She listened with big round eyes to the story of the brave Emperor who saved the baby from the medicine, and the wicked Empress who killed him before he could save Cho as well. But when Divine Endurance came to the moral – that because Wo had helplessly broken the rule it was *obviously* right for Cho to follow, now she was old enough – the child's eyes just got rounder and rounder.... Divine Endurance cautiously retreated.

She came back, again and again, like water dripping on a stone: Cho's brother, torn away from his home without a proper education, needed Cho urgently by now. How much the two of them would be able to do for the world, when they were together. Sometimes there are overriding imperatives.... But for a long while the dripping did not work at all. The child became distressed, but more and more obstinate. Divine Endurance began to be seriously worried about her secret plan.

But the weather continued to deteriorate. The air was oppressively thick and warm, and small earth tremors rattled through the palace daily. They stayed under the western walls now all the time. And one day there was a dark blot on the grey plain of the wilderness. It did not seem to move, but it grew, little by little. Cho saw it and was filled with a strange excitement, but at the same time she felt compelled to get up and go and hide behind her boulder. The Cat came too. Together they watched as the blot came closer and began to pass by. They saw animals, stumbling and huddling together in the foul, dusty wind. And they saw the others ... wrapped to the eyes in crusted rags, striding along. Some of them were sitting on top of animals, to comfort them. Strange sounds came to the boulder, sounds that Cho had never heard before.... She saw dark eyes, laced in patterns of blue; she saw one blue hand outside a mantle, and her heart began to beat very hard.... Not one of the train even glanced up at the boulder, and the strange excitement faded. Cho and Divine Endurance got up.

'He isn't with them anymore,' whispered Cho.

'He can't be everywhere,' said the Cat. 'It would be different if you were with him.'

Cho was looking after the train, with a slightly puzzled expression. 'Were they happy?' she asked shyly.

14

Divine Endurance answered, honestly. 'I don't know. I think it is more difficult to tell than you would think.... Obviously it would be different if there were two of you. But they were doing the right thing. We must make a move ourselves very soon.'

'Perhaps things will get better?'

'I don't think so, child. I have seen these fits before. It is working up to a climax, and this time we have no Controller.'

'You mean, we might not be able to keep ourselves mended?'

'Indeed we might not,' said Divine Endurance grimly.

The end of Cho's resistance came abruptly. One sultry, ominous morning they went walking into the palace, to see how it was surviving, and they found their way blocked. There was a huge split in the ground between them and the inner buildings. It was wide and there was something shining deep down inside – the Controller's entrails, split open. They stared into the pit. The hot ground shivered menacingly underfoot.

'Divine Endurance,' said Cho suddenly, 'you are right, and we should leave. We should go now.'

And so, without any farewell, without any ceremony, they left the palace forever. They simply returned to the western walls, climbed them again and went on. When they had come down the first slopes and were out on the level ground in the wilderness Cho looked back. But already her special boulder, where she had watched the little mouse and dreamed her dreams, was just another rock on the hillside.

2 Living on the Ground

Cho and the Cat ran on and on tirelessly over the barren plain. Sometimes the pumice dust was skinned over the little red plants, more often it was bare, and they were wading knee-deep as if in cloudy water. 'I remember,' said Divine Endurance as they ran, 'the day this wilderness was made. There were great trees, as tall as the Controller; they all jumped in the air and disappeared. Rivers and lakes were stirred up with the hills, making mud that boiled, and the rocks began to run about in streams. We were inside, of course, but the Controller let us see what was happening. Afterwards we found that all the other palaces had vanished in the confusion. Then we started waiting for the people to come back. But they never did. It was not so bad to leave us, we could have been quite happy. But they should have told us, shouldn't they, that they were going for ever. It would have made such a difference.'

'Perhaps they meant to come back,' said Cho. 'Perhaps they've been busy.'

Above them, the sky had begun to swell and darken. As they ran on a wind started to rise, and then the clouds opened and poured on them a flood of thick, rust coloured rain. 'It has picked up sands from the glass basin – ' said the Cat. In front of them now the grey plain was giving way to a more rugged terrain of old lava, but they could feel new tremors coming, and the dust seemed safer. Cho found a scrape of a hollow in a patch of stunted bushes, some way before the rocks began, and they crept into the middle of this to try to hide. They crouched close together, feeling the tenseness of the earth as it shuddered towards another convulsion. They could tell this one would be very strong. 'An occasion for sleep,' said the Cat. So they lay down, the way Divine Endurance had been taught was correct

16

for 'sleeping' a long time ago, and made themselves still. Because there was nothing they could do. They could only hand themselves over to the earth wave and hope that it would bear them up and not drown them.

Cho woke. She lay alertly considering what was around her. She had had no dreams and she was grateful for that, but she wondered what it meant. Everything has changed, she thought. The sky was at a different angle. She sat up and found the left side of her body was caked with red mud – because on that side the screening bushes had been torn away. She was on the brink of a great churned pit of earth that had not been there before. The water in it steamed. She looked for Divine Endurance and saw that the Cat must have woken earlier. She had climbed into the remaining bushes and was now apparently asleep, perched weirdly between two branches. The leaves and twigs were charred black. The Cat opened her eyes.

'How long have we been asleep?' asked Cho.

'As long as necessary, I suppose.'

She climbed down from her perch and together they peered into the red, evil-smelling gloom that hid the wilderness plain. 'Everything has changed,' whispered Cho. Now they knew for certain they had left their home forever. For ever and ever. After a while they got up, and began to pick their way through mud and clinkers and steaming puddles, on into the west.

For a long time the two fugitives wandered in a daze. They were continually harassed by small after-tremors and by cloud-bursts of the thick, abrasive rain. But worse than anything else was the sense of that emptiness behind them. Divine Endurance suffered just as much as Cho. In spite of all her schemes she probably would never have been able to leave the palace without the urgent threat of the earthquake. After all the plotting and persuasion they had both been simply obedient in the end, running away from something that would damage them. Now they were orphaned, and there seemed no purpose in life. It was almost by accident that they journeyed westward at all.

But eventually the tremors faded, and the air calmed and cleared. They found themselves above the wilderness in a land made of glittering slivers of shale, interrupted by heaps of strange-coloured boulders. As the clouds and fog began to melt

17

away they saw this country stretching endlessly ahead of them, climbing onwards in broad, gleaming terraces. They stopped their mindless trudging and began to appreciate their surroundings: there was blue sky, which Cho had never seen before. The crystals that grew in the boulders were charming, and away on their right-hand side was the fascinating clear line of the glass plateau. There was no water, no plants or animals, but there was plenty to enjoy. At night the rocks produced their own light; a rich, changeable, flickering glow. Lingering in this shining country they recovered from their loss. It was like the pleasant life Divine Endurance remembered. She introduced Cho to sunset watching, and the art of appreciating a warm stone or a cool shadow, and she told her interesting stories of the Empresses and Emperors she had known. But they did not watch the dawn, and they avoided looking in that direction. And always as they wandered about, finding themselves new temporary homes with different attractions, they kept moving towards the west.

At last Divine Endurance began to talk about the future again. She talked about Worthy to be Beloved – or Wo, as his sister should call him, and the delightful prospect of being helpful, and useful, with Wo. The Cat knew that if she was to get her own way, she had to watch out for certain features of Cho's nature: she warned the child repeatedly against the danger of attaching herself to one particular person. That would be selfish. The end of the quest was to join Wo, and be *truly* useful. . . . She began to teach Cho how to behave in the world: 'Remember you must not be lazy. And don't push yourself forward. The people don't like it, it embarrasses them. Be helpful when you are asked, and not before – and then be discreet about it. And you'll have to change your manners. From what I can remember, they're a complete disgrace at present.'

The first lesson in manners was going to sleep at strictly regular intervals. The second lesson started when they came to a land where mosses and lichens began; trickles of water and gradually more and more activity. One day Divine Endurance suddenly jumped into a bush and did something very strange to a little animal, rather like Cho's mouse. Cho was shocked.

'It's all right,' said Divine Endurance. 'They enjoy it really.'

18

She did not manage to teach Cho to kill the ground squirrels prettily, but the child became quite competent, and they were able to practise eating nearly every day. Cho would have prefered to nibble leaves and seeds.... 'Certainly not,' said Divine Endurance. 'They might be poisonous. Eating poisonous things is a waste of maintenance and very naughty.' They wasted none of the squirrels. After eating it was manners, Divine Endurance explained, to dig a small hole in the ground and post the eaten things into it. 'The people keep some of it back,' said the Cat, 'we needn't. We just post it in and cover it up nicely.' She found this hole business quite delightful, but Cho thought it no more than mildly pleasant.

Because of the routine of hunting, eating and sleeping they began to travel more briskly. They started to notice the changing moon, and to measure time. At last one clear night, about the end of a month of steady westward progress, brought them to the very last of the climbing terraces. They sat waiting for the moon. Divine Endurance had been remembering more of the world's manners, so there was a little fire, and the current squirrel was toasting over it on sticks.

'What does your name mean, Divine Endurance?' asked Cho idly.

'It means,' said the Cat 'that I come from the early days of the palace. Later on, it was thought unnecessary and even unwise to dwell on some of our special features.'

'Does it mean you don't mind about time? It's strange isn't it? In the palace time was like air, I never thought of it.... But now it seems to pass and pass. Do you think we will ever find them? Do you think they have all gone?'

Their campfire was on the top of a cliff. Beneath their feet, blue-black in the starlight, plunged an endless cataract of rounded hills. Without a thought, they had known which way to run when they left the palace, and that way was south and west. But they had been running a long time with no encouragement, not even a trace of the gypsies.

'It is not time to give up yet,' said the Cat. 'Everything has changed, but eventually we must reach the southern margin of this landmass. Then we should find a long Peninsula running into the sea. Our feeling is, isn't it, that they've trickled away, to the edge of things, south and west.'

19

'Yes. They've slipped away.'

'So, probably they are on that Peninsula. Resting, or retiring or whatever it is they've been doing all this time. And Wo is with them.'

The moon came up, slowly lifting its thin yellow finger-nail into the sky behind them. They ate the squirrel, and the Cat told Cho to go to sleep. But she did not. She lay down with her eyes open dreaming all through the night, about the Peninsula, and the end of the quest.

3 Day of Blood

It was too warm in the courtroom. Hand-turned fans slapped the air with languid palms; tack, tack, tack. The people pressed against each other, whispered and scuffled; some giggled hysterically. The criminal stood with his head bowed, the Rulers' agents at their long table spoke to each other very softly, and one of them wrote something down. Outside in the sun the streets of the city were quiet, shops empty, markets shuttered. It was a Hari Darah, a rest day. Prince Atoon in his canopied chair sat like a delicate statue, but his eyes hunted the crowd. There was not one veiled head, not one attended figure making a space around itself. They were all boys, boys and men. Atoon had not expected the women to protest or intervene in any way. But he had prayed for a miracle, he had prayed that they would be here. They were not. They had abandoned Alat to his fate.

The noble criminal stood accused of indecent assault on a young boy in his family's household. It was the custom of the Peninsula to change the majority of male children at birth or in infancy: the 'boys' thus created did society's menial work and deserved in return to be cherished and protected. In happier times, the native council would have harassed the noble family into paying a huge fine, almost as much as if Alat had killed someone, if the charge were proved. But the facts in this case were irrelevant. Alat might very well have buggered the witness. How many men live lives of perfect chastity, whatever their families claim? Equally, he might never have seen the boy until today. Alat, a nobleman of Jagdana, had been writing letters to someone in another state, that was the real offence.

The Peninsula had been controlled by foreigners for several hundred years. The Rulers came out of the southern ocean, claiming to have left behind an enormous country that was no longer habitable, and settled on artificial islands off the south-east coast. Gradually, on various excuses, they began to take

21

over the world. The process was now complete. Peninsulan independence had been dead for a hundred years, since the mad, ruinous Last Rebellion. There was no High Prince any more, presiding over the patchwork states, for the family of Garuda the Eagle was deposed and vanished and the Eagle Palace lay at the bottom of a reservoir. The Rulers stayed on their islands but their agents, the Koperasi, renegades who had 'co-operated' with the oppressors, controlled every state. Jagdana was the only princedom to retain some shreds of self rule, at the cost of a rigorously maintained appearance of docility. Atoon had been assured that the letters really existed, and when he knew that he knew Alat was lost. The Rulers' agents themselves might relent before the Dapurs of Jagdana: *Thou shalt not risk lives* is the greatest law. The palace had rescued conspirators before, but this time Atoon's family could not interfere, for reasons far above Alat's head. Poor man, he had chosen the wrong moment to get caught out in his little meddling.

The crowd waited, simmering urgently. Occasionally a head turned furtively to see what was happening in the marble-latticed gallery above the inner end of the hall, where the Pertama Dapur, the first ladies of the land, were supposedly presiding. Atoon knew there was no one behind the thin, dark curtain, behind the pierced stone, yet he found himself staring too. But it was all over. An elderly boy in black and indigo livery came out, rapped with his staff for attention and bent his old tortoise back to heave the cord that raised the draperies. The women of Atoon's family had officially departed, satisfied with justice. And Atoon, although he had known there could be no other issue, felt his head begin to spin.

The Rulers' officer left his place and came up to the dais, glanced over his shoulder at the body of the court and said in a muted tone: 'We'll give the prisoner as strong an escort as we can, Sir.'

It was you, thought Atoon, you and your kind, who robbed the people of their self respect and turned them into savages. How did you do it? God knows, I don't. It's done, and we would all be better off dead than living like this. You will give him up at the corner of the street.

'If you're ready to leave, Sir,' prompted the officer, respectfully, weighing up and down Atoon's calm, graceful silence: 'We will give you an escort back to the palace.'

By sunset the streets were quiet again. The palace, which spread in a maze of courts and gardens through the heart of the capital, had heard the noise start up, rise to a tumult and at last die away. Now there was only the stillness of a rest day evening. The prince Atoon, and a guest of his family, were sitting in an audience room, deep inside the maze. It was a vast apartment; long unused. Little groups of stiff furniture stood about in its dim expanses, looking prim and desolate. The blue and gold of Jagdana was fading from everything, and the garden, neglected, grew up to the verandah steps. The prince sat propped against one of the slender pillars that supported the inner roof, staring at nothing. His companion, sitting a little distance away, watched the last rays of the sun gleaming on Atoon's ordered braids, making the worn gilding on walls and pillars burn. The light slipped away, and indigo shadows gathered. A boy came pattering through the dim depths of the room, bringing a lamp. He wished to prostrate himself before Atoon's companion, but she caught him in the act with a quick frown so he simply bobbed a curtsey to the prince, and fled.

She was the reason why Alat could not be saved. She was the granddaughter of the last High Prince: the young prince Garuda who was rescued after the rebellion and the murder of his family, and hidden in the hills. The prince was accepted by the outcast mountain people and became one of them. He had a daughter and Derveet was her child, the only thing the last Garuda saved from the wreckage of his defiant attempt to renew the struggle. He smuggled the baby away from the Peninsula and brought her up on the Black Islands in the eastern sea, among the diving people. But the Rulers decided to evacuate the diving colonies, which were losing population and could not support themselves. The exiled prince set sail for nowhere, with other despairing islanders. He would not return to the Peninsula: he was old and sick and his time had passed. But Derveet, though still very young, escaped and managed to get back to her country, alone. The Hanomans, the Royal family of Jagdana, were loyal – Hanoman the Ape had always been the Eagle's great ally – and they would have sheltered her

23

for the rest of her life. But Derveet was not looking for shelter. She had come to the Peninusla to start a new rebellion.

She knew that the women had placed a ban on armed revolt after the last disaster: she did not want to repeat her grandfather's defiance. She wanted the Dapur's support in a new kind of warfare, a desperate kind to suit the desperate straits of the country. She spoke of disruption and subversion, secrecy and trickery. She wanted to use women's powers of wisdom, cunning and hidden knowledge in the man's domain of war. But her ideas were unacceptable. The Hanoman ladies informed her that all overt resistance to the Rulers or their servants was suicidal. When the country was stronger the men's honourable outbursts were permissible as a safety valve, but now no longer. To involve them in sheer banditry would be to degrade them for no purpose. That women should be concerned in such things was simply unthinkable. In reality there is no recourse for us, they told her, but patience and endurance. It is up to you whether you understand that sooner, or later.

She left the court of Jagdana and went into the mountains, to her grandmother's people. Peninsulan society loved beauty and order, and hated any kind of deformity – the central mountains had always been a refuge for misborn, grotesquely coloured or misshapen creatures. Derveet thought no one could dispute her right to teach and inspire the *polowijo*, the people the Peninsula rejected. She set herself up as a dealer in the illegal achar weed that everybody smoked, and she endured the humiliation of being taken for a man as she explored the south of the Peninsula beyond Jagdana; the country that had once been the Kedaulatan, the Garuda state, and was now the Sawah – occupied territory. She made friends with bandits, brothel-keepers; the fringes of the Koperasi. And it was all to show the Dapur what she could do, and how her plan would work.

But the outcast community had suffered like all the other states. The polowijo were weak and frightened. Finally, Derveet's attempts to organise her guerilla campaign blew up in her face, literally. She had been experimenting with home-made explosives, alone, because nobody dared help her. The polowijo in a panic sent for help, and Derveet was smuggled back to Jagdana.

So the young rebel returned to the Hanoman court,

defeated. She was very ill: the Dapur saved her sight, and patiently brought her back to health. But Derveet was now a known outlaw, and though she had not used the name Garuda of course there were whispers. Her presence in the palace compromised her friends, threatened the very existence of independent Jagdana and incidentally had destroyed one foolish man.

In the faded hall the prince and the outlaw sat together – a strange contrast. Derveet's grandfather had done his best, but the child had taken after the mountain people. She was too tall, her features were harsh and her skin was black, not golden. It was bizarre to see this lean, ugly young woman move and glance exactly like a Garuda; beside the Hanoman prince she seemed like disorder incarnate. The exhausted silence continued. There was nothing to say. Atoon had come straight from the court and asked Garuda, his eyes blackly dilated, his beautiful face calm as a jewel, *if he might be relieved of his duties*. (Atoon's father had asked his Dapur that question, some years ago. And they had released him, knowing a man can take just so much shame.) He wanted to borrow a long knife, he was not allowed to bear arms himself, of course. She had refused, and reproached him bitterly. Now she watched him – leaning gracefully against the pillar, glowing in the lamplight like something painted on silk: an exquisite work of art, gold to the waist, white brocade below. But behind the façade – *emptiness*. She put up her dark hands suddenly, and covered her face.

Atoon stirred. 'Is your eye bothering you?' he asked softly.

'No, it's very well.'

'We retreat in order to advance, we curve in order to go straight,' said the prince. 'We fight no battle unless certain of victory, we never engage against superior force. They are right.'

'Yes.'

'They keep us alive.'

Across the uncut lalang of the deserted garden they could see lights coming out in the blue of the evening: mellow lemon and amber, patterned by marble. It was the Dapur, the women's quarters. The silence behind those fretted walls ruled Jagdana, as the silence in the centre of every household ruled the Peninsula. Women did not care for talking; it did not suit their

25

way of life. In all her long contention with the Hanoman Dapur, Derveet had never seen their faces, nor heard them speak. She had knelt in the antechambers waiting, for a message pushed under a screen or whispered to her by one of the boys they kept in their service. Silence, and the rustle of silk, the chime of an ankle chain. . . .

She could not go in. When a young woman is judged old enough, perhaps two years after the *darah pertama*, the first blood, she is entered by the men the Dapur have decided are most suitable. If she fails to conceive after a certain time she must leave the Dapur, which is the garden of life. Derveet had failed. Circumstances were against her (it happened on the Black Islands) but rank imposes obligations: Garuda couldn't complain. So the Royal ladies of Jagdana, and any Dapur women anywhere, could keep Derveet at a distance and bar her from that 'hidden knowledge' she had so rashly demanded.

Derveet knew more than most people outside the walls about some of the Dapur's mysteries. She had studied history that was discarded as myth and found glimpses of an incredible world, where control of life did not mean making boys or deciding who should enter a young woman – it meant that the very elements that made living creatures could be manipulated at will. The stories that were not completely fabulous were ugly, even though they were surrounded by wonders to match any rumours of the Rulers' shining islands; ugliness that explained perhaps the Peninsulan horror of human deformity. But long, long ago the women had turned their backs on those design and control roads, and on every kind of false control of the world. Derveet was glad, though that revulsion had led, inevitably, to the endless defeat. She would not have wanted to revive that knowledge.

The Dapurs of the present had different secrets: their boy-making; the *jamu* – drugs – they used for healing, which somehow no one outside could discover; their uncanny way of communicating with each other – their way of knowing, when they chose to know, what the Koperasi were plotting. Derveet's grandfather had hinted to her about some enormous mystery concealed in the silence and stillness of the garden. She did not really understand. When she asked for 'hidden knowledge' she was asking for the hoarded wisdom of scripture and memory,

26

and the skill and foresight of trained minds tempered by seclusion. . . .

But now she knew. They had treated her burns in a kind of suppliants' house, outside their walls. She remembered blackness, pain and a voice – inside the pain, not outside – *You are not a man or a child*, it said. *We will not overrule your mind. You will heal yourself. . .* and then they made her search her own seared tissues, from the inside, tracking down the damage and persuading the connections to reform, to grow back to wholeness. . . . *Be warned you may still lose your sight on that side*, the voice said, before it left her in the end. *Nothing repaired is ever quite the same.* They meant secrecy.

Derveet understood that if she had been a boy or a man she would have slept and woken with the burns healing, relieved to find they were really quite minor. Because the Hanomans wouldn't do that to a woman they had been forced to trust her after all. In a way they were safe. She would never be able to go where they had taken her on her own. They said 'you will heal yourself' but she realised that that was impossible. She had not been brought up in the Dapur way, and her mind was fixed now, she was shut out. *Why* do you keep it secret? her heart demanded. Why can't you use this power the way I've asked you to? It would save our lives – But she knew the answer: *Reach for the wholeness*, said the voice in her mind, and she reached out, for the small purpose of recovering the small miracle of her own eye, and she glimpsed, only glimpsed – only touched with her fingertips – the wholeness, the brightness, the real mystery that kept the Dapur wrapped in stillness and silence, beside which war and destruction passed like the flicker of an insect's wing. . . .

And now she accepted that the Dapur of Jagdana was never going to give way. She had done nothing but harm with her meddling here: it was just cruel of her to pester the poor mountain people further. How often had her grandfather told her: *Submit – it is the Dapur's only word. And it is true. Believe me child, I swear it. You will never know a day's happiness in your life, not an hour's, until your will is broken.* (Supposing I don't want to be happy? she had demanded angrily. But he only smiled.) She got to her feet restlessly and leaned against a pillar with her cheek pressed to the worn gold, gazing with wide black eyes full of rebellion and longing at the quiet lights in the dusk.

'What will you do?'

Atoon did not know exactly what had passed between Derveet and his family, but he knew that she was leaving, and would not be going back to the polowijo.

She had already decided. At the southern tip of the Peninsula there was an island called Ranganar, where a colony of women from several states had built a city. They called themselves the Samsui. They had started out as reformers, apparently, trying to recover the purity of ancient customs. But they had fallen under the sway of the Rulers and the Koperasi long ago. The city was built on vice and shame, and was hated wherever independence still flickered.

'I will go to Ranganar.'

Atoon looked at her, and then glanced away. 'Oh, of course,' he agreed softly. 'Why not? You could always become a night-club entertainer.'

There was a short silence. Derveet stared into the garden. Atoon bowed his head and rubbed his hand across his eyes wearily. 'I beg your pardon, madam. I forgot myself.'

It was getting very dark. At last the boy came back and fidgeted in the shadows. It was time for Derveet to leave. Atoon stood up.

Derveet looked at him, standing in his frame of faded blue and gold. She smiled crookedly. 'The chained,' she said, 'are luckier than the unchained. If you are chained, it means you have a place to sleep. You'll have to find yourself a new dealer, I'm afraid.'

The prince did not smile. He went down on his knees and touched her feet and stayed there, bowed, in a graceful gesture of loyalty and mourning for the lost cause.

To the south of Jagdana capital a thick wood, the sacred monkey forest, grew almost to the city walls. Just inside the trees, by the roadside, was a glade where a giant waringin, or banyan, grew. It was a famous creature, endowed with a powerful personality by the Jagdanans: unguessably ancient, hollow as a rotten tooth. It was a meeting place and landmark. Lovers and children hid themselves in the arches and caverns of

28

its trunk; old boys sat and gossiped in the shade of its hanging branches, surrounded by the endless cool whisper of its leaves. . . . In its old age the waringin had acquired a new significance. The *amuks*, the mobs, always seemed to find their way here, whatever they were up to.

There was a hari darah moon, a left-hand sickle rising bluish-yellow and crooked. Hidden in the trees beside the waringin glade Derveet sat smoking a green skinned cigarette, on horseback. The horse was a young black gelding called Bejak: a present from one of the achar dealer's customers. A fine-looking beast, he would have been kept as a stallion, but black all over was considered hardly decent in a male animal: it was the woman's colour. The night was uncannily quiet. Not a sound from the city, so close at hand. Peninsulans worked twenty-four days a month and rested on four. This had been the first rest day. The citizens had a breathing space, to keep in their houses and recover. They would have forgotten everything when they came out again, or so it would seem. They had a miraculous way of getting over these outbursts.

Derveet rarely experienced the flow of blood that should mark hari darah days. She had no magic to protect her now. She shivered in the warm night and slipped from Bejak's side. He was trembling, he did not want to go any nearer to the glade. She put her arm round his neck.

'Oh Jak, dear Jak. Trust me – '

Alat was still alive. They had tied him to the tree and left him. Blood, black in the moonlight, was on his face and ran in caked rivulets down his pale outstretched arms and sides. A blot of darkness masked his groin and thighs but he moved. She saw the body shift, trying to ease itself. Not a sound – She took the knife Atoon had wanted and stepped forward, crossed the space. She couldn't look at his face, she couldn't speak. She put herself against his side to take his weight when he fell, and attacked the thongs. The eyes just beside her face gleamed as they stirred, the caked lips parted.

'Who are you, Sir?'

'No one,' said Derveet shortly. She had no womanhood, and no name now in this country. Let him call her what he liked.

'Then, no one, in God's name set me free.'

'I'm trying.'

29

'No. *Set me free.* Have you no pity?'

She stopped sawing at the thongs and looked into his eyes. She wanted him to live. Mutilated, tortured, humiliated beyond bearing, she would *make* him live if she could. But there was his question, and the darkness, and an agonised human spirit trapped behind the mask of death.... She stepped away from his side, and turned the knife around.

'Ah – ' said Alat. Something scraped hideously, and a gush of warmth fell suddenly over her hands.

Uncertain what to do with the knife, she left it at the dead man's feet. She walked into the trees. Bejak followed her, tossing his head a little and sniffing at jutting roots as he picked his way. She found a little runnel of water by the sound, knelt down in its soft bed of rotten leaves and rinsed her hands. So that's what blood feels like, she thought.

Where was this cause leading her? Farther and farther from the gates of the garden of life. Shame and bitter self-reproach, that she had kept to herself for Atoon's sake, flooded over her. She bowed her head on her knees and sobbed, without tears, for a few moments. She loved the Dapur. She understood it in her heart. The silence and the stillness, to live in the world like a leaf or a stone, innocently at one. It would not be easy, it would not be nothing to do that – it would be immensity.

But why could they not see what was happening? All over the Peninsula there were these horrible fits of mob violence; and the suicides of the gentry. And young women, failing to conceive, were leaving the garden and going, in despair, to Ranganar and other sore-spots – Koperasi bases. Was it because the Rulers had abandoned their property? They left everything now to their hateful and destructive agents, the Koperasi renegades. The disease was not new. She believed it had started after the last reckless war of rebellion. It was after that that the Rulers retired to their islands, and were never seen on land again. And then what had been a sore but still a bearable predicament changed, insidiously. It was as if some vital restraint had been removed. Chaos was spreading through the princedoms like cancer and gathering speed now, all the time. Too late for acceptance and the long view. *It was too late.*

She stood up. Bejak came to her at once and snuffled noisily against her shoulder.

30

'Hush dear. What are we thinking of, hanging around near the walls like this? We'd better be on our way.'

Away they went into the deep blue forest night, into the south. She would not despair. She would go to Ranganar.

4   Gress

In the morning Cho got up, and went to look over the cliffs
again. The country ahead looked the same as it had done at
night, a riot of tumbling hills pouring downwards and onwards
apparently without end, without any hint at all that might mean
people. They have gone, they are far away – murmured Cho to
herself. And then the sun came up, jumping into the sky behind
her. Its light beamed down the hills, and Cho cried out. She
had seen something down there, something bright.

'A palace! Divine Endurance, I can see a palace!'

There was a tiny, perfectly regular diamond of brightness
lying in a valley far down below them, and beside it was a
straight line, cutting the endless green.

'A road!'

'Don't get your hopes up. It might be a natural phenomenon
of some kind,' warned the Cat. But Cho was already scrambling
down the cliffs.

It took them quite a while to find a way to that diamond.
Only the twist of earth that had reared up the great cliffs, over
the waterfall of hills, had made it visible even to Cho and the
Cat's sharp eyes. The soft-looking carpet of treetops was a
savagely entangled jungle that seemed to cover the whole world
from now on, without a single break. They gave up living on
things and simply travelled, but still the moon had come back
to the same phase again before they knew they had completed
the descent. Divine Endurance decreed another sleep till the
end of night, since it happened to be night-time. She was trying
to be strict about practising regularly.

The next morning there was daylight through the tangle
ahead. They pressed on eagerly, and then they found out why
the thicket had ended. They were on the brink of a huge, deep
cleft in the ground, slicing straight across their path.

'It's like the day we left,' said Cho. 'But giant.'

32

'Cho,' said Divine Endurance, 'I'm sorry, but I'm afraid this is your road.'

'I am not turning back,' cried Cho. She knelt down at the edge. The farther wall was very sheer. It could have been made by people. Suddenly she swivelled round and was hanging by her fingertips over the chasm.

'Child! That's very naughty!'

But Cho had disappeared. In fact it was quite easy to get to the bottom. There were several foot and handholds. It would have been even easier just to jump, but her conscience wouldn't let her. She stood on the floor of the canyon looking around, and there was a soft thump beside her.

'Cats are meant to be lazy,' said Divine Endurance. 'Now what, child? This is just a natural crevasse. You must see that.'

But Cho wasn't listening. She could hear a lovely soft sound, like the sound of running water but softer and more regular. 'I can hear *music*,' she declared. She began to run. Up ahead she soon saw a blank rock wall, as if the canyon was shut like a box, but before she had time to be disappointed she realised that the cliff on the left gave way: the crevasse turned a right angle. Cho raced round the corner and saw smooth brightness. The palace! But it was not. A little way further, and the illusion vanished completely. In front of her lay only a great, bright, silver lake, with wild jungle all around it, and the little waves lip-lapping quietly on the shore.

That evening, Cho and Divine Endurance were sitting by a fire on the margin of a small, blind inlet of the enormous water. They were not alone. With them was a bundle of wet knotted cord. It sat on a flat stone, steaming in the heat of the flames; inanimate but with a definite presence. Cho had found it as she wandered desolately along the shore. There had been people here. They had made the lake. She imagined lake-admiring parties going up into the hills to stand on the crags and see the diamond shining. But it was long ago, so long that she could detect no trace here. It was only in her heart that she knew. Then she saw it, like a bunch of weeds in the shallows. She knew at once it was the work of human hands.

'It was part of a fishing net,' said Divine Endurance.

'Yes. They must have been playing with the fishes. I wonder why it does not mend itself into a whole net again?'

Divine Endurance kept quiet, and the child soon found her own answer.

'Perhaps it's Art.'

Their supper was a rat, not a squirrel; thicker in the head, with different teeth and a thin tail. Cho turned it on its sticks and smiled at the fire. She felt very peaceful now. She would be happy to wait for the people to come back here, no matter how long.

Divine Endurance was not feeling so contented. She had never worried about the state of the gypsies – the poor we have always with us – but this fishing net disturbed her. Was it a general indication? Could it be that all the people had turned into gypsies now? She had never thought of that. She wondered what sort of place Wo might have, in such a forgetful world. Be careful, said the scrap of flotsam to her. Approach with caution. They dutifully ate the rat, and then lay curled together by the embers, listening to the water music and the quiet night.

'Don't move – '

Cho felt Divine Endurance's nose touch her cheek. She opened her eyes, which had been shut to appreciate the delicate touch of early sunlight. The tonguing water near her face was rocking wildly; and soon she saw why. Thirty-four heads on thick necks were forging through the silver surface. Their ears were placed right on the crown like a cat's or a rabbit's, but the muzzle was long and the whole a lot bigger. All seemed to be moving in concert. For a moment Cho thought she was going to see something stupendous, but the heads approached the far side of the inlet and separated, shouldering water aside, producing long legs, glistening backs and trailing tails. 'Horses,' said Divine Endurance. 'Exactly what we need. Come on.'

'Oh please let's not. We did eating last night. And they're so *big*.'

'Idiot child,' said the Cat. 'I'm not talking about food. I'm talking about information. And local colour. Come along, and bring that net.'

They set off round the lake. The Cat said it would be foolish to get in the water. The horses would not like being copied and followed. On the way, she explained what was on her mind. The bit of fishing net said they were now approaching the places where people lived. She knew what Cho was feeling: lazy

34

feelings that there was nothing more but to wait to be fetched. It wasn't good enough. Suppose the people never came back? They have a way of never coming back. No, the right thing to do was to go on and seek them out. People admire horses, horses often live with people quite intimately. One of these thirty-four would be the ideal companion, to guide Cho and the Cat into the world and make them look just like everyone else.

The animals had settled where the lake, in some past retreat, had left a tract of rich, black mud that was now growing good grass. Cho and the Cat watched.

'Divine Endurance,' said Cho, 'I'm sure your idea is good, but it won't work. If you ask creatures like mice and so on to play with you they never will. They always have things to do – I've tried.'

'Hush! They are wandering on, aren't they? There is more grass on the other side of the next bit of thicket.'

When the horses began to pass through the neck of tangled trees that separated two grassy beaches, Divine Endurance and Cho were there already. The Cat had made Cho lay a trap on the path, made of the unknotted fishing net. Cho argued about breaking the peoples' Art: by the time she gave in she had to be very quick about undoing it and hiding the snare. The horses came through. Divine Endurance picked a little yellowish mare with black legs. She looked different from the others. She had rubbed places on her shoulders and her tail and mane, though free now, had once been cropped. Cho tugged her cord. The little mare stumbled. She struggled, while the other horses passed by indifferently, but not for long. She knew she was well caught. She bent her head and bit at the snare.

'Good,' said Divine Endurance. 'A bright one.'

They went away and left the mare to think about things. The rest of the herd began to leave the lakeside and gradually disappeared, moving south and west. Two days passed. The prisoner could reach grass and water but she could not get free, and her friends had abandoned her. Eventually the Cat decided it was time, and she and Cho went back. Cho wanted to apologise and explain it was only to get her attention, but the Cat wouldn't let her. The little mare heard them and faced the rustling truculently, determined to sell her life dear.

'Hello,' said Cho. 'Do you know anything about people? We

35

are looking for some, and we thought you might be able to help us.'

Divine Endurance sniffed at the knotted cord, warily because it was near those sharp little hooves. 'You seem to be in trouble,' she remarked. 'What happened to your friends?'

'It's only to be expected,' said the mare. 'I'll attract anything nasty that's around, won't I? Speaking of which, don't you think you'd better get away yourselves? There are big cats and so on in these hills.'

She had a kind face, and her sturdy calm made Cho ashamed, but Divine Endurance wouldn't let her confess. 'If the child sets you free,' she said quickly, 'which she can easily do, what will you do then?'

The mare looked puzzled. 'Follow the herd of course.'

'Really? They'll think it strange that you escaped, won't they. And you aren't well liked.'

It was clever of Divine Endurance to have guessed that time spent with humans would be a blot on a horse's career. Cho would never have thought of it. The little mare blinked at the Cat, then dropped her head, pretending to graze to hide her feelings. 'It's true,' she said stoically. 'And there's no use anyone travelling alone. You may as well leave me. Off you go.'

Cho got down on her knees and undid the snare. 'You could come with us,' she said.

The mare's name was Gress. She quickly decided that Cho must be a poor, lost gypsy child.

'They come from the end of the world,' she said. 'Over the glass mountains and round the edge of the poison deserts. They've been passing through. We've seen them, over the years, moving this way. Away from something bad that's happening over there. Did you get lost?'

It did not strike Gress as strange that she could talk freely to Cho. She knew from experience she could usually understand and be understood to some extent, and this was an unusually patient and attentive child. She told them that the fishing net must have belonged to gypsies. But she didn't think they were coming back.

'They go west and south, but they don't come back. Not in our memory. I've got a sort of feeling they've all passed now. It feels very empty over there now, doesn't it?'

Cho and the Cat agreed. The east felt very empty to them. The places where people lived and stayed, said Gress, were still far away. She knew, because she had been born near there; that was how she came to spend time in service.

'We can follow the road.'

'A road!' cried Cho, delighted. She had always wanted to see one.

So they set off together. For a while Cho was continually expecting the wonderful road to appear, and then the people round the next corner. But after a few days even the printed trail left by the herd grew vague and fragmented. Gress lost interest in it and wandered, looking for food and pleasant terrain. To Gress a 'road' was what the herd did: it travelled eastward into the empty lands until unnerved by rumours of poison and earth tremors, and then it moved westwards to the luxurious fields of the humans until driven away by horse-catchers and resentful farmers. A lifetime could be spent in either direction without seeing the turn. It was a way of life, in fact, and Gress did not live in a hurry or a straight line, unless under duress.

Cho and the Cat did not press their guide. They were satisfied to be moving in the right direction. Cho felt the journey ahead expand again in her mind. She learned how to assimilate things from Gress and all her herd-memories. She saw the road; mountains and desert and wilderness, still stretching on. Gress told how she had left the people who caught her when she was a yearling, running with her mother. High up in the passes of the hills on the people's borders, she was tired one day of rushing over bare rocks and scree with things banging on her back. 'Someone forgot to tie my legs up, so I left. I came down, and fell in with those others, and we lived east. But it is true, I wasn't really one of the family.' Whenever Gress mentioned humans she always added 'no offence?' to her remarks. She grew fond of Cho, and often tried to persuade her to become an honorary horse and stay on the road and forget about humans. Her high opinion came partly from the fact that Cho never showed the slightest desire, or need, to ride. As for Divine Endurance, she held herself rather aloof, in case the coincidence of their both having four legs gave Gress incorrect ideas.

37

A new development was that they always halted now from dusk to dawn. This was Gress's idea, and Cho thought it was a good one, though it slowed them down. Stillness and the night seemed to suit each other. If the weather was appropriate they looked for shelter, but they all preferred the open air.

One night, when Gress seemed to be asleep, Cho asked the Cat quietly:

'Divine Endurance, what do you suppose happened to the gypsies *we* saw? I *liked* the "desert", but I can see it must be nicer to be up in those shining mountains. Only, they weren't going very fast. What do you suppose they did when the earth wave came?'

Divine Endurance did not answer at once. She was sitting in a neat, round hump, with her paws tucked away. But her ears and whiskers attended delicately to the night. Cho lay beside her, and watched the gleaming half-circle of the Cat's eye, perusing the darkness.

'Divine Endurance?'

'I don't know,' said the Cat. 'I can't tell.' Then, after a pause, 'It would be different, of course, if you were with Wo.'

The gypsies nagged at Cho, but she put them out of her mind because there was nothing to be done. The journey went on; wandering and delaying but always onward, out of the empty lands, towards the distant goal.

5 The Green Ricefields

With Gress the journey was much more interesting. A big river was something to ponder about for weeks, and sometimes she would stop and say, 'Oh, this is South-West Wind. We never travel in South-West Wind' – or some equally curious announcement. It seemed to be something to do with the weather, but it was a mystery to Cho. To her, *bad* weather meant poison rain, earthquakes and scouring sandstorms, and there was never anything remotely like that.

One day they turned from the west forever. It was a dry time, in a country where the dust puddled like red water underfoot, and the great trees stood like skeletons with flowers of red and yellow scattered strangely over their bare, heat-scoured branches. And they turned south. It was quite uncomfortable at first. It felt like walking sideways. They travelled on as before, and it was some weeks later before Gress happened to remark that they had been in the people land ever since they took that turning.

'We're almost through Gamartha now,' she told them. 'This is the beginning of the real Peninsula. Look, you can see the sea – '

They were on a ridge of springy turf, in a country of abrupt white rocks and hanging greenery. Divine Endurance and Cho looked, and saw far off on their right a blue that was not the effect of distance. Cho barely spared it a glance. She wanted to turn back instantly.

'What is Gamartha like?' asked Divine Endurance.

'It's very good,' said Gress. 'Fruit trees and good fields, though a bit slanting. Have you ever had white mulberries? In the middle and down to the sea it is a bit swampy. That's why the people have to keep leaving their cities.'

'They leave their cities?'

'Oh yes, so I'm told. They build one, and then it gets wet,

39

which is bad for the feet, so they go off and build another one. Or there might be other reasons, I suppose.' She added, as her friends seemed suddenly depressed, 'Of course, it's different now. The Rulers have built a city called Nor on the sea (over on the other side, we can't see it) – a special kind that doesn't get boggy. I don't think it matters what the Gamarthans do anymore.'

Gress was relating gossip from her service days. She didn't really know what she was talking about, it just sounded knowledgeable and impressive. But Divine Endurance stared back down the turf, where the ridge was lost in the hills and wide valleys of rich Gamartha. The tip of her tail twitched. After a moment or two she said:

'Let's get on.'

They were now in Negara Kambing, inhabited by goats and curly goats, and bordered by Gamartha, Timur Kering and other places Gress could not remember. Cho was amazed at the number of names; so much detail after the blank empty lands. The next afternoon they saw a bunched parcel of the curly goats in the distance, and something taller moving among them. Cho's heart leapt. Gress promptly trotted off in another direction.

'It's all right,' she said. 'There aren't terribly many of them anywhere, you know. We won't get caught.'

It seemed to Cho that she and her guide had a serious difference of opinion to sort out, but Divine Endurance told her to be patient. 'A city, which, as you know, is a large collection of palaces, is what we want. And it should be one that belongs to people who "matter", don't you think? Let's wait a while.'

Gress spoke of a place called the Sawah down in the south, which she had heard of as a promised land. The people in the fields weren't catching; they didn't matter at all. They were looked after like captured horses themselves, by other people who had things they'd made to ride on and carry goods. The word 'Rulers' featured again in her description. Divine Endurance told Cho this sounded like a good place to start looking for her brother, so Cho resigned herself to wait again.

But Gress had no will of iron. She failed, eventually, to resist the temptation of cultivated land. One fresh, bright morning

40

Cho and Divine Endurance found themselves in a strange place. It was grassland. The grass was all the same height, but it had not been cropped. This was strange because there were little paths in it which Gress followed daintily, one foot after the other. There was a sound of running water in the air. Why didn't what made the paths eat the grass? wondered Cho. Gress seemed to like it. Then she noticed that the little streams they kept crossing were not all running in the same direction. They went up and down and round corners looking playfully busy and organised.

'Is it alive?' she whispered.

It was all around them. She felt it as one entity – the talking brown water and the fervent greenness and the little footways. Divine Endurance said:

'Cho, I think you ought to climb onto Gress's back.'

'Why? To comfort her? She's not unhappy, are you Gress?'

But Gress, admiring the Cat's cunning, thought it was a good idea too, so Cho did as she was told. From her vantage point she saw a thin, reedy sapling with one odd red leaf sticking out of the green – and another, and another. They passed one, and at its foot a stream was changing direction.

'Oh! It *is*! They are here! They are here!'

Journey's end.

The boys and men of Jagdana did not go out into the fields, even near the city walls, without the protection of numbers. They were not allowed to carry weapons, and there were bandits throughout the mountain chain that looked down on the capital, not to mention Koperasi. Besides which there were other marauders, no less savage, where the fields lay close to the hills. As Cho was gazing with rapt delight at the wonderful, mysterious being the people had created, trouble was closing in on the lone child and pony – six large mountain cats and their mate. They were hungry. Gress had been feeding well and looked most appealing.

Suddenly Gress stopped walking, and began to shiver. Something was stirring in the grass. Divine Endurance, lying across Cho's shoulders, made a soft noise in the back of her throat, and began to rise. The grasses parted. A cat stood there, a giant cat.

'Hallo,' said Cho. It did not reply. 'Ah – excuse me, you are in our way.'

41

The giant cat moved a little, fluidly from the shoulder, and suddenly Cho recognised the dreamy expression in its eyes. She pushed at Gress with her knees and managed to turn her. The terrified pony began to run. But there were tawny flashes in the green ahead.

'Surrounded,' growled Divine Endurance. 'Turn back. That was the man, we might be able to bowl him over.' Again they twisted round. Gress was now in such a state Cho had to do everything for her. But the male cat was not alone. Two great loose-shouldered savages barred the way now... 'Can't be done. One gets our backs while we go for the other. You'll have to – '

She said what Cho would have to do. Cho could not take it in. In her panic, with the pack of five chivvying her on, Gress was now running straight at the eldest cat and her mate. Up they leapt together, tawny, mottled, red mouthed, breathing blood....

'Stop!' cried Cho, but they didn't. So she did what Divine Endurance had suggested.

There was not much left of the two cats. 'Good work,' said Divine Endurance. The other hunters had vanished. 'I don't think we need worry about them anymore.'

Cho was not listening. *She had done wrong.* She must not do things for herself; only to help people. She could have saved the situation in any number of ways, if she had thought.... She had no ability to slip under locked doors like Divine Endurance: *Wrong – not allowed, not allowed....* It swelled in her mind, it swelled until it burst. Gress suddenly cried out wildly and bolted. Divine Endurance leapt clear almost at once. A few pounding strides later Cho's body came off the pony's back and flew through the air like a broken doll, landing half in an irrigation ditch, its face buried in the chuckling water.

There was another traveller in the green ricefields that day. Derveet, sometime friend of a prince and suppliant of a Royal Dapur, had been on a journey. She was riding back to Ranganar: a hard-faced, dark-skinned ruffian with a patch over one eye, mounted on the kind of horse only a gangster would ride – long legs, flashy lines and black all over. She travelled discreetly and kept away from roads and Koperasi presence. But

42

indeed the sight of that figure, in the distance, or at dusk in a lonely place, was enough to dissuade most people from rash curiosity.

It was four years since the moonlight in the glade of the waringin tree. They had been bad years for the Peninsula, but good years, in a way, for Garuda. To her own amazement she had found supporters in the collaborators' city, and she was now the leader of a small band of secret rebels, spreading confusion and disruption just as she had dreamed. This journey marked an important decision. The group had proved that the wild idea could work, and they had been anonymous long enough. It was time for their leader to declare herself. Derveet knew the others were right but she didn't want to take this step. Every move she made was still intended for that silent audience watching from within the garden walls, and she was still waiting for the blessing that would never come. While the rebels were preparing for their declaration a rumour came that someone important wanted to see them. Derveet rode at once into the north of Jagdana . . . but it was nothing, only another bandit. He did not meet Derveet, only a brigand like himself, and she rode south again, to keep an appointment.

Derveet had a friend in Ranganar who had wonderful plans for an imaginary future: emancipation, social equality, land reform. . . . But she herself only thought of the Dapur. Any orthodox Peninsulan would tell you: the world outside, of words and actions, is just an illusion. Only the women's life is real. But what would it be like, if that life came out of the garden not in fragments but entirely, and spread over the world . . . ?

Her hands were loose on the reins, she had forgotten her gangster face and was just Derveet, her angry eyes growing quieter as the years went by and the absurdity of everything wore down her rough edges. She was feeling tired and lonely. Ranganar was still an alien city, she could not understand her friend's ideas, and no one shared her vision. . . . But what would it be like? What would it *mean*? To be in touch with reality . . . ?

Bejak shied at something and stopped dead. Derveet woke up and looked to see what had startled him. What she saw was the remains of the two big cats.

43

What did that!

Bejak backed sideways off the path, splashing in the muddy field margin, treading the bright grain. When she had quietened him she got down, with a dry mouth, and looked closer. Then she scraped up the scraps of bone and hair and threw them in a ditch, and scooped water up to wash down the path. She did this very calmly, as if tidying up such litter was quite ordinary. She remounted and went on. But a little further down the path she suddenly said to Bejak – 'I'm tired. I think I'll rest for a moment.'

She sat down on a strip of grass between the path and a stream. Bejak wandered a few steps and browsed. Derveet made herself breathe slowly until she could see – the gold and green and blue and the brown, clear water. Surprised small locals popped into or out of the channel, affronted by her shadow. A slender yellow snake propelled herself down stream, head in air, her scarlet tongue flickering.

Land reform! thought Derveet.

What did it mean? Impossible to tell what the things had been, except that they seemed not human: animals of some sort. That did not seem to make the destruction less frightening. It was meaningless and bizarre, like something done by the Rulers themselves. The Koperasi had not, to her knowledge, any weapon that could wipe away like that. Was this a new development? Or was it, she thought, something worse: a kind of warning. . . .

She stayed beside the stream for a while, letting the great, quiet, living machinery all around reach her and calm her. Old as time, always new. It was like the best of dancers, she thought, whose movements you can hardly see, they are so inevitable. Of course, this could not be a 'warning', not in any direct way. Now that her heart had stopped thumping she could see that. She would go on.

The heat of the day had begun. The indigo mountains, that seemed from here to stand on the edge of the fields, were rapidly being buried down to their knees in cloud. She sat up and gazed, frowning, towards the red walls of the city, glimpsed through the glitter of a grove of palms. She wondered if her friend would sense that she had passed close by. Perhaps he might feel it. She had come so near to Jagdana capital meaning to try and send a message to the prince, but now she dared not approach any closer. On an impulse, she emptied her breeches' pockets and looked over the small collection of objects. In another moment she called to Bejak and was on her way.

6   A Sea Shell

In the coolness of the sunset hour Atoon of Jagdana went out walking. It was a whim: the prince had been feeling out of sorts and had thought it might refresh him to go on foot into the green fields. The young courtiers strolled informally in twos and threes, making a splash of brilliant colour in the rural scene with their sashes and silk *kains*, flowers in their intricate braids, jewels on their golden arms and breasts. Only Atoon wore white; it was not the custom to distinguish between other male offspring of the Royal Dapur and noble youths sent to court by their families. The heir the Hanomans had chosen for Atoon had been sent away from the capital as soon as he was old enough to leave the Dapur. The Rulers' agents insisted on this 'to prevent intrigues'.

Ragged children played with paper kites, wallowing buffaloes stared with solemn eyes, water hyacinths tumbled in mauve crowds in the ditches. The young men admired everything, and pretended to talk knowledgeably about the state of the grain. Someone said the prince was like a still flower in a crowd of butterflies, or like a white stone among quick-coloured flowers. Laughing at each other, some arm in arm and whispering, they began to extemporise little verses about the flowing rivulets and the standing grain, the busy clouds held in the quiet sky. . . .

Prince Atoon moved a little apart from the rest; their chatter seemed unusually irritating. Most of the time there was nothing else he wanted in life except the company of pretty and sweet-tempered youths, but occasionally his own good temper would fail him, and his thoughts would start to wander down the long forbidden paths. The ladies had schooled him well now. He lived from day to day and did his best to ignore the disintegration of his country, of every state in the Peninsula. It was only on rare days like this that something took hold of him, and the very sky and earth seemed full of aching meaning. He knew that the lost cause was still not quite dead, not yet. He had heard of the trouble the Koperasi were having in the occupied south. Brigandry, vandalism – the Rulers' agents tried to conceal any political motive, but the people knew better. These bandits did not rob for gain or destroy out of malice. They were mysterious, they were magical. . . . Others said the outlaw Anakmati was just a criminal, cleverly preying on the peoples' fantasies. . . . It had been going on for two years or more, which would be about right. Atoon had heard a lot about 'Anakmati', that black-skinned villain with the eyepatch, fearless as a demon, riding a big black horse. He wondered exactly what kind of madness she was stirring up in the Sawah. But most likely he would never know. He would only hear, one day, a garbled story of how Anakmati died. And the Dapur would think of an excuse for the court to go into mourning.

His thoughts turned, as he paced unseeing through the lovely grain, to an ugly phenomenon that was spreading from the north. It had started in Gamartha, that country of passionate extremes. Young women, when they failed, were mutilating themselves with acid and scalding water: 'the scouring', it was called, a kind of self-immolation. Could it happen in Jagdana? The idea of the Dapur, *of his own family* perhaps, giving up reason and restraint, cut through his resignation, made his flesh creep. But it was all one of the endless falling, down into the abyss.

A youth dressed in a pattern of deep rose, with a sash of rose and silver, came to Atoon's side shyly.

'Look, prince,' he said, 'look west. See how the sun's colours run through the sky, to be stilled in the arms of evening – '

'Sandjaya,' Atoon smiled, and took the youth's hand absently, but his eyes still brooded on an unseen distance.

'How old am I, Ja?'

'I'm not sure,' said Sandjaya tactfully, afraid this was not a cheerful subject.

'Ah well. They say life is short, but I think it is long enough.'

The young man's hand, which Atoon had forgotten and released, rested for a moment at the prince's waist, on the elegant hilt of a dagger tucked into his sash. It was not a weapon; it was an imitation, made of wood. In other courts nobles refused this mockery – and paid fines for not being 'appropriately dressed'. But the Dapur of Jagdana did not encourage wasteful gestures. Ja touched it as though it were a wound.

'How can I comfort you – ?'

At that moment there was a sudden outcry. All the young nobles and their attendants rushed together to the bank of one of the irrigation channels. Atoon, at once alarmed, went quickly to see what was the matter.

Someone had found a body. It was beyond help. It had evidently been in the water several hours. Two liveried boys lifted the limp bundle onto the bank and the young men all exclaimed. Atoon's first thought was to wonder why whoever had seen it had not had the sense to look away. The child, boy or youth, was dressed in a blouse and trousers of some indeterminate colour. His hair was pale, his skin light. The eyes, wide open under delicately pencilled brows, were dark but had a strange upcurved shape. (Cho's appearance, inevitably, reflected a collision of tastes.)

'What a little oddity,' said someone, and then a silence fell.

Atoon's first thought was now coming to everybody. In these times any little incident could lead to trouble. And though they had had an illusion of freedom for an hour, at the end of the field track the Koperasi escort was waiting to take them back to the palace. The courtiers eyed each other uneasily, and Atoon, watching their faces, felt bitterness and anger rise in his throat. Then someone, having noticed a curious change in the dead face, bent down over the body again, and cried out in astonishment.

'Why – he's breathing!'

All waifs, strays and runaways had to be handed over to the Rulers' agents. This was a very strictly enforced rule. Obviously, the unfortunates went straight to the brutal farm camps in the Sawah, but what could anyone do? Saving one miserable slave or other would not help the thousands, would not change the Koperasi. And this child was not even appealing; sold by his own family no doubt, to give a better chance to the rest. It is the way of the world. . . .

Atoon said calmly, in a voice that invited no questions: 'Someone wrap this child in a shawl. I want him brought back

48

to the palace. My family will take charge of him until his friends can be traced.'

The escort, taken by surprise, clearly didn't know what to do and so ignored the incident for the present. Atoon had the child carried to a room in his own apartments that was not occupied, and then banished everyone. He was smiling as he sent them all packing. He looked so cheerful they were quite amazed. The palace began at once to rattle with stories of the mysterious foundling, whose ugliness soon changed to ravishing beauty. People began to sigh and shake their heads. Poor Sandjaya. The prince, if he had little *rencontres* with the lower orders, was usually so discreet.

Atoon, left alone, smiled even more. He had good reason for his odd behaviour. The Koperasi were devious and never used their claws on the prince himself; they made him suffer by punishing his servants or his friends. He was determined to keep this provocation to himself. But he knew how wild the gossip would be in an hour or two. He was also smiling at the thought of trying to explain to the Dapur this irresponsible whim, this act of reckless daring. He went to the low bed, and began to unwrap his shawl-swathed bundle. The child's eyes were closed now, the features, though spoiled by the light colouring, were delicate and pure. I wonder, is it hurt? he thought, and began to take off the blouse. The material was dry, he noticed with mild surprise, and felt odd under his fingers – probably matted with dirt. He slipped the child's arms carefully out of the sleeves. . . and then discovered the truth. As he stared in consternation, there came a gentle scratching at the door, Atoon jumped up, pulled the shawl over what he had found, and went to answer it. It was Sandjaya.

'What is it?'

'Near where the child had fallen,' said the youth, 'there were hoofmarks. A tall animal, and well shod. And this.' He held out something on his palm.

It was a small sea shell. It had an innocent look, as if it did not know how far it had strayed. Who could have dropped it and left it lying there? Atoon took the little thing and stared at it blankly.

Sandjaya said, after a moment: 'A sea shell, you know, is supposed to be the sign of the bandit Anakmati.'

Atoon had never seen the sea. But somebody had once shared with him her dreams of an island shore: the green, glimmering tide on the black sand at a scented nightfall; the glaring ocean at noon creased by fins like sails. His hand closed on the talisman. . . . Sandjaya bowed and slipped away unregarded. Atoon shut the door and turned to face the couch, and found the child was awake, sitting up and gazing at him with a face full of naked joy.

The prince, his head spinning, said the first words that leapt into his mouth.

'You belong to Derveet!'

The child smiled beautifully. And then, as if suddenly remembering she was not a child, but a young woman, she bowed her head at his confusion, and began to fasten up her dirty blouse again.

Something must have gone badly wrong. He must have been supposed to know all about this. Cold fear gripped him. Had messages been intercepted? But no – the Dapur would have known it. He saw the plan at once. The foundling was to be taken in by the Royal ladies, and plead Derveet's cause for her. It was a good plan, a clever plan. The Royal family could protest quite reasonably against giving up a lost young *woman*, to the slave camps, supposing such a creature came their way, and no matter how unprepossessing her appearance. And that very appearance would lull the Koperasi. They would not suspect the palace of conspiring with such an outcast little creature. A good plan, a clever plan. Supposing, of course, that the ladies would agree. . . .

'There is something I must know,' he asked. 'Before we consider anything. Are you – are you grown up?'

The young creature gazed at him, placidly puzzled, still full of that mysterious joy. 'I don't know,' she said. 'You'll have to measure me.'

There was no mistaking her utter ignorance.

Atoon said, 'Please excuse me. I must – ' and left the room abruptly.

On reflection, he saw why the emissary was such a child. Derveet must mean to get her out again before the complication of entering arose. He paced his rooms, telling himself he was in the grip of a fit of madness. He might be leaping to wild

50

conclusions. And if he was not – it was hopeless. He must go back and tell the child it would not do. The ladies should not even be asked. But his blood was singing.

He went back and found the stranger and a small brown cat that had got into the room somehow. They were both examining his dress dagger, which he had left behind, with what seemed the most lively interest.

'I know what *this* means – ' said the child, holding up the twin edged wavy blade. It was carved in dark wood and inlaid with ripples of silver in a shimmering, ascending double coil.

'Yes,' he said, taking from her hands the symbol of manhood, made into a mockery for so long – '*Yes.*'

She was a well-schooled secret agent. She told him her name, but any other questions were effortlessly deflected with riddles and confusion. And she was careful. At one point he took out a cigarette and absent-mindedly offered his case. 'I think that's medicine,' she remarked gravely. 'I'm not allowed.' He went to her determined to have her whole story and then tell her it was impossible to go on with this scheme. He left her, having learned practically nothing, quite convinced that she *was* Derveet's emissary. He found an old faithful boy, who knew everything about the Hanomans, to wait on her, and shut himself up to concentrate on composing a very important letter.

Of course, before the night was old the new version of the foundling story was about. The palace gossip had to change its tone entirely.

7   Cho in Jagdana

Cho sat on her bed and watched Hanggoda outside in the courtyard. He curtsied to the west, poured a tiny river of water from a silver jug and set red and white flower petals floating. He had told her that this was a greeting to Father, who had gone over the sea long ago. In the evening the flowers and the water were poured the other way, for Father's child, who would come back one day and fetch everyone away to a beautiful place. He did not say whether Father's child was a woman or a man; perhaps it was a boy like Hanggoda himself. The tiny river sank into the white combed sand. Hanggoda arranged the rest of his petals around the feet of the statue of Hanoman the Ape, talisman of the Royal family, and shook the silver gilt bells on Hanoman's stone dancing ankles to draw his attention to the offering. Jing! Jing! Jing! said the little bells. Cho turned to Divine Endurance with a smile of delight.

The Cat shrugged her whiskers, unimpressed. 'Let's go and explore.'

They were allowed to go where they liked so long as they stayed in the balé, the prince's private apartments. Someone had taken Cho's clothes away, because the ladies wanted them, but Hanggoda had given her a long, loose blouse and a sarong – boy's clothes, but they would do for now. They were too big. Cho waited for them to alter themselves, but they seemed rather lazy. Divine Endurance said Gress was hiding, and would not go on without them. She declined to take a message telling the pony not to worry. She said, 'You never know –'

Cho was delighted with this palace. She loved the way all the novelties like *lamps* and *beds* and *curtains* were only a delicate screen between her and the night and day, rock and earth, heat and shadow of the world. Divine Endurance had worried her sometimes by describing something very different. Now she heard real music at last. She knelt on stone by the prince's small orchestra pavilion listening with rapt attention to the patterns chiming and singing, late in the warm night and going on till dawn. The musicians, having heard that the child was a young lady, politely ignored her, and Cho thought they were like the mouse on the hillside, getting on with their own business happily. Dance was rare in Jagdana palace now, but she heard the word often, and once she saw a young man dressed in rose and silver, in a pavilion all alone in the middle of the night, moving about with a strange, sad floating precision that held her entranced, like the music. . . .

From Hanggoda Cho learned – That there were two languages: High Inggris for the gentry, the Koperasi and the Rulers, and Low Inggris for boys and servants. She learned that Atoon really was his 'father's' son (it usually slips out, unless the ladies seriously want it kept secret) but the present crown prince, who could not live at court, was sixteen years old and probably Atoon's half-brother, or else a cousin. . . . The prince wore white because he was the prince. Other men wore the man's colour only to visit the Dapur. Or to go to war, if we did that anymore. She learned that only country people dance with bells on their feet; bells are vulgar – except for the Hanoman prince. (Not that our prince ever dances. But if he should care to he would wear bells, and it would be very dignified.) A sarong is a length of cloth with a seam and must be folded like *this*, around the waist. A kain has no seam, and the loose end must be arranged gracefully, but only men wear it, or failed women. It would be indecent for men to do certain things, so boys look after them. Ladies can do anything, but they are too important to serve anyone; it would be too frightening.

She took in the confused mixture of information and gossip and trivia and sorted it carefully. Just as she had understood at once that she must talk to people in a new way, not the way she talked to the Cat, the moment Atoon addressed her, so she understood she must learn all she could, so that she would be ready to be helpful. The only thing that made her anxious was the *ladies*. Atoon could not be bothered now, because he was 'engaged with the ladies'. Hanggoda had a little pompous way of drawing himself up when he said 'ladies' but Cho felt a shiver behind it. Atoon shivered too, a little bit. She felt the position of the Dapur through walls and corridors and gardens as a large

53

cloudiness. Everywhere around her there were people bustling with needs, making her tingle with the possibility of usefulness. But in that cloudy place it was different. She could not define exactly how, but it made her feel strange.

Atoon conferred with the Dapur. He tried to consider why they had asked for Cho's clothes, but his heart was still singing too loudly to let him think. He went about his normal duties in his usual exquisite calm, but behind the mask he felt reborn. Whenever he thought of the dusty-headed child, who walked into such danger, smiling so beautifully, a new spring of joy rose up. The ladies kept him waiting, sending for him every few hours to continue a graceful, indirect, temporising exchange. But he was sure the balance had fallen. They never played cat and mouse with his ideas. No was their swiftest answer.

Cho and Divine Endurance pattered around their corner of the palace, looking into everything. Without nagging or bothering people they managed to find out a good deal about the social life of the Peninsula, and its politics. They also found a name. It was spoken very quietly, with an eye over the shoulder. Hanggoda never used it, he was far too discreet. But Cho knew it was sometimes just behind his lips: *Derveet*. A boy mason, who was patching up a garden wall, squatted on his heels and muttered.

'They won't have you, you know. They don't like the sound of the word Derveet. Not after the last time, when they put her together when she'd been playing with the things that go bang. You know what I mean.'

'She'd been making fireworks?'

The mason squinted sideways, and nodded. 'If you like.'

Then he heard someone coming, and earnestly attended to his work.

In the room that held Atoon's private library the librarian watched Cho wandering about, peering at the pictures, and said quietly.

'*She* was always in here you know.'

'Who?'

'You know who I mean. Derveet. She used to spend hours, quiet as a mouse, reading fairy tales and scribbling.'

'Ask him about the "Rulers",' said Divine Endurance, jumping on the boy's desk.

54

But Cho said, 'What is a fairy tale?'

'A fairy tale? Well, a fairy tale is like the story of Roh Betina, our Mother, refashioning the Peninsula out of chaos, making the mountains out of clouds and so on. It is an explanation, when the truth is too complicated or people have forgotten. Derveet was always searching for the deep past, before the Rulers, but that's a time of fairy tales. Perhaps the truth is we were dressed in leaves and grunting, as the Koperasi say.'

'Is that what she was writing about?'

'Oh no. Poetry mostly, I believe.'

The librarian was neither old nor young. His Hanoman livery had gently faded from sun and sky to quieter indoor tones; his face was smooth and sad. He looked at Cho with a strange, grave, hungry expression.

'Some of us know and guess more than the family would like,' he said, 'we people of the palace. It is not disobedience, we just can't help ourselves. We can't help remembering her. When she left, you see, she took with her something that we couldn't do without, nor could we live with it: something precious and deadly – '

'What was it?' asked Cho, puzzled by his hungry eyes.

'Hope,' whispered the librarian. 'It was hope.'

Cho and Divine Endurance sat on the floor in their room, sharing Divine Endurance's supper. Neither Hanggoda nor Atoon thought of giving a young lady meat to eat, and Divine Endurance would not let Cho eat leaves or fruit or roots in any disguise. Hanggoda thought the child was fasting for some ladylike reason, and politely pretended not to notice. But he had seen one of the palace cats had made friends with his charge, so they were able to keep in practice from Divine Endurance's dish.

'It's as if we have walked into one of the stories the Controller used to tell me,' said Cho.

' 'There was bound to be some game going on. This is quite an ordinary one.'

Having considered the facts, they had decided Wo must be with the happy people – the Rulers, and not with the unhappy Peninsulans. Divine Endurance urged a quick exit from Jagdana. She thought it was time to go on with the journey and hurry to the Sawah and the place called Ranganar, where it seemed the Rulers were regarded as friends.

'From the distaste these Jagdanans show for the name,' she remarked dryly, 'I imagine it will be much more like the world one was brought up to expect.'

'But Divine Endurance what about all the things these people here want?'

'Exactly,' said the Cat. 'Obviously, the sooner we get you to Wo, and the whole thing is sorted out, the better. We will have to think of a way to make these people tell us to go.'

Cho was puzzled. Of course, Divine Endurance was not present when Atoon told her the wonderful news, but it was strange that the Cat had not noticed anything different. She did not argue: she felt a little shy. But she was convinced, deep in her conscience, that she was right and Divine Endurance, strangely enough, had got things wrong. The Cat went away, to check up on Gress. Cho sat on her bed through the flower-scented night, wondering and dreaming about *Derveet*, who spent her days here once, making fireworks and writing poetry, and reading fairy tales.

In the morning prince Atoon came to take Cho to the Dapur. Hanggoda had poured water over Cho, and rubbed it off again: a pleasant game that he was very fond of. It had been more austere this morning: 'Ladies do not use scent,' said the boy. He dressed her in thin underclothes, and then a pair of thin, soft trousers in a pale violet colour and two blouses, the same but slightly different shades. The top blouse went almost to the ground and covered her arms and throat completely. Then he wrapped up her hair and ears and forehead and mouth and nose. She peeped interestedly out of hiding, wondering what would come next. Prince Atoon was there. He was dressed in white as always, but it seemed a heavier and a richer whiteness. His hair was wonderfully braided on a filigree silver frame behind his head; his eyes and mouth were painted dark and rose in his pure golden face. In her veils, she felt rather than saw how the lovely prince knelt, and put something delicately round her.

'This is the sash of silence,' he said gravely. 'Hyacinth colour, for your childhood.'

The long, fine cloth was bound around her closely, from

56

breast to thigh. Then he took out from his own sash something that chimed and glittered. It was a silver chain, with a plain anklet attached to one end.

'This is the –' The child did not stir. The sudden strange hesitation was his own. 'It is symbolic,' he said. 'We men, we are the chain. We hold you back.'

He saw the expression on Hanggoda's homely face and recovered, bent forward fluidly from the waist and fastened the shackle on her little ankle.

Now began the journey to the Dapur. They went very quietly, by the private ways of Atoon used for his own night visits. Hanggoda, Cho knew, was thinking of the 'great occasion' when a young woman, before she is entered, parades all round the palace. The initiate would be under a veiled umbrella, the crowd would see only her feet, but it was a great feast day. Throughout the entering the celebrations went on: music and dancing and puppet shows. Later, the lady would either go to another court (if she could get permission to travel) or stay in Jagdana and receive the usual decorous visits – depending on what the Dapur decided. Unless, alas she had to go away. . . . Cho kept seeing on the passage walls that sign, the twisting silver lines that she had recognised in Atoon's ornament. She knew what it meant, it meant life. All life comes from the double helix. *Even me* she thought, and she was stirred and thrilled. She had discussed this with the Cat, she knew that really it was like that lake shore: only the sign remained. The people had lost interest and gone away from what it used to mean. But still she hoped: in the cloudy place there might be someone –

She walked with tiny steps beside the prince, the chain held in his hand. Through fretted windows she glimpsed a pair of white oxen pulling a mowing machine over a smooth lawn, a group of courtiers strolling like slow butterflies on a terrace of coloured stone; a secret spire of some hidden pavilion rising out of dark jewel-flowered trees. . . . How strange, she thought, that just a piece of cloth makes the world so much bigger. Hanggoda had told her that the sash and veil were to protect people from the frightening importance of a lady, but now she understood that they were a discipline, to help the wearer to concentrate so she would not lose her sense of proportion in the

57

confusion outside the garden. Inside is the greater world. Outside is the real constriction.... She remembered Hanggoda telling her as he did his little ceremonies: 'Father is imaginary really. We all know that. But it would be wrong for us to try and go any further, out here....'

As they came close to the Dapur more and more of this new information and explanation came to Cho. But to her distress she found she couldn't take it in very well, because of the strangest feeling – But it must be all right. People were bringing her here. Atoon stayed in the outer garden, it wasn't the right time of the day or month for him to come further. Cho, with Hanggoda carrying her chain, walked down a cool shadowy cloister with sunlight at the end of it.

She saw flowers, and two children playing with a white monkey. Their small bodies were so long and pliant in the binding sashes they looked like two pretty caterpillars. At the far side of the small courtyard a gauze curtain moved in a doorway and Cho saw a slender golden hand, the fingers banded with silver. And then – nothing more.

Hanggoda saw her fall to the ground. He ran forward with a cry of horror and indignation – quickly stifled, and dragged her away.

'It is nothing,' said Atoon, very calmly. 'No need to be alarmed. The poor child has seizures. We will apologise to the ladies for the disturbance, and no doubt they will send someone to give her attention –'

But he knew, and the faithful old servant knew, that this was a disaster.

By noon it was all over the palace and out into the streets, that the foundling prince Atoon had tried to introduce to the Dapur was a failure, not a proper woman at all. In fact, probably a monster. The ladies, in their indignation, had struck her down with a flash of lightning. Before noon, Atoon had done what he could. He had sent a message into the hills, to the only people within reach who might help Cho. He hoped they would come in time. When he had done that he sent, grimly, to the Koperasi office. But they could not reinforce the street patrols, they said. They were willing to take the foundling into protective custody, but otherwise ... 'Big brother suggest little brother fix-up fix-up him clean the house boys.' What a jargon they always made of the 'lower language'. Atoon read the message with a cool smile, and set to work to marshal his unarmed courtiers and frightened servants. That evening and the night passed quietly enough.

Cho was left alone, entirely alone. No one even brought her a tray of roots and leaves. They had fastened the door. They had put her away and didn't want her again. What had she done wrong? There was a lot of muttering and running about in the palace but she didn't like to try and find out why. At last, as a heavy twilight fell suddenly on the second day, Atoon appeared. His hair was dressed plainly, all his richness was gone. A boy with a tray did not want to come in until Atoon spoke sharply. He drew down the blinds, lit a small lamp and left again. It had been a hot, close day. The heat remained but now a wind was rising.

'I am sorry that you have been neglected,' said Atoon. 'I did not know. I could not come to you myself, and the household has been disturbed.'

She was sitting on the floor, wrapped in her bed cover. Hanggoda had taken the Dapur robes away, and she felt the need to hide –

'Can you tell me what I did wrong?' she asked sadly.

But Atoon could not. He said, haltingly. 'The people believe – well, a young woman who finds when she is entered that she cannot bear children has to leave the Dapur. The people believe that you are like that, and the ladies knew it, and – rejected you.'

'Oh.'

Atoon could well believe that his family had the power to knock someone over without touching them. But *why* would they do that – even should they feel insulted – especially in such a delicate situation, and after long and careful consideration of Cho's mission. And yet, he could not imagine Derveet, crazy though she might be, using a child subject to fits as a secret agent. Nothing made sense. And the worst aspect was that the ladies, since the incident, had not communicated with him in any way. But for now there was the child –

'Cho,' he said, 'Don't blame yourself. You did nothing wrong. Perhaps you were not better from that fall in the stream, perhaps that was it. You did your best anyway. It was just a

59

twist of fate. But now I have to get you away. I have sent a message. We will leave in the night and just hope the people I sent for make the rendezvous.'

The child's face had brightened considerably, but she looked puzzled.

'What does *entered* mean?' she asked. 'Like entered in a competition? I've learned about those.'

Atoon could not deal with this. He jumped up: 'We must get you some clothes –'

And then he saw on the couch a blouse and trousers like the ones she had been found in. The stuff was pure white, the make and weave unmistakably fine.

Prince Atoon stared. 'So this is their answer –' he murmured. He still did not understand. And yet, he began to see –

'A boy brought them,' said Cho. 'But he didn't tell me to put them on.'

'You are honoured,' said the prince softly. 'Put them on now.'

It was no time for ceremony: he just turned his back while she dressed. Then time passed. They both ignored the tray of food. Atoon sat and looked at Cho wearing her white clothes with a beautiful expression in his eyes that made her forget all the upset. She knew that she had been useful, to this person at least. The scent of the lamp rose sweetly, darkness deepened, the wind rattled the blinds.

'What are the things,' asked Cho, 'that men are not allowed to do?'

'To light a fire,' answered Atoon, automatically. 'To prepare food, to weave, to work in the fields, to build a house, to rear children. The essentials of life. But the ladies don't want to be too involved with us, for various good reasons, and so they make boys.'

'Then what *may* you do?'

'Oh there's sport, literature, various pastimes. And we are allowed the Dance, if anyone had the heart for it nowadays. And there was war.'

A troubled murmur had begun to grow, somewhere outside, like a muttering storm.

Atoon smiled – 'And of course, I govern –'

60

'Couldn't you get your friends in the Dapur to teach you the "essentials"? When you visit them?'

Atoon stared. He thought of curtains, veils, darkness: a brief event, at first alarming, then made acceptable by repetition. What world does this child come from? he thought. But all he said was, gently, 'No, Cho. I don't think so.'

Divine Endurance came bounding through Cho's door.

'You're not supposed to do that,' said Cho. 'You're supposed to get someone to open it for you.'

'There was no one about,' said the Cat. 'Come quickly. I have Gress waiting. The crowd is coming. They want to mistreat you, and unless you have more control over your maintenance than I imagine we are all going to be seriously embarrassed when they try. They wish to perform an operation called *scouring* –'

Atoon had been looking the other way when the Cat came in. Cho turned to him and asked:

'What is scouring?'

But he did not have to answer. A deep sound had begun to ring and ring and ring.

'That is the great gong,' said the prince calmly. 'It means the mob has entered my family's citadel. Come –'

He took the wooden dagger from his sash, dropped it and picked up from by the door things he had left there as he came in: dark, wide shawls to cover their clothes, a short bow, beautifully carved, and a wicker quiver of arrows. Out of the prince's apartments, through deserted gardens and a hall of faded blue and gold; they left the palace by the same route the young Garuda had taken, one unhappy night. All was quiet: the trouble was behind them in the great forecourts. They went underground, and came up in a private house, apparently empty, that leaned against the south wall of the city. A dark figure whispered, and they slipped through a wicket gate. Forest trees tossed their branches over the southern roadway. Atoon took the carved bow from his shoulder and listened to the darkness. But there was no one. They ran into the trees, past the glade of the great waringin and on, through the earth and leaf-scented darkness and the stirred, stormy air. At last they came to a junction where a ragged track went off uphill behind an enormous fig tree.

61

'Up here –'

Cho and the Cat went ahead of him, and they crouched together on a natural platform, the birth of three huge boughs. There was a moon somewhere in the rocking clouds. It glimmered on Atoon's eyes, wide and dark as he knelt with his arrow ready.

'I do know how to use this,' he remarked, grinning. 'In competitions.

'I am twenty-nine years old. I have an heir. God knows the cause is hopeless but what does that matter? Thank you, Cho. I can never thank you enough. You have not failed. I was a corpse walking and you brought me to life. You made me act –'

Cho said, anxiously: 'Twenty-nine *what*?

'Years.'

There was no time for more. Below them great lights suddenly jumped in the dark. The Koperasi patrol, knowing the habits of fugitives, had left the riot to look after itself and come to check the south wall. At the same time there were hoofbeats down the steep track. Atoon groaned, afraid the rescuers would turn back when they heard and saw the Koperasi. But they did not. Shapes milled under the tree. Somebody whistled, and Atoon replied. Someone shouted – 'Quickly – jump!'

'Goodbye Cho,' said Atoon. 'Remember me to her –' and then Cho was down on the ground among large plunging bodies. Someone cried: 'There's another pony –' 'Grab it then. The more the merrier –' Cho heard Gress's voice and cried, 'Oh, please don't. She doesn't like being grabbed –' Something faceless swooped then and grabbed *her*; flung her over a horse's shoulders and cuffed her wickedly hard on the side of the head. It was quicker than a blindfold.

The night of the wooden daggers ended in the early morning hours when the storm finally broke in thunder and torrential rain. Apart from material damage and many injuries of the kind unavoidable in street fighting, the only Jagdanan casualty was the noble youth Sandjaya. He had been too convincing with his wooden weapon, and persons unknown had defended themselves in earnest. The Dapur had his body brought to them, and arranged his funeral themselves. Perhaps it was time for the wall and the garden to pass away, but still they honoured him for remembering his purpose in life.

8   Four Sacks of Rice

Cho woke up. She had been sleeping for most of a long confusing journey that had lasted more than one day and night. Every time she stirred, because it seemed she was wanted, they growled *go back to sleep*, or smacked her again, which she took to mean the same thing. She lay with her cheek pressed against dark, gritty sand, considering. The journey had been in two stages. First they stopped in a murky cramped place, and she glimpsed through the door wooded hills all around. The people discussed Atoon's message, and wondered what to do with Cho, but they didn't want her, so she went back to sleep. Now they've brought me to somewhere else, she thought. They've brought me to someone who knows what to do. I'm wanted again now. She felt excited.

The sand extended in all directions with humps and twists of rough dark rock cropping out of it. There were several people sitting about looking very like the rocks. There was not much light but somewhere nearby red flickering flames jumped and danced. Her eyes followed them upwards into solid darkness: she was in a cave.

Someone said, 'It can't have run after us all the way from Jagdana –'

'Well, who carried it then?'

Cho rolled over and found Divine Endurance sitting beside her coolly washing her ears.

'You've upset them,' she whispered accusingly.

'They'll get over it.'

The people noticed that Cho was moving, and a boy came and took her by the arm and led her to the fire, which was shut in a box with a red hole for the flames to get out. He found a little three-legged stool, looking shy as he produced such a treasure, and invited Cho with smiles to sit down: enjoy the hearth. She tried to talk to him in Atoon's way, but he could not. He showed her his mouth. It was like a snake's, with smooth sharp gums and a little ribbon of a tongue.

'That's an interesting idea,' said Cho. 'Can you catch things like a snake? Can you swallow squirrels?'

The boy only smiled. Then he stood up, and crouched down in a curtsey. Cho saw someone coming towards them: a tall woman. She had a scarf tied round her head, but the hair that escaped was a bright, harsh, yellow colour. The skin of her face was red, and her eyes were blue. Cho stared, she couldn't help it. Somebody prodded her in the back and muttered, 'This is our Annet. Show respect.' But the yellow-haired woman laughed. She squatted down and looked at Cho carefully.

'So, "Derveet's emissary". Well, what can I do for you, Derveet's emissary?'

The rock people gathered round. The snake boy had picked up the leg of a dead animal that our Annet had dropped by him and was singeing off the hair, turning the thin shank over the escaping flames. He smiled encouragingly. Divine Endurance hurried up, and jumped onto Cho's knees.

'Ask her –' she began firmly –

But Annet laughed again and said, 'Don't bother now. Eat. Sleep. I want to think about you.'

She stood up, prodded with her fingers at a pot steaming on the stove and walked away, pulling up her sarong to wipe her hands and revealing long legs that were the same hot brick colour as her face.

So Cho ate and slept with the rock people. They touched her clothes and murmured, and gave her a kind of coverlet. Cho didn't know what to do with it; it was not decorative, and she didn't want to hide, but the rock people laughed at her and said, 'Don't you feel the cold?' They were all out of the ordinary in some way, like the snake boy and Annet. Some of them were very odd indeed: she could not think that all the interesting ideas were good ones.

Eventually Annet appeared again. This time she took Cho out of the hearth cave and along a rock passage that opened on daylight. Below them lay an enormous basin of black sand, patterned with tiny pale paths and scattered patches of vegetation. Steep cliffs rimmed it, small and sharp far away, dark and rugged here. The sky above was a thin clear blue, like

Annet's eyes. A path led down from the cave entrance to the sand.

'Am I in a different country from Jagdana?' said Cho. 'Is that why people are different?'

Annet was looking into the basin. She glanced at Cho, and laughed. 'You're in another country all right. This is Bu Awan, the Sky Mother. You're in the capital city of the country of the polowijo. Prince Atoon sent to my people, to get you out of Jagdana, and of course they brought you to me.'

Divine Endurance had been nagging and was now sitting at Cho's feet staring insistently. So Cho asked politely, 'Excuse me. You did ask what you could do. Please could you tell me how to get to the Rulers?'

Annet stared, and laughed again. 'You'll never see one,' she said shortly. 'They're like God. You can't touch them, see them, smell them. All you can do is try to endure whatever they decide to throw at you – The Rulers, ignorant little Derveet's emissary, live on their "shining islands" off the coast of Ranganar and haven't set foot on land for a hundred years. Are you making fun of me?'

'No,' said Cho gravely.

Annet gave her a glance of lingering suspicion and stared down at the sands again.

'Perhaps it's the Koperasi you want to get to. You know who they are, those big brutes in uniform. A lot of them look like me, don't they? The Koperasi are much more important than the Rulers.'

She smiled bleakly. 'Listen, little Derveet's emissary, since you're looking at me as if you never heard the word "polowijo", or "Koperasi" either, for Mother's sake – I'll tell you. All proper Peninsulans hate anything deformed. They always have. Red skin or three legs, it's all one, except red skin's worse, it's not even pitiable, just disgusting. They always, always have. And so, when the shining islands people came, they found a whole little nation scattered about the Peninsula, with nothing to lose and ready and willing to co-operate. Where would the Rulers be without them? So you see, even though our families abandon us, or sell us to the camps, we polowijo are not to be despised.... It means *weeds*, in case

65

you didn't know. The things the Dapurs root up and throw away. What do you think of my garden of weeds, little one?'

Cho was listening seriously. It was not the first time she had heard 'polowijo' or 'Koperasi', but Annet seemed to know this anyway, so there was no need to explain. She tried to be polite, so far as her conscience would let her.

'Well, I didn't know it happened to people, but perhaps these ones were designed wrong, a long time ago – ?'

Annet looked up, startled. She peered at Cho with a puzzled expression that changed to a scornful smile.

'Oh yes, I remember. That's one of Derveet's crazy stories. Don't be ridiculous. You can't design people. There's no mystery about it, we're just mother earth's little mistakes. I'm a mistake. And you are too. You're a polowijo yourself.'

'No I'm not,' said Cho.

Annet would have laughed, but the childish innocence in those peculiar little eyes was too much for her. She shrugged, and turned back to the wide black sands.

'And so's Derveet,' she murmured. 'She's one of us too.'

There were some people, tiny in the distance, down in the basin. They crept out from the farther cliffs a little way and then crept back. Not wanting to interrupt anything – for clearly this was what Annet had come out to see – Cho waited until they were gone before she asked diffidently –

'Is Derveet here now?'

'No,' said Annet. She seemed annoyed, she didn't look at Cho. 'No, Derveet isn't here. She left us.'

Then they went in. The yellow-haired woman became more cheerful when they were back in the caves.

'That white outfit,' she said to Cho. 'It's cute. I like it. Suits you.'

When she had gone away, leaving them with the rock people again, Cho asked Divine Endurance about what Annet had said. The Cat reminded her that once there had been several different makes of people. The red-skinned ones, or other shades, were simply left over from that time.

'What about the others? *Did* someone design them wrongly?'

'This world isn't like our palace,' said Divine Endurance. 'Mistakes are normal. If there are more than usual now, it could be the remains of something people did to each other. Or it

66

could be something to do with the way things broke down, that time when they went away and left us. It doesn't matter. You can't expect such an old world to run the way it ought to.'

They were silent for a moment, thinking of the age of the world.

'Of course, when you get to your brother, the two of you will be able to sort out all these problems.'

But Annet did not come back, and the polowijo clearly didn't want their visitors to leave. They watched Cho carefully, and showed by signs she was not to go near the passage to the outside. The disappointment Cho had felt when Annet appeared increased. These people were definitely the *outcasts* who had once helped Derveet to make fireworks. But most of the polowijo who had known her had gone away, it seemed, and anyway no one wanted to talk to Cho. They managed to explore a little and found Gress in a rock corral with a few other miserable ponies. She wasn't happy. She had heard that these people sometimes needed meat more than they needed transport. Or visitors.

'I've seen them looking at you in a funny way,' she said. 'We ought to leave at once.'

'This isn't getting us to Wo,' grumbled Divine Endurance.

But how could they leave if the people wanted them to stay? Cho wanted to try and explain that she really wasn't a polowijo, but Divine Endurance pointed out that insisting on this could only give offence.

Cho sighed. 'If only some of the Derveet people were here still. Things seem to change and happen so quickly in this world. Which reminds me Divine Endurance – what can prince Atoon have meant by saying he'd only been alive twenty-nine years – ?'

'Ah,' said Divine Endurance. 'I was going to explain about that.'

But she didn't. Snake boy appeared then, and took them back to the hearth.

The problem was solved in an unexpected way. Another night passed, with a very small amount of eating practice and the undecorative coverlets. Early in the morning Annet came back and took Cho to the rock corral. She fetched Gress, with a rope tied round her head, and gave the end to Cho.

'Come on,' she said. 'Bring the cat, if it is yours, and anything else you had with you.'

They went by different passages this time that sloped uphill. Cho knew they were climbing inside the black cliffs and through the rim of the basin. Gress's hooves clopped and stumbled on the smooth rubbed lava. Soon the air freshened. It was hard to tell when they were underground and when not, for it was scarcely light and they were at the bottom of a stirred pot of frozen rock waves, of fissures and twisted grottos; the jagged, dim sky coming and going in splashes overhead. There was a smell of sulphur in the air. At last they emerged in the open. Peaks stood all around, coloured rose and purple in the dawn. 'Pencak Biru,' said Annet. 'Obeng, Bahtera – the attendants of Mother Sky.'

Cho looked behind her and saw the caldera of the vast sleeping volcano, wider and greater than from the cave's mouth and veiled mysteriously in morning cloud.

'And now look at this –'

Annet tucked up her sarong and scrambled over the bare ridge of ground, and stood looking down. They were on the edge of a secondary crater. But there was no black sand, no vegetation, just bare red screes, steams and shining clays. The far wall had gone, and in the jagged gap a red wilderness fell away, fading in the distance into a tumble of brown and greenish hills. It was an impressive view. Cho sat down and stared.

'Mangkuk Kematian,' said Annet. 'The Bowl of Death. The states meet here. In the west, Jagdana: in the east, Timur Kering. Those hills are the north of the Kedaulatan, that was the Garuda state, the sovereign land. It's called the Sawah now, it's just one big Koperasi farm camp. There was a battle here in the last Rebellion. You used to be able to see bones, before the hot springs dyed them. Half the princes were fighting on the Koperasi side by that time, for various stupid reasons. That's the way the Rebellion ended – we all went mad. The Rulers just looked on, and then left us to the Koperasi. So the Dapurs say: never more. If we go to war again the earth will turn to poison and the sun will no longer shine. Which makes people stop and think, however little life is worth now, because the ladies generally keep their promises.

'Now I'm going to tell you a story. After the Rebellion the Garuda family was destroyed. The Garuda palace was sacked before they built the dam, and most of the Dapur died there. Some escaped, but ten years after the Rebellion the Koperasi were still hunting, and the Garuda remnant finally surrendered themselves and their boys and men, and they were murdered. Only the crown prince survived, a little baby they'd sent secretly to Bu Awan. He grew up with the polowijo, but unfortunately the servants who brought him here gave him a ridiculous education – taught him he was a prince, the Garuda, the last hope. And I suppose the polowijo believed it too. When he was grown up he started trying to plan another Rebellion. He was going to set the polowijo against the Koperasi, that's a joke, isn't it? Worse, he'd got an idea into his head, about certain things the Dapur likes to keep hidden. There is no Dapur on the mountain, we have no secrets here. But talking was bad enough. The Hanomans of Jagdana, who knew all about the polowijo Garuda, sent him a warning that he'd better stop. He did, more or less. Now ever since the prince was old enough for entering, the polowijo had been trying to get children by him, because men are rare up here. But it's hard for a weed to bear fruit. The prince was well past forty, when someone finally managed to give birth to a daughter. The effort was too much for the poor weed, and she died. But having a daughter changed everything for the prince. As soon as she was rational he started his rebellion plans again. He didn't have to listen to the Hanomans, he had his own Dapur, and she – apparently – was as mad as he was. He called her Merpati, the dove, which is an old family name. When she was fourteen years old, a woman, but not old enough to be entered, the Koperasi raided Bu Awan and took her away. They'd found out about the rebellion plans, you see. The Koperasi had learned to be a bit more subtle. They didn't kill our "last hope". They offered him his daughter back. And he accepted the offer. When she died, he left for the Black Islands – but not alone, as you know. Only one thing the shit-eaters hadn't reckoned on: the bloody-mindedness of a young Garuda. They had no idea she'd have conceived from what they did to her. But of course she knew there was no other chance. . . .'

Wisps of steam drifted across the Bowl. Annet, squatting on

her thighs, shifted her weight a bit. A thin ribbon of dust-coloured track curled across the red rocks. There was something moving on it.

'I've told you that story, because there's something about it that always strikes me: the Hanomans must have known. They've always got their feelers out, keeping track of the Koperasi. I'm not saying they organised it but they *knew*. And they let it happen – to save lives. What I mean to say is, if you've got people to look after you have to do whatever you can.

'It isn't the same up here as it was a hundred years ago. Something's happened to the Peninsula, since the Rebellion. It's not that the Koperasi have everyone in their camps: it's more that people take things out on the polowijo the way they never did before. They stone babies, if you can imagine that. The whole area around Bu Awan used to be our sanctuary. Not anymore. We're few, we're hungry, we get sick, and none of us lives long. There's not much I wouldn't do for half a dozen *senjata* less than fifty years old.'

She glanced at Cho sardonically: 'That means guns. Firearms. To shoot animals – I am not interested in shooting the Koperasi. Nor am I interested in any messing about with black powder, white powder, garden cleaner and sugar. I never was. All that business is pointless.

'It's hard enough just to stay alive. My family sold me, a slave camp reared me until I ran away. That's the story for all us Bu Awan people. What are the Koperasi to us? Only the ones who didn't escape. Remember my story. I don't want to betray anyone; I wouldn't betray *her*. At least I hope not. But this won't do her any harm, she's too clever. Times are hard you see. It's all very well for prince Atoon, but he's just got no idea how hard times are. . . .'

She stood up. The movement on the path had been replaced by scrambling noises. As she stood, a head appeared above the rim of the bowl. The figure clambered up and was followed by three more. They gathered together and approached. They were all holding things that were obviously weapons somewhat different from Atoon's bow and arrows, and their faces had a hard and hungry look. One of them was wearing canvas boots with laces, another a sort of jacket with the sleeves torn out and some very tattered ribbons on the shoulders. . . . Annet clearly was not surprised to see them.

They came forward, slowly and warily. Annet nodded to them, and one, shifting his weapon carefully from hand to hand, tossed down a heavy small sack. Each in turn did the same. Annet folded her arms and smiled. And then, with a cool indifference that had something fine about it – even in these circumstances – she picked up two of the sacks of rice, turned her back and walked calmly away. The four renegades came up to Cho and Gress and the Cat and stood around them staring. One of them licked his lips.

'I *told* you,' said Gress, shuddering on the rope's end. 'I *told* you they were looking at you in a funny way. We should have made a run for it –'

But even she could see it was too late now.

9 Crossing a River

Just after dark on the second day they came to a big river. The bridge was a floating one; a raft that was winched across the water on great thick hawsers by a gang of boys. The raft was nowhere to be seen when they arrived, just the hawsers reaching out towards the farther shore, where there were no lights and no one seemed awake. The river was thick and high and smothered, like the whole landscape, in pouring rain. Far away behind them Bu Awan and her attendants had vanished at last; they had been hovering in the northern sky like mirages, high above the lowly wilderness.

The road spread out into a vague area of broken stones, puddles and litter where various vehicles and beasts stood dismally in the wet dusk. Under a big dripping lean-to shelter, travellers of all kinds were waiting for the turnaround. Lamps stood on benches, each white blot of light a smudge of tiny insects, and an unpleasant smell of stale food and rancid oil rose from the hawkers' braziers. The renegades put Cho on a damp unlit bench just under the crazy roof, and sat themselves further inside, keeping an eye on her occasionally. But they had learned that she was very docile, so they didn't bother much. Gress left the pack animals, and tried to join Cho and the Cat, but there was an outcry, so she had to stay outside eyeing the four ruffians threateningly through her dripping mane. But it was clear by now that they were not going to be eaten. Nor were they, as they had first thought, in the hands of the Koperasi — who might have taken them to the Rulers, and Wo. Divine Endurance and Cho had soon realised the truth. They had been sold to a gang of bounty hunters. Cho was the bait in a trap.

The other travellers under the lean-to were a mixed bunch. There was a party of Commercers from Ranganar, looking prim in waterproofs and galoshes; a small detachment of Koperasi in uniform; some more or less respectable-looking boys alone on their families' errands; a few men, commoners or small gentry, watchfully surrounded by servants. Everyone seemed equally ill at ease: travel could be perilous in the Sawah. A handbill tacked to a roof prop near Cho's bench warned that the infamous Anakmati was still at large. Cho looked from group to group. For two days the gang had been talking about getting back to the Koperasi world; the delights of civilisation, but there was nothing delightful here. She didn't like the strong-smelling white lamps, or the borrowed-looking scabby litter that seemed to cling to everything. All the travellers were gloomy and silent. The only sign of life was in a distant corner, where a boy was running to and fro feeding the Koperasi's vehicle from a big tub of fuel. There was someone sitting over by the tub, in the dark, apparently indifferent to the sickening smell of hydrocarbon. This person was playing a game: trying to light a cigarette in the rain and flicking sizzling matches at the fuel boy. He laughed delightedly as he dodged with his splashing jug. Cho saw one of the waterproofed people go over and remonstrate.

The figure in the darkness suggested, in an easy, smiling voice, that the good woman might go and lick herself. The Commercer, startled at being answered in such an idiom up here, backed off. But she had glimpsed the ruffian's face. She retreated to her friends, and muttered. The Commercers moved further away.

One of the bounty hunters had gone off, in a furtive way, to talk to the ferry boys under the winch hut. Evidently arrangements were being discussed. Divine Endurance crouched on the bench by Cho's side, grumbling continuously. It was all Atoon's fault. Of course the outcasts had been bound to sell Cho. 'The man has no understanding of his own world. He might as well have given us to the Koperasi in the first place.' She stared angrily out at the streaming night: 'Why *do* they let it rain like this? They do it out of spite.'

'This is North-East Wind,' said Gress dolefully. '*Nobody* travels when it's North-East Wind –'

The Cat had been trying to get Cho to escape ever since Bu Awan. Now she said hopefully: 'Those red ones in uniform are going south.'

'You're eavesdropping,' complained Cho half-heartedly.

73

'They're not allowed to take that vehicle of theirs across the causeway. It's called an "hc treader". Ah, this Ranganar place is on an island. Perhaps there's another causeway to the Rulers' islands. They live next door, don't they. . . . The red creatures have decided this bridge is broken. They think they'll try another crossing. . . .'

'What about Gress?' said Cho.

The Cat gave her a scornful glance.

Cho was occupied by a strange feeling that she was being looked at. She answered inattentively: 'We were told to sit here. And anyway, Divine Endurance, I don't like that treader thing. It is *messy.* . . .'

Divine Endurance contemplated the hc treader, easily identified in the huddle of bullock carts and scraggy pack ponies. It was a long, squat box of rusted metal, mounted on continuous tracks of articulated treads, with a dented cab in front for the driver and guard. It would be dry inside that box.

The fourth bounty hunter came back and there was an animated discussion. The other travellers eyed the gang resentfully. They felt that 'mountainy' people shouldn't be allowed, but it was obviously pointless to protest. Cho was here to be looked at. A representative of the quarry was somewhere about, incognito, examining the goods. Was she exactly as found? The small cat, the pony, the clothes: nothing interfered with? This was very important. The gang studied Cho and arranged her, and exhorted her to smile, to look pleased, pleased or else they would smack her. They wondered who the connection was and stared hard, with bursts of giggles, at the rubber-coated Commercers. They wondered what Cho, whom they took to be a boy, was to the quarry and poked, graphically, their thumbs into their fists, winking at her. . . . Bzzz Bzzz, they told her lewdly.

The fun was interrupted by a hawker boy, who was going round herding up lamps. Suddenly they realised that the scene around them had changed. Instead of distant uneasy groups, benches were being drawn together to form a single huddle of travellers in the middle of the shelter, ringed with lights. . . . The hawker whispered. The bounty hunters listened, but they were not impressed. They laughed. 'Anakmati!' they cried derisively, right out loud. The other boy winced and flapped his hands; the nervous travellers glared out of the lamplight.

74

'Anakmati is not here,' said the boy in the sleeveless jacket. He put his fists in his sash and strutted, with a complacent wink or two at his bold companions. 'I am telling you. He is not here. Not himself, oh no.'

But the tight, brightly lit huddle did not seem reassured. And something else was happening. The uniformed Koperasi, scenting trouble, had made up their minds at last. They were off to find another ferry.

'Come on – ' said Divine Endurance.

Cho was thinking – Who *is* it that's watching me? The treader started up with a growl, farting gouts of black smoke. Carts jostled and beasts stumbled: it thrust itself out of the parking lot backwards and began to turn, noisily. The bounty hunters suddenly stopped laughing. They had realised their plot was at risk, if something unusual seemed to be going on. The treader, with a final roar, vanished into the dark. Cho jumped up: 'Oh!' The bench beside her was empty. The boys pushed her down again. 'Sit there! Sit! Sit!' they cried like birds, and flapped off in a panic to the winch hut.

Cho was alone. She could hardly believe that Divine Endurance was gone. Divine Endurance had *always* been there. Surely she would come trotting back in a minute, out of the black rain; grumbling and nagging. . . . No one came. The rain dripped from the eaves on the little figure left uncared for out in the dark. So now the journey was really over, and there was nothing between Cho and her childhood's dream. She had upsetting thoughts, of death and brief lives, mysteries and misunderstandings. But she let them come and go. They were not her business. Her business was to make a move. It was hard, it went cruelly against her nature, but it had to be done.

Cho had followed the details of the game she and the Cat had fallen into with attention. She knew she was in a very awkward position just now. She had been worrying ever since Bu Awan. What was she to do? It hurt her to think how upset the bounty hunters would be. They had told her to Sit! Sit! She shivered. She was beginning to learn, in her heart, what chill and coldness meant. She looked down at her white clothes; they were damaged and had lost their brightness. The travellers were engrossed in their fear, there was nobody

75

now in the corner by the fuel tub. She felt very lonely. Quietly, she got to her feet and slipped out into the rain.

Gress had not let herself be tied, and she followed faithfully after. So did someone else. Cho crept through scrubby bushes on the river bank, heading away from the road. In spite of the noisy rain, she soon realised she could hear the crunch of hooves.

'Gress? Is that you?'

It was not Gress, it was a tall stranger, so dark she felt rather than saw him. Someone was at his head holding the bridle to stop it chiming.

'Please don't be alarmed. I've been watching you, and I thought you might be in need of help. Is there anything I can do?'

The voice was quiet, but something about it made Cho shiver again. The rain and the river water beat together on the darkness.

'Who are you?' she whispered.

The horse's bridle clinked and a light sprang up. Cho saw – the ruffian from beside the fuel tub. And now it was clear why the waterproof woman had started an alarm. A dark skin, harsh features and a black patch over the right eye: it was the bandit on the poster.

'It is a kind of pigeon,' said the quiet voice. 'It sits in the woods endlessly saying plonk, plonk, plonk on a descending scale, which sounds so miserable they call it the dead baby bird – Anakmati.'

'Oh. You were looking at me.'

'Yes.'

The one brilliant eye stared at Cho now, again. First at her face and then – with a sudden soft exclamation the light came forward:

'You've torn your blouse,' said the bandit, in a strangely hesitant tone, touching the place with one dark finger.

'I know, I've been waiting for it to mend itself but it hasn't yet.'

'What – ?'

Cho had just realised that the small flame still fizzing in the rain was not a match. It was a firework. Suddenly there were shouts. White light splashed out of the lean-to: people were running and yelling.

76

'That's for you,' said Anakmati, tossed the lightstick into the bushes and jumped onto the horse. Cho felt her wrist grasped strongly and up she went in front. They got down to the water with the hue and cry still milling in disarray around the parking lot. But the floating bridge had started to move at last. The tall horse saw a monster rushing at him. He reared up, into the glare of the raft's big lamps.

'Disini! Disini! – Here! Here!' yelled the ferry boys. The hue and cry came running, yelling, 'Stop! Firearm here! Senjata bullit!' The bounty hunters could be heard shouting that no one was to damage their goods. The senjata were home-made and horrible. One of them went off, vomiting chunks of resin, nails, broken crockery – flinging its owner backwards. Anakmati's mount struggled and jibbed half in the river and half out of it, more panicked by the crowd than by the makeshift bullits. The riders would have been overwhelmed when suddenly, with a wild inhuman cry, someone else thrust into the mob, sending ferry boys and the bolder travellers flying.

'Gress!' cried Cho. 'She was following me –'

In another moment they were in free water, with the dun pony plunging gamely beside them. Anakmati pulled the horse round to the raft and lunged – the boys saw a long knife and all leapt for the far side, but it was the hawsers that were slashed – sliced almost through with two fierce strokes, and the unbalanced weight did the rest.

Uproar and chaos left behind, the two horses thrust strongly into the current and pulled themselves up at last on the farther shore, a safe distance below the crossing.

'That is an extraordinary pony,' said Anakmati. 'How did you teach her?'

'Teach?' said Cho. 'I think she just lost her temper.'

The tall horse slowed to a walk and stood, breathing heavily, getting over the excitement. After a moment Anakmati's arm stopped holding Cho.

'You may as well get down,' said the bandit, 'and ride your own pony.'

So Cho got down.

10 Anakmati

In the hilly north of the Sawah at least as much achar grew on the meandering terraces as any legal crop. Lawless little towns of the weed-farmers sprang up and quickly faded. They were rootless without the Dapur, but new spores were always drifting in. The Koperasi either would not or could not control this land. Much of the low grade 'sawah plant' found its way to the slave farms and helped to keep them quiet, and besides the gangsters controlled themselves, one way or another.

A traveller arrived at Adi's hotel, late at night, alone but for one small servant. A whisper and a shiver of excitement went round the courtyards as the black horse was led away. The desk clerk presenting the nightstay book (for Adi's had pretensions) nearly swooned when the traveller briefly smiled. He wore drab rough silk, well cut, a sash of dull scarlet. His hair in a short braid dangled scarlet cords on his shoulder. So gentlemanly – only canvas Koperasi boots and perhaps too many rings on the long dark hands, gave away the gangster. The clerk pursed his lips faintly at the boots and sighed. They were in a spreading pool of water.

'Sir has been in the rain tonight.'

Sir volunteered nothing.

'May we send a brazier? A small meal?'

'Thank you, nothing. I am tired and do not wish to be disturbed.'

He reregistered; a perfunctory scrawl with his right hand. He had been born left handed and had been trying dutifully to unlearn it for fifteen years. The people considered it, though wrongly, a woman's trait. The boy made a hissing noise at the servant – shooing him off to the kitchen instead of standing dripping in the guests' hall.

'No. Sleeps with me.'

The clerk smirked, and inquired if another bed was needed. He was quelled by a hard glance from that one glittering eye.

Adi kept the best room in the house for Anakmati. The lamps were trimmed and bright, the bed curtains only a little ragged; the rattan screens that gave onto the verandah were in good repair. Adi's personal boys, the junior management of the hotel, carried in Anakmati's one small bag, and left reluctantly fizzing with suppressed excitement. The bandit's servant seemed worried about something.

'I know,' said Anakmati. 'I feel it too. But I would rather not have anything hanging over me.'

The Sawah world had loved and respected Anakmati for years and the bounty hunters were stranded by the crippled ferry. But everyone knew about that project, and the change it meant in the Koperasi's attitude. It would be a shame, but if Anakmati's luck was over, then it would be something to have shared the idol's most exciting moments.

'Let's wait a little.'

He took out a cigarette. He had smoked about half of it, wandering round the room in his wet clothes, when a member of the junior management appeared with a tray: 'Please, please take something. Or we'll be ashamed –'

Anakmati laughed, and accepted the appetising little meal. The boy was a lovely young thing. He gave Cho a sulky look as he went out.

'I hope you are not very hungry,' said Anakmati, and taking the tray into the private washroom disposed of the food. Cho was still standing: 'Sit down –'

She crouched on the floor, and watched the bandit sit on the end of the bed and peel off the sodden canvas boots, and the eye-patch. The eye was not blind. It blinked at the light. . . and there was a subtle change in Anakmati's presence and bearing.

'*Derveet*,' said Cho softly.

Derveet smiled. 'I sometimes have trouble with that eye,' she said. 'I hurt it, years ago. Besides, the patch – er, helps me.'

'It's a game,' she went on. 'Just a game.'

She undressed no further, but sat with her chin on her hands, frowning. Cho examined a dark face with a long firm mouth, angular cheeks and jaw, and a sharp curved beak of a nose. The skin near one of the beautiful eyes was a slightly different texture. Anakmati-Derveet grew restless under this steady appraisal. She got up, and prised something out of her breeches' pocket.

'When I came to Adi's yesterday,' she said, 'I heard that someone was offering something that belonged to Anakmati for sale. Anakmati was to send a friend to look it over, and arrange the transaction. I was curious, so I went to the crossing myself.' She opened her hand, and showed a little round silver gilt object, delicately engraved. 'Do you know what this is?'

'Oh yes,' said Cho at once. 'It's one of prince Atoon's bells. He wears them when he dances and it is very dignified.'

Derveet's eyes widened; her mouth twitched, fractionally. 'Where *did* you get those clothes?'

'It was before I went to see Annet. The ladies gave them to me, when I was staying in prince Atoon's pabrik.'

'His what?'

'Pabrik. Factory? A place where you live. I've never said it out loud before. Is it not the right word?'

'It is not quite the usual term,' said Derveet gravely. 'So, Atoon had trouble, I know that. He passed you to Annet. Who promptly sold you to those playboys. Oh well, I suppose she couldn't help it. I'm lucky she didn't tell them another name for Anakmati, aren't I?'

'Do you have a lot of names?'

'One name. Various titles,' Derveet smiled. 'Which is quite usual, of course, for a person in my position.'

The child, kneeling in delicate composure on the dirty floor, seemed to have no intention of explaining herself. She radiated a bewildering innocence, just as in that sordid riverside shelter. In the neck of her torn blouse pale flesh curved like the petals of a flower. Derveet got up and put the tray out in the corridor. She stood by the door and said, 'Where do you come from?'

Willingly, Cho started to tell. Derveet soon stopped her. She remarked, sounding a little dazed, that people love to exaggerate. She had always heard the east of the landmass was one poison desert. . . .

'Yes. That's true. It's pretty though. It shines.'

'Oh. I see. So – so what did you live on?'

'On the ground.'

For the second time in a few days Derveet felt her affairs

entered by something forceful and mysterious. This was very different, a different order of invasion entirely, but the sense of helplessness was the same. She left the door, and sat down by Cho's side.

'When I was passing through Jagdana a few days ago,' she said, 'I saw a horrible thing. Someone had dealt with some animals in a way – I can't imagine how. There was nothing left but blood.' She meant to say: that she knew these were frightening days, she could understand the evasions, it was hard to trust anyone. She didn't get so far. The quiet face was suddenly wide open, flooded with a child's anguished, abject shame –

Derveet got up at once and moved as far away as possible. 'I'm sorry,' she said. 'I'm sorry –'

A long silence fell. The hotel bustled a little, and settled for the night. Derveet smoked another cigarette and moved around quietly, making some preparations. Her companion was curled up on the floor like a little cat. Derveet thought she was sleeping; it seemed best to leave her alone. She put out the lamps and lay down. Eventually, there was a tiny sound. Derveet opened her eyes. The door was not bolted. Anakmati rarely fastened doors: it was part of his fearless style. The latch rose with a tiny plop and the door floated open. Derveet had left the bed. She walked into the last two intruders – burst a firestick in the eyes of one, and kicked the other in the face. She turned on the one who had come in first. He was big; a man, by the look of him. She was afraid of firearms. The Sawah made its own bullits out of untempered resin that shattered in a ghastly way on impact. But this assassin had a weedcutter. He swung it in an arc – she dropped to the floor. There was a smell of fused sawdust and an angry whining as the blades met some of Adi's furniture. She kicked up into his crotch, took his weight and he fell over her. She followed, rising in a fluid curve, left the ground and brought her heels down savagely on his face. The whining stopped. She hoped he had not fallen on the cutter, or broken his neck. The other two seemed to have vanished. She rolled over, and saw the child, her head raised alertly but not looking at the fight, looking at the garden screen. She herself could hear nothing. She got to her feet and picked up two small

81

armed quoits that she had left on the end of the bed. The screen slipped open.

'Habis?' said an unwary voice in the slice of cool night – 'have you finished?' There seemed to be three or four of them. Silence, and the soft sound of purposeful movement: they took the point, and fled. Derveet sent the quoits after them, and someone crashed in the bushes, howling. Then all was quiet. She went and prodded the first assassin. He was curled into a ball, and groaning. She lit a lamp, and began to pull hard and steadily on the bell-rope by the bed.

The management perhaps thought Anakmati was clutching it in his death throes. For a long time no one stirred. When at last they came running, they found the bandit, eye-patch in place, sitting cross-legged on his bed, playing with the blades of a weedcutter and looking at a corpse. The hotelier himself, a paunchy, ageing boy full of easy good humour, was first in the room.

'Ah, Adi,' said Anakmati. 'So sorry to disturb you all, but could you please remove this?'

The one who had fallen in the bushes now ventured to moan a little.

'– And see to whoever that is in the garden, would you?'

The younger boys, giggling and whispering nervously, began to drag the groaning corpse away. Two of them were the intruders she had singed and kicked at. Adi looked at the floor, and his sliced furniture, and the calm amused face of his guest. He smiled sheepishly.

'Adi, I'm afraid you've been cooking with meat fat. I'm sure there was something in that meal you sent that kept me awake –'

The hotel owner was Jagdanan, originally, and hated any sort of a scene. His expression became pained and reproachful –

'Oh all right Adi. Goodnight.'

When he was gone she closed the screens and fastened the door. She stripped off the gangster's finery at last, and the silk sash that bound her breasts. She sat on the bed wrapped in a sarong with her hair unbraided and falling heavily to her shoulders, and put her face in her hands.

How very far she was from the garden now. The antics of the Sawah made her laugh, when she was afraid they ought to make her cry. She was frightened sometimes: Anakmati might murder or maim someone one day, on the grounds that it was wrong to try to be different from the people. And here in the Sawah was the mirror of the entire Peninsula: flaring loyalties and unreasoning treachery – the whole proud, passionate imbecile entanglement. How can I lead them? she thought. Am I doing right? She had had to learn to tolerate that question in her mind's furniture; like a bad memory or a useless regret, it would never go away. She lifted her head, suddenly remembering the child, and found herself looking straight into those strange and quiet eyes. For a moment she forgot herself and gazed. It was as if a cool hand had touched her fever.

'I am sorry about that. I hope it didn't upset you.'

'Was it something that you are not allowed? Never mind – at least you didn't fall down.'

Derveet smiled. 'I am glad you do not think so. But you've been sleeping in wet clothes. Take them off, and come and sleep up here. Don't mind me. I'm going to stay awake.'

The child undressed without fuss and slipped under the coverlet. 'Excuse me,' said Derveet, just as she was closing her eyes, 'but you haven't told me your name. Would you like to?'

The rain was over, the clouds had broken. The moon had set, but a scatter of stars lit the sky over Adi's garden. Anakmati, dressed in dry clothes, sat on the verandah, unmoving but relaxed. Extraordinary things had been happening to Derveet. After leaving that shell in Jagdana fields she had travelled on, with a strange feeling not so much of uneasiness as of portent: something was happening. She was in the south of the state when she heard of the big riots in the capital, the 'Night of the Wooden Daggers'. The garbled story had an odd effect on her. What had Atoon been up to? Of course, probably he had done nothing: it was just the usual meaningless trouble. She went into town looking for information. There was a disturbance in the streets; she never reached her rendezvous. But someone pushed her in the crowd – a boy, she didn't see his face. She found in her hand Atoon's little silver bell. She held it now on her palm. Atoon – It was an answer to her sea shell. He had woken up. And more than Atoon himself. . . . She thought of Cho's white clothes and a shiver ran through her. It was as if the world, that had always turned obstinately against her, a stubborn, dragging force against all she attempted, had suddenly shuddered under her feet and majestically begun to roll the other way.... 'Chosen Among the Beautiful,' she said, out loud, and smiled. She was still sitting there on the verandah, breathing quietly, only her brilliant eyes awake, when the dawn came and the chickens wandered out and began to scratch around thoughtfully on the dew-pearled lawn.

11   The Sovereign Land

Anakmati and his servant left Adi's shortly before noon in another downpour, and rode away from the earth-walled settlement, with its senjata in the thatch, pungent bales in broken sheds and boy-brothels for month-ending Koperasi. The late rising Sawah world paid no attention: only the boys of Adi's hotel came out, and watched until the tall black gelding and the dun pony had vanished into the misty rain.

At sunset Derveet halted. The sky had cleared. They had left the road soon after leaving Adi's and were in a gully of red sandstone on the side of a hill, facing south with the achar and tea terraces behind them and ahead, apparently without end – a green barrier of savage wilderness. Derveet unsaddled Bejak and sat down and took off the Koperasi boots.

'Now then,' she said. 'I'm late. I have an appointment with my friends near Ranganar, but we're going to miss it because I daren't go by road after this excitment. We'll just have to trust them to rearrange themselves. We'll stop here. It's better to start on the forest by daylight, and I need some sleep.' She frowned at the unpromising green wall: 'Don't worry. I know a good route from here. We won't get lost. . . . I'm sorry. I have just realised that I have not asked you. You do mean to travel with me, don't you?'

Her companion looked up, and smiled and nodded as if the question was scarcely necessary.

'Will those boys chase us?'

'Oh no. There's no malice in it you know. They haven't the concentration.'

She had so many questions to ask this bewildering stranger, it was hard to know where to begin. The interrogation so far had hardly been satisfactory –

'If this is our camp,' said Cho, 'we ought to have a fire.'

Derveet shook her head: 'I'm sorry child. I'm afraid I can't.'

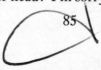

85

'Oh I know about that. Because of not being properly female. But can't I do it for you?'

She looked up cheerfully; she had already collected a little pile of damp twigs. No one had ever put the unfortunate truth to *Derveet* quite like that. She laughed. 'Of course –' she said, fumbling for her lighter, with her face turned to hide her feelings. There was a faint crackling; a wisp of smoke and a flicker of miniature flames rose from between Cho's hands. Derveet looked stupidly at the cigarette lighter she was still holding.

'Oh, that's from prince Atoon –' cried Cho delightedly. It was a worn knot of silver monkeys, with tiny ruby eyes.

In the morning they left Bejak's heavy harness, the canvas boots and Anakmati's rings in a neat pile for anyone who might find them. There were several hideouts in the Sawah and over the border in Timur Kering where Derveet was accustomed to keep the bandit's black horse, between adventures. But this occasion was different, and she wouldn't leave Bejak as a burden on frail loyalties if the Koperasi were hunting; he had better come to Ranganar.

'The bandit disappears,' she said thoughtfully, looking down at the discarded possessions without regret. 'And this time, I wonder, is it forever?'

Down to the sea on either hand the former Garuda state had been stripped and razed, replaced by endless tracts of copaiba, rubber and cane, the farm camps and the straight roads. But Derveet's route kept to the spine of the Kedaulatan where untamed forest, never touched by the Garudas, still defied *co-operation*. The wild green world that terrified the Koperasi was quiet and peaceful and still. The travellers moved quickly. Riding was impossible, but Derveet set a hard pace. Sometimes they had to make long diversions, submitting to the forest's casual obstacles. When the night was clear they walked until the moon had set, following the sound of a stream or one of the mysterious footpaths that appeared, along green ridges of bamboo and grass that rose and fell among the trees. Derveet was as firmly against meat as Divine Endurance had been against plants, but she promised Cho they would not eat anything poisonous. She had dried fruit and sticks of pressed rice with her, and when these ran out they ate what the forest offered. Cho was delighted, she felt just like the mouse by her boulder nibbling its seeds.

Sometimes Derveet talked, as they walked along with Bejak and Gress behind them, about the Peninsula and its history: Snakes and Cranes and Buffalo and Mouse-deer – a whole menagerie all gone now, under the Rulers; and the remainder – Hanoman the Ape of Jagdana, Garuda the Eagle and Singa the Tiger of Gamartha.... 'The Singas, the tiger-cats of Gamartha, ruled before my family took over. They've never forgiven us for being in charge when the shining islands came. *They* would have managed much better, they wouldn't have stood any nonsense.... There are three powers in what remains of the traditional Peninsula, Cho. You've made a great impression on two of them. I wonder what the third will think? We'll have to wait and see.'

Sometimes her voice changed, and Cho would realise joyfully that a story was beginning: a fairy tale.

'There was once,' said Derveet, 'a child who was born to rule. She lived in the garden, within the beautiful walls. She was taught by the wisest women, and excelled in everything, or at least everybody told her so. She was always happy and she never worried about her future, because she thought to rule such a perfect world must be very easy. But there was one path in the garden that she was told she must not follow. One day, when she was already a grown woman, she said to herself: Whatever is down that path, I ought to go and see. So she went down the path. It led to the city gate, so she went to the gate and looked out and saw the world. She was fascinated. She wondered why this important view had been kept from her. But then she saw something lying by the road. It was a human figure, lying in pain. The lady had never seen sickness like that before. She was bewildered. She could not understand why the other people just hurried by, as if the strange apparition was invisible to everyone but her. She went back into the garden and was very thoughtful; she said nothing to her friends. But the next day she went again down the path. When she looked out, she saw the figure that had been lying by the road being carried off, wrapped in a cloth. She stopped a passer-by and asked, "What is the matter with that boy?" "Madam," the citizen replied, "nothing is the matter. He was sick, and now he is dead." Then the lady decided she could not stay in the garden. She could not rule the people unless she could find a way to overcome sickness and death. That night she went to the nurse's room, where her baby son was lying, and she said to him: "I will name you before I go and I will call you Rahula, a shackle, because if anything could keep me back from my duty, it would be you...." Then she left the beautiful walls, and wandered over the world. But since that time, all ladies have worn the *rahula* in memory of her.'

They were following a small river, that ran between cool dark rocks in a narrow gorge. Derveet lay on a big boulder to look into the stream.

'And what happened to her?' asked Cho. 'In the end?'

'In the end? Oh, there was a shaven-headed nun whom I missed out because we do not have them nowadays, we have nightclub entertainers instead – and there were many adventures. They say she came back to the garden at last, by a different way....'

She told stories too about Ardjuna, the exiled prince, who was so elegant and well mannered ladies not of his own family were always wanting him to father children. This lead him into an endless series of absurd scrapes, with pretty youths and boys sent out to entrap him, as he wandered the princedoms.... 'In real life,' said Derveet, grinning, 'Ardjuna hates travelling. He says it makes his feet spread, and he can never get his hair done properly.'

Once, passing through an open glade, they came too close to a nesting place and were suddenly assaulted by a storm of colour: a whirl of gold and indigo plumes. 'Chack –' said the forest hen, sitting quietly and resolutely in the shadows, and the cockbird arced his wings and offered his throat of violet, his breast of crimson; just as he had paraded them in the other glade where he was chosen, not understanding then what it was for, his beauty.... 'God bless you,' said Derveet softly, and turned to hide the frightening glint of her eyes. 'Yes –' echoed Cho, thinking Derveet might be God, by another of her titles, and they went on. Cho listened, and remembered everything. She knew that Ardjuna was Atoon, and also that other prince, the baby called Rahula, was Atoon, and also in a way the rainbow bird. And the Dapur, cynical and tricky in the

Ardjuna stories, was also the desired garden, and the resolute waiting eyes in the shadows. She thought of these things and pondered them, in the black darkness of the night, when the two horses shifted about like invisible monsters: insects sang; a leaf fell with a sigh like thunder, and Derveet lay sleeping, her head pillowed on her arms on the soft ground.

For six days and nights they moved quickly southwards in perfect security. On the fifth night, the moon that had been thin and young when Cho left Jagdana came to the full, and Derveet missed her appointment, for she was supposed to meet her friends on the morning of the fourteenth of the month. But she assured Cho there would be no problem, perhaps also reassuring herself. This had happened before, and things had worked out. After that, however, the peaceful journey ended. On the seventh day the forest, which had been growing less dense, had changed completely. The great trees were still all around, but they seemed unsure of themselves and the silence was broken by a faint disturbing murmur: the Sawah at work in its camps, on its roads. That night Derveet tethered Jak for the first time.

The next morning they breakfasted on earthy groundnuts and a hand of wild bananas with pink seedy flesh. Derveet seemed sad and not only, Cho thought, because of the end of the forest. They had not been walking long that day before they came out of the trees into a broad open ride. It vanished, to their right, into swamp and elephant grass but to their left it led away, straight and true, with deeply incised banks rising on either side, half lost in young trees and undergrowth.

Cho stood, feeling the heaviness in the earth underfoot. 'Is this a Koperasi road?' she asked.

'No,' said Derveet.

The road was green, its pavement buried deep. But there were shapes among the trees on the valley sides, and there was an atmosphere Cho recognised. Several other rides intersected. Cho looked down them curiously but Derveet was uneasy. There was a feeling now that people were close by, and might appear at any moment. At last they came to a place where two pillars stood frankly at the top of a green ramp by the side of the road. Derveet led Bejak up and Cho and Gress followed. They entered a square space. It had been walled in wonderfully faceted black stones, most were fallen now, but there were rough repairs of stakes and thatch, so the sanctuary still had some privacy. There were platforms with steps, some of them roofed in thatch to protect the remaining carvings: Cho stared.

'Roh Betina,' said Derveet, 'The Mother of Life, directs Hanoman the Ape and Gardua the Eagle in remaking the Peninsula out of chaos. That pointy thing under her left foot is Bu Awan –'

The mother of life was carved like a hideous demon, to give some sense of her terror and her power.

'They are dancing.'

'Of course.'

Derveet was looking round the sanctuary, on the sculpted altars and in the niches of the walls, but she couldn't find what she was searching for, and gave up, frowning a little.

'Come on. We'll leave Gress and Bejak here.'

As they went up the road, the atmosphere Cho had recognised quickly gave way before a very different feeling. The straight way had been gently climbing. They came to the top of a rise – ahead of them the vista was cut off. The green road vanished under a wide expanse of stone chippings; a chipping road curved away to one side. There was a huge, angry-looking wire fence, and inside it buildings with hc treaders in front of them. Beyond the buildings a great white wall with yellow water stains on it stopped the mouth of the valley. A small amount of water moved from two vents at the bottom of this wall. There were people walking about.

'Are you going to blow it up?'

Derveet had slipped to her knees, below the skyline. She said without looking at the child: 'No. I hope not. Ranganar depends on this place now. I need Ranganar, we all do.'

'*Without the water the fish will die,*' murmured Cho. Derveet turned to her, and smiled.

They took a path into the undergrowth, came to a wide drain that took the outflow of the reservoir and crossed it paddling through the stream. They climbed over the pipelines, rearing like great snakes through the greenery, and arrived at last on a hilltop. The heat of the morning was already bright up here. Under a vivid blue sky spicy scents rose from shrubs and bushes; tumbled stones sprawled about. Derveet and Cho lay

90

looking into the lake. To their left was the retaining wall, topped with a narrow walkway and two small towers.

'They control the outflow.'

In spite of the sky, the long oval of water looked grey. All the way round it, halfway down the slopes, there ran a white track interrupted by pointed domes which were clearly big lamps. But next to some of them were blackened patches, and the track was not clear of weeds. Both the towers had broken windows.

'Day is better than night,' said Derveet. 'It is easier and safer then to stage a diversion. And at night they *do* patrol: armed. It is to stop the camp people climbing in and fishing for the treasure they imagine is down there.'

She watched the empty scene a little longer, then they slipped across to the other side of the hill. Just beneath them began the collective fields. Quite near at hand was a group of long huts, fenced in: a farm camp. Immediately below a figure with a long switch was seeing over a gang of workers, clearing mud out of a ditch. They had no tools but their hands. They were in rags; most of them were no more than children. They moved listlessly. Even the seeover had a shabby, apathetic look.

'It is not that our Rulers are greedy,' said Derveet quietly. 'It is worse. It is that they just don't care. There is nothing anywhere in the Sawah but what you see here: neglect, wastage, decay. How it is possible to bring the Peninsula to the brink of starvation beggars the imagination. Mother Sky has given us so much; even in Timur Kering all you have to do is add water. But the Koperasi have managed it.'

'I suppose they don't have the Dapur.'

Derveet was silent for a moment. 'We say not,' she said at last. 'We say the women of the Koperasi families destroyed themselves, in shame after the Rebellion. That is, they took jamu to prevent themselves having daughters, and then quickly died of grief. But as you can see, the Koperasi have plenty of children still.'

'Will those down there grow up to wear uniforms, like the ones I saw at the river?'

'That's a good question. No. The uniforms are brought up in cadet schools in the coastal bases. They come from a different source, mainly. The girls down there probably will not grow up

91

at all. You see, on the Peninsula most male children are changed into boys. The Dapur decides, when they are born or before. Whoever nurses babies who are to be changed takes jamu to alter their milk and also meditates, I mean thinks in a certain way about the children. One of the treatments is ritual, one practical: the ladies won't say which. Anyway, the male organs do not develop, and at three, when the difference begins to show, the little men have to leave the Dapur. . . . Because of this custom, the Koperasi are mortally afraid of Peninsulan women, and hate them. They're afraid of losing their "manhood". Which is sad. Manhood without the Dapur is useless and destructive but they don't see that. They just live it.'

The seeover stamped up and down, cutting at thin shoulders in a bored way: 'He'll keep them near the camp. He's afraid of the terrorists, who have been breaking into store compounds and ambushing supply convoys and so on –'

'I've heard of them. Do the things to eat go to the people?'

Derveet smiled. 'Not directly. Knowing the Peninsula, that would be too much to ask. All the produce of the Sawah you see, as in all states, goes into places called Welfari stores, where most of it rots. The terrorist attacks do very little damage, but afterwards the officers are able to report big losses, and sell the loot. Meanwhile, the achar gangsters lend the people Koperasi *cash*. The people are therefore able to buy "damaged" goods. So the *cash* goes back to the Koperasi, who spend it on achar. . . . It all fits together quite neatly. In fact, I thought the Koperasi liked the arrangement as much as anyone, until a few days ago.' She glanced at Cho thoughtfully. 'But things have changed. Yes, perhaps things have changed. There was no sign at the sanctuary, so I am taking it that my friends have not yet arrived. We'll check the dam compound again in the morning.'

They spent that night in the sanctuary of Roh Betina. Derveet told Cho to go to sleep and sat up with her back against a slab of carved stone, to watch. She had a great deal to think about.

She had guessed the moment she touched Cho's clothes by the river crossing that something momentous had happened. By now she had no doubt that Cho had been used by the Dapur of Jagdana to carry a message: a response at last. How like the Hanomans to choose an answer so elegantly simple, and complete. She felt suddenly certain, tonight, that all was well; tomorrow the others would arrive and the declaration would be made. There stood Roh Betina, on her dark wheel of stone, giving the twisting dagger of life to Garuda: Will you give me a blessing too? she asked, silently. But the immense stillness of the carving said nothing. It was just stone. Derveet smiled at herself: God is not a partisan.

The message was one thing, but what about the messenger? It was strange, but it seemed Cho had had no idea she was an emissary. In fact, the Hanomans, according to Cho, had behaved very oddly. But it was hard sometimes to understand the child; she had odd turns of phrase. Cho knew a great deal, about Peninsulan affairs among other things, but there were bizarre gaps in her knowledge. Her whole story was bizarre. Was she lying?

No. Her story was not the only strange thing. The journey from the achar hills, peace and beauty apart, had been extremely hard. It had pushed Derveet almost to the limit. Admittedly she was not strong, only obstinate: any long effort was likely to leave her ill and exhausted afterwards. But Cho, apparently about fifteen years old, and looking as delicate as if she had never been outside a house before, had come through it without a scratch, without a sign of fatigue. Derveet told her not to mind the leeches, their bites do no harm on a short trip. 'All right,' said Cho gravely. 'I won't mind them. I didn't know you liked them.' But she didn't need to. The leeches left Cho alone, as did every other small unpleasantness. . . .

She turned to look at the slight figure lying beside her. Cho's light skin gleamed faintly in the moonlight: *'Did you lose all your belongings?' 'Lose? The ladies took my clothes away. I hope they aren't missing me.'* Empty hands. Had she really come out of the impossible east, just so? There had been a time when people knew more about the landmass, when wanderers were not unknown, reaching the Peninsula with curious stories and trophies. But the world was growing smaller: in a hundred years it had collapsed inwards at an alarming rate – almost impossible now to sort out truth from fiction. Was Cho the last survivor of a forgotten race? Perhaps. . . . I wish we could stay in the forest, thought Derveet. I'm afraid for you, outside. But she could not say, even to herself, exactly what she feared. Cho

93

stirred in her sleep and murmured, and the blouse that was being so slow to mend itself fell open. Derveet looked down on the child's dreaming face; the rise and fall of flower-petal flesh. After a moment she gently tucked the blouse closed, and settled once more to watch the dark.

There was a further complication, a troubling fountain of joy. Derveet had fallen in love with the bewildering stranger: loved her the first moment she saw her, at that river crossing in the dark and the rain.

12 The Previous Heaven Society

The painted tricycles came careering along the last stretch of the causeway in a pack, scraping wheels and jolting over the tran lines. The drivers yelled at each other joyfully, their hard brown legs going like pistons, and the crowd outside Straits Control began to laugh and cheer as the herd stampeded up to the fence and crashed to a halt. The women got out smiling sheepishly and all went through the gate marked for clan papers only.

Handai stood at the desk and looked at her number overhead: 424. Is that lucky? she wondered. There was no sign of the other four hundred and twenty-three citizens, only an empty, glaring, concrete square, with Handai's party standing about in ones and twos looking bored; and behind the fence the chattering boys' queue. She could see through the barrier that their desk seemed to have shut already, but in the mystic, ever hopeful way of boys the crowd probably would not give up and go away for hours. The Koperasi read the forms. It is a historical society, thought Handai. We call ourselves Previous Heaven because we Samsui believe there was once a golden age. . . . If we work hard and don't drop litter Mother will let us have it back someday. . . . But the Koperasi did not speak, though he kept glancing up at her as he read, or pretended to read. She saw herself through his eyes, she knew she had a childish face – rosy cheeks and curly hair and innocent round brown eyes. It depressed her. She was sometimes pulled up, speechless, at a political meeting by a sudden inner glimpse of what people saw – an earnest twelve-year-old haranguing them. . . .

Cendana the dancer strolled about the yard, idly graceful. She perused the faces of the Koperasi at the gates with detached interest, just on the edge of insolence. The crowd of boys had

95

recognised her. Cendana! Cendana! they called – Sandalwood girl! and reached through the wire. Sandalwood was not the name Cendana's family had given her. Cendana claimed to have forgotten what that was. She had a glance that would cut glass for unwanted admiration but she smiled on the boys benignly.

'Hey you girl, get away from there –' shouted one of the Control guards. 'Stop causing excitement – !'

Cendana drifted away. Siang and Soré, who were also dancers, lolled against the fence arm in arm and laughed at the guard behind his back. Pabriker Kimlan, a tall, thickset woman with grey in her hair, took out her pocket-watch and groaned. Cendana made a circuit of the yard, silently, sometimes exchanging a look or a sigh with one or other of the waiting women. She stared up at the bright morning sky, and stood for a while gazing through the clan papers' gate, back at the road that ran across the Straits. No one offered to examine the women's belongings. Smuggling was rife, even among the most respectable, but the Koperasi seemed to have forgotten.

Handai's thoughts were wandering, fatally, to a little girl left behind in Ranganar. She had tried to teach herself never to think of her daughter. The idea of Dinah orphaned, abandoned by a mother who died in prison, turned her to jelly. *Mustn't* she muttered inaudibly, and hoped the Koperasi didn't see her lips move. Then her eyes were drawn to the crowd of boys. She imagined she caught a glimpse of a dark, distinctive face. . . . This was ridiculous she knew – a sign of nerves. I mustn't stare, she thought, or they'll all come running over, thinking I'm going to give them something.

Cendana came back. 'Hello dearest,' she said, touching Handai's shoulder. 'How are you getting on? We're all fine. Nobody has anything on their mind.'

'Sign here,' said the Koperasi.

'What?'

'Put chop here. This place.'

'Oh – Oh yes. Sorry.'

'I'm fine too,' she said to Cendana, but when she looked at her hand signing the form, she saw to her horror that it was shaking.

The Samsui colony of Ranganar was founded by women who wanted to reform society. Samsui means three springs. The three springs were to be: one, rediscover physical labour; two, abolish boy-making; three, treat men as equals. The Garuda family gave the project reserved support, the island was leased from the Kedaulatan lands. Radical ideas fell victim to economic necessity: the riches of Ranganar were in extraction of metal from the sea, and the colonising ladies put off reforming the native islanders, the Ranganarese, because they needed their boys' unskilled labour for the dredging. In the end the island was not much different from any other state, except that instead of by hidden and secret power, the Dapur governed by a host of practical conveniences. The Samsui never co-operated. In the face of great hostility from the traditional Peninsula, especially the north, they refused to quarrel with the Rulers, and maintained they could see good in the government of the shining islands. But they would never take part in the subjugation of their mother country.

Then came the Rebellion, and at some point in the war, because of their isolation; because, perhaps, of an overwhelming atmosphere of defeat and fear, the Samsui let the Koperasi in. They never regained their independence. The East Coast barracks dominated the city: although nominally the committees of the clan elders still governed everyone knew they were just puppets of the Administration Compound. The practical Samsui had always reused all their resources: they had a sea-water sanitation system that pumped human and other suitable wastes to a recycling plant that turned the refuse into gas power. So traditional Peninsulans called the women 'shit-eaters'; after the Rebellion the term was used universally, with hatred, for the Koperasi as well, as if Koperasi and Samsui were one and the same.

The Butchers, the clan into which Handai was born, remembered the 'three springs' more than most. They put their daughters to work at an early age in the meat yards and the market; they treated their Ranganarese boys fairly. They resisted the insidious *cash* – the Koperasi paper money that was taking over from communal interdependence. They refused to buy Peninsulan produce sold off in Ranganar. Handai was called 'Miss Butcher' because her mother had been head of house, but she was never likely to serve on any Koperasi-ruled committee.

As she grew up, Handai could no longer be satisfied with her family's mild and quiet dissent. She became a young radical, struggling angrily against the corruption of her city. She hated the way respectable Samsui treated Peninsulans who had failed at entering and came to Ranganar. Before the Rebellion these young women would have been adopted into clans. Now they were shunned, because of what went on in the nightclubs around Hungry Tiger Street.

Handai was enraged at Samsui hypocrisy. She knew, everyone knew, that it wasn't only 'tigers' who did secret, shameful things in those dark alleys. She could not make contact with the woman-whores. They wouldn't talk to her. But there were a few Peninsulans who did not end up in nightclubs. They worked at the Classical Theatre: Dance, the great art, was revered – ironically – in the collaborators' city, and the performers had to be Peninsulans because nothing could replace Dapur training. Miss Butcher sought out the dancers, and found anger like her own.

The Samsui had an old custom of exchanging daughters. It was a practical arrangement for strengthening common interests, but it was called 'getting beloved', not without reason. Miss Butcher Handai got beloved with Cendana the dancer, and it did not only mean that she loved Sandalwood, it meant that they believed in each other, Peninsulan and Samsui. . . . The group organised meetings, handed out leaflets, made attempts (unsuccessful) to rescue Ranganarese boys from the ritual excision, got into trouble with street patrols and were fined and threatened. Handai tried to teach the dancers the three springs. But they were half wild, even Cendana. It was hard to get them to take anything seriously: they laughed when they should cry. She sometimes wondered if there was any point in going on, her efforts seemed so petty and useless in the face of the complacent blindness all around her.

Then one night (it was a cool rainy night in North-East Wind) a shabby old boy diffidently led her to a seedy coffee shop. There she met a gaunt, ragged person with skin so dark it was almost a deformity, with an incongruous air of utter self posession and speaking the most beautiful Inggris – High Inggris – Handai had ever heard.

Derveet was a sophisticated savage. Handai could imagine

rough splendour in her past – eating from gold and crystal, but with her fingers. She never wore shoes. She couldn't write properly – she printed in wobbly letters like a child. She didn't even know what year it was. . . . Derveet did indeed eat with her fingers. She never said what she thought of Samsui table manners, but after a while, Handai wondered. It turned out she did know what year it was, but it was a different year: not 489 Ranganar, but 2031 SS. 'What's the SS for?' said Handai, watching Derveet print this for her. She was bemused, she thought the Peninsula used all sort of petty reckonings, and that was why the Koperasi had made them conform to Ranganar-time. 'Sukarelawan Selatan,' said the other casually. 'Accession of the South.' Handai looked at the severe yet delicate dark profile and had thoughts that silenced her. Two thousand years.

Derveet would not be re-educated. She didn't laugh, she contradicted and answered back. She admitted Dapur government was secretive, autocratic; often utterly ruthless, but she seemed to think the women had a right to behave that way. To Derveet men were *ksyatria*: essentially marginal, a wall around the garden of life. Why did Miss Butcher want more of them? What for? Derveet politely detested the 'contrivances' of Ranganar. Miss Butcher informed her the only way the Peninsulan ladies could maintain their exquisite unencumbered lifestyle was because they had a slave culture. Boys are *slaves*. 'Aren't we all slaves, in the end?' said Derveet, with a maddening smile. Then there was the horrible ceremony: the excision of young boys at twelve or thirteen to give them a kind of darah pertama. Forbidden by Ranaganar's statutes it went on everywhere: generally performed by older boys themselves. . . . Derveet shocked Handai profoundly by saying she 'could understand' the excision. She meant the boys' honour. Women have the darah, men have their first entering. What ceremony can boys have, to pass into adulthood? But pride and honour, though she was full of them, were lying words to Miss Butcher; they made her furious. So did religion.

'I think you ought to know,' said Handai firmly, 'I don't believe in God, or Mother or whatever you want to call her.'

Derveet thanked her for the information. 'Don't – ' said

Sandalwood afterward ' – Say "her" when you mean God. Not to Derveet anyway.'

'What should I say then? "It"?'

'No pronoun at all. Just don't Dai. You're embarrassing me.'

But it was Derveet, after all the sparring, who turned Handai's group into the Previous Heaven Society. Handai was scandalised when she first heard the plan; it was pure suicide. Then her friends told her about the secret of the Dapur: the secret even her beloved, Cendana, had kept from her. Derveet had at last, in Ranganar, found a way in to the mystery. The dancers like all failed women had kept silent and suppressed their faculties, partly from loyalty to the Dapur and partly to protect themselves. But for Garuda they put their powers to work. They could dream lucidly, and get glimpses of the future or present events far away; they had intuitions, premonitions about safety and danger that could be relied upon; they could sometimes read minds and they could shield themselves and their affairs from hostile attention. And so the Previous Heaven Society passed to and fro over the causeway unsuspected, while the mysterious terrorists plagued the southern Sawah.

The failed women had left the Dapur at fourteen and fifteen years old; the power in them was undeveloped and erratic. But Derveet wouldn't let anyone try to train the mystery into a better weapon: she had a horror of that idea. Previous Heaven remained a disorderly hybrid, mixing the deep secrets of the Dapur with most un-Dapur-like devices such as illicit crystal sets, and home-made explosives cooked up on the sly, to the recipes Derveet had first tried on Bu Awan.

It was hard to tell if the dancers shared Garuda's mysticism. They only discussed their faculties, if at all, in strictly practical terms. But once or twice Cendana spoke to Handai about something she called 'the floating world' – 'I touch it when I dance,' she said. 'Sometimes. It's hard to reach –' And she spoke then as she never did of the Peninsula; like an exile remembering the beloved country – lost forever, only visited in fleeting dreams.

There were no other tourists. 'It is dead,' said the boy at the gates of the ruins, when he emerged at last from some sleepy interior. 'Mati – the trade is dead these days.'

They found the green road, and the ramp with the carved pillars at the top. Quietness surrounded them, the grass and the stones mourned for great things buried and forgotten. Handai drew a breath and stepped through the gateway. The sanctuary was empty, but behind one of the thatched platforms stood a tall black horse and a small dun pony. Miss Butcher stared. Kimlan looked at her watch again, and shook her head in disbelief. The dancers glanced at each other – and began to laugh, half in triumph, half in relief.

'But why the pony?' said Kimlan.

Then they all turned, hearing some slight movement. Derveet was standing between the pillars. Beside her was a young girl dressed in white. The dancers stopped laughing abruptly.

Derveet put her hand lightly on Cho's shoulder. 'Cho,' she said. 'This is the Previous Heaven Society, a group from Ranganar who are interested in relics of the past. They have crossed the Straits on one of their regular outings. My sisters, Cho is a friend.'

She stepped briskly into the open space, and at once a change came over the group. All trace of excitement and tension vanished. Cho backed off a little and sat down by Gress, and watched Previous Heaven going smoothly into action. There was no discussion, everything was planned. The different elements knew, from long practice, how to play their parts.

'Kimlan?' said Derveet.

The big woman glanced up and nodded. She was busy laying out her equipment on the stone plinth under the carving of Roh Betina, with her assistant, a young Samsui called Cycler Jhonni. Pabriker Kimlan was the head of a bicycle factory. The Koperasi controllers got on well with this big, easy-going woman. They didn't mind if she did a little 'night-market' fiddling with illegal chemicals (supposedly for work on resin quality improvement) or other small supplies.

'It's good stuff,' she said, prodding the wads of explosive. 'We've improved it a lot. It's even fairly safe.'

The dancers were dressed in dark cotton blouses and trousers like the Samsui, but they had long, shining, braided hair and beautiful golden faces. Some of them were carrying baskets, as if for a picnic.

101

Derveet said, 'Cendana, go back to the gates. Take the path across two fields to what is called the Elephant Stables, though it was nothing of the sort. You will find a boy there. Tell him you want to hire ponies to tour the ruins. He'll provide you.'

Cendana and the dancers took their baskets and left.

On the hillside on the outer flank of the great dam there was a pyramid-like boulder of glittering granite, strange to the region. Legend said a Gamarthan lady had fetched it there as a present for her Garuda prince, who had never seen a mountain. Derveet slipped between tangling vines into a dark hole underneath. Pabriker Kimlan went after her, and Cho, who had followed them from the sanctuary. Derveet knew all the secrets of the lost Garuda citadel, she had learnt them far away and long ago, and checked her lessons since on solitary expeditions to this place. She led them halfway through the hill to a place where what seemed to be a black underwater canal ran between carved walls. Their path was a ledge on its side. The water disappeared, and the path too, under fallen masonry. Poked into a crack in the wall, one of Derveet's lightsticks glowed, waking up eyes and flowers in the night drowned stone.

'How long can you hold your breath?' asked Kimlan. 'A minute?'

'Little bit longer than that.'

Kimlan tucked the headpiece of her crystal set over her ears. Derveet was naked, her hair braided again, the explosive and its accessories strapped to her waist and thigh.

'Bit nerve-racking, isn't it?' remarked Kimlan. 'Like waiting to have your first shit, after you've had a baby –'

'I never knew you had children, Kimlan.'

'Oh yes, I had three,' said the big woman evenly. 'Then I gave up.' She shook her head as Derveet winced at her own clumsiness. 'No, no don't worry. It was years ago – Anyway, did you have a good trip? I know what travelling's like: room without fan, dirty hawker food –'

Derveet and the young girl exchanged a glance, a private smile in the darkness.

'What's the joke?' said Kimlan. 'Oh well, don't tell me. You're in good health though? I think you lost weight.'

102

'Of course I lost weight,' said Derveet, mildly irritated. 'I've been travelling.'

And now – Handai and Kimlan's assistant, Cycler Jhonni, were on the spicy hilltop above the dam compound. The sky over them had turned blue-black, the heat was oppressive. Down below something was happening – a threat from outside: a panic-stricken seeover from the farm camp was at the gates, jabbering. Derveet had told Cho: for the four nights of the full moon the watch is lax. Koperasi like to take their leave then, instead of at hari darah. . . . The depleted guard began to race to and fro, screaming faintly and dealing out weapons to technicians and orderlies. The duty patrol came running down from the walkway towers to join in.

'All right,' said Handai to Jhonni, bent over her set, the twin of Kimlan's. She had to be quick; she didn't want to be picked up on the Koperasi's Wave network.

'That's it,' said Kimlan.

Derveet crouched, flickering in the shadows, her eyes intent; the smooth muscles under her shoulders rising and falling.

'You're sure all this stuff is *waterproof*?'

Kimlan laughed. Derveet was gone.

There was a strange world under the water, lost and dream-like. Derveet ignored it and swam steadily. She climbed the cracked discoloured inner face of the retaining wall, entered the first tower by its broken window, laid her charges and opened the sluices wide. She climbed out and ran along the walkway to the next, ducking low under the parapet of the wall. But the staff and the guards were still trying to get organised, to deal with the gang of terrorists or brigands who were about to attack. . . . Derveet appeared in the window of the second tower, and dived into the lake.

· Down in the compound the loud disarray halted: the boys and men had suddenly noticed, above their own row, the outflow changing from a hiss to a roar. The duty patrol ran for the steps to the walkway. But when they reached the first tower, the door seemed to be jammed. They looked at each other. Then one intelligent person turned and fled, and the rest pelted after.

Cho and Kimlan, in the dark, heard nothing of the explosions. At least, Kimlan did not. Cho smiled to herself and murmured 'Fireworks – '. They had to wait a long time before Derveet reappeared. She had stopped on the way back, she said, to do a little domestic chore.

'Oh, of course,' said Kimlan. 'Good thinking. Lucky you remembered.'

Rain raced down on the flat fields. Derveet, Handai, Kimlan, Cho and Cycler Jhonni watched from the hilltop, while excitement jumped about like a firecracker, sizzling in the downpour. The guards at the dam had Waved to Sepaa, the nearest base, for help, but here there was panic. The slaves darted about staring at the sky, or flung themselves into ditches or made off for the horizon, while the seeovers struggled vainly for control.

'Everyone keep their heads down,' said Kimlan. 'And let's keep quiet – if we can, with all these farting vegetarians about.'

Derveet was crouched under a bush trying to smoke a damp cigarette. She smiled.

'Are you talking about me? I never fart.'

Now the dam is broken, thought Handai, and the river pours out and spreads through the thirsty land. Unstoppable. We're unstoppable. Cycler Jhonni squatted beside Miss Butcher. She was a daughter of the rich, respectable Cycler clan; a sturdy prosaic-looking Samsui child with reddish skin and thick ankles. But she had fallen in love with the Peninsula; this drenched hillside was the height of romance to her.

'Here they come –' breathed Kimlan.

Out of the trees at the base of the hill came the brigands. They raced across the drab landscape, moving as one. Their shining braids and bright ornaments made the rain glitter, and the last rider carried a pure white-streaming banner. They were fifteen. Rumour made them a small army: the White Riders who appeared and disappeared like ghosts. Who were they? *What* were they? They dressed in white, the colour of war, but they had never been known to use the weapons they carried: and yet, effortlessly, they defeated the Koperasi. . . . Derveet watched, as always, with a feeling of slight unease. The dancers gave themselves lovely arrogant airs, and lovely new names:

104

Nyala, the flame; Pelangi, the rainbow – Sandalwood. But they had *failed* and she knew that was not something a Peninsulan woman could forget. They had kept out of the nightclubs, but they were too fond of danger.

Suddenly, the watchers on the hillside gave a concerted gasp of alarm. The riders had done their work, it was time for them to vanish. But instead – they had wheeled and were coming back. The slaves were in a mass now, the riders clearly meant to snatch a way between them and the long huts. The space looked small but Cendana had not misjudged it. The troop swept into the centre of their stage. . . . But some of the audience were not attending. They were staring at a thing like a pink moon that had risen in the grey sky over the eastern horizon, and was swelling silently, enormously. It was an airship. Inside the spherical envelope the shadow of the gondola could be seen, carrying reinforcements from Sepaa. Cendana had not seen the bubble, nor sensed it.

'What's wrong with her?' cried Handai. 'What's got into them?'

At the last possible moment one of the riders turned her head. Her cry rang in the air. The women on the hill recoiled in shock – for a moment it seemed as if the White Riders charged straight *at* the bubble as it landed. . . . But no. The horses spun around on their heels in a flashing display of skill and streamed away. The bubble settled. Close up it could be seen that it was rather battered, it had trouble making a steady descent. The troop from Sepaa poured out, but it was too late. The slaves milled, and the seeovers ran about smartly like chickens with their heads chopped off.

In the sanctuary again, Previous Heaven gathered. The ponies that drama had made into warrior steeds were back at the Elephant Stables. The dancers had changed into street clothes.

'You shouldn't have taken a risk like that, Cendana,' said Derveet.

But the dancer was unrepentant. Her eyes burned. 'There was no risk,' she answered. 'None at all. We had them in our hands, Garuda. *We had them in our hands!*'

Derveet looked around and saw that every face was alight. Even Pabriker Kimlan was grinning broadly. She wanted to bring them back to earth, but just now it was clearly useless to try. She laughed instead, and put her arms round defiant Sandalwood, and hugged her.

After all, there was some reason for excitement today, even without the news she had not yet told them. A declaration had been made, a signature had been added to the strange warfare of the White Riders that would be understood from one end of the Peninsula to the other. The sky cleared as Previous Heaven quietly left the ruins. The Sepaa troops fanned out in the thin jungle, the seeovers locked up their hysterical slaves, and Koperasi technicians already began to tinker with the damaged sluices. But in that deep, secret, lovely valley, of hanging woods and whispering cascades, where the Garudas had built their palace long ago, the water was still falling – falling away from galleries of pierced marble, pavilions and towers. Silt and weed blurred the outline of the emerging dream, but not where it most counted. On the topmost pinnacle, clean and bright, the golden wings of the Eagle lifted into the air, soaring and burning in the sunset light.

13 Among the Ruins

There was a resthouse at the gates of the part of the Garuda ruins open to the public. The Samsui visitors had a permit to stay the night there, because obviously they couldn't cross the causeway until it opened in the morning. All through the evening treaders rumbled and clattered past the Garuda gates, up and down the white road to the dam. There were voices, sounds of people running, occasionally the loud report of a weapon discharged aimlessly. The hotel boys went about giggling and clinging to each other. The Koperasi officer from Sepaa came to the resthouse with a small detachment and walked through the shabby courtyards, but he saw nothing: only the women, sitting on their verandahs, brushing their endless hair and staring at him with eyes like black stones.

'Tell them to stay in their rooms,' he said to the boys. 'No wandering about. Not allowed.'

When everything was quiet at last, Miss Butcher went for a stroll. The back of the resthouse blended imperceptibly, in the darkness, into ornate broken walls and weed-grown empty spaces. She sat down on a fallen lintel. The moon was coming up: the night was clear, the air as soft as milk and faintly silvered. Insects chanted gently. An angular shadow figure silently approached, and sat down near-by.

'We had a panic this morning,' said Handai after a moment. 'The tran girls were on strike again. None of us knew. It was only by chance we had enough *cash* between us to pay for trishaws.'

Derveet for a moment wondered what her friend was talking about. Tran girls and strikes confused her, she had been so far away from Ranganar.

'You know the Trans hire all sorts of girls as drivers, well now they're striking – for less pay and longer hours, needless,

107

to say. I wish I could think it meant something but they won't even talk to me. They're just a bunch of red-backed kites.'

Derveet always wondered what harm those useful and handsome scavengers had done to the Samsui.

'I hate that rotten city.'

The moon strengthened, they could see each other's faces. Handai remembered another cause for indignation.

'Do you know, those troops made the boys at the ruins, the caretakers, go out and beat the jungle with them. There could have been armed bandits in there –'

'But there weren't.'

'But it's the *principle*!'

Derveet smiled. Handai scowled – and suddenly they both burst out laughing, partly at each other, partly in sheer elation.

Before they left the Garuda ruins, Derveet had told her friends the good news. Acceptance by the Royal Hanomans and their prince was a dazzling change of fortune, made even more dazzling by the fact that it came on the day – as it were – Derveet announced that the name Garuda was behind this new, stealthy, undercover rebellion.

'What now, Derveet?'

Derveet had taken the silver bell out of her pocket and was rocking it on her palm, carefully; not letting it chime.

'Nothing much changes,' she said softly. 'Not yet. As we'd decided, Previous Heaven will keep quiet for a while after today's show. The dancers have protected us so far, but we shouldn't push our luck. Later, I suppose we'll go back to work, without the dressing up: that's served its purpose. And not alone. I don't know what the Hanomans will decide to do, but I imagine life will become mysteriously uncomfortable, for the Koperasi in Jagdana. . . . But there is something I have to do urgently and that is get in touch with the Singas. They must not feel left out.'

'You're going to Gamartha?' exclaimed Handai, dismayed.

'Oh no. No need to go as far as that.'

She frowned a little and put the bell back in her pocket. 'I'm glad the masquerading is over. I wasn't seeing things, was I? They did, for a moment, mean to attack that bubble?'

'They do get fairly keyed up. Peninsulans are all a bit wild.'

108

Derveet grinned, and took out her cigarettes. 'What do you think of Cho?' she asked abruptly.

'Oh she's *very* nice.'

Derveet was amused, for the little girl in white had hardly looked at Handai, or anyone. She had chosen, for some reason, to efface herself completely. Miss Butcher must be being tactful: Garuda, though unaware of it, must have been absurdly transparent.

'Cho's rather mysterious,' she said. 'She's been alone all her life. She says she's an art person – I don't know what art she means unless it's the art of living as simply as – oh, a leaf on a tree. A cat brought her up. It travelled with her from their home, until it decided to run off with the Koperasi.'

'She had a pet cat?'

'Mmm. They lived very far away. She gave me a bearing – north by north-east, roughly, right into the landmass. I was rough I mean – she wasn't. She told me the distance; an extraordinary number, lots and lots of them – digits, I mean. It went on forever. I think she meant steps.'

'What an odd story,' said Handai. 'I'm going to bed.'

She judged this was not the first strong cigarette of the evening. It was a difference of opinion. Derveet did not find drunkenness funny. Miss Butcher detested that cloudy look, and the rambling nonsense. They had learned to avoid each other when necessary.

'All right,' said Derveet. 'Never mind – Oh, no. Wait, wait a minute.'

She had remembered the trishaw story. She pulled a roll of Koperasi *cash* out of her pocket: 'You'd better have this.'

Handai peered at the greasy bundle, and looked mutinous.

'Come on, take it; take it. The last thing we need now is for Miss Butcher to be picked up for being "without visible means".'

The resthouse room was warm and sticky, not a breath of air came through the verandah screens. Cendana knelt on one of the thin mattresses unrolled on the floor, plaiting up her hair.

'Siang,' she said, 'dreamed of the rendezvous. She saw us at Straits Control; she saw us going into the sanctuary, and what hour it was by the sun; and Bejak and that dun pony that no one could explain. She knew something was wrong, so did we all, but we couldn't tell what. Then the news of the riot in Jagdana came through on the wall bulletins, and we guessed it meant Veet was delayed. So we told Siang to dream it again and she did, and read the date on the board at Straits Control. And here we are.'

'I know all that,' said Handai. 'But what happened to you on the field? You terrified me. What made you do that?'

Cendana laughed. 'It was joy,' she said. 'Joy made me do it. I knew there was no danger.'

Handai looked at her solemnly. 'I'm glad you won't be doing it again. You know you shouldn't use those "powers" more than you have to.'

The dancer smiled. 'That's Derveet's conscience, not mine.'

'Cendana – ?'

'But she's our Garuda. I love her. I believe in her.'

She shook her head and laughed, and came to join her beloved on the other mattress. She peeled back Handai's blouse and kissed her shoulder, rubbed her face against the soft skin: 'Do you know what I like? I like it when you forget I'm here, and think of nothing but your own pleasure. Because when you cling to me then it's *pure*. D'you see?'

They put out the lamp, not wishing to entertain any in-somniac hotel boys with shadow play on the screens.

In an outer court of the dead palace two black stone demons guarded a roofless room. Cho was kneeling in the doorway, using a massive ankle as an armrest, admiring the moonlit ruins. Derveet stepped in, and sat down beside her.

'You've been very quiet today, Cho.'

'Wasn't that what you wanted?'

'Was it? Perhaps it was. Do you always mean to do exactly what I want you to do?'

'Oh yes.'

'Dear me. What a responsibility.'

Cho looked up with a flashing smile. She put her hands in her blouse pockets, and laid out on the doorstep a little heap of groundnuts: a mouse-meal.

'Let's pretend we're still in the forest.'

'Good idea.'

110

Derveet cracked nuts and ate thoughtfully. 'That bubble was in a poor state, wasn't it. And the dam. The Koperasi just cannot maintain this world the Rulers handed to them.' She frowned, and propped herself against a demon. 'I think I know something about the Rulers. It explains their fatal indifference, and the way they have withdrawn so completely. I think they are dying out. After all, they were old when they came out of the ocean long ago: survivors of something dead and gone. The Dapurs always said we would outlast them. Patience, submission, has always been their message: Don't risk lives, wait for the wheel to turn, as it always does. I would believe them, I am not such an idiot as to go to war for "independence" or any other word of that kind. But something *different* has happened to the Peninsula, Cho. The Dapurs won't see it; they've shut themselves off, since the last rebellion. But the truth is we are not just oppressed, we are dying. And those left alive call each other "shit-eaters", "natives", "polowijo", "collaborators" and so on – too busy hating each other to see what is happening to us all. The collapse is coming quickly now. In a few years there may be no government at all. If I don't find some way to unite the peoples before that happens, the Peninsula will just disintegrate.'

She sighed. 'I am a fake, you know. My lovely manners and my accent – everything that Miss Butcher most objects to, is just a reproduction of a reproduction. The original is gone forever. But I can still call myself a Garuda, and that means a great deal, in spite of my looks. One failed woman is a meaningless fragment: even my grandfather had more authority. He had a daughter – Still, I am sure I could have called out half the country, boys and men. That would have been exciting. But I'm greedy. I wanted more than excitement, I wanted – reality. That's what makes you so important, Cho. I didn't want to defy the Dapur. It isn't a game, these things I have persuaded the dancers to do: peering into the future, and into peoples' minds. God knows where it will lead us in the end. To God, perhaps. . . . But I am desperate, so I must use it.'

She leaned over and touched Cho's white sleeve. 'This doesn't only say the Hanomans know and accept the truth about the famous White Riders. It says yes to my heresy: using what the Dapurs have hidden so carefully, to save our lives. It is

111

more than generous of Jagdana. I was such a nuisance to them in the old days. And I know they have a horror of that dying monster. . . . Oh Cho, perhaps it's all ridiculous. Perhaps the Rulers are still all-powerful, and everything will end in disaster. But I have to try. I have to give the people hope. What do you think, Cho? Can you help me – *Am* I doing right?'

'Of course I'll help you,' said Cho.

Derveet smiled.

Outside the demons' brandished daggers there was utter stillness. Only the moon and the dimmed stars were moving, slowly, slowly, overhead in the profound blue. Derveet arranged herself more comfortably, and lit a cigarette. She grinned, catching Cho's eye.

'More medicine. I'll come to a bad end, I know.'

She relapsed into silence. The end of her cigarette glowed and faded like a little pulsing red star.

Cho had discovered, when she first opened her eyes in this world, that she belonged to Derveet. She had never troubled to wonder how. She found that she knew, deep in her heart, that this was the way it happened: One day somebody said, 'You belong to –' and everything was settled. She had almost given up thinking about her brother from that moment – she couldn't help herself. Divine Endurance must be wrong. *Evidently* this was the real end of the quest. She had remembered all the Cat's lessons: not being lazy, not putting herself forward, waiting to be asked. She had learned to eat and sleep for pleasure now – nothing seemed strange since she had found Derveet. But tonight she was aware of a puzzling tension in the atmosphere. She had been aware of it, growing, all the time that Derveet was talking.

Now, as the silence lengthened, she could feel Derveet's eyes on her in the moonlight – the same insistent gaze she had felt at the river crossing, like a hand touching her. But the eyes kept slipping away. Was she to turn around, or not to notice?

'Cho –' said Derveet suddenly. 'Would you – ?'

Cho turned. Derveet stared at her, seemed about to speak: but instead she threw the end of her cigarette into the darkness, angrily, and put her head in her hands.

'Cho,' she said, with her face buried. 'I've been wrapped up

112

in this cause of mine too long. Delight seems alien to me, happiness seems like an invasion. I don't know what to do –'

Silence. The moon moved, the stars moved. Cho knelt, waiting. At last Derveet looked up. The moment of absurd panic had passed. She propped her chin on one hand and smiled, and reached out to touch Cho's face with her fingertip, tracing the pure outline tenderly as if she was giving it up forever.

'You go to sleep,' she said sadly. 'I'll, I'll sit up for a while, I think.'

But her hand stayed. Cho did not move. At last Derveet sighed. Her hand slipped under the rim of Cho's hair to the nape of her neck; she drew her forward gently and bent and kissed her strange crescent eyes.

'Well?' she whispered 'Well – ?'

To Cho it was like the moment when Atoon first told her who she belonged to. Suddenly she felt completed, as if everything was explained. She said *Yes*, without words but with all her heart, and gave herself up joyfully to Derveet's embrace, Derveet's searching, ardent mouth and hands.

Cho woke up, hours later, in a soft world of pearl-coloured mist and coolness. She lay looking at Derveet's left hand sleeping where it had slipped from her shoulder: dark, supple, long fingered and slender. She thought: '*Entered*. Ah – !' Among other confused feelings, Derveet had been afraid it was wrong of her to fall in love with someone so young and childlike, and she meant to be very careful not to demand too much of Cho's inexperience. Her awakening that pearly morning was a revelation.

PART TWO

Wide, wide flow the nine
streams through the land

Dark, dark threads the
line from north to south

I pledge my wine to the
surging torrent

The tide of my heart
swells with the waves.

Mao Tsedung

I am very angry with Cho. First she refused to follow me at that river, and now I find she has formed the sort of association I particularly warned her against.

The place I went to in that dry but unpleasant smelling vehicle was a farm camp. These people, it seemed, use their preoccupation with a large scale and exceptionally unlovely kind of landscape gardening as an excuse to gather numbers of themselves in very small palaces. I suppose it keeps them from spreading all over the place but I found the arrangement irritating. I did not announce myself. I soon realised that the Koperasi, though they think differently, are not to be included in the category of people who matter.

The Rulers, most sensibly, have as little to do with anything that goes on on this Peninsula as they possibly can. And yet, I was aware of their influence. I am aware of it even more now that I have come to this place: Ranganar. Everything is running down. This is the great natural process of course; I have known it all my life. But I must admit it gives me a peculiar satisfaction to feel these Rulers gently, without fuss, giving the process their assistance. I am now quite certain Wo is with them, helping them in this smooth descent. It is pleasant to watch the thing, slowly rolling, but I wonder what will happen when there are two of them acting on each other, as Em said. I am eager to find out.

The Rulers are eager too. They are already aware of Cho's arrival. They must have been watching out for more of us since Wo came to them. They don't fade away and drop off as quickly as the Peninsulans, so they don't forget things so easily. They have contacts, naturally, in the palace of Jagdana (even that very private part, that thinks itself so special). Anyway, something alerted them. Messages passed to and fro quickly – the Rulers do not share the Peninsulan passion for the simple life – and we could have been safe and sound, but for the stupidity of those bounty hunters. It was Cho they were supposed to be fetching. But they were greedy, and foolishly imagined their local celebrity was a much bigger catch.

All this I have picked up here and there. Essentially, it means that there are people waiting to take us to the Rulers (they don't, of course, know what Cho is – that would be silly). The only problem is the association Cho has formed. I will try to get her to see reason, but these attachments were designed to be very stubborn. An added difficulty is that the ones supposed to be fetching Cho now are just as impressed by the local celebrity as

116

the ones up in the Sawah, and nagging them does not seem to help. The Koperasi 'authorities' are no use, they are far too lazy and timid. But I am sure I will find a way. I have learned a great deal from Wo already, though I have never met him, and I find I can do many interesting things, if I take the right approach, without being pulled up by my conscience.

14 What I Find
I Can Do

The west side of the Ranganar river was the home of the native islanders: the Ranganarese. The river itself was no more than a black tidal creek on the edge of the Samsui city: beyond it a confusion of mud alleys and board walks over silted waterways trailed away into the encroaching salt-water swamp. The area had none of Ranganar proper's amenities: no water, no gas, no tran, no streetlights, no recycle. It was a squalid place, a warren of secret creeks, eyes and boltholes: the natural haven of low life criminals. The Koperasi left it well alone.

But the island of Ranganar had a long history, stretching back before the Samsui colony was thought of. The West Bank slums sprawled over ancient ruins, mostly buried in swamp; sometimes jutting out above the hovels. In one place the water-gardens of a great mansion remained almost intact, with one bathhouse still standing. It had been reclaimed. Clear water gleamed again in the square pool; the dirt and debris of centuries had been cleaned away. Blue stone pillars stood around the water from which a crumbling but polished stairway of rose marble led to the gallery they supported, and an upper room where long gone youths and gentlemen had rested and amused themselves after bathing. Stone wings were carved everywhere: both the Garuda symbol and another, gentler kind. Merpati, the Dove, said Derveet, had been the original name of her family. They adopted Garuda at the accession, so as not to seem hypocritical.

Derveet's boys had been waiting for her after the dam incident, hiding down on the Straits with a wasp-tailed smuggler's boat. They were Jagdanans: they had mysteriously turned up in Ranganar right at the start of Derveet's exile, and insisted on becoming her household because it was too shock-

118

ing for Garuda to have no one at all – Petruk, Gareng, and old Semar. Derveet periodically tried to send them back to home and safety, but they always refused, and so she felt, distantly, that the Hanoman Dapur had not yet quite abandoned her. Previous Heaven passed innocently across the causeway. The boys took the horses, decorating Jak with white splotches that horrified and depressed him so that he became a completely different animal; led them over the Straits and stabled them safely in the warren. Derveet and Cho took the boat, slipping along the coast and across to the western tip of the island in darkness, and so they reached the security of the West Bank, and Dove House.

A wide bed was the only piece of furniture in the upper room, apart from a chest of clothes and a few curios. The floor was cool bare stone, patterned in blue-grey and rose, the tall windows were open to the air in all but the worst of weather. The carved inner roof had gone, of course, and rain dripped at times. The boys put pots under it, and remarked that madam really ought to get something done.

Cho watched through the bed curtains as the room quietly reappeared: it was dawn again. She disengaged herself softly from hard smooth thighs and dark arms that had lost their cradling strength – Derveet had fallen asleep. She reached down beside the bed and picked up a round box made of a grey raspy material. When she dipped her hand in it came out full of glimmering blue-whiteness. The pearls were from Pulau Sinar Bulan, Moon Island – the place where Derveet grew up. She thought of Derveet, alone in a boat sailing on the enormous ocean and let them slip through her fingers, smiling. Then she heard something land on stone with a soft *plump*. She looked through the curtains and there was Divine Endurance sitting in the window. . . .

'No I won't,' said Cho. 'I think you're silly to ask me. You must know I have to stay with my person now.'

To her relief and suprise the Cat did not begin to nag. She settled her paws under her and said, 'Well, how are you getting on, anyway?'

'Pretty well. But there's a lot to learn about making them happy.'

Divine Endurance narrowed her eyes, and her ears pricked.

119

'It's no good giving them things to eat, and making the weather nice. It's more subtle. You have to go by their inside feelings, and sometimes it's a complete contradiction.'

'Ah,' said the Cat. 'You've noticed that.'

'It's strange how ignorant they are, too. The Peninsulans, I mean. They don't seem to know about fading away, and how sad it is; nicely sad, you know. They say all the time "everything's passing, everything's over soon – " but they don't seem to realise that it's themselves they're talking about. But the Rulers too, and – well, everything. You know what I mean, Divine Endurance.'

The Cat looked at her foster child thoughtfully.

'What about – er – Derveet?'

'Oh, Derveet's different. She knows things. The divers on her island used to bring relics up from the sea, that they couldn't even recognise. The Rulers collected them. And she's heard of the Blue Nomads bringing things from the landmass, though she never saw any of them. It was world-wide, she says; the Peninsula was part of it too; you can tell by things like High Inggris, which was *always* the second language, long before the shining islands came. She wonders if the Rulers are the only survivors of that other creation. Perhaps something could have lived on elsewhere, through the long ages, preserving ways and knowledge that would seem very strange now. . . .'

Divine Endurance heard the voice of her adversary, and felt annoyed. Cho *would* have to pick a bright one.

'I told her there were no people where we lived, except for the nomads: only me and you. She seemed a bit disappointed.'

'No people at all?'

'Well, there weren't.'

'Does she ask you a lot about yourself?'

Cho frowned slightly. 'At the start she did. But then she stopped. I think it made her upset for some reason, and she's given it up.'

'Ah yes,' said Divine Endurance, and looked across at the long dark body spread out on the bed, sleek and relaxed inside the cloudy curtains. 'That's what happens. I told you: they get embarrassed. I wouldn't press the subject.'

'Of course not.'

The Cat yawned. 'How difficult these Peninsulans are. They

have so many things wrong with them. They've got infestations in their lungs, they've got worms in their guts, they never get enough to eat. And yet if you cured all that would they be happy? No. They'd still be longing for something. They know it Cho, deep in their hearts. They know what they *really* want. In fact, you could say all their little troubles are a sort of manifestation, of the longing that they hide away. . . . It is a shame they are in such a muddle. You and Wo together could soon help them sort it out.'

Cho did not seem to be attending. She looked back into the room where Derveet lay, and she smiled. 'Divine Endurance,' she said, 'you know what you ought to do. You ought to find a person for yourself. Then you'd understand.'

Divine Endurance stood up, twitching her tail in exasperation. The child was besotted; this was just wasting time. Now I've annoyed her, thought Cho. But suddenly the Cat changed her mind.

'Hm,' she murmured. 'Hm. That's an idea.'

She vanished.

Cho looked down into the yard. The boys were outside the kitchen house, thumping coffee beans for Derveet's breakfast. They waved to her and smiled broadly. There was a smell of roasted coffee, and no sign of the Cat.

Derveet had woken, and seen Cho at the window with a visitor. 'Was that your pet?' she asked sleepily as Cho came back to bed.

'Yes, it was Divine Endurance.'

'I wonder how she found you. How clever – '

'She's gone again,' said Cho. 'I think she has things to do.'

15   A Fan on the Ground

Handai was in the covered market, ordering dry groceries. Her little daughter, Dinah, leaned on a sack of onions, picking absently at a bulging seam. She was three years old and extraordinarily like her mother except that her hair was straight, not curly. From under a thick fringe her round eyes peered out, staring down the other customers with a fine non-conformist disdain. The stallholder was very friendly with Miss Butcher, but when she'd added up the goods she frowned. She leaned over and whispered that the Butchers had not enough hours left.

'D'you want to make it up with *cash*, or borrow it from somewhere else and give me a chitty?'

Handai's family was always short of hours. They had no more credit with any other clan than with the Commercers at the moment. She blushed, annoyed at the whispering. She was not ashamed of being poor.

'No thanks,' she said firmly, and rather too loud. 'Give me the list and I'll take some things off.'

The stallholder sighed. 'You Butchers are crazy. Why spend everything you earn on fines? You never achieve anything. The Koperasi just laugh at you. They dismiss you completely.'

'I know,' said Handai. 'I know they do.' But for once she did not explode. She only smiled.

Out in the street it was a glaring hot afternoon. The road was up along the market front, as it had been for months, because of a sanitation problem. Overhead a tattered banner flapped, a reminder of North-East Wind Drill:

> ASK YOUR SISTER DOES SHE KNOW
> WHAT TO DO AND WHERE TO GO

In the eleventh to the thirteenth month the city centre was often flooded.

The water supply had been down for twelve days, and Straits Control shut. Giggling boys queued at standpipes, and people argued bitterly with a few triumphant market gardeners. No one panicked. An explosion in the Sawah was hardly news. The excitement was nearly over now: the causeway had opened, soon the taps would be working again. 'They think they can forget all about it,' thought Handai. 'They'll be amazed when they look back and remember this "little incident" – '

What would the support of the Dapur mean? Handai was not comfortable about the 'powers' – that whole business reminded her, embarrassingly, of an idiotic song often heard at drunken meetings of the stockbreeders club:

> Well, first I made a bunny
> I made it up so funny
> It had three ears!
> It had three ears!
> It had three ears!
>
> And then I made a ducky
> The duck was not so lucky
> It had no feet!
> It had no feet!
> It had no feet!

She did not like the idea of changing into a new kind of animal. When she saw Cendana, talking seriously to Dinah about the little girl's dreams, it gave her a strange feeling –

The Dapurs run things, she reminded herself. That's their real importance. The hot street was reassuringly solid and familiar, even down to the hole in the road. 'When I'm old,' she said to Dinah. 'There'll be young women *and men* gathering on these street corners, telling each other the revolution's gone to seed: it stinks, it's time to get rid of the old women. . . . Oh Mother,' she added fervently, under her breath. 'Oh Mother, let me live to see that day – '

Handai had got a lift into town with one of the Butchers' delivery boys, in his trishaw – her bicycle was off the road. Now the trans seemed to have vanished. At last the lines above the street started to hiss, and the tran appeared – but there was a Koperasi uniform in the cab. The tran hired girls wanted to be‍

123

paid in regular hours again, and *cash* only for extra time. Their quarrel was purely mercenary, nothing to do with the destruction of communal life, but it was still vile of the Trans to get the Koperasi in – another step downward for the rotten city.

'It's all right, Mummy,' said Dinah resignedly. 'I can walk.'

Sitting in the shade of the five foot way near the transtop there was a brown cat, with unusual blue eyes but otherwise merging perfectly with the Ranganar street. Divine Endurance saw the sanitation pump, cracked and seeping into the fresh water pipes; she saw the rain damage of not one but many seasons patched or left unrepaired. She had already seen the abandoned fishing quays; the metal-dredging plant shut down 'temporarily'. She had been eavesdropping: she noted with amusement Handai's desire for sweeping changes, so long as everything stayed exactly the same. 'This has possibilities,' she thought. 'But how they do blind themselves. Or is it Wo who blinds them? The truth about this city and its street corners is really very simple.' She slipped down from her doorstep and briskly followed Miss Butcher and her little daughter.

Handai went back to the house in Red Door Street, where First Aunt, the old lady who had taken over when Handai's mother died, ruled absolutely over the sister, cousins, nieces of three generations, and their various attachments. Because of the coming New Year, the family conversation was all about accounts. They had to pay fines for not carrying *cash*. They had to pay low-spending tax for not buying Koperasi 'imports'. They had to pay punitive fees for the servant boys' and labourers' citizen papers (second class). They wanted to keep more live meat in stock, but could they possibly afford to? Divine Endurance was extremely bored.

When Derveet first came to Ranganar, she was puzzled about an important aspect of Samsui life. She saw little Samsui daughters everywhere; she saw her new friend Miss Butcher becoming obviously pregnant. But she never heard the arrangements mentioned, never a hint of discreet visitors tapping at night at a side door. The Ranganarese kept their men enclosed, they had nothing to do with the 'renegade women' nowadays. She asked her friend at last – Handai, please tell me: do not eat me, I can't help being ignorant. Where do babies come from?'

Handai's face flooded instantly, darkening painfully. 'I thought you knew,' she muttered. 'We go to them.' The answer to the riddle was in Hungry Tiger Street.

The people called what the Koperasi did in nightclubs *kejahatan rajah* – the Rulers' vice, but there was no proof of that. More likely they had taken up the practice as a kind of oath between them, sealing themselves off with finality from all other Peninsulans. Derveet had known about nightclub entertainment, and that the Koperasi didn't grow their élite officers in slave camps, but absurdly enough she had never seen the connection. Now she knew the real shame, that even Handai in her fierce radical anger could not bear to discuss. . . . What if Handai had had a son? Derveet didn't ask. Samsui male children were never mentioned. She felt heartsick. Our enemies don't need to touch us, she thought. We hate ourselves, we destroy ourselves. The nightclubs of Ranganar were the very heart of the Peninsula's despair.

Hungry Tiger Street was in the Singa quarter, but it was a bad Ranganar joke that 'whore' and 'northerner' were synonymous. The failed women came from all over the princedoms. Women do not commit suicide, but the *tigers* had found something more expressive: serving the Koperasi themselves and arranging the Samsui business with them. The most famous nightclub was at the corner of the Pasar Diluar, the open market, and the Street. It was run by two sisters who were the undisputed rulers of the tiger world. It was Leilah, the more forceful of the two, who had instituted the brilliantly shameless and cynical dress now worn like a uniform by all the women-whores. Big Simet wore the silver anklet of her childhood embedded in her muscular flesh with a few blackened links still trailing. How she had come to bring it away with her was a mystery, but the gruesome gesture was much admired in that world. No one knew where the two came from. The tigers pretended nothing mattered to them, but as among the dancers it was an impossible crime to ask someone's family.

The day after the causeway opened, Derveet left Dove House for the first time since the adventure. At sunset, she was playing chess with Handai in the garden in front of Nightclub Leilah's, Cho observing with mild interest. The real business of the club had not begun; only a few sleepy tigers sat about, looking sordid as nightlife does even in twilight. The Koperasi were still on duty, the customers were Ranganarese boys drinking beer out of teapots, and a few respectable Samsui, come to look, at this hour, not to do business. The nightclubs had their own horrible fascination.

Soon Leilah appeared: a small woman, still young, with rich hair in artistic tangles down her back. Years of tigering had coarsened her, but she still had a look of sullen pride especially in her eyes, which were extraordinary. They were light grey, flecked with chips of gold and green and amber, like splinters of burnished metal. She had come out, ostensibly, to see the place was in order for the night, but as she wandered about, snapping at the girls in an undertone, she had her eyes on Derveet's table.

Derveet watched her with an almost guilty expression. She knew Leilah quite well, in a way. There were two powers, mysterious and tiresome to the Koperasi, in the disreputable or 'native' side of Ranganar, and for the last four years Leilah had been only one of them.

At last, Leilah came over and flung herself in the chair beside Derveet. She wore the sash, bound from her breast to her thighs, in a bright silk batik: an interesting combination of constriction and nudity. She sprawled so Handai had to look quickly away: grinned at this, and watched the game.

'Her prince's horse,' she said to Handai, after a moment or two.

'Thank you Leilah,' said Derveet, smiling. 'Don't you think I can lose on my own?'

The nightclub owner laughed, took a cigarette from the case at Derveet's elbow and leaned over her shoulder to get the silver lighter.

'I think I'll keep this. It's pretty.'

Derveet bore these intimacies patiently. She had never intended to become Leilah's rival in the city, but it was hard to explain this to the tiger. Leilah did not like competition.

'How's your little girl?' she asked Handai. 'Does she take after the stud at all, or don't you remember?'

Handai's face went stiff; she stared at the chess pieces

126

angrily. Leilah chuckled, got up and left them, lifting a handful of cigarettes and rumpling Derveet's hair in passing. But she left the lighter.

Handai said, 'Oh – It's that cat again.'

A brown cat had jumped onto the table, and was gazing with interest at Nightclub Leilah as she strolled away.

'It came home with me and Dinah yesterday and this morning it went off with Cendana. It must have followed me from the theatre just now. D'you think I've been adopted?'

Derveet shook her head, 'You must be dreaming. That's Cho's pet. The one I told you about. It found her again. I know it by the eyes – '

Cho said, 'Why have you been following people about? It's rude.'

Divine Endurance slitted her eyes benignly. 'I'm just taking your advice. I'm choosing one.'

'That's the wrong way round.'

Handai and Derveet lost interest in the minor puzzle of the cat. The chess game was abandoned. Now that Straits Control had relaxed they could expect news from other places; perhaps emissaries. 'How will they know?' asked Handai. 'All over the states, I mean?' 'They'll know,' said Derveet. 'Word like this has a way of spreading, among my people – '

'Well I don't think much of yours,' said Divine Endurance to Cho, 'I must say. Its colour doesn't match. And listen to it – '

Derveet was coughing a little, resentfully: the humidity of Ranganar never suited her.

'Oh hush,' said Cho. 'She particularly dislikes you to notice that.'

The blue dusk had grown dark and bright with lamps, the respectable element in the clientele had left, and the tigers looked different now.

'We ought to go,' muttered Handai uneasily. 'I don't know why we came here anyway.'

'To show Cho to Leilah,' said Derveet quietly.

'Yes, I gathered that. And did you get what you wanted?'

'No.'

'Well, of course not. It was you who told me, there's no

127

point in trying to reach the tigers. They're dangerous, that's all – '

Derveet sighed. 'I'm afraid Leilah is dangerous to no one but herself. But I owe her something.'

'What?'

'Discretion, if she won't have anything else.'

In the lighted doorway of the club Leilah stood talking to her big sister, with sharp little gestures.

'I wonder what sort of family she came from. Do you think they mistreated her, because of those funny eyes?'

Derveet was putting away the chess. She glanced across at her rival: that cloudy wild cat stare hidden now in the darkness.

'Oh no, I don't think so. There are places where eyes like that are quite well thought of.'

Since the lamps went on, the little stage in the centre of the garden had presented fairly good dancing, and mildly simulated love-making by tigers still clothed, if you could call it that. But now the scene changed: unusually, for there might still be decent people walking by. A boy, almost naked, danced swooningly with a muscular young man. He flexed his knees and swayed backwards; his spine arced wonderfully and the young man, supporting him with a hand in the small of his back, parted both their clothes and began to treat him 'as the bee treats the flower – '

'That's *disgusting*,' said Handai. 'And it's not what bees do to flowers anyway.'

Leilah was watching them from the doorway.

Derveet smiled faintly. 'I think it's a hint. Let's go.'

There was something in the air that New Year, not only on the city island but up and down the Peninsula from Gamartha to the sea. Even Sepaa and Nor were affected – by something that puzzled many, but made others eye each other in the street, and secretly smile. Rulers' agents in several places noted, reported, and decided it would go away. They made no connection with events surrounding a minor attempt on the Ranganar reservoir.

The Classical Theatre was a steep half circle of stone tiered seats under a sweeping roof, open on three sides to the humid darkness. It was a gala night, the first of the New Year.

Ticket-holders climbed to their seats, the Ranganarese packed themselves in front of the stage. (There were no Ranganarese women: they rarely crossed the river because of the contamination of the Koperasi.) The theatre's famous orchestra began to test patterns in the air; coughs and ripples were struck from the ancient moony bronze. This historic gamelan had been salvaged from the old Garuda palace, its name was Drifting in Clouds. The stage remained empty. Down in the pit, a tall black-skinned woman appeared, causing a stir. Her colour was nothing in the city, where all hues rubbed along – but she turned heads; she obviously meant to. She was dressed formally, in an exquisitely cut jacket of thin silk; a fan at her wrist, her sash and kain panjang patterned sombrely in the prized, rich colours 'of blood and clouds'. By her side was a young girl in white. Handai, up in the dancers' guest row, thought: She's not so *very* tall. Kimlan tops her by a head. It's when you realise that, you start to wonder *who does she think she is?* Nightclub Leilah, late as always, arrived while Derveet was still standing. She was in her best clothes too; more of them than usual. For a brief moment they looked at each other, and the boys began to shiver with anticipation – Derveet sat down. A Rulers' agent, making himself comfortable up above, laughed and said to his neighbour: 'Gangsters – '

Handai put her chin on her hands, and tried to understand Drifting in Clouds. Derveet said this gamelan was 'one of the few justifications for the existence of the human race', Cendana thought it was good too. In the middle of the floodlit stage a fan lay on the ground, picked out by the light: gold filigree over dark silk, waiting for somebody to come and pick it up, as a sign that the Dance had begun.

16   At the Dance Theatre

In the rehearsal courtyards behind the Theatre, violet water-lilies stood over their deep reflections; dragonflies wandered glinting across the fountain pools. Inside a pavilion a class was going on and the blurred images of the dancers swayed under their feet, in dim waters of polished wood. Outside, the Previous Heaven Society, or most of it, sat about on the steps or the cool pavement, turning out a chest of properties. Gareng and Petruk of Dove House were lending a hand, rubbing things up with metal polish and folding silks. There was no news yet. Derveet asked the dancers if they had seen anything, but no one had anything striking to tell.

'There is danger ahead,' said someone.

General laughter. Of course there was danger ahead. Dinah dressed herself up with care, tying mangled knots in exquisite scarves and sashes Cendana had just smoothed and folded. She was observed, belatedly, and ran off round the fountains shrieking like a factory whistle, with Sandalwood in pursuit. Siang took her little iron off the brazier and tested it with a licked finger singing softly, glancing at Soré –

> ... bruised coriander leaf
> my sweet
> my kelapa muda,
> milky coconut...

Cho was puzzled by the stage daggers: 'Are they meant to be like the one Atoon wears, except that his is made of wood?'

'That's right.'

'Derveet, everybody knows what *this* means' – she sketched a double helix in the air – 'If that is what the daggers are to mean, isn't it a bit odd to have a straight one?'

Derveet smiled at Cho's 'everybody knows'. She glanced at the toy that Cho held. It passed, at a distance. It was, yes, straight as death. . . .

Siang looked up. Nyala the flame, Pelangi the rainbow, turned as well: 'What's the matter? Did I say something?'

But the dancers shrugged, and went back to what they were doing. The moment passed, it was only the briefest ripple.

'They have to be straight,' she said, 'or they would be facsimile weapons. Besides, it's hardly worth the trouble. Those curves are not easy to produce.'

Handai came to sit beside Derveet, who was stretched out lazily on the pavement. She was slightly embarrassed by the presence of Semar, who was massaging her friend's neck and shoulders with his clever old hands.

'Are you worried because there's no news yet?'

'Not really,' said Derveet. 'I still feel dazed, I think. I'm used to fighting. I am not –' her mouth tucked itself up wryly at the corners – 'used to winning – '

'I suppose it will be all over pretty soon once the big Dapurs get started.'

Derveet shook her head. 'Oh no. Don't start thinking that, Handai. I only meant winning *relatively*: not losing so badly anymore. And even if the Dapurs could somehow forge a weapon to hammer the enemy, they wouldn't do it and we mustn't want them to. We must borrow from our future as little as we can. Don't you see? If a people were growing wings, they might find the bumps on their shoulders useful for hefting things, but then they never would fly. . . .'

'You look a tiny bit tense, madam,' said Semar to Handai, kindly. 'Shall I give you a rub?'

'Oh no – I mean no, er – thank you – '

It was a while before anyone noticed that Cho was gone. Was she in the pavilion? No: the class had broken up, the polished floor was empty. The rehearsal gamelan sat swaddled in its canvas wraps; hunched animal shapes in the shadows.

'Oh wait,' said Nyala. 'I saw her. She was talking to a boy, by the gates.'

In the alleys round Dove House Cho was always vanishing: disappearing into some ricketty hovel; playing with the children in dirty little gangways over the mud. Everybody loved

131

her. Derveet liked to see her go, to the people. 'Oh so that's it – '
she said slowly. The afternoon had worn away unnoticed, the
theatre compound had grown quiet, before the burst of activity
that would herald the evening performance. Petruk and
Gareng put away their rags and polish and stood up.

'Derveet,' said Nyala, 'I've just remembered. I've seen that
boy before. He comes from Tiger Street.'

'*Bodoh* – ' whispered Derveet – *fool* – The dancers glanced at
each other, the atmosphere suddenly sharp: *No*, she said, in
the same language, *I'll deal with this*. And she ran to the gates,
with the boys hurrying after her.

Down near the waterfront Ranganar river ran blackly; under
derelict godowns on the Samsui side, West Bank boardwalks
and huts on the other. There was no bridge, the length of the
city. The Ranganarese were quite happy with their boats, and
who else wanted to cross over? Derveet stood in the flower
market where the lowest ferry plied. In the city behind her the
bell in the Commercers' clock tower clanged the sunset hour.
The flower boys gathered around the roots of a waringin tree,
threading garlands and creating petal confections in little leaf
baskets, for people to send down the river to Father across the
sea. They were busy, trade was brisk; it was still New Year.
Heaps of scarlet and white, blue and yellow, tiger stripe and
violet, poured on the worn cobbles.

Derveet had sent Petruk and Gareng to Tiger Street's alleys,
to spy out what they could. She had sent Semar to a place on the
East Coast road, near the barracks. It was called the Assistance:
both a convent and a place for unruly people whose families
couldn't manage them – so the Samsui put it. Nowadays a
Koperasi cadre worked beside the nuns. It was possible Cho
had been taken there.

Derveet paced the waterfront waiting for the boys, thinking
of all the hiding places there were in Ranganar. But what did
she fear, really? Not that Cho had been handed over, for
revenge or spite, to the city Koperasi. Not that someone had
taken the child for ransom. No. It was more than that. She had
given up asking Cho about her past. Why? She had given up
thinking about the extraordinary stir that had attended the
child's arrival in this world: the riots in Jagdana, the bounty
hunters. She had managed to put out of her mind that lingering

132

sense of something very strange. . . . It had been easy, so easy she felt dizzy now to think how much she had blithely put aside. But Cho was so dear, made every moment so sweet. And yet. . . .

She leaned over the river wall, and watched a shower of petals falling, spinning down bravely from sunlight into moving darkness. She had not been able to forget, not entirely. She had been afraid, from the start, that she would not be allowed to keep her treasure. Oh the poor child, dear child. What would they do to her?

Cho was in a room with painted walls. She could see out of a small window a herd of bicycles corraled, minus their metal chains and gear wheels. They did not have crossbars, they were for export, but trade was slow just now. It was the back of the pabrik (which was not, after all, the same as palace) where Kimlan worked. *Kimlan* she thought, but she didn't like to press it. Kimlan was probably busy. She knew where she was: the pabrik quarter merged into nightclub land. She looked at the paintings on the walls. It was a *wayang* room – thin, gold, ornate people surrounded her, acting out a legend. Sometimes the customers liked a touch of grandeur. Cho gazed at the golden puppets solemnly, and looked down at her own tied hands and feet. She had something poked in her mouth as well: sign language again. Someone opened the door and she looked up to see who it was.

Derveet was still by the riverside, under a darkening sky. She did not know where to go, how to start. But as she stood there, suddenly there was a brown cat in front of her, sitting on the cobbles; sniffing at the flowers. It turned and stared with brilliant blue eyes, then stood up and trotted away. Derveet, without thinking, without questioning, followed.

The Cat led her down to the seafront, and out of the city centre by the East Coast Road, jogging along the five foot way; hopping over storm drains. The East City had no nightlife, it was too near the barracks, the streets were empty. The Cat did not pause at the barracks, or at the Assistance walls. She led Derveet on, to where there were no more buildings and then left the road, slipping through a fringe of coarse shrubs down onto the sand. The Straits of Ranganar; the forgotten, abandoned ocean lay dark and empty. There was a small jetty, once used by fishing boats. Divine Endurance jumped onto it, walked to the end, and sat down.

Derveet followed. She stood and looked out to sea. Far away, standing out black against the dim evening sky, there was a skeleton tower, heavy swell rocking around it. The Rulers had left several of these things behind, when they moved further out after the Rebellion. Smugglers used them. Divine Endurance looked up at Derveet. Her eyes, glinting in the dusk, spoke very simply. Derveet measured the distance. It was about half an hour's swim: nothing. But she had not been well; it was taking her time to get over that last escapade.

'Cat – ' she said. 'You – whatever you are. I don't think I can do it.'

'You could at least try,' said Divine Endurance's eyes.

Derveet took off her jacket and sash and kain. She rolled up the kain and twisted it round her waist, because nakedness puts you at such a disadvantage. The tide was full, so there was plenty of water. She dived into the sea.

17 Wayang

Derveet reached the tower, but she could not climb into the scaffolding. A hard rib between two columns slammed against her knuckles, she fell onto it gratefully and hung there, with the dark bitter water slapping her in the face. Stupid, she thought. It was nothing. You did it too fast. In a moment or two she had her breath back and pulled herself up. She sat crouched against one of the columns. The surface of the sea glowed faintly with a reddish colour. She had never swum off Ranganar before: so strange, to live on an island that ignored the ocean. The Ranganarese said the Rulers had frightened the fish away, the Samsui said they were letting the waters 'rest' and blamed the Peninsula for over-fishing. Rest? she thought, tasting it in her mouth and feeling it on her body: it is dead. The image of a whole ocean dead, surrounding everything, came to her – she closed her eyes and shook it away.

There was not a star in the heavy sky. Ranganar was a vague blackness, with a city shape of lights. She felt better. She coughed to clear her throat – suddenly her mouth was full of liquid. It was warm and salt; it came out on her hands black in the darkness. . . . Derveet knew about this weakness of hers. It was a plague the Dapurs had wiped out at least once in history, but it was back now, more stubborn than ever and beyond even their power. She was prepared to bear it like the common people, and just try to take care. But she had never had this particular experience before. She sat still, wide eyed, and the waves lapped. It doesn't mean anything, she muttered, and bent to rinse her hands and mouth. When she looked up, she saw the brown cat, perched in the framework above her head. She was not even surprised, or only for a moment.

'The only wonder,' she murmured, as she wrapped the dripping kain round her and knotted it over her collarbone, 'is, what do you need *me* for? Lead on.'

High overhead was a black roof, the underside of the solid part of the tower. The Cat led Derveet nimbly, occasionally glancing back with some scorn, to a ladder which took them up to a railed walkway. Derveet pressed herself against the inner wall, and stood very still: where the walkway turned out of sight round the curve of the tower was a glow of light, and a huddle of figures. She could make out five: boys or men. A sixth figure, a little apart from the rest, made her stare; she thought it was a woman. Then she saw what they were watching. A bubble was coming, a small one. It floated just above the water, making a trail of glimmering reflected light on the little black waves. It was rose coloured and silent; she could see that it would dock in a bay designed for it, below where the people were standing. It had come for Cho. . . . Her nails dug into the palms of her hands. But her guide wanted her attention.

There was an entrance, a blot of deeper darkness in the wall across from the head of the ladder. She could not see the Cat but she knew she was being led on, into the centre of the tower. Everything she touched felt like the scaffolding; smooth and hard and curiously cold. She realised it was all made of metal, all of it. There was no sign of decay. The sea-washed ribs and spars she had climbed had been sleek and bare too, after a hundred years. She had a feeling that she did not want and could not use: it was not decent fear, but a failing of the heart. . . . Luckily this is the Cat's rescue, not mine, she thought. The corridor ended in a blank wall. But as she sensed this, and stretched out her hands, the wall glided away. Divine Endurance slipped past her. The room in the middle of the tower was not large. It had a trestle table in it, benches, some old sacks: incongruous flotsam. The air glowed with a dim, pale light. The Cat trotted to a section of the curved wall and stared at it. Derveet approached: the wall opened and a light came on inside. The Cat was gone. Cho was sitting on the floor of the cupboard, with her back propped against the wall and her head hanging limply. Derveet stood looking at the little figure, her heart full of love and pity; tears pricking her eyes. Cho raised her head, and her face lit up in welcome.

'Don't come in,' she said. 'There's no catch on the inside. I was just coming. I was, really.'

It was like the first bounty hunters: she had delayed trying to think of a way to satisfy everybody, and wondering a little if she really ought to go to see her brother. But now Derveet was here there was no dilemma. She got out of the cupboard.

'Wait – ' said Derveet. 'The Cat – where's she gone?'

'Did Divine Endurance bring you?'

Derveet was looking under the table.

'Oh, I don't think we need her,' said Cho, a little embarrassed. She was going to explain; it was rather awkward – but there was no time. There were people in the corridor. Derveet snatched Cho's hand and together they made for the farther wall. It opened and they fled into the dark. But this was not the Sawah river crossing: everything around them was hostile and there was no confusion. The passage end was blank and would not give way. There was no sound of pursuit but they could feel someone in the room behind them: someone in control. Cho turned quickly, after a flicker of thought, and the side wall opened. 'It's a storage space,' she said as she ran. 'It doesn't lock up, you can only change the doors about.'

They ran, not noticing the darkness; knowing by senses other than sight that a room had become a dead end corridor – a corridor's walls had fallen away and left them lost in space. They ran round and round the tower: Derveet lost all sense of place, the maze could have been endless. But they could not get to the walkway over the sea. Whoever was playing with them was too good at this game.

'Stop!' cried Derveet. The room they were in stayed still. 'We can't get out!'

'No, I don't think so,' said Cho, so composed, so perfectly at ease. She looked at Derveet expectantly. And Derveet at last, suddenly, realised the meaning of what she imagined: what she guessed. . . . Light fell on them abruptly. The passage behind them closed. Doors on each side opened together, and another straight ahead. The boys surrounded them. The woman Derveet had glimpsed turned out to be Nightclub Leilah. She faced them smiling, and the boy beside her levelled a Koperasi *stop*.

Koperasi did not often use things like that law and order weapon now. As the years passed they fell more and more to a conventional armoury: various firearms, fairly sophisticated but not different in kind from what the Peninsula could understand. And so people said the Rulers had sunk down; were powerless. But Derveet thought no: It's just that we are not the only ones who are being abandoned. . . . The sight of that sleek thing worked on her like the tower itself. Bitter and defeated anger exploded in her. She shouted, 'Cho! – ' and flung herself at the boy.

The sound pistol flew to the floor. Leilah, for a fatal instant, forgot she was not a lady and recoiled in disgust from this crudity – she had never played the Anakmati game. The boy was on the ground, gasping. The others grabbed Derveet as she came up, but by that time Cho had the stop, and was pointing it at all of them. The boys instantly, carefully raised their hands. They knew it was a soothing myth that this thing was 'only to stun', you could die weeks later or lose a limb, from the vibration damage. But Leilah cried fiercely –

'Oh, you shit-eaters! She's only a slave. She daren't use that thing. She can't do it – '

Cho was looking at the weapon, with a faintly puzzled and unhappy expression.

'You're right,' said Derveet sadly. 'She cannot.'

White light shone on the makeshift smugglers' furniture. One of the boys stood over Derveet, tied by the wrists and held down on a bench at the table, the stop nuzzling her throat. The rest of them sat on the floor in a corner, whispering occasionally but keeping their heads bowed and their eyes lowered. Leilah stood apart with her arms folded, her face a cool mask. Derveet admired her: shameless, degraded, traitor she might be, but she was *not* going to be impressed. She thought of the Cat (where is she? what happened to her?) but with scarcely a flicker of hope. A panel in the wall by Cho's cupboard was open, showing a mysterious nest of what must be controls for this place. On the other side of the table a stranger, strangely dressed, was examining Cho.

The Ruler was large, larger than most Koperasi, which struck Derveet as odd for the Dapur always worked for smallness, considered long bones, big bodies unsuccessful. The head was a bare shining globe, not shaven she thought but naturally hairless, the face smooth except for many tiny, tiny lines when it moved, around the eyes and mouth. The body was

138

dressed in baggy coveralls, carefully fastened – no doubt as protection against this alien, abandoned world. She could not say if the Ruler was a woman or boy or man, there was no sign of anything like that. Perhaps this person had left behind such distinctions, as very, very old people do. . . . Large smooth hands moved confidently, encased in glistening film; applying various devices to the subject. Derveet had to watch: the procedure was grimly absorbing. Finally, the Ruler put everything else away, and wrapped a web of flexible glass tubes around Cho's head.

'Look at the tabletop please.'

It was the first time the stranger had spoken. The Inggris was oddly accented, naturally enough. The battered tabletop went white in a square area, and Cho's face appeared in transparent detail of bone and moving blood. Then an enlargement of her eyes. 'Ah – ' The image showed something strange. In the centre of each eye, as if on the retina or the lens itself, there appeared tiny silvery lines. The Ruler adjusted for more detail. And now the silvery engraving stood out plain and clear. Each eye the same – a group of minute patterns of crossed lines, and then four letters: ACGT.

'Adenine, Cytosine, Guanine, Thymine. The tumbling dice. That settles it.'

The web was removed; all the instruments were folded away and slipped into some deep pocket of the coverall.

'Those – ah, chemicals are the final building blocks of life. They were synthesised, and changed incredibly. This is a product of the Tumbling Dice Toy Factory, Beijing Province, Rising Sun World State. The most advanced model they ever made, for it was soon after this particular range came out that – the party was suddenly over, as it were. Ah well.' A glistening finger tapped Cho on the shoulder: 'There is no doubt about it. This is a meta-genetic android.'

'No I'm not,' said Cho. And the whole room was startled to hear her speak.

'Oh, I'm sorry. Gynoid, I meant of course. That's all I wanted to know, anyway. We were pretty sure, but we thought we'd like to confirm it. It's very satisfying. A very satisfying turn of events.'

Derveet stared at what was Cho: awe greater than horror;

139

greater than any feeling. So far to go up, so far to come down. . . . She felt the vast weight of the past for the first time, truly. It seemed too much for the world to bear.

The Ruler looked across at her and asked, conversationally, 'Did you know?'

'I knew . . . fairy tales, folklore; rumours, of the *wayang orang*, the doll people. They belonged to another age of the world. No story imagined they had survived into this creation. The very best of them came from a special pleasure city in the east. They were called "wayang legong" – angel dolls. They were not machines but perfect lifelong companions. They were invulnerable to fire, disease, any kind of weapon – time. They protected. They had power over animals, the elements, the minds of enemies. But they were always good and gentle. They would do no harm.'

'All that and more. There has never been anything like them. An angel doll can grant, *will* grant, every wish of the human heart.'

The boys kept their heads down. Leilah stood as before, preserving her cold mask with a great effort. She had thought she was recovering a stolen farm camp slave.

'But how did *you* know?' asked Derveet.

'Oh, that's easy. We have one already. We've had him for about a hundred years: picked him up, it doesn't matter how, at the beginning of your last troubles. We've been looking out ever since, in case there were any more. . . . He has helped us so much. I'd try to tell you, but you wouldn't understand. You will though, you will.'

Derveet had some idea of keeping the creature talking, as if she might in a moment think of a way out of this. But no more words would come. The Ruler was perfectly relaxed; watching her face, smiling a little. . . . It was strange. She could not see, when she looked into her enemy's eyes, any sign of enormous evil and power. There was only an immense, immense weariness: the vast weight of the past. She stared, for a long moment of curious intimacy, trying to understand.

Suddenly the large person sighed, and then leaned forward with a new expression.

'Oh dear. You are going to lose the sight after all I think. It happens: even the best repairs are never quite the same. How

140

do they do it by the way. . . . Fascinating. Still, it serves you right for those bold bandit antics of yours in the Sawah. That'll teach you to wish things on yourself.'

Derveet had only an instant for dismay, at this mocking glimpse of knowledge she was given – and to remember it didn't matter anymore now. With the last words the Ruler moved: a faint, almost imperceptible nod, and the boy turned his stop and brought its butt crashing down.

'There,' said the Ruler. 'I was wondering just how long before she realised all she had to do was to say a word to the doll. But it is a habit one has to develop, I suppose. Ours, now, has gone far beyond needing someone to tell it what to do all the time. But they too have to develop, to reach their full potential. Which is *enormous*. . . . Open one eye for me. Yes, she's safe for quite a while. But tie her up thoroughly please. Do things properly – '

Leilah had not moved or made a sound since the revelations began. The Ruler smiled at her pleasantly, rivers of tiny lines rippling.

'Now then. I will give you all a lift to the shore and put you down somewhere quiet; it's safer that way. The price, I'm afraid, remains what it was. This other person is really Koperasi business, not mine. Just one word of advice madam: it might be better to leave Ranganar for a while. "Tongues wag", you know. I'll collect these two on my way out.'

The gang of boys shuffled to their feet. What kind of servants would the Rulers use: who would work for the monsters themselves, with no disguise? The dregs of the dregs, obviously. Can dirt that you walk on be insulted? Leilah went with them, still expressionless, and the Ruler was close behind her.

Divine Endurance had not been far away. She had followed all the proceedings, while at the same time looking curiously around the rig. She was soon aware that the plan was rather different from what she'd thought. And yet, and yet. . . . It had its own elegance. She was content. As soon as the Ruler's bubble had gone she bounced into the centre room, jumped up on the table, and sat there licking her ruff.

'Why *did* you bring her?'

'I should have thought that was obvious. I wanted you to

141

come to the Rulers and you said you wouldn't leave her. Anyway, I didn't bring her. I just helped her to come.'

Cho gave the Cat a rather quizzical look. Two small figures, crouched on a cold bare floor, on either side of a body lying motionless. The walls had dimmed again, the nest of controls had vanished: the room was still and empty. Cho touched the dark face – Derveet awoke to see the child bending over her.

'Cho?' she said, and put her hand to the back of her head.

She sat up and saw the table, the benches in the grey gloom. The Cat was back, and where were the rest of them? She looked curiously at the rope-ends lying beside her, carefully unknotted and neatly coiled.

'Do you want it to hurt or not?' asked Cho. 'I wasn't sure.'

'Come on,' said Divine Endurance.

The walls opened with eerie obedience: the Cat led them to the ladder on the walkway, and down. She disliked climbing *down* things, but she knew Cho would only start fussing. . . . At the bottom of the ladder a smuggler's boat was moored, painted black inside and out.

'It's the one they brought me in,' said Cho.

Of course. Derveet stared. She turned her head and looked back, up at the bulk of the tower. Nothing stirred. No great eyes opened in the blackness, nothing reached out. . . . The child and the Cat were sitting in the boat looking up at her. She got in the stern and started up the illegal wasp-tail engine.

When they reached the shore the Cat hopped out neatly, shaking her paws at the wet sand. 'Goodnight,' she said. 'I have a feeling your friend is going to stand about *talking* and I'm sure it's going to rain. Besides, I have to get back to my person.'

Derveet let the boat go, to take its chance. She looked around: 'Where's the Cat?'

'She's gone back to her person.'

The beach stretched dimly: quite near to them was the jetty Derveet had dived from, between the black sea and the dully glowing sky. The palms and pandanus hiding the road rustled and tossed harshly; the sea bumped against the sand in heavy blind waves. Out over the ocean the sky cracked suddenly with light, revealing cloud capped towers of storm piled up into the dark –

'They let us go,' said Derveet. 'Why did they let us go; let *you* go? Cho, why did you never tell me there was – someone like you, with the Rulers. Didn't you know?'

Cho said nothing. She was in tears. It was not that she had not known exactly what she was. Of course she knew. But the knowledge had been so simple she had never looked at it, never thought what it meant.

'Oh no – ' cried Derveet. 'Dearest child – '

She put her arms round Cho and held her tight. Cho sobbed.

'Child it doesn't matter. What difference does it make? We are all *wayang*; all – I, yes, even that creature with the gold head, all *wayang*. What else is there?'

But Cho had been listening to Derveet intently, lovingly, for all the time she had known her, and she knew that the Dapur, which held Derveet's heart, had been striving all its life to leave Cho behind, to get beyond Cho entirely. And now here she was: wrong, wrong, the very thing that wasn't wanted. How could she make Derveet happy?

'It's why,' she sobbed. 'It's why I couldn't go in the Dapur.'

Thunder rolled like a rockfall over the sea and the rain came down with a roar; invisible one moment, a white forest of falling stars the next. They ran up the beach, Derveet pulling Cho by the hand, and took shelter in the ragged, trailing undergrowth; wet bodies huddled together, comforting each other.

In the cabaret room of the nightclub Leilah sat with her sister. It was evening again. Leilah had returned from her adventure in the early morning, and shut herself up all day. Tonight the club was closed. The dull lit room smelled of stale beer, old achar smoke and sweat.

'You going to do this often?' asked Simet, grinning sardonically at the empty tables. Leilah flashed a glance at her and said nothing. The brown cat that had come to live in the club recently jumped on her knees and curled itself comfortably.

Something had got into Leilah. It was entirely unlike her to chase after adventures at all. She had detested the interloper Derveet for a long time without doing anything but snipe. It was Leilah's way, to hate and be disgusted and yet at the last moment get sickened at the idea of action. Some time ago they had investigated the squatter who had taken up residence in the

143

old Merpati ruins, now called 'Dove House', and found her out; even found out the trail that led to Bu Awan, and the lost Garuda prince. Leilah did nothing, but sneer and hint: Derveet never turned a hair. Now suddenly she had done this thing, in spite of the people she had to deal with. 'Why not?' she said. 'I *want* to do it – I wonder what they'll do with the little girl.' Simet thought it was mad, but she didn't interfere. But Leilah had come back in a very strange mood.

'What are you going to do then? Turn her in?'

'You don't listen, do you? *They know.*'

The most mysterious part of all this was that Derveet was *not* a prisoner of the Rulers, with her little girl. Simet had sent over to the West Bank: Derveet was at home, alive and well, as of this afternoon. Leilah, when told this, stared with enormous eyes. But she did not seem surprised. Simet was jealous.

'The truth is you've always been a bit trickly for her,' she said. 'What you really want is to get your hand in her pocket.'

'You talk like a five-year-old,' said Leilah. 'Her father was the Koperasi, her mother was a polowijo. She has *no* rights: none. She's going to set herself up with that "little girl" of hers, seduce the common people, persuade everyone the Dapur is on her side – big lies are best, aren't they, and bring the country out. Her friends are the Samsui, the Koperasi, the polowijo on Bu Awan. It's unbearable.'

'She's never done anything like that before.'

'Don't you listen to the news? Don't you know someone sank the water in the Garuda dam just before New Year, and set the Eagle flying again? The whole Peninsula knows it.'

Simet said stupidly, 'But you're not interested in politics.'

Leilah glared: her sunset eyes took on the blank, cat-look that meant trouble.

'All right,' said Simet quickly. 'I'm listening.'

'Obviously it is coming soon. Everything points to that, especially this thing she's got hold of. But she doesn't know how to use it properly. They'll take it when they want it, even if she got away this time. . . . Don't make any mistake, Simet. There is no hope. All we can do is hate them. We can't win. I've always known it, and I know it better now because I've seen one. I've been in their world.'

She fell silent. How many years had she lived this life? She had come to Ranganar to escape from unbearable reminders, and found she had to live on Tiger Street. She had been in a mood to laugh at that, at the time. Why had it taken her so long to find out that she need not laugh, sneer; swallow vomit? She could do something else. Her hands soothed the cat's sleek fur: Divine Endurance crooned gently.

Simet looked at her sister's aroused and vivid face. She wondered. She wondered what 'this thing she's got hold of' referred to, but obviously she wasn't going to find out.

'What do you want to do?'

'I'm going to do what the Ruler told me to do,' said Leilah. 'Leave Ranganar.'

She raised her head and their eyes met, but Simet soon gave way. She sighed.

'Anything you say, madam'.

Then she took a bottle of Anggur Merah from behind the bar and brought it over, with two glasses. The wine smelled of mountains; its colour was bright as blood.

18   Atoon in Ranganar

Derveet was sleeping in the sun. She lay on a flat roof at the back of Dove House, one arm behind her head, the other outstretched on worn stone. A tray with the remains of breakfast lay beside her, and the bold mynah birds, rolling their sulphur-circled eyes, stalked grandly from one fragment to the next. At the end of the red mud alley, a little flock of boys appeared, ragged and excited; clinging and jumping like kittens round a sedate figure in their midst, a stranger to the West Bank. The flock halted, pointing and explaining, and then their chattering faded. The visitor came down the street alone, between tumbledown shacks and pungent heaps of refuse. He wore white, his hair was coiled in shining braids; his perfect golden shoulders were bare. He did not seem to feel in the slightest degree out of place.

When he came to the end of the alley she sat up. They looked at each other gravely – it was a long time since the sunset, the day of Alat's trial. She reached down to him, he grasped her wrist and came up onto the low roof. They knelt face to face, strangely tongue-tied, then Atoon took something out of his sash; she smiled when she saw it and opened her left hand. She had been sleeping with the dancer's bell tucked in her fist. Solemnly, they exchanged tokens and then, at last, embraced.

They had never quite given each other up. The link between them was very tenuous: no Dapur power, only the more mysterious bond of friendship, but it had never quite broken.

'So,' said Atoon at last. 'You have become a Samsui.'

Derveet looked at herself – black trousers and blouse. She often wore the city women's clothes now, she had forgotten it was strange.

'Why yes,' she said. 'After all, in the end, I think I have. But you, my dear, are still a prince I see.'

She was laughing at him. 'But this is your territory isn't it?'

146

said Atoon – he meant the West Bank – 'Naturally I tidied myself up. Why ever not?'

Derveet frowned. 'It's true you're probably safe from the Koperasi here, but they are not the only problem. Shall we go inside?'

She stood up, lifting the breakfast tray. Atoon looked again. The face of his angry young friend had changed, it had grown; it was strong and calm, and yet –

'Derveet,' he said. 'Have you been ill?'

She had her back to him, stepping through the window she was using as a door. 'I'll? – Well, perhaps a little different from usual. It is hari darah, Atoon. Are you trying to insult me?' She flashed a smile over her shoulder – 'Now I've made you blush. How sweet. Watch out for holes, and beware of falling lizards.'

She was lying, of course. Atoon followed her, frowning slightly.

In the upper room, Cendana the dancer and Miss Butcher Handai were waiting. They had not seen Derveet since she left them at the Dance Theatre several days ago, they had only had a message passed on via the Butchers' hired boys, that the kidnapping had been foiled and Cho was safe. Meanwhile the big nightclub on the corner of the Pasar Diluar suddenly had its shutters up: Leilah and her sister had disappeared, no one knew where. But all was not well, the dancers knew it though they had no clear picture of what had gone wrong. Handai and Cendana had been waiting, ready for any kind of disaster, when the summons came, through the boys again, that they were to come to Dove House. The prince of Jagdana had travelled down the coast in secret, crossed the Straits with smugglers and was now on the West Bank.

Handai stood up, nervously. 'How do you do?' she managed to say, in a strangled voice.

'How do you do?' returned Atoon gravely, offering his hand. Miss Butcher took the elegant golden thing gingerly, as if terrified that it would break. Cendana bowed correctly over her folded hands, for a moment not brave Sandalwood or the great dancer but a failed woman of no particular family, meeting the Hanoman prince –

Derveet sat on the end of her bed and watched them. 'An important meeting of four conspirators,' she remarked, 'coming together to discuss how they will take over the Peninsula –'

Her voice was strange – irony without a hint of laughter. Handai and Cendana glanced at each other.

'I wish it was,' said Derveet. 'But I'm afraid it isn't. I don't even know why Atoon is here, I haven't asked him yet. And there is something else we have to discuss.'

Then she told them the real story of Cho's kidnapping: the truth about the child Jagdana Dapur had dressed in warrior white, who had come to change their fortunes, and the cool familiarity the Ruler had shown with certain Peninsulan affairs. She left nothing out, except that she was a little vague and dismissive about the 'gangster' who had been the Ruler's instrument.

When she had finished there was a long, stunned silence in the upper room. At last Handai stood up and went to the window, irresistibly drawn there. Down in the courtyard the Dove House boys were playing tag with a brown cat and a piece of string. Cho sat on the kitchen doorstep and laughed, showing her small white teeth. It was incredible. She turned away.

'I was going to tell you,' she said huskily. 'I was trying to get up the nerve to tell you – that she was too young for you, it wasn't right.'

That made Derveet laugh.

She looked at Atoon. 'Well, why *are* you here? Of course I am pleased to see you, but it is a long and dangerous journey for someone as precious as the Hanoman prince. Why didn't they send a good boy, whatever their message is? Your family has been behaving very strangely, from the start.'

Atoon sighed. 'I think,' he said, 'that I was sent, principally, to carry a warning that could be trusted to no one else. But I have come too late.'

The Hanoman women knew at once that Cho was not 'Derveet's emissary'. They did not reveal this to Atoon, because they sensed that something very important was happening that should not be discussed prematurely. They were curious about the circumstances of Cho's arrival: her clothes, her sojourn in the irrigation ditch and remarkable recovery, Atoon's instant conviction that she had been sent to call him

148

back to the struggle; to call him back to life. They had acquired these details carefully, through the screens, without showing their astonishment to the outside palace, which was, Atoon included, so strangely ready to ignore everything strange about the visitor. . . .

'But if all this, then why the white clothes Atoon? Why send her to me? I don't understand.'

The prince shook his head. 'You must know what happened when I tried to send her inside: my family never actually examined her. Then there were the riots. I think it was only afterwards that they studied the past and so on, and became quite sure of what she must be: that she is a wayang legong – ' He paused. It was a name out of a fairy tale, with only the vaguest of associations; either wonderfully good, or wonderfully bad, but certainly not real –

'I believe that in one way they sent her to you quite simply as you and I accepted it, to recognise your work. But it was Cho herself, Cho's arrival that made them decide it was time to give up neutrality. This angel doll is very dangerous, very fateful, they told me. She changes everything. But they couldn't tell me how. I think they are still trying to find out themselves.'

He fell silent. After a moment Derveet prompted him quietly. 'Anything else?'

'I was to tell you: Set thy heart upon thy work, never on its reward. Let your thought be for the good of all, and then do thy work in peace. . . . '

Handai whispered to Cendana – 'What's all that about?'

'It's scripture.'

Atoon exclaimed, 'Why *didn't* they take her into the Dapur?'

Derveet smiled. 'Oh, I can explain that. It was nothing to do with your family, it was Cho's conscience. It won't let her go where she's not wanted. And I imagine, Atoon, that the Hanoman Dapur, in its heart, does not have much use for – machines.'

Handai said firmly: 'Of course we can't give up Cho. We simply can't do that.'

Derveet was studying, with concentration, the rose and smoky pattern in the marble floor. She glanced up at her friend obliquely, but said nothing.

'What about the rest of the Peninsula?' she asked Atoon. 'We have heard so little in Ranganar, except rumours and what comes filtered through the Koperasi airwaves. How are people reacting to the dam message, and the Hanomans' child in white? How far have things gone?'

'The signs have been read, definitely,' said Atoon. He hesitated – 'There's a certain amount of visible excitement, Derveet. Especially in the north.'

'Oh no!' The soft exclamation was involuntary. 'You mean Gamartha, don't you?'

'Derveet, they can't help it –' Handai remembered the *two thousand years*, and felt for the excitable Gamarthans. 'They don't know what's happened. I thought you wanted other people to take up the initiative.'

'Yes – But not like this.'

Derveet got up and began to pace the room restlessly; touched the pearls and put them down again: 'Jagdanans hate to exaggerate Miss Butcher. If the prince says there is "a certain amount of visible excitment" you can take it from me the whole country is bubbling. Boys and men bubble. If the Dapurs had allowed themselves to become involved, there would be nothing to see on the surface ... just some unexplained changes, developing. So, we have the women holding aloof, in spite of the Hanomans' declaration, and danger in the north.'

She had come to the window and stood there. 'The trouble is, Dapur government isn't meant to impose authority: it is meant to give the ladies peace and quiet and time for more important things. It's an arrangement that has worked for a long time, whatever you may thing about "covert manipulation", Handai. But it tends to make some people – outside the walls – irresponsible. And there is so much hatred about nowadays. We were very careful in our game with the Koperasi. There were no losers, I think Anakmati has as many admirers in Sepaa as anywhere. Even so, it was going to take us all the time, all the patience, all the restraint in the world to keep our factions together. Think of the possibilities. I'm sorry to bring this up, Handai, but where do the Rulers' agents come from ... for one thing?'

'And there is Cho –'

The boys had gone away and Cho sat quietly with her pet, she looked up at Derveet and smiled. Derveet smiled back.

150

She spoke half to herself. 'I can accept that the Rulers have known everything, that they have been laughing at my amusing antics all along. But why did they let us go? They have not stirred from their islands for a hundred years, but they came for Cho. *Why* did they let her go again?'

'You escaped –' Atoon reminded her.

'So we did,' said Derveet dryly. 'It was very easy. It had not occurred to the Ruler that the angel doll might rouse me. The boat left behind was no doubt a simple oversight.'

For a while no one spoke. Petruk was banging pots and pans in the kitchen house, and singing tunelessly.

'Cho is dangerous, Cho changes everything because the Rulers want her and we've got her,' said Handai. 'That's clear enough. They're playing some kind of cat and mouse game, that's all.'

No one commented. Cendana glanced at her beloved with a brief smile, like a mother a little embarrassed by her child. No one could think of anything else to say, under the shadow of that one bewildering fact: the Rulers knew. They should draw back, they should undo what had begun – but how? In fact, it was impossible.

At last Atoon said, 'We have never been able to understand them. We have always lived in fear, and we would none of us have started on this enterprise if there had been any other choices left. Nothing has changed. We must go on, as best we can. When Ardjuna the perfect archer takes aim the world disappears for him. He sees nothing, no distractions; nothing in his way – only the point on his target where the arrow will strike. We must be like Ardjuna.'

Derveet smiled, the dancer's eyes glowed. Handai wondered why the prince was suddenly talking gibberish.

When Cendana and Handai had gone, over the river, Atoon turned on Derveet immediately.

'Who is she?'

Derveet pretended not to understand. She lit two cigarettes, and gave him one, and stretched out on the bed.

'Who is who? And why? We have so much to talk about. Have you forgiven me, for refusing to let you disembowel yourself that time?'

'I mean the person who kidnapped Cho.'

151

'Oh – I thought you gathered. Just a nightclub owner. Afterwards, as I said, I sent the boys to see what had happened to her. She got back safely, apparently, but then vanished. Probably afraid of what my "gang" might do to her.'

But he had seen her reaction to the mention of trouble in Gamartha. 'I somehow got the impression,' he said obstinately,' that your enemy is a northerner.'

Derveet was silent for a moment. Then she said, 'No, Atoon. I won't tell you the name or the family of a lady whose bad luck brought her to Hungry Tiger Street. She was someone who should have been my friend, it must have been partly my fault that she wasn't. You may find out who she is soon enough, but not from me.'

'What do you mean by that?'

'Nothing,' said Derveet. 'I hope – nothing.'

Cho and the Cat were enjoying the warm stone. The Cat licked her flank indolently, relaxing after the amusement – something she enjoyed once in a way – of making the boys jump about and squeak.

'Divine Endurance,' said Cho. 'Why *did* you come back with me and Derveet? I thought you wanted to get to Wo, and take me with you.'

'I changed my mind,' said Divine Endurance. 'It's a cat's prerogative.'

Cho looked sceptical, so for peace the Cat explained.

'I've realised there is no point in nagging. This world is so small you and Wo are bound to meet sometime. Meanwhile I think you are doing quite well at helping to help people just where you are. And I will help to, of course.'

'But what about your person? Where is she? Have you lost her?'

'No I have not lost her,' said Divine Endurance crossly. 'She has gone somewhere she likes, and I am still helping her. You don't *have* to get in their pockets to make them happy you know.'

Cho laughed, delighted to have caught the Cat out for once. 'You don't know what that means,' she said.

Derveet might as well have told him. Her discretion was about to become quite pointless. On the same day that Atoon arrived in

Ranganar, prince Bima Singa of Gamartha stood in an ante chamber, waiting. He was in the northern palace, where the Singas were discreetly contained by their enemies. He gazed through a high fretted window of grape-bloomed stone at citrus gardens and mulberry groves; and beyond, the steep emerald terraced hillsides and the sudden brilliant sky. He was a handsome young man, with the wide cat-face and pointed chin of the Singas, and the notorious 'tiger eyes'. The Gamarthan Dapurs had a passion for close breeding. Eyes and face at the moment were full of pride and a new feeling: a fierce, reckless joy. He loved his country very much.

In Gamartha things had always been different. People of high caste ate meat and drank wine, and the ladies were far closer to the world of men. This was not the Dapur, but behind Bima a light screen, veiled with draperies, had been put across the room as a mark of respect. He heard the rustle of silk and turned, drawing a deep breath of happiness, to kneel and greet his long lost sister.

19 The Black Horse

The rising in Gamartha sent shock waves all through the Peninsula. There were outbursts everywhere: even parts of Sepaa mutinied and took to the hills. Garbled bulletins on the Administration Compound walls told a grim story of lives wasted and savage, ineffectual reprisals. In a matter of days it was as if the delicate, careful work of the White Riders had never been. The people of Ranganar knew nothing of that of course. All they knew was that fugitives were pouring into the city: hordes of starving slaves from the camps; seeovers barely distinguishable from their charges; Sepaa mutineers, brigands; and even whole families from the near parts of Timur Kering. The city was in an uproar. The Samsui were indignant that *their* Koperasi failed to control the influx. The truth was the men could not do it. They were no longer capable of doing the job for which they had been hired, and so bitterly paid.

The black horse struggled as Derveet led him into the yard. He was afraid of the dark and the flaring lamplight.

'Hush, Jak – hush –'

Cho put her arms round Gress's neck and whispered to her. The horses had to be moved. Tonight, suddenly, their hidden stable was in danger, it was too near the river.

'He'll be all right,' said Gress. 'He's just a bit highly strung.'

Bejak stood still, pressed his face into Derveet's shoulder and sighed heavily. He was bitterly disappointed. He had thought when they came to fetch him that the horrible imprisonment was over.

'Console him for me Cho,' said Derveet. 'I can't think of anything to say.' The journey through the forest seemed like a lost paradise – far out of reach now.

Cho led the animals away. Petruk turned his lantern out and studied the fireclouds over the city. It looked as if the trouble had moved, since midnight, into the Commercers' quarter.

'Madam, could you not possibly cross the river? This is disgraceful.'

'No Petruk,' said Derveet. 'It would only mean some of the rioters would be shouting my name, and that would give me no pleasure. Besides, the Koperasi might arrest me.'

Petruk grinned. The red creatures were showing them-selves sadly incompetent at arresting anyone. It was nearly a month now since the news from Gamartha. Street fighting had broken out among the fugitives quite early in the crisis: every-body said the Sepaa mutineers were mainly to blame. Now every day and night brought more violence. And overcrowding was weighing heavily on the city's resources.

Handai was standing at the window, staring. 'Where is it?' she asked anxiously, as Derveet came into the upper room.

'Commercers, the boys think.'

Miss Butcher and the dancer had come over to talk, uselessly, about what could be done, and been stranded when the night's trouble broke out. Little Dinah lay on Derveet's bed, oblivious. Beside her was prince Atoon. He had been caught in the city, with no word from his family. He was still waiting for a safe chance to leave.

When the news first broke that prince Bima Singa had declared *merdeka* and launched an armed uprising, most of Previous Heaven had felt something uncontrollable: a start of joy. No one spoke of that now. Derveet was grimly silent. Prince Atoon said openly, ruthlessly, that the sooner the Koperasi pulled themselves together and stamped it out, the better he would be pleased. The name of Leilah of Gamartha had appeared frequently now on the Koperasi walls, and it was fairly common knowledge where this lady had sprung from. Derveet had given up etiquette and told Handai a story.

There was once a young lady, a jewel of a young lady; accomplished, spirited, clever. One of her blood brothers was the crown prince. This being Gamartha he knew it, and naturally was drawn to her. They wrote long letters. The Royal Dapur were worried about the influence of this one daughter of theirs. They did not want their prince to be inflamed with sad, stupid fantasies about merdeka – freedom. They could not send her to another court or household because of 'movement restrictions' in that subjugated country. . . . The dilemma was solved when the fiery young lady, and her most faithful companion, failed at entering and went away to ruin. They did not need any papers for that. Nor – the big base on the gulf of Gamartha – was not far enough for such a fallen star, so they came to Ranganar.

If it was true that Leilah's failure was arranged, those hard-hearted, careful ladies had sown the wind, and they were reaping now. 'Why don't they stop her?' demanded Handai. 'Because they can't,' said Derveet. 'Anyway, some of them probably don't want to.' It was evident from the bulletins that the Singa Dapur had taken a very Dapur-like decision. They had withdrawn from the action, abandoning Leilah and Bima to their fate, which was inevitable. . . .'How did she find the courage to do it?' wondered Derveet. 'For better or for worse – I thought she was lost. I thought nothing could move her.'

Derveet's room had changed. The boys had infiltrated its austerity with mats and cushions, for the prince's sake, and there were several lamps burning. It was very quiet. Dinah slept. Atoon tried to answer Handai's questions about what would be happening in Gamartha now. She made a point of talking to Atoon seriously: she disliked a way Derveet had of treating him lightly, like an amusement; like something she owned. Cendana took down her hair and began to brush it out.

'Let me do it,' said Derveet. The dancer was right: talk was pointless. She knelt on cushions, and Cendana sat at her feet. Her hair was very different from Derveet's slick, heavy stuff. Opaque and insubstantial it spilled on the air, and twined itself self destructively around the brush.

'Did you ever have long hair, Derveet?'

'Oh yes. All divers did. Only men cut their hair on the islands. Silly, really, but it was tradition. I had a great thick plait – negative buoyancy, I suppose.'

'It was cut when you were entered?'

'No,' said Derveet, working gently on a tangle, 'that couldn't be, because I couldn't have dived with cut hair, and I had to earn our living. It was not a great occasion, the ceremony. Only my grandfather entered me, there was no one else. Perhaps I was too young. We couldn't wait because he was ill, and the evacuation was hanging over us.'

Hush, hush, said the smooth strokes over Cendana's shoulders. The sound was like the sea, sighing on that lost, dark shore. Derveet felt adrift. She had the sensation every day now that she must act – urgently. But what could she do? Atoon's wise words about Ardjuna the archer had come to nothing. They had had no chance to 'go on' with whatever action or restraint, before the Singas' merdeka exploded. Such a destructive explosion: Miss Butcher had said more than once that at least the Gamarthan outbreak showed there was no need to worry about the Rulers. Whatever they knew, they were letting the Koperasi do their dirty work, as inefficiently as ever. We don't have to be afraid of them suddenly striking us down in some awful way – Don't we? thought Derveet. Perhaps they've just done it. She did not believe that Leilah was the enemy's tool now, not consciously; she had seen a revulsion of feeling in the tiger-cat, that night on the rig, and been afraid even then of what it might mean. Leilah was sincere, like all the other thoughtless rebels; sincere like the rioters. . . . But while Derveet tried doggedly to think of this disaster as a setback; a reverse to be weathered – we lie low and then try again – something monstrous and shadowy was taking shape in her mind. What had she disturbed?

These frantic outbursts were not new. In a milder form they had plagued the Peninsula for a hundred years. A few nights ago, alone here with Cho, she had asked the child about the other angel doll, her brother. What could *Wo* do? What sort of thing would he do for the Rulers? And Cho answered with her usual impenetrable candour. 'How many people?' asked Derveet. 'How many people could someone like Wo "make happy"?' Cho said, apologetically, 'Well, there isn't really an answer.'

She had asked the dancers what they could see ahead when things first started to go wrong, before Gamartha came out. But they could not help her; they still could not. They offered her obscure fragmentary dreams, vague feelings that something tremendous would come out of all this trouble. And they did not seem to care that their intuition had deserted them: 'Too much is going on,' they said. 'The present's too important just now.' She did not ask, but she had a feeling no one had glimpsed the 'floating world', that painful memory, for quite a while. . . .

157

She tamed the filmy masses of Cendana's hair into one sheaf, and began to put them into a thick braid. Are you hiding something from me? she thought. Do you see something you are afraid to tell me, is that it? I am Garuda: perhaps I could make you tell. If I dared. . . . But Cendana was listening to Atoon and Handai talking about the price of violence; the cause of the Gamarthans.

'Derveet,' she said softly, 'does everything always end and fail and come to nothing?'

Suddenly there was a great crack of dry thunder out in the dark. It came from the east. Handai jumped to her feet.

'You may as well sit down,' said Derveet, after a moment. 'Whatever it was, there's nothing you can do.'

Cho came up from consoling Gress and Bejak and settled by Derveet, nestling down among the cushions. Derveet finished her plaiting and Cendana moved away. Darkness stood around the lamps, and no one felt like sleeping. Suddenly, Cho lifted her head.

Handai said, 'O it's *raining*. Mother, what a relief. It'll put out the fires —'

Derveet looked at Cho and got quietly to her feet. A moment later and they could all hear, above the sudden rush of the rain, Semar's voice raised querulously at the yard gate. Atoon moved away from the sleeping child and glanced around the room, assessing. Frightened footsteps thumped up the stairs. 'Madam —' But Derveet said, 'Don't be rude, Petruk. Bring the visitor in.'

It was Cycler Jhonni. She stood dripping, twisting her hands in her wet sleeves.

'Jhonni!' cried Miss Butcher. 'What's happening? What were the explosions?'

'Well — someone set light to some raw rubber that we hadn't moved. The river caught fire for a bit —'

'Is *that* what I could smell —'

'The explosion was probably the Clock Tower. It was very hot, all the windows burst. . . . That was the worst, actually. The Clock Tower was the only big thing, and it was, it was an accident. . . .'

It was difficult for Jhonni now. Her clan and family blamed the radicals for everything. She was forcibly kept away from

158

her Previous Heaven friends and she was afraid they didn't trust her anymore anyway. She looked at the prince, and couldn't speak for embarrassment.

'What is it Jhonni – ?'

Finally, she managed to tell them. Yesterday, the major clans led by the Cyclers had decided the mass of fugitives had to be expelled. They were to be given an amnesty, to leave peaceably. After a certain day, the Koperasi were going to round up any remaining aliens and see them off.

'I thought you ought to know. I don't know what they're going to do about the West Bank. I didn't know how to – to get here, but tonight the firefighters had boats on the river you see –'

Once it had been the dream of Jhonni's life to come to Dove House, and sit in this room. 'I'd better go,' she muttered. 'I'm sorry –'

'See them off where?' cried Miss Butcher. 'They won't go. It's mad! It'll make things fifty times worse –'

But Derveet was staring intently at Jhonni's bent head, the rim of wet hair plastered pitifully on her reddish nape. Her eyes grew wide and black.

'Atoon, I know the answer. I have been wondering all along, why did your family send you into danger. Just that late warning wasn't enough reason. Now I understand. I know what we should do.'

Twelve days after the Clock Tower riot, it was deportation day. The playing fields that covered the old reservoir, which the Samsui had filled in because of salt-water seepage, were thronged with people in the grey darkness before dawn. Many of them had been camping for days in makeshift shelters. Samsui organisers hurried about, their voices ringing in the air. There were bales, carts and animals. Of course, the 'causeway people' were getting what supplies could be spared. On the perimeter of the crowd hc treaders from Straits Control snarled up and down. The Samsui ignored this infringement, they knew the Koperasi were nervous and touchy.

Derveet was at the playing fields' foodstalls, standing *behind* Atoon in the way Handai so disliked, her hand just

159

touching his shoulder. For once the prince was not in white: he wore drab riding clothes.

'Here he comes. Now don't smile. They don't like you to smile, unless you are saying something very simply humorous.'

The speaker for the mutineers said, 'G'day.'

'Good day,' said Derveet.

He was red, big. 'We're for Anakmati,' he said aggressively. 'If Anakmati stays, we stay.'

'Anakmati is staying. But I think you should not.'

His blind-looking eyes followed the hc treaders uneasily.

'They won't touch you if you go.'

The mutineer stared at Atoon, who remembered not to smile.

'This is your man?'

'This is my man.'

The red creature at last shrugged, and nodded. He vanished into the crowd. Derveet and Atoon sat down together.

'Derveet change your mind. Come with me. I don't like the feel of this city —'

The Samsui imagined that Ranganar would be 'back to normal' in a day or two, with all its prized amenities, but the prince of Jagdana knew better. It was not just the riots. He had learned, painfully, to know the insidious marks of final decay. Derveet shook her head.

'No. I can't. There aren't any Samsui listening are there — ? After all, this is part of the Garuda state; it's my place to stay. Besides —' She smiled shyly. 'I'm not really fit for a camping holiday. You must have noticed.'

He had noticed. There was nothing to say; the uncertainty ahead swept over such minor concerns.

The noisy crowd milled around. Atoon said quietly, 'Tell me about the angel dolls.'

He knew she had some theory she was keeping to herself. She had refused to discuss it until the deportation was arranged.

'I once saw something Cho had done by accident,' said Derveet, looking into the crowd. 'Some mountain cats had attacked her and Gress: there was only blood left. I didn't know what I'd stumbled on, but then I met Cho and told her. She was very embarrassed. I thought – hm – she was embarrassed about something else, but I realised later. . . . They're not supposed

160

to be weapons. But perhaps they could be perverted. The Rulers could have left Cho to us so we'd quarrel over the marvellous toy, but they know we quarrel anyway. More likely they think we'll try to *use* her, and come to grief. Well, we will not. I think Cho was bound to gravitate to some power or other. By "coincidence" she came to you, and to me: both far too Dapur-ridden to be tempted by that kind of experiment. We are safe.'

'So what is it you are afraid of?'

Derveet glanced at him, and away. 'That it may be enough for Cho just to be here.'

'Oh Derveet –'

'No, no; not doing anything on purpose. But – Suppose the wayang the Rulers have, has some kind of harmful influence? Cho could affect that – a sort of catalyst. . . . Of course, this may be nonsense. . . . Or if not, I'll find a way round it.'

Atoon looked at her steadily, and said nothing. Derveet suddenly shook her head, dismissing the subject.

'For now, the point is you have a safe passage. Ranganar escapes the fun of a Koperasi round up, and you will keep this dreadful rabble out of mischief.'

'Yes. I had thought – I could travel via Bu Awan and talk to Annet, maybe stay there.'

Derveet frowned. 'No. Don't do that. Leave Annet alone – I've a feeling she has troubles enough at the moment. Stay completely in the wilds. Here – I want you to have these.'

She gave him a small padded bag. It was the pearls from Sinar Bulan.

'Derveet,' said Atoon. 'My family is not rich nowadays, but I think we can support people who are really in need.'

'But you'll have to go into the hills. Not to the capital. These people are displaced *anywhere* Atoon. I'm trusting you to keep them safe.'

'Until?'

'Until you hear from me.'

The Samsui must have been aware that some unseen force had taken over their ignoble decision, so that the trouble-makers, the mutineers and strays, came quietly and willingly. Nothing was declared. But there was an incongruous air of purpose in the ranks of the unwanted. In fact, there were many

161

in the lines who had not been asked to leave at all. An impression had spread that this docile departure was really, secretly, a great adventure.

It was time for Atoon to leave. The treaders snarled and distant voices shouted. Everything began to move. As he stood up, a line of carts passed and out from behind them two boys led a big nervous animal with a hide like black glass.

'Derveet –'

The boys whipped off a saddlecloth of cloud colour and blood rose, and flung over the horse's shoulders the blue and gold of Jagdana.

'Don't get on,' said Derveet grinning. 'Might attract too much attention.'

Some people shouted out – some knelt down: for Garuda's steward, their prince and leader; and then the moment was covered in the surging crowd.

'Go to the hills. Go far. Don't go back to Jagdana; don't go to Bu Awan, or anywhere near trouble. Stay away from Bima Singa. Stay away from the sea –'

The sea. It was her last word. The ranks pressed forward and she disappeared. A Sawah boy ran and snatched the blue and gold and stuffed it into his blouse. He took the bridle and proudly led the black horse after the prince, into the ranks of the people.

The cavalcade passed away, flanked by Koperasi vehicles, down the causeway road: mutineers and seeovers and slaves; Samsui and Ranganarese; veiled peasants from Timur Kering with their whole families trailing, and the senior boy holding up the rahula. . . . Derveet watched with Cho from the foodstall. 'Do you remember,' she said, 'I once said I had to find a way to unite all the peoples?'

Handai arrived, in a hurry.

'Have you seen Jhonni: Cycler Jhonni?'

She looked after the crowd with a helpless, angry expression and turned on Derveet: 'You know what you've done. You've amputated the men. Typical Dapur tactic: when in doubt send the men off to kill each other. What d'you think's going to happen to Atoon up there, and all those poor people?'

Cho looked at her reproachfully. Cendana, who had caught up, said savagely, 'Dai, shut up.'

It was the fourth month. The flame of the forest tree that stood over the little tables had a crown of scarlet in the morning sunlight. Handai stared down the road.

'What's Jhonni's mother going to say now?'

20 The Arousing

The audience made a tight circle around a young woman, dancing. Evidently she had been a tiger; she still painted her face and had her hair loose, but she wore Samsui clothes. Her partner was the same, she stayed still in the centre while the other moved round her. She danced wonderfully. The air near her shook with faint after-images or anticipations: it was the effect called thunder-and-lightning; people said Sandalwood had it, if you had eyes to see. The ring had reached a high pitch of tension. It was impossible to tell now whether the dancer was moving so fast or so slowly that she seemed to stand, while the earth spiralled round her. Suddenly the girl in the middle cried out. She fell to her knees, palms pressed into her eyes.

'Oh! I see it – It's like a cloud. A branch – unstretching –'

Something rose up from the ground between the dancer and the other; a figure flickering, glittering. Its hair fell down its back; its face was the face of both young women. The blind one spoke again, a throaty unintelligble muttering. The audience gasped and began to whimper.

'Stop her! –'

Handai and Derveet crashed through the bodies. Handai launched herself after the dancer, but the devotees were running in panic, and the young woman vanished with them. There was nothing left but a patch of waste ground in the Pabriker quarter, and Derveet holding the other girl by the shoulders. She was still muttering, but her eyes rolled up whitely.

'We'll get nothing out of this one for a while.'

Handai came and crouched down; peered into the empty face. 'We've got to get to the source of it.'

The streets of Ranganar had been quieter since Atoon left, but not more peaceful. Of course, it was only the healthy, able-bodied fugitives who had gone. The rest remained, and

164

more kept coming. The round-up had been cancelled as impractical, the prison the Samsui called their 'Assistance' had become, helplessly, a packed pauper-camp, and still the city seethed with homeless strays. Ordinary services like water and the recycle were strained already by riot damage. Produce looted by the Koperasi from the Peninsula disappeared from the markets, and the once self-sufficient colony had a horrible shock. The city, everyone agreed, was suffering a plague of *red-backed kites*. There were shortages, there were infections. This was one of them. It must have begun just about the time Previous Heaven lost their prescient dreams. Whores had abandoned tigering and were taking to this cult; a crude indulgence of the faculties Derveet had tried so hard to keep secret, and not to misuse. Previous Heaven were breaking up the meetings wherever they found them. The Ranganar Koperasi were in a bad state of nerves. If they realised the talk about women's magic loose in their streets was true, they might panic horribly.

The Pabriker quarter was very quiet. It was noon, but no crowds of workers hurried to the foodstalls round the Pasar Diluar. One whistle shrieked, at a distance, faintly. There was broken glass in the street. On the waste ground, tangled morning glory vine had crawled over a pile of factory waste that was waiting to be recycled. On a blank wall plastered with old bills, one of Handai's 'Don't Eat Rice!' posters, with the skeletal Peninsulan child, hung in tatters.... What had happened to Ranganar? Outside taps, heaps of refuse; people locking their daughters up at night, for fear of weird orgies. Miss Butcher shuddered, unwilling to touch the tranced body.

While she went to search for a trishaw Derveet stayed with the girl. She looked down at the body in her arms. It shivered occasionally, the way something rotten moves, with a life that is not its own. Her expression was bleak. She had sent the causeway people into hiding because of a terrible suspicion: it was more than a suspicion now.

She was thinking of something she had seen a few days ago. She had come across a small crowd in the Open Market. When she went up quietly, she found there was no dancer, instead there was Cho. She was talking to an elderly boy, and everybody was listening seriously, it was a religious meeting. The boy asked Cho a question that had been around for some years, an anxiety often expressed by the people. When was the Father's child coming back? The trouble was, everybody knew there was something wrong with the sea now. Perhaps it was quite dead, and then how could it carry that Emissary? How long are we to wait? Has God, who is really all the people we pray to, forgotten us?

Cho thought for a moment. Then she said, 'Once upon a time there was a Ranganarese lady. Her sisters and aunties and daughters had gone away to an entering in another part of the Bank, and all the boys had sleep-in jobs with the Samsui. So she was living alone with the man of the family and she had to go to market herself, holding up her own chain. She left the man to mind the house and went out. Well, evening came, and it was raining hard. The man sat in his own balé, his own little house, at the back of the compound, and smoked achar and played music to amuse himself. He was sleepy and a bit fuddled. He remembered to bar the gates, but he forgot the lady was outside. And so when our Semar came along that gang just when it was dark, he saw a lady standing in the rain –'

The boys were always with Cho: Derveet had told them never to leave her alone. Old Semar was squatting in the front row, he grinned delightedly at his own appearance in the story.

'Semar was very embarrassed,' said Cho. 'He hid his eyes and ran past.'

The crowd, which contained more than one veiled, escorted Ranganarese, laughed and nodded –

'But he came back later, and there she was still. He peeped from behind a tree and wondered what was happening. Then he decided that he must do something, so he went up with his eyes lowered and banged and rattled on the gates. But the man inside must have been asleep. The lady didn't even look at Semar, so he had to go away. But he was worried now, so he kept coming back, it was near our house, you see – and it went on raining and there was the lady still standing there in the rain and the dark, right into the middle of the night. Now the man had woken up. When Semar came close he could hear him stirring about inside the compound, searching for his lady and getting frightened when he couldn't find her. Semar knew a lady wouldn't shout, so very boldly he shouted for her: "Open

166

the gates! There's someone waiting here!" But the man was upset and the rain was noisy; he was afraid, obviously, that it was robbers outside and he didn't dare come. So then Semar, who soon runs out of patience, crouched down to the lady and said humbly, "Madam, after all times are changing. I know it's rude to shout, but why don't you touch this man's mind as I am sure you can do, so he can let you in. It's too disgraceful for you to stand here all night." Then the lady, without hurrying, turned to him at last and said: "The gate is barred and I am not within. No doubt the significance of this will come to him in time. . . . "'

Semar saw Derveet in the crowd. She shook her head at him and walked away, she did not want to speak to anyone just then. Cho understood the Peninsulan mind too well.

And so do our enemies, she thought, kneeling on the waste ground. How can we resist a poison that's so alluring? – recklessness, abandonment, giving up everything; opening the gates – She remembered being seriously worried, as Anakmati, about how she would reclaim her identity as a woman, if the time should come. How absurd that seemed now. Bandit or Garuda lady: nightclub owner or leader of the Singas, no one cared. And the power of the Dapur had turned into something anyone could understand: no longer awesome, no longer out of reach. . . . Everything we ever wanted. Derveet smiled thinly. She had carefully understated her fear to Atoon, otherwise it would have been difficult to make him go away. She shared her hardening dread with no one now: it would do no good, it would only help spread the poison.

She saw the morning glory flowers and watched a pair of orioles in their lilting flight, from tree to tree in a factory garden across the street. The birds called to each other blithely and clearly.

At least there was no news of Atoon in the Wave bulletins, only reports of the Koperasi trying ineffectively – or was it unwillingly – to control the spreading violence. The causeway people had vanished. There was hope for them. In her worst moments Derveet was afraid there was not much hope for anyone else.

Handai came back and they piled the girl into the trishaw. She was still unconscious, or making a good show of it. Derveet

167

would not come back to Red Door Street, she thought she had been away from the West Bank long enough. She was determined not to break down and start behaving recklessly herself.

'How is Dinah? Is she eating now?'

'Oh no. *She's* not stupid. She knows if she doesn't eat her bean cake today we'll be forced to give her chicken rice tomorrow.' Handai laughed. 'I think the little brute's going to starve herself to death if this goes on,' she said casually.

Derveet tried to make herself say something reassuring, but she could not.

The trishaw boy wanted Handai to get into his cart but she refused. It was against her principles to have a boy pedal two adults, except in an emergency. Derveet left them arguing, totally at cross-purposes. The sound of Miss Butcher's voice, raised in anger, that pursued her, was strangely heartening.

Cho was in the monkey quarter. Once, before the days of Pabrikers and Commercers, the city had been named after various princedoms. In this area there were still battered shrines of white apes, called 'monkeys', on some street corners. In front of one of them was a crowd. A Sawah boy was chanting in a loud voice about the dream he had had. He saw a great battle, the warriors had breasts – the enemy fled, and melted into a mist. . . . The people gasped and swayed, stirring themselves up to see what he had seen, and make it real. . . . But Cho was frowning. She saw Divine Endurance slip neatly from between the shuffling feet and hurried after her.

'You shouldn't encourage them! It's wrong of you. They're going to wear themselves out!'

The Cat turned her head coolly. 'I believe you are right,' she said, with a blink of satisfaction. 'And about time too. It is very proper and right.'

'They shouldn't be behaving like this. I know they shouldn't.'

'You and your Derveet. Such a passion for the simple life. Why not let them enjoy themselves? They're soon going to be wearing out very rapidly indeed, anyway – by the way things are going over the causeway.'

Koperasi bulletins, and rumours, told a bleak story. Prince Bima's followers had not been able to get into Nor or the other bases, so now they were out of control; attacking towns in

Gamartha and neighbour states that hadn't 'come out'. There was no united front: the Gamarthans would have nothing to do with the brigands and mutineers who were running wild in other parts. The Koperasi, it was said, had orders from the Rulers to keep the rebels from each others' throats. Cho knew that this particular piece of news had not made Derveet less anxious. . . .

'Derveet says,' she said firmly, 'that they will stop. The Dapur, I mean the idea-Dapur, the real one, will stop them. It says that no one must go to war, not properly. You remember: Annet told us.'

'Ah yes. A not-allowed.' The Cat looked cynical. 'They seem impressive at first, I know. But in my experience there isn't anything these Dapurs and Controllers can really *do*.'

Cho sat down on a doorstep, her chin in her hands, a frown of concentration on her face. 'Divine Endurance,' she said, 'I'm not sure anymore. It was right for our palace and everything to fade away, because we are the very very last of something, aren't we. But these people are the very, very first of something, I think –'

The Cat gazed at her blandly: 'Idle speculation. But – So?'

'So, we ought to help them more than we are doing, somehow. We ought to get them out of this trouble.'

Divine Endurance smiled with slitted eyes. 'Oh, don't upset yourself,' she purred. 'I think we'll soon have them out of it, you and Wo and I.'

She had gone too far. The child was staring at her curiously.

'Hm,' said the Cat. 'Ah well –', and jumped, just the moment before Cho grabbed her. For the next few seconds the patch of hot pavement was an interesting sight, because the child and the Cat were both moving a good deal faster than usual. They flickered like the trance dancers, only more so. But Cho quickly realised that the Cat was too good at this game. She left off and walked away, without the explanation she wanted, still looking worried.

Back at Red Door Street, Handai asked Cendana to see if she could get anything out of the captive. But no source emerged, and they had to let the girl go, like the others. The Classical Theatre was temporarily closed. Cendana, restless

169

and idle, started staying out late in the evenings, to see her dancer friends.

Atoon found that the causeway people could not stay in Jagdana, not even in hiding. When he had brought them safely through the Sawah he sent ahead to tell his family what he was doing and soon a messenger from the capital arrived at the camp. The ladies praised Atoon's altruism for taking on this task, but suggested it was not wise, just now, for the Hanoman prince to sit up in his hills with a large band of followers, however secretly. So the deportees marched on, fleeing every rumour of trouble, farther and farther up the Peninsula. Atoon was dismayed to find how little he liked the sacred tasks of women: it depressed him to have hard dirty hands, and his hair never dressed properly. He wondered how Derveet had managed to hypnotise him into this extraordinary position.

They avoided all roads, all towns, all Koperasi presence; crossed state borders without ceremony on unmarked trails. They bartered all sorts of things with the hill women; notably, of course, the pearls of Sinar Bulan. Customs around them changed: in wayside shrines a many-armed, fierce creature presided; the spirit of life was not Bu Awan, the sky mother, here in the north, but Bumi, the seed-swallowing earth. Boy-making was not so common. They passed families of young men at work in the steep fields, astonishingly lovely, loaded down with gold and coral. Dreamy eyes beckoned boldly, the whites tinged with a brilliant blue to accentuate their beauty. Atoon took care to walk beside Breus, the leader among the ex-Koperasi, and warn him:

'Don't approach them, however welcoming they look. They tend to defend each other's chastity vigorously.'

'I'll pass it round,' said Breus. 'Why *are* their eyes like that?'

'Their ladies give them jamu, to make them more interesting.'

Right from the start, there was an element that disturbed Atoon very much. People, all sorts of people – Samsui and mutineers included – said they were dreaming dreams, and seeing things. Some said they could hear what was going on inside each other's minds. Some could hear or see what was happening in Ranganar. Several people saw a woman with a fierce face and many arms, dancing round the camp at night. . . . Atoon did not disbelieve any of them, but he was sure this sort of thing could only cause trouble, outside the Dapur. He tried to keep it down.

Another dark, drenching day. It was the end of the sixth month, and South-West Wind was in full flood at the landmass end of the Peninsula. The causeway people had gathered together and made camp in a hollow of the hills where there were caves for shelter. Atoon was down by the river with Koperasi Breus and Cycler Jhonni, on watch. Breus was a strange character. He considered it enormously good of himself to have forgiven Anakmati for being a woman. That had been the hard thing, much harder than breaking out of Sepaa. Atoon laughed – and Jhonni turned on him indignantly, absurdly defending the mutineer: 'You don't *try* to understand – '

'Look at that, Atoon – ' said Breus softly.

Lying concealed, they watched a small armed band traverse the scrub-covered slope on the other side of the stream. One of them was carrying the merdeka flag: a red dagger on a white ground – many of the insurgents used it. The sentries were not alarmed. Peasants had told them there were other 'freedom-dreamers' about: this time a parley seemed unavoidable. The band marched up to the water and stared around.

'Monkey!' yelled the one with the flag.

Strange manners, murmured the prince, but they all stood up. 'Come across – ' called Jhonni. 'It isn't too deep – '

The next moment six senjata were levelled over the stream. Atoon and the others slowly lowered their own unready weapons.

'But we're friends,' said Jhonni blankly.

The flag-bearer ignored her. 'Monkey,' he shouted. 'You'd better get out of here, and your renegade whores and shit-eaters. We know all about you, and this is Gamartha, in case you didn't know.'

'I have no quarrel with my brother Bima Singa,' said Atoon mildly, because he would rather lose a little dignity than be torn up with bits of old iron. 'Or with his family.'

The boy, or youth, laughed loudly. '*Your brother Bima Singa,*' he mimicked, 'is cleaning up Jagdana state right now, monkey. Our lady and our prince are cleansing the whole

171

Peninsula of corrupt southern elements. Where have you been? Don't you know what's going on?'

Silence. Breus and Jhonni gaped. The Gamarthan grinned. Atoon, his face calm, his eyes dark with rapid thought, said coolly: 'I do not have to worry about those two. If I am in Gamartha I am under the protection of the Singa Dapur.'

But the flag-bearer laughed again. 'Out of date, monkey. The Dapur is with us now. All nations, all ladies together against the menace of deformed criminals, renegades and dupes of false Garuda Koperasi-whore – '

'You little rat turd!' shouted Breus. 'You stupid bugger *we're* not the enemy! We know about *your* lady – She'd have had me as well if I did it with women, the way you all do – '

Atoon turned and kicked Jhonni to the ground, Breus was too big for him to tackle. The flag-bearer had a self righteous expression. It was not *his* fault that the enemy carried no flag of truce. . . . All this in a fraction of a fraction of a moment – there was something happening behind Atoon's back – 'No!' he yelled. Kimlan and the people she had brought up held their fire. The Gamarthans ran away, unharmed.

Atoon had been ignoring the bad dreams, keeping strictly to Derveet's rule and refusing to be drawn by ugly rumours among the hill people. But this he could not ignore. He sent down scouts, cunning ex-Sawah bandits, to the towns and the roads. The 'freedom-dreamers' stole a few horses, unless that was the locals, but did nothing more. The scouts came back. It was all true. The Singa Dapur, for whatever reasons, now supported Leilah and Bima. Bima was moving with an army somewhere down in the small states of Timur Kering, purging 'corrupt elements' among the insurgents there, and gathering allies. Leilah, officially in residence in the northern court, was really in the Sawah collecting her own special fighting people to fall on the starving city of Ranganar and leave no one alive. . . .

'She may be there already,' whispered the boy, awed, transported by the magnitude of his bad news. 'Ranganar is lost . . . Anakmati, *Garuda* is lost – '

Rain drummed on the canvas awning in the mouth of the cave, where the leadership of the causeway people were gathered. Those who couldn't get in were pressing and crowding in the sodden mists outside.

172

'What about the Koperasi?' said someone.

The boy who had been speaking glanced at the other scouts, lowered his eyes and shrugged his shoulders a little: 'Nobody is talking about them.'

Late in the night, the rain ceased. Atoon walked out of the cave he was sharing. He sat by the entrance and lit a cigarette, and watched the smoke float away in the darkness. The camp was very quiet; even the sound of the animals shifting in their lines seemed ominous and strange. He thought of the long journey; its trials and losses, and the people who had joined the ranks on the way. Seventy days since deportation morning, nearly two months since that calm letter in Jagdana moved them on into the wilds. He wished he could conjure Derveet or his family here, to tell him what to do now. He tried to remember all she had said at the last moment, but the situation had made her words meaningless.... The scouts reported that the small towns where they looked for news were strangely empty. The ordinary people who had not been infected by the fever of this rising were leaving and taking with them their boys and men, into the wilderness. *What are they afraid of?* Atoon had asked. *Rebels sweeping through? Koperasi punishment? No, it is more than that,* whispered the boy. *I spoke to a wise woman, she took me into her hearth. Scatter and hide, she said, is the word now. The end is coming....* If that is the only advice the women here have to give, then I must refuse it, thought the prince. I will stay with my own inferior vision, which shows me no reason to give up hope.

Even if everything the boys reported was true, if the situation on the Peninsula was so terrible it could not be right to run any further. Derveet could not possibly have meant them to disappear into the desolate lands and never be seen again. The boys said Bima was supposed to have an army of 'six hundred thousands – ' Six hundred thousands was substantially more than half the population of Gamartha. Still, it could be assumed that prince Singa had a lot of company.... He put out his cigarette and stood up, with the starless dark all around him. He had made up his mind. He would turn back, and parley with Bima Singa.

And he remembered, as he made his decision, that the words

173

from scripture sent by his family to Derveet, months ago, were spoken on the edge of a battlefield.

The life of Ranganar ebbed in slow waves. First there were the riots, then the magic and the weird enthusiasm. That business seemed to fade about the same time that they heard of the prince of Jagdana, suddenly appearing on the Peninsulan stage 'with an army'. The next wave was more boring, it was just sickness and tiredness. *Cash* in quantity was the only currency for any comfort, decent food or medicine. The fugitives still coming in reported big war bands of some kind roaming in the Sawah: the Koperasi wouldn't guard the causeway properly and everyone was afraid.

Derveet had been out all day, alone. Now she lay on the bed in the upper room beside Cho, staring into the sunset light at the window. She shaded her left eye with her hand for a moment, and smiled a little. 'Tiger Street is nearly empty,' she said. 'I suppose they have gone to other Koperasi bases, I hope they will be safe. But I went looking for my friends as well, at the Theatre and at their homes. Where have the dancers gone?'

'Perhaps Atoon has got them?'

Derveet smiled again. 'That doesn't comfort me any more, child. I tried. I failed.'

A strange thing had happened to Derveet. Her right hand had lost its skills. It had forgotten how to write even, she had had to revert to the left. Every injury she had suffered in her life seemed to be coming back to haunt her: a place on her side where Anakmati was knifed once ached and ached, though there was hardly a scar. She sat up to slip out of her clothes.

'And where's that Cat? Has she deserted us too?'

'I don't know,' said Cho unhappily. 'She isn't letting me know.' She had not seen Divine Endurance since that day in the Monkey Quarter.

Derveet said suddenly, fiercely – 'Do you understand what is happening? We cannot bear a war, a civil war. We are too weak. The Dapurs have turned inward; imagining the future's already come they can't or won't deal with this crude situation. The princes are idle puppets, they've never been trained to think of the consequences of anything. And the people – We will be destroyed!

174

'And I'm so tired – '

She put her arms out and held Cho hard. 'But it won't happen,' she said, intently. 'Here are Atoon, and Singa and Leilah, all hanging on the edge of disaster, and on the edge they stay. They *cannot* fall. Stillness, Cho. It is our only weapon, but it will win. It must.'

Her skin was hot. She made love as if she was burning and wanted to burn Cho too. Then she slept. Cho lay with her cheek on Derveet's hair, that smelt of cocoa butter and flowers, and watched the room grow dark.

Cendana was cooking in the kitchen house at Red Door Street. She murmured to herself *hot wok cold oil, hot wok cold oil* – She had given up the affectation of refusing women's tasks long ago, but she would never be good at this. She could not open the sliding wall because the courtyard was camped out with sick fugitives, she opened the windows as wide as she could. There was music playing somewhere in the compound; not classical, just Samsui popular tunes on three fiddles and a horn. Aunt insisted everyone had to keep cheerful –

> Every day we used to meet
> In the garden
> You gave me a flower –
> Where have you gone?

As she listened, the dancer suddenly felt an odd little stab of happiness. Life had been good after all, in so many ways. She began to sway and then to move fluidly, with perfect artistry, around the kitchen floor. A small black kitten that had crept in looking for scraps sat back on its heels amazed, privileged to be Sandalwood's sole audience. She laughed at its round eyes and gave of her best, until the music ended.

The wok and the steamer had been included in her choreography so there was no harm done. She left most of the food under covers, for the family couldn't possibly eat all together anymore; some she put in a tiffin carrier and took away to Handai's room. Dinah woke up: something smelled good. Handai lifted the lid off the carrier and looked at her beloved reproachfully –

175

'Eat up,' said Cendana. 'And don't ask silly questions.'

While they were eating she said suddenly – 'Dai, I won't let them hurt you.'

Handai and Dinah, with full stomachs, fell asleep instantly like babies. Cendana took the tiffin carrier back to the kitchen. She did not do the washing-up because there was no water ration left and she had not managed to acquire the art of doing without. She walked softly between the bodies in the courtyard and slipped out of the back gate, closing it very quietly behind her.

PART THREE

The wayang on the left side represent an evolutionary phase which has already completed itself and is bound to become extinct, and those on the right side the next phase to come. Nothing can ever stop this process. Nature cannot have regard for individuals, and thus it arouses our sympathy to see the blameless characters on the left fulfilling their duty and keeping their vows, though they know there is no chance of success for them.

Hans Ulbricht, *Wayang Purwa*

21   A Deputation

Cendana had vanished, and in her place was a city daily more clearly given over to death. 'It's ridiculous,' sobbed Handai angrily. 'She's a *dancer*. She's never handled a real weapon in her life!' It was impossible to find out what had happened to anyone who had left the island. On the Peninsula prince Bima and Atoon moved about, according to the Wave bulletins, like tom-cats getting ready to fight. Some rumour attributed scruples to one prince; some gave protestations to the other, but at this stage it was meaningless. Now the mood of Ranganar changed again. Koperasi reappeared as a presence in uniform on the streets. Bubbles from Sepaa and further away were seen landing at the East Coast barracks; this activity was not mentioned in the news.

Handai had given up reproaching Derveet for sending the causeway people to an unknown fate long ago, she had shared her friend's dismay when Atoon turned around. Now she followed the bulletins slavishly; knowing they were mostly lies, and days old anyway, and waited like everybody else for the inevitable. But Derveet, bleak and withdrawn as she was, stubbornly refused to give up hope. Life is stronger than death, she said. In their hearts they know what is really happening. They *will* draw back. And day by day Singa and Hanoman hovered on the brink, as if held apart by a mysterious invisible force.

At the start of the second twelve days of the eighth month, a deputation of the major clans wanted to see the Butchers of Red Door Street. The Butchers cleared away some of their house guests from the big dining room and put out tables and chairs, wondering what the clanswomen had to say.

Everybody sat around a row of tables pushed together. Overhead the fans said clack, clack, clack; sometimes whirring for a few seconds and then slowing to clack, clack again. It was a

179

very hot day. Noises of the sick and homeless came through the thin walls, fine lines of gold crept between the slats and lay burning on the floor. Mrs Cycler, without much polite preliminary, began to read out a long account of everything that was wrong with Ranganar: sickness was spreading; piped water had to be boiled. The tran system was completely shut down; gas for light and power unpredictable, sanitation failing. Fresh food was almost unavailable; dried food adequate but for how long? Industry was at a standstill, children missing their education.... Unknown powers in the Sawah were liable to attack at any time –

'What is this leading to?' murmured one Butcher to another. 'The "roundup" idea again?'

And apart from all else, because of lack of drainage maintenance North-East Wind floods would be the worst ever known. Mrs Cycler gathered herself and her papers and came to the point. The Rulers had offered, through the Koperasi, to evacuate the whole of Ranganar to a safe place for the duration of the present disturbances. Knowing the Butchers' great influence over the native population, the clanswomen wanted their help to get the idea accepted and organised smoothly –

The great influence Mrs Cycler spoke of was sitting apart, at the end of the row of tables. The deputation had covertly requested its presence: no names, no problems. They were all now pretending Derveet was invisible.

Uproar! First Aunt jumped to her feet, shouting angrily. Mrs Builder and Mrs Printer jumped up too and yelled back at her: shouting that it was all the Butchers' fault anyway. With their sympathies they ought to be in the Assistance now, not sitting at a meeting –

'Quiet!' roared Handai. 'Quiet! Aunt *please* sit down –'

Calm was restored. Mrs Cycler said, 'Mother knows I have enough to reproach you with. Where is my child? But we need your help. I will tell you something that must not leave this room. The Koperasi themselves are evacuating, from Nor and from Sepaa.'

The Butchers stared at each other and muttered. Handai looked at Derveet, sitting quietly as if nothing could shock or surprise her anymore. How thin Veet had grown. She knew her friend was spitting blood: Derveet insisted the haemorrhages were very slight, nothing serious. . . . She needs rest, thought Handai. Rest – when will any of us have that ? . . . Incredulous and suspicious murmurs died away. Derveet said (and all the clanswomen started involuntarily, at her beautiful High Inggris):

'Where exactly are they going to put you?'

'On one of the big islands. They're making a camp.'

'A camp. Ah. May I smoke?' She rolled a cigarette and lit it; pungent fumes of the mixture of achar cake and tobacco she was reduced to rose –

A Butcher called Pao suddenly burst out: 'Anyone can see through this. They don't care about you. They just want to flush out the few people who could still save the Peninsula!'

'All right,' said Mrs Cycler. 'I'll tell you. Three days ago Mrs Leilah of Gamartha was travelling through the Bu Awan region to er – to join her brother. Her escort was attacked by a band of – deformed criminals and mutineers, of the other party. It was a massacre. So now it is war. No one's going to save the Peninsula. And we are getting out.'

Again the meeting was upset in shouting and angry exclamations.

Early on that same morning there was a small disturbance at Causeway Control. The Koperasi were in their blockhouses, indifferent. The traffic was as usual; partly stumbling, haggard fugitives; partly people who were making regular trips, somehow finding produce and meat to bring back to the hungry city. Some charitable Samsui women were at the gates. They did what they could for the fugitives, and tried in a kindly way (and without success) to get the traders to give up their goods to the fair market. Empty handed, with bundles, handcarts, leading animals, the morning entry came down the grey road on its piers that stretched away across the shining water. Among the people was a creature they did not like. Even the bewildered ex-slaves pushed it away. It had not a human face but a blunt calf's muzzle. It had no proper fingers on its hands. Its body was a lump of muscle clothed in a coarse hairy blouse matted with old dried blood. It stank. Get away, you mountainy thing – they said, and they began to shove it and kick it as it reeled about, grabbing at everyone; trying to find a friend. 'A-a-ati?' it sobbed – 'A-a-ati?' Suddenly one of the charitable Samsui, a

181

young girl, gave an exclamation and ran through the gates. She took the calf's grotesque hoof-hand. Its ox eyes stared at her. A-a-ati? it begged: Anakmati.

The deputation had gone. The Butchers still sat around the tables.

'The whole population –' said Handai. She tried to imagine this, packed into bubbles. 'How can they do that?'

'Oh, it will sort itself out,' said Derveet softly. 'People will hang themselves, jump into the sea and so on, before embarkation day. The ones who finally line up will be the sensible type, so there'll be no trouble. I've seen it before.'

They did not believe what Mrs Cycler had said about Bu Awan. Leilah was in Gamartha. The mountain people were harmless; incapable of massacring anyone. The past few weeks had produced a succession of incidents like this – probably outright invention. All of their thoughts were on how to deal with this threat of evacuation, when the sliding wall opened, and the young woman from the causeway came in with the calf who was still sobbing for Anakmati.

The creature had been running on its thick legs for days and nights, it did not know how long. It gasped out a bubbling string of sounds the Samsui could not follow. It was Low Inggris of a kind: hantuhantu-bertempur... mati, dihukum – ghosts, and a fight, and death. But Awan's child squatted on the floor, he hardly knew what a chair was. The Samsui girl crouched beside him, holding his stumpy hand: 'They killed them all!' she cried. 'They killed all the poor polowijo!'

Derveet got up from her place and knelt down in front of the monster. 'Child,' she said gently. 'Why *dihukum*? – Why "punished"?'

'It was wrong to fight them.'

The creature made a great effort: these words were quite clear.

A strange silence fell over the room.

At last Handai said, 'Derveet, we've got to do something, we'll have to get you away. Pao's right, this evacuation is aimed at you – and, and Cho. You can't stay in Ranganar.'

For a moment she had fallen, she could see from their faces that the others had fallen too, into the relief of being able to give up at last, to give up hope. But only for a moment. There was still work to do (*she is dead, then,* she thought. *If not now, then very soon –*).

'Yes,' said Derveet. 'Yes. You're right. Of course.'

Late that night, one of the Butcher boys came and woke Handai up. She had not been sleeping in fact, just lying with her mind going round and round: it was that hour of the night when you know you are incapable of thinking, but you can't stop. She followed the boy's breathy whispers and soft tugging hands to the kitchen house. He vanished and she made out a figure, sitting very still, down on the floor by the doorway. She thought it was one of the fugitives at first.

'Veet! What are you doing here? – It's dangerous! What's happened?'

'Hallo dear,' said her friend quietly. 'I couldn't sleep, I thought I'd come and see you.'

Handai went and fetched a lamp, muttering, and stumbling over the gas line as she pulled it out across the tiles. She lit a match and Derveet's face appeared in a sepulchral blue glow.

'– Not supposed to have it on at night now. You didn't really come over here for no reason did you? That's just bad morale –'

'I love that lamp,' said Derveet. 'That factory-made lamp, and that hose thing that so offends my sensibilities.'

Handai stared at her, bleary and half angry.

'What?'

'I wanted to tell you: It is you. You Samsui women with your shrill voices and ridiculous ideas. You have no dignity, you're not *ladies*. But you are alive. Dapur women know so much – but you can't teach human beings without being human yourself, without joining in. You see the trouble with women is that they are so sure. They are born sure. Their purpose is certain, their value is certain, and so they naturally dismiss everything else – as unimportant. If we had listened to you Samsui we would not be facing what is coming now crippled and divided. . . .'

The lamp hissed. Handai stared at her friend with a dull, bemused expression.

'Oh, Derveet,' she said at last. 'What does it matter? What does any of it matter now?'

183

22   The Mountain Top

Derveet was not fit for the wilds, so she travelled by road to Bu Awan. The South Sawah was alive with Koperasi: bubbles in the sky; vehicles snarling – no sign of the roaming war bands in an empty land. She was not surprised. She knew she was seeing the wheels go round, behind the scenes. No one saw her. She was invisible, among the people. She set out alone. She knew her friends would try to stop her, and she did not want anyone, not even the dear child – (Ah no, above all not Cho –) But on the second night she was sheltering in a shack by the roadside, haunch to haunch with other fugitives. Rain streamed down and gathered in cold pools round their feet and buttocks; the treaders crashed by in the dark splashing white light across blank and fearful faces, and Derveet suddenly knew someone was watching her. She looked up and thought she saw something move; a rat perhaps, in the criss-cross of poles under the tattered thatch.

After that she was haunted. She knew all the time that something was beside her, though she never saw it move again. The treaders swept up wanderers on the roads, and carried them off to 'collection points'. They picked up Derveet with the rest more than once, and she saw the Sawah from the back of packed Koperasi boxes, rolling on their jolting tracks. Endlessly the plantations, the rows of trees and melon vines and maize fell away – rotting and derelict. Blackened shells of farm camps rose up and disappeared; Koperasi standing over heaps of strange fruit at the gates. . . . She could not take her eyes away. She heard the voice of whatever was haunting her whisper: 'All this is very good –'

The clanswomen had been right, the Koperasi were clearing up and getting out. She never found out what happened at the 'collection points'; she managed always to give her lifts the slip before the final destination. On the fourth day she was beyond most of the action. She hitched a lift in a treadie flying the merdeka flag. The brigand in charge dropped her on the western edge of the Bu Awan wilderness, and drove north to find Singa. She walked to the last village on the mountain, and found a few boys still hanging on. She hired one of them and two ponies for a great deal of *cash* and the ruby and silver lighter; her last negotiable possession. That night, lying out in the open on the mountainside, she woke. The boy was asleep a few paces away. Near her face in the darkness gleamed two diamond blue eyes. Derveet sat up. 'Ah, it's you –' she said softly. 'I might have known.' The Cat made a small dim shape against the stars, low on the stony ground. Derveet was not surprised, not surprised at all. 'Why are you here?' she whispered. But Divine Endurance was gone.

Derveet did not need a guide. She assumed the boy was with her to keep an eye on his pony, she didn't care. When they came to the rim of the caldera he became very reluctant. The dead, he said, had not been attended to –

' – There is no need to be afraid of them.'

The boy huddled his shawl round his half-naked shoulders and shivered nervously. 'The Koperasi have been here,' he muttered, and his eyes flickered; shamefaced and uneasy: 'They might, I think they might come again. . . . It is dangerous.'

She left him at the foot of the descent and went on alone. The caldera was terribly silent. When she saw what she was coming to as she approached the polowijo caves her mouth filled with bile and her vision began to swim. But she would not turn back.

All the way up country she had heard of *the massacre*. The boys on the flank of the mountain had spoken of it with awe: fire on Bu Awan; blood and the cries of the dying – No one had exaggerated. There were hundreds of bodies lying under the cliffs. They had been untouched for days. There was a smell of death; sickly, hideous, throat-catching. She walked to and fro between the stark images, over ridges of fine black silt that crumbled underfoot. She was not the first on the scene. Some of the bodies were torn or gnawed, others showed signs of looting; some had been stripped and laid out in rows. Sticks, stones, knives – senjata lay around, but the bodies showed evidence of worse weapons, she noted grimly – The Gamarthans were dressed for their part as a lady's escort, in white linen stained and filthy now, with silk sashes bound high on their breasts; some had bright ornaments or marks where they'd been torn away. It was hard to tell the ragged polowijo and the mutineers apart, except that the men had bigger bodies even in death, which makes everyone look smaller. . . .

The broken outline of the cliffs rose up, terribly familiar. Here she had lived, bullying the poor outcasts with her dreams. She had left them vowing she would never forget them, her own family. By her black skin she was marked like them – Bu Awan's child. She had promised them she would make them part of something wonderful one day. And they believed. She remembered Annet's angry, hungry cynicism . . . *never betrayed me, never. . . .*

Did the Gamarthans attack, or did the polowijo? It made no odds, though some might pretend to ask the question, for a little while. The rent was big enough to let chaos in. She stood in the hideous silence, her mind empty. What had brought her here? Only the knowledge that it didn't matter any more, so why should she not mourn her dead. But oh, how was it done? She had been so sure, as the long battle of wills dragged on, that the Dapur rule was going to hold after all. The enemies would have to try another way; they couldn't make the Peninsula destroy itself so easily. How was it done? What boy or man, renegade or noble, could have raised his hand to this – ?

It was then that something glinting caught her eye. She looked down: a Gamarthan lay at her feet. On the warrior's forearm, smeared with black blood, was a bracelet Derveet knew quite well; incised silver, sprinkled with little crystals – very pretty. Soré made it. She stared for a while, without comprehending. Then she went down on her knees. The smell of decay was strong, but it was strange how all revulsion left her as she lifted the thing's head. She cried out aloud: 'Siang!'

The sun slipped away below the great crater, and the caldera grew vague under a veil of vaporous cloud. Derveet was sitting by the path that led to the rim, where she had left the boy, holding a silver bracelet in her hands. She had forgotten about the ponies, and her guide. She was weeping. She felt someone approach and raised her head. The brown cat came neatly down the slope and settled itself beside her.

Derveet said nothing, but the Cat could see that she had at

last begun to realise a few things. The mists crept over the bowl, the shadows deepened. Divine Endurance began to speak: 'A good many Koperasi so-called mutineers had come to live with the polowijo. One morning before light a host of warriors came over the rim and attacked without warning. It was illusion, of course, part of the special weaponry Leilah has been finding out. The girls were very pure in their use of these weapons. They knew they would all be killed. It was their sacrifice, for the good of the Peninsula.

'The tigers had been gathering to Leilah for a while. She was what they wanted when they began to feel alive again. As I think you know, she did not have to send clumsy messengers to fetch them. The others came later, it took them time to realise what they wanted. They taught the tigers to masquerade, of course. You see, Leilah was afraid it was all going to grind to a halt, with you sitting in Ranganar disapproving of everyone and embarrassing them. And the Dapurs were getting at her brother's armies. If something dreadful had been committed by the renegades it would bring Atoon and Bima together, and strengthen them to go on. . . . The girls all hoped you would understand in the end. It was you, after all, who dressed them in white and told them women must step down into the sordid world, to save it.'

A muffled sound came from the woman. Her hands covered her face, Siang's bracelet rolled away in the dust.

'I'm glad you understand me,' said the Cat. 'I thought you would. I've always suspected those noises were quite superfluous.'

'You did this. You, and the wayang that the Rulers have. You drove people mad – '

Divine Endurance parleyed briefly with her conscience. But it would be unkind to leave the woman desperately trying to deceive herself.

'Not I,' she said. 'Not Wo. We have been interested, but in the end our part has been quite small. You humans are very odd. You don't even recognise your own dreams when you see them coming true.'

'See – ' she purred 'See how still they lie, how simple they are now. No more divisions. Stillness, simplicity, the leap into the eternal. You asked, and she has performed, and it will go on. . . . '

Derveet whispered, '*No. I did not. I never asked her anything. I was afraid –*'

'Oh yes you did,' said the Cat. 'Cho told me so, and Cho does not tell lies. You wanted her help so she has been helping you, right from the start. She is hardly more than a child, for she has led a very sheltered life, and she doesn't understand some of her own effects, but it makes no difference.'

The dead were out of Derveet's sight in the dusk and the distance, but Divine Endurance could still contemplate them, with quiet satisfaction.

'You should not be surprised,' she murmured, half to herself, 'if what Cho has given you is not what you thought you wanted. She did her very best, so naturally this happened. As I told her, but she wouldn't listen, every desire of the human heart is just the real desire in disguise, the desire of the world. Wo's people understand; it's what they've been trying to teach you. It is all over. It was settled long ago. I saw some of it happen – most impressive. . . . There is no point in fighting, Derveet. It's natural, it's right and proper. What does the Dapur say? *Submit*, it is the only word.'

'*The desire of the world, which Cho and Wo and I, and our kind, have always served.*'

The sky cleared and turned black. Divine Endurance, pleased with the effect she had produced, slipped away for a while. Derveet watched the night. She saw the fountain of joy, and Previous Heaven playing tag with death the day the Eagle rose, and now it seemed it was true: she must have always known. Strange fruit by the Sawah roadside, Alat's blood on her hands in the waringin glade long ago, it was all the same. She heard her own voice – telling Atoon that by God's grace or good fortune the angel doll had come to someone above temptation.

She tried to tell herself that there was hope still; that the new world might live even if the old was utterly destroyed. But she could not. She had seen how the strange, frightening beauty of her vision had been belittled and degraded: there was no safety. Nothing is assured, *nothing*. The gate was open and it was not God who was waiting, only emptiness. She had come to the centre of the mysteries and here the Rulers disappeared, the Dapur vanished, even Cho herself meant nothing. Cho did not make the darkness, the universal darkness, swallowing the stars.... A ragged moon rose and arced slowly over the caldera. Derveet sat on unmoving, hour by hour. She could not pray, or weep anymore. But after a while a pain began, deep and insistent, somewhere around her heart. It seemed physical and real. She was glad of this pain, and hoped that it would stay with her from now on. And it did.

The day after the deputation, Handai went to Dove House and realised at once what Derveet had done. Horrified, she left everything to First Aunt and started in pursuit. She made Cho come with her, because she knew she wouldn't reach the great mountain alone. Cho didn't want to leave Ranganar: Derveet hadn't told her anything. She said: *I don't know what to do to help Derveet now.* But she was obedient. They travelled fast. The Koperasi never touched them. Gress, Cho's hard little pony, came with them all the way – a succession of others served Handai, straight up the great west roads, right through Koperasi country. Handai was past caring how any of it was done. She was thinking of her city and all that was gone for ever, for ever and ever and ever. The words of that stupid old song kept running through her head, pitifully –

> Oh, then I made a moo cow
> It was meant to be a blue cow
> But it died
> But it died
> But it died –

She hardly hoped that she would get to Derveet before the enemy did. But something in her would not let her give up. She would not abandon her friend now, no, nor the dream they had shared.

On the fourth night they were in a peasant's hut or cave, high on Bu Awan's side. The polowijos' speech was animal noises to Handai. She set Cho to question them while she crouched by the dapur, the hearthstone, blinking in the smoky firelight. How strange to find people still living here. Nothing is ever complete, she thought – not even destruction. She watched the boy-creature who had brought them in with his mother, or his sister. They sat close together, touching gently, stroking each other's faces, holding hands. As the firelight flickered their eyes seemed to brim with light. She remembered how she had always hated the way Derveet behaved with the Dove House boys – fondling them and petting them all the time. She wondered, if she tried hard now would she understand at last? The shining eyes turned to her. For a moment, perhaps, something stirred in her mind – shapes and colours; intimations, but then it was gone again. Perhaps it was only a trick of the shadows. She was very tired.

When it began to be light Derveet stirred and looked around, vaguely at first; then she stood up sharply.

Divine Endurance interrupted her morning toilet to remark – 'He's gone. He took both ponies. They left yesterday afternoon in fact. Didn't you notice?'

Derveet stared blankly.

'I can see it's going to take a while to sink in,' said the Cat. 'Well, I know you'd hate me to help you down from here, so we won't bother about that. Come on, I'll show you something of sentimental interest. It'll take your mind off things.'

The brown cat trotted away. Derveet hesitated, then followed. Divine Endurance led her south, to where the crater wall broke up in grottos and fissures; through the paths where Annet had once led her and Cho, and up into the dawn beauty of the peaks, etched in rose and indigo against a shining sky. The Mangkuk Kematian, the Bowl of Death, was at their feet.

'Officially the attack was only on the Koperasi element,' said the Cat. 'An absurd story, when you consider the excitement of these things. The tigers knew better anyway. But some of your friends were shocked at what really happened, and quite changed their minds again – '

In a hollow below them white vapour eddied over a bubbling pool, with a strong mineral smell. There were two bodies in the sulphur mist. Derveet went down, and found that one of them was Leilah's sister, Simet, the blackened silver chain still trailing from her ankle. The other was Cendana. Death had

190

caught her in the act of twisting the knife that killed her out of Simet's hand, and burying it in her throat.

'There now,' said Divine Endurance. 'Isn't that nice to know.'

The bodies were not decayed, the mineral steam had preserved them. Derveet carefully drew Cendana away from her enemy. She gathered branches from the thorns that grew near the hot pool, and put them around her friend. She searched her pockets in vain for her lighter, but found some matches. It was not much of a pyre, but it was all she could do. There lay Sandalwood – still lovely; no longer reckless, no longer passionate. She remembered the night in Dove House, when she brushed the dancer's hair. Had it already begun then, even then – ? How lonely Cendana must have been, with hope burning her up; struggling towards this adventure. But it was all over now. She held across her hands something she had found under the two bodies: it was a dagger, made of gilt and base metal, straight as death. Not your fault, Sandalwood, no blame to you. I wish I could tell you so. *Happy the warrior to whom the just fight comes, that opens the doors of heaven. . . .* She did not know much about lighting fires, but the thorns caught and crackled.

Derveet sighed at last and said 'Divine Endurance, why Bu Awan? A hundred years ago perhaps – but who but the converted would believe such a thing of Annet's poor shiftless thieves? And it is so out of the way. Couldn't Leilah have found herself a more convincing atrocity?'

The Cat was on the other side of the hollow, watching the funeral rites dispassionately and occasionally glancing down into the great bowl, where it seemed there was something that interested her.

'I was wondering when you'd come to that,' she remarked composedly. 'It's quite simple. The polowijo are your mother's people, Derveet. Leilah thought it would fetch you out, and she was right. She, and other interested parties, who are now advising her, have been looking for a way to get you out into the open – before you made off to some desert island, leaving the idea of you behind to hold things up, if you see what I mean. They have been watching the mountain, and paying the remaining peasantry, who are quite hungry I'm afraid, to give information.'

She was not sure how much of this got through, but conscience told her she ought to make the gesture, and it could do no harm.

Derveet heard nothing. The voice in the night had gone: there was only the thing that looked like a brown cat, with its strange, implacable eyes. But as she knelt there, watching the flames, suddenly something fell away from her, and she realised – That the boy had disappeared. That she had given him Atoon's lighter, in case anyone needed any help. That she had been quite mad for days, ever since she heard that Bu Awan was dead, and she had walked, simply and co-operatively, into a trap. She stared at the fire, that was waving a flag of smoke now; above the vapours, high into the clear blue air. . . .

'You have not won,' she said, finally, in a firm voice. 'You are so clever, but you have made the same mistake as always. I'm no loss. I was half on your side already, as you so cunningly realised. Your real enemy is a woman in Ranganar, who chops meat in the market, minds her child, and gets into stupid arguments in the street. She'll go on doing all of that; and there are thousands like her – in your desolation; even in your evacuation camps. Fight you? She doesn't know how to stop. You will never destroy her –'

The brown cat gazed. Something in Derveet's mind said: *Most inspiring. I am impressed. But after all, there's Cho.*

'Cho is innocent!'

Silence. Divine Endurance turned her back and peered into the bowl again, her tail twitching pleasantly, like a cat that is watching little birds through a window. Derveet got up, slowly, and went to see what the Cat was looking at.

Handai climbed the scree on a narrow path, tugging her pony's bridle with one hand; the other fastened on the grip of her knife. She was afraid. She did not know what she would find above the ominous rim of red and black: Derveet arrested? Derveet a prisoner? The scale of these mountains appalled her. How could she begin to search them? When she came over the edge and saw Derveet, standing there quietly, she was confused. She couldn't understand it – Cho came up too, with Gress. Derveet said nothing. Cho hid her face in the pony's mane.

Divine Endurance had disappeared.

192

In silence the friends faced each other. Protests, reproaches died unspoken. Handai began to cry. She let go of the bridle and stumbled down into the hollow, into Derveet's arms, and they stood together, tears mingling. So this was how it ended, all that fuss about uniting the Peninsula, and women and men being equal. Here it came to rest; here in the bleak red rocks and the sulphur steams it lay down – and it seemed, like the dead, so much smaller.

Handai pushed herself away – 'Derveet!' she cried. 'You've got no time. The Koperasi have Wave down on the mountain. A boy has given you away. We'd better hide – there are caves aren't there. We aren't finished yet, Veet. We'll get you over the sea –'

Derveet said, 'Cho brought you.'

'Well – yes. I had to have help. I couldn't leave you alone.'

Miss Butcher had been under the edge of the scree. She had not seen the bubble quietly descending. It had come down on the Bu Awan ridge, just out of sight above them.

'Derveet – *come on!*'

'Now listen,' said Derveet. 'They won't touch you, you're a Samsui. Just go quietly, and afterwards do what you can. If there is anything to do, now they have Cho. You have been used Dai. Don't worry, so have we all.'

Handai couldn't understand. There was such a look in Derveet's eyes – it was horrible.

She said suddenly, 'What's that fire for –?' It flashed into her mind that her friend, in despair, had deliberately –

'Ah – wait. Dai!'

Handai struggled. She felt the brittleness of Derveet's arms; fleshless bone beneath the cotton sleeve. But just as she escaped, a group of people appeared, and came quickly down into the hollow: a troop of Koperasi, armed, and with them was Leilah of Gamartha. Leilah was dressed in riding clothes. She had lost weight, and her tiger eyes were very bright. She looked beautiful and strong. She stood in front of her enemy: *Yes. Look at me. I am the coming race that you prophesied. You could have been me but you didn't dare. I dare anything.*

'Arrest her,' she said briskly to the Koperasi. 'She's responsible for all this.'

193

At Derveet's feet was the tawdry dagger. She glanced at it, and bowed her head.

Handai cried, 'Derveet! Don't let her say that! Don't give up!'

She started forward. . . . But the Koperasi did not give her a chance to speak. They shot her. At a range of some twenty paces their hardened bullits tore great holes in her chest and body, and she fell back, bewildered, into Derveet's arms. 'Ah – ' she said, and no more.

The echoes that the shots had raised rattled slowly away. Handai lay on the ground, and did not know her beloved was beside her. Derveet had fallen to her knees; and the Koperasi closed in solicitously. The fire around Cendana's body was dying down. Leilah stood apart from all this. She watched the tableau for a few moments, but then turned her face away coldly. It was nauseating to have to work with the shit-eaters. And yet she felt very satisfied that her stratagem had succeeded. The massacre was never, of course, meant to reconcile Atoon. It was to strengthen her brother. It was just a little present, because she had seen he needed something to help him make the plunge. They had not been together since the event but she knew how he would take it: shyly, a little coyly, pretending he didn't know who it came from. . . . She smiled, thinking of the man's weakness and feeling her own power course through her to her fingertips.

The Koperasi thought Leilah was being used, but she knew exactly what she was doing. She had known from the beginning.

Thinking of all this, she saw the two ponies, and the slight, childish figure beside them. Cho had not moved since Handai ran from her into Derveet's arms. She had not made a sound or a sign all through the little drama. Leilah's eyes widened. She did not want the angel doll, but she knew the Rulers did. Their agents never mentioned it, and nor did Leilah, but she was well aware that the toy was at the back of everything. They had let her kill all the people on Bu Awan; they had let her stick her fist up Garuda, all for the sake of the angel doll. She had not cared. When she turned on her 'advisers' in the abyss after that, what difference would it make if they had one more machine or not? But she had not imagined such an opportunity. She glanced at

194

the Koperasi who were still occupied. *They'll kill me* she thought. The consideration had no weight at all.

'Come on madam, up you get,' said the Rulers' agent to the prisoner, 'And count yourself lucky we're here with that lady, and not some of the "tigers". Don't you see her eyes? She's mad. Completely off her fucking rocker.'

Leilah unslung her own senjata and moved casually round to the ponies. She noticed that, unfortunately, the better one was unbridled. The Koperasi suddenly woke up to the presence of the angel doll. They spoke to each other; some of them stepped cautiously forward –

'You'd better not touch it!' shouted Leilah. 'It's poisonous!'

The men stopped. She laughed out loud, made a dancer's lunge across the remaining space, and grabbed Cho by the arm.

'I'll take this –' she cried. 'It belongs to the people, not to you. This child in white is our sign: purity, war, womanhood. It had fallen into the hands of the corrupt south, now I'm claiming it. Merdeka! Daulat untuk Gamartha!'

She bundled the doll onto the bridled pony, flung her firearm away and jumped up behind. Cho did not resist. She only cried, 'Derveet –' If Derveet answered, no one heard. For a moment Leilah faced the Koperasi, her eyes blazing. Then she bent over the doll, down to the pony's neck and whispered, or touched it. The poor, starved, jaded creature reared up. It bounded over the rim of the hollow and the noise of it, plunging recklessly down the screes, thundered all around the great bowl.

The Koperasi came to life. Some of them rushed to see where Leilah had gone. They reported to Wave, but it seemed there were no orders to cover this development. No one wanted to go in pursuit anyway. The woman was mad, and reputedly possessed of appalling Dapur powers. They marshalled themselves and the prisoner; and soon the bubble went swinging into the air and glided away, leaving Bu Awan to the dead.

23   A Sharp Knife

Leilah was pursued down the screes by the riderless pony. Some madness had got into it; as soon as the path allowed it was up beside her, shouldering her and showing its teeth. 'Get off – ' she shouted, and lashed at it with the end of her reins. The toy, that she was holding in the crook of her arm, raised its head then and perhaps did something, for the pony gave way. It still followed. Leilah kept looking back and seeing it, the only thing moving besides herself in the great theatre of the bowl. She decided to take no notice.

It was hot down in the wilderness. The screes stood against the sky, dimmed in a haze. A singing silence, bare lava, cracked earth; a scorched aromatic scrub that rasped against the pony's legs as it stumbled between the rocks. There was nothing in the sky but the sun, there was no one following. Leilah let the pony slow down; it was exhausted now. She rode slackly, hardly pretending to hold the doll. She began to smile, and then to chuckle, and then to laugh. The pony stood still. Leilah slipped from its back with a sly look at her companion. It was very hot. She found a boulder and sat herself beneath it. She began to chuckle again.

'Merdeka! – They didn't know what to do –'

The doll had come after her.

'Go away,' she said to it. 'I was lying. I don't want you. Go away, do what you like. I don't care.'

A small brown cat came trotting down the dusty path, and sat beside Cho. Leilah did not seem to notice.

'This is your one isn't it,' said Cho.

'Oh yes.'

'There's something very wrong with her.'

Two pairs of eyes, dark and brilliant blue. Leilah watched them both, indifferently.

'What can we do for her?'

196

'Don't waste your time,' said Divine Endurance. 'I've been helping her and helping her but it's as you said. They simply wear themselves out.'

'I have killed my sister,' said Leilah. 'I have corrupted my brother, I have betrayed Garuda. It's all done. The armies don't need my help anymore. Nothing will stop it now.'

Her eyes moved dreamily. She thought of pushing the doll, live but unresisting, into some crevice of the rocks, or pressing it down into a pool of bubbling mud. She knew it would only climb out again. She had made her gesture, that was enough.

'Don't think I've changed my mind,' she said. 'It was right, all of it. Oh, I knew we had a chance, don't think I didn't. I could see we might be *patient*, we might be *reborn*. But I couldn't stand that. It is disgusting. To survive on top of all the dead. . . . Too many filthy things have been done, just to keep on living. Living now is swallowing vomit, eating shit. . . .'

'Perhaps they'll forgive you,' said Cho. 'If you say you're sorry.'

Something flickered in Leilah's eyes for a moment, but it didn't stay. Her hands took out the knife she carried in her sash. She tested the point against her thumb, and then on the underside of her left wrist. It went in very easily. She had stayed alive so long from the thought that it would be so hard, it would hurt . . . what a waste of time. A bright, chuckling stream. She felt herself growing dizzy, but she wasn't satisfied.

'Not enough,' she muttered, and took the dripping point up to her throat.

There was a long silence. It was broken by the sound of Gress's hooves, clip clopping in the dust of the path. She didn't like the smell of blood but she came up anyway. Cho went to the other pony. It was a brindled, mountainy roan, its coat all patchy with sweat, its miserable flanks still shuddering. She took off its harness and stroked its face. 'Go on,' she said. 'She doesn't need you anymore.' The puzzled beast looked around for a moment, then tossed its eased head and slowly trotted away.

'Would you like us to go and help your one now?' asked Divine Endurance sweetly.

Cho gave her a long look.

'She didn't want me.'

197

Then the three companions left that place, and vanished into the wilderness.

On the night that Derveet watched over the dead, Annet of Bu Awan woke from a pain-filled dream and found herself in a place with a high roof and a few squares of moonlight. She missed the smells and closeness of the caves. Then she tried to move, and remembered. She was in the barracks of a derelict farm camp, under the Mountain on the Jagdana side, being kept alive. She closed her eyes in helpless bitterness. After the battle, so she'd been told, she had been dragged from under a pile of bodies by the snake boy. She remembered coming to herself in one of her peoples' boltholes in the side of the Bowl of Death; she remembered the suffering, dying polowijo. There was no food, no water, no fire. The Koperasi were hunting on the Mountain, there was no hope. She remembered her own voice sobbing – 'No, no. We'll stay here. We'll join no factions....' After that, everything was confused. Help had come; too little, too late, and so in the end there was this place.

Snake was dead. He had been hit by a stop, and when he began to bleed internally on the dark journey no one could keep him alive. Annet had been hit by a stop too. She had been burned by some kind of flame-thrower down one side and thigh, but also when they found her there was a black stain of broken blood vessels on her back. Now she could not move or feel her body from the waist down.

When Annet first saw her rescuers, the robes and veils, she thought it was part of her ugly dreams. She didn't understand. The last thing she had heard, before the horror, was that Jagdana – even Jagdana, had abandoned their prince, instated Atoon's heir and gone over to Bima Singa. She hated all Dapurs. Derveet had done this with her meddling, but the women were worse, letting it happen. She didn't want their charity. All she wanted was death, and she couldn't see why they were holding her back. She thought of a small figure dressed in white, gazing at her solemnly in the hearthcave. She knew, obscurely, that it had all begun with that little girl. But she couldn't remember how....

She woke again. She was still in the derelict camp, lying on a string bed on the verandah of one of the long huts. Her mind

198

was clear, but she had the feeling that days and nights had gone by. Furtively she slipped her hand down to her side and felt clean scabs under the dressings, no scar tissue. I am alive, she thought. But she could feel in the air, all around her, the enormous menace: the end was still to be faced. Everything was very quiet. She could hear polowijo voices, somewhere nearby. On the steps of the verandah a woman sat paring mangoes into an enamel bowl. She wore soft trousers, her cropped head and golden breast bare as if she were safe in her own garden.

Annet said, 'Why are you healing me? I don't want to be healed.'

The woman raised her head and smiled. 'You are healing yourself Annet. Are you not aware of that?'

She stared sullenly, refusing to answer. 'Why couldn't you have left us alone. We could have died just as well in our own place.'

The Jagdana lady went on with her work. 'Why did Garuda give their son to Bu Awan?' she said quietly. 'What use is a prince without a family? we asked them. The Garuda, though dead, answered: the polowijo are the prince's family. We have learned to understand that message. A polowijo is disorder, it makes cracks in the patterned walls of life and thrusts itself through. So – the prince, that is, the Peninsula, can only survive by embracing the polowijo: that which breaks down the walls, abandons the patterns. It has been hard for us to learn, but we see now the truth the Garuda left us. We could not leave you to die. You are our hope.'

The lady's voice came from a cool, still distance; it was utterly without inflection. Annet looked at her with hatred.

'You can leave that out,' she said roughly. 'What's happening outside? What's happened to Derveet?'

The Jagdana lady bowed her head. And so Annet understood that it was really all over. She accepted the news blankly. It didn't seem to matter much.

'Oh no,' said Jagdana lady. 'She is not dead. We sent her our prince. Like the rainbow bird in the forest he was meant to outface the enemy, while she took her nestlings into hiding. But she sent him away instead and he became entangled, and she – was in greater danger than she knew. Who can tell? Our way might have prolonged the struggle, probably it could have done

199

no more; this enemy is so implacable. But she is not dead. She will rejoin our prince on the field of battle, and who knows what may happen? The poet says: As the flower and its scent and the fire and its flame, the flower is Krishna and the scent Ardjuna, the fire is Krishna and the flame Ardjuna. . . . '

Annet turned her face away. Jagdana lady must have forgotten that scripture is not taught in farm camps.

'Oh, what's the point,' she muttered. 'You don't care, anyway. You'll come out and make a new Dapur world, with nothing human in it, when you've cleared us all away. None of this affects you. I bet you set it all up. You've even cleared the Koperasi out this time, God knows how. I'm sure you can deal with a few senile old Rulers –'

There was a silence so intense Annet could not stop herself from looking round. Jagdana lady's golden hands, banded with silver, for she was a mother of children – had closed convulsively on the paring knife.

'The senile few,' she said softly, 'are in the grip of a purpose far greater than they. Their only blame is, because of clinging to the past, they have put in the hands of that Purpose things that should not –'

The lady could not find words. Words often failed her, that was why she had retired from them. She opened her hands.

Annet saw drops of scarlet, falling on the bright flesh of the fruit. She understood. The lady said, silently, *We are mortal.* She said, *There is no protection, nothing is secure. This is not the end of your world only.* It is the end.

She had thought she would never feel anything again, but suddenly an abyss of fear opened in her heart.

24 Sunset

'This is it – '

Two people were crouched at the foot of a small, scrub-covered rise near the southern boundary of the Pancaragam, the holy city of the west. Behind them stretched the ruins: field on field of half-buried streets; shrines, meeting halls, nunneries.... The Pancaragam was far greater and far more ancient than the drowned Garuda citadel. The Gamarthans first built it; a monument to the unity of their everlasting empire. The early Garudas had kept it up for a while. Now it was a barren plain, halfway down the coast of Jagdana, forgotten by the peasants of the Hanoman countryside, haunted by the never ending mournful sighing of the sea.

The causeway people had been outmanoeuvred by prince Bima, who would not talk but led them and followed them in an uneasy dance up and down and across the princedoms until, like the last outnumbered piece on a chequer board, they had no choices left. So here they were. The Pancaragam was on a rough peninsula; it should cost even Bima's great army dear to dislodge the defenders. But the causeway people had their backs to nothingness. For more than a month there had been a kind of stalemate. The fields beyond the neck of the Peninsula were covered with the tents of princes and warriors – but Bima would not strike or actively enforce the siege: neither side made any hostile sorties. Meanwhile the Rulers' agents, like children playing a callous game, kept on delivering to Atoon's camp the *recalcitrants*: the sick and old and defiant who wouldn't leave Ranganar, and fugitives rounded up on the roads. The noble allies claimed they were being patient and merciful, but it was evident that the real enemies were gradually making it impossible for Atoon to defend his people. When they had achieved this aim, they would let Singa off the leash.

Pabriker Kimlan stopped digging and watched as Atoon

grubbed in the dry soil with his hands, uncovering long folds of shiny, dark cloth. They had come out to look for buried treasure, hidden here by Atoon's family in some nervous time years ago. He peeled back the treated silk, and laid bare long serpent necks.

'Very pretty,' said Kimlan. 'Still working, eh?'

'I don't know much about field guns. Probably they'll only blow our own heads off. We'll get them carried back and I'll load them up with black powder and see what happens.'

'Atoon, Atoon,' said Kimlan. 'You *must* learn to delegate.'

She sat back on her heels and stared at the western horizon, where the land ended. 'I've got a plan,' she said, 'for making kites. We could make kind of *winged* flying devices, with little hatcha engines to get them up into the currents: I've been drawing pictures of one in my head. Then we could all fly away.'

'That would be nice.'

'Breus says if he can have someone who can start a treadie he can walk past the corral guards. There are Welfari supply sheds, untouched; medicine and food, just down the road. He's very good, you know, at that sort of thing.'

Atoon shook his head. 'No. They would call it truce-breaking if they caught him with the vehicle. We are *not* going to give them their excuse.'

'Of course he won't get caught.'

'Besides, it is misuse.'

Kimlan looked at him thoughtfully. 'And what would be the *right* use, Atoon, of being able to read people's minds?'

Atoon was silent. All through the long march there had been an understanding among the causeway people that something strange was happening to them. It was an uneasy subject. People joked about it, or said nothing. The prince was one of the many who resisted and refused, insisting that it was wrong; horrible, to let changes like these grow on a battlefield.

'I wonder what it will be like,' said Kimlan at last. 'The new world. It'll be very weird, it'll take some getting used to. No more ignoring misunderstandings and getting by on the surface. No more pretending the people you hurt aren't really human. . . . I think I could have got to like a life like that. Oh

202

well – never mind. It's a causeway's job to lie down and be walked over.'

A pebble dropped on a stone. Atoon looked up and saw her walking away. He did not follow. He stayed where he was, chin on his knees, eyes blank and dreaming. He was a different creature from the whiteclad aristocrat of long ago. He wore Samsui blouse and trousers nowadays, much faded and worn. He had dug ditches and tended fires and minded children and sucked wild pigs' bones for the marrow when he could get them. He had shorn off the long braid of his manhood for convenience, and couldn't even remember the occasion of this life-changing act. His cropped hair sprang up above his brow in obstinate vitality, making his tired face look strangely young.

He knew the end was not far off. The camp was crowded now, and supplies were dwindling. At the beginning of the stalemate Bima had suddenly announced terms for a settle-ment: Peninsulans could go free, if they would give up 'corrupt southern ideas' and the false Garuda, and return to their families. Samsui and ex-Koperasi would be taken care of by the Rulers, who realised the people would no longer share their country with such elements, and were making new arrange-ments. Atoon, knowing he was hopelessly trapped, could only answer, to the repeated offers: that they were all Peninsulans. That prince Singa couldn't possibly expect him to behave so despicably.

News of the massacre at Bu Awan had come quite soon. It did not have the effect – supposedly – intended. The causeway people saw through the lie at once, and were horrified by whispers about Leilah's methods of warfare. And Bima wavered – Even while his emissaries and allies were pro-claiming the official version, Atoon *felt* him struggling. . . . But the flicker of hope passed. Leilah had disappeared (how wise of her, or someone) and become a martyr. Worse, a story had begun that the renegades now had in their possession the *anak khusus putih* – the 'child in white'; talisman of hope and freedom. Having heard the various stories, Atoon believed Cho was gone for ever. She had escaped, poor innocent – she wouldn't stay to harm her friends. But the rumour persisted. And it was said the idea of the child affected the princely allies and their followers with a kind of madness. There had been no embassies now for several days.

He gazed into the west, where the sun was going down in scarlet. Even that wide gate, Derveet's beloved ocean, was not open anymore. Soon after the causeway people reached this ancient place they had woken up one morning to find a row of shining half circles lying on the line between sea and sky. It was the Rulers' islands. They had come from the eastern sea. No one knew how they had travelled, whether they had come instantly, or whether the Rulers had known for a long time that this was where things would end. But everyone in the camp felt that presence all the time now: watching, waiting to be satisfied.

Some of the renegades were bitter about the great Dapurs and said the ladies had betrayed the Peninsula. But Atoon understood. It was the correct Dapur decision: Singa was stronger, therefore Hanoman must not be encouraged – *Thou shalt not risk lives.* In desperate danger it is right to ignore the rules. But if there is no way out, not the most crooked; if the calamity descends inexorably, then it becomes right to give up all machinations and let fate find you, if it must be, doing your duty – no matter how irrelevant. And so fate finds us, thought Atoon. Even Bima is doing what he ought, in serving his sister. Together we will appease those watchers on the horizon, with a blood sacrifice.

He remembered something Derveet had told him once, about the Black Islands. Some decadent communities there had forgotten how to give birth. When someone came to term, and began to struggle, her belly was opened with a knife. Conditions were poor, many people did not survive: it was considered the most honourable death. Is this our role? he thought, and he shuddered. Not for the causeway people but for the others; the old and bewildered and especially the children. Atoon had seen death now: death by disease, death by injury, in a way he had never known it while he lived in the palace of the Hanomans, not even at the end when the mobs were running wild. He understood as he had never done how the Dapur shielded their people, and he knew that the end here would be hideous. But the new world would survive, in hearts and hidden places, and rise again. *Someday we will be remem-*

204

bered – He knelt for a while, listening to the grieving murmur of the sea, then got up suddenly and began to walk back to camp.

'There. He's gone.'

'And a good thing too,' said Divine Endurance. 'You'll have the whole pack of them onto us.'

'I was only looking.'

They had scratched out a den for themselves among the roots of the long-legged bushes – behind them lurked Gress in a little dimple among the rocks, bare and hot and very uncomfortable, but the pony never complained. Divine Endurance complained all the time. Now she said sharply:

'You've looked enough. We must go, before we find ourselves trapped here. Or have you changed your mind again?'

At last the child had given up her wrong-headed ideas and agreed to return to the original plan. Divine Endurance was delighted, for the time was ripe. But she could not help wondering how much Cho understood.

'You do realise it is only by joining Wo that you'll help these people, and end their troubles?'

Cho's eyes took on an inward and impenetrable look.

'Yes, I see that,' she said softly, resignedly.

'You're only upsetting yourself now,' said the Cat. 'It'd be better to get on with it.'

'I will see Derveet,' said Cho, and turned to creep back through the roots to Gress's dimple.

Atoon walked through the outskirts of the camp. The red and white merdeka flag was fluttering above the ruins; somehow it had changed sides over the months . . . the allied leaders flew their own banners, under the colours of Gamartha. Behind him scarlet faded to clear, lovely, nameless hues; around him countless little parties huddled around cooking fires. He felt a strange stirring of his spirits. Each little fire was an affirmation. *Yes*, he thought. *We will be brave.*

He saw a treadie arriving in the great square, by the tumbled bulk of the sanctuary of Roh Betina. Who have they brought us today, he wondered. He saw the Dove House boys there. They had arrived in one of the first batches, very distressed because their lady had fled without them. But Atoon was glad: she was

205

safer alone. The garbled stories of how Cho suddenly appeared and escaped had no mention of Derveet: in the other camp this was supposed to be a cover-up – the Rulers were actually holding Garuda in special confinement. But every time a treadie arrived, Atoon's heart lifted defiantly – Derveet and the ocean had always been friends. The crowd seemed excited; there must be someone from Ranganar. Not many of those who had escaped and vanished were still on the loose – 'Handai!' he cried suddenly, and broke into a run.

It was not Handai. The Koperasi said, 'That's your lot, you won't see us again,' and jolted away with grins on their faces, pleased at the joke. The rest of the treadie's load squatted on the ground, trembling and half senseless, and in the midst of them a gaunt dark figure swayed, and was caught in someone's arms. Soon the prince and the causeway people knew the worst, and understood that this was the finishing touch which their enemies had been saving to the last.

When the bad news had been delivered, people began to drift away again. There was nothing anyone could think of to do or say. On one side of the big square was a ruined hall of vast proportions. Around the walls stood stone figures of the heraldic animals; in the middle of the chamber, where the roof had vanished completely, there were trestle tables and benches with a well-used air, under a makeshift thatch shelter – the centre of the camp. Butcher Pao stayed when the crowd had gone, but Garuda did not seem to know her.

'You'll need somewhere to rest,' she muttered. 'I'll – I'll arrange it – '

Now they were alone, Atoon did not know how he would dare speak to her. He thought she didn't know where she was, or what was happening. And then, while he struggled, she raised her face and smiled, the same smile as ever: wry and warm and sane.

'It suits you,' she said. 'You should have done it ages ago.'

A moment of pure relief – but just then there was a sound behind them. Two Samsui women, one small and bent with curly cropped grey hair, stood with a little girl. It was clear they had told Dinah. The Samsui never keep important news from children.

'Aunt?' said Derveet, sounding frightened. 'Don't bring her to me, please – '

206

'It's only fair. Who else is her mother now? She has a right to remember you.'

Derveet stared, wondering perhaps how long Dinah's memories had to live.

'All right,' she said abruptly, 'Don't leave me too long.'

In the hall of the nations the evening grew dark. Derveet lit a lamp. Little Dinah had been crying, but nothing that had happened to her recently seemed very real. She was sleepy now. She rested her cheek on her arms on the table-top and told Derveet helpfully, 'If my mummy was here she would sing to me – ' So, when Atoon came back Derveet was singing a lullaby. He waited in the shadows, listening to her voice: it had been a dark, soft voice for singing; it was cracked and faint now, but still true.

> I know a river
> Where the water runs
> Runs runs ever
> Through the green green trees
> And the sun shines on it
> And the leaves dapple it
> And the rocks and the branches
> Stand still in the water
> But the river runs forever
>
> I know a little girl
> Who ran by the river
> And put flowers in the water
> And the flowers danced away
> Like a disappearing rainbow
> But the river runs forever –

Derveet realised she had lost her audience, stopped singing and drew the child up against her shoulder. Two Butchers appeared; they had been waiting for the right moment. The child opened her eyes.

'Finish?'

'Finish,' said Derveet. 'Go with your people, dear.'

Dinah's hair brushed Derveet's chin, her small body was relaxed and warm and heavy. After a moment she sighed, and got down and trotted away, forgetting to say goodnight.

Atoon stood looking at his friend, sitting alone with the

207

single lamp beside her. The patience and quiet of her face was intolerable. Something had happened to him, when he first saw Garuda. He stared at her, imprisoned and defeated, everything lost, and suddenly, in a moment, he understood what he had done. The thoughts of a few minutes before filled his mouth like bile. *What am I doing here?* he cried to himself. *Oh God, she told me to keep them safe –*

She glanced up, and saw him.

Atoon said: 'You should have let me kill myself, the time I asked you. It would have been better.'

She had told him to go far, and not come back until he was sent for: to take away the seed of life, and save it. His own family had told him the same. Was that too hard for him to understand? Was simple obedience so difficult?

Derveet smiled. 'No,' she said at last. 'Don't blame yourself Atoon. Sit down. Let me tell you a story.' The lamplight flickered. From the camp outside came muted sounds, of various preparations. 'Once upon a time – ' began Derveet.

'Once upon a time there was a people who lived in a poisoned land. They had to leave it, so they came and became neighbours of the Peninsula. Naturally, they took over the government of this benighted country. But there was always an antipathy; a clash of philosophies. The neighbours had kept hold of a certain kind of civilisation, and it seemed to them the Peninsulans were wilfully throwing away everything of value. So their government was strict and angry. Finally it got to such a pitch that the Peninsulans revolted. We'll never know what really happened. But in the turmoil something came to the Rulers – in the form of a delicate and lovely youth. Perhaps one of them, one of the emissaries they had on our soil then, met this youth one night on the road, and felt his life changed for ever. From then on, the Rulers were not strict or angry anymore. All their resentment ended.

'Now to understand why, you have to realise the Rulers had been dying for a long time. I don't know if the old poison was really, physically, killing them. It seems to me more likely it was because they would not let go of the past, that death had got hold of them. Anyway, by the time of the Rebellion at least, the question was academic. Their population had passed the point of no return. They knew all about this death, they were used to

208

the idea. What filled them with conflict and distress was that our *alien* life would continue.

'I do not know how openly they have admitted to themselves what has been happening. It doesn't matter. Wo works from the longings of the heart. He has certain restrictions; rules built into him that he can bend but not break. But he has found ways around them. For all these years the angel doll, with its great powers, has been helping the Rulers: soothing them so the neglect and abuse of their rule did not seem shocking, and at the same time quietly persuading us, in many ways, towards self destruction.'

Atoon stared. A bitter chill suddenly ran through him, as if his blood had turned to water. He wanted to tell her to stop, but Derveet went on.

'It isn't even their fault, Atoon. *It was written*, as they say. There is nothing that the angel dolls can do but bring chaos and death. They give us our desire, and *desire* is not a little thing. It is one of the powers that hold the universe together – set free it must tear things apart, one way or another. . . . Even, even the desire for hope, to turn the people from despair, will end in destruction – '

Her voice shook, she put a hand up to her face: 'Remember, Atoon, she has always given us what we wanted. She brought me quietness when I was playing Anakmati. She brought you action, when you were pampered and idle and despairing. When I sent you away, her vigour in your heart brought you back. And I, while ruin was plotting, kept my *stillness* in Ranganar. And finally, when they wanted me they took me. It wasn't hard. Like everyone else, I had surrendered already.'

A breath of air from somewhere stirred the darkness, making the lamp-flame shiver and bow. The quiet voice began again, relentlessly:

'When I entered this struggle, I put my faith in the mysterious flower our women found in their garden, who knows how long ago. They used it for what seemed most important: medicine, surveillance – control. They nurtured it and kept it secret at any price, so it could grow, believing it to be the hope of the world. Even I only turned to it in desperation. We were wrong, I believe. I now think the flower is really more like a spark. It needed a wind to make it bloom, not a shelter. Well,

209

the wind came.... But it is no use. Leilah of Gamartha has proved that even the mystery can be corrupted. The Dapur power may approach to God, but it is rooted in our humanity, and our humanity, ours, not the Rulers', is *wormeaten* now. I don't think we have had a chance, since Cho set foot on the Peninsula.'

Silence. Then Atoon said – 'Cho disappeared. We know Leilah of Gamartha stole her, but Leilah never came back to her brother. The Koperasi might have overtaken her in the wilderness. But we wouldn't be waiting here now if the Rulers had Cho....'

He stopped. Derveet was looking at him with a half smile in her eyes, and shaking her head.

After a moment he said in a defeated voice: 'We think Leilah killed herself.'

'Yes.'

She shivered. 'I was very low, up on Bu Awan. The Cat, Cho's cat you know, did a really good job on me ... very professional. I am better now. But things have been different since then. Have you had dreams Atoon? I know they haven't got Cho. She is near this camp. I know it. I don't think it is her fault. I don't think she can stay away. Her brother draws her. They are twins. They act on each other, do you remember I once told you that? He is coming to her, she is going to him. We can't keep them apart. I've been thinking ... but wayang legong can't be destroyed. Oh, Atoon, I couldn't do it anyway. I couldn't do it....'

Her face, by the end of this, was resting on her outstretched arms; the jagged eagle profile and the black long curve of lashes grazing her cheekbone. Atoon asked no more. But at last, as the dead gods listened to the night and the shadows sighed and whispered, he reached out a shaking hand to touch her hair.

25   Midnight

Daylight strengthened. Atoon had been watching it grow. He had not slept, but he thought maybe Derveet was sleeping now. He was propped up in a corner of the bed shelf in the cell, the old nun's cell Pao had given Garuda, so she could lie against his shoulder and have some support for her difficult faint breathing. His arm was round her, his hand over her breast. He'd been in starts of terror all night, imagining the dark flesh cooling against his palm, the shallow movement ceased. But now it was morning, and he knew she was still with him, for another day. The last day. Would there be a final embassy, or were all ceremonies over? The camp, he knew, had been preparing for defence as far as possible. And part of his night terror had been to listen for a swift and wild alarm. But he was not afraid now.

The grey dawn was calm and still. What a fool I have made of myself, he thought. Swaggering around the country after Bima Singa, posing in romantic attitudes. . . . Well, it was all over now. Just a weary wakening from a wild dream, no need for remorse, no place for recriminations. He knew something that Derveet had not told him last night. He knew that he had ignored the visions and portents sent to warn him on that first journey; sent to warn the people from the depths of their own hearts, and he had kept down the mystery, when, if it had flamed, the sparks might have reached Bima's army, making war impossible. . . . It was hard to believe that nothing would have made any difference. And yet, in the empty silence that filled his heart, he did believe it. . . . Suddenly – had his eyes closed for a moment? – he realised that he and Derveet were no longer alone.

'How did you get in?' he said, without surprise.

'Through the window,' said Cho. There was a tiny square of pallor, high in the wall, not big enough for a cat –

Derveet awoke and felt Atoon's arm round her. She opened her eyes, and it was like the dreams she had had in prison: a blazing instant of joy, and then the understanding dawning, that if Cho had come back there was no hope left at all. But this time the dream went on. She sat up.

'Please don't be angry,' cried Cho. 'Please – I couldn't help it. I had to see you again.'

Derveet left the couch and went to her. Atoon picked up his blouse and slipped quietly out of the door.

In the centre of the camp of the princedoms was a large space of carefully smoothed earth, guarded by beautiful youths armed with senjata, dressed in white with sashes of the mountain colours; green and purple. Here stood Bima Singa's tent. Beside it, under the steady rain that had begun soon after dawn, hovered a rose-coloured sphere, parked on a cushion of air just above the ground. The dust that was being kept dry under it danced incessantly with a faint hissing sound. Bima had been up all night with the adviser from the shining islands. The youths were yawning. No one was allowed near the prince's quarters while the adviser was on shore, not even to change the watch.

Bima had never liked the connection with the Rulers. His sister had always dealt with them herself; she understood his repugnance. To her strong soul accepting *their* help meant nothing, because she knew she was going to turn on them in the end. But Leilah had disappeared. Since she had left him, a horror had been growing on Bima. He could not take the 'official version' into his heart; he realised there the things she had done, with her strong soul. He had announced her murder, but they had been so close he knew the truth, of course. What could he do now? Not, certainly, abandon responsibility for her rising. He could not give up the terrible venture that he and Leilah had begun together. He must go on. But there was no honour left in this war. It disgusted him.

The adviser from the shining islands had come to offer prince Bima a solution. The suggestion was that Bima should give the renegades one last chance. If that failed, the Rulers were prepared to provide what their ambassador called 'a sort of demonstration'. The prince's sister had wanted decisive

212

weaponry, but the Rulers had given up that sort of thing long ago. What was offered was a relic, left over from the Rebellion.

Bima and the adviser sat opposite each other on the plain canvas floor with a low map table between them. The tent was big but rather bare; Bima liked to live simply. Its walls were tightly closed; a pendulum fan scarcely stirred the air. The prince's visitor was closely encased in a strange sort of coverall garment, but showed no sign of discomfort. Bima found it hard to swallow his revulsion at the smooth, hairless skull and the unreadable bland features, all wrapped in some kind of caul like a newborn animal. He did not want to accept this creature's help. But the Peninsula was in desperate straits. The adviser had been going over with him all the trouble spots – the empty towns; ruffians and criminals harassing Timur Kering; defiant rebels hiding in the Sawah. And *all* the Koperasi had been evacuated. . . . It was a symbol of good faith, said the adviser. To Bima the causeway people were not a last stand, but a place for a decisive stroke to end the bloodshed.

'I must stress,' said the adviser, through the caul, 'that the offer we are making has *no military value.*'

'But it will impress?'

'Oh yes. It will impress. Please understand we don't want to force anything onto you. This must be of your own free will. But you know, it's only as a last resort. The first suggestion may well succeed, and then everything will be settled.'

Bima passed his hands over his face. He could see, yes, that making them give up the child-in-white would break them.

'What – er – what are you going to do with her?'

The Ruler shook that grotesque head gently. 'Now, now. I told you, you mustn't worry about that.'

'The people won't like it when they realise she is to go to you.'

'These mob fancies pass.'

Silence fell, but for the murmur of the rain, and the sigh of waves breaking somewhere. Bima tried to think. They had been talking for hours, but what exactly had been said? There were times when the Ruler's High Inggris was difficult to follow. Some things didn't make sense. Just what was he being offered?

'Try to make up your mind. It's quite important we get this sorted out now. North-East Wind is coming soon.'

Bima was alone, without his family or his sister. How many lives would be lost, in the taking of Pancaragam? If everything could be ended at a stroke did he dare refuse?... And now the Ruler did not look so alien. There was sympathy in that strange face – sympathy and understanding. A moment of intense quietness, then Bima sighed, and the balance dropped. 'So be it,' said the prince.

Somehow people knew that Cho had appeared. When Atoon emerged that morning he found the camp buzzing with the news. Friends and strangers kept coming up to him and congratulating him on his great good fortune, that changed everything. Not long before noon emissaries arrived, to deliver Bima Singa's ultimatum: Forget all other conditions and former terms. Give up the *anak khusus putih*, the child-in-white, or the truce will be ended with all possible force, tomorrow noon. Of course, there was no question of giving up the child. Atoon told the ambassador so, and the Gamarthan nobleman, who did not know he was addressing the so-called former Hanoman in person, looked up and down the trestle table of shabby figures and said something disgusting about monkeys and girl children. And the last embassy broke up in near violence as the representatives of the people all jumped up shouting around Atoon.

All that day, as the rain streamed down, the Pancaragam was alive with purpose, under the red and white freedom flag. The causeway people had been growing quieter and quieter as they realised what was going to happen to them and watched hope trickle away. But now the long awaited moment had come they were suddenly filled with excitement. The return of Cho was being treated as a miracle. It was not clear exactly what was expected – but even victory tomorrow was not impossible. *See*, said Kimlan to Atoon, *we're all volunteers. How many of those masses over there are only here because they're forced, and don't understand what's going on at all? But every one of us few is ready, is willing to die –*

The dishevelled township of tents and shacks was dismantled and brought into close order. The non-combatants were supposed to be packed into the vaults under the ruins, because no one knew what weapons the princes might produce. But there were so many there was not room and shelters were hastily constructed behind the thickest walls. . . . The *naga* guns – the buried treasure – looked very fine rubbed up and trundled around on wheels quickly made by the smiths. Derveet and Cho walked about together, letting themselves be seen. Atoon pitied them; it seemed a shame they could not have these hours in peace. But the show was necessary.

Derveet and Atoon had fixed on one frail, final plan. They would let the ultimatum run out and the fighting start, and under cover of this send Cho away up the coast by sea. There was a boat available; a smugglers' prahu in which some enterprising Samsui had fled from Ranganar. The Dove House boys would take her, and leave her somewhere to disappear in the desolate lands. The prahu had been well hidden, and sea-going was unknown on the Jagdanan coast because of religious taboos and poor fishing. There was a faint chance that Singa and his advisers would overlook this possibility. . . .

At the meagre night meal people came together. They brought out their last little hoards of achar, beer and spirits and sang and kissed each other and were very emotional. Atoon imagined identical scenes in the other camp; he could not bear it, he hid away. When the night had quietened he came out, and found Derveet sitting alone again in the hall of nations, drinking weak achar tea over a small red brazier, for the rain had made the air quite cool.

'Sit in front of me,' she said. 'Or I can't see you. Haven't been able to see anything out of my bad eye for weeks.'

'I'm sorry.'

Derveet smiled.

'Where's Cho?'

'Gone to fetch Gress, her pony, from where they were hiding. Don't worry, she has an escort.'

'Who?'

'My boys.'

'Derveet,' said Atoon. 'I can't do it. I cannot fight. It is too terrible. It will make no difference, they'll catch Cho anyway, or her brother will pull her back. Why don't we just surrender? We are in God's hands –'

Derveet gazed into her bowl. 'That would be nice, wouldn't it,' she said softly. 'You should have heard Cho's parable, Atoon. I'm afraid it's rather the reverse.' Her words were bitter, but her face was strangely quiet. She looked up: 'No. We can't stop trying. With or without hope, it is never right to give up.'

In the shadows the dead stone animals gathered round: Garuda with the human head lost and crumbling wings, the posturing white ape faceless. A limping stone centipede, token of some long vanished state, seemed to caper weirdly. . . .

Atoon whispered, 'I cannot see any *right* in killing my own kinsmen and making my friends murderers, knowing they are all helpless puppets. . . . I would rather lose heaven –'

'Bima is your brother, Atoon,' said Derveet. 'Don't put yourself above him. . . . Such a mass of contradictions, in the end our only resort is to do what seems to be our duty. Come here.'

When he came she drew him down beside her, and kissed his face, his eyes, his lips.

'There. Have you forgotten? "Thy tears are for those beyond tears, and are your words words of wisdom? The wise grieve not for those who live, and they grieve not for those who die. Life and death will pass away. . . . " Be strong. Arise and fight. Now, go and sleep, my dear. You will find that you can.'

Derveet was dreaming. It was a room in the Samsui house, an inner room with windows into other rooms and courtyards. There was a pleasant low murmuring of other people's lives going on, within the undividing walls. There was a lot of light in the room. Handai was sitting on a square stool with fat claw feet; there was no other furniture. There was a lot of light. She watched Handai feeding her baby – one shoulder bare, the other clothed, the creature fumbling reproachfully at the dark, swollen nipple. It was strange to see Handai's little round breasts so heavy and strained. And yet she was fascinated, all the same.

'You're distracting me,' said Handai.

'But you're not doing anything.'

'Yes I am,' Handai bent her face with a sly smile. 'My uterus is contracting. I can feel it.' She knew Derveet was ridiculously shy about remarks like that. 'It almost hurts,' she said, and laughed at her friend's doubtful expression.

There was a lot of light in the room. As Handai laughed there came a sudden convulsion of that light – no sound. It passed, and Derveet realised there was a storm going on somewhere: a storm of light. She got up and came to stand behind the young mother. The white floor seemed a long way away; another of those soundless invisible spasms, but Handai settled back, accepting Derveet's support. Her body felt warm and solid leaning there, she turned her rough head – you don't trim your hair when you have a newborn baby, for some reason – and looked up.

What had happened to Handai's face? Hollow eyes – from lack of sleep of course, but more. The golden, rosy curves were shrunken in, drawn and drained; only bone and shadow remained under the glowing skin, no substance left. The virtue has gone out of her, thought Derveet. But where to? Not into that purplish, hairless thing with the squirming limbs. . . . Surely not. But where to? . . . . where to? Handai's cheek was pressed against Derveet's bare side where her jacket had fallen open – the touch had such a warmth, of reassurance. The room contracted again in another of those silent convulsions.

'It is the sort of thunder one feels rather than hears,' said Handai.

And Derveet woke up. Her open eyes saw straight away the figure of Cho kneeling beside her but there was something odd – 'Ah,' she thought. 'When I dream I see with two eyes.'

'Have I slept long?'

'Not long.'

The brazier was dying. Derveet thought of pouring herself another bowl of tea, but it was a huge effort to raise her arms, she decided not to bother. Cho, who had been feeding the crumbling fire delicately, as if it was a small animal, looked up and saw that Anakmati had come back; the person she had met by lamplight at Adi's hotel, so long ago it seemed – drab jacket and breeches, and a dark, harsh face alive with vivid energy. But the energy was quenched now. And we did not let them give us a brazier then, thought Cho.

Derveet gazed, on where there was nothing glowing now, only a lingering glimmer under the ashes.

'Derveet,' said Cho softly. 'Do you love me again? Will you always?'

'Dearest, I loved you the first moment I saw you,' said

217

Derveet. 'I never, never stopped. I am so sorry that I hurt you. I will love you till I die.'

'That's what I thought,' said Cho.

A faint sigh, of the grey charcoals settling. Derveet stirred: 'Where are those boys?'

'They are not coming,' said Cho sadly. 'I am not going with them. I am going out to sea, to my brother. Don't be angry with them. I told them it was your orders.'

She stood up.

'Cho! –'

The child trembled. 'Even if you think I am betraying you, I still must go.'

'Cho, what can you do? What power have you – ?'

'I have none now. But I will have.'

'What –'

'Derveet, I knew you didn't want me to do anything about your being ill. So I never did.'

Time seemed to stand still. Then Derveet suddenly moved – to get up, to cry out. But she did not move, nor make a sound. Something had touched her, it was as if her body had turned to stone. Cho stood with her hands pressed to her heart. 'So it's like that is it?' said Derveet, silently. 'Well, goodbye then. I love you.'

Cho darted forward and kissed that mouth – the strong, clever, gentle mouth that had been so sweet, briefly, once, and fled.

Three figures hurried through the ruins. The pony's hoofbeats echoed, the cat bounded dangerously underfoot. No one saw or heard: the whole camp was frozen in a dream. At the last wall the two-legged one stopped, and suddenly turned and flung herself against the stone, her arms before her face. No sound came from her. The pony rubbed her soft mouth against the little one's shoulder.

But the Cat chivvied impatiently: 'Come on, come on. For *that* you will find, one has all the time in the world.'

There was a boat waiting for them on the dark shore, nosing the sand. Not the black prahu, but another smaller vessel, gleaming faintly as it rocked there.

'I'll be waiting,' said Gress. 'Don't forget me –'

'Now you have got your way,' said Cho to the Cat. 'After all this time, how does it feel?'

Divine Endurance looked up at her sharply and said after a moment, 'I believe you have been doing what you shouldn't. I believe you've been prying into things. It won't do you any good, you know, whatever your plan is. It is too late. I promise you.'

Cho did not answer. She knelt gazing at the shore as it fled silently away, and soon the little shining boat was swallowed into the vastness of the sea.

In Pancaragam Butcher Pao, whose watch it was, did not know that a small piece had gone from her night, and neither did her sentries. At dawn she walked into the hall of nations with two of them and they found Derveet apparently asleep at a table. They spoke to her, but she did not answer.

'Fetch Atoon –'

When he came, she was on a stretcher wrapped in coverlets. She was shivering, her skin was burning to the touch.

'Sitting up all night in the chill and the damp – and in her condition –'

Atoon knelt on the ground. She grasped his wrist with hot fingers, the skin scurf and dry as a snake's.

'Atoon you must go out now. Go out *now*.' He could hardly hear the words.

'Don't let her talk –' said Pao.

'It's Cho. I can't tell you why. Not enough – ah, breath. You must take their attention away from what is happening out at sea –'

Her hands fell lax. Her eyes were not quite closed, she murmured but not to him. She would not speak to him again.

'Get her away from here. And come back, quickly. Call all the representatives –'

He turned his back.

'Well, tears won't help,' muttered Pao. 'Now then, you two: lift.'

219

26   Morning

The shining islands jumped between sea and sky but finally they were visible all the time. They grew enormous. Some had projecting arms reaching down from their flanks. The boat went to one in the middle of the row, and approached a smooth ramp lowered at the end of one of these arms. It was hollow inside: a great, round, climbing tunnel, dimly lit. The ramp sucked the boat to itself, Cho and the Cat climbed out. The seal a little way up the tunnel quietly irided itself, and they stepped through.

The floor cuddled their feet and carried them up into the island world and then, as if sensing they would rather be alone, it left them to walk by themselves. They passed through streets and halls and squares. In some places there were images of trees and flowers built in the air, with convincing blue sky overhead; other places had coloured lights falling and talking like water. There was no one to welcome them. Sometimes Cho heard the murmur of voices, or saw a figure crossing a street in the distance, but no one came near. There was a feeling of peace, long undisturbed. It was a lonely place, but not unhappy.

Without needing to be directed they moved into the centre of the maze. Divine Endurance trotted busily, her tail up and her whiskers pricked forwards. Cho walked with care, her eyes absorbed as if she was concentrating on carrying something precious. It was as if she had a present for her brother, which she held in her heart, and she was afraid it might break and spill over before she could bring it to him.

Finally, in the middle of the island, they came to a private-looking but unassuming hallway. The wall at the end of it unfolded as they approached. They stepped into a small room, very well lit. It contained a table with a chessboard on it, the quivering crystal pieces in disarray, and a sort of string bed; a good imitation of the kind of thing night-watch boys used to use in Ranganar. There were no windows. One of the walls was holding a suit of some elaborate uniform, including a peaked cap with gold braid. On the bed frame, lying on the bare netting, was an old, old man, quite naked. His arms and legs were spread-eagled and tied to the four corners with black ribbons. Kneeling over him was what seemed to be a slim youth, with hair the colour of dust.

The old man turned his head. 'Yes, do come in,' he said. 'I have to admit company does not make much difference nowadays, one way or the other.'

Cho looked at the youth's face and arms, which were covered in blue, whirling, tattooed patterns.

'What happened to them?' she asked. 'The nomads, I mean.'

'Oh, they were taken care of,' said the old man. He frowned slightly, trying hard to raise the spark of pleasure.

'Well, I've come,' said Cho.

Her brother glanced at her sideways, with dark eyes that mirrored her own, and went on with what he was doing.

'He doesn't talk much,' said the old man. 'Never did. You mustn't disturb him at the moment anyway. He's doing something rather hard.'

Divine Endurance jumped up on the chess table, crooning softly in her throat. The pieces fell into the air and were deftly caught and swallowed by it. She began to wash her face.

'Yes. He's managed it at last. He could never have done it without your help and your friends', especially the coloured lady. You see just now everybody, all at once, is longing for an end of some kind. So now it can be done, and none of us will feel bad at all. Of course, he's had to cut through a bit of red tape. He's not *breaking* the rules, but it is a rather delicate piece of interpretation, and on top of all his usual load it's a bit of a burden. That's why you mustn't bother him. He is only doing this for me because I'm the king you know, and I ought to have special attention.'

On the Pancaragam, Cho thought, it was morning now, and the battle had begun.

'Is it true then?' she said slowly. 'Have I really come too late?'

The king said kindly, 'Never mind. I'm sure he'll be glad to meet you anyway.'

Divine Endurance tucked up her back leg, and began to lick inside it contentedly.

On the morning of that day, a party of riders came galloping out of the south. They pressed urgently westward down the old road to the holy city, through stripped fields and deserted villages. In sight of the ruins they reined in and stared. They were in a grove of coconut palms; some hacked and seared, some still standing in tall, graceful curves. There was a smell of brine in the air, but it was mixed with acrid smoke. The horses fretted, frightened by the noises carried on the sea breeze, the riders hesitated. Then one figure broke away, urging her horse onward, her black veils flying, not looking to see whether her companions followed.

She rode blindly, until the battle was all around her: screaming faces and blundering bodies flashing out of the turmoil and vanishing. Once someone grabbed at her bridle and yelled at her, 'Get that horse back behind the lines! This is no place to bring a poor dumb animal –' She saw a woman's face, haggard and furious, topped with thick greying hair – The face fell back and she rode on. She was aiming for the red and white banner she had seen, flying high above the battlefield.

When she reached the spot she got down and stood uncertainly. The uproar was all behind her. She found herself in a courtyard paved in stone, quiet and hushed, surrounded by mouldering carved walls. The white flag with the red dagger, which she knew was freedom's banner, hung on a bamboo pole looking like something forgotten. Old women and boys came in and out of dark doorways carrying linen and trays. They glanced at her and ignored her. She could hear children chanting a lesson, somewhere close. She had been told by the women at the derelict farm that she must reach this place today; that she was needed for an important duty. Her back still tired easily, she wanted to lie down.

At last a woman went past, younger than the others, and looked at her brightly.

'Excuse me –' she said. 'I'm Annet.'

'Ah,' said the woman. 'Who? I don't know all your names. Come to sit with her? What are you – convalescent? Is that why

222

you're not fighting? Come on then. That other girl's worse than useless.'

She was a Baker. She wasn't political at all; the troubles had just thrown her in with 'this lot' by accident. But she'd always been good at sick-people duties, which was lucky. So she told Annet, leading her along a passageway and up a little stair.

'It's the fluid on the lungs now, and the fever, that will settle it,' she said. 'I daresay she could have had a few more months, living quietly, but I can't be sure. When this disease turns nasty, it is pretty quick –'

Annet was bewildered. In the door of the room they were entering was a very young woman, with reddish skin. She was sobbing. Someone murmured – 'Jhonni –' and she ran and crouched beside a mat on the floor. The person lying on the mat stroked the girl's hair with a weak, awkward hand, and said something to Annet's guide.

'Don't worry,' said the Baker. 'I'll find her plenty to do.'

Then Annet was left alone, looking down at the dying woman.

'*Garuda* –' she whispered.

Derveet had closed her eyes for a moment. She opened them and saw the leader of Bu Awan, wearing the black and indigo robes of the garden. She was splashed with mud and dust, her startling hair was tumbling out of the veil in a flood of gold.

'Annet,' she said, as if they had parted yesterday. 'Annet, I'm so glad to see you. Do you think you could call me by my own name? I'd prefer that.'

Annet knelt down, biting at her lips. She put her arm gently under Derveet's burning, wasted shoulders and turned the sweat-soaked bolsters, propping them up higher. She saw fresh sheets lying on the floor, abandoned by the weeping girl presumably. As gently as she could she stripped off the stained and clammy bedding, and replaced it.

'Ah,' said Derveet. 'Thank you.'

'They would not let me lie with other people. Bad for morale, I suppose.'

The room had a floor of boards and a roof of tiles: at some recent time people had lived in this part of the ruins. It was very still. There was nothing in it but Derveet's mat, and a tin

223

bowl placed under a hole in the roof. Through a long arched window in the thick wall came a distant threatening murmur.

'Derveet, what is happening?'

Derveet looked up. Her mouth quivered. 'They are fighting,' she said gravely. 'Didn't you notice, as you came in?' Then she repented. 'Annet, please. I'm sure someone will explain. But not me. I really can't.'

Then she could not speak anymore. She lay listening to the ragged, careful noise of her own breathing. Annet moved closer, and offered her hand. Skeletal dark fingers closed over it gratefully.

'Think I'll sleep for a bit now. You'll stay?'

'Oh yes.'

'Dreadfully hot, isn't it. . . . '

It was midmorning. The heat of the day had begun. The air around the Pancaragam was full of the smell of blood and black powder, and horrible confused sounds. Atoon, once prince Hanoman, rode the black horse, Bejak, along a ridge of higher ground above what had been the Timur Kering lines, and looked down on the battle. The few thousands of the causeway people were still holding ground. The fierceness of their reckless sortie had thrust them into their enemies' ranks, sending great masses of the immaculate warriors reeling. Now the two parties were locked together in an inextricable embrace. The princely armies did not see how pitifully small the forces of the renegades were. The causeway people took no account of the vast numbers against them. They would all of them slash and blast and kill as long as they could stand.

Atoon could not see the banner of sunlight and blue sky anymore. He wondered if his heir, the young prince of Jagdana, was alive or dead. Perhaps I killed him myself, he thought. He had been deep in that chaos, he had only left it briefly to make this survey. He did not remember much of what he had done there. Suddenly, as he sat Bejak's trembling shoulders, staring at the butchery, it seemed to him that his mind was cleared of madness. He knew what he must do. He called someone to come and take Bejak: he was going back to the field.

The rosy sphere had been forced to move a little out of the way of the fighting. Now it rested lightly in the feathery shade of a grove of casuerina trees on the edge of the battlefield, and just above the seashore. Bima was there, with the adviser, when his bodyguard brought the renegades to him. There were three of them: a big, red, brutal-looking Koperasi, one of the Samsui women and a third; small, with cropped hair. They were all dressed in shabby blouse and trousers, smoke stained and bloodied. The woman and the deformity seemed puzzled, almost angry. The small person looked resolute. Bima had difficulty recognising prince Atoon. But when he did he rushed forward and grasped his brother's hands.

'I prayed you would come,' he cried. 'There must be a way to end this. We must find a way. God will not forgive us if we fail –'

'You don't understand,' said Atoon, 'I have come to surrender.'

A few paces away the warriors of the princedoms were still thrusting against the renegades. The bubble's inner and outer apertures were open: glimpses and sounds of the battle came in by the connecting passage, through the smooth opening in the outer sphere. But within all was calm. The adviser was sitting before a bank of instruments, gazing with mild interest at some dancing dots on a screen. Bima dropped Atoon's hands. He turned round sharply.

'Call it off,' he said.

'I'm terribly sorry,' said the creature. 'But I can't do that.'

'It's not noon. Call it off, damn you –'

The large figure in its sleek, alien clothing turned with a tired smile. 'Ah, but I'm not controlling it. Our young friend, who does everything for us, is in charge. I don't know a thing about it. I certainly wouldn't know how to stop it now, or from here.'

For the benefit of the three newcomers the Ruler began to explain. 'The princes wanted something that would bring all the disturbance to an end. Now this has never been made public, but we've had some – ah, devices, in site on shore for a long while. They were put in place just before the Rebellion, up along the edge of the landmass. We never used them: we realised in time we would never have forgiven ourselves – we are not monsters after all. But the situation is different now, isn't it, and prince Bima freely consented. Don't worry. The blast area is, so far as we can find out, quite unpopulated, and the explosion will be in the air, so there's not much risk of triggering earthquakes. Of course, you won't believe what has happened at first, but you'll soon understand, when North-East Wind sets in. And then you'll join us on the islands. . . . Life will be so much more pleasant when we're "all in the same boat".

'Our agents, the – er "Koperasi" have already had all this explained to them. Likewise the "Samsui". There's a medical examination: those who need it, probably not too many if I've followed your recent history, will have treatment to make them suitable for a contained environment. And that's all there is to it.'

Prince Bima stared. The blood had fled from his face. The bones stood out of his handsome flesh as if he were already dead.

'Didn't you understand?' said the adviser, with a worried look. 'Oh dear. It can't be helped you know. Even from here the event will be extremely impressive, just as I promised. It will stop people in their tracks all right. But I'm afraid it is going to be *rather* dirty –'

Prince Bima stood for a moment, as if puzzling what this strange term 'dirty' might mean. Then he said to Atoon, calmly, 'Brother, we are betrayed.' He was carrying no weapon but a knife in his sash. He threw this on the floor and ran out of the bubble's side, unarmed into the mêlée. His bodyguard ran after him, and Breus, and Pao. The Ruler turned back to the screens, smiling tolerantly. One of the instruments counted out numbers.

'Ah – we're leaving in a minute.'

But Atoon stood transfixed. His hands hung empty at his sides. He could neither move nor speak.

The courtyard underneath Derveet's room had been very busy: full of running footsteps and urgent voices and sobs and cries as the injured were brought in. But to Annet all these sounds seemed far away. She knelt at her friend's side, waiting and watching. Someone had brought a bowl of water, she soaked a cloth and cooled Derveet's face and hands with it every few minutes. Slowly, the morning passed by. Several times Annet thought she found herself alone. But not quite yet.

At last, Derveet stirred and opened her eyes again. 'Hallo,' she murmured.

'Hallo. There's some water here. Do you want to drink?'

Derveet moved her head a little: No. She was silent for a while, then she whispered: 'Is the fighting still going on?'

'Yes.'

'Not much longer –'

Annet saw she was smiling, faintly and sweetly. But her eyes were very sad. A few minutes later she spoke again; Annet bent close, she could barely make out the words.

'Dear, I have not said. I'm sorry – forgive me?'

'What? what?'

'Bu Awan –' breathed Derveet.

Annet could not speak. Her eyes filled, her throat was closed with tears. When she found her voice she cried, 'Ah no, no blame –'

Too late.

In the small bright room, far away out at sea, Cho stood waiting for her moment, a look of listening concentration on her face. The moment came. For an instant she felt as if great wings were beating round her, holding her in love and sweetness and strength. The eagle rose shining into the light of the sun. Cho was alone, forever.

She said to her brother, 'You help people don't you?'

The youth with the dust-coloured hair raised his strange face.

'Well then, help me.'

Wo felt pain. It was not like the crying of the world, which he had learned so well how to soothe. It seemed to belong to him; it seemed to be inside him. When he tried to help, in his usual way, he found himself in peculiar difficulties. The mind was like his own: it was his own. It couldn't deceive itself, it couldn't forget, it couldn't die, it couldn't be offered the prospect of a meeting in another world. It couldn't destroy itself either: *that's not allowed.* The youth frowned. A ripple of dissatisfaction, even uneasiness, passed over the blue whirling lines of his face, for the first time in many years. All the other things that he was doing, and people he was looking after, were like juggler's eggs forgotten in the air. He made one more determined effort. . . .

227

There was a sudden, palpable change in the air of the bright room.

'Now look what you've done,' said Divine Endurance. 'You've broken him, you naughty girl.'

Annet in the upper room dropped the lifeless hand and stared wildly around her – 'What's happening!' she cried. . . . And on the battlefield above the seashore spitting firearms were dumb, long knives fell from lax hands. The warriors and the renegades stood in dazed attitudes, gazing about them in bewilderment.

Cho went to look at the youth's body, which had fallen from the bed and lay on the floor.

'He is gone.'

The king, who had been woken from a peaceful little doze by the bump, twisted round to have a look.

'Why so he is,' he said. 'My goodness, isn't that clever.'

Cho stared.

'Well, he isn't just dead you know,' he told her. 'He couldn't die, you know that. He's ceased to exist. He has left the Wheel. It is called Nirbhana. It's held to be quite an achievement.'

'For human beings,' said Cho. Then she said, 'But I am still here. I wasn't sure about that. I wonder what happened in the olden days. I hope there was some humane arrangement.'

Divine Endurance had got down from the table and now stood looking up at Cho. Her scheming was all over, and nothing had turned out as she had planned. Not even her curiosity had been satisfied: now no one would ever know what happened when you fastened the bad babies together again. But to her surprise none of this seemed to matter, beside the desolation in the child's face.

She said, 'We'll go away. We'll go somewhere nice. And anyway, you can't tell. For ever's a long, long time. There might always be a big earthquake. Or we might wear out –'

Cho was not comforted. 'Divine Endurance,' she said, 'How old are you?'

The king, getting restless, coughed to attract their attention and plaintively requested that he be untied.

228

The sky had cleared over the battlefield. The sun stood at noon and then moved on serenely westward in its usual course. Some people tended the dead and wounded, making no distinction between friend and enemy. Large groups stood looking out to sea. A little pale disc had appeared, between the shore and the shining arcs on the horizon. It was a kind of bubble. It approached very quickly and stopped suddenly a little way down the beach, hovering above the gently breaking waves. Cho got out, carrying Divine Endurance. The king followed with dignified care, dressed in his uniform, holding his braided cap under one arm. But at that moment someone came pushing through the crowd: a woman in dishevelled Dapur robes. She ran to prince Atoon, spoke to him; bowed her head and wept. And then a wave of grief, shot through with glory, broke from those two and swept through all the people.

The king had wanted to give his hat to someone; he thought this would be the correct thing. But he could not see anyone who looked interested. So he left it in the water, rolled up his trousers and pottered off by himself along the sand.

But later he came looking for Cho again. He found her crouched with Divine Endurance under the casuerina trees behind the empty bubble.

'Ah, there you are. I wanted someone to help me off with these things. And I thought I'd like to say goodbye too.'

'Where are you going?'

'Oh, anywhere.'

She helped him to shuffle off the heavy clothes and watched him wind a long swathe of saffron cotton around his shrivelled body. He did not seem sure how to handle this garment and ended up with some odd patches of nakedness. The peace celebrations were a background presence.

'Well, well,' remarked the king. 'So it is all over. I am not sorry you know. We only wanted this, really – for it to be all over. So you see, you two angels did manage to make everybody happy, after all.'

Cho said nothing.

The king smiled at her. Behind an irrepressible look of utter carelessness his old eyes were compassionate. 'Wo taught me a lot,' he said. 'And not all of it bad, whatever they may say. In this game of ours your achievement is great, greater than his, even. For you turned back, with your foot on the threshold of heaven, because you heard the cry of the world.'

'I am a wayang. I had no choice.'

'No? Ah well.' He had produced a small wooden bowl from a pocket of his discarded finery and was examining it fondly. A moment later he was gone, the pat-pat of his bare feet fading into the sound of the murmuring sea. Gress came out of the trees, and stood close to her friends.

'Shall we go away soon, child?' said Divine Endurance.

That night the victorious army spread themselves generously to entertain those who had surrendered. No campfire or outside kitchen of the princes' forces was complete without at least one renegade to fete. It was like a great banquet, spreading all over the shore and spilling into the ruins. Distinctions were blurred: the warriors and the causeway people were so mingled, so light hearted it was as if they had known all along that the battle was just a game.

Atoon walked alone in the darkness that surrounded the flowers of light. He had excused himself from the company of the other princes. Bima, of course, had tried to disclaim the victory, saying that it belonged to the causeway people, and the part that he and his armies had played was simply shameful. But Atoon had no desire to share this triumph. Today life had been saved from the terrible gifts of the wayang legong. One of them was destroyed; the other harmless because her motive force was gone. All around him were women mingling freely with men and youths: fastidious gentlemen and bigoted peasants eating from the same dishes as outcasts and Koperasi. The new world was beginning. But his heart ached. It seemed so little to gain: '*merdeka*', and a new social order. He knew the people were making legends already: Anakmati who feared nothing and despised no one, not even the most degraded. . . . Garuda weeping upon Bu Awan. . . . It is not enough! he cried out silently. Nothing, nothing could make up for Derveet, alive and human as she would never be again, never again –

Then suddenly he noticed something. In his blind grief he had walked past, already, fires where a strange quietness reigned. There were not many. They were scattered all over the shore. He did not know how he could pick them out, but he could. Stillness, silence; eyes moving like stars – mind to mind and heart to heart, just as Kimlan had said . . . (Ah, where was Kimlan now?) Atoon stood. In the morning they might forget; they might hold on to the old ways for a while. But the spark was leaping now with nothing to hold it back. He had a vision of that fire: spreading, spreading, until it overwhelmed the world and swallowed up everything he had ever known, ever loved. . . . His loss was greater far than he had imagined. It was so great that, after all, he was satisfied.

Derveet's boys brought out the black prahu, which was meant to carry Cho away. They draped it with silks abstracted from the tent of a rich nobleman and all night it lay on the sands, bearing its slight freight. They had dressed her in the plain breeches and jacket of Anakmati. They had combed her hair on her shoulders and folded her dark beautiful hands on her breast. Just before dawn the tide turned, and Garuda was sent out on her last sailing, the way the dead used to be sent by the diving people, on the islands where she spent her childhood. The sail was set; the breeze caught it, Garuda flew away. And up behind the watching crowds rose the white rim of the morning.

When it was over, Atoon and Annet rode down the shore with Cho.
    'Stay with us,' said Annet. 'At least for a while. You can't do us any harm now. I'm sure of it.'
    Cho shook her head. 'It's time I was going.'
    'Where will you go?' asked Atoon.
    'I will go north,' said the child. 'If you go far enough north, the ice and snow I saw once in the distance on the glass plateau comes down from the peaks and covers everything – all the land and sea. I've never been very cold. It might work.'
    Atoon looked into her eyes. He said softly, 'Well, there is a new prince in Jagdana. I don't feel like disturbing him. Perhaps I'll follow you one day.'
    Someone came running up breathlessly; she had been following them, not sure if she dared approach.
    'Here –' said Cycler Jhonni, shamefaced and awkward. 'I thought you might like to have this.'
    She had been crying again. The package she held out fell open, revealing a lock of glossy black hair. Cho looked at it. She could

231

feel the harsh silk on her palm. Her hands, not wanting to be rude, tried to reach out – but they could not.

'Thank you,' she said politely. 'It was nice of you. But please keep it. Come on Gress.'

She scrambled up, and Divine Endurance came lightly after and settled in the crook of her arm. The little waves sighed, the sea breeze whispered in the casuerina trees. Cho left the people behind and began her travels again, with the pony Gress and the Cat, Divine Endurance.

Acknowledgements

My thanks to Maud Casey, Bryan Loughrey, Chris Magness, Anne and Graham Holderness and Shantini Sockanathan. I must also acknowledge my debt to Bill (the bible) Dalton's Indonesian Handbook (Moon Publications, Michigan, USA, 1977), the best traveller's book in the world. The poem by Bettina Pfoestech appeared in *Emphasis*, the college magazine of UWCSEA, Singapore, 1978. The Mao Tsedung poem comes from *Mao Tse-Tung Poems*, Foreign Language Press, Peking, 1976.

KING ALFRED
1683–1760

FREDERICK
Prince of Wales
1707–1751

MARY
1723–1772
= Frederick II
of Hesse Cassel
1747–1837

A Simplified family tree
of the
DUKE OF CAMBRIDGE'S
relations.

Except for Augustus Fitz-
George and Francis Teck,
who never married, all
the Princess Royal's gen-
eration had issue.

GEORGE
Duke of Cambridge

GEORGE III
1738–1820

 ADOLPHUS = AUGUSTA
Duke of Cambridge   1799–1889
1774–1850

GEORGE
Duke of Cambridge
1819–1904
= Louisa Fairbrother
1816–1890

AUGUSTA
1822–1916
= Frederick, Grand
Duke of Mecklenburg-Strelitz
1819–1904

MARY ADELA
1833–1897
= Duke of Te
1837–190C

QUEEN MARY
1867–1953

FRANCIS
1870–1910

AUGUSTUS
FITZGEORGE
1847–1928

ADOLPHUS
FREDERICK V
1848–1914

The Royal George

H.R.H. The Duke of Cambridge

The Royal George

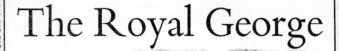

1819-1904

THE LIFE OF
H.R.H. PRINCE GEORGE
DUKE OF CAMBRIDGE

Giles St. Aubyn

CONSTABLE LONDON

LONDON
PUBLISHED BY
CONSTABLE AND COMPANY LTD.
10-12 ORANGE STREET W.C.2

Printed in Great Britain by
Butler & Tanner Ltd., Frome and London

This book
is dedicated to the memory of Mrs Mary Nayler
who for many years helped me with my writing
and who assisted with this biography which she did
not live to see finished.

THE biographer in his choice of a victim is confronted with a dilemma. Either he writes about famous people of whom little new can be said, or he selects a lesser-known person, the subject of a mass of unpublished documents, who nevertheless is too obscure to catch the public's fancy. How well known the Duke of Cambridge is today is difficult to tell, but of three things I am certain. First, as Commander-in-Chief of the Victorian Army for thirty nine years he occupied the centre of the political stage at one of the greatest moments in our History. Secondly, the material for his life and times, much of it unpublished, is important, extensive and exciting. Thirdly, the Duke enjoyed a fascinating and momentous life. It is customary, I know, to leave such extravagant claims to the Publisher, it not being thought proper in an author to advertise his wares, but having stumbled on an historical Treasure Trove I am anxious to share my discovery. Merely because the Duke of Cambridge is no longer a household name, I hope it will not be thought that this biography is only of interest to scholars.

To prevent this study of the Duke becoming a two-volume work like its predecessors, I have purposely omitted much which the official lives included. For example, I have said little of the Duke's travels, of his German relations, of his Staff, of his concern with colonial wars, of his correspondence with the Commanders-in-Chief in India, or of his interest in a number of military matters, which, however absorbing they might have been in the Victorian Age, have lost something of their relevance in the mid-twentieth century. Besides intentional omissions, there are gaps which proceed from ignorance rather than choice. Despite an overwhelming mass of evidence, parts of H.R.H.'s life escape the Biographer's trawl. While it is possible to discover from the Duke's Diary the exact time he left Gloucester House for the War Office on the morning of 12 November 1884 and with whom he dined on 7 September 1901, it is not possible to find out where he first met his wife. When the story becomes disjointed, the charitable reader will I hope assume that the evidence is wanting rather than the Author.

I am deeply indebted to Her Majesty the Queen for permission to use the Royal Archives at Windsor. I owe the loan of the FitzGeorge Papers to the kindness of Princess Galitzine and Brigadier Balfour. For leave to study Lord Wolseley's letters at the Royal United Service Institution, the Cardwell papers at the Public Record Office, and various nineteenth-century political collections in the British Museum, I must gratefully acknowledge the permission of the authorities concerned. Whoever has worked at any of these institutions, or in the Library and Archives at Windsor, or in the War Office, will know how much help, patience and knowledge are ungrudgingly bestowed on researchers.

I should like to thank Mr James Pope-Hennessy, Mr Michael Howard, Mr Peter Townend and the Reverend Charles Tomkins, who, after reading the book in manuscript, made many valuable suggestions and helped me to avoid some serious errors of fact, judgement and style. Finally, I owe an immense amount to Miss Rosemary Stopford, who helped in countless ways, and who contrived to translate an illegible draft into a faultless typescript.

GILES ST. AUBYN

St. Tudwal's Island
1963

CONTENTS

The sketch on page 121 is by Lieutenant Hobday and
belongs to Captain C. G. Chichester, D.S.O., R.N.

A PRINCE IN THE MAKING

T HE sons of King George III were disconcertingly reluctant
to marry. Moreover, they were disposed to regard as unattractive alliances which their advisers assured them were
alluring. Some even indulged in the delights of matrimony without incurring its legal liabilities. Consequently it was not until the
fifty-ninth year of his father's reign, that Adolphus, Duke of
Cambridge, the favourite son of the King and a young man
unblemished by scandal, produced a boy whom the law could
recognize as a Prince of the Blood Royal. In honour of his grandfather the child was christened George. Before the birth of his
cousin, Princess Victoria, the infant Prince was heir presumptive
to the throne.

Prince Adolphus was born in 1774 and in 1801 was created
Duke of Cambridge. The title had originally been bestowed upon
four of the sons of James II, all of whom died in infancy. It was
revived by Queen Anne for the Prince Electoral of Hanover, later
King George II, and became merged in the Crown when he

ascended the throne.¹ Prince Adolphus played a gallant part in the
Revolutionary War. In 1794 he was captured by the French in
Flanders but contrived to escape unrecognized. One of his Staff
Officers spoke as highly of his amiability as of his courage, and
described him as having 'a countenance beaming with benevolence
and goodwill towards all.'² In the following year he was wounded,
ordered back to England, and after a few months sent to Hanover,
a part of Germany he knew well since he had been educated
at the University of Göttingen with his brothers, Ernest and
Augustus. On Napoleon's annexation of the Electorate the Duke
retired to England, but when in 1813 the Emperor was compelled
to withdraw, Adolphus was sent to Hanover once more as
Commander of its Army. At the Congress of Vienna the Electorate was raised to a kingdom and the Duke was appointed its
Governor General.

The death in 1817 of Princess Charlotte, the only child of the
Prince Regent, and the wife of Prince Leopold of Saxe-Coburg,
made it urgently necessary for the Duke to marry if the Hanoverian line was to be preserved. On 5 November, the anniversary of a great deliverance, Princess Charlotte gave birth to a
stillborn son. Early next morning she herself was dead, exhausted
by protracted labour and weakened by dieting and bleeding. The
Royal Dukes, conscious of their duty to their country, and not
unmindful of the prospect of Marriage Settlements, began to
look about for wives. Unfortunately they were scarcely attractive
suitors. Their mistresses, their natural children, their formidable
debts and their advancing years, were defects which might be
considered overwhelming by any but the most despondent of
Princesses. The Duke of Cambridge alone was unscarred by
scandal and still comparatively young.

The Duke of Clarence commissioned the Duke of Cambridge
to explore the German Courts to find him a bride. Soon Adolphus began sending his brother back glowing descriptions of the
wit, beauty and charm of Princess Augusta, daughter of Frederick,
Landgrave of Hesse-Cassel. The Duke of Clarence was greatly
amused by these letters. 'By Heavens!' he said. 'He's in love with

her himself. I'll write and tell him to take her, bless him!'[3] The wedding accordingly took place at the castle of Hesse-Cassel on 7 May 1818, and was subsequently also solemnized in England.

In March 1819, at the Palace in Hanover, the Duchess was confined with a child, which, if it survived the attention of her medical advisers, would become the only lawful descendant of George III. So important an event needed to be observed by witnesses of undisputed integrity. Amongst others, the Duke of Clarence was present. Scrupulous precautions were taken to ensure that all was in order, and that no grounds could be entertained for alleging that anything spurious had taken place. Henry Rose, Envoy Extraordinary at the Court of Berlin, reported the details to Castlereagh, then Foreign Secretary.

Having been apprised by His Royal Highness the Duke of Cambridge at a quarter before one o'clock of the morning of Friday the twenty-sixth day of March in the year of Our Lord one thousand eight hundred and nineteen that Her Royal Highness the Duchess of Cambridge's labour pains had commenced, we repaired forthwith to the room adjoining to that in which Her Royal Highness was to be delivered, in Cambridge House in the City of Hanover, the door between these two rooms remaining open during the whole of our attendance; having been previously informed by His Royal Highness that Her Royal Highness would be confined in Her Bedroom up one pair of stairs, and that free access must remain from that room to Her Dressing room immediately contiguous to it, and these rooms having been previously shewn to one of us, the Right Honourable George Henry Rose, the seal of the said Right Honourable George Henry Rose was affixed so as to close it, upon the outside of the outward door of the dressing room under the directions of His Royal Highness, the Duke of Cambridge, who locked the door and gave the key of it to the said Right Honourable George Henry Rose, so that no communication with the bedroom could take place from without, but under Our eyes, we remaining in the room adjoining to the bedroom, and through which all persons entering that bedroom must pass; sharp labour continued until ten minutes past two o'clock of the morning aforesaid, when Her Royal Highness the Duchess of Cambridge was safely delivered of a male child, whose sex we determined by actual inspection.[4]

The boy was christened on 11 May, in Hanover, according to the rites of the Church of England. He was called George, William, Frederick, Charles. Royalty are disposed to be prodigal with Christian names and for a Prince of the Blood to possess so few was to send him almost naked into the world, but as most of his relations bore one at least of these names they forgave the parsimony. The Prince Regent, represented at the ceremony by the Duke of Clarence, and the Duke of Clarence, represented by the Earl of Mayo, were the child's Godfathers.

Prince George was fortunate in his parents. His father was by far the most agreeable of all the King's sons, although, considering his heredity, his eccentricity bordered on the disturbing. Wellington, in a moment of exasperation, told Mrs Arbuthnot that Adolphus was 'as mad as Bedlam.'[5] As a young man he read widely, was interested in Science, loved Music, and proved himself an industrious and efficient soldier. He played the violin expertly and had an impressive voice: invariably audible if not inevitably melodious. Many of his friends were scholars, musicians and artists, who shared his tastes. In the Victorian Age he appeared a pleasant survival of the eighteenth century, courteous, cultivated and robustly religious, displaying the charm of that vanished era without betraying its vices.

Sir Charles Bagot met the Duke of Cambridge at Brussels in 1825 and found him volubly affable. 'Yesterday,' he wrote to a friend, 'I dined with His Lowland Majesty to meet the Duke of a place called Cambridge somewhere in the English fens, where they teach arithmetic. This Duke, with his Duchess and Dukelings, set out for England this morning. He is just the same good-humoured rattle that he always was, and she, I think, is a very personable body for a Princess.'[6] Other people, however, found the Duke's explosions of goodwill overwhelming. Lady Lyttelton met him at Windsor in 1839, while she was in waiting on Queen Victoria, and described the encounter in her letters.

. . . The Cambridges arrived yesterday, and enriched our dancing evening. Queen's headache quite gone, luckily, for it requires a sound head to listen to the Duke . . . I was so *bestürmt* with questions, one hundred in a breath, close to my eye, by the Duke on his first arrival that I was fairly bewildered, and answered, 'Yes, Ma'am'. After dinner, during the dancing, he came and sat by me, and to be sure how he did shout and cross-examine! but he never wants any answer, so it don't matter. 'Where do you *habitually* reside, Ma'am? Oh, Hagley, you *did* live there. I see, I see—your son lately married—how long? a few months? I understand. *Now* where do you mean to live? At Richmond for the winter? Oh, I see! Where have you been since your son's marriage? Leamington? Why Leamington? Oh, your brother—I understand! Your brother, Captain Spencer! I remember—I perfectly recollect. A naval man, I believe. Yes, I saw him in 1825 at your father's in the Isle of Wight. Yes, yes, I know—Frederick Spencer, to be sure! *Your* father-in-law, Mr Poyntz? No, surely not so, Ma'am. Oh, his father-in-law? Oh, I see, I see,' and so on for half an hour. I was quite out of breath with listening, and could hardly stick in a word in answer here and there, and all as loud as a very sonorous voice can reach . . .

When the Duke left Windsor it was like the silence of night after a battle.

. . . The Cambridges are gone, and the Castle is still as death, for want of the Duke. Think of his asking *me* if I had 'any commands' to town? Think if I had told him I wanted a small parcel carried! He shouted on to the last, singing the quadrilles while they danced, and 'God save the Queen' while we dined, rather than be silent . . .[7]

Wherever the Duke went he spoke so loud and incessantly that it was impossible to be unaware of his presence. He had, moreover, inherited his father's trick of repeating everything three times: a habit described by Horace Walpole as 'triptology.' He often thought aloud, sometimes with disquieting candour. The stories of his absent-minded comments in Church are legion: some are even true. Like the sayings of Dr Spooner, the authorized version is very much shorter than the Apocrypha. That he shouted 'encore' after a preacher had delivered himself of a particularly eloquent peroration is too improbable to be believed, but the following reminiscences are authentic. The Duke of Cambridge 'constantly attended the Sunday Morning Services at St Paul's, Knightsbridge, in the time of the Rev W. J. E. Bennett, and occasionally was pleased to express in an audible tone his approbation of the proceedings, and his opinion of the sermon. I remember on one occasion when the officiating clergyman pronounced the exhortation—"Let us pray"—the Duke bravely responded from his pew:

' "Aye, to be sure; why not? let us pray, let us pray, let us pray!"

'On another occasion, while the commandments were being read I heard him remark—

' "Steal! no, of course not; mustn't steal, mustn't steal, mustn't steal."

'At the opera, this eccentric habit betrayed itself in a still more marked and frequent way. I remember once hearing him all across the house, exclaim, as he moved his opera-glass round the circles—

' "Why, I declare there are not half a dozen pretty girls in the house; not half a dozen, not half a dozen, not half a dozen."

'One night when a young pupil of Molique's, a mere boy, was playing in the orchestra from his master's desk, the Duke, who was very observant and also had a keen ear for music, struck by his precocity, sent between the acts for the boy to come up to his box, which was opposite ours, and taking him on his knee entered into a lively conversation with him, the Duke's share in the dialogue being heard pretty well all over the house. All that generation of the Royal Family were in the habit of talking in what we will call a *cursory* way, employing expletives rather expressive than choice.'[8]

Towards the end of his life the Duke became increasingly deaf, so he decided to move from the gallery of the Church at Kew, which he frequently attended, into a pew near the pulpit. Close by were some local schoolboys and every Sunday he counted them. If any were missing he would lean over the pew and say to the schoolmaster: 'Simpson, there are two or three boys not here today.' 'They are ill, Your Royal Highness,' Simpson would reply. 'Send to my house for soup for them' was the welcome answer. During a very dry summer, the Vicar read the prayer for rain; at the close the Duke joined fervently in the 'Amen,' adding, in exactly the same tone of voice, 'but we shan't get it till the wind changes.' One Sunday, during the reading of the offertory sentences, when the words, 'Behold, the half of my goods I give to the poor,' were read, His Royal Highness astonished his fellow-worshippers by exclaiming, 'No, no, I can't do that; a half is too much for any man, but I have no objection to a tenth.' Again, on hearing the text, 'For we brought nothing into the world, neither may we carry anything out,' he ejaculated, 'True, true—too many calls upon us for that.'[9]

Such stories of eccentricity present a distorted portrait of the Duke, for he was a very ordinary person, little inclined to stand on his dignity, friendly to all and admired for his integrity. He showed scant regard for pomp and officialdom. When he was taken to visit a cricket match on Upper Club at Eton, he broke away from the escorting Provost, preferring to be shown round by a small boy of his acquaintance.[10] It was because he so little resembled the common conception of a Royal Duke that he was so much better liked than his brothers.

Although Prince George owed many Hanoverian characteristics to his father, his mother was the more profound influence on his life. The Duchess died at the age of ninety two. She survived her husband by forty years and lived long enough to congratulate her

son on the anniversary of half a century's service in the British
Army. Like Prince Adolphus she was a great-grandchild of King
George II. Without being especially clever or highly educated, she
was interested in politics, enjoyed music, loved the theatre and
read widely. She had been brought up in the traditions of the
eighteenth century and was wholeheartedly conservative. Her
dignified and somewhat austere manner was lightened by flashes
of humour. Those who remembered her only in old age thought
her forbidding and terrifying. Queen Mary never felt wholly at
ease with her querulous grandmother, although Ella Taylor, a
Lady in Waiting who knew the Duchess from earlier days,
described her as 'a Duck of a Duchess. I never met with anyone
with whom it is so easy to get on . . .'[11] Princess Augusta spoke
to the last with a strong, guttural, German accent and never
became entirely reconciled to English ways.

'The Duchess of Cambridge,' wrote her daughter's biographer,
'was a handsome, stately lady somewhat above the average height
of women . . . When in repose her face wore rather a severe
expression, but directly she spoke her countenance lighted up and
a charming smile at once betrayed the gentle nature within . . .
Dignified in bearing and manner, as became a great lady brought
up in the sentiments of the *ancien régime*, the Duchess was invariably kind and gracious to those about her. . . . Punctuality was a
strong point with Her Royal Highness, and she never allowed the
carriage to be kept waiting longer than was necessary. Method
and regularity were seen in every department, and it would have
been difficult to find a household better ordered. . . . Her Royal
Highness had much ability, and was a good conversationalist,
while her keen sense of fun and humour made her a most delightful companion . . . The Duchess was a thorough musician,
possessing a beautiful soprano voice, and greatly enjoyed the
opera. She was also warmly interested in politics; she was a
frequent attendant at the debates in the House of Lords, and never
missed reading her daily paper.'[12]

The early years of Prince George's life were spent with his
parents in Hanover. While still very young he caught scarlet

fever and the doctors despaired of his life. His father was at dinner when a message was sent to him that the Prince appeared to be dying. The Duke, in a frenzy of agitation, seized some Steinberger, a Rhine wine which he particularly relished, and rushed to the sickroom. Heedless of all protests, he forced the child to drink a glass. From that moment the boy revived and the fever abated. For many years Steinberger was always drunk on Prince George's birthday to commemorate this marvellous recovery.

Prince George, having been saved from fever, only narrowly escaped being murdered. His first tutor, the Rev Henry Harvey, finding his task too arduous, employed a Mr Welsh as his assistant. From the first, Welsh proved eccentric, but nobody actually suspected him of madness until he was discovered one night kneeling by the Prince's bedside, armed with a knife, exclaiming loudly that he had been called upon to cut the child's throat and 'send him straight to heaven.'[13] Fortunately he was overheard and overpowered before being able to fulfil his pious intention. Harvey's selection of a tutor was a poor testimony to his discernment, and in 1828 he was replaced by the Rev John Ryle Wood, who took charge of the Prince for the next eight years.

Wood was a strong, upright man, severe in his judgements and a strict disciplinarian. He believed in leaving little to chance. His pupil's work and leisure were minutely supervised, yet he entirely won the confidence of the Prince, who later referred to him as 'my beloved preceptor.' Wood subsequently became Chaplain to Queen Adelaide and a Canon of Worcester Cathedral. His old pupil never forgot him. When the Kaiser visited England in 1874, Prince George, then Duke of Cambridge and Officer Commanding-in-Chief of the British Army, gave an official banquet to welcome the German Emperor. The Prince of Wales and all the foremost generals in England were invited. Amongst these eminent guests was Canon Wood, a little out of place in so glittering an array of military men, his clerical dress somewhat drab in that flurry of gold, silver and scarlet, but very proud to have been invited. When Wood died, Prince George recalled in

his Diary the many years they had known each other and the
fervour of their friendship.

> 8 November 1886. Heard today of the death of my dear old
> friend and tutor, Mr Wood, after a very painful and somewhat
> protracted illness. He died early this morning. He is a friend
> of fifty-eight years' standing, and was very dear and good to me.

Wood encouraged his pupil to keep a Journal, which, with
some interruptions, H.R.H. continued to the last year of his life.
The early volumes are a mixture of pious observations, evidently
dictated, or at least suggested, by the Master, and comments
which could only have come from the boy.

> I fidgeted on my chair whilst learning my lesson, until
> coming to the edge without knowing it, I slipt off and fell to
> the ground pulling the chair over me and causing it to give
> me a hard blow on the head.
>
> I cried for an orange! How silly. I think it must have been
> my third or fourth Birthday which I last celebrated and not
> my *ninth*!
>
> I told a lie, saying that I had not spoken to anyone, when I
> had spoken to the upholsterer. I tried, when found out by Mr
> Wood, to explain away my falsehood, arguing and equivocating,
> pretending that I did not know *when* he meant. Oh! that I
> could leave off lying and shuffling. It always gets me into
> trouble—is so unlike a gentleman and so wicked.

When the Duke of Clarence ascended the throne as William IV,
he decided that his nephew should be brought up in England. The
boy's parents seem to have been allowed no choice in the matter.
So in 1830, at the age of eleven, Prince George, under Mr Wood's
care, set out from Hanover for Windsor. What prompted the
decision is a matter of conjecture, but Queen Adelaide loved
children and, having lost her own in infancy, may well have
encouraged her husband in his belief that the boy should live
with them. Both the Duchess and her son found the separation
painful. 'Since I love you so unutterably my good George,' she

wrote to him, 'I do not like a single day to pass without my having written you at least a few words.' Her very first letter to him, dated 9 August 1830, showed her despair on losing him.

My precious George,—These are the first words I have to address to you by the help of pen and paper, since it is the first time we have ever been separated. Did I not, my angel boy, well keep my promise to you to make the parting very quick and short? God grant that you have not grieved too much, and had no return of your severe bad headache, for then you would have sadly needed poor Mama, who knows her George so well and knows best what he needs and likes. Ah! could I but hasten to you every two hours to exchange a couple of words! But that happy time the good God will soon restore to us! Be of bright and good courage, we shall soon meet again. Already three days have passed in which we have not seen each other, thus one slips away after the other, and before long the bright day of our happy reunion will shine for us. . . . You must write to me very fully—all details, my dear good George! Also how you like your new home—all, all, everything. I want to know! No secrets from me. *Make* plenty of time to write, it is my only consolation . . .[14]

To leave home and to live with the King was a daunting experience for so young a boy. His mother warned him to be 'respectful' to his uncle, 'but not shy and nervous, which makes you appear quiet and formal.' She advised him to be 'very open and confiding with the Queen,' and to 'tell everything and all that you wish, very openly and frankly.' The Duchess's confidence in Queen Adelaide was justified for she soon became devoted to her nephew, who ever remembered her with gratitude and affection.

The Queen had a gift for entertaining children. It gave her a chance to escape for a time from the formality of regal life and to be entirely natural. Prince George of Cumberland, later the blind King of Hanover, spent much of his youth in her charge, but the royal residences at Windsor and Brighton were poor places in which to bring up children, and the gaiety of court life was blighted by the King's outbursts. His marriage had begun unpromisingly as he was thirty years older than his bride, and had scarcely troubled to conceal from her that he proposed to marry out of a sense of duty and for money. Moreover there were times when William IV seemed to have inherited his father's insanity. In 1828, according to Princess Lieven, he became violent and had to be put in a strait-jacket.[15] At George IV's funeral, instead of walking solemnly behind the coffin and making some gesture of grief, the new King waved and smiled at the congregation, and excitedly shook hands with several of his friends. He behaved at his brother's funeral with an exultation he had not displayed at his own wedding. Indeed some of his observations were so startling that the Duke of Cumberland at one time contemplated having him put under restraint and ascending the throne himself.

Queen Adelaide acquired a certain skill in humouring her husband's outbursts and repairing the wreckage of his witless indiscretions. But tact was often insufficient to restrain him and her sheltered life and her natural timidity and diffidence left her without resources to weather the storms. The Queen distrusted anything unfamiliar, and her husband's unpredictable temperament introduced the very uncertainty into her existence which she always strove to avoid. So scared was she of innovation that when she first took up residence at Windsor, she had the gas cut off, despite the fact that George IV had only just installed it in the Castle.

One of the principal reasons given for taking Prince George from his family was that it was essential for him to be given an English education. Queen Adelaide, however, although she lived in England for many years, always remained very much a foreigner. From the first, she regarded Prince George as her 'special property,' and he took the place of the children she longed to have. On 27 March 1831 she wrote: 'The birthday and death day of my first child was very much softened for me by the possession of Georgy, for he is a consolation for my loss in this world.'[16]

William IV was himself extremely fond of his nephews and

niece, but the Duchess of Kent was determined that Princess Victoria should have nothing to do with the Court. She was very jealous of any rival authority to her own, and she refused to permit her daughter to associate with the King's natural children. This virtually deprived the Princess of the company of her uncle and aunt, since they were surrounded by FitzClarences wherever they went. The King felt the rebuff deeply for he was of a generous, friendly and hospitable nature. When the Court was in residence at the Royal Pavilion, Brighton, he used to send to the principal hotels to ask for the Visitors' Books. If he saw the name of any one he knew, or had ever met, an invitation to dinner followed. Mr Leveson Gower, describing his life as a schoolboy at Brighton, wrote: 'We saw a great deal of the royal cousins, Prince George of Hanover [the Duke of Cumberland's son] and Prince George of Cambridge. They were put under the care of their Uncle the King in order that they might be brought up with English surroundings, and were staying with him at the Pavilion. We liked them both; they played with us at our school, and we were often summoned to the Pavilion to play with them. We were delighted with the King, who was very kind to us, and told us sailors' stories, sometimes rather coarse ones, which amused us very much.'[17]

Prince George preferred Windsor to the Royal Pavilion. 'We can make little use of the hounds,' he complained in his Diary on 3 November 1834, 'and this adds to the disagreeableness of Brighton.' Later in life he discussed the days of William IV with Lord James of Hereford, a fellow guest at Sandringham. William IV, he recalled, 'was a most determined fellow. Of course he used absurdly strong language, but was a good King for all that. He used to post from Brighton to London and return the same evening, to have a row with his Ministers . . . He would tell me what he had said and done in London with great satisfaction.'[18]

As a boy Prince George lived at the centre of political excitements and intrigues. At the time of the Reform Bill agitation he was riding in the Queen's carriage when it was attacked by a mob and he was slightly injured by a stone.[19] As an old man he retained a somewhat confused recollection of the defiant courage of his much-hated uncle, the Duke of Cumberland. Lady Geraldine Somerset, Lady in Waiting to Prince George's mother, whose Diary is a prolific source of information about the whole Cambridge family, records that 'the Duke told us à propos of our evening here [St James's Palace] yesterday, he had been discussing with Sir Charles Wyke the various scenes they had witnessed in this house! The Duke remembered coming as a child, to lunch with his cousin, George of Cumberland, in the room we dined in last night, and the Duke of Cumberland making at the same time an early dinner of it, because he was going down to the House of Lords for the debate on Catholic Emancipation. [Was it not rather the Reform Bill?] He was then at the height of his unpopularity, the whole courtyard and street *crammed* with ill-conditioned people awaiting him, everyone *implored* him not to go out and expose himself to their insults, perhaps ill treatment! Nothing would dissuade him, and he *rode* boldly down through them all to the House of Lords! yelled at and hooted all the way!! He had pluck enough for anything!'[20]

Life at Windsor was more placid than at St James's. Apart from long hours of study under Mr Wood's vigilant eye, Eton boys would be invited to the Castle to amuse the Prince. Miss Clitherow, a friend of Queen Adelaide's, saw him 'at gymnastics with half a dozen young nobility from Eton, who came once a week to play with him.'[21] On his sixteenth birthday thirteen Eton boys went out hunting with him. The Prince was a sensitive, nervous child, not over-endowed with Hanoverian bravado, and his Diary is full of self-criticism on the subject. Evidently Mr Wood was caustic about cowardice and bestowed on his pupil the sort of commonsense advice which unimaginative people suppose sufficient to dispel irrational fears. 'The day before yesterday,' admitted Prince George in his Diary on 14 August 1834, 'I went out shooting for the first time, had three shots, but, as might be expected, killed nothing. I, however, at first behaved very ill indeed, and was quite alarmed lest the gun should kick, and therefore lost many good opportunities of firing. I feel dreadfully ashamed of what I have done, and have made up my mind to try to get the better of every kind of useless fear.'

Again on 24 July 1835, there is a characteristic entry. 'I regret to say that my conduct yesterday morning was such as to cause Mr Wood to order me to breakfast in my own room. After he had had a long and very kind conversation with me relative to my conduct, particularly about my riding, and had said that Papa and Mama were so very anxious about me, I said, "That is my look out!" an expression which is anything but proper on such an occasion.' Even in the company of two of his Eton companions, the young Prince was unable to conceal his terror of a frisky horse. 'Yesterday,' he noted with regret, on 9 March 1832, 'two Eton boys came to see me. Their names were Ward and Compton. We rode together and then played at hockey. During the ride I am afraid I showed some marks of cowardice. I do hope this will soon be over.'

Despite moments of fear and panic he grew to enjoy riding and hunting, and became so knowledgeable about his mounts that, many years later, an astonished cavalry officer declared, 'The Commander-in-Chief knows as much about horses as any veterinary surgeon.' Although the society in which he moved preferred chasing foxes to pursuing culture, he was permitted to indulge his inherited love of music. In his youth he played the piano and organ skilfully, but on joining the Army he gave up performing for fear of being thought effeminate.

Early in 1834 Prince George returned home to Hanover for the christening of his younger sister, Princess Mary Adelaide, later Duchess of Teck and mother of Queen Mary. His other sister, Princess Augusta, who was to marry the Grand Duke of Mecklenburg-Strelitz, was born in 1822, and being a girl was permitted to live with her parents in Germany. Prince George's Diary during this visit was only passingly concerned with the great event which occasioned it.

10 January 1834. Yesterday evening the christening of Mary took place. A most solemn and beautiful ceremony and the

service was well performed by Mr W[ood]. The little baby did
not cry at all. I signed my name as witness.

A fortnight later a great ball was given to celebrate Princess
Mary's birth. All her brother remarked about it was, 'The
Hanoverians are great eaters of supper.'
The Hanover visit was no holiday. Mr Wood had not accompanied his pupil merely to conduct the Baptismal Service. Work
went on as usual, as did the *contretemps* between the Prince and his
tutor.

25 January. Though I got up late yesterday I did my lessons
after breakfast as usual. First some Cicero to construe, and then
I did my German . . .
6 February. Yesterday I fear some more bad behaviour
showed itself. I have not remembered so many bad days following so soon after each other for some time . . . I was
violent, hasty, and indeed might almost say did everything that
was wrong. I shall however to-day give myself the greatest
pains to behave well.
9 February. Did not behave very well in the morning, but
better afterwards. A constant desire to chatter which always
brings me into trouble.
19 February. Last night I got rather a disagreeable letter
from England. The Queen writes me word that I am to return
soon after Papa's birthday, probably therefore in a fortnight.
1 March. Another month gone by. Have I been diligent
enough, or behaved in it as I ought? I fear that but too often I
have not. Chattering is one of my chief faults.
4 March. My most glaring fault now is that I desire to argue
with everybody, and then after all I generally am in the wrong.
I must now however make up my mind to conquer it.
12 March. Mr Wood was very angry with me in the
morning for my always standing near the stove. He said it was
very wrong because Mama as well as he himself had so often
told me of it, and on my saying I could not help it, he explained
to me the necessity of my conquering myself, because if I

could not do it in trifles, I should not be able to do it in much greater things.

13 March. Yesterday I again fell into that bad fault of mine to form hasty opinions and speak hastily rather than first thinking them over in my mind, and saying my ideas quietly. I am then generally obliged to retract them, which will become a very unfortunate thing hereafter. I must really take great pains to avoid this.

Prince George returned to England in April 1834, and soon began an arduous course of preparation for his Confirmation. His mother, who came over for the ceremony, wrote proudly to her father, the Landgrave of Hesse-Cassel, telling him that her son had been examined by Dr Blomfield, Bishop of London, who 'was very pleased and even astonished, and said to others he wished that all young candidates for Confirmation could pass as well as George did.'[22] Possibly this tribute was somewhat exaggerated. Mothers are quick to seize on such compliments, and Bishops of an established Church seldom go out of their way to insult the Sovereign's relations.

The Queen herself examined the boy.

30 March 1835. I understand from Mr Wood that it is the Queen's intention to-day to examine me in the thirty-nine Articles and other branches of scriptural instruction relative to my Confirmation. I feel rather nervous, particularly as Lord and Lady Howe have asked to be present likewise, and I only hope it will go off well.

31 March. I am happy to say that my examination went off very fairly yesterday, and I hope and think that the Queen and Lady Howe, who were present, were satisfied. Once or twice my attention failed for a few minutes, but I soon recovered it. The whole lasted about two hours and a half, and I must confess that at the end of that time I was very tired.

Prince George was given little opportunity to take Confirmation anything but earnestly, and fortunately the zeal of his instructors, far from producing the opposite consequence to that intended, as sometimes happens, was triumphantly rewarded.

8 August. The solemn day is come and my Confirmation is to take place this day. May God give me grace to enter upon it with proper feelings, and may He enable me to give all my attention to the ceremony before me, and not to those vain forms of this world which are as nothing, when compared with Eternity.

9 August. I am delighted to say that my Confirmation yesterday went off remarkably well, and I thank God that I am now admitted among His real disciples. May He this day give me grace to enable me to receive the Sacrament worthily, and may I henceforth behave in such a manner as to prove that I have attended to and duly appreciated the good advice the Archbishop gave me.

10 August. Yesterday morning I received for the first time the most comfortable Sacrament of the Body and Blood of Christ. God be praised that I am now admitted into the number of His people, but I trust also that I am admitted worthily, and that I have made such good resolutions as to be able to abide by them. I think that the whole Ceremony of the Lord's Supper is a most solemn one, and one that ought not to be entered upon without preparation.

The Duchess of Cambridge, during her visit, hoped to persuade the King to let her take Prince George back to Hanover, but, for the moment, her pleading was overruled. 'I am afraid,' she wrote to her father, 'I shall not be allowed to bring him away with me; the King, alas! will not yet part with him . . .' The prospect of his mother's return to Germany depressed the Prince exceedingly.

25 August 1835. The nearer Thursday is approaching the more I feel the misery I shall have to endure at parting, and I only pray to God that it may not be of long duration, and that we shall soon meet again in health and happiness. I now begin

to feel that very natural desire of entering once more the house of my Parents.

28 August. Yesterday I regret to say I was obliged to take leave of my most beloved and respected Mother, and of my two darling sisters. God grant that I may soon—yes very soon—see them again. This prayer is very short, but it is most true and fervent, and nothing would give me more real satisfaction than to see it accomplished. . . .

Prince George's prayer was answered sooner than he could reasonably have expected. The very next year it was decided that he should return to Hanover. Nor was that all. Mr Wood was to become Chaplain to the Queen, and Colonel Cornwall was appointed in his place as a Military Governor. The Prince, and Colonel Cornwall, left England on 21 July 1836. The Duke of Wellington had been consulted by the King about his nephew's military education, and this arrangement was in part the consequence of his advice. Although Prince George was naturally delighted to be reunited with his family, he left England with mingled feelings of pleasure and pain. 'I love this country dearly,' he wrote while still at Windsor, 'and I shall be very sorry to have to leave it for long!' Moreover he dreaded parting with his 'beloved preceptor,' for despite his severity, Mr Wood, as the Prince said, 'has ever been my friend in all circumstances.'

Notwithstanding Mr Wood's departure, Prince George's routine in Hanover was still partly academic.

3 February 1837. My days here in Hanover are spent on the whole very quietly. In the morning from seven thirty till one p.m. occupied with my studies. Then I generally ride in the School till three, and then I have another lesson till dinner-time. We dine at four thirty, and in the evening I either go to the play, the concert or some party. Three times a week I have a music lesson in the evening. Wednesdays and Saturdays I have more time for myself.

While in Hanover the Prince met many German Royalty, most of them in some way related, part of the time he travelled, there were balls, and occasionally he hunted and went shooting. But far more important than any of these activities was the start of his military career. It is true that since the age of nine he had been a colonel in the Hanoverian Guards, but the position, as might be imagined, was honorary. It was not until he reached the age of seventeen that he was expected to perform any martial duties, and these were no more arduous than mounting guard. He took a great pride in his work and loved to drill his men in front of his parents' summer residence. He described his first guard duty as one of the happiest days of his life, 'for I, for the first time, felt as if I was really a soldier.'

Late in June 1837, Prince George received news of the King's death from Mr Wood and in response to the suggestion contained in the letter he instantly set out for England, travelling day and night with Colonel Cornwall. 'My dearest Prince,' ran the letter, 'God's will be done! Our dear lamented King expired this morning at twelve minutes after two—calm, resigned, happy and without a struggle. The transition from life to death was so easy as to be almost imperceptible to those who stood by and solaced His Majesty's last moments. He had been gradually sinking during the whole day. Towards night the near approach of death, of which he himself was quite conscious, became more evident. He remained, however, sitting in his dressing-room till one o'clock, when he was moved into his sitting-room, where, in consequence of his extreme weakness, a small bed had been prepared for him. On this the dear King was laid, the Queen, as she had done for hours before, continuing on her knees by his side, gently rubbing his hands and striving thus to restore the rapidly departing warmth. Under these circumstances, with his hand within those of the Queen, our beloved King calmly breathed his last, the Archbishop, who had been summoned a few minutes previously, pronouncing a prayer as his spirit returned unto God who gave it. Our lamented Sovereign's dearest friends could not have desired a happier, easier death. May the Almighty grant that it may be blessed to him and to ourselves.

'The poor Queen remained some time on her knees in prayer

1A Adolphus, Duke of Cambridge
from a portrait by Sir William Beechey

1B Augusta, Duchess of Cambridge
from a portrait by Von Angeli
Reproduced by gracious permission of Her Majesty the Queen

2 H.R.H. Prince George of Cambridge
from a portrait at Windsor Castle

by the bedside. She then went to her room, and slept for some hours. She got up, however, soon after eight to receive Lord Conyngham, who with the Archbishop had been to announce the sad event to the Princess Victoria. . . .

'Of our dear Queen's conduct throughout the trials which she has undergone, few persons can speak with composure. Dr Chambers, a perfect stranger, can mention neither the name of the King nor the Queen without tears. . . .

'On the immediate effect of this great loss of one who was with so much sincerity a father and benefactor and friend to you, my dear Prince, for so many years, as regards your plans and those of the Duke, it would be almost presumption in me to speculate. But I should be much to blame, if I did not inform you of the opinion which Sir Herbert Taylor has just expressed, that you ought to lose no time in hastening to this country, to be present when the last sad offices are performed to our departed King. It is probable that your own affectionate heart has anticipated this suggestion of public duty, and that the Duke and Duchess, even if necessity should detain His Royal Highness in Hanover, will have already proposed to you to come over. . . .'[23]

When the Prince reached Windsor he found the Queen Dowager more composed than he had expected, and indeed it must be admitted that the loss was not without consolation, for her marriage had been beset with troubles, and there had been agonizing moments of trial. In after-years the memory of her husband, hallowed by discriminating forgetfulness, gave Queen Adelaide greater happiness than she had ever enjoyed during the King's lifetime, for he was a monarch bursting with ill-conceived enthusiasms, and, at best, an unpredictable companion.

The funeral over, the whole Cambridge family were obliged to leave Hanover, a Kingdom in which the Salic Law prevailed. On the accession of Queen Victoria to the English throne the Duke of Cumberland became King of Hanover and the position Prince George's father had held since 1815 became superfluous.

12 July 1837. The death of our poor dear King, besides the sorrow we all feel for his personal loss, is in another way a

c

most severe blow to us all, particularly to my own family,
for by his death and the accession of Queen Victoria, the
kingdom of Hanover is separated from the Crown of Great
Britain, and my father is therefore removed from the Government of that country, where he has lived for these twenty-four
years, and where we have all been born . . . Alas! our connection with it is now suddenly broken off: for though we are
still, and by God's blessing ever shall remain Princes of Hanover,
yet we shall live for the most part in this country. My Uncle
the Duke of Cumberland has now become king of that country,
and my cousin Princess Victoria is Queen of England. I am thus
nearly allied in blood to two great and happy families that are
governing two happy and prosperous nations.

On returning to England the family took up residence at
Cambridge House, Piccadilly, now the Naval and Military Club
(the 'In and Out'); and at Cambridge Cottage, Kew, a building
of some forty rooms, which they regarded as a country retreat.
In the spring of 1838 Prince George was introduced to the London
season, the first of the new reign. He was not altogether convinced
of its delights. On 28 May he observed in his Diary: 'I am now
quite a gay young man, leading a regular London life, in a quiet
sort of way nevertheless. Really, pleasure sometimes becomes
quite a business . . .' The Queen watched her cousin's social life
with concern. She spoke to Melbourne 'of George Cambridge's
being somewhat in the hands of the fashionable ladies; Lord
Melbourne said his (George's) age was a very awkward one, and
that he remembered it well himself; that living only for amusement in London was very tiresome, if you had no pursuits besides.'[24] H.R.H. was wholly sceptical about a fancy dress ball
he attended, finding that 'there were a great many most extraordinary and, at the same time, vulgar looking people present,
who had on the very oddest costumes I ever saw.' The Queen's
Drawing Rooms displeased him. He refers to one at which there
were over two thousand people present, among whom 'there was
a considerable collection of ugly ones.' Even a ball at Buckingham

Palace, which he admitted was 'magnificent,' had gone on too long, and by four o'clock in the morning 'almost everybody was gone before the Queen retired.' Prince George opened the ball with Her Majesty, and 'thought she danced really very nicely, and seemed to be very much amused.'

The Coronation provided the climax of a dazzling and fatiguing summer. Prince George, a tireless if not profuse diarist, evidently felt so great an occasion required an expansive technique. His account of the ceremony reveals a royal eye for detail, and one can visualize him taking in the scene with an intense Hanoverian stare; the unyielding gaze of one accustomed to being looked at and determined on revenge.

28 June 1838. To-day was a very busy day for all of us, and at the same time a most important one for the Country at large. Queen Victoria was crowned Queen of England. God grant that her reign may be happy to herself, and glorious to the nation . . . At a very early hour of the morning people began to assemble along the streets through which the procession was to pass, and the carriages rolled to the Abbey. At seven, the troops and the police made their appearance . . . My sister, Miss Kerr, Colonel Cornwall and myself started from hence at a little before nine, when we drove down to St James's Palace . . . and then we all went together down to the Abbey. The effect on entering was magnificent. The Cathedral was already quite full and looked most imposing. On the right of the Throne were the Peers, on the left the Peeresses, and in front the House of Commons. To the back of the Throne was the Orchestra, and all the rest of the places were filled by the public. We were close to the Altar, and opposite to us were the Bishops. Just above us was the Queen's private box, and above the Bishops were the boxes for the foreign Ambassadors and Ministers. In our box, which was exceedingly small, besides our party, the three Duchesses and their respective attendants, were the Duke of Nemours, the Duke of Coburg, the Duke of Nassau (who had just arrived), Prince Christian of Glücksburg,

the Princess of Hohenlohe, daughter of the Duchess of
Kent, and the Prince of Leiningen. The Queen arrived a little
before twelve, and the ceremony was conducted in the usual
manner and without any remarkable occurrence. The Archbishop of Canterbury performed the Service, assisted by the
Sub-Dean. The Bishop of London preached a most beautiful
and appropriate sermon. The Queen, I think, looked less well
than usual, but on the whole was very graceful and dignified . . .
The ceremony lasted till near four. Before it was quite over, the
party with which I went started off for Cambridge House,
where we arrived without the least difficulty. We here had
time to take our luncheon comfortably, and had to wait two
hours before the procession came past. It was exceedingly
beautiful and indeed I think one of the finest parts of the spectacle. All the foreign Ambassadors, the various members of
the Royal family, the Queen's attendants, and at last the Queen
herself, had a most imposing effect. Some of the foreigners had
most beautiful equipages, and of the Royal carriages I think
my father's were the handsomest. My parents did not return
till after six . . . After dinner I walked all over London to see
the illuminations, which were quite beautiful. At eleven there
were some splendid fireworks, in the Green Park and also in
Hyde Park. We, of course, saw the former. Soon after twelve,
I went to a great full dress ball, given by the Duke of Wellington, and did not get to bed till near three o'clock.

Owing to insufficient rehearsal, the ceremony in the Abbey was
not without awkward incidents. The coronation ring had been
designed to fit the Queen's little finger, but the Archbishop,
insisting on precedent, forced it on the fourth finger: an agonizing
procedure. During the homage Lord Rolle, an old man of eighty-
eight, slipped and fell on the steps of the throne. A foreign
visitor was assured that the roll was intentional, seeing that his
Lordship's family held their title on condition that they performed
this acrobatic feat at every coronation. Towards the end of the
service, the Bishop of Bath and Wells turned over two pages at

once without noticing and told the Queen that the service was
over. She consequently retired to Edward the Confessor's Chapel.
After prolonged consultation, she was summoned back. The first
thing the Queen did on her return to Buckingham Palace was
to give her poodle, 'Dash,' a bath.

The London season was only a brief interlude in Prince
George's military career, and at the end of the summer of 1838
he was sent to join the military garrison at Gibraltar. He set sail
from Falmouth on 24 September with Colonel Cornwall in
attendance. As he was a poor sailor even in calm weather he
spent the early part of the voyage in his cabin. At length the ship
reached Portugal where the Prince, much to his relief, was able
to spend a few days ashore. Part of the time was occupied visiting
the battlefields of the Peninsular War. At Caldes he stayed in an
inn which was 'very uncomfortable, and the animals of every
description, such as bugs, fleas, flies, etc. were so bad, that I did
not undress at all, but lay down in my clothes.' While in the
country he paid an informal visit to the King and Queen at the
Palace of the Necessidades. He had determined to travel incognito,
under the name of Lord Culloden, and was most aggravated to
find that, owing to some misunderstanding, a state carriage with
an escort had been sent to collect him from the Consulate where
he was staying. The Queen of Portugal was near confinement,
and for this, or for other reasons, hardly spoke a word. The King,
however, was pleasantly conversational and 'exceedingly good-
natured,' but 'unfortunately has his hair so long he looks almost
more like a woman than a man.'

From Lisbon the 'Royal George,' as his contemporaries dubbed
the young prince, sailed direct to Gibraltar, where the Governor,
Sir Alexander Woodford, a soldier who had distinguished himself in the Peninsular Campaign and at Waterloo, ordered a
ceremonial reception.

> 9 October 1838. At about seven a.m. Colonel Bridgeman,
> military secretary to the General, came off in a boat to ask at
> what hour I should wish to land, and we then settled to do so

at eight o'clock. The General wished that I should come on
shore in uniform, and so I put on my regimentals, and at eight
a boat came off for me with Mr Morret, the Governor's
Aide-de-camp. When we landed there was a Guard of Honour
of the 33rd Regiment to receive me and several of the principal
officers of the Garrison. The Governor's carriage was waiting
for me, and I got in with Colonel Cornwall and drove to the
Convent, where I was very kindly received by Sir Alexander
and Lady Woodford. I breakfasted with them, and then the
General took me to my quarters. . . . I dined in the evening at
the Convent, where there was a large dinner, and I was introduced to several people, which is not the most amusing thing
in the world.

Prince George contrived to conceal how bored he was by the
restricted social life of Gibraltar, although Colonel Cornwall was
sometimes hard pressed to invent or discover amusements for
him. In a letter he wrote to the Duke, the Colonel refers to 'the
ennui and consequent depression of spirits to which the Prince I
regret to say is liable.' However, the gallant officer was not
utterly at a loss. 'I have succeeded in procuring a Piano Forte.'
Music was to provide a diversion to relieve the tedium of garrison
life. Wherever the Prince went he was followed by 'Nelson,' a
black retriever, who swam in the sea at every opportunity and
who slept in his master's bedroom. While based on Gibraltar,
H.R.H. made a number of short journeys to Granada, Tangier,
Cadiz and Seville. But most of his time was spent in parades,
drills, and guard mounting, occasional hunting and shooting of a
meagre kind, and frequent receptions and dinners in which the
same small circle of officers and their wives met at each other's
tables and exchanged trivial gossip. A severe attack of measles,
during which he lost almost all his hair, provided a rare, if
unwelcome, change from this monotonous routine.

The Duke not only received news of his son's progress from
Colonel Cornwall, but also from General Woodford, and all
reports were gratifying. 'My dearest George,' wrote the Duke on

24 October 1838, 'We were all delighted the day before yesterday at the receipt of your letter from Gibraltar, which contained the welcome information that you had not suffered at all on your passage from Lisbon and that this time you really had enjoyed your voyage by sea. I was also very glad to hear that you were pleased with the house that General Woodford had got ready for you, and that you felt sensible of the attention he and Lady Woodford have shown you on your arrival. Sir Alexander writes me word that he is delighted at the manner in which you had received the officers of the Garrison when they were presented to you, and that every one was pleased with you. This I mention to you, my dearest George, in the hope that this will encourage you to go on as you have begun. You are now beginning your military career, and I do not doubt that with proper application you will soon learn your duty under so experienced an officer as Sir Alexander Woodford. By your being placed on his Staff, you have the great advantage of being employed in any way in which he thinks is best for you, and which would not be the case if you were attached exclusively to one Regiment. During the time you are learning the Regimental duties, you will of necessity be commanded by officers who are of an inferior rank to the one you hold in the Army, and of course you will be bound to obey them.'

The Duke's letters were full of good advice. Just before Christmas he warned his son of the danger of officers interfering in politics. It was a temptation Prince George never wholly resisted. Later in his career he constantly professed an impartiality he never quite achieved. Fervently believing, in later years, that he was personally above faction, as in theory the Commander-in-Chief was bound to be, he nevertheless used language which betrayed his Tory principles. Conservatism was so ingrained in his nature that he grew to identify it with constitutional propriety. 'In my opinion,' his father told him in a letter dated 22 December 1838, 'no soldier or sailor should have anything to do with politics. His duty is to obey the orders he receives from his superiors, be they Tories or be they Whigs.' A soldier, he maintained, should keep his political opinions to himself, and certainly in a garrison there could be no obligation to divulge them.[25]

In April 1839, Prince George left Gibraltar for a tour of the Mediterranean. He had been exceedingly popular with the garrison and Sir Alexander was able to report most favourably on him to the Government. 'It is very gratifying to me,' he wrote in an official despatch, 'to be able to add that Prince George has entered upon all the duties assigned to him in the most exemplary manner. H.R.H.'s conduct throughout has been highly praiseworthy; the quickness of his perception and taste for the profession give a fair promise of his becoming a distinguished officer in the service.'[26]

After visits to Malta, Corfu and Athens, H.R.H. returned to England in November 1839. It was rumoured that the whole purpose of his going abroad was to avoid being forced into marriage with the Queen. Within three months of her coronation he left for Gibraltar, and only returned home a little before her marriage to Prince Albert. Lord Melbourne is said to have spoken to the Queen suggesting the cancellation of Prince George's appointment. When she asked him whether her cousin wished to go, the Prime Minister replied: 'He is very distressed at the idea of leaving his parents—and friends—Ma'am!' Certainly Prince George betrayed relief at the news of the Queen's engagement. In his Diary he wrote on 15 December 1839: 'After dinner Papa got a letter from the young Queen, in which she announces her Marriage with Prince Albert of Coburg. Nothing could have given me greater pleasure than this intelligence.' His congratulations are so enthusiastic that the Queen noted in her Journal on 18 December: 'George quite different towards me, much less reserved, and evidently happy to be clear of me.'

Rumour needs scant nourishment and gossips can make a meal of a morsel. Tongues had begun wagging when it was noticed that the Queen at court balls nearly always started dancing with her Cambridge cousin: a fact which a casual acquaintance with rules of precedence would have shown to be inevitable rather than significant. For a time the Duchess of Kent favoured a match. Prince Albert, who watched all intrigues with personal concern, reported to his father that the Duchess of Kent 'is always full of complaints against her daughter, which she repeats to the horrible Royal Family, who use them for their own ends; at present she is said to have taken George Cambridge under her wing.' It was his opinion that 'cross-currents of cabal and intrigue run in every direction' united only in opposition to the Coburgs: 'the stud farm of Europe' as Bismarck once described the family.[27] In her Diary the Queen records on 13 June 1838, 'Spoke of George [the conversation was with Lord Melbourne] who I said I did not like—though had nothing to say for himself and was particularly stiff with me; but that I believed his parents teased him about me, and that Ma got into the Duke and Duchess's favour, by saying she would promote a match between us; all which Lord Melbourne thought very likely.' The Duchess was eager that Prince George should be invited to Windsor. 'I then spoke with Lord Melbourne,' wrote the Queen, 8 September 1838, 'about the Cambridges, and about George, and if I ought to ask him to stay, which Ma hinted at.' Melbourne was rather disparaging about the family. According to the same diary entry he told the Queen that the Cambridges were foolish people. ' "The Duke is the foolishest man I ever saw"; all which, God knows! is most true . . .' Again on 17 October 1839, the Queen mentions a discussion with Lord Melbourne on the subject of her cousin. 'Lord M. talks of their wishing George for me; "It was clear *he* did not wish it," said Lord M., "by his distant manner"; and I said I never could have thought of taking him—ugly and disagreeable as he was.' On 23 October she refers to him as 'an odious boy,' and when Lord Melbourne pointed out what a success he had been at Gibraltar, he was told that Prince Albert 'disliked him very much.'

The Queen was often the victim of sudden and substantial prejudices and at least one of her objections to Prince George was manifestly perverse, for she listed among his shortcomings the accusation that he was 'ugly.' Contemporary verdicts agree that he was strikingly handsome. As the Queen grew older and more inclined to charity she revised her opinion: indeed her early

hostility towards her cousin may have been expressed so vehemently in order to disguise an affection she was anxious to conceal,
or to fortify a change of heart. Towards the end of her life,
Ponsonby, her Private Secretary, remarked on her 'great affection'
for the Commander-in-Chief. 'It was noticeable at a drawing
room when she came into the ante-room where the royal parties
were assembled, she would single him out for a word of conversation before turning round and proceeding to the Throne Room.'[28]

On 10 February 1840, the Queen's wedding day, Prince
George was in the highest spirits. 'The Queen,' he records in his
Diary, 'was married at the Chapel Royal at twelve in the day,
and we all attended in State, and walked in procession from the
State Apartments to the Church. After the Ceremony there was
a great breakfast at Buckingham Palace to which we went, and
then the young couple went to Windsor, where they were to
stay till yesterday and then return to town. We, the family, went
to dine with the Queen Dowager and afterwards I walked out
for a short time to see the illuminations, which was exceedingly
good fun, there being an immense crowd of people in the streets!
I concluded this long day by going to a full dress party at the
Duchess of Sutherland's, which was a very handsome thing
altogether.'

On the Queen's wedding day Prince George met his own
future wife. His Diary for the year 1840 is now lost, as are several
volumes covering this period of his life, but a subsequent entry
enables us to fix the date of the meeting precisely. '10 February
1899. This is the anniversary of my first acquaintance with my
dearest wife Louisa, also the anniversary of the Queen's Wedding
fifty nine years ago.' As Louisa was an actress, it seems unlikely
that they met either at the wedding service itself, or at the
ensuing royal festivities. It is more probable that they saw each
other for the first time at the Duchess of Sutherland's ball,
although the newspapers of the time make no mention of Louisa
in what appear to be complete lists of guests.

Even before he met his future wife, Prince George made no
secret of his views about marriage. He believed, reasonably

enough, that 'arranged marriages were doomed to failure.' He asserted that he would wed whom he pleased, if necessary in defiance of the Royal Marriage Act of 1772, which, among other provisions, made the consent of the King and Parliament necessary for the marriage of Princes under twenty five. He was ready to devote himself unsparingly to the service of his country, but his private life he maintained was his own. Although the political advantages of various possible alliances were urged upon him, he remained obstinately unconvinced of the wisdom of marrying some princess whom he did not love.

Louisa was the ninth child and fifth daughter of John Fairbrother, a partner in a family printing firm in Bow Street where she was born and lived. She took to the stage in 1830 and acted at Drury Lane, the Lyceum and Covent Garden Theatre. She was a woman of classic beauty and elegance, an accomplished actress, and a graceful dancer. Moreover in private life she possessed captivating charm and was an admirable conversationalist.[29]

There is a tradition that Louisa's father was bitterly opposed to her going on the stage, believing the theatre to be a disreputable calling. He told her that actresses were wanton women. She did not attempt to deny that some of them were, but simply observed that he had not as yet contemplated abandoning his own profession merely because there were villainous printers.

The marriage eventually did not take place until 8 January 1847. As later there was a controversy about this date it is necessary to examine the evidence supporting it. In a letter he wrote Louisa on 8 January 1851, Prince George talks of 'writing *on the day itself*. . . . You alone know love, or *ought* to know, how blessed and happy I feel that *this day* (four years) made you my own and me yours . . .' Moreover the records of St John's Church, Clerkenwell, despite some inaccuracies, establish that the marriage was solemnized there on 8 January 1847, by the Rector, Doctor Hughes. A letter written to Louisa begging for money, mentions in passing the fact that she was married by this clergyman. No less a person than King Edward VII thought the date

incorrect and the entry in the register false. The King detected
three errors in the records, but the inference he drew from the
discovery was invalid. Sir Almeric FitzRoy tells the story in his
memoirs.

'Sheppard [H.R.H.'s Official Biographer] was very anxious to
verify the time and place of the Duke's marriage, which he had
always understood, from the old Duchess of Cambridge, took
place on the eve of his departure for the Crimea, but he had
never been able to trace it, when one day in a train he overheard
some men talking of the Duke; he interrupted them with the
remark that he was intimately associated with events in the
Duke's life, and they might therefore perhaps think it as well to
be cautious in what they said. One of them thanked him and
replied that they looked upon the Duke as a public character
about whom they might talk as they liked, but in fact they were
discussing the subject of his marriage; upon which Sheppard
told them of his anxiety to obtain information about it. "Oh,"
said one of the men, "I can tell you where it took place, as I
have seen the register at St John's, Clerkenwell." Sheppard
accordingly paid a visit to the church, and there, sure enough,
was an entry purporting to be the register of the Duke's marriage;
but the date given was 1847, and he noted with surprise that the
Duke's signature was entered as George Cambridge. A few days
after he acquainted the King with what he had seen who expressed
a strong desire to look at the register. Sheppard obtained it from
the Vicar and submitted it to His Majesty, who, with that extraordinary precision he has in matters of personal detail, at once
exclaimed, "There are three errors in this. In the first place, the
Duke never signed himself as George Cambridge—one was his
name and the other his title; and, in the second place, he never
was at [Clerkenwell] in his life; and thirdly, his father's names are
given inaccurately." Whether these inaccuracies, taken with a
date so much at variance with the Duchess of Cambridge's
statement on the subject, suggest that the register is a bogus one,
Sheppard cannot determine.'[30]

After Prince George's death in 1904, Lady Geraldine Somerset discussed the marriage date with Sheppard, then Sub-Dean of the Chapels Royal. She made a note of the conversation in her Diary on 30 July 1904.

'He also showed me a most *incomprehensible* mystification!! At the time of Mrs FitzGeorge's death fourteen years ago, when the Duke was as fresh as ever he was, and his memory far better than that of most men of twenty five! one evening the Sub-Dean was spending alone with the Duke speaking of her and his past life and he told him he married her the night before he started for the Crimea to give her a better position with the status of a wife in case it should ill befall him in war.' Lady Geraldine goes on to say that Prince George's sons now 'declare that he married her in 1847!!! at St John's Church Clerkenwell. The Sub-Dean wrote to the vicar to ask for a copy of the Register and the vicar sent him it and he showed it to me!! All duly *entered*: *his* signature George Cambridge! and hers Louisa Fairbrother! witnessed by her sister. It passes understanding and is impossible to believe! The vicar incidentally says the Duke's signature is in a small, "apparently faint hand." Now this is so *very* unlike the Duke!!! If he did the thing at all he was the last man to dream of disguising his hand and to my mind it is the clue to make one believe the register is a false one! Why should the Duke speaking openly of his past with the Sub-Dean volunteer to tell him this version of his marriage? If it were not true how could he with his fabulous memory be mistaken on such a point? . . . It is of profound mystification and I am *convinced* the true story of the marriage is before the Crimea.'

Prince George's family consisted of three sons. The eldest, George FitzGeorge, was born on 27 August 1843. The next child, Adolphus, was born on 30 January 1846, and the youngest, Augustus, on 12 June 1847. There were two other children who lived with the family: Louisa Katherine, and Charles Manners Sutton. Louisa was born on 22 March, probably in 1839, and Charles on 5 August, three years before. If the years of these births are given correctly, Louisa and Charles were born before Prince George met his wife. All that is certain is that Mrs

FitzGeorge was Louisa's mother: a letter signed 'your affectionate daughter Louisa' is among her papers. Charles also was in all probability Louisa's son. She left him most of her property in her Will: a document in which his surname is significantly given as 'Fairbrother.' The Duchess of Cambridge presented George, Adolphus and Augustus with five thousand pounds each,[31] and saw a good deal of them at St James's, but she gave Charles nothing and there is no record of their ever meeting. When in 1869 Adolphus was travelling as the Duke of Edinburgh's A.D.C. in the East, he asked his father what he should say to the Duke if they happened to meet Charles, who was then a serving soldier in India. H.R.H. was 'rather at a loss what to say' and advised Adolphus to use his good judgement, 'and whilst not offending Charley you need not say more to the Duke than is absolutely necessary to explain matters.' A month later he wrote again: 'If you see Charley be very kind and affectionate to him and do not on any account give him any offence. If you are asked who he is, of course you must say he is your half-brother.'[32] When in 1875 there was trouble over Adolphus's marriage and his mother declined to attend the wedding, he wrote to her saying, 'Of course as you refused I have not asked Charles.' It is improbable that Prince George was Charles's father as he was only seventeen at the time of his birth. Moreover in many of his letters to Louisa H.R.H. refers to George as 'our eldest boy.'

Although Prince George and Louisa postponed the marriage ceremony until 1847, they regarded themselves as man and wife long before that; as is apparent both from the existence of their family, and from a sentence in a travel diary Louisa kept in 1844. 'I hope,' she says, 'I shall see my dear George waiting for me, tomorrow night. I hope to God to be in his arms and when once there, I care for naught else, bless you for tonight my dear husband.'

What Queen Victoria thought of her cousin's marriage is largely a matter of conjecture, for she did not commit her views to paper. Obviously she strongly disapproved of the match. Her fondness for the theatre hardly extended to welcoming actresses as members of the Family. Besides, she was unlikely to look with favour on any arrangement in which neither her opinion nor consent had been sought. Publicly she pretended to be ignorant of the marriage, and Louisa was never invited, or even mentioned, on official occasions. The Queen, however, went further, and kept up this pretence in her private life and with her own relations. When George FitzGeorge was sent back to England by Wolseley, with the news of the victory of Tel-el-Kebir (1882), he took the despatches to the Queen at Balmoral. She was exceedingly curious to see him and noticed a strong family likeness, but never a word passed to suggest that they were in any way connected. She told the Duke of Connaught in a letter: 'We had Major FitzGeorge here from Saturday to Monday. Of course I made not the slightest allusion to his being Uncle George's son. He is very gentlemanlike and unassuming.'[33]

There is a tradition in the FitzGeorge family that the Queen finally relented and agreed to meet Louisa. The encounter, it is alleged, lasted two hours instead of the few minutes originally proposed. It was followed by many more such visits and even by a grudging admission that Mrs FitzGeorge was so enchanting that H.R.H.'s marriage was justified.[34] Neither the Queen nor the Duke refer to any such meetings in their Diaries. Moreover on 12 January 1890, the day Louisa died, the Duke noted 'I received a most affectionate letter from Her Majesty which I highly appreciate, and which would have been such a joy to my beloved one had she known the fact.' Presumably this implies that the Queen had at long last relented and was prepared, now that Louisa was dead, to admit that she had existed.

Louisa lived in a house given her by Prince George, Number 6, Queen Street, Mayfair; and later she had a place in the country, Cambridge Lodge, Horley. As Mrs FitzGeorge, she lived her own life with her own friends, and in her company her husband entered another world. It was a commonplace world, inhabited by very ordinary people, including Louisa's old theatrical friends. To H.R.H. it was a happy escape from the confined splendours of royal life, and he was enchanted by the snug, bourgeois comforts of the little house in Queen Street.

To what extent Louisa was accepted by Prince George's own family is difficult to decide. She was at least known to her father-in-law. Writing to her husband in 1848 she mentions that she saw Prince Adolphus on Constitution Hill, and 'he kissed his hand to me for no person was near.' There is no evidence that the Duchess of Cambridge ever saw Louisa; indeed all we do know is that she was mistaken about the date of her son's marriage. There is a story that while Princess Mary, Prince George's youngest sister, was driving in Hyde Park, her lady in waiting suddenly exclaimed: 'Why! There's Mrs FitzGeorge.' 'Where?' asked the Princess excitedly, 'Which is she? I have never yet seen her.'

If the marriage was frowned on by his own family, it was very popular with most Englishmen. An old soldier's widow, who had been housekeeper at the Horse Guards, summed up popular feeling. 'Ah, well,' she said, 'he loved a fine woman and he married her and stuck to her, and said he would rather be buried with her in Kensal Green than with his own family in the royal vaults at Windsor.'

Prince George was exceedingly sensitive about Louisa's position and there are many stories of the vigour of his resentment when he imagined that his wife had been insulted. A young Prince of Mecklenburg was reputed to have been flung bodily into Piccadilly for showing disrespect to Mrs FitzGeorge. Even the Kaiser William I, it is said, was not spared. Ignoring the marriage, he kept proposing alliances with German princesses. Finally Prince George lost his temper. 'His wealth of invective nearly paralysed the Emperor. In bluntest terms he described Germans in general, Prussians in particular, and Teutonic princesses in detail. No gentleman, he stormed, would ever advise another to desert a lady to whom he had pledged his word in the sight of God and man.' Prince William, later the Emperor William II, fared little better than his grandfather, although he at least attempted, somewhat clumsily, to be courteous. When he

3 Mrs FitzGeorge
from a portrait by Winterhalter
Reproduced by kind permission of Princess Galitzine

4 Major General H.R.H. Prince George of Cambridge, K.G.,
in 1847

from a portrait by John Lucas

was visiting London in 1885 he enquired after Mrs FitzGeorge's health, adding, if it would gratify her, he might find time to visit her. 'I am afraid, Willie,' was the crushing reply, 'that my wife will not be able to spare the time to see you. She only sees friends. But I will mention that you asked after her.'[35]

THE PROFESSION OF ARMS

IN 1840 Prince George was attached as Lieutenant-Colonel to
the 12th Lancers. His new duties took him no further afield
than Brighton. Two years later he was gazetted Colonel of the
17th Lancers and sent to Leeds to command the regiment. Here
he was engaged in his first action: fought against the inhabitants
of the town. The magistrates obsequiously thanked him for his
assistance in suppressing riots. It was during these years with the
Lancers that H.R.H. acquired his detailed knowledge of cavalry.

While serving with the Lancers, Prince George became the
innocent victim of a most unfortunate scandal, the details of which
Greville records in his *Memoirs*, not without a suspicion of sancti-
monious relish. The story went that Prince George had fallen in
love with Lady Augusta Somerset, a daughter of the Duke of
Beaufort, and that she was about to have his child. It was alleged
that both the Prince and the Duke agreed upon a belated marriage
but that the Queen refused her consent.

'This story with many trifling variations has been in all the newspapers and been circulated with incredible success not only all over England but over the Continent also. The whole is false from beginning to end, except that He did flirt with her and She with him last year at Kew, where she was staying while her Father was abroad—flirtation such as is continually going on without any serious result between half the youths and girls in London.' A formal contradiction of the rumour was published in *The Times*, but Greville doubted it would succeed, since 'the appetite for scandal is so general and insatiable, there is such a disposition to believe such stories and such reluctance to renounce a belief once entertained, that it is very improbable that what has been done can be entirely undone, and this calumny will affect the Lady more or less as long as She lives. Though it is totally false that she was ever with child, and P. George certainly never thought of marrying her, it is probably true enough that She behaved with very little prudence, delicacy or reserve, for she is a very ill-behaved girl, ready for anything that her caprice or passions excite her to do. Fortunately He is a very timid unenterprising youth, not unwilling to amuse himself but by no means inclined to incur any serious risks, as he has abundantly shown on other occasions. His vanity prompts him to make love to the Ladies whom he meets in his country quarters, and as Princes are scarce his blood royal generally finds easy access to rural and provincial Beauties. But when he finds these affairs growing serious and the objects of his admiration evince an embarrassing alacrity to meet his flame with corresponding ardour, I am told that he usually gets alarmed and backs out with much more prudence than gallantry.'

The matter might have ended there had the Queen not declared that she knew the story was true. Her habit of believing scandal without troubling about evidence had already led to tragic consequences. As Greville justly observed: 'It is really incredible that after the Flora Hastings affair and the deplorable catastrophe in which it ended, the Queen should not have shrunk instinctively from anything like another such scandal. Anybody would imagine that after the grievous wrong she had done to one woman She would have been especially cautious never to run the least risk of doing the same to any other; but between the prudery of Albert and her own love of gossip and exceeding arrogance and heartlessness this tracasserie arose.'

The Duchess of Cambridge, possibly quite unaware of the gossip, took Lady Augusta with her on a visit to Windsor. Soon after, the Queen, in a violent outburst, told the Duchess of Gloucester, 'that she knew the stories about Lady Augusta were all true and that She was only brought there for the purpose of getting rid of the scandal, and that it was very wrong of the Duchess of Cambridge to have brought her, with a great deal more in the same strain. The Duchess of Gloucester told her that this was a very serious charge not only against the girl but against the Duchess of Cambridge herself, and asked her if She intended that she should tell the latter what the Queen had said. The Queen said She did.' Prince George's parents were furious when the charge was made known to them.

'Both the Duke and Duchess of Cambridge immediately took the matter up in the warmest manner and one of them wrote to the Queen, complaining of such an imputation having been cast on both the girl and on them, and that H.M. could not suppose they would either bring her, if She had not been innocent, into Her Majesty's presence, or allow her to continue at Kew as the associate of their own daughter. The Duke of Cambridge said that he considered himself bound to protect and defend her as much as if he were her Father. To this expostulation a very unsatisfactory answer came from Albert, in which he said that "as Prince George had given his word of honour that the story was untrue, He supposed they must believe that it was so." This letter by no means satisfied the Duke of Cambridge, and still less the Duke of Beaufort, who was by this time made acquainted with what had occurred and who was not at all disposed to submit to such an indignity. The Duke of Beaufort wrote to Sir Robert Peel on the subject, expressing what he felt and announcing his determination to demand an audience of the Queen. Peel endeavoured to pacify him, and represented to him that he would gain nothing by an audience, as the Queen would infallibly say nothing and bow him out, just as she formerly did Lord Hastings. The Duke however desired Peel to communicate with the Queen on the subject and to let her know what his feelings were. But the Duke of Wellington (who is always appealed to on these occasions) told the Beauforts Peel was so afraid of the Queen he did not think he would venture to speak to her. Peel, however, had some communication with her and, after a great many pourparlers and much negotiation amongst them all, Peel wrote a letter to the Duke of Beaufort (or to the D. of Cambridge, I forget which) in which he said that the Queen had desired him to say she was now entirely satisfied and she begged there might be no further discussion on the subject.

'This is a tolerably correct account of the incident as the Duchess of Beaufort told it to me yesterday. They are however boiling with resentment and indignation, and anxious to show their sentiments, if they only knew how.'[1]

In 1843 Prince George was sent to command the garrison of Corfu, where he remained until 1845. Louisa, who at the time of his departure was about to have a child, felt she was being deserted. She never quite appreciated the need for her husband to obey orders. In a letter written on 27 August 1854, while H.R.H. was at Varna waiting to embark for the Crimea, he recalled the night he left for Corfu. 'This day, or rather night, eleven years, our dear child Georgy, our eldest boy was born. Well do I recollect that dreadful, that painful night, when I was on the point of departure and left you in the middle of your misery.' Next door to H.R.H.'s residence in the Citadel stood the Artillery House, occupied by Colonel Gordon, 'a dull, heavy, common-looking Scotchman,' whose son, the General, was to become a national hero, and whom Prince George in later days remembered well as a small boy.[2]

Lord Seaton, High Commissioner of the Ionian Islands, who had been Sir John Moore's Secretary in the Peninsula, reported 'to the Duke of Wellington, Commander-in-Chief of the Army, that Prince George had by his exertions and his unremitting

attentions to the discipline of the troops under his immediate
command, effected a great improvement in the several Corps,
both as to their general conduct and appearance under arms.'³

At the age of twenty seven, H.R.H. was promoted to Major
General and sent to Ireland, first in command of the troops at
Limerick, and in April of the following year, 1847, of the Dublin
District; a position he held until 1852. Although he took his
duties seriously enough, they were not so demanding as to prevent
him spending considerable periods on leave in England, from
whence he conducted the business of his command by post. In
1848, however, he remained nearly the whole year in Ireland,
because, as in most countries of Europe, Revolution threatened.
H.R.H. followed events in Germany with a personal interest, and
was disposed to blame its rulers for precipitating unrest by
opposing all reform. 'The news from Germany,' he wrote to his
mother on 15 March, 'is at this time not pleasant, and unfortunately the Princes are now forced to do what they would have
done very much better to have yielded voluntarily long ago. I
am not at all for giving way in everything, and in the way it is
now being done, certainly not, but to set oneself sharply against
all changes that time brings—that does not do at all, and causes
much eventual misfortune.'⁴

In Ireland, Revolution seemed probable, but despite the people
arming themselves, Prince George believed no serious outbreak
would occur, and he maintained that if one did, the troops would
prove 'faithful, true and good.' One reason trouble was averted,
was the successful arrest of William O'Brien, a most dangerous
Irish rebel. H.R.H. in a letter to his mother described his own
part in the event. O'Brien was recognized 'in a village called
Thurles and seized, which was effected without the slightest
trouble. Thereupon he was brought here to my quarters under
an escort of police. It was at two a.m. in the night of Saturday
and Sunday. Everyone here was in bed. I alone was sitting up.
Suddenly I heard a violent knocking and ringing of the bell. All
my servants sleep at the other end of the house and they heard
nothing. I did not want to wake them, and as no one came I went

2

myself to the door and opened it. Imagine my astonishment at seeing a number of constables, all armed, with the information that it was Smith O'Brien standing before my house. I could not believe my ears. I admitted the A.D.C. and shut the door, as I would not let Smith O'Brien himself in (although the stupid newspapers say I had a long interview with him, in which there is not one word of truth). I should have much liked to see him, but I thought it would have a bad effect and therefore I let it alone, of which now I am doubly glad. I then sent the fellow and his escort to the prison, where he is now happily confined. I myself then quickly got my horse and rode off to Phoenix Park to announce the fact to the Lord-Lieutenant who also was in bed, and whom I had some trouble in getting at, as his people likewise never heard my knocking. Jim [Macdonald, H.R.H.'s Equerry] told me he never saw a man so quiet and collected in so critical a position. He is prepared for everything, and says he did not succeed because it was six weeks too early, that had he had those six weeks longer the whole country would have followed him. Well, Heaven be praised we have got him and everything is quite quiet. . . .'[5]

The Prince was not happy in Ireland. Writing from Windsor, he described England as 'a charming country,' and added, 'would that I could get some appointment that would keep me on this side of the water.' In another letter he speaks of a 'sort of oppression which rests upon me in that unfortunate country.'[6] He grew increasingly unsettled, hankered after politics, and was so critical and outspoken on military matters that he ran into trouble. Despite official rebukes he remained unrepentant. 'The real fact is,' he wrote to a friend, 'a General Officer should make a point of saying *nothing* and he will always be well thought of. But that is not my system, and, in spite of annoyance and rebuff, I shall continue to say what I think and shall freely give my opinion.'[7] There can be little doubt that throughout his life he remained as good as his word. Even when he became Commander-in-Chief, H.R.H. felt himself free to criticize the Government whose servant he found it difficult to believe himself to be. His

opposition to the Army reforms of Mr Gladstone's party, were
so vigorous and unrestrained that the Queen, who sympathized
with his views but felt that they should be more reticently expressed, administered a tactful rebuke. In a letter written from
Osborne, 24 July 1871, she warned him to be 'very careful in
conversation lest opinions which you express may, perhaps in a
distorted manner, be quoted by persons who do infinite harm in
society by retailing gossip. It is to be remembered that a conversation is hardly ever repeated exactly as it takes place. Party feeling
at this moment is unfortunately very bitter. People who feel
strongly . . . and who may consider that you have not been
fairly treated, are only too ready to catch any expression of yours
which may confirm this view, forgetting that by reporting what
you may have said . . . they are doing you a great mischief,
and are giving a handle to those who wish to affirm that you are
not acting cordially with the Government.'[8]

The Queen and Prince Albert paid one of their rare visits to
Ireland in 1849 and H.R.H. was responsible for all the military
arrangements. The visit was a flawless success. Prince George
delightedly informed his mother that 'the grace and favour and
affection for me shown by the Queen and at the same time the
friendly and hearty tone of Albert, were such that I can only be
flattered. . . . My efforts and military arrangements are very fully
appreciated here, as the Queen herself proved by expressing it to
me on every occasion . . . Lord Clarendon and Sir George Grey
also very expressly told me it would have been impossible to
have made better dispositions than I had done, and that the Queen
had specially imparted to them her very great satisfaction with
all I had done, and how she felt "greatly indebted to me for the
manner in which I had conducted everything, which had greatly
added to the comfort and pleasure she had experienced during
her visit to Dublin." . . . Albert also was very friendly and made
me the finest compliments upon my military knowledge, which
is a fresh proof that he is kindly disposed towards me. And he
said to others he had never seen prettier manoeuvres and that the
troops were magnificent under my leadership. It certainly all

went extraordinarily favourably, not a mistake was made, not an escort, not a guard of honour was faulty, and the troops of every arm behaved excellently and did their utmost. The enthusiasm of the people it is impossible to express in words, and it is impossible any longer to doubt that Irishmen are at heart thoroughly Royalistically inclined, if only the agitators would leave them in peace. . . .'[9]

During the preparations for the Queen's visit, Prince George made a decision of the greatest importance to his career, for he turned down a somewhat mysterious invitation to become Regent of Hanover. He explained his reasons for so doing in a document dated April 1849 in which he argued that, despite the fact he had been born in Hanover, he had been educated in England and had acquired the habits and outlook of an English Prince. He believed it would be folly to exchange a secure position and great prospects for the uncertainty of German politics.[10] Although almost wholly German by birth, he had come to love England more than anywhere else. 'I can perfectly understand,' he wrote to a friend who had just returned from abroad, 'your feelings on landing in dear old England after so long an absence, as I have experienced them myself on several occasions. The fact is however one likes seeing foreign countries and however amused and interested one is in seeing the various customs and habits of others, still upon returning to England one feels that everything here is so very superior to what one has seen that one is doubly proud of being an Englishman and of belonging to a nation that has such a country to live in.'[11]

On hearing that his father was ill, Prince George came over to England in June 1850. It was after visiting the Duke, at Cambridge House, that the Queen was attacked by Lieutenant Pate, late of the 10th Hussars. On 30 June, the day Sir Robert Peel fell from his horse and received injuries from which he died, the Duke had a violent stomach attack which left him exhausted and feeble. Prince George's Diary records his father's gradual decline.

3 July. My father continues much the same, but without any material improvement. The gloom cast over London by Sir

Robert Peel's death overpowers everything. 5 July. My father
to-day not so well, and the medical men not satisfied. Great
debility . . . 6 July. My dear father was moved on a sofa into
his sitting room for a few hours. This, however, rather exhausted him. 7 July. Dr Bright saw my father to-day and
evidently had a very bad opinion of him. . . . Towards night
my father, who had been progressing favourably and tranquilly
during the day, grew much worse quite suddenly and about
eleven o'clock the medical men did not think that it could
last much longer. By help of stimulants, however, he got
better, after one o'clock, and towards morning was so considerably better that the pulse had regained its composure and
firmness, and his mind which had been very languid, had quite
regained its energy. We sat up all night with him—and a fearful
night it was. . . . After one o'clock, he seemed to get more
quiet and better and we moved him on to the sofa and he
rallied wonderfully and got quite himself again, very collected
in thought. 8 July. At about seven all things were so much
improved, and he appeared going on so well altogether, that
I went to Gloucester House to carry the better tidings to my
dear Aunt [the Duchess of Gloucester]. We sent for Watson.
I called Dr Bright myself. They came immediately and were
astonished at the rally that had been made. . . . The dear
Duchess of Gloucester came at eight, and took me to Buckingham Palace, when I saw the Queen, who was most anxious
and much affected. Returned to Cambridge House and went
to see my father, who spoke kindly to me and blessed me.
Went down to dine. At nine fifty I received a message to say
I was wanted immediately. I rushed up without a moment's
delay, but ere I got there all was over. My dear Father had
expired quite unexpectedly and most calmly and quietly. . . .
My poor mother had just gone out of the room. Suddenly he
opened his eyes wide, uttered a faint exclamation and fell back
lifeless without a struggle. . . . I have lost the best of fathers,
the most sincere and kindest of friends. May we meet again in
Heaven. After all was over we had prayers by the bedside of

the dead, which was the only consolation left to us. . . . This
is the most fearful blow that has ever come upon me.

Princess Augusta, who in 1843 had married the son and heir of
the Grand Duke of Mecklenburg-Strelitz, and consequently spent
most of her life abroad, travelled night and day to reach her
father before he died. She arrived seven hours after all was over,
and sank down by his bedside, sobbing 'Too late, too late!'
During the Duke's last days her sister, Princess Mary, spent
many hours at Cambridge House. 'I feel so grateful to God,' she
wrote, 'that I was permitted to be with him during his illness. . . .
The last day I never left him for he liked to have me with him,
when Mama was for a moment called away, to fan him and to
bathe his temples with eau-de-Cologne; and then he would press
my hand and whisper, "charming," "Dear." The same evening
all was over, and the spirit had returned to God who gave it.
His will be done.'[12] The Duke was buried at Kew Church, which
he had so often attended, and the funeral over, his son returned
to London in an agony of grief. 'I cannot tell you,' he wrote to
Louisa, 'how miserable I am. Every minute makes me more so
and I feel that I have lost the dearest and best *friend* not alone
Father that I possessed on Earth. My only prayer is that I may
meet him again in Heaven. Bless my dear children. May they at
my last end have as much cause to be grateful to me, as I have to
be so to him.'

On Prince George's succeeding to the Dukedom, the question
arose of a parliamentary grant. Prince Adolphus left his children
less than £30,000 between them, a sum which in his circle
amounted to destitution. If the Government did not come to the
rescue they would be left royal paupers.[13] Lord John Russell
proposed an allowance for Prince George of £10,000 a year,
but the Queen, taking up the cudgels on her cousin's behalf,
declared this sum insufficient and proposed £12,000.[14] Prince
Albert then sent for various ministers, ostensibly to sound their
opinions; in fact in the hope of gaining their support for the
larger allowance. Sir James Graham, an austere economist, told

the Prince Consort, 'that there might be some danger in allowing
the Duke to have the £12,000 rather than a smaller amount now
and the hope of an increase on a marriage.' If the Duke's eventual
income were to depend on his choice of a wife, the Queen would
be given a powerful means of influencing such a decision. Moreover, Sir James feared that 'the religious part of the House' might
well attack Prince George's moral character, since his 'connexion
with an actress or dancer, and his having several children of her,
was very notorious.' Prince Albert, who some years before had
suspected that his brother Prince Ernest of Saxe-Coburg was being
led astray by Prince George,[15] appreciated the force of this
argument, but replied that it would be better to show confidence
in H.R.H., and 'to lay hold of his affection and gratitude.'
Seizing the opportunity thus offered, the Prince Consort brought
up the whole matter with the Duke. He told him 'he might
consider the point [the larger allowance] as gained' and took the
chance 'to hint at the fear entertained on account of his relations
with that woman, but said at the same time that Victoria had the
fullest confidence in his never bringing dishonour on the Royal
Family by making a disgraceful marriage. George was embarrassed but made the strongest professions of regard for his
position, and gratitude for our exertions to help him.'[16] Considering that the Duke was already married to Louisa, his embarrassment, under the circumstances, was understandable. As
predicted, the House of Commons voted him an allowance of
£12,000 a year, and his sisters £3,000 a year each; an arrangement which H.R.H. described in his Diary on 20 July 1850, as
'very satisfactory at the present time.'

On his mother's birthday, 25 July 1850, the Duke took his seat
in the House of Lords, sponsored by the Duke of Wellington and
the Duke of Beaufort. Prince George had a great regard for
Wellington, and this was almost the last occasion on which he
saw him, for two years later the great Duke died suddenly, at
Walmer. The Queen wrote to her cousin from Balmoral, 22
September 1852, deploring her personal loss. 'My dear George,
You will, I know, join in the grief of the whole nation at the loss

of that great and immortal man, whom it has been my privilege, I may truly say, to have known intimately. The dear old Duke's loss is an irreparable one in every sense of the word, and one cannot realize at all the possibility of his being no longer amongst us, or think of *England without him*.'[17]

On 18 November, the day of the funeral at St Paul's Cathedral, H.R.H. was given command of the troops and made responsible for most of the arrangements of the procession. By a strange chance, his father had supervised Nelson's funeral. In his Diary he wrote, 'Up and dressed by six fifteen and out by a quarter before seven. Though most unpromising in the morning, it turned out a most beautiful day. I had the entire command and responsibility as regards the troops. Everything went off to perfection and without an accident. The masses of people enormous: their conduct dignified and admirable in the extreme. . . . Got home safe and sound, though a good deal tired, by five thirty.' Princess Mary came up from Kew to watch the ceremony from the Duchess of Gloucester's house in Park Lane. She was full of admiration for her brother's arrangements. 'From the balcony we saw the military part of the procession pass soon after eight o'clock. Infantry, artillery, and cavalry, all looked so magnificent! and George, commanding them, *so* well! that there was a sort of melancholy pleasure in seeing them march slowly by, while the bands played funeral marches by some of the *old* composers. They were chosen by Albert, and were very appropriate.'[18] The Queen on the evening of the funeral wrote to congratulate the Duke for his part in the ceremony. 'It was a most touching and impressive sight,' she concluded, 'which never can be forgotten, may *his* example ever live in *our* hearts, Dear great Duke. I cannot yet believe it was *him* who was borne with all his country and honours and all his nation's tears—to the grave! Albert says the ceremony in the Cathedral was most affecting.'[19]

Wellington's death made it necessary to appoint a new Commander-in-Chief. His own view, expressed in 1850, had been that the Prince Consort should succeed him. The Queen seriously considered the idea, for no choice in her eyes could be wiser, but

Prince Albert himself rejected it, rightly judging it would be bitterly resented. He saved the Prime Minister, Lord Derby, possible embarrassment by telling him at once that he did not himself wish for the appointment. Lord Derby next suggested the Duke of Cambridge but the proposal was rejected. He was only thirty three at the time and his rank of Major General was regarded as insufficient to qualify him for the post, yet to promote him over the heads of senior officers would cause intense ill-feeling. Despite the desirability of having a royal Commander-in-Chief—a proposal originally advocated by Wellington and wholeheartedly endorsed by the Queen—it was finally decided that the Duke was too junior in the Army, too young, and that 'he would have carried no weight with the public' at a moment when as Prince Albert foresaw, 'many attacks on the Army, which have been sleeping on account of the Duke, will now be forthcoming.'[20] Another possible candidate was FitzRoy Somerset, later Lord Raglan. Greville thought he would have been a very popular choice, and was inclined to attribute the eventual appointment of Lord Hardinge to court favouritism.

Lord Hardinge, even if he did owe his promotion to the Queen, was an admirable choice. He was gazetted as General Command-ing-in-Chief, a lesser title than his predecessor's, and a formal recognition of the unique position Wellington had held. Hardinge had purchased a commission in 1804, had stood by Sir John Moore when he received his fatal wound at Corunna, and was himself injured at Ligny so badly that his hand had to be amputated. In 1820 he became a Member of Parliament in the unreformed House of Commons, in 1828 he was appointed Secretary at War, and in 1844 was sent to India as Governor General, to replace his brother-in-law, Lord Ellenborough. Eight years later he re-entered Parliament and was appointed Master General of the Ordnance, a post which he only held for a few months. He at once discovered that there were only some fifty cannons fit for service in the entire country, the most recent of which had been made before Water-loo, so he persuaded the Government to manufacture three hundred guns and two hundred ammunition waggons, without which the Crimean expedition would have been disastrously hampered.[21] His military and parliamentary experience, combined with his administrative ability, energy and commonsense, were qualities well suited to the office he now held.

Although the Duke of Cambridge was rejected as Wellington's successor, he had earlier in the year been appointed Inspector General of Cavalry, a position which he retained until he was given a command in the field during the Crimean War. His new duties placed him at the centre of military and political affairs, and by requiring him to live in London ended his weary separation from Louisa which had caused them both such grief. Moreover he had grown to rely upon her judgement and he missed being able to consult her immediately. 'There are so many things going on,' he wrote on 22 September 1850, 'in which I want advice, that I am quite at a loss without you, my dearest beast.'

Since the Duke wrote to Louisa every day that they were separated, a considerable part of his correspondence refers to his longing to be reunited. Louisa was a more erratic writer than her husband, but her theme was the same. Life, he constantly assured her, was never the same or so happy without her. Again and again he tells her how much he loves her, how he longs to 'press her to his heart,' and how his affections are given to her alone: the word 'alone' sometimes being underlined as many as three times. She, in reply, longs to 'lie in his arms,' to see 'his dear old face again,' and to have 'a good cuddle.' 'Ah! my beast, my own darling George,' she wrote in an undated letter, signed 'Your affectionate wife, Louisa Cambridge,' 'I shall be so glad to see your dear face again and to lie in your arms and to be pressed to your heart where I have lain for so many years, so many happy years, and you darling have often said how intensely happy and blessed you have been in mine, and that you would not change wives with anybody, for that you loved me with all your heart and soul—praise be to God that it is so.'

When the Duke went away shooting, or staying at country houses, Louisa pined for his return, and such visits sometimes

provoked quarrels. 'How I wish I was with you,' she once wrote
from Brighton, 'paying visits. There is nothing I dislike more
than your remaining away so long. I most sincerely hope soon
all secrecy will be at an end, and then I shall be rewarded for my
patience, and you must say I have behaved well upon that point.
Oh George what a beast you are! I do not think I can continue
to love you dearest . . . I hate these separations, to me they are
detestable.' 'Believe me, my own love,' the Duke assured her,
'that had I my own way, I *never* should leave you even for a day,
but there are little duties that one must do now and then, and
these you my love are the first to acknowledge in your heart,
however much they may bore and annoy you at the moment.'
In another letter he admits that 'he does not object now and then
to a shooting expedition,' but he adds consolingly, 'I am always
far more pleased when it is over, and I can get back to you my
dearest wife.'[22]

When the Duke was away, Louisa was inclined to grow suspicious. She hints in many of her letters that there must be
somebody else in the background: a possibility either suggested
to her by her imagination or by ill-natured gossip. There is no
truth so disagreeable that some mischievous friend cannot be
found to broach it. She admitted that she had a jealous nature
but attributed it to 'excess of love.' 'I think dearest,' she wrote,
'I ought to be a little angry with you. You left London without
having a cuddle. I do not think that was very kind of you. I
suppose you were reserving yourself *for your friends.*' It seemed in
vain that her husband assured her, 'I like nothing so much as to
tell you how much and how devotedly I love you, and you *alone*,
for you and the children are all in all to me.'[23]

The Duke never forgot anniversaries, and many of his letters
to Louisa reminded her of them. The day of their wedding was
never allowed to pass unnoticed. 'My own Louly,' he wrote on
the fourth anniversary, 'my dearest wife, need I assure you how
I thought of you on awaking this morning, and how I wished
you were by my side? Need I assure you dearest, that my love
for you now is greater, if possible, than it ever was? I love you

better dearest than anything on earth, than life itself.' Later in the same year, 1851, when he was visiting Germany, he wrote on 15 October, from Hanover, a characteristic letter, full of love and longing for Louisa.

Hanover, 15 October 1851.

My own Louly, My dearest Wife,

I have but a free moment to myself today dearest, but I must just send you one line love to tell you, that I think my calculations are correct, that I intend to start from hence on Friday and hope to be with you, my dearest beast, my darling love, in the night from the Saturday to the Sunday. There is a charm in that thought dearest, which to me is perfectly delicious and so I am sure dearest it is also to you. I feel confident of this not only because I know it, but also because you say so in your dear letters. So my darling you may expect me and I hope as I said in my last that you will leave the street door unlocked and will let me find a lamp in the passage, to creep up into my own Louly's, my dear wife's arms. Oh! God how I long to press you to my heart, that heart, which beats only for you. I have bought some beautiful pocket handkerchiefs for you. And now my letter must go by the post, so God Almighty bless you love, and our dear children. That I may soon press you to my heart, is the fervent prayer of

Your most loving and affectionate husband,

George.

While the Duke was serving in Dublin, Louisa paid him occasional visits, but separations were long and frequent. After he began working in London in 1852 he saw her almost every day, although the duties of Inspector General of Cavalry were more demanding than those of the Dublin Command. The Army in 1852 was in urgent need of reform, having been absurdly neglected ever since Waterloo. 'If unreadiness for hostilities,' wrote Fortescue, the great historian of the British Army, 'be any furtherance of the cause of peace, then assuredly the English cannot be blamed for leaving the experiment untried.' After every

E

great war in our history we have treated the Army as if it would
never be needed again. 'Marlborough's troops marched from
victory to victory, and returned to be cursed as the plagues of the
nation. Thousands of officers and tens of thousands of men were
turned adrift.' When in 1914 Britain declared war on Germany,
the War Minister said of his Cabinet colleagues, 'They at least
have courage, they pit themselves without any army against the
greatest military power in Europe.' The mania of the Government
for economy after 1815 led them to consider military problems
exclusively from the point of view of the Exchequer, and to
pursue, in Fortescue's phrase, 'the time-hallowed policy of
striving to purchase a good Army for the price of a bad one.'[24]
    Ever since the days of Cromwell, the military have been looked
upon with suspicion. After the restoration of Charles II such troops
as he retained were a source of bitter controversy, and James II,
by filling regiments with Catholics, increased ill-feeling. The
Whigs—the tradition was inherited by many nineteenth-century
Liberals—regarded professional soldiers as dangerous reaction-
aries, ever ready to fight in defence of despotism. They declared
that the Militia was the surest protection of English liberties,
recruited as it was from volunteers; unpaid, untrained, and probably unusable in a serious emergency. Indeed military ineffective-
ness, rather than the fact that it consisted of ordinary citizens
doing part-time service, constituted the best conceivable guarantee that it would never overthrow a government. Nor, of course,
would it have repulsed an enemy. When members voted for
reductions of military estimates, they persuaded themselves that
the Army could always be expanded as necessary in times of
emergency: an utterly false premise. 'A shocking waste of blood
and treasure was involved in the improvisation of forces to meet
each crisis as it arose.'[25] Even if we lose the opening engagements
of a war, it was argued, we always win the last battle. Moreover
the sea is England's best defence against a foreign foe, and the
Navy may always be relied on to ward off invasion. Standing
Armies were characteristic of continental states, as was the absence
of that 'freedom in speech and action which every Englishman

claims as his birthright. Why, therefore, should parliament both hazard the loss of these benefits and exhaust the national treasure by maintaining a Standing Army as a defence *at home*, when the Navy, as the first, and the Militia as the second line of defence, were not shown to be unable to secure our shores?'[26] It was such arguments as these which encouraged otherwise responsible statesmen to disregard the Army in peacetime, to reduce its establishments, to deprive it of weapons, to ill-treat its officers and to neglect its men. Then, when inevitable disaster followed in time of war, as the direct result of their own incompetence, their own ignorant interference, and their own inveterate frugality, they complacently heaped abuse on the commanders in the field. Soldiers soon learned what to expect. Kipling was to express their feelings in a caustic couplet:

Tommy this and Tommy that, and turn him out the brute,
But it's thin red line of heroes when the guns begin to shoot.

So little regard was shown for the military profession that convicts were given the choice of enlistment or gaol.

Despite the defects of Army organization revealed in the war against France, little was done after 1815 to improve its administration. Business was conducted by thirteen different departments, not to mention several boards and commissions, virtually independent and mutually jealous. Nearly all communication was in writing. Florence Nightingale, who knew something of the inertia of the War Office, described it as 'a very slow office, an enormously expensive office, a not very efficient office, and one in which the Minister's intentions [she was writing to Sidney Herbert] can be entirely negatived by all his sub-departments, and those of each of the sub-departments by every other.'

To escape the notice of hostile politicians, troops were hidden away in distant parts of the Empire, and had little opportunity for effective military training in such scattered detachments. Battalions abroad were seldom relieved. To be posted was to start a life sentence. Soldiers in distant stations soon became part of the landscape, married, grew vegetables, mounted a few guards, and if an inspecting General threatened—a rare disaster—polished their drill and their uniforms. The Army, in Prince Albert's phrase, was 'a mere aggregate of battalions.' There were no manoeuvres, no waggon train, no divisional organization. Except for officers who had taken part in the French war, nobody had seen a larger collection of men than a brigade. Wellington fought hard to retain even the nucleus of the transport system he had built up in the Peninsula, but Parliament swept it away. No Staff existed accustomed to deal with the three arms. Sir Thomas Picton was popularly supposed to have shot the last commissariat officer for incompetence.[27]

Attempts were made to blame Wellington for the deficiencies of the Army, despite the fact that he spent much of his time denouncing reductions. 'The Government,' he once complained, 'will not, they dare not, look our difficulties in the face and provide for them.' In 1847, much to his annoyance, part of a confidential letter he wrote to Sir John Burgoyne was published in the newspapers. In it he described his fruitless attempts to induce the Government to improve the country's defences. There was not the means, he maintained, to resist an invasion anywhere along the South Coast. This disclosure provoked Cobden and the Radicals to deny the need for military expenditure and to ridicule the Duke for proposing it. Even so perceptive a statesman as Peel shared the views of the Manchester economists. 'We should best consult the true interests of the country,' he told the Commons, 'by husbanding our resources in time of peace and—instead of a lavish expenditure on all the means of defence—by placing some trust in the latent and dormant energies of the nation . . . to defy the menaces of any foreign power.'[28]

Such was the condition of the Army and such the climate of political opinion, when the Duke of Cambridge was appointed Inspector General of Cavalry. The Duke's name is not ordinarily associated with reform. Towards the end of his career as Commander-in-Chief he became increasingly conservative as the years passed, and his obstruction and opposition to change became notorious. It would, however, be wrong to imagine that the proposals he resisted were invariably enlightened: many were inspired by ill-conceived notions of economy. In 1852 he was only thirty three, and was every bit as anxious as Lord Hardinge to fit the Army for war. So vigorous and even ruthless were they in their efforts, that Sir George Brown, 'who cordially hated all change whether good or bad,' resigned his appointment as Adjutant General. The departure of this martinet from the Horse Guards was not greatly regretted by those, and they were many, who found his insistence on the letter of Army regulations oppressive.

In the brief period between the death of the Duke of Wellington and the beginning of the Crimean War, many improvements were made, 'largely due to the energy and administrative ability displayed by a young member of the Royal Family . . . An energetic, tall, slim young man, a crack shot and keen hard rider to hounds, a young officer who had taken pains to perfect himself in every branch of his profession, and was impatient of inefficiency in any form.'[29] In the first year of office the Duke produced four important memoranda, which between them exposed the deficiencies of the service. The first was entitled 'Observations on the Organization of the British Army at Home' (December 1852), which was followed by 'The Organization of British Infantry' (January 1853). Next he produced a paper on 'The Organization of British Cavalry' (October 1853), and he concluded his survey with a document on 'The Age of General Officers' (December 1853). These memoranda were the result of considerable experience, informed commonsense and a passionate regard for the interests of the Army. The Queen and Prince Consort read them with concern. 'My paper,' wrote the Duke to Louisa on 14 January 1853, 'was well received by the Prince and he has asked me for a copy of it which looks well. They are very full here [Windsor Castle] of the defences and what ought to be done, and I am in great hopes that something really will be done at last.'

The Duke's memorandum on the state of the Army constituted a distressing revelation of military unpreparedness which

was soon to be further exposed by the events of the Crimean
War. It insisted on the need for divisional organization, and proposed annual manoeuvres of all three arms to give officers and
men experience which they could not gain in their regiments.
H.R.H. predicted that there would be chaos at the start of a war
unless this were done. 'It will no doubt be generally admitted,' he
wrote, 'that no army can be considered as in a proper state to take
the field, however good its component parts may be, unless it
has some organization on a more extended scale than the mere
formation of regiments and batteries, in fact, unless a brigade and
division system be introduced, which is to be found in every
continental army. The British Army alone is . . . not at present
subject to any such organization, the result of which must be
inevitably that, however excellent the regimental system existing
in it may be, and which no doubt cannot be surpassed, still the
confusion and uncertainty on the first outbreak of a war or an
attack from without would be most lamentably and seriously
felt.'

The Duke's memorandum on the retirement age of senior
officers revealed an astonishing state of affairs. 'We have hardly,'
he reported, 'a single general officer in our service who has not
attained or will shortly attain his sixtieth year. It must be admitted
that this is far too advanced a period of life to *commence* upon the
arduous duties of active military command . . . A system of
retirement must sooner or later be adopted.' He recommended
that this should take place compulsorily after fifty years' service,
and then 'younger men could be brought forward in the vigour
of life and physically capable of filling satisfactorily the higher
grades of the Service.' Wolseley, writing to the Duke from
Dongola on 11 December 1884, told him, 'when I was a very
young man I was brought into intimate relations with generals
and staff officers of high position, who were absolutely useless,
many of them worn out old gentlemen, as brave as lions, but
whom physical infirmities alone prevented from being more
than an encumbrance to the Army they served.'[30] The Duke himself was only thirty four when he wrote so incisively on the need

to retire elderly Generals. His youth gave him a certain detachment from the problem, but when in 1895 the question of his own retirement at the age of seventy six was raised, he insisted that he still felt perfectly equal to the performance of his duties.

One practical result of all this paper work was the decision in 1853 to hold large-scale manoeuvres. The novelty of the 'Camp of Exercise' held at Chobham excited great interest in the newspapers. *The Times* devoted many columns to describing the military operations in 'the wilds of Surrey.' Unfortunately it was a particularly wet summer and the troops were exposed to fearful discomforts. *Punch* declared that the Camp established that the Army 'could not only stand fire but also stand water.' The manoeuvres certainly proved how necessary they were. Exceedingly few soldiers had the remotest conception of military tactics, and some regarded 'the whole damned thing as a waste of time.' Distracted staff officers were kept busy searching for lost units, or persuading over-zealous commanders that they were attacking their own side. ' "This Army," remarked an officer in the Royal Artillery with angry exasperation, "is a shambles." '[31] Shortly afterwards the Government agreed to purchase nine thousand acres of Hampshire moorland—the present Aldershot—to improve future manoeuvres, little anticipating that in the following year the Army would be engaged, in earnest, on the heights of Sebastopol.

THE CRIMEAN COMMAND

EARLY in 1854 the Crimean War broke out, and the price of the neglect and apathy of successive Governments was to be paid in blood. The Army's administrative system, such as it was, collapsed under the strain, and British troops endured sufferings intensely provoking because evidently avoidable. The briefest visit to the French Camp at Sebastopol showed what could be done. In February the Guards Division sailed for Malta in holiday mood. A series of farewell banquets constituted the most energetic preparation of an otherwise leisurely departure.

At first H.R.H. was uncertain whether he would be given a command in the field, but on 16 February he was able to write in his Diary, 'At 2.30 the Duke of Newcastle [Secretary of State for War] came, who announced to me my good fortune in being appointed to a Division in the expeditionary force. Overjoyed at this news. Communicated it to all my friends.' At the age of thirty five, he had been given the First Division, consisting

60

of Guards and Highlanders. The Supreme Commander of the Expeditionary Force was Lord Raglan. Under him were four Infantry Generals: H.R.H., commanding the First Division, Sir De Lacy Evans the Second Division, Sir Richard England the Third Division, and Sir George Brown the Light Division. The Duke's Division consisted of two Brigades. The First, commanded by General Bentinck, was composed of the Third Battalion Grenadiers, the First Battalion of the Coldstream Guards and the First Battalion of the Fusilier Guards. The Second Brigade was commanded by Sir Colin Campbell, and consisted of the forty second, seventy ninth and ninety third Highlanders. All the other Infantry Divisions were given to Peninsular veterans, some over seventy, none under sixty.

The decision to give the Duke a command was partly a consequence of the Queen's advocacy. In her Diary she wrote on 13 February: 'George came to see Albert (and I afterwards went to see him) in a great state about his going with the troops, and having a command, about which, between the danger of placing him in too responsible a position, and his being so high in rank, a hitch seems to have arisen. He said he would feel himself disgraced, were he not allowed to go. We agreed with him and promised to do all we could.' 'My heart,' her entry concluded, 'is not in this unsatisfactory War.'

The instant he received definite news of his appointment, the Duke wrote to Louisa. 'Knowing as you do,' he told her, 'that I thought my military reputation was at stake if I did not go out with the First Division, you will easily conceive how much I have been gratified at hearing today officially that I am to have the First Division . . . To leave you is *almost* death to me, but with God's blessing I shall get back all safe, and then if I have done any good I am a made man and my military career is really open to me. I am sure you will feel this as I do.'

Louisa, to whom the separation was to be almost unendurable, was at least delighted at the fulfilment of her husband's ambition, and wrote him a letter quoting a most favourable newspaper article.

                                           18 February 1854.
My Darling,

   I have copied this article out of the Papers, it is charming. 'The
Appointment of the Duke of Cambridge to a divisional command
has excited much satisfaction among military circles, by whom he
is greatly esteemed. Though an extremely young Major General,
there are very few of his Military grade, though double his years,
who can approach him in a thorough knowledge of his profession
in every department down to the minutest details. Those who
have had the pleasure of serving under him in garrisons will readily and strongly bear testimony to his extraordinary activity, zeal
and devotion to the service, as well as to his quickness, clearness,
dexterity in handling troops and marvellous memory.' Just write
a line to say you are pleased. I am delighted.

                                           Your loving wife,
                                                     Louisa.

   Before leaving England the Duke left a sealed letter with his
mother, only to be opened if he was killed in the war. In it he took
a last farewell of her, and told her, what he said he could not and
would not disclose verbally, or except in the event of his death,
that he had *married* Louisa. He begged her to think of him with
affection, and to look after his three dear boys, for nobody else he
knew would take a loving interest in them. Although he had done
all in his power to leave them independent, her protection would
help them in the world. He asked for her forgiveness, and hoped
that his last letter would perhaps explain much which might have
seemed strange to her.

   Instead of sailing with his Division for the East, the Duke, at
the special request of Napoleon III, accompanied Lord Raglan to
Paris to discuss the coming campaign with the Emperor. He
stayed at the Embassy with Lord Cowley; while Louisa, her son
Augustus, and her sister Georgina, put up at the Hôtel de Londres.
The Ambassador was doubtless somewhat surprised that his royal
guest spent so little time under his roof; while the Duke, for his
part, must have found it increasingly difficult to invent plausible

excuses for leaving the Embassy. Some days he visited his wife before breakfast, and at other times late at night, when Georgina's presence was a little frustrating, for as Louisa later complained, it made it 'hard to have a cuddle.'

The Duke was impressed by the Emperor, nor did he fail to observe the charm of the Empress, who, he grudgingly admitted, 'is certainly very handsome.' On 12 April there was a great review, but most of the time was spent in detailed military discussions. In his Diary the Duke comments on 13 April, 'The Emperor is most interesting. He is extremely judicious in his remarks.' Napoleon strongly supported an idea, initially proposed by Francis Joseph, that the Duke should travel to Constantinople by way of Vienna, where he would be in time to attend the Emperor's wedding. The British Government, anxious to seize any opportunity to persuade the Austrians to join the war, endorsed the plan. Taking leave of Lord Raglan, who travelled direct to join the expedition, the Duke on 18 April left Paris for Vienna. There was a more important farewell to be taken. 'Went to the Hôtel de Londres to say goodbye to dearest Louisa, having fully made up my mind to start for Vienna that evening. The parting was a fearful moment and I shall never forget it as long as I live, and I confess had I known what it would have been before, I am doubtful whether I should have been so anxious to have gone on this expedition. But the die was cast and it must be done and so at six o'clock I kissed the boy, my dear child Augustus, and then Louisa, and was off.' Two days later he wrote to his wife from Prague. 'Dearest love, if you knew how I suffered when taking leave of you. Oh! darling, to look at your face, and dear Augustus's, and then to think how long I should probably not see it again, was the most painful moment of my life.' On reaching Vienna on 22 April, he wrote a further letter full of despair and misery. 'Ah! My dearest dear Louly, I feel daily, hourly more and more how impossible it is for me to live or exist without you. You are all in all to me and life is positively not bearable when it is spent away from you. A short absence is a most serious annoyance, but a long one is intolerable. I shall set all my will to work to get near you love, be it by arranging for you to come out to join me, or be it for me to return to you.' On his way to Vienna, his sister Augusta, the Grand Duchess of Mecklenburg-Strelitz, met him at the station at Dresden. 'She said,' concluded the Duke's letter, 'she would consider it a duty and a sacred trust to look after and befriend our dear boys should anything occur to me.'

The Duke's conversations with Napoleon, and his appearances in public, helped recommend the English alliance to the French nation; both countries being more accustomed to regard one another as enemies than allies. The Foreign Secretary, Lord Clarendon, wrote on 15 April to congratulate H.R.H. on the success of his mission. 'I consider that the visit of Your Royal Highness to Paris has been a great political success as it has given the French people an opportunity of publicly ratifying the policy of the Emperor, while on the other hand His Majesty will be more confirmed in that policy and more bound to the English alliance by receiving such unmistakable proofs of the advantage he derives from it at home. Permit me to add, Sir, that much of this good effect is due to Your Royal Highness individually, to your personal bearing and courtesy, and to the manner in which you appear to have satisfied all classes.'[1] But delighted as was Lord Clarendon, and he was in an unrivalled position to judge the importance and success of the visit, it did not commend itself to the British Press, which ignorantly condemned the Duke for dallying in the French Capital, allegedly for his own entertainment, instead of hurrying to the war. *Punch*, at the end of April, published a cartoon representing Hector (Mr Punch) chiding Paris (H.R.H.) for not hastening to the East. The Duke in fact joined his Division at Constantinople over a month before it embarked for Varna, and four months before it set foot in the Crimea. Such unjust and inept attacks encouraged H.R.H. to form a rather embittered view of newspapers.

The journey from France was very disagreeable. Although only April, it was exceedingly hot, and the Duke travelled 'in the worst possible carriage' in which he was 'completely shaken to pieces.'

The mission to Vienna was even more important than the visit to Paris, for Napoleon was already an ally, whereas Austria had yet to be won over. 'Lord Clarendon,' observed the Queen in her Diary on 6 March, 'agreed with us in the great importance of George going to Vienna, which is desired by the Emperor of Austria, and which both from a military and political point of view, is most important.' H.R.H. stayed with Lord Westmorland, the Ambassador, and was well rehearsed for his encounters with Francis Joseph. Their first meeting took place on 23 April. 'After breakfast at eleven a.m. was received in state by the Emperor. He is a young man, full of life and energy, and appears also full of talent. He conversed long on the important topics of the day, and all that he said was most just and true and, as far as it went, satisfactory. I congratulated him, on the part of the Queen, on his approaching marriage. As this was my first interview with him, I did not wish to press him too much, but I am confident his intentions are with us.' The following day he attended the Emperor's wedding, and before leaving Vienna had 'a most interesting talk' with Metternich. His daily letters to Louisa told her his most confidential news, for he trusted her with all his secrets. He complained that he was obliged to pay visits to countless Austrian royalty, 'which is a great plague here with a family of *twenty* Archdukes.' But H.R.H. regarded the visit he received from the veteran Marshal Radetzky, as 'a real honour and happiness,' and he described him as 'a delightful old man of eighty nine, as fresh as ever, full of energy and life.' In another letter, written three days later, dated 30 April, he speaks of Francis Joseph as 'a charming young man of great ability,' and says that his discussions were more successful than he expected, for Austria was clearly favourable to England, but proposed to 'wait till they think it judicious to join us.'

Lord Clarendon again wrote to congratulate H.R.H. 'It would have been impossible,' he declared, 'for any experienced diplomatist to have conducted matters with more judgement and ability.' The Queen, Prince Albert, and the Government were 'greatly pleased' with the Duke's despatches. The Foreign Secretary told Lord Westmorland, with whom he had no need to be obsequious, that the Government were intensely 'gratified by the reception given to the Duke of Cambridge,' who they considered had performed his mission 'admirably.'[2] So did the Queen. 'I am anxious,' she wrote on 3 May, 'to express to you our pleasure and satisfaction at the manner in which you acquitted yourself of your delicate mission at Vienna. We and the Government think your letters most interesting, and the news they contained very important.'

The Duke left Vienna on 1 May, and after a brief visit to his old quarters in Corfu, reached Constantinople on the 10th. On the day of his arrival he met the Sultan, and was received in an audience he described as 'neither long nor interesting.' 'I cannot say,' he admits in his Diary, 'I was very favourably impressed by his appearance or manner. In fact he seemed to me to be a most miserable creature.' The Sultan arranged for the Duke to stay in apartments in the palace of Ferez, 'very nicely furnished for the sort of thing, but inconvenient to me from its great distance from the troops.' Before the day was out, H.R.H. had visited the Ambassador, Lord Stratford de Redcliffe, with whom he had a long conversation. Wherever he went 'he was most enthusiastically received by the troops,' whom he found in 'the best of health and spirits.'

While at Constantinople, the Duke was tireless in his efforts to drill his Division, so much so that some of his more lethargic officers regretted he had not been detained longer in Paris and Vienna. 'The Duke of Cambridge,' wrote a colonel under his command, 'is full of zeal. We are out every morning at seven o'clock and either march into the country or have a field day in camp. The Duke is a capital fellow, nothing escapes him, and some of the mounted gentlemen have brushed up very much.'[3] Prince Edward of Saxe-Weimar, writing to the Queen, said, 'George is very popular both with the officers and men.'[4] Nevertheless, his excessive enthusiasm for field days, essential as they doubtless were, put a considerable strain on the soldiers under him. 'Our life,' wrote one of them, 'is not an idle one . . . Our royal chief is far too fond of field days, and keeps us out five hours under arms so that we return pretty well knocked up while the day is yet young.'[5]

The Duke with his Division embarked for Varna on 13 June, where they landed the following day amidst heavy rain and thunder. The town struck him as 'a most miserable place and the fortifications very poor.' As he became better acquainted with this part of Bulgaria he liked it even less. 'The town of Varna,' he told Louisa, in a letter written on 18 June, 'is a most wretched place. The most miserable village in Ireland or Germany is better than this place, which is full of squalor, filth and disease . . . The fact is this country is really not worth fighting for, and the people less so. The sooner we can get out of it the better.' He blamed Lord Stratford de Redcliffe for involving England in a war on behalf of an utterly worthless ally.

Soon cholera broke out at Varna, particularly among the Grenadier Guards, and the hospitals became overcrowded. 'We are doing everything we can for them, but it is most distressing and the men are a good deal frightened.' Towards the end of June, the Duke himself developed a fever. Besides suffering from stomach spasms, he became crippled by gout. Throughout much of August he was in great pain, and only able to move about on crutches. Lord Raglan lent him his coach so that he might visit the camp. The summer heat was fearful and he longed to be home. He told Louisa in a letter of 4 August that it was too late in the year to land in the Crimea. By the end of the month it was known at Varna that a landing was in fact to be made, and the Duke feared that he might not be well enough to take part in the expedition. However he recovered sufficiently to join the fleet anchored off Varna Bay. Writing to his wife on 4 September, he told her that the transports were on the point of sailing, 'I presume for Sebastopol.' 'If God in his mercy spare me,' he concluded the letter, 'I shall have had enough and more than enough of soldiering, and the rest of my days shall be devoted to making my dearest wife happy and to looking after our children.'

The Crimean expedition was decided upon by politicians who

ignored both the inherent difficulties of the undertaking, and the
advice of their own Generals. Raglan warned the Duke of Newcastle that he doubted it would be possible to winter in Russia,
and was told for his pains that the Crimean climate was 'one of
the mildest and finest in the world.' Against such invincible
ignorance there was no hope of sense prevailing. Without a
proper base, without land transport, without ambulances, without
winter clothing, and without even maps, the Army was launched
against one of the strongest fortresses in Europe. It was an insane
enterprise.

The Duke was utterly opposed to an expedition so late in the
year, but, as he observed in his Diary on 8 August, 'public opinion
in England is to be satisfied at any hazard, and so the attempt is
to be made.' In the letter he wrote Louisa on board ship at Varna,
he told her of a conversation he had had with St Arnaud, Commander of the French Army. St Arnaud was very much amazed
at finding so many people against the expedition, 'amongst others
myself, and said it was very odd and he could not make it out.
I told him I believed the whole of his Army was against it and he
acknowledged this to be the case.' Louisa agreed with her husband
that the attack on Sebastopol was rash in the extreme, and rightly
foresaw that if things went wrong 'All blame would be thrown
upon the Chief [Lord Raglan] the Ministers of course creeping
out of the affair.'[6]

After several delays, the huge fleet of transports and warships
set sail on 7 September. 'Got under weigh for the great expedition.
It was a lovely morning and everything looked propitious. At
about twelve all were fairly off and certainly it was a most
magnificent sight.' Five days later the coast north of Sebastopol
was reached, but landing was delayed until three o'clock on the
morning of the 14th. The day before disembarking, the Duke
wrote to Louisa describing the voyage and a conference which
nearly ended the invasion. 'I must just scribble a line to you my
dearest wife to prove to you that amidst the bustle and confusion
of the moment, I am thinking of you, my soul, my life, and of our
dear, dear, little children . . . We heard that there had been a

conference at sea, that Marshal St Arnaud was very ill' and that his Generals 'had handed in a protest against the expedition.' But Lord Raglan, believing that the allies were far too committed to withdraw, persuaded the French to go on with the landing. 'Of course I do not know more than anybody else so am all in the dark.'

Some despondency was caused when it appeared that disembarkation was to take place within close range of Russian guns. It was with relief that it was discovered that what at first had appeared to be formidable batteries were after all only windmills. The landing was carried out successfully although it rained heavily the first night. 'If opposed we should have had a very tough job of it,' was the Duke's comment. 'To me it was quite marvellous why the landing was not opposed, for it was a tremendous confusion. Though the infantry landed very fast, hardly any artillery and no cavalry whatever were landed the first day.' As the baggage was also left on the transports, the Duke had to sleep under a gun carriage, and the letter describing that wet and restless night was written sitting on the ground. Fortunately, as not a Russian was seen, 'all went off to perfection,' except that the Navy refused to bring their ships near enough inshore, and consequently the soldiers had a long wade through deep water.

From the moment of disembarkation the Army began to suffer for the improvidence of the Government in failing to provide a Land Transport Corps. Indeed the House of Commons had deliberately destroyed the last vestige of a waggon train. The English nearly always forget the lessons of war the instant peace is signed, and the constancy with which the same mistakes are repeated proves how faithful we have ever been to this astounding practice. Already at Varna the want of horses had been seriously felt, and the Duke on 20 June complained in his journal: 'the difficulty of moving or getting anything is very great and the commissariat extremely bad and helpless in every respect. It is difficult to see how we are to move at all.' Writing from Constantinople on 20 June, he told Louisa, who loyally affected to take a professional interest in military matters, 'the want of horses

F

is dreadful, and where they are to be got I cannot tell . . . The stores are in a sadly confused way and many of the most important things have not arrived.'

After repeated delays, for which English staff work was largely responsible, the allied armies began their march on Sebastopol, and on 20 September engaged the Russians at the battle of the Alma. It was an extremely confused engagement. Sir George Brown, a stickler for the drill book, was driven almost to distraction when it proved impossible to scramble through vineyards, to ford the Alma, and to ascend the steep slopes on the further side, as if still on the barrack square. Groups of men, from different regiments and even Divisions, got so mixed up that they offered their services to any officer prepared to accept them.

Lord Raglan's strategy was not unduly elaborate. He simply launched a frontal attack on the strongly entrenched Russian positions holding the heights of the Alma. The Duke's rather vague instruction was to advance in support of the Light Division, which was on the extreme left of the British line, and which had been ordered to cross the river Alma and capture the enemy guns in the Great Redoubt. This apparently simple plan was complicated by the nature of the ground to be crossed, and the great strength of the Russian defences.

The Light Division, under devastating fire, crossed the river, gained the heights and stormed the batteries; but the Russians brought up reinforcements and drove them out. The casualties of the Light Division were very heavy, their formation was broken, and some regiments 'retreated in disorder. The Duke, only too aware of the responsibility of having the Brigade of Guards under his command, and lacking clear orders what to do, was agitated and bewildered. His progress was consequently hesitant, and more than once he had to be urged to hurry. At one moment he is said to have considered retiring, but was prevented from doing so by Sir Colin Campbell. 'No Sir, British troops never do that, nor ever shall while I can prevent it.'[7]

At long last, with the Guards Brigade on the right and the Highlanders on the left, the First Division began its attack, moving with splendid precision in unbroken lines, as if on parade. Halfway up the hill, the Fusilier Guards in the centre were thrown temporarily into confusion by some retreating remnants of the Light Division, but the advance continued, and after a withering volley of rifle fire, the Russians were driven from their position at the point of the bayonet. The day was won. Soon after, a Russian General, with both legs shot off, was found dying near the crest of the hill. So amazed was he by the courage of British soldiers that he begged to see the officer who had led them to victory. The Duke, on hearing of the request, hurried to the scene. '*Mais je veux voir le Général,*' exclaimed the wounded man, '*pas ce jeune homme-ci.*'

Louisa was staying in Brighton when she first heard news of the battle. She spent two wretched, sleepless nights, thinking of her husband and praying for his safety. 'Ah! George,' she wrote to him on 4 October, 'if it has pleased the Almighty to bring you out of all those dangers that have encompassed you, the *first* thing we will do when we meet shall be to thank our Almighty Father for his great mercy towards us . . . I dreamt of you one night. You walked into some room where I was, you looked so pale. I spoke to you, you leant your head upon my shoulder and after some little time lifted up your hand and showed you had lost the tops of your fingers. I kissed them, you smiled and I know nothing more.' So long as his heart was the same she assured him, she would not care if he was disfigured.

Two days after the battle, while Louisa was anxiously waiting for news, her husband found time to describe it for her. The engagement, he told her, began at seven o'clock in the morning. The village of Alma was in flames when Sir George Brown's Division crossed the river and began to attack. They were hard pressed and soon in confusion. 'I was ordered up to support.' While advancing through the vineyards and crossing the river 'the Division was exposed to a most murderous fire of grape.' The Light Division was falling back. 'The moment was an awful one. I had merely time to ask Sir Colin Campbell, a very fine old soldier, what was to be done. He said the only salvation is to go

on ahead and he called to me "put yourself at the head of the
Division and lead them right up to the Battery." I followed his
advice.' After the Russians retreated from the Redoubts, 'We
then and there halted and, Lord Raglan coming up, the whole
line cheered from right to left. I think to me it was the proudest
and noblest moment of my life. Everybody rushed up to me,
seized me by the hand and congratulated me. I could not help it
but cried like a child . . . I feel I owe all to the excellent advice
of Sir Colin Campbell, who behaved admirably and had a horse
shot under him. Finally I firmly believe that the First Division
carried the day and the whole army admit it. How often have my
words to you my love come across me, when I used to joke to
say, that I should like some day to see in the papers "The Division
led by the D. of C. now came gallantly forward and the day was
gained." This has now I flatter myself literally taken place . . .
Yesterday we spent in riding over the ground, collecting killed
and wounded both Russian and English, and burying the dead.
This was an awful sight and I shall never forget the horror of it
as long as I live.'

The Duke had confronted fire unflinchingly, and mounted
general officers were always dangerously exposed, providing, as
they did, select and conspicuous targets. But although heedless of
his own life he was almost too careful of the safety of the troops
he commanded, and was reluctant to commit them to action.
It was a most amiable failing but not one shared by the world's
great generals. 'Dogs! Will ye live for ever?' was how Frederick
the Great addressed his hesitant troops. The Duke, however, was
neither hardened against remorse, nor, if he could avoid it,
prepared to accept its pangs. Lacking initiative, fearful of committing himself, and inclined to be over-anxious, he was not a
skilled commander in the field. Indeed he would have required
exceptional military genius to have overcome the disadvantages
of his youth and inexperience of war. But H.R.H., although
seldom consulted, was not without strategic insight. He pressed
for a *coup-de-main* against Sebastopol immediately after the
Alma, which Russian historians later agreed would probably have

succeeded. Three weeks before Gortchakoff tried to raise the siege by attacking the rear of the British lines, H.R.H. anticipated the possibility of such a move, and begged Lord Raglan, unavailingly, to strengthen the position.

The congratulations he received for his part in the battle, in which, in fact, he had been jostled into victory, were somewhat extravagant. His son George, writing from school, attributed the success entirely to his father's efforts. 'I am very glad,' he wrote, 'to hear that you escaped unhurt and were the cause of the battle being won. I hope that you will not be hurt in besieging the fort of Sebastopol. I wish that you would tell me how to spell it. I think that you had better be quick about taking Sebastopol as the winter is beginning.' Mrs FitzGeorge's congratulations were scarcely more restrained. 'To think,' said Louisa, writing on 14 October, 'that you should with the Light Division have had to bear the brunt of the battle, for it appears that had your Division hesitated the English army would have been cut to pieces. Ah! My love how well I can conceive your feelings of pride and triumph. It must have been a proud moment for you and God knows from the innermost recesses of my heart I congratulate you my own dearest George. . . . What you have often said in joke is now a reality and almost your own words.'

Grateful as Louisa was for her daily letter, she chaffed to join her husband in the Crimea, and to see what was happening for herself. Lord Errol, who commanded the 60th Rifles, was accompanied throughout the campaign by his wife and her French maid. Indeed her ladyship's tent was pitched directly behind the Duke's. It was very small, so Lady Errol slept on the ground and her husband occupied the bed. But it was generally known that she was with the Army, and Louisa thought it was a precedent to follow. 'Other people,' she told H.R.H., 'have their wives out, agreeable or otherwise to the authorities, and I am determined that if you do not join me, or I you, I shall make some arrangements for myself. As to your thinking for one moment that I am to continue to lead this lonely life, this dull monotonous existence, *I will not do it upon my soul*. If you have the great love you profess

for me, you will not make any excuses. If you can live in discomfort so can I.' It was a constant theme of her letters that she
must be allowed to come out. 'I promise you,' she writes, 'I will
not be troublesome. You never shall feel that I am in the way.
How I envy all that are near you, and I who love you the most,
and am most beloved, cannot share what your servants are
allowed, the pleasure of being near you.' Lady Errol is alluded to
frequently. 'You tell me Lady Errol is the only person who has
been permitted to follow her husband, and that on account of his
being mad. If he is so, why is he allowed to remain in the Army?'[8]

The Duke, eager as he was to be reunited with Louisa, knew
that a camp was no place for a woman. He promised her he would
either return home, or send for her the moment he moved into
regular quarters. 'As regards my own individual feelings and
wishes,' he assured her, 'I cannot tell you how dreadfully I miss
you every hour of the day and how I long to see your dear old
face again.' As for Lady Errol, it is true she came out, but 'all
from Lord Raglan downwards agree in thinking that it is very,
very wrong.'[9]

Louisa was not to be silenced by talk of the hardships of cam-
paigning. 'No discomfort can be so great,' she told her husband,
'as that of being separated from you.' Only when he was sent to
Corfu had they been parted for more than a month. 'I know
dearest that I am most wretched and miserable *without* you and
had I my way I would leave England and join my own dear
husband. Oh! George, do you suppose that I would not rather
put up with every sort of inconvenience and discomfort than be
separated from you.' As the weeks went by, she became less sub-
missive. 'If you will not send for me I shall leave England and go
to the East. I cannot bear it any longer. One day is so like the
other, work, read and drive and see no person scarcely. It is
beyond everything miserable.' She even suggested that she should
cut off her hair and dress as a private soldier. 'I could pass as a
friend of yours. I think I could manage to disguise very well and
be always *near* you.' In the same letter, she described her utter
loneliness. '. . . . About six o'clock I cannot help feeling very low

spirited, it is your usual hour love for coming home, but alas no dear beast makes his appearance and we get on as well as we can, and then at night when I go to my room, ah! how lonely and deserted it appears. It breaks my heart to think that you are no longer there to press me to your heart and bless me before going to sleep. Oh! George dear George what misery would I not undergo for your sake, you my darling husband who I love better than any creature in the world and without whom I should not care to live. I really sometimes can scarcely tell how I can go on without seeing you, you are so necessary to my existence, for I have given to you every feeling of affection, of love, of adoration, my whole heart is entirely yours, and should the war last long I *must* see you, I *will* see you, let what may come.'[10]

Although the Duke discouraged the idea of Louisa joining him, he held out hopes that he might himself return home. He thought it improbable that the Army could winter in the Crimea. 'To remain here,' he wrote, on 3 October, 'would be awful and quite impossible I should think, for as it is one can get nothing to eat but what is supplied by the ships . . . Should it please God to spare me I am fully determined to go home, for I am dreadfully tired and sick of this sort of life, which is a desperately hard one, and for my part love I have had quite, quite enough of it.'

Despite the approach of winter, the prospect of the arrival of further Russian reinforcements, and the almost hourly strengthening of Sebastopol's fortifications, valuable time was wasted and nothing whatever was done. Lord Wolseley, writing to H.R.H. in 1892, after a visit to the Crimean battlefields, said, 'I have always thought . . . we should have taken the works, then just begun, on the South side at the Malakoff . . . We unfortunately halted to wait for our siege guns to be landed to knock down works that did not exist upon our first arrival, and which were actually built during the time we squandered in landing guns.'[11]

As the weeks passed, the Duke became more and more exhausted. Nearly every night there was some alarm, and the noise of gunfire was incessant. On 12 October, he confided to Louisa his intention of returning home. He hoped that Sebastopol would be taken, the troops re-embarked for Constantinople, and he would be free to hurry back. 'My darling, I cannot tell you how miserable I feel and how I long for the end of this dreadful campaign, for I am thoroughly worn out with fatigue and so are we all, and the misfortune is that we see little or no progress made . . . As to our holding this country I conceive that to be madness and unprofitable. This is the opinion of all, but we dread our Government insisting upon it, and our Chief possibly thinking it necessary to obey. Should this be so I for one shall do *my utmost to get home* and think it cannot well be refused me. . . . If it pleases God to spare me upon the taking of Sebastopol home I go, either with the army if we are all to go, or by myself, if the rest must remain, which for their sakes poor fellows I trust may not be the case, for there is not one of them who does not require thorough rest and reorganization both bodily and militarily.' The gay, picnic mood in which the expedition began had given way to despair. 'War is indeed a fearful thing,' wrote the Duke to Louisa, on 31 October, 'And the more I see it the more dreadful it appears.'

If Louisa had reason to be distressed by her husband's hardships and depression of spirit, he was made uneasy for his part by references in her letters to suspicions and jealousies, inflamed in part, by anonymous communications. 'I am so sorry to tell you I have had several anonymous letters respecting you and your intrigue. If I could prove it, not that I have taken the least step in the matter, God! how I should hate you.' 'You know I am a jealous person and I must confess it gives me great pain, for I love you dearly George and I cannot understand why all these allusions should be made. I cannot suppose you would prove inconstant or false to me.' 'Dearest child,' came the reassuring reply, 'I cannot imagine who annoys you with anonymous letters but of this you may rest assured, that the accusations against me of which you speak are infamous, and wholly and entirely unfounded, that I swear to you.'[12]

The anonymous letters continued and Louisa was made wretched by them. 'You must feel,' she wrote on 27 June 1854, 'that accusations like these make me very unhappy, I having thought you truth and honesty itself, and flattered myself that when you pressed my hand at the altar so fervently at the words "until Death do us part" that nothing could force you to break that Oath . . . I now ask you (and much, very much will depend upon your replies) have you ever directly or indirectly supplied her [a Mrs Burton] with money, visited her unknown to me, been criminally known to her, or taken liberties with her, or she with you?' Louisa required a separate answer to each question, 'as though you were standing in the presence of your God.'

The Duke's repeated affirmations of innocence left his wife none the less disturbed by shadows of doubt. Unfortunately he had occasionally lied to her, and had been discovered doing so, which, naturally enough, reduced his credit. On 25 October she wrote to say, 'There is one thing I trust you will never do again, that is to tell me a *falsehood*. I have no wish to prevent your going where you please, but I should soon have a thorough contempt for a person that did so often. You must remember after I found you out in the first, you promised you would not do so again, how you kept that promise you well know.' Such deceits were not forgotten, for a year later Louisa again referred to them. 'Had you not twice told me little stories I should never for one moment have thought you could deceive me and in my heart I do not think you would, for I am sure dearest love that you are a good and dear husband and love your dear wife with all your heart and soul.' But this confidence was not always sustained, and a letter from the Duke to his wife, written on 21 November 1855, after he had returned from the Crimea, showed how offended he claimed to be by her suspicions. 'I found your letter here,' he told her from Paris, 'and I confess to you dearest I am quite *broken hearted*. Is it credible that you my wife, my love, can write to me your dear husband, such a *cruel*, such a dreadful letter, and that after having known me for nearly sixteen years, after having had the greatest confidence and trust in me, and knowing that I have ever been the most true, faithful and devoted husband, and that the first and great object of my life has been to make my wife happy, as she has ever made me so . . . As there is a God in heaven I swear to you that I am a good and faithful husband.'

These expressions of doubt and questioning were rare, compared with Louisa's constant protestations of devotion and love. For the Duke in the Crimea, the entire world of Queen Street was little more than a momentary escape, a dream soon enough shattered by the war around him. After the Alma the allies advanced to Balaclava, a convenient base for the siege of Sebastopol. On 25 October, the Russians made a sudden, surprise attack. The First Division was not engaged, but the Duke records in his Diary what happened that eventful day, having, soon after the charge of the Light Brigade, received accounts from survivors. 'The first thing this morning we heard heavy firing towards Balaclava and I immediately rode off to see what had happened. It was soon evident that it was a serious attack on the part of the whole Russian Army on Balaclava, as the enemy was seen in heavy masses of Infantry and Cavalry with a good deal of Artillery before the village of Kemara. An order came for the First Division to march to Balaclava. On reaching the telegraph in our rear we were horrified to see that the Russians had attacked and carried all the fortified points occupied by the Turks, who had fled in the most shameful manner without hardly firing a shot and leaving the guns in the hand of the enemy. At that moment heavy bodies of Russian Cavalry were pressing them and coming into the plain just below us. It was then that the Heavy Brigade of Cavalry, admirably led by General Scarlett, attacked the Russians, the Greys leading in splendid style, and though far outnumbered they cut through and entirely defeated the enemy who fled in wild disorder leaving vast numbers of dead on the field. We then continued our march and reached Balaclava where we found that the enemy's cavalry had attempted to enter the town, but were repulsed by the 93rd Highlanders in line, the Turks again shamefully running away. General Cathcart moved down with a Brigade towards the mounds held by the Turks . . . I moved to the left to connect Cathcart with Balaclava and support him if necessary. The Russians held the further mounds and there we stood all day looking at one another. Meanwhile a fearful disaster occurred. Our light Cavalry was by some mistaken order directed to charge the enemy. The order was in writing and rather a vague one. Unfortunately it was carried by Captain Nolan, the first man almost who was killed. He made such offensive remarks both to Lords Lucan and Cardigan, that though doubtful what was intended and foreseeing what would happen, they allowed the orders thus given to be carried out. The Light Cavalry advanced right into the head of the Russian army. A battery of ten guns was to their front and batteries raked them on both flanks. Into this destruction they rode nearly two miles ahead of any support. Most nobly did they behave and a more gallant act never was done, though at the same time an utterly useless and senseless one. They rode right over the guns, took them all, cut down the gunners, but could not bring them away as they were completely surrounded. The Brigade returned destroyed. Only one hundred and eighty nine men mustered on their return. I personally escaped the horrors of this fearful sight and I am grateful that I did. There lay our noble fellows all amongst the enemy and we could not go forward to assist them. Oh, it was heartbreaking . . . Miserable and dejected we returned to our quarters after dark.'

After the failure of the attack on Balaclava, the Russians, on 5 November, made another attempt to surprise the allied camp, attacking at five thirty in the morning in drizzling rain and dense fog. The fiercest fighting at the battle of Inkerman centred round a position known as the 'Sandbag Battery.' For a time it was held by the 41st and 49th Regiments, who, heavily outnumbered, were eventually forced to retire. The Guards were then ordered to retake the position. The attack was made with bayonets and the Russians were put to flight. But soon reinforcements arrived and the enemy re-formed. With reckless bravery, and outnumbering the defenders five to one, the Tsar's troops at length recaptured the position. When the Guards eventually retired, H.R.H. galloped in front of them and ordered them to stand firm and fire, but their ammunition was exhausted. The Duke was surrounded by the enemy in the midst of a hailstorm of bullets and shells. His horse 'Wideawake' was shot in the leg, and he had to use his orderly's mount. A ball passed through his sleeve, but only grazed his hand as it was deflected by a pair of gold buttons containing his sister's hair. His A.D.C.s, Captain Clifton and Major Macdonald, both lost horses under them, and indeed so conspicuous were mounted officers, that of seventeen Commanders on Inkerman Ridge, six were killed and only two escaped without wounds. At one period of the battle, the Duke entirely lost the Brigade of Guards, and was driven almost to distraction. With a nonchalance which did little to dispel H.R.H.'s anxiety and irritation, a young officer cheerfully reassured him, 'The Guards, Sir, will be sure to turn up.'[13]

Although the Russians were repulsed at Inkerman it was an expensive victory. At the close of the action British soldiers lay on the ground utterly exhausted and hardly able to speak. Nobody escaped the general feeling of depression and discouragement. Lord Raglan was advised to evacuate the Crimea, and officers openly discussed sending in their papers and going home. Lord George Paget actually gave up his command and returned to England. Few in the Crimea blamed him, but the Queen was so outraged by his conduct that he bowed before her displeasure and returned to winter on the heights of Sebastopol.

'The Duke of Cambridge,' according to a letter from the Crimea, 'behaved uncommonly gallantly at Inkerman. No private soldier or officer behaved better than he did that day. He was the only man who looked after our interests. He is one of the best hearted men going. Nobody I think could have made himself much more popular than he did amongst us.'[14] The Duke of Newcastle, writing to Lord Raglan, told him how delighted the Queen was to read the favourable account in his despatches of the conduct of her cousin. 'Her Majesty has received with feelings of no ordinary pleasure your Lordship's report of the manner in which His Royal Highness the Duke of Cambridge distinguished himself. That one of the illustrious members of Her Royal House should be associated with the toils and glories of such an Army is to the Queen a source of pride and congratulation.'[15]

H.R.H. was undoubtedly a great favourite with the men. A sergeant in the 63rd Regiment wrote, 'No officer was more truly beloved by the Army than was the Duke, from his constant attention to their welfare, his identity with them in their dangers and sufferings, and his ready acquiescence in anything likely to add to their comforts.'[16] The Prince of Wales, after the war was over, discussed the campaign with Sergeant Major Edwards, and asked him who was the favourite general with the soldiers. 'The Duke of Cambridge,' was the reply. 'He was what we called our number one. He took great care of his men—and was very brave —in fact I used to think he was too brave and exposed himself too much.'[17]

Two days after Inkerman, Dr Gibson ordered H.R.H. to rest. In a letter written to the Countess of Westmorland on 30 November, the Duke speaks of 'having been very ill with dysentery and typhoid fever.'[18] He was moreover worn out by camp life, overwhelmed by the anxieties of command, and 'quite unequal to work.' Consequently he was sent aboard H.M.S. *Retribution* at anchor off Balaclava. 'I am dreadfully out of spirits,' he wrote in his Diary on 10 November, 'and cannot at all recover myself.' The day he left camp he wrote to Louisa telling her, 'I am worn out with fatigue and anxiety and am really completely done.' He described the battle, compared with which he assured her 'the Alma was a joke,' and told her of the fearful English losses. 'Broken-hearted with sorrow and fatigue, though grateful to God for his providential mercy, I returned to camp with my handful of men.' He could not see how the war would ever be won. 'We shall always beat the Russians when we meet, but our army is diminishing while their army is continually reinforced.' He ended by saying how disheartened he felt, and that he was determined to get home as soon as he could possibly do so 'with honour.' In another letter, written ten days later, he told Louisa, 'I have got a sort of ague which is very disagreeable, being at times extremely cold, at others equally hot, and then my nerves, which as you know are never of the best, are quite shaken and everything fidgets me and puts me out.'

For one suffering from battle fatigue, H.M.S. *Retribution* was the worst possible place to have chosen to rest. On 14 November it barely survived the storm which destroyed so many ships off Balaclava, and which wreaked such havoc in the Army encampment. Tents were scattered in all directions, barrels bounded along 'like cricket balls,' trees were uprooted by the hurricane, and many ships, loaded with everything that was most needed, were dashed to bits on the rocks.

The storm broke at five o'clock in the morning and a thunderbolt struck *Retribution*. At first, those on board thought it was a Russian shell. 'I prayed to God to forgive my sins,' the Duke told his wife, 'and was quite prepared to die.' According to one account, H.R.H. grasped a steward's hand, and bewailing his fate, moaned, 'Oh! Is it come to this? Oh! We shall be lost.' Several gossips and some newspapers reported that the Duke had gone out of his mind as a result of the war and the gale. 'I suppose you are aware,' wrote Richard Cobden to a friend, 'that the poor Duke of Cambridge lost his head at the last battle. I mean the little reason that was in it . . . The Slaughter of his Guards drove him mad. He showed the usual courage of his family, but the excitement was too great for him.'[19] Angered by accounts in the English papers of his having gone out of his mind, and after reading in the *Daily News* a story of his alleged quarrels with Lord Raglan, H.R.H. hastened to assure Louisa 'I am quite as sane, if not more so, than the writers of these abominable aspersions.'

After the storm, H.R.H. wrote a letter, addressed to all his immediate family, in which he described his deliverance from shipwreck. 'God's gracious and protecting hand has once again spared me, and I have been saved from a most awful calamity . . . The Morning of the 14th, a most fearful gale set in, and so suddenly that in about an hour's time there was no possibility of getting away. There we lay outside the harbour with quantities of ships all around us, which of course increased the danger. It began about six in the morning, and continued to increase momentarily in violence. The other ships and transports were dragging their anchors and passing us in rapid succession, some so close that we thought they must have been upon us, in which case we must have gone with them. These poor creatures drove on the coast, which was of perpendicular rock, and in a moment all perished, the ships regularly breaking or blowing up. At ten o'clock our rudder was carried away and there we were perfectly at the mercy of wind and waves. Our Captain, Drummond, a fine fellow, behaved most nobly, and by his coolness, courage and determination, certainly saved us under God's blessing. He threw all his heavy guns overboard, and all his shot, and kept her up to her anchor by the steam. We had three anchors down. At twelve, however, two of these anchors went and we had then only one left, and this one saved us . . . At two a thunderbolt came down and struck the ship. We thought at first it was a Russian shell . . . and then there came a tremendous shower of hail . . . I being unwell at the time lay in my cot all day, it was in fact impossible to sit up, and the decks were streaming with the water which was coming in every moment. The men brought us in accounts every now and then how things were going and by their countenances one could see how ill they thought of it. Tho' I did not give up all hope, I confess I thought all was lost and was fully prepared to die, I prayed for you all and thought much of dear home. Had the last anchor gone I had made up my mind to go on deck, prepared to try to swim with the rest, but I suspect that not many of us would have had a chance . . .'[20]

The experience of the storm, 'worse than even the most fearful action,' did nothing to improve H.R.H.'s health and spirits, and so he decided to go on leave to Constantinople. 'Lord Raglan,' he told Louisa, 'sent me a very good natured message to say that he hoped I would not go about much at Constantinople as otherwise disagreeable remarks might be made, though he, for his part, thought my going there quite natural.' Even in Balaclava Bay H.R.H. had thought it wise to keep to his cabin so as to prevent comments 'as to my not being with the troops.' What troubled the Duke far more than his fever was that he had grown utterly weary of war. He had witnessed it 'in all its horror, and a most dreadful thing it is. The more I see of it the more I think it would be well if it could be avoided.'[21]

Before H.R.H. left for Constantinople he was visited on board H.M.S. *Retribution* by Prince Edward of Saxe-Weimar, who wrote to the Queen after seeing him, giving her an account of his health. 'I went a few days after the storm to see him on board, his nerves of course were not in a better condition after the storm than before it, he had also a little fever or ague upon him but was otherwise well. He has now gone to Constantinople. There are plenty of ill natured people who make remarks about his going, although I firmly believe it was necessary for his health, but he was indiscreet in not disguising his joy at going away from this in no way enviable abode. George showed a great deal of courage and sangfroid, but he lost his head, he did not know what to do at the critical moment and the responsibility was too much for him; he is popular, amiable and kind, but has no decision whatever, and has certainly not shown the talents of a general which had been expected of him.'[22]

From Constantinople, the Duke wrote to Louisa, telling her he was still afflicted with fever and sick of the 'dreadful war, which has fairly worn out my nerves and spirits. I feel an altered man, twenty years at least older than I was.' If he were free, he told her, to follow his own inclinations he would immediately return to England, but she must not depend upon his coming home, his health had improved and he could not appear to desert the troops. 'I shall do all in my power to get home to you my wife, my life, my all, but I must not do so at the expense of my *honour* and this I know you will yourself admit.'[23] On 27 December H.R.H. was examined by a Medical Board and ordered home on sick leave. Three days later he remarked in his Diary, 'I received a significant letter from the Queen as to my return to the Crimea, which put me out a good deal.' 'I hope,' it ran, 'you will be back in the Crimea by this time. Forgive my telling you frankly that I hope you will not let your low spirits and desponding feelings be known to others; you cannot think how ill natured people are here, and I can assure you that the Clubs have not been slow in circulating the most shameful lies about you. It is for this reason that I, as your true friend and affectionate cousin, wish to *caution* you for the future not to let your very natural feelings be known and observed by others. To your own relations of course this is another thing. Your kindness to all around you and your thoughtfulness for the poor wounded has touched and gratified all.'[24] On the same day the Queen recorded in her Diary, 'A letter from George, saying that as he could not shake off the fever, and the Doctor said he was not fit for a Winter campaign, he had asked Lord Raglan to come home on sick leave. We were horrified as I am sure this will have the very worst effect!' In the end, at the suggestion of Lord Stratford, he decided to go to Malta, either to recover sufficiently to return to the Crimea, or to negotiate his return to England.

Before leaving Constantinople he visited the Hospital at Scutari, accompanied by Lady Stratford and shown round by Florence Nightingale, 'a most unaffected nice looking person.' 'I was very well satisfied with all that I saw there,' he wrote in his Diary on 29 December, the day of the visit, 'and think they really have done as much as they possibly could to make it comfortable. However it was a sad sight. Such a fearful number of sick and wounded men, many in the very last stages of disease.' Miss Nightingale herself later in life recalled this visit. 'What makes "George" popular is this kind of thing. In going round the Scutari Hospitals at their worst time with me he recognized a sergeant of the Guards (he has a royal memory, always a good passport of popularity) who had had at least one-third of his body shot away, and said to him with a great oath, calling him by his christian and surname, "Aren't you dead Yet?" The man said to me afterwards, "Sa feelin' o' 'Is Royal 'Ighness wasn't it m'm?" with tears in his eyes. George's manner is very popular, his oaths are popular, with the army. And he is certainly the best man, both of business and of nature, at the Horse Guards: that, even I admit. And there is no man I should like to see in his place.'[25]

G

The Duke ever after this visit supported Florence Nightingale, although complaints about 'The Queen of Scutari' were often enough made to him. 'It is a pity,' ran one, 'that the Army should be dictated to by a young lady who has not lived in the first Society.' Her reluctance to go through proper military channels, and her preference for direct contact with civilians at home, although essential if anything was to be effected, enraged the officers she ignored.[26]

The Duke left for Malta on 3 January 1855, and in the last letter he wrote Louisa from Constantinople, dated two days earlier, he told her he was broken-hearted about 'the shameful lies that have been circulated about me.' Some suggested he had behaved badly at Inkerman. Others complained of his taking sick leave, entirely ignoring the fact that a Medical Board had passed him unfit. 'Now love, I have received such a host of letters praying me on no account to think of coming home, that I confess I have been quite perplexed and staggered . . . I will tell you in the strictest confidence what I have decided to do by the advice of Lord Stratford himself, who really has behaved most generously and kindly to me. I shall go to *Malta*.'

In Malta the Duke stayed at a small family hotel, and much of his time was spent in writing letters home negotiating his return, 'never dreaming of the extraordinary excitement that would be caused in England by the return of any officer from the Crimea.' 'I got quantities of letters,' he told Louisa, 'from the Queen, my mother and aunt: all begging and praying me not to think of coming home. Even you, quite against your own interest and inclination, give the same advice. The fact is I am not ill enough to be in bed, nor do I look ill, but my whole nervous system has had a great shake from continued anxiety.' He told Louisa he was going to send strong letters to the Queen and his mother, although 'if I return, it is not impossible I shall be banished to Kew for a time.' Three days later, on 10 January, he wrote again. 'I have sent a very firm reply to the Queen to say that she could hardly expect my return [to the Crimea] after having passed a Medical Board, and that though I hoped to improve greatly here, it would be with a view of returning to England, as I could not go through a winter campaign . . . To my mother I have written a very long letter and entered into full particulars, I have told her all, that I was unhappy there, that everything was going to the dogs, that nobody was listened to and that it broke one's heart to see it . . . Thank God that I had a good and *honourable* cause for getting away on the very natural plea of health.' This was the first letter in which the Duke admitted that his difficulties as a General contributed to his desire to return home. 'I told you from the first we ought not to have gone to the Crimea, we knew nothing of what we were doing and were not prepared for it. How right I have been. From first to last nothing but blunders have been committed, and now . . . us poor devils out here who have worked like slaves, have fought for the honour of the country, are to be made to pay for the follies and mistakes of the Government.' Despite H.R.H.'s friendship and loyalty to 'the Chief,' he confessed that some of the Crimean follies were of his making. 'Poor dear Lord Raglan he is an honourable man and gallant to a fault, but he is no *General* and those about him are not, and the whole thing is such utter and hopeless confusion, that I thank my stars I am well out of it and don't want to be mixed up with it again for the world, for he will not listen to us . . . Oh! it is so awful and breaks one's heart. You can now easily understand why I was so anxious to have so good an excuse to escape as that of health, which is *real* and *not put on*, that I can swear to you. Had I thought that I could have saved a man of those fine noble fellows, I would willingly have stayed with them . . . It has quite broken down both my spirit and my heart.' The letter concluded by insisting that Louisa must not repeat one word he had said in criticism of Lord Raglan.

In another letter, written on 16 January, he defended Raglan against ignorant press criticism. 'The fault lies with those who sent out the expedition inadequately prepared for so great an enterprise.' He again referred to newspaper rumours that he had quarrelled with the 'chief,' and although he objected to their tone, he admitted that they were partly true.

H.R.H.'s correspondence with his mother was similarly filled with hatred of war and despair at casualties. 'I am now dejected in mind and body and overwhelmed with our dreadful losses.' 'I am completely worn out with fatigue and anxiety of mind and want of rest. I have not had my things off my back for weeks.' He complained of the difficulties of a General. 'Lord Raglan is an excellent man certainly but I admit I do not think he is up to the job and is not the man to be in command of an army . . . Lord R. is too reserved, he does not reveal his views to anyone and we generals are not treated by him as we should be in our position. . . . He listens to no one and gives no information . . . I am making all these observations to you, dear Mother, but they should not and must not go further . . . Please, please not a word of all this to any living soul. . . . Of course if I went home I should put it all down to my health needing rest through the winter which indeed it does . . . As to my nerves it is better not to say too much about them, so I am writing this for *you* alone, so that you really may understand me and not be upset on my account. I must put everything down to the fatigues and the fever, and this is the absolute truth, for you have no idea how many of us are in the same condition, all broken down . . . England is so unjust . . . Once this War is over for my part I shall *never* serve again, that I swear by God.'

The letter which finally overcame the Duchess's resistance to her son's return home was written on 7 January. It was an indignant epistle. 'And now at last I must open my heart to you, dearest Mother, because I cannot hide my indignation at all this from you. It is possible then that you, my family and friends, wish to bury me with this wretched expedition so lamentably undertaken, and which, as you all realize by now, cannot and will not succeed . . .? God knows I was not commanding it but I did all in my power to defend and uphold England's honour . . . If I could save the Army I would stay until I went to my grave, but I cannot help them because nobody listens to me . . . He [Raglan] is an upright and honourable man and that is all you can say about him, but as a general he is a *nonentity* . . . Sleepless nights, hard, continuous work, all so exhausted my nerves that if I had stayed any longer I should have had a nervous fever; I was already well on the way to it . . . Now that I am ill and finished they [the Queen, Prince Albert, etc.] will not even grant me what every poor soldier finally obtains, because hundreds of officers and men are being sent home sick . . . Look at Evans, Cardigan and all the many others. They have all gone home, but I mustn't go because I am the Duke of Cambridge and as such must personally make good the mistakes of Albert and the Government. A thousand thanks, but I shall not lend myself to this . . . What do I care about Albert and the Duke of Newcastle? They can explain their own mistakes but they won't have me die as a victim, that I swear.' If he returned to the War, he argued, the Army would think his illness a fraud. He was determined to come home but he must be supported by his own family. 'If you and Aunt [the Duchess of Gloucester] welcome me kindly then *everything* will be alright, and the Queen, Albert and the Prime Minister can say what they like. Why doesn't he [the Prince Consort] come himself and have a try? He wouldn't stay *twenty four hours* I know, the fine gentleman . . . I always said it was no use going to the Crimea and who was right? I was insulted for it and now look at things. All good soldiers are on my side and would go through fire and water for me. That is my sole satisfaction . . . Just let me come back quietly, I am only returning to recuperate and not to *amuse* myself, for none can think of doing so in these sad days. But I repeat, I must and will have rest and I shall only find it in England. The ridiculous rumours that I have become insane are all humbug, but if they want to drive me into an asylum then let them send me back to the Crimea because that will really finish me.' The Duke thought that the Court and Government's opposition to his return was 'so that I cannot say anything at all (which however was never in any way my intention) and to sacrifice me, so to speak, for their mistakes and blunders . . . I must ask you, dearest Mama, to stand by me with the Queen.'[27]

In a letter to Lord Raglan, the Queen explained her objections to the Duke's return. 'The Queen has been much grieved to hear

that the Duke of Cambridge has asked for *sick leave*, and means
to come home; she fears the effect of his leaving his division at
the moment, when the siege seems really to be drawing to a
close, will be very unfortunate, and she still much hopes that
he may remain at Malta, whence he could return quickly to
his post.'[28]

The Duchess relented, and indeed it was chiefly fear of public
opinion which had first led her to oppose her son's return. What
influence she exerted on her niece is impossible to say, but on 19
January, writing from Windsor, the Queen at last gave the Duke
the encouragement he sought. 'Pray set your mind entirely at
ease about your return, and believe that neither we, or your own
family or the Country, think otherwise, tho' we all *regret* the
necessity, than that you are *entirely* justified from your broken
health, and the decided medical advice you have received, in
coming home on sick leave. Be assured my dearest George, that
we *all* fully appreciate your devotion to your country and the
service, and *fully* acknowledge your unflinching participation in
all the danger, privations and anxieties of this very trying campaign. You have every right to be received as you will be, as one
of *our* Heroes.'[29] When the Queen saw H.R.H. at Windsor she
thought him improving in health, but, as she told Lord Raglan,
'he is much shaken and certainly would have been quite unfit for
duty in the Crimea.'[30] Louisa was also converted to the view that
it would be acceptable for her husband to return. Just before
leaving Malta on 22 January he wrote to tell her he was coming
back, although he admitted as far as his fever is concerned he had
nearly recovered. 'But I say nothing of this, as it is better to give
out that one is still far from well.'

'The first quality of the soldier,' said Napoleon, 'is constancy
in enduring fatigues and privations. Courage is only the second.'
In the heat of action, the Duke had displayed a gallant disregard
of danger and sought the thick of the fight. But he did not possess
the sustained fortitude which enables men to endure discomfort,
fatigue, nights without sleep, cold, hunger and the sight of
suffering. Overwhelmed by responsibility and worn out by

anxiety he succumbed to fever and depression. Moreover he longed to return to his wife and children, and he knew that a Crimean winter might kill him. Disillusioned and sickened by a war whose strategy he was powerless to influence, he accepted medical advice and returned home to recruit his strength.

The Duke was always overwhelmed by grief after a battle. On the evening of the Alma he described in his Diary the awful sights he saw. 'When all was over I could not help crying like a child.' After Inkerman, he was even more deeply affected. 'We went over the field of battle to behold a field of blood and destruction and misery, which nothing in this world can possibly surpass. After dinner I had to ride to Lord Raglan to consult with him, and on my return I was so overpowered by all I had gone through, that I felt perfectly broken down.' Writing to the Queen about the battle he told her, 'Our loss has been awful and I cannot deny that seeing all my good friends and fine fellows falling around me, has quite broken my heart.'[31] Kinglake in his book *The Invasion of the Crimea* says of H.R.H. that he was brave enough himself, but too reluctant to risk his men, and too easily overcome by the horrors of war. 'He was liable to be cruelly wrung by the weight of a command which charged him with the lives of other men. He was of an anxious temperament; and with him the danger was that, in moments when great stress might come to be put upon him, the very keenness of his desire to judge aright would become a cruel hindrance.' He preferred to act on orders than to be thrown back onto his own judgement. In view of the Duke's later conservatism, it is interesting that Kinglake describes him as having 'no dread of innovations; and the beard that clothed his frank, handsome, manly face, was the symbol of his adhesion to a then new revolt against custom.'[32]

Lord Wolseley, with whom H.R.H. was to have many notable encounters, the two men representing opposed schools of military opinion, was contemptuous of the Duke's courage. 'I am heavily handicapped,' wrote Wolseley to his wife in 1884, 'in having to contend not only against ordinary prejudice and obstruction, but to overcome those difficulties presented to me in the form of a

fat, clever, royalty. . . . It is amusing to read the Duke of Cambridge on his own doings in Ireland. He fancies himself very much
over what he did there, and being personally—as I have often
told you—a man of the most *timid* nature he is *as* proud of having
dispensed with police protection in Cork and Dublin as if he had
led a storming party.' Elsewhere he says that Lord Airey often
told him that 'H.R.H. is quite as great a coward morally as he
is physically.' In a letter written in 1884, in which he discussed
sending Augustus FitzGeorge into the forefront of the battle, he
says it would be interesting to see if the son could 'stand being
shot at' as 'the father could not.'[33]

Such accusations are strangely at variance with all other
evidence. Colonel Gordon, writing to General Grey, Prince
Albert's Private Secretary, said: 'The Duke of Cambridge behaved
very well indeed [at Inkerman] and I wonder how he escaped.'
Lord James Murray declared: 'The Duke of Cambridge was
everywhere [again at Inkerman] in the thickest of the fight, doing
his best to direct and encourage his men, and you know how
soldiers love and admire an officer who does so.' Colonel Phipps
told the Queen, 'There is not a braver soldier in the Army, officer
or man than the Duke of Cambridge. I believe that there is not
a man . . . but would lay down his life for him.'[34] These tributes,
written during the war by those close to H.R.H., have a better
claim to credit than the secondhand recollections of a declared
opponent of the Duke. Wolseley's correspondence with his wife
was written in a vigorous, entertaining and often highly exaggerated style. He did not need to weigh his judgements carefully,
consider the feelings of others, or even to bother overmuch
about the truth of what he said. H.R.H. was the consecrated
obstruction who prevented Wolseley, an impetuous and self-
willed reformer, having his own way, and therefore nothing that
could be said about him was too uncharitable. But when all
allowances are made, the conclusion can hardly be resisted that
the Duke's return from the Crimea, if it was not disgraceful, for
he was broken down in body and mind, was scarcely heroic.

H.R.H. left Malta on 22 January 1855. The ship was very

crowded, and the noise made by the children aboard proved 'a great annoyance.' On the way home he again visited Napoleon III at Paris. He made little effort to conceal his gloom about the military prospects of wintering in the Crimea. Nor did he hesitate to attribute the responsibility for disaster to the French and English Governments. '*Le Duc de Cambridge est arrivé à Paris exaspéré contre son gouvernement, découragé et décourageant a l'excès.*'[35] On 30 January he landed at Dover and took the first train to London. He had written to Louisa from Malta on 21 December, telling her 'not to meet him at the Railroad for fear he might break down in public.' Instead, he arranged to go to Queen Street as soon as he possibly could. 'Reached Town at six,' he wrote in his Diary, 'and drove at once to St James's, where I found my dearest mother and Mary, looking both very well. Then hurried up to Queen Street and was once again in the arms of my dearest Louisa and our beloved children. Never shall I forget the happiness of that meeting after all I had gone through. . . . Ramsthal [H.R.H.'s steward] was enchanted to see me, but so are all, wherever I go.'

The day after his return he saw the Queen and was relieved to be well received. Her Majesty 'having come to London in consequence of the defeat of the Ministry and their resignation, sent for me and received me most kindly and graciously, together with the Prince. I was some time with her, and I lunched with her. Being still far from well and anxious to keep quiet, I did not go anywhere else excepting to see my own family.' 'George arrived and lunched with us,' wrote the Queen in her Diary. 'He only reached Dover yesterday, and looks ill and much broken, bent, very thin, a haggard look, and wearing a huge beard. Poor fellow, it is sad to see him like that, and he was a good deal affected when he first saw us, but cheerful enough afterwards, though rather agitated.'

Louisa was displeased that she saw so little of her husband on the first day of his return. She wrote him a letter on 11 February saying she could not bear partings, however brief. 'Ah! how glad I shall be when Tuesday comes. I am so anxious to see you again.

I cannot bear being separated from you for more than a few hours. I do so love you my dearest heart and have been separated from you for so long a period that I feel quite low and wretched. I hope you are enjoying yourself and that you like your visit, but I am quite certain you thought of me and will not be sorry to return to one who loves you with the greatest truth and sincerity. Fifteen years yesterday since we met and eight of those we have been married, what happy ones they have been (except for the last). I have been one of the happiest of wives and you say you have been the happiest of husbands and when you returned home you said you would not change for anyone in the world, for I was dearer to you than life itself. I was your all on earth. You know that must please me loving you as I do, and I therefore was much annoyed we could not spend that day together, it was most unfortunate, but generally happens that the Queen invites you upon days that I am anxious you should pass with me.'

After a few months in England the Duke completely recovered and wished to rejoin the Army in the Crimea. 'On saying to George,' wrote the Queen in her Diary on 6 June, 'that I thought he ought to go out again, found that he was most anxious to do so, as he was not at all happy in inactivity.' When he heard the news of Lord Raglan's death, and again later of Simpson's resignation, the Duke aspired to the Chief Command himself. Writing to Louisa on 30 September he says, 'I want so much to command that Army. That would be the height of my ambition, for if successful I should be a made man and no power on earth could shake me then. Ah Lu, what a glorious thing that would be would it not?'

Much of the summer of 1855 H.R.H. spent in trying to obtain a command. He had several interviews with the Queen, who did what she could to 'pacify' him, for she regarded him as 'agitated' and 'excitable.' 'After luncheon,' she wrote in her Diary on 31 October, 'in spite of the rain, we took a walk with George, who talked very eagerly about himself . . . He aspires to be Com-mander-in-Chief, for which honour, he said, he must show his fitness. He wants to go back to the Crimea, but has not been chosen for a command. I am very sorry for poor George and feel for him, but much is his own fault (which he now sees) at not having gone back to the Crimea, as he ought to, six weeks after being home.'

Early in 1856 the Duke wrote to Lord Hardinge, explaining the difficulties he had encountered in obtaining a command, and seeking the assistance of the Commander-in-Chief. 'The kindness,' he wrote on 4 February, 'I have ever received at your hands, prompts me again to address you on a subject, which we have before several times spoken about. It is now more than a year, that I have returned home and have been unemployed. Since that period I have made several efforts to be again placed in Command, and my anxiety was great to receive an important trust.'[36] His insistent efforts all proved vain, for although nobody was prepared to tell him so directly, the Government had decided early in 1855 not to give him another command. Lord Panmure, Newcastle's successor as Secretary of State for War in Palmerston's administration, wrote in March to Lord Raglan to tell him not to expect the Duke to return. 'I may tell you in confidence that you will not see the Duke in the Crimea again, as I have advised him not to return. What effect this may have on you I know not, but I trust it may not disarrange any of your plans. I shall likewise endeavour to persuade Cardigan that his health is insufficiently reinstated, for his temperament is not such as to make him looked up to as a C.O. should be. All this, however, I communicate in the strictest confidence.'[37]

Lord Panmure himself bore the brunt of most of H.R.H.'s importunity. There were times when he received almost daily visits. On 3 October the Duke 'went to the Horse Guards, where I saw all the authorities and heard a great deal of news of various sorts and kinds. Simpson has certainly resigned, but his successor is not yet known. I wish they would send me.' Two days later he was back again at the War Office. 'Saw Lord Panmure, with whom I had a long conversation about myself, and my anxiety to command the Army in the field. He seemed to fear there were great difficulties, but was very kind in all he said.'

Lord Panmure, in considering a successor to General Simpson, wrote the Queen a review of all possible candidates for command. 'Lord Panmure presents his humble duty to Your Majesty, and has the honour to forward to Your Majesty copies of despatches which have arrived by this mail. Lord Panmure cannot conceal from Your Majesty that in General Simpson's letter there are grounds for anxiety as to the present state of things with the Army. It is quite evident that General Simpson thinks himself unequal to the task of commanding the Army, and is anxious to be relieved from so weighty a responsibility. With this feeling so strongly expressed, Lord Panmure is of opinion that it would be unjust to the Army to leave it in trembling hands, and unfair to tax General Simpson's powers of mind and body beyond what he states himself able to endure. Under these circumstances Lord Panmure asked Lord Palmerston to hold a conference with Lord Hardinge at the War Department on this momentous crisis. They went over the list carefully and discussed the following selections as being possible.

'1st. Lord Seaton. His age is seventy six, and though his frame is robust for that period of life, he is unfit for exposure to such a climate as the Crimea.

'2nd. Lord Hardinge. He stated that, if ordered by Your Majesty, he would obey, but he represented that he was physically unfit for the task.

'3rd. The Duke of Cambridge. Your Majesty will, I trust, forgive me when I state that, admitting all His Royal Highness's hereditary courage, he might fail in self-control in situations where the safety of the Army might depend on coolness and self-possession.'

To find the Duke occupation, and to divert him from commanding in the field, Panmure offered him the Governorship of Gibraltar. H.R.H. 'anxiously considered the proposal,' and 'consulted two military friends in whose judgement I could confide, as also one or two members of my immediate family.' In the end he came 'to the conclusion that however honourable the post is that you have thought of for me, it is not exactly one that would suit my views and feelings. The fact is that the sphere of action is, if I may be permitted to express myself, rather too confined for a person of active habits like myself . . . Of course, I am perfectly prepared to take my share of active duty in the field, if it should be thought desirable that I should again join the army in the East, but otherwise I should wish for some employment at home, where I think I might perhaps be useful at the present moment in superintending the levies of various descriptions that are preparing for active service.' When he heard the news of the fall of Sebastopol, the Duke again wrote to Panmure begging to be sent out to the front. '. . . Poor Lord Raglan! how I wish he could have seen this great work accomplished under his own eyes! I am in despair, as you can imagine, at not having been present; this is a most painful feeling, really at times quite unbearable, and, indeed, I feel daily more and more ashamed at leading an idle life when the Army and my gallant and dear friends and comrades are all in the field. If this war lasts, I do beg and pray of you to employ me actively in the field.'[38]

The active command for which he longed was denied him, but early in 1856 he was sent on an important mission. After the fall of Sebastopol it was decided to hold a conference in Paris to discuss how best to prosecute the war against Russia. H.R.H. was appointed as Senior Military Delegate representing England. Before the Conference, however, reached any decisions, the enemy came to terms, and one of the most futile and incompetently conducted wars ever fought was joyfully concluded.

As is customary after most campaigns, a good deal of acrimonious discussion took place in an effort to discover what went wrong. Kinglake's early volumes, published seven years after the Peace, provoked bitter controversy, and the Duke became involved in the disputes. *The Invasion of the Crimea* is in all respects monumental, but its author, in attempting to make sense of conflicting accounts, sometimes depended upon unreliable evidence. 'I have heard old officers of the Guards,' wrote Fortescue, 'who were present at Inkerman discuss with much amusement

Kinglake's account of the Brigade in that action, knowing well the individual from whom he derived most of his information.'[39] Sir George Lewis, Secretary for War at the time of Kinglake's publication, wrote to H.R.H. to say that he had just read the book, which he regarded as 'a nasty pamphlet, or rather a collection of nasty and personal invectives, in the form of a history. I fear it is calculated to do the country much harm.'[40] The veteran martinet Sir George Brown sent the Duke a detailed synopsis of the work, which he told him he read 'with some *strain* on my patience . . . I have no hesitation in declaring it, so far as it has gone, one of the most injudicious and mischievous productions that has appeared in my time!' He described it as 'quite unreliable,' and he believed it 'impossible that this work can ever be considered an authority on which any rational man could safely attach his belief.' Brown thought that Kinglake's 'vituperation and slander' would reflect on Lord Raglan, and he wondered who had advised Lady Raglan to put her husband's papers into such hands.[41]

The passage in Kinglake's history which particularly incensed the Duke was one in which it was suggested that the First Division had been so dilatory that it had failed to give effective support to the Light Division. There was too much truth in the accusation for it to be anything other than objectionable. The Duke wrote round to other Generals who had fought at the Alma, asking if they agreed with Kinglake's account, and, not surprisingly, none of them did. 'In Mr Kinglake's very detailed account of the battle of the Alma,' he wrote to De Lacy Evans, 'at the bottom of the three hundred and forty first page, it is stated that you sent me a message, pointing out to me the danger of not advancing more rapidly in support of the Light Division with my Division the First. I certainly have no recollection whatever of ever having received such a message . . . I should therefore feel much obliged to you to let me know whether it was your impression that you sent me such a message, by whom it was sent, and to whom it was delivered. You can easily imagine if you have looked at the passage in question, that I am anxious to understand on what grounds Mr Kinglake asserts that the First

Division did not give effectual support to the Light Division, a view of the case I entirely deny the correctness of.'[42]

De Lacy Evans sent back a most diplomatic answer, saying that he was in fact indirectly responsible for sending a message to H.R.H. suggesting that he should advance. However, being on higher ground than the Duke, he could see more of the battle, and gave his opinion that with the necessarily restricted view of things which the First Division had, it was perfectly reasonable for it to have halted. 'Strictly speaking I sent no communication in my own name to the First Division, but as will be seen, I caused a communication of importance to be made ostensibly from a higher source. . . . Colonel Steele, Military Secretary to the Commander of the Forces, a most active officer, came to me twice during the battle to ask how I was getting on with my attack . . . I asked him if he would undertake to go to the First Division and state that he was the bearer of orders from the Commander of the Forces, that that Division should forthwith pass the river and proceed as rapidly as possible to support the troops of Sir G. Brown.' The second day after the battle De Lacy Evans sat next to Raglan at dinner in his tent and Colonel Steele was opposite. He asked Steele if he had delivered the message. Steele said he had done so. 'Lord Raglan then placing his hand on my shoulder said—"But I also sent the same order." Your Royal Highness expresses anxiousness to understand on what grounds the effective support rendered by your Division could be questioned. I trust it has not been questioned. Because in my judgement no troops could have eventually more nobly performed their duty than those under your Royal Highness's command.'[43]

The Duke also wrote to Sir Colin Campbell, created Lord Clyde in 1858, about this alleged delay of the First Division at Alma. The Field Marshal replied that 'there can be no doubt that an interval, to some extent, did elapse,' but he described it, with some reservations, as 'justified and inevitable.'[44] Sir George Brown, the most outspoken of Generals, who would never have hesitated to be offensive had he believed the facts warranted it, and who, as commander of the Light Division, was in the best position to judge how effective the Duke's support had been, told H.R.H. 'I have always considered that the Guards came up *precisely* at the right time. Had they come earlier they would have been exposed to a heavy fire in passing through the vineyards and crossing the River . . . I did not look for nor see them until I wanted their assistance and then I found the Grenadier Guards formed and ready to come to my aid. H.R.H. would in my judgement have done very wrong to have advanced earlier and thereby compromised their order by getting his troops prematurely involved in the attack.' Brown could not speak savagely enough of Kinglake's book: part of the reason he had for believing him to be misinformed was that he had never once consulted the General commanding the Light Division. 'He seems to have preferred placing faith and relying upon camp gossip, and on the idle reports and statements of irresponsible individuals to the more authentic information that he might have received from the General and superior officers of the Army.' This 'most atrocious book cannot fail to do endless mischief amongst ourselves and in the French Army and nation at large.'[45]

The Duke finally saw the culprit himself. At twelve o'clock, 17 February, 'Mr Kinglake came, and I had a long interview with him on the subject of his book. I discussed with him such parts as I thought unjust towards myself as commanding the First Division at the battle of the Alma. No one could behave better or in a more gentlemanlike way than he did, and I firmly believe it was not his intention to do me any injury. He seemed well disposed to set matters right as far as he could. He was with me an hour.'

The confusions and blunders of the Crimean War necessarily led to a prolonged post-mortem. Some said it was the Duke of Wellington's fault, some accused Lord Raglan, others the Ministers. But the most persistent and unjustified efforts were made to blame Raglan's staff; in particular the Commissary General, Lord Airey. He was attacked by the Press, and the Government attempted to blame him for its own shortcomings. The Duke of Newcastle even tried to drag Raglan into the conspiracy but was

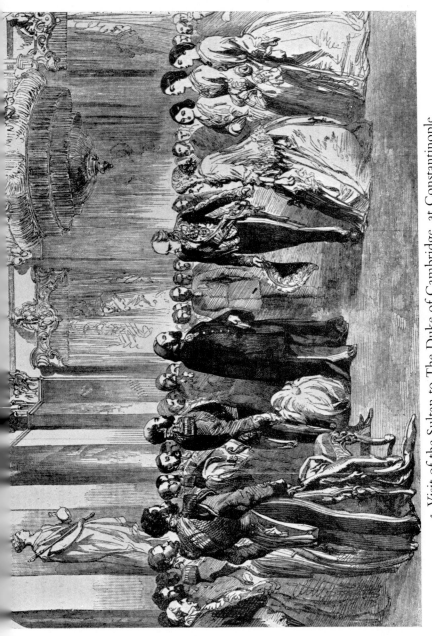

5 Visit of the Sultan to The Duke of Cambridge, at Constantinople

Illustrated London News

6 The British Troops on the Heights of Alma

Illustrated London News

firmly rebuffed. 'Am I,' he asked the Secretary for War, 'or are the writers of private letters in the best position to pronounce upon their [the Staff's]merits?' General Simpson was sent out to investigate Raglan's staff, and unobligingly reported 'The Staff here at headquarters have, I am convinced, been very much vilified. They are a very good set of fellows—civil and obliging to everyone who comes. I am speaking of the personal Staff, who have no responsibilities further than being generally useful. Nor have I any fault to find with Airey and Estcourt.'[46]

The Duke of Newcastle next attempted to persuade Raglan to agree to Airey's being transferred to a command in the field, but was told for his pains that 'If he be removed from the appointment of Quartermaster-General, a very great injury would be inflicted on the service and myself personally.' Idle gossip was thought sufficient evidence to destroy Airey's reputation. Newcastle told Raglan, 'This very day, an angry relative of an officer dying from sickness said to be brought on by avoidable causes, asked me how a Quartermaster-General was likely to attend to his important duties who found time to write long private letters to at least half a dozen fine ladies in London.' Lord Raglan answered: 'I can, of course, give no reply, to the charge of an officer dying from avoidable causes: but I can say this, that the Quartermaster-General can have nothing to do with these causes. He has not the charge of sick officers. General Airey pleads guilty to having written to Miss Hardinge who was in great anxiety about her brother, then confined by illness to this house, and to Lady Raglan to let her know how I was; and these are the only ladies he has written to except his wife. I really cannot understand any gentleman venturing to intrude upon you such an insinuation . . .'[47] Wolseley regarded Airey as one of the most capable soldiers he knew. The despicable attempt to blame him for almost half a century of parliamentary neglect was very much resented by H.R.H., who himself knew too well how ignorant chatter could be repeated as if it were Holy Writ.

Arguments over Kinglake, and the search for scapegoats, were the least profitable aspects of the vigorous re-thinking on military matters which followed the war. After 1856 a constructive period of reform ensued, and the Duke of Cambridge, who in that year succeeded Lord Hardinge as Officer Commanding-in-Chief, wholeheartedly gave his support to a number of important changes, many of which he is ignorantly supposed to have resisted bitterly.

COMMANDING-IN-CHIEF

O N 7 July 1856, a great review of troops who had returned
from the Crimea took place at Aldershot before the Queen.
The Duke attended with his mother and Princess Mary
Adelaide. As it rained the whole afternoon, H.R.H. 'therefore
showed Mama and Mary the Camp, and we went to all the old
Regiments of my Division. All looked admirably well and
received me with the very greatest cordiality and good feeling.'
It was so wet that the parade was cancelled and the Duchess
returned to London. In the course of the afternoon, Lord Hardinge,
while talking to the Queen and Prince Albert, was struck down
by a stroke. The Queen at the time merely thought he had
slipped, for his mind remained perfectly clear, and he apologized
'for making such a disturbance.' Two days later the Commander-
in-Chief resigned, the whole of his right side being paralysed,
and he died in September, killed, according to Queen Victoria,
'by the Press.'

The Prime Minister, Lord Palmerston, discussed the matter of

Hardinge's successor with the Queen. She recorded in her Diary on 9 July, 'Talked of Lord Hardinge's illness and our fear indeed knowledge, that he would resign, which places us in a great difficulty, for his loss will be immense. Lord Palmerston fully appreciates his great qualities and merits and the seriousness of his loss, for a man of his experience, cannot be replaced. Then we discussed his possible successor. Sir William Codrington we agreed would be the best, but he is so much junior, that unless he had gained a victory in the field, it would be impossible to put him over the heads of others. Talked of George, of his great regimental knowledge, his experience of different armies, his devotion to the Army, and popularity, and all pointing to his being the *most* suitable. Albert truly observed while for the Army it would be an advantage to have a Prince of the Blood at their head, for the Crown, it might not be a support, as any attacks against him would reflect to a certain extent on the Crown, and the Commander-in-Chief ought to be a support to the Crown. We then went through the whole Army List, and with the exception of Lord Seaton, who would be quite the right man, were it not for his great age, we could find no one worth considering.' The next day the Queen received 'poor Lord Hardinge's resignation,' and sent it to Lord Palmerston, expressing her 'opinion, that George was almost without a competitor.' On 12 July she heard 'that the Cabinet, after due consideration, had concurred in advising me to approach George, as successor to Lord Hardinge. They say that the Army expects and wishes it.' 'Viscount Palmerston presents his humble duty to your Majesty,' ran the letter recommending the Duke's appointment, 'and begs to state that he has consulted with his colleagues as to the advice to be tendered to your Majesty in regard to the appointment of a successor to Lord Hardinge as General Commanding-in-Chief; and upon a full consideration of the subject, the Cabinet are of opinion that your Majesty's choice could not fall upon any General Officer better suited to that important position than His Royal Highness the Duke of Cambridge, and Lord Panmure will have the honour of taking your Majesty's pleasure upon the matter officially. It seems quite clear that there is no General Officer senior to His Royal Highness the Duke of Cambridge to whom it would in all respects be desirable to entrust the duties of the command of the Army, and there is no General Officer below him in seniority who has claim sufficiently strong to justify his being preferred to His Royal Highness . . .'[1]

On Sunday, 13 July, just as he was about to dress for an early dinner, the Duke received a note summoning him to the Palace. 'The Queen saw me in the Garden, and in conjunction with Albert announced to me my appointment to the Commander-in-Chief of the Army. She was most gracious and most kind in her expressions of pleasure, as was the Prince. Thus I am placed in the proudest military position that any subject could be placed in: it is an onerous one, but I will do my best to do myself credit. I saw Lord Hardinge, who was aware of the appointment, and who I found rather better, but still very feeble.' The Queen took the opportunity, as she recorded in her Diary, to impress upon the new Commander-in-Chief the need for consulting her before taking any important decisions. 'George came at seven, and I informed him of his appointment, and *embraced him*. He had just received Lord Palmerston's letter, announcing it, and is much pleased . . . We tried to give him good advice as to appointments and begged him always to consult us, before anything definite was done.'

On the day of his appointment to supreme command of the Army he wrote two notes to his mother. 'Although nothing is yet known, I think I can tell you that it is decided and that I am Commander-in-Chief. I have received the following letter from Lord Panmure. "I have much satisfaction in informing your Royal Highness that the Cabinet has cordially concurred in recommending you to the Queen as Lord Hardinge's successor. This is a step to which I rejoice in having been a party, and I have no doubt that it will be beneficial to the Queen, the Country and the Army to have your Royal Highness at the head of the latter." ' A few hours later on the same day the Duke was able to write: 'So it is all settled and I am Commander-in-Chief. I

heard from Lord Palmerston, and the Queen sent for me to come
to her this evening and announced it to me in the presence of
Albert. She was very much moved, and I saw it touched her very
nearly, but she was exceedingly gracious and friendly and kind to
me, and we had a very nice conversation together, with which I
was very well satisfied. It is a tremendous undertaking, but yet I
am quite of good courage, for all are for me.'

The Duke's aunt, the Duchess of Gloucester, who was especially
fond of her nephew and deeply appreciated his kindness to her,
indeed so much so that on her death she left him her house, wrote
an excited letter to her sister-in-law, the Duchess of Cambridge.
'You may judge, by your own feelings what mine are at our dear
George's distinguished appointment . . . He is so looked up to
and beloved by the troops, and the Queen is so fully sensible of
all his merits, that the moment she could make him Commander-
in-Chief she has done so. Dear sister, as you doubted when we
parted that I should see you to-day, I write this note to wish you
joy of this great and joyful event, which I know you have been so
long looking forward to with so much anxiety, and it must make
you feel very proud to be the mother of a son who has made
himself so popular and beloved by all classes, and that the confidence of the Queen has so clearly shown itself as to have given
him this responsible situation. From my heart I wish you joy, and
dear Mary also. George wrote me a kind little note last night to
inform me of this event and of the Queen's great kindness to him
when she saw him on the subject. I could not fly to Kew at
eleven o'clock last night, or I would have done so, and having no
notice of when you might come to town to-day I put off writing,
hoping you might call in passing Gloucester House . . . I wrote
of course to the Queen the first thing this morning to express my
joy and happiness, and I have had a letter from her full of affection
and feeling for him. God bless you.'[2]

The post of General Commanding-in-Chief, the highest in the
Army, which the Duke held for the next thirty nine years, was
one for which he had longed since the death of the Duke of
Wellington. When Louisa heard the news of his predecessor's

death, she wrote to her husband, 'So poor Lord Hardinge is dead. I am very sorry, for I think he was a man who was blamed for the fault of others. What an excitement you would have been in, had you not received the appointment some time ago, but that is now over and you have what you consider the greatest blessing in life.'[3]

Since the very earliest times an important part of the Crown's authority was its control of the Army. The office of Commander-in-Chief is the oldest in the military hierarchy, some writers have traced it back to 54 B.C. when Cassivellaunus put himself at the head of the English forces collected to repel Julius Caesar's second invasion of Britain. St John, who defended Hampden in his resistance to Ship Money, was reluctantly forced to admit that Charles I had wide powers to defend the realm, and that 'inherent in his Majesty as part of his crown and kingly dignity' was 'his primitive prerogative of Generalissimo and Commander-in-Chief.' At the Revolution of 1688 an attempt was made to subordinate the Army to Parliament but it was far from successful. Officers still regarded themselves as serving the Crown, and as deriving their authority from commissions signed by the Sovereign. The history of the office of Commander-in-Chief is largely the story of the struggle between the Crown and Parliament for control of the armed forces.

Various titles have been used to describe the Chief Officer of the Army: Captain-General, Field Marshal on the Staff, and General Commanding-in-Chief. Monk, Duke of Albemarle, was appointed Commander-in-Chief by Charles II. On his death the King personally assumed control of the Army, and from 1670 to 1793, except temporarily in the emergency of war, the office remained dormant. In the eighteenth century the Secretary-at-War, a politician subject to the controlling authority of the Home Secretary, and unfortunately even more subject to the influence of those officers who possessed powerful friends in Parliament, assumed responsibility for army discipline and the disposal of patronage. In 1793, on the outbreak of war with France, Lord Amherst was appointed Commander-in-Chief, and two years

later was succeeded in the office by the Duke of York, who delivered the Army from political jobbery, restored its efficiency
and reformed its administration. The power exercised by the
Secretary-at-War, or by the Commander-in-Chief, in the opinion
of successive sovereigns, was a delegated authority belonging to
the Crown; and for a time George IV contemplated assuming the
office himself, until Lord Liverpool convinced him that the Duke
of Wellington had a superior claim.

   Although the Duke of Cambridge has been referred to as
Commander-in-Chief, he did not officially assume that title until
it was conferred upon him in 1887, the jubilee of his fiftieth year
of military service. In 1856 he was gazetted as 'General Commanding-in-Chief,' the distinction being that his name was not
at the top of the Army List, and since he had been promoted over
the heads of his seniors, he was the chief but not the first officer in
the British Army.

   Queen Victoria, 'a soldier's daughter,' was always intensely
interested in Army matters. She frequently referred to 'her Army,'
and the troops thought of themselves as 'soldiers of the Queen.'
Writing to Lord Panmure on 28 February 1855, she alluded to
'her noble, brave, and unequalled soldiers (whom she is so proud
to call her own).' 'You never saw anybody,' wrote Lord Panmure
to Raglan, 'so entirely taken up with military affairs as she is.'[4]
Believing the Army to be her own possession, she was sensitively
jealous of any threat to her prerogative. She insisted on signing
every officer's commission, and would not contemplate suggestions for reducing the labour, because she was anxious to
retain the 'personal connection between the Sovereign and the
Army.' The Duke of Wellington had always told her that 'it was
of the utmost importance to the stability of the Throne and the
Constitution, that the command of the Army should remain in
the hands of the Sovereign, and not fall into those of the House of
Commons.' For this reason he had urged the Prince Consort to
become Commander-in-Chief.[5] At the close of the century, Lord
Roberts maintained that the Sovereign 'stands far above the
exigencies or influence of party,' and hence was the proper person

to dispense Army patronage, and to inspire the devotion and loyalty of the troops.[6]

H.R.H. took over command of the Army in an age of vigorous reform, and certainly there was ample scope for improvement in the soldier's life. As Lord Wolseley said, 'to enlist was to be disgraced,' and the low grade of recruits was made an excuse for not improving their conditions. Barracks were ill built, overcrowded and insanitary. One pump was considered enough for a battalion. Beef and potatoes were the only meals provided. Abroad conditions were worse and the mortality rate was shocking. At Sierra Leone a soldier's chance of surviving his term of service was four to one against. Even in England the death rate in the Army was five times higher than in civilian life. Pay, after various reductions, was about threepence a day, and discipline was maintained by branding and flogging. Parliament took better care of convicts 'who were public enemies than of soldiers who were a public safeguard.'[7] The Duke, by his constant efforts to improve the conditions of the troops, became exceedingly popular with them, and earned the epithet 'The Soldier's Friend.'

A year after H.R.H.'s appointment, Lord Clarendon, then Foreign Secretary, told Greville how pleased he was with the Duke of Cambridge, who had shown 'a great deal of sense and discretion, and a very accurate knowledge of the details of his office.' He had given 'great satisfaction' when summoned to Cabinet meetings, and was a better Commander-in-Chief than Lord Hardinge had been. The Queen, who was not always easy to please, was delighted with her cousin's energy and zeal. On 29 October 1856, she remarked in her Diary: 'Remained talking with George, after breakfast, for some time, about military matters, and also when we walked out with him later. I must say I think he is much devoted to his office and very active and energetic, in getting things into good and proper order.' Again on 23 October 1857, she wrote: 'The Army much talked about at breakfast. George understands his business well, and he is very keen about it. He spoke of the bad system of the Government in not telling him *beforehand*, what is intended to be done, merely taking sudden decisions, which he could not always carry out.' Certainly he was conscientious and scarcely ever let pleasure interfere with business. 'I was to have gone today on a visit to Belvoir,' he says in his Diary on 2 January 1868, 'but thought it right to give it up, as I did not like to be absent from my post while these Fenian threats were going on.'

A great deal of H.R.H.'s time was spent writing to Generals all over the world, with whom he liked to correspond personally as well as officially. He told Sir Hope Grant, sent out to command the China expedition of 1859, 'I think that it is very desirable that privately and confidentially you should keep me well informed of all your proceedings . . . I find this the best mode of dealing with all the General Officers in Command in various parts of the world . . .'[8]

The Commander-in-Chief's letters, often several pages long, and all written in his own hand, are a formidable monument to his industry. If he had had no other occupation than keeping up this correspondence, he would have been hard worked. It did not matter what distance lay between a commander in the field and the Duke at the Horse Guards, his interest in the minutest details of organization would be evinced by a constant flow of letters.

One of the very first of the Duke's reforms was to improve Army music. At a parade to commemorate the end of the Crimean War, the massed bands struck up 'God Save the Queen.' The sound was so painful that H.R.H., who loved music and spent many of his evenings at the opera, was overcome by the noise. He immediately instituted a standard pitch, and founded a School of Army Music at Kneller Hall, once the home of Sir Godfrey Kneller, the artist and courtier who painted ten reigning sovereigns. The Royal Military School of Music set standards admitted throughout the world, and outside the school gates to this very day stands a public house: 'The Duke of Cambridge.' On 13 August 1857, H.R.H. went by train 'to see the new Musical School I have formed. It seems admirably established and is working most satisfactorily . . . A charming locality and they play and sing wonderfully well.' Nearly thirty years later, on 28 May 1886, he took Sir Arthur Sullivan to visit Kneller Hall. 'Heard the band in the chapel first, and then a fine and powerful band on the Parade Ground. Was very much satisfied with the whole condition of things, as was Sullivan, who said he had no sort of suggestions to offer for improvements.'

Many proposals suggested by the Commander-in-Chief were not so successfully accomplished. The trouble was nearly always the same. Successive governments, committed to retrenchment, did all in their power to reduce Army estimates, and little could be done without money. In January 1857 the Duke pressed upon the Government the need to train men for the Commissariat, but despite the lessons of the recent war, he was told that military expenditure had to be curtailed and that what he proposed would be too expensive. 'The supplies of the Army,' said Lord Panmure, 'will have to be obtained in the most economical manner, in order to keep John Bull in a good humour.' In one of the most prosperous decades in our history, and with the warnings of the Peninsular and Crimean Wars before them, Palmerston's Ministry wilfully allowed the Commissariat to become once more a token force. The crippling expenditure necessitated in war by perverse economies resorted to in peace suggests that parliamentary control of the Army has not always been exercised with undeviating wisdom; and the resentment felt by soldiers against ignorant and short-sighted political interference was based on heart-breaking experience. The Duke's career as Commander-in-Chief involved a ceaseless struggle against reductions in military expenditure, and he made many enemies in the fight, but his efforts saved the Army from much of the havoc wrought by ill-judged economies.

Both Tory and Liberal politicians regarded military matters primarily from a financial standpoint. Disraeli, as Chancellor of the Exchequer in Lord Derby's Ministry, thought Lord Hardinge 'very prone to expenditure,' and wishing to produce a popular budget, resented the expense of the 'damned defences.' The Liberals, the party of 'peace' and 'retrenchment,' ever suspicious of the political threat of an Army, ceaselessly preached and

practised every form of economy; but how peace could be promoted, 'by denying to the Government the means for suppressing
disorder,' Cobden and his followers never explained. Both
parties, moreover, were anxious to extend parliamentary control
over the armed forces. 'I fear,' wrote the Queen to the Duke in
1857, 'the Cabinet have been dabbling in military details again,
for which they seem to have a singular predilection, and for which
they are eminently unfit.'[9] H.R.H., writing on 8 June 1858, to Sir
Colin Campbell, complained of constant attempts to extend civil
control. 'A restless spirit is abroad and a great desire for constant
change . . . If we want any change it should be with a view of
putting more military element into our organization, but I am
afraid that is not the spirit of the age, which wants to introduce
further civil control which must lead to harm, for an army never
can be commanded or controlled by civilians. . . .'

The Queen supported her Commander-in-Chief in opposing
reductions. 'Only be stout and determined,' she encouraged him,
'and you may rely on our backing you up.' Every year the Duke
submitted his estimates to the Secretary for War, and every year
he pleaded that ill-considered attempts to save revenue only cost
more in the end. 'What a deal of money,' he told Sir Colin
Campbell, 'our economy fits have cost the country.'[10] In 1858
he protested 'that in the present state our armed force is most
deficient in number . . . I cannot answer for the consequences if
something is not done at once to add to our military forces both at
home and abroad.' Again in 1860, he stressed the inadequacy of
Britain's defences. 'I am strongly impressed that in the present
state of the world, England ought never to be in so deplorable a
military position as she is at present for the want of troops, more
particularly Infantry. I am well aware that it is a most difficult
matter to find a remedy, as any additional force must require increased expenditure; but, on the other hand, the question we have
to put to ourselves is, Are we justified in leaving matters in such
a condition? I think we are not, and therefore I feel bound to bring
the subject to serious notice.' The following year he informed the
Secretary for War that 'I have no hesitation in saying frankly and

unreservedly, that I consider this force [the Army, after it had been reduced by 14,000 men] *totally inadequate* for our present work and requirements.'[11] Sometimes his own Generals, anxious to placate the Government, would suggest economies or agree that they were feasible. Lord Mansfield, Commander-in-Chief in India, whose political loyalties were suspect at the Horse Guards, was warned by the Duke that he would not acquiesce in reductions in the Indian Army. 'The proposed reduction in rank and file in European Regiments of Cavalry and Infantry serving in India have not reached me officially, and though no doubt they will be accepted and approved by the Government, and consequently carried out, I shall feel it my duty to warn the authorities of the danger which in my opinion is incurred by making them. I am well aware that the financial difficulties are great, and that these have induced you to make these proposals, but looking at the vastness of our Indian Empire, at the extent of our frontier, at the distance of India from support, or at the suddenness with which difficulties have arisen before now, I cannot but think the economy is altogether a false one, and that the present European force serving in India ought not to be reduced by a single man for many years to come. In fact the financial difficulty ought to have been met in some other way than by the reduction of the army.'[12]

The support the Queen offered the Duke in resisting cuts in the Army was, in the estimate of some of her Ministers, given too generously. She very properly complained to Palmerston in 1857 that the Government did not appear to have learnt the lessons of the War against Russia. 'The Queen is anxious to impress in the most earnest manner upon her Government the necessity of taking a comprehensive view of our military position at the present momentous crisis, instead of going on without a plan, living from hand to mouth, and taking small isolated measures without reference to each other.' The Prime Minister, suffering from a surfeit of regal advice, neatly contrived to administer a rebuke to his Sovereign. 'Viscount Palmerston . . . has had the honour to receive your Majesty's communication . . . stating what your Majesty would have said if your Majesty had been in the

House of Commons. Viscount Palmerston may perhaps be permitted to take the liberty of saying that it is fortunate for those from whose opinions your Majesty differs that your Majesty is not in the House of Commons for they would have had to encounter a formidable antagonist in argument . . .'[13]

The Queen and Prince Albert attributed the difficulties and sufferings of the Crimea to the 'miserable reductions of the last thirty years.' They protested that economies were being made even before peace had been signed, and the Queen told Palmerston that she 'expected' retrenchments to be carried out 'with great *moderation* and very gradually.' In 1857 she referred to the position of the Army as 'pitiable' and assured the Prime Minister that the measures taken to deal with the Indian Mutiny were 'by no means adequate to the emergency.' The Prince Consort, writing to Stockmar, told him that the disasters in the East showed what befell an Army 'which rests upon civil government and the Press,' and he complained that while politicians made 'grandiose speeches' they let 'our poor little army be wasted away.' In 1869, hearing rumours of further economies, the Queen informed Lord Derby that if England were to be listened to in Europe she must be powerful and not regarded as 'despicably weak in her military resources.'[14] She enthusiastically endorsed Palmerston's precept, which was more than in practice he did himself: 'For a country great and rich to leave itself without the means of defence is not a method to preserve peace in the long run.'

In 1859 two events occurred to awaken the public to the inadequacy of Britain's defences. The first was an invasion scare. Orsini, the year before, had thrown a bomb at Napoleon III, and many Frenchmen held England responsible for the outrage, partly because she had harboured the conspirator, and partly because she was reputed to desire the death of the Emperor. The Duke, anxious to appease, and believing that revolutionaries should be deported, suggested that Lord Panmure should persuade his colleagues to reconsider their attitude to immigrants. Panmure, however, remained defiant. 'While quite prepared to make the most searching investigations for any breach of our laws on the part of those whom we harbour, or, more correctly speaking, who came to our shores, we must maintain the high position which we so proudly occupy of giving shelter to the unfortunate, of which shelter there is not a *party* who now attacks us who have not from time to time, availed themselves.'[15] The danger of a French invasion was, in reality, remote enough, but had Napoleon seriously contemplated an attack, our military preparations would have proved ridiculously insufficient. The second event which increased awareness of danger was the publication in 1859 of Sir John Burgoyne's pamphlet 'Observations on the possible results of a War with France under our present system of Military Preparation.' Although written as a confidential memorandum in 1846, little since had occurred to modify it. If the French invaded, Burgoyne predicted, the English army would be out-numbered ten to one. We were so weak militarily that we would have to surrender. The British Empire, in Palmerston's phrase, 'existed only by sufferance,' and unfounded optimism about perpetual peace obscured the need for effective defence.

The Commander-in-Chief was sensitively aware of England's vulnerability. Parliament, in an emergency, was always inclined to place excessive reliance upon volunteer forces, although the greater part of the Militia 'served no purpose except to inspire the negligent and ignorant with a false feeling of security.' British patriotism, it was thought, was a sufficient substitute for training and organization. Fox in 1804 had advocated 'an armed peasantry' as 'the great defence of a country' against invasion, but Sir John Moore was not so confident in the effectiveness of untrained forces. He once told Pitt, Lord Warden of the Cinque Ports, that the place for volunteers would be on the cliffs, where they would have a good view of the battle being fought on the shore. In 1856 the coast was completely undefended, and Wellington's dis-closure that, except immediately under the fire of Dover Castle, infantry might easily be landed anywhere had inspired moment-ary panic rather than appropriate action. H.R.H. took the matter up in 1861 and managed to persuade the Secretary for War that money must be spent on defences. Sir George Lewis, who in 1861 succeeded Sidney Herbert, accepted the Duke's advice, with certain reservations. 'I quite appreciate the advantage of fortifying our arsenals and naval stations—but I cannot see the benefit of dotting little forts, like the old Martello towers, along our coasts. We have been building a little fort on the coast of Aberdeenshire of which I am unable to discover the use, unless it is to prevent the Norwegians from kidnapping the Queen from Balmoral, and it is now proposed to fortify the Scilly Isles—in order, I presume, to save Mr Augustus Smith to the Nation.'

H.R.H. agreed about the absurdity of some of the proposed fortifications but thought that the great dockyards and arsenals needed some protection. 'At the same time there are parts of the coast which cannot be quite overlooked, and these must be attended to. For instance, Newhaven in Sussex, where a landing could easily be effected, and where there is a small port of disembarkation just opposite the French coast. I would certainly have a work there, and I hope you will allow it to be proceeded with. Then again I think the mouth of the Humber and of the Mersey are points which cannot be altogether overlooked, as they are the great emporiums of our trade. The Clyde again would be another point. As for Aberdeen, I say nothing in its favour, and I have still less to say for the Scilly Islands.'[16] Resisting dangerous economies, and urging the Government to look to the defences of the country, occupied much of H.R.H.'s time and energy, even without wars and campaigns on his hands, and there was hardly a year of unbroken peace during the period of his Commanding-in-Chief.

The Duke of Cambridge as an old man was reputed to have a very low opinion of the Staff College and its products. Wolseley once suggested that a vacant appointment should be given to a Staff College Officer. 'Staff College Officer,' grunted the Duke, 'what does he want a Staff College Officer for? I know those Staff College Officers. They are very ugly officers and very dirty officers.'[17] This outburst, gleefully treasured by regimental officers who had suffered at the hands of objectionable students from Camberley, was not directed at all graduates, but against a

7B H.R.H. Augusta, Grand Duchess of Mecklenburg-Strelitz
from a photograph by Ellis and Walery

7A H.R.H. Mary Adelaide, Duchess of Teck
from a photograph by Ellis and Walery

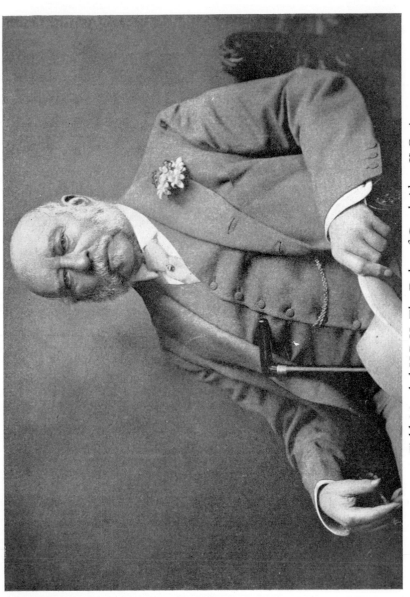

8 Field Marshal H.R.H. The Duke of Cambridge, K.G., in 1900

minority who viewed the College solely as a means to promote their careers, and who took insufficient trouble to master their regimental duties. But towards the end of his time, the College 'developed into a nursery of missionaries' who condemned H.R.H.'s convictions and set less store than he did on the importance of the Regiment. As a result, he still regarded 'those Gentlemen who have been at the Staff College' with 'the very best feeling' and considered that they had always 'done remarkably well; but I prefer for the staff to have regimental officers.'[18]

When he was in playful mood he often pretended to abominate the Staff College. 'One time when he was inspecting a district at home and when the gala feast in his honour at the general's house, which all the staff of the district are invited to, had arrived at the port and walnut stage, he was heard to lift up his voice and to remark to the general in loud-toned guttural accents which sounded all over the room, "I'm glad to know, Sir ——, that you have no Staff College officers on your staff. [The staff were nearly all Staff College men, as he was perfectly well aware.] I don't like Staff College officers. My experience of Staff College officers is that they are conceited, and that they are dirty! Brrains! I don't believe in brrains. You haven't any, I know Sir, and as for my Military Secretary over on the other side of the table, and a damned good Military Secretary too, he's the very stoopidest man I ever came across." '[19]

As a young man, with the experience of the Crimean War vividly in his mind, H.R.H. was strongly in favour of maintaining a considerable Staff and training it rigorously. 'It is preposterous,' he told Sidney Herbert, 'to go back to the Staff we had before the War. Is it really wished . . . that we should again fall into this fatal error? I can be no party to such a plan, and I trust you share my views.'[20] After the Duke had hardly been a month in office, he began to impress upon Panmure the need for a highly trained Staff. 'I am sure you will permit me to remark that it is really essential to the new formation that we should have a thoroughly efficient staff, for it was in this point we formerly failed so much, and it is necessary that Staff Officers should have opportunities

for studying their professional duties, and how can they do so if a
certain increased number to the old establishment be not appointed?' The Secretary for War in his reply made the usual
excuses about cost, and H.R.H. begged him not to 'give in too
much to the cry against the Staff, for, believe me, if we have not a
very efficient Staff during peace, we cannot have a really good one
during war.'[21]

Ever since Le Marchant opened his school at High Wycombe in
1799, some attempt had been made to train Staff Officers in their
duties, but the reconstituted Staff College at Camberley—then
named Cambridge Town—owed its existence very largely to the
efforts and enthusiasms of the Commander-in-Chief. On 14
December 1859, the Duke laid the foundation stone of the present
Staff College buildings. The Sandhurst Cadets formed a guard of
honour. It was a sunny but piercingly cold day, and as they stood
knee-deep in the heather, their toes felt like falling off from frost-
bite. H.R.H. laid the first block of masonry, instructed in the task
by the architect. In a brief speech, the Commandant thanked him
for the honour he had accorded the College, and said how fitting
it was that the Duke should have undertaken the ceremony,
since 'the College has been your Royal Highness's actual creation.'

H.R.H. was an advocate of every form of military education.
Mr Gleig, the Chaplain General, who was also Inspector General
of Military Schools, was delighted with the interest shown in his
department by the new Commander-in-Chief. In the old days,
Gleig had been a close friend of the Duke of Wellington, but they
had become estranged because of the Inspector General's introduction of schoolmasters to the Army. 'By God!' exclaimed
Wellington, 'if there is a mutiny in the Army—and in all probability we shall have one—you'll see that these new-fangled
schoolmasters will be at the bottom of it.'

In 1862, not long after the opening of the new Staff College
buildings, the Sandhurst Cadets mutinied. In the grounds of the
Military College stood an old fort, originally constructed to give
practical instruction in gunnery. After an enthusiastic start, it had
long since fallen into disuse. Exasperated by irritating discipline,

and provoked by the food offered them, the Cadets secretly provisioned this old redoubt, withdrew behind its solid defences, and refused to come out until their grievances were redressed. The authorities attempted to open negotiations but were warned to keep their distance. Eventually the Governor agreed to consider the Cadets' complaints, on condition they surrendered. He then proceeded to arrest the ringleaders before any redress was offered. Furious at this treachery, and refusing any talk of terms, the Cadets returned to the fort, which they held against all onslaughts. 'Local fire was completely ineffective, and it was necessary to employ ordnance of the heaviest calibre: the Duke of Cambridge, whose weighty and lurid verbal metal reduced the fort. He saw that justice was done, restored the broken corporals to their rank, and left for London, the cadets' cheers ringing in his ears.'[22] The episode was characteristic of the paternal nature of the office of Commander-in-Chief.

At the end of every year the Duke appeared at the Staff College and inspected the Cadets. There were certain features of the visit which froze into ritual. After hearing the Director General of Military Education read a report on the attainments of candidates for the Staff, H.R.H. was shepherded into one of the lecture halls, where 'specimens of the work done during the year were submitted for his approval. "Verr gude, verr gude," the Duke used to grunt, as he passed some exercise along to the Adjutant General and the other big-wigs brought along in his train, who murmured their admiration. It was the practice in the second year for the seniors to carry out a survey of a considerable tract of country, each of them doing a different area representing perhaps a square mile or so. Colonel Richards then pieced these different sketches together, pasting them on to a vast board—no mean achievement, and one that called for much erasure, for a good deal of give and take, and for a liberal expenditure of pigments. Some officers would have coloured their woods the tint of cooked spinach, while others had preferred the hue of a young lettuce. Some would have depicted buildings in a delicate pink; others would show them like clots of blood. But in the Colonel's cunning hands these crudities disappeared, the work of his pupils appeared as one harmonious whole, and when the vast board was hung up on the wall the result, at a distance at least, was pleasing to the eye.

'A regular programme was always followed. The Duke's attention was drawn to this work of art, and while he was gazing at it somebody, put up to it or knowing his cue, remarked in an undertone, "But it surely must have taken an officer a long time to map out all that country all by himself." "Tut, tut," interrupted H.R.H., "you don't understand. It's the work of a whole lot of these officers each doing his separate bit. See here." And he would peer and would point to some spot where the joinings of two bits of paper were particularly conspicuous. After that he went off to his lunch in high good humour, and all was well.'[23] On one occasion an irreverent cadet inserted on the margin of the combined map: 'To the Grouse Moor.' 'Humph! Grouse Moor,' grunted the Duke. 'By Jove, you're lucky fellows having grouse shooting at your very doors. Didn't know you had grouse in these parts.'

Luncheon provided the culmination of the ritual, although unfortunately in an unimaginative desire to please, not wholly foreign to military catering, the main course was invariably the same. The Duke having once rashly expressed delight at being offered pork chops, word went round every mess in the Army that no dish was more appreciated by the Commander-in-Chief. Consequently, for forty years, he lived on a never-ending succession of pork chops, until he grew to dread the appearance of the once-relished delicacy. H.R.H.'s visits to the Staff College grew more frequent when his own sons were passing through the nearby Military Academy. On 13 December 1864, he 'spoke to the Sandhurst Cadets on the impropriety of their conduct at Blackwater Fair . . . Dear Gussy [Augustus FitzGeorge] carried the colours and looked very well. He has passed a most excellent examination, eighteenth on the list without purchase out of the forty vacancies.'

On the Parade Ground, the Duke of Cambridge was often 'priceless.' 'His comments on his inspections were a joy to the select few who heard them. He once reviewed in Hyde Park the three battalions of Grenadiers who, after a long interval, happened to be in London together; and summed up as follows: "In all my experience of reviews in England, Ireland or on the Continent of Europe, I have never witnessed such a damnable exhibition of incompetence as has been shown by the Grenadier Guards to-day.

When the Cease Fire sounded, the First Battalion was firing at the Serpentine; the Second Battalion was firing at the Marble Arch; and God Almighty knows where the Third Battalion was firing. I don't." '24 Once on parade he was storming against the habit of swearing in the Army and wound up his tirade by saying, 'I was talking it over with the Queen last night, and her Majesty says she is damned if she will have it.'25 H.R.H. was almost too expert in drill, and few deficiencies escaped his unyielding gaze. 'Where are the pioneers?' he asked the Colonel of a defaulting battalion. 'I don't see them.' 'In front of the leading company, your Royal Highness.' 'Have they got their picks and shovels with them?' 'Certainly, your Royal Highness. Do you want them to do anything?' 'Yes,' said the Duke. 'I want them to dig a very deep and very wide hole, and then bury this battalion in it.'

The Duke did not confine his energies merely to inspecting. On field days he often personally took command, and it was a rare occasion if victory were conceded to his opponents. In 1861 H.R.H. was appointed Colonel-in-Chief of the Royal Artillery. On the morning after dining with them, a field day was held, the Commander-in-Chief taking over half the garrison with which to launch an attack, and Sir Richard Davies, the Commandant, who had commanded the Artillery in the Crimean War, taking up a defensive position on high ground with the other half. 'The Duke advanced his force straight at the enemy's position, no cover was utilized, and when the position was near, a magnificent battalion of marines, without taking the trouble to deploy, charged and captured it, having heroically disregarded the fire of three batteries, which slated them for some hundreds of yards across the open. Little attention was paid to tactical considerations and taking cover in those days. The decision arrived at by the Umpire . . . was that the Duke had been successful in his entirely direct attack, and that the honours of the day rested with him. We, on the opposing side, who had poured artillery and infantry fire for half an hour into the serried masses of His Royal Highness, were of an opposite opinion. Since those days I have been fortunate enough to acquire a large and varied experience as regards manoeuvres in other countries than my own, and I can recall no single instance in which a prince of the blood royal, who happened to be in command on one side, was not adjudged to have been successful.'[26]

The Indian Mutiny was the first campaign with which H.R.H. was concerned as Commander-in-Chief. News of the outbreak reached England at the end of June 1857. In July, Sir Colin Campbell, who had served under the Duke in the Crimea, was appointed Commander-in-Chief of the Army in India, to succeed General Anson, who had died of cholera. 'Colin Campbell came,' wrote H.R.H. in his Diary on 12 July, 'and I took him to the Queen to take leave of her, and she was most gracious to him. He then took leave of my mother and sister, and then I said goodbye to him, with really a very heavy heart, for I love that fine soldier and respect him more than any words can describe.' Sir Colin, despite forbidding difficulties, managed to restore order in India, not without the help of an abundance of advice from the Horse Guards. As always, H.R.H. was concerned for the welfare of the troops, and pressed Sir Colin in May 1858 to go into 'summer quarters' and not risk exposing his men to the savage heat of the Indian sun. His anxiety did not end there, for he rebuked Sir Colin himself for moving about, as Wellington had done in Portugal, with an insufficient escort. Nobody, except the Duke of Cambridge, was in a position to criticize a commander in the field to his face. 'I think that you exposed yourself a great deal. I cannot say anything against this, but I do hope that you will always bear in mind in this operation that the country looks to you to carry out the great work in hand, and that if anything were to happen to you I really do not know what we should do, as I know of *nobody* who could replace you efficiently . . . I have almost a mind to be *angry* with you. . . . Remember, my dear friend, you are not simple Colin Campbell, but Commander-in-Chief of Her Majesty's forces in India, and that the latter is a very different personage from what the former may wish to consider himself.'[27]

In the year of the Mutiny, the Duchess of Gloucester became ill. 'No old nurse,' she told Princess Mary Adelaide, 'could have taken more care of me than George did.'[28] On 30 April at five o'clock in the morning, the Duke and his mother watched her die. 'After sitting up during the whole night, at two o'clock the end of our dearest Aunt was evidently approaching . . . Towards three all were in the room and Hawkins and Hills watching attentively said that it would not last many minutes. Still the struggle, without being apparently painful, was a long one, and at five fifteen after a deep sigh our beloved Aunt breathed her last without pain or suffering. It was an awful and most distressing moment. All behaved nobly . . . We had a short prayer before death and another after it. Nothing could surpass the solemnity of the moment . . . Dined alone at my home, and felt most wretched, for I have lost the best friend I possessed on earth.' The whole Cambridge family were deeply moved by her death. 'We young people,' wrote Princess Mary, 'that is to say, George, Augusta, and I,' loved her 'as a second mother.' She was an angelic being, and 'I trust that one day I may follow her bright example, and resemble her in mind and heart as well as in name.'[29]

The Duke had several meetings with the Queen and Prince Consort to discuss the funeral arrangements. On 8 May, the sad day arrived, although it 'had the advantage at all events of fine weather. At eight fifteen I went to Gloucester House. Everything was ready, and at nine punctually the procession started for Paddington Station. It was a most dreadful moment to see the body of the beloved one carried lifelessly out of the house she had been mistress of and loved so well . . . Returned home to the Palace to breakfast, and at ten fifteen drove to the Queen's Private Station of the S.W.R. Thence by special train with the Prince of Wales to Windsor. Mama and my sisters joined us at Richmond. We were at Windsor at eleven thirty. Prince Albert had already arrived. At twelve the mournful procession began to arrive from Slough. All was admirably conducted. The funeral ceremony then commenced and was beautifully performed by the Dean reading and the Choir singing. Nothing could be more beautifully impressive, and not a dry eye was to be found in the Church. As to myself, no words can describe how I felt on the occasion. I was conducting to its last resting place that being whom I most respected and venerated on earth. May God have mercy on her soul, and may I have the happiness of joining that blessed soul in Eternity, however miserably unworthy I am!'

The following day, as one of the Duchess's Executors, he went to hear the reading of the Will. 'It is a beautiful Will, not anybody forgotten, and her kindly feelings of charity expressed throughout all quite beautifully. There are things left to everybody: annuities to the servants, the plate to Mary and a good many jewels —and all that is not willed away to myself as her absolute heir. How beautifully she has ever behaved to me, really in a manner for which I can never feel or prove myself sufficiently grateful.' Gloucester House, which the Duke occupied until his death in 1904, stood at the west corner of Park Lane. Although the house contained many fine apartments, he used three small rooms at the back, where the prospect was mainly roofs and chimneys. He also inherited from the Duchess many possessions which had belonged to her father, George III.

Another royal death, which took place in 1861, had a profound influence on H.R.H.'s career, for the Queen's protracted widowhood left him to perform many of her duties. In December the Prince Consort caught a feverish cold. Some attributed it to a hasty visit to Cambridge, undertaken after he had received the news of a romantic escapade in which the Prince of Wales had been involved earlier in the year. Others blamed the Eton College Volunteers, who held a review on the South Terrace at Windsor, which Prince Albert, despite a chill, felt obliged to attend. It was a mild enough day, but although wearing a fur-lined overcoat, he felt as though cold water was being poured down his back.

The Duke was kept closely informed of the progress of Prince Albert's illness. Every day, sometimes even twice a day, he was sent a note by Sir Charles Phipps, the Prince's Private Secretary. 'The Prince,' he wrote on 7 December, 'I am sorry to say is not any better, indeed his disorder has again declared itself as a fever of the kind sometimes described as Gastric Fever. Symptoms are I am glad to say all favourable, but it is a very tedious disorder, and we must not expect improvement for a fortnight yet. Your Royal Highness knows the Queen well enough to be aware that Her Majesty cannot bear to be alarmed and therefore if Your Royal Highness writes to Her Majesty it should be in a cheering tone. I do not think that Her Majesty could at present see anyone, but she is perfectly calm and cheerful.'

11 December: The Queen is quite well and keeps very cheerful, looking always at the bright side, but she is constantly, except when she takes a drive, attending the Prince, and if I am to speak sincerely to your Royal Highness would, I think, not be disposed to see anyone at present. The Prince is of course quite unequal to receiving anybody.

13 December: Although the Prince had not a good night last

night the material symptoms have not, I am assured by the
doctors, been prejudically affected by it, and His Royal Highness is not considered worse than he was yesterday.

13 December: Your Royal Highness will believe with what
unspeakable grief I have to announce to you that the Prince
Consort's illness has taken a very unfavourable appearance, and
the doctors are in much and deep anxiety. They are not without
fear for the night.

So alarmed was the Duke by the news, that he took the seven
o'clock train to Windsor on the morning of 14 December.
'Found the Prince had got over the night and was a shade better,
but I observed from the countenances of the medical men that they
entertained but little hope of real amendment. Saw the Prince of
Wales, who had arrived from Cambridge during the night. Did
not see the Queen, but saw Alice who has behaved most beautifully throughout.' H.R.H. returned to London the same evening,
only to be awoken that night with the news of the Prince's death,
brought to him in a message from Sir Charles. 'The most dreadful
event that could, I believe, occur to this country has fallen upon it.
My beloved master expired at ten minutes before eleven, so
peacefully and tranquilly that it was hardly possible to say when
his last breath was drawn. . . . The Queen, the Prince of Wales,
and the Princesses, with the Prince and Princess of Leiningen,
surrounded the bed and watched the last moments of the best man
that I ever met with in my life. The Queen has shewn herself to be
possessed of great strength of mind. Overwhelmed, beaten to the
ground with grief, her self-control and good sense have been quite
wonderful. If aid and support and assistance can be given her by
those far below her—how many thousands there are who would
give their lives up to such a task. But I am not fit to write to your
Royal Highness for my heart is broken—though my feelings at
such a time should not be mentioned.'[30]

On the 15th the Duke returned once more to Windsor, still
too dazed to realize how fearful was the blow which had fallen.
'Nobody can have any idea of how great the loss must be to the

poor dear Queen and to the Country. I went to Windsor by eight o'clock train, arriving soon after nine. Found all at the castle in an awful state of consternation and despair, though as calm and resigned as it was possible, under the circumstances, to conceive. . . . I attended prayers in the Chapel at twelve, and after that saw the Queen for a moment. I found her fearfully affected, but still able to give vent to her feelings in a profusion of tears. She is behaving nobly in her heavy affliction.'

The Duke was so agitated by the calamity that he took to his bed, and was forbidden to attend the funeral, although for a time he declared he would go, in defiance of the doctors' advice. His sister, Princess Mary, thought that 'the worry and excitement had well nigh driven him into a fever.' Grieved as he was by the Prince's death, there had been moments when little love was lost between them. The Duchess of Cambridge 'abhorred' the Prince Consort, possibly for supplanting her son in the Queen's affection; and Prince Albert was always suspicious of the Cambridges, and of their influence on the Prince of Wales. The Queen, writing to the King of the Belgians in 1863, recalled her husband's fear that 'Bertie' would be led astray by his 'Uncle' George. She refers to 'a mad and very imprudent idea' of her son joining the Cambridge family in Germany, 'the very *worst* society for Bertie possible, which my Angel said he must be kept out of.'[31]

The death of the Prince Consort left many offices vacant, and although the Queen felt unable to fill such posts immediately, she let the Duke know through Phipps that she proposed to appoint him to the Colonelcy of the Grenadier Guards. Writing from Osborne on 6 January 1862, Sir Charles said, 'The Queen with a feeling which Your Royal Highness will well understand and appreciate feels an insuperable objection to an immediate filling up of the offices which have by so lamentable a misfortune become vacant. Such a course would be repulsive and intolerable to Her Majesty. But the Queen thinks it may be satisfactory to Your Royal Highness to learn that it is Her Majesty's intention, whenever the time for such an appointment shall come, to offer Your Royal Highness the Colonelcy of the Grenadier Guards. This is a subject upon which you may well imagine the Queen finds it impossible to write herself, as realizing the loss which makes all the rest of her life a blank to Her Majesty.'[32]

Fortunately the life of the Royal Family was not all sorrow and mourning, and the wedding of the Prince of Wales in 1863 was, as the Duke described it, 'a great day for Old England.' The Cambridges were delighted with Princess Alexandra of Denmark and thought it 'a charming marriage.' The Queen also formed a high opinion of her daughter-in-law. 'Dear Alix' was frequently employed to reform her husband. She was instructed, for example, to prevent him smoking cigars after dinner, in which, if she ever made the attempt, she was far from successful. 'Beloved Albert so *highly* disapproved it, which ought to be enough to deter Bertie from it.'[33]

For the Duke an even more important wedding was that of his sister Mary. The Prince of Wales met Prince Teck at the court of the King of Hanover, and invited him to Sandringham. Further visits to England followed, and he became engaged to Princess Mary in March 1866, the proposal being made in the garden of Kew Cottage. The Duchess of Cambridge and the Duke were both delighted, for there had been anxious times when it seemed possible that no suitable offer would ever be made. Princess Mary was generous, impulsive and entertaining, but she was a 'mountain of a girl,' and her massive proportions scarcely hinted at the attraction of her character. Prince Teck, however, was undaunted. 'The young couple,' wrote the Duke on 6 April, 'looked and seemed supremely happy. It is a great event in my family, and I must say I think it is a *very happy one*. He is a charming person and likely to make dear Mary an excellent husband. It is a real pleasure to see Mary so thoroughly satisfied at the resolution come to.'

The wedding was arranged for 12 June, but very nearly had to be postponed, because the date did not suit the Queen, who insisted that she must have 'full three weeks rest' at Balmoral, and could not therefore return from Scotland until 13 June. In the end she grudgingly changed her plans and attended the ceremony, which though 'very trying,' was nevertheless 'a satisfaction,' and she trusted 'the beginning of many years of happiness.' On 26 May 1867, 'dear Mary was confined at one minute before twelve o'clock,' and gave birth to 'a charming, healthy little girl with powerful lungs.' This child, destined to become Queen Mary, was christened at Kensington Palace. Her Godfathers were her uncle the Duke of Cambridge (who was one day to become God-father to her eldest son, the present Duke of Windsor) and the Prince of Wales, later Edward VII.

The year of his sister's marriage saw the defeat of Austria in the six weeks' war, and it became evident that the Prussian Army, with its magnificent General Staff under Von Moltke, could not only win wars with lightning rapidity, but provided a lesson in organization and tactics which it would be dangerous to ignore. The Commander-in-Chief fully appreciated the importance of studying the methods of other armies. In 1864 he wrote to the Secretary for War, telling him that the Horse Guards were insufficiently informed about what was going on elsewhere, and suggesting that the expense—for he rightly anticipated objections on that ground—of Military Attachés was completely justified by their value. 'In the present most disturbed state of Europe, when military operations and preparations are going on in so many states, I think it really would be of the greatest importance that we should have a Military Attaché at all our principal missions, such as Berlin, Vienna, Copenhagen, St Petersburg and indeed I think it would be as well to extend this system even to America.'[34]

One thing which made the Prussians' military system so effective was their vast trained reserves for use in emergency. The Duke in 1866 wrote a memorandum on the subject for the War Minister's consideration. He began by pointing out that in England there was 'no sort of Reserve to fall back upon with the exception of our Militia.' On the other hand, most continental powers were 'in a position to expand their forces at the shortest possible notice through the powers of conscription.' His suggested remedy was to allow regular soldiers after seven years' service to go on unlimited leave, on condition they returned to the colours in time of war. Furthermore he proposed that soldiers on enlisting should engage themselves to serve on the Reserve if and when they left the Army.[35] The plan for forming a Reserve by introducing a seven-year enlistment period was later taken up by Cardwell, who inaugurated a scheme for short service.

In his old age the Duke acquired the reputation of obstructing changes and of suspecting anything which even hinted at reform; and it cannot be denied that with increasing years he became more conservative and retrograde. 'I am an old fashioned person,' he wrote in 1883, 'and though fully prepared to go to a certain extent with the spirit of the age, I am for letting well alone unless the necessity for change is very clearly demonstrated.'[36] But in his early years as a soldier he was wide awake to the faults of the Service and eager to make improvements. 'Probably there has been no short period more fruitful in Army reforms than the two years from 1859 to 1861, during which Sidney Herbert, as Secretary of State for War, and the Duke of Cambridge, as Commander-in-Chief, laboured shoulder to shoulder for the good of the Service.'[37] The period of military reorganization following the Crimean War owed much to his inspiration. Officers were made to realize that soldiering was 'something more than filling in the time between breakfast and lunch.' Even the Cavalry, that sacrosanct arm in which H.R.H. had received his early training, came under his restless scrutiny. He told the Queen, 'I have long felt a great anxiety about making some change in the Cavalry to simplify matters in that branch of our Service in which at present there are a good many anomalies.'[38] During the first twelve years, from 1856 to 1868, in which the Duke was Commander-in-Chief, he set up a department of Military Education, he revolutionized the Staff College, he pressed for joint manoeuvres of all arms so that 'officers and men should be thoroughly trained and prepared for war,' he called attention to the need for a trained Reserve, and he conducted a continual struggle against reductions.

The Duke's financial problems did not end with the Army

estimates, for his own sons showed a capacity to spend money which would have been wholly admirable in a Secretary for War, but which was disturbing in Officer Cadets. In 1858 H.R.H. had to send one of his A.D.C.s to Sandhurst to 'pay George's bills and blow up the tradesmen for giving him so much credit.' Five years later George was in money troubles at Malta, and in 1866 he had 'lost at the Gibraltar races and is in great difficulties. It is too sad, for in every other respect he is a nice, intelligent and gentleman-like lad.'[39]

Adolphus, who was an officer in the Navy, frequently distressed his father by threatening to leave the Service. 'Adolphus expresses a wish to leave the Navy,' wrote the Duke in his Diary, on 31 March 1863. 'This I have refused, but have got him transferred to the Flag Ship of the Channel Fleet . . . which will give him a change from the dull station of the Cape.' Later his ship took him to Australia where his father warned him to be 'prudent.' 'A young fellow is easily laid hold of by a nice and pretty girl, but it would be such a disadvantage to you to commit yourself in any way in this respect.'[40]

Adolphus's wild oats were sown prodigally, and an angry correspondence ensued between father and son. The young man was accustomed to purchase extravagant presents. 'You give no sort of reason,' writes the Duke, 'for buying those earrings worth £27 for some common woman, who would I should think have been well satisfied with the present of *one pound*, if not less . . . I regret the loss of that beautiful pin. Probably some other female friend of yours has walked off with it. It is most sad.' In another letter, H.R.H. enclosed two extracts, 'one from the *Morning Post*, the other from the *Army and Navy Gazette*, and I need hardly tell you how much I have been pained to find your name thus publicly noted in so discreditable a manner. Of course everybody talks of these things and instead of my sons' names being creditably brought to public notice, it comes before the world in the most unsatisfactory manner it is possible to conceive. This is now the second time that your name has come to public notice discreditably, and I confess to being both disgusted and very angry.

I hear from every variety of quarters that you are most unprincipled in the non payment of your debts and in fact you owe money in every possible direction.' He refers to a bill of £19 at a cigar shop, and mentions the earrings again. 'Certainly they have not been bestowed on anybody at home. You have left heavy debts at Portsmouth. But even worse than all this you have borrowed money of Charles who in the kindness of his heart lent it to you, and who can ill spare it himself . . . Have you not actually had the meanness to owe ten shillings to a billiard marker who poor devil has not sufficient to live from day to day? Is this gentlemanlike, is this honourable, is this not enough to disgust and enrage the most indulgent Father . . .? I will stand it no longer . . . I shall not again be found to listen to any of your excuses and subterfuges, which you may have thought have thrown dust in my eyes. Who is this person to whom these earrings have been given? You are ruining yourself by the bad company you keep. You think this very fine no doubt, let me tell you it is most dishonourable, very ungentlemanlike, and will not be tolerated by me, or indeed by Society at large. A man who behaves without honour to his neighbours in the payment of his just debts, must be ruined not only in purse, but in character.' The Duke threatened to stop Adolphus's allowance if he did not mend his ways. 'If you do what is right you know you will be well supported by me, if you do not, but continue in the sad course you now alas seem to have adopted, I shall decline to disgrace myself by having any share in your discreditable acts. Your very annoyed father, George.'[41]

Despite his father's threats and entreaties, Adolphus continued to run up debts, and tradesmen, desperate for money, complained to the Duke. 'It is utterly impossible to go on in this way,' he told Adolphus. 'I am more wretched about you and George than words can describe. If after this payment you do not keep out of debt . . . you must go to the wall and take the consequences of your folly. I am not going to ruin myself for you, of that you may rest assured.' A letter arrived at Queen Street from a money lender. 'Mama opened it by my advice and found it contained a threat that if you did not repay what you owed at once he would declare you an outlaw!' Distinctly declining to assist again, the Duke cleared £800 of debt as a twenty-first birthday present for Adolphus, telling him, what was only too apparent, that he had no idea of the value of money, and that 'you boys will be the death of me if you go on in this way.'[42] These troubles, however, were only a beginning. Before he had finished H.R.H. was to pay over £100,000 to rescue his sons from financial disasters.

Apart from absences at shooting parties, and short visits abroad, Louisa and her husband lived happily together in Queen Street, with only an occasional cloud to overcast the radiance of their marriage. Louisa's jealousy sometimes erupted. 'I have always thought,' she wrote on 8 December 1856, 'and still believe that there can be no love without jealousy.' True to this maxim, she became suspicious of the length of a visit her husband paid to Sir George Wombwell at Newburgh Park, and provoked from him a protestation of innocence which must have left him feeling most uneasy. 'I swear to you my darling by everything most sacred, that I have ever kept the oath I swore to you that I am yours and yours only and ever have been so, and that I have *never* made love to any other woman or wished to do so.'[43]

Louisa, although Society ignored her marriage, was nevertheless expected to behave as if she were Duchess of Cambridge. H.R.H. was horrified to hear that she had even momentarily contemplated acting in private theatricals. 'As regards the question you put to me about your taking a part in some private theatricals, I never thought darling that you put that question to me seriously, but now that I find you do, I must confess that I have a *very great objection* to it and hope you will *not* do so.'[44] But generally she was free to live her own life, entertain her own friends, and give parties at which her husband was more a guest than the host. Queen Street was strictly her establishment and Gloucester House was his. 'Went to Queen Street,' wrote H.R.H. on 20 December 1865, 'where Louisa had her annual little Christmas dinner, which went off very well. We had about thirty people, a very good sit down supper and kept it up till past three o'clock.'

K

In 1867 Louisa became ill and was so crippled that she had to be carried from room to room. For the rest of her life she remained something of an invalid and bore her sufferings with unprotesting courage. 'Louisa, though perhaps better on the whole, is in a very suffering state and really perfectly helpless. It is painfully sad to witness, and she bears her misfortunes with wonderful resignation.'[45]

While Louisa was recovering at Buxton, the Duke was left to look after the house in Queen Street, and a crisis soon threatened. Writing to his wife from the Library of the House of Lords, he told her that there was servant trouble. 'Ramsthal tells me that a very awkward thing has happened in Queen Street. The Cook told him this morning that Julia [a maid] had had a man in her room last night, and on her remonstrating with her, she refused to open her room door till she threatened to call a policeman.' Then both the man and Julia went out all night. 'When Ramsthal spoke to her this morning she said it was her *cousin*, which he explained to her made no difference, in his opinion, but Cook says it was a *Captain* somebody.' H.R.H. asked Louisa what she would like done, warning her that if Julia were dismissed the cook might go too for fear of being left alone in the house.[46] It was a domestic experience from which Royal Dukes are customarily sheltered.

Louisa, wishing to amuse herself in Buxton, asked her husband to send her the Queen's *Highland Journal* which had recently come out. He replied that he had not been given a copy and had been unable to buy one as it was already out of print. 'It is a pity,' he added, 'that it was ever published.' A day later, on 11 August, he received a handsomely bound copy, 'with a very pretty inscription in the fly leaf, "To dear George in recollection of his dear friend and cousin, from his affectionate cousin." Very nice I think, don't you?'

A FLOOD OF REFORM

I N the autumn of 1868 Disraeli decided upon a General Election. The Conservatives, despite having extended the franchise the year before, were heavily defeated, and Gladstone was returned to power with a majority of one hundred and twelve. The Duke watched the campaign with mounting anxiety. 'The elections,' he wrote on 21 November, 'are going most horribly against the government and I fear the next Parliament will be a most mischievious and radical one. God knows what they will not do!' The next day he heard rumours about the names of the new ministers. 'Mr Lowe they say is to have the War Office. This would be *awful* for me.' Writing to Adolphus FitzGeorge on 4 December, H.R.H. told him 'it is generally understood that Mr Gladstone is at this moment forming a new government. What this may lead to, Heaven only knows, but I presume it must end in considerable reductions in both Army and Navy . . . I regret all this deeply, though as you know, I take no share in politics. I confine myself to the duties of my office.' On 7 December the new Ministry was announced. 'Mr Cardwell is the new Secretary for War, a most gentlemanlike man, with whom it will be pleasant to act. I confess, however, that I am under considerable apprehension that large reductions of establishment may be contemplated . . . although we have not a man or officer more than we really want or require.'[1]

The new War Minister was educated at Winchester and Balliol, and derived from those institutions an invincible conviction that his high-minded liberalism involved a unique revelation of ultimate Truth. His Oxford career was impressive. He achieved a first in Maths and Classics, and was President of the Union. He was called to the Bar in 1838, entered Parliament four years later, and at the age of thirty two was appointed Secretary to the Treasury by Peel, who greatly admired his ability. Subsequently he became President of the Board of Trade, Chief Secretary for Ireland and Secretary of State for the Colonies. At the time of his appointment as Minister for War he was fifty five, six years older than the Commander-in-Chief.

During his political career he had formed an unfavourable opinion of the workings of the War Office. He was a man to whom economy and administrative competence were an end as much as a means, and whatever else might be said of his new Department, it could not be claimed that it was either cheap or efficient. Cardwell believed that the Commander-in-Chief at the Horse Guards should be subordinated to the Secretary for War at the War Office. The Army, he argued, was a parliamentary army, and he, as the Minister responsible to Parliament, could not tolerate a divided authority. His party had been elected 'to obtain the greatest amount of efficiency at the smallest cost,' and this could only be successfully accomplished by means of 'a complete reformation of a system now universally pronounced to be unsatisfactory.' In a paper submitted to Gladstone,[2] Cardwell outlined his plans for subordinating the military element to the civilian; for abolishing Purchase and with it the aristocratic principle so offensive to the Liberal party; and for making the Board of Admiralty a model for the government of the Army.

It was an attractive enough programme to radical minds, but calculated to inspire the boundless indignation of the Queen, the hostility of the majority of the Army, and a stubborn rearguard action on the part of its Commander-in-Chief.

Until he was appointed Viceroy of India in 1872, Cardwell's Under-Secretary of State was Lord Northbrook. He was a very much more diplomatic person than his austere master, and skilfully sugared the bitter pill which H.R.H. was required to swallow. The moment the Liberals came to power, Northbrook was appointed chairman of a committee instructed to report on Army organization and to recommend improvements. It followed in the footsteps of an enquiry headed by Sir James Graham, which in 1860 had reviewed the relationship of the Secretary of State to the Commander-in-Chief, and had investigated War Office organization. Graham told Cardwell, 'I assure you the only word which will describe it properly is "chaos."' The War Office had developed piecemeal over the centuries as a result of changes and compromises in which temporary exigencies had only too often obscured basic principles. It was haunted by the ghosts of extinct offices and Cardwell found himself curator of a constitutional museum. Northbrook advocated the ending of the 'dual control' of the Army, the passage of legislation confirming the Secretary of State's complete responsibility for all military matters, and the transfer of the Commander-in-Chief and his staff from the Horse Guards to the War Office. These proposals, not surprisingly, were modelled on those which Cardwell had also outlined to Gladstone.

The Duke of Cambridge fought desperately to prevent his removal to the War Office, then situated in Pall Mall. It clouded the issue to pretend that it was merely an administrative simplification. The prestige of the Commander-in-Chief, even the prerogative of the Crown, was threatened by the move. For the Duke to be turned out of the Horse Guards 'would be a degradation which would altogether alter his status in the estimation of the Army and public,' and would, in his opinion, he told Cardwell in December 1869, 'be most injurious to the interests of the Crown, the real head of the Army . . .' It was largely because what the Duke said was true that the plan appealed to the War Minister.

The Duke, in fact, never denied the Secretary of State's sole responsibility to Parliament, but what he claimed was that the Crown delegated to him the 'active command of the Queen's forces,' which could scarcely be undertaken by a civilian. In a letter to Cardwell he wrote: 'It may be urged, and truly urged, that the Secretary of State for War is responsible to the country for all matters connected with the Army, and is also the adviser to Her Majesty on all military matters. I do not for one moment deny this; and you will do me the justice to say that I have ever held this to be the correct and constitutional view of the case. But the Secretary of State, being a high political functionary and a civilian, cannot, as such, take any active command of the Queen's forces, and these duties are consequently delegated to the Commander-in-Chief appointed by the Crown, and to whom the Crown, under the advice of her Ministers, delegates the supreme military authority.'

Finding Cardwell stubborn, the Duke proposed a compromise. The Commander-in-Chief, he suggested, should have a room in the War Office and the Secretary for War should have a room at the Horse Guards. 'There would be more give and take in the arrangement . . . We have now a telegraph between this office and yours. The most instantaneous communication can thus go on between us, and the touch of this magic instrument would bring me to you in less than five minutes . . .'[3] It was an ingenious suggestion, but Cardwell was reluctant to be accommodating, although under bombardment from the Queen as well as the Commander-in-Chief. One concession he could not avoid. While suitable quarters were being prepared for the Duke in Pall Mall, a building with fewer amenities than a workhouse, a section of the War Office had to be sent to the Horse Guards. Lord Haliburton was chosen for the unenviable task of heading the intruders who were painfully aware of the frosty welcome in store. 'To an absolute fearlessness Haliburton united that peculiar blend of tact and force which is only found in strong men. He was one of those fortunate people, who, without being thick-skinned in the vulgar sense, are impervious to hostile atmosphere. He marched his staff of clerks into their new surroundings as if they were merely moving from the west to the east wing of the old buildings in Pall Mall. It was not a case of smoothing over difficulties; they simply ceased to exist. On the morning upon which the transfer was effected the Duke came down in choleric mood, prepared to criticize the new department as if it were a regiment with a black mark against it paraded for annual inspection. He found everything working with the smoothness of a well-oiled machine. H.R.H. was an outspoken prince, and he ever gave frank expression to his feelings. "Well, I'm damned," was his only commentary.'[4]

The new War Office quarters were first used in 1871, the Commander-in-Chief, on the Queen's insistence, being provided with a special entrance. 'Went to War Office,' wrote the Duke on 23 September, 'where, alas! the dear old Horse Guards are now established. It is a sad change, and the state of discomfort from all being unfinished is something really quite dreadful, and makes me feel very unhappy.' As an act of reverent, some called it childish, defiance, H.R.H. asserted his independence by heading his correspondence 'Horse Guards,' despite the move to Pall Mall. After preliminary protests, the Secretary for War let the matter rest. 'I hear that Mr Cardwell foresees difficulties about dating letters from Horse Guards when we are at the War Office, but I hope he will give way. It is all very well to break up old traditions but these are the very life and soul of an army . . .'[5]

In order to complete the subordination of the Horse Guards to the War Office, Cardwell drafted an Order-in-Council defining the Duke's duties. The Queen, on 28 June 1870, signed it with much reluctance, for it removed the Commander-in-Chief from his sole and immediate dependence on the Crown. *Blackwood's Magazine* described the measure as 'the severest blow that has been struck at the monarchical principle . . . since the times of the Long Parliament.'

Cardwell, with his Treasury experience behind him, was

expected by his colleagues to effect large economies in Army estimates, and this he achieved by making the Colonies responsible for their own defence, and by reducing the size of the forces at home. Such reductions were effected despite vigorous protests from the Queen. She told Cardwell that she had serious misgivings about 'the extent to which it is proposed to withdraw troops from the Colonies.' She trusted the matter had been discussed and considered by the Cabinet. 'The Queen could never forgive herself if she found that she had inadvertently given her assent to anything that could risk the safety of her colonial possessions.' When this policy of denuding the Empire of regular troops involved the country in the Kaffir and Zulu wars in South Africa, the Queen wrote to Disraeli in 1879 underlining the lesson which 'is again taught us,' but which is so seldom heeded: '*Never let the Army and Navy down so low as to be obliged to go to great expense in a hurry* . . . We had but small forces at the Cape; hence the great amount having to be sent out in a hurry . . . All this causes great trouble and expense afterwards. If we are to maintain our position as a first-rate Power . . . we must, with our Indian Empire and large Colonies be prepared for attack and wars somewhere or other *continually*. And the true economy will be to be always ready. Lord Beaconsfield can do his country the greatest service by repeating this again and again and by seeing it carried out. It will prevent war.'[6] General Airey, writing to the Duke of Cambridge during the Franco-Prussian War, said that events in Europe led him to consider the condition of the British Army, and despite the Government's complacent assurances, he personally believed it lacked 'everything that constitutes an army ready to take the field . . . The consolation is that everything is remediable with money—but money is wanted at the beginning—not in profusion at the end which is our usual plan.'[7]

The Commander-in-Chief implored Cardwell to reconsider the wisdom of these economies. In 1870, when the defeat of France underlined the dangerous depletion of our military resources, he insisted on an interview with Gladstone. 'I felt the necessity,' he told Cardwell, 'of telling him how strongly I feel the need for an increase in men and horses.' The Duke warned the Minister of War of the perils of reducing the staff. 'I hope the Staff may not be cut down too much. When we went to the Crimea we had no staff and felt the serious want of experienced officers for staff duties. If a thoroughly efficient staff be not maintained in peace, you cannot have one when War breaks out, and your army is thus rendered very helpless and inefficient.'[8] But despite the Duke's entreaties, the estimates, far from being increased, were reduced by over a million pounds.

In a memorandum prepared for Cardwell on 22 December 1868, H.R.H. emphasized that emergencies were often unheralded, and it was useless to reduce the Army in times of apparent peace, thinking, if the need arose, that it could at once be expanded. 'There cannot be a doubt in the present state of the world, and more especially of Europe, that, should troubles arise, they are likely to come upon us suddenly and when we may least expect them. All history leads us to this conclusion. Such was the case of the breaking out of the Crimean War, which found us completely unprepared for so great a contest. Such was again the case in the Italian Campaign of 1859, and more recently in the great German contest of 1866. Even our great Indian Mutiny came upon us quite unexpectedly, so that we have two instances affecting the very existence of our Empire, the Crimean War and the Indian Mutiny, in which the absolute necessity for instant vigilance and the power of rapid increase of our forces have been clearly and palpably demonstrated. It is to meet such sudden contingencies that the great Continental Powers have of late largely increased their already enormous means of military power . . . It would be impossible for us entirely to overlook what our neighbours are doing in this direction without taking warning ourselves in time . . . When it is considered that the whole of our Infantry of the Line at home amounts to only 49,291, of that in and on passage to and from our Colonial possessions to only 31,144, and of that in and on passage to and from India to 44,196, making a grand total of 124,631, and that at present we have nothing in the shape of a proper Reserve Force to fill up our battalions in an emergency, it can hardly be thought prudent or wise to diminish this force still further till some regular system has been devised and adopted to meet the very peculiar requirements of the present state of the world.' How unavailing were these protests may be judged from the frequency with which they were repeated.

The Duke found it hard to become accustomed to the cataract of changes in which Cardwell plunged him. 'I am endeavouring to reconcile my mind,' he exclaimed, gasping for breath, 'to the numerous changes which are proposed on so many subjects connected with Army matters, and I hope you will do me the justice to say that I have given every assistance in my power to carry out these changes. There are, however, two points to which I cannot reconcile my mind, the one is the large reduction in Establishment, the other the removal of such a large portion of the troops from the Colonies, and the actual military abandonment of some of these colonies by the entire removal of their garrisons. These two points are to me so serious that I feel bound once more to entreat of you to consider whether something could not be done to mitigate these two evils.'⁹

History is so much orientated to the parliamentary point of view that, although events proved the Duke's predictions right, he has nevertheless been represented as a retrograde whose incessant obstruction prevented Ministers reforming the Army. Military setbacks, instead of being blamed on the politicians who failed to anticipate them, were often ignorantly attributed to the Duke, although he unavailingly demonstrated to successive Secretaries for War that reductions would lead to disaster. He committed the unforgivable enormity of being right and he paid for it by being made a scapegoat.

Once a decision had been reached, the Duke loyally carried it out, although he felt it his duty to do all in his power to prevent mistakes being made while matters were still under discussion. To his own sons, for example, he was prepared to admit that he 'fought' Cardwell in the hope that a Conservative Government would regain office. Writing to Adolphus FitzGeorge on 18

March 1870, he says: 'We live in most anxious times, everything is being changed, everything is being cut down in a most frightful manner. In short nothing can be worse for both Army and Navy. I hold on and am determined to do so in the hope that better times may come.' In another letter to Adolphus written on 1 May 1869 he observed: 'Change is decidedly the order of the day, and our old institutions, which have made us the great nation as thank God we have hitherto been, seem to be a good deal threatened . . . The onslaught on the Army and Navy is very fierce, particularly on the former, but I am fighting a good fight and hope I shall get off victorious.'

The Duke found the Queen a sympathetic audience when discussing Cardwell's shortcomings. As usual, she thought her cousin 'agitated.' 'Saw George,' she records in her Diary on 15 August 1870, 'and found him greatly excited. He told me of all his difficulties, of the obstinacy of Mr Cardwell and want of knowledge of military matters in detail.' Even Wolseley, who greatly admired Cardwell, admitted that the Secretary of State 'was absolutely ignorant of our Army and War.'[10] This, however, he reckoned was not such a handicap as might appear, since the Minister availed himself so freely of Sir Garnet's advice.

The Duke of Cambridge, as Commander-in-Chief, worked with eighteen Secretaries for War. Their ignorance he soon took for granted, but the merit of civilian rule of the Army was lost on him. When regiments had to be sent out to Africa in 1879 they were so depleted that they had to be made up with volunteers. He discussed the matter one evening with his mother, and Lady Geraldine, who, as always, was present, and who recorded the conversation in her Diary. 'The Duke returned from Aldershot where he had this morning [18 February 1879] inspected the troops under order for Africa; every day shows more the abomination of idiotic Cardwell's system!! Every regiment for service having to be brought up to its full numbers by 300 or 400 volunteers from other regiments, destroying all esprit de corps and solidity, starting on a campaign and then not knowing each other, not the officers their men, not one another's names!! The *idiocy* of the English constitution taking an ignorant *civilian*, a stupid *lawyer* full of theories, to organize the Army!!!'

Both the Duke and Cardwell at times thought themselves ill-treated by the other. Cardwell complained that the Duke sabotaged him, expressed his criticism of the Government too freely and too publicly, and was liable to say one thing to his face and something quite different behind his back.[11] H.R.H. believed that the Secretary of State was too inclined to consult everyone but his official advisers, that he failed to obtain the Commander-in-Chief's sanction in circumstances where precedent required him to do so, and that he was always endeavouring to circumvent the Horse Guards. The Duke discussed his ill-treatment with the Queen. 'I sat under the trees where George came and talked with some excitement of the state of affairs, considering that he had not been well treated, and I counselled moderation, calmness and great discretion.' Previously she had spoken to H.R.H. on this vexed subject and agreed that the Government had behaved badly to him. 'After luncheon saw George C. who talked very sensibly, but to whom they have not behaved very well.'[12]

While Mr Delane, Editor of *The Times*, was dining at Marlborough House with the Prince of Wales on 15 July 1870, a note was slipped into his hands. The Duke, who was present, was as disturbed as his host to learn that France had declared war on Prussia. Hostilities could have been prevented, declared Sir Robert Morier, an expert on German affairs, 'if for twenty four hours the British public had been furnished with a backbone.' This was too much for the Commander-in-Chief, who for over a decade had insisted that power politics presupposed the possession of power. 'What the hell,' he asked, 'is the use of a backbone without an army, which we have not got?'[13] The next day H.R.H. received a telegram from Osborne. 'Have telegraphed to Mr Gladstone that steps ought to be taken for our safety and that Parliament ought not to separate without some measures being taken to increase our efficiency in Army and Navy, as no one can tell what we may not be forced into. The conduct of the French is too Iniquitous.'

The outbreak of hostilities nearly produced a crisis at Mecklenburg-Strelitz. The British Ambassador at Berlin, Lord Adolphus Loftus, telegraphed to the Duke on 21 July: 'Persuade Grand Duke of Mecklenburg-Strelitz to return forthwith with his son. If his Royal Highness delays in joining Prussia and National movement he risks his throne . . . Young Prince should at once offer himself to King of Prussia for military service.' Two days later the Ambassador enlarged on his telegram in a letter. He was relieved to hear that the Grand Duke and his family were returning at once to Germany. 'I learnt,' he told H.R.H., 'that national feeling was becoming very strong in the Grand Duchy, that the prolonged absence of the Grand Duke was being ill viewed, and further that unless the Grand Duke came forward to give his adhesion to the popular movement, it was to be feared that some very stringent measures might be resorted to, and we have experience on such occasions Count Bismarck is a man of action. . . . I am happy to learn this morning that the Grand Duke has telegraphed to the King of Prussia, offering the services of the Hereditary Prince [Prince Adolphus] in the Army, and that the Grand Duke and his son are to return immediately.' The Commander-in-Chief telegraphed to the Queen on 24 July asking her to find out through her daughter, the Crown Princess of Prussia, whether the King had received the Grand Duke's offer of help. 'It would be most gracious of you if by some means through dear Vicky, or otherwise, you could ascertain if this offer of service has reached the King, who otherwise might assume that no such offer had ever been made.' In the end it transpired that the Strelitz family were well received in Prussia, were invited to dinner by the King, and Prince Adolphus was attached to the staff of the Crown Prince. Loftus told Granville, the Foreign Secretary, that unfortunately the Grand Duchess had returned to Strelitz without seeing either the Queen of Prussia or the Crown Princess. 'It would have been more politic for her Royal Highness to have done so.'[14] Princess Augusta could never forgive the Prussians for conquering Hanover in 1866, and her loyalty to the German Empire, established in 1871, of which the Grand Duchy became a part, was unenthusiastic. When she died in the winter of 1916, at the age of ninety four, she sent George V a last message from the country with which he was at war. 'Tell the King it is a stout old English heart that is ceasing to beat.'[15]

The Duke, soon after encouraging Prince Adolphus to join the Prussians, had an angry interview with a young English officer who had offered his services to the French and had fought with the army of the Loire. On returning to England the offender was summoned to the Horse Guards and severely rated by the Commander-in-Chief. He was informed that he had behaved abominably, broken countless Queen's Regulations, disgraced the Service, and was fortunate not to be court-martialled. After this fierce rebuke the Duke paused and then muttered under his breath, 'I am bound to say in your place I should have done the same.' The young man's name was Kitchener.[16]

The Duke followed the events of the Franco-Prussian War with a professional interest and kept a special Diary of the Campaign. His letters were full of the battles raging on the Continent, and when he heard of the proclamation of the Third Republic, he prophesied untold trouble for France and Europe. In a letter to Lord Napier of Magdala, 8 September 1870, he wrote: 'The extraordinary events of the past week really surpass all belief and expectation. Marshal MacMahon's army, having got into a most unaccountable corner near Sedan, between the Belgian frontier and the Prussian Armies, has been defeated in three successive battles, and was driven into Sedan where the Emperor surrendered himself as a prisoner of war to the King of Prussia, and the whole French Army there assembled, about 80,000 men, have laid down their arms. There never was such a catastrophe befell a great country since the world began. The Republic has been proclaimed at Paris, and accepted apparently by France, which says it is determined still to hold out, and to stand a siege of Paris. The Germans are now marching on the French Capital, and according to all human calculations, I should say they would enter it within one week. What is next to happen, God only knows, but the events are certainly most grave and I fear it is the commencement of many wars and conflicts throughout the world.'[17]

The success of the Prussians in 1870 was attributed to a bewildering variety of causes, but nobody disputed that conscription, and the large reserves thereby made available, played an important part in their military system. The Duke had already pointed out in 1868 that the English Army lacked any adequate Reserve. In 1870 Cardwell introduced an Army Enlistment Act, which provided that after a period of short service with the Colours, initially six years, men could join the Reserve: a nucleus of trained professional soldiers recallable at a moment's notice. As H.R.H. admitted at the Royal Academy Dinner of 1878, when Short Service 'was first introduced by my noble friend Lord Cardwell, I had some doubts whether it would answer,' but 'I am happy to say that the success of the measure has been complete.' Sometimes setbacks encouraged the Duke to revert to his former suspicions of Cardwell's plan, and certainly he did not always speak of it so enthusiastically, but as he had himself emphasized the urgent need for a trained Reserve, his criticism was confined to deploring the loss of the old, veteran soldiers, and doubting the value of new, untried recruits.

The Queen was even more doubtful than her Commander-in-Chief of the merits of Short Service. When in 1882 she telegraphed to Wolseley after his victory at Tel-el-Kebir, she 'squeezed a drop of lemon juice over her honeyed congratulations.' 'The Queen,' ran part of her message, 'is glad to hear that Sir Garnet entertains such a high regard of her Household Cavalry; she would remind him they are the only Long Service Corps in the Army.'[18] Lord Roberts, a more knowledgeable if less vociferous critic than his Sovereign, who was one day to be Commander-in-Chief, made a speech, after his Kabul campaign in 1880, opposing Short Service. 'Young soldiers,' he said, 'of eighteen or twenty, may be, and probably are, individually as brave as their comrades of maturer age, and as well able to fight when everything is *couleur de rose*; but I will never admit that young soldiers, or those new to each other, are as reliable, in times of difficulty, as old and tried soldiers. What is it that has enabled a comparatively small number of

British troops, over and over again, to face tremendous odds, and win battles against vastly superior numbers? The glorious annals of our regiments give the answer—discipline, *esprit de corps*, and powers of endurance—the three essentials which are absolutely wanting in the young soldier . . . The origin of the short service system was, I understand, the necessity of having a reserve of trained soldiers in England. I fully admit this necessity, but, even after the experiences of 1878, I take leave to doubt whether we can always depend on securing the services of the reserve we are slowly forming, and of this I am quite certain that we are sacrificing our army to obtain a reserve, which, except in the case of a great national danger, it is evidently not intended to make use of.'[19]

On 21 February 1871, the Commander-in-Chief was denounced in the House of Commons. 'Mr Trevelyan brought forward his motion to-day in the shape of an attack upon myself, and my administration. Nothing could be more satisfactory than the debate, which was entirely in my favour, and in which many friends spoke out well, nobody more so than Bernal Osborne. The Division gave a majority of one hundred and eighteen against Mr Trevelyan, the numbers being two hundred and two against eighty three, so I hope this disagreeable question is now disposed of.' Trevelyan's motion was that: 'In the opinion of this House no scheme for military organization can be regarded as complete which does not alter the tenure of the Commander-in-Chief in such a manner as to enable the Secretary of State for War to avail himself of the best administrative talent and the most recent military experience from time to time in the British Army.' Trevelyan, the biographer of his uncle Lord Macaulay, was one of Gladstone's more radical subordinates, and despite courteous references to the Duke's good intentions, his insistence that the Commander-in-Chief should not be a permanent official was something of an indiscretion. The motion provoked speaker after speaker to rise in H.R.H.'s defence. Lord Eustace Cecil claimed that if the officers of the Army were asked if they wished the Duke to continue in his command, an immense majority would say that there was no better man to be found. Cardwell declared that 'if there is one thing which would be more mischievous than another, it would be to have the smallest suspicion of politics' introduced into the office of Commander-in-Chief. Mr Osborne, whose speech H.R.H. particularly appreciated, suggested that Trevelyan had merely regaled the House with a dissertation he had many times starred in the provinces. 'I believe,' he said of the Duke, 'a more honest and conscientious man and a man better fitted for the post, never presided at the Horse Guards.' Turning with scorn to Mr Trevelyan, he continued: 'He endeavours to raise a cloud around the Horse Guards; he talks of purchase, Army agents, flogging, marking with the letter "D," and contagious diseases.' He puts all these together, and he endeavours to blame them on the Duke of Cambridge.[20]

The Secretary for War was informed that his Sovereign trusted the Commander-in-Chief without question. 'The Queen,' she told him on an earlier occasion, 'cannot shut her eyes to the fact that a disposition exists in some quarters (she fears even among some of the subordinate members of the Government, as, for instance, Mr Trevelyan), to run down the Commander-in-Chief, and generally to disparage the military authorities as obstacles to all improvement in our Army administration. So far from this being the case, the Duke of Cambridge has always acted most cordially, as the Queen is sure Mr Cardwell will already have found, with successive Secretaries of State, in promoting and giving effect to all well-considered measures of improvement, and ever since he has been at the head of the Army H.R.H. has deserved the Queen's entire confidence, and is entitled to her best support.' Cardwell himself was not so fortunate. When Queen Victoria heard that the Speaker of the House was about to resign, she at once suggested Cardwell as his successor, because he was 'disliked by the Army,' 'knew nothing of military matters,' and was unfit for his post.[21]

Of all the military measures of Gladstone's Government, the one which provoked the fiercest storm was the abolition of Purchase. 'The system,' as Fortescue observed, 'being utterly illogical, iniquitous and indefensible, commended itself heartily to the British public.' Purchase had arisen in the seventeenth century as an attempt by Colonels charged with raising regiments to recover, in part, the expense of so doing, by requiring the officers they appointed to buy their commissions. These, in their turn, sold their commissions to their successors. Although William III attempted to abolish the practice it was energetically supported by vested interests, and Parliament, ever eager to maintain an Army cheaply, did not feel inclined to terminate a system which saved the taxpayer money.

There were a number of powerful arguments in favour of abolishing Purchase. It was inevitably an aristocratic system, and soldiers without money, whatever their ability, became 'bent and bald under that cruel game of golden leap-frog of which they are the eternal victims.'[22] Many officers hardly troubled to learn the rudiments of their profession, not caring a farthing what their superiors thought of them. Promotion was by bank balance. Guards officers would take hansom cabs to join their battalions in Hyde Park, and considered themselves overworked if their day did not end with luncheon. A Cavalry officer was reputed to have remarked: 'Soldiering would be all right if it only consisted of the band and the Mess; no damned men or horses.' Yet it was such people who in times of need performed feats of staggering heroism, and subalterns, should fate so decree, crushed rebellions and ruled empires. When Purchase was abolished, *Punch* published a notice to 'gallant but stupid' young gentlemen. 'You may buy your commissions in the Army up to the thirty-first day of October next. After that you will be driven to the cruel necessity of deserving them.'[23]

The fact that so many officers were Gentlemen sufficed to condemn the system of Purchase in the eyes of radicals. The author of 'A Letter on Army Reform,' published in 1855, analysed the various reasons why schoolboys joined the Colours. 'The reasons,' he discovered, 'which procure commissions for boys desirous of entering the army are various. One obtains his commission because he has a friend at court, another because he is a neighbour of the Commander-in-Chief, a third because his mother is a very agreeable woman, a fourth because his grandfather lost a leg at Barossa. But in no case are the personal merits of the applicant considered for one single moment. Whether he is robust or puny, intelligent or dull, well educated or ignorant, is never inquired; if he has "interest," he gets his commission; if he has not "interest," he does not get it . . . It is also a *sine qua non* at the Horse Guards that all applicants for commissions shall be "gentlemen,"—i.e. that their parents shall never have been actually engaged in any retail trade, or in any mechanical or agricultural calling, by which they have earned their bread. No previous military education or training, no long and good service as a non-commissioned officer, gives an applicant for a commission in the British army without "interest," a preference over the idlest and dullest school-boy with "interest," who ever sought refuge from the Greek grammar in a red coat; on the contrary, the latter is certain to succeed in obtaining it—the former to fail.' Gentlemen might well be 'gallant fellows, ready and anxious to fight but averse to face vicissitudes of those climates which kill many, many more British soldiers, than the bullet or the sword, and too much accustomed to the luxuries and amusements of home society either to bear their fair share in the tedium and peril of colonial service, or to look upon military life otherwise than as a dashing and casual pastime, rather than a serious and permanent profession. And these are the men who claim to have given a high tone to the British army, and who invariably carry off its prizes; they aver that it is to the leading of "gentlemen" like them that our military renown is due, thereby implying that without them that renown would never have been achieved. To show the utter absurdity of such a claim we need look no further afield than to the records of two of the most distinguished brigades in the British service—the Guards and the Marines—the one the most, the other the least, aristocratic corps in her Majesty's pay. Is there a pin to choose between them; and, if there be, in whose favour is it?'[24]

In 1856 a Royal Commission had enquired into 'The Sale and

Purchase of Commissions in the Army.' It found there was 'little inducement for officers to acquire proficiency in the science of War' knowing, as they did, they might 'look forward with confidence to the attainment of high military rank' so long as they had 'a sum of money available to purchase promotion.' The subaltern without the means to buy himself advancement might serve 'during all the best years of his life in distant stations and in deadly climates,' and yet however enthusiastically he performed his regimental duties, however industrious, experienced, or gifted he might be, it availed him nothing, unless he was 'able to buy the rank to which his qualifications entitled him.' The system was prejudicial to discipline because old officers could hardly be expected to show deference to young men promoted over their heads because they were rich enough to buy seniority. The report concluded by describing the system as 'vicious in principle, repugnant to the public sentiments of the present day, equally inconsistent with the honour of the military profession and the policy of the British Empire, and irreconcilable with justice.'[25] Despite this striking condemnation, nothing whatever was done.

Even before he became Secretary for War, Cardwell had censured the system of Purchase. Indeed he said that to mention it was to condemn it. 'It is not known in any other country; it would not be tolerated in any other service; and it is not admitted in the Artillery, the Engineers, the Marines, or the Navy.' Abolishing the system would do exactly what his opponents said it would: give England a professional officer class, which was what the country needed. 'My impression is that if we pass this bill . . . its effect would be to attract to the Army the aristocracy of merit and professional talent, which is after all the true aristocracy.' Those who argued that Purchase was the very life-blood of the regimental system were answered by a series of pointed questions. 'Is there no regimental system, no *esprit de corps* in the non-purchase regiments? Is there no *esprit de corps* . . . in the regiments of Prussia? Is there none in the Navy?' Cardwell admitted the heroism and gallantry which had always been displayed by

British officers. 'But if there is one lesson which we have learned from the history of the late campaign it is this—that the secret of Prussian success has been more owing to the professional education of the officers than to any other cause to which it can be ascribed. Neither gallantry nor heroism will avail much without professional training, in these days when arms of precision shoot down soldiers at immense distances.'[26]

The Commander-in-Chief held very different views on Purchase to those of the Secretary for War. 'I should, of course,' he told Cardwell, 'deeply regret any change in the system of Purchase, for, however theoretically objectionable, I think it has worked favourably in the interests of the service. It has enabled us to officer our army with gentlemen, and it has kept our officers comparatively young in years compared to the other armies of Europe.'[27] In advocating Purchase, although admitting it to be 'theoretically objectionable,' most Army officers regarded the Duke as defending their interests, and some of the arguments they advanced were not without substance. Promotion by selection, they feared, might cause 'ill-feeling in the Army and encourage officers to hate each other.' A professional Army would make England like Prussia, 'neither more nor less than a military despotism.' Moreover, this 'out of date Army' had secured an Empire on four continents, had humbled the pride of Napoleon and had forced the Tsar of All the Russias to sue for peace. Was it wise to tamper with a system which had proved so triumphantly successful? The Treasury, if Purchase were abolished, would have to find huge sums in compensation, retire officers on pensions, and might even be compelled to consider paying them adequately: the existing rates being much the same as they had been in the reign of William and Mary. A subaltern's expenses were reckoned at £157 annually and his pay at £95, leaving a deficit of £61. The net pay of a lieutenant colonel, after deducting income tax and interest on the price he had paid for his commission, amounted to the magnificent sum of £170 a year. Besides, if promotion were to be by merit, alleged or actual, the Commander-in-Chief would be exposed to intolerable pressures. Yet if it were arranged by seniority, the stagnation which existed in the non-purchase Corps would pervade the entire army. What would happen to the Cavalry, in which youth and daring were imperative, if it were commanded by elderly officers? Finally, it was asserted that men of property, men with a stake in the country, were a perpetual guarantee against Army dictatorship and military adventurers.

The purchase of commissions was defended by many eminent people. Wellington had argued that it brought into the service 'men who have some connection with the interests and fortunes of the country besides the commissions which they hold from His Majesty. It is this circumstance which exempts the British Army from the character of being a "mercenary army," and has rendered its employment for nearly a century and a half not only not inconsistent with the constitutional privileges of the country, but safe and beneficial.'[28] Palmerston believed that it was 'only where the Army was unconnected with those whose property gave them an interest in the welfare of the country . . . that it could ever become formidable to the liberties of the nation.'[29] When Sidney Herbert had considered the possibility of modifying the system, he encountered strong opposition from the Queen, the Prince Consort, the Commander-in-Chief, and Lord Panmure, who in 1871 resisted Cardwell's bill when it was debated in the Lords. 'In so doing, he was actuated by a sense of the political security which is afforded to a State by having its army officered by men belonging to the higher classes, or, at least, having a stake in the country, and in this connection he recalled the dictum of De Narbonne, War Minister in France during the Revolutionary Period, who declared that the effect of giving promotion solely for merit would not in reality be favourable to political liberty, because a Staff composed of soldiers of fortune would be much more likely to support a Dictator than would a body of officers who were already bound to the ancient institutions of their country.'[30] Lord Salisbury predicted that the principle of 'seniority tempered by selection' would soon resolve itself into one of 'stagnation tempered by jobbery.'

The Duke of Cambridge, in resisting the abolition of Purchase, opposed it so energetically that he came into serious collision with the Government. Gladstone was anxious to force H.R.H. to support abolition in the Lords, partly because he knew what harm was done to the cause by its opponents suspecting that the Commander-in-Chief shared their views. 'There is a general feeling,' Cardwell told the Duke, 'that the measure of H.M.'s Government, if not actually deprecated, is certainly not cordially supported by Your Royal Highness.' This impression is 'strengthened by your not having taken an opportunity of saying anything publicly in its favour.' The Secretary for War reminded H.R.H. that he had spoken in the House at the time of Trevelyan's motion, of the Duke's 'cordial assistance.' 'Is it right,' he asked, 'that I should defend you in the House of Commons on the ground that you have given us your cordial assistance . . . and then find that we are impeded in carrying out measures by an impression that they are not cordially supported by you?'

To require the Duke to deny publicly what the Ministers privately knew he believed was to precipitate a crisis. The Government purposely placed him in a dilemma, because, as they saw it, he must be compelled to co-operate or to resign. He, however, maintained that provided he loyally endeavoured to carry out the Government's policies once they had become law, he was under no obligation to support measures in the Lords which he believed ill judged. On the contrary, his office required him to maintain a strict political neutrality, which was hardly compatible with delivering partisan speeches at the crack of the Government whip. He maintained that it was unusual for Princes to vote, and that not only was the Commander-in-Chief not a politician, but there was no necessary reason why he should be a member of either the Lords or the Commons.

On 3 June 1871, he wrote to Cardwell defending his refusal to speak or vote on Purchase, and argued that this refusal was consistent with loyal support of the Government. '. . . It has ever been understood by myself, and certainly been admitted by all previous Governments, that the officer holding the position of Commander-in-Chief could have and ought to have no politics, and I have consequently most scrupulously abstained from ever taking part in any political discussions. . . . Whatever measures Her Majesty's Government may decide to adopt in conjunction with Parliament, it will be my duty and my desire cordially and loyally to carry them out, and so long as this line of conduct is adhered to by me, I do not see how it can be assumed that I am not, to the fullest extent, carrying out my duty by the Sovereign, by the Government, by the Country, and by the Army.' Cardwell replied, through Airey, that whatever may have happened before, the view of his colleagues now was that 'after fairly discussing and combating all measures with opinions and advice' it would be regarded as the Commander-in-Chief's duty to 'acquiesce.' If he failed to do so, 'the Government are *more* than prepared at once to remove him.' The gloves were off. Either the Duke must surrender, resign, or be dismissed.[31]

In this emergency H.R.H. turned to the Queen for support. 'I understand,' he wrote to her, 'that you are likely on Saturday to see Mr Gladstone, and I would venture to suggest to you that it would be a great assistance to me in maintaining the neutral position I have always tried to keep as Commander-in-Chief of Your Army . . . if You would strongly impress upon Mr Gladstone the absolute necessity of not pressing me on the matter of support in the House of Lords when the Army Regulation Bill comes up for discussion . . . If ever the Commander-in-Chief is required to depart from his strictly neutral position, his tenure of office would inevitably have to depend on every change of Government, and by this means the office would become a political one, and with such a change the interests of the Army would be handed over to political interest.'

A few days later he wrote to say that he had seen Gladstone and Cardwell, but that they had remained adamant that he must vote and speak for the bill. 'Mr Gladstone added that he considered the responsibility of the acceptance or rejection of the measure by the House of Lords would now be in a great measure on my shoulders, and if the Bill were rejected in the House without my having voted or spoken in its favour, the result would have very grave consequences to myself and to the Army, for as he expressed himself the ground would be cut away from under his feet, for he could not defend me against the attacks of his more advanced followers, and that not only would he be compelled to abandon me, but also he feared the office of Commander-in-Chief would go with me . . . The interests of the Crown are deeply involved. They must not suffer from any false step on my part.' The Duke added that Lord Russell, Lord Dalhousie, and he believed to some extent, Lord Grey, although Liberals, 'take a view adverse to the Government plan.'[32] The Prime Minister in fact threatened that if the Commander-in-Chief failed to support the Government in Parliament, he would either be dismissed, or his office would be modified. Some of the Duke's friends thought that Gladstone, by this high-minded blackmail, had put himself so thoroughly in the wrong that H.R.H. would be justified in threatening to disclose the whole proceedings unless the demand was withdrawn.

The Queen, as requested by her cousin, wrote to Gladstone expressing the hope that the Commander-in-Chief should be allowed to remain outside politics. She told him that she thought it would be wrong for the Duke to be forced to support the Government in the Lords. 'The Queen thinks that few more serious evils could arise, both to her as sovereign, to the Army, and to the country, than the fact of the position of the Commander-in-Chief, and indeed of other officers holding high military commands, being looked upon in any way as political . . . That the Duke will honourably and cordially assist the Government in carrying out any regulations which may be enacted, the Queen cannot for an instant doubt, but she strongly deprecates any course of conduct being expected of him, which will place him in open antagonism to the opposition and thus render his position nearly untenable in case a change of Government takes place.'[33] Gladstone, however, replied that there were several precedents for the Commander-in-Chief voting in the manner suggested, and he predicted that if the bill were rejected without H.R.H. supporting it, there would be 'an immediate movement in the House of Commons against his Royal Highness; nor can your Majesty's advisers undertake to answer for the consequences . . . It is, in the mind of the Government, clear that the influence of officers connected with the Horse Guards has been used adversely to the measure: and that public opinion even ascribes a similar use of influence, by the expression of unfavourable sentiments, to his Royal Highness. Doubtless this opinion is erroneous; but it is much to be desired that the effects produced by it should be removed.'[34] On 9 July the Queen had an interview with Gladstone 'and talked of George C. and what Mr Gladstone had written to me. I begged him to see George, which he said he was most willing to do, protesting most vehemently against any intention of making George depart from his neutral position; but it was not wished he should in the slightest degree give his opinion now, or in favour of the Bill, only advise its adoption. On my urging he should not be pressed to vote, Mr Gladstone said . . . for George's own sake, it will be better that he should vote.'

The episode ended in anticlimax. The Duke made the required speech, which Granville in a telegram described as 'skilful as to his own position, and fair towards the Government.' The Queen wrote in her Diary on 15 July, 'read George's speech, which is extremely good. While maintaining the neutral position of the Commander-in-Chief, he gives the Government that support which it is wise he should. I have written to compliment him and tell him so.' As the Prime Minister had suggested, H.R.H. contrived to advocate the passing of the bill by his fellow peers, without supporting the measure itself. It was a piece of sophistry which came naturally enough to its proposer, but which did not so readily recommend itself to the Duke. And then, after all this flood of controversy, the Lords destroyed the bill by amendments, and the sale of commissions was finally abolished by Royal Warrant, not Act of Parliament. All the excitement, high words, even menaces, turned out to be merely much ado about nothing.

Had the Duke not spoken in favour of the bill for abolishing Purchase, the Liberals, by their own admission, would have blamed him for its defeat. But the very Government which was prepared to hold him responsible for reverses was happy enough to take upon itself credit which was rightly his. Cardwell's biographer, Sir Robert Biddulph, an admirer and subordinate of the great reformer, speaks of the Secretary for War determining to 'introduce' manoeuvres into the British Army; as if the plan was the product of his own, unaided genius. In fact, of course, the Commander-in-Chief had been stressing the need for large-scale exercises since 1852, and the manoeuvres held at Aldershot in 1871 owed more to the Duke's inspiration than to all the Members of the Cabinet put together.

The Aldershot manoeuvres were the first to be held since 1853, and they were repeated the next year, but, owing to the expense, no further exercises on such a scale were contemplated again until 1898. Manoeuvres were so exceptional an undertaking in the British Army, that special Acts of Parliament had to be passed each time they were held. The military operations of 1871 were planned for September, and lasted about a fortnight. The Duke resided at the Queen's Pavilion at Aldershot and considerable numbers of military observers from abroad attended. They expressed themselves delighted by the civility and hospitality with which they were received, but most refrained from commenting on the technical aspects of the proceedings, except that 'many foreign officers unhesitatingly declared that the Duke of Cambridge thoroughly understood his business as a General in the field.'[35] Three Divisions were involved. The Prince of Wales commanded a cavalry brigade 'with an interest and vigour,' according to the Duke, 'which it is truly gratifying to observe.' Both officers and men displayed bewildering ignorance of the rudiments of fieldcraft. It was with the greatest difficulty that they pitched their tents. The horses of the First Life Guards stampeded before operations ever began, frightened by a flock of geese. Carts broke down, rations were mislaid, and harnesses fell to pieces. The *Quarterly Review* described the manoeuvres as 'a shameful performance,' proof of administrative deficiency, and 'a spectacle of open humiliation.' Nevertheless it was far better to discover such shortcomings during peaceful exercises than in time of war. The following summer manoeuvres were held on

Salisbury Plain and Cardwell managed to persuade Gladstone to attend. He hoped that if the Prime Minister were seen taking an interest in the Army it might help to dispel military hostility to the Government. The success of this device was not conspicuous. It needed more than a brief glimpse of the great statesman to persuade most soldiers that the Liberal party was not their enemy.

Towards the end of 1871 the Prince of Wales caught typhoid at Sandringham and his life hung in the balance. The illness followed the same course as had his father's, and the Queen dreaded her son would die on 14 December, the day of the Prince Consort's death. Sir William Jenner warned the Royal Family that the Prince might succumb at any moment, and the final crisis arrived on 13 December, the eve of the dreaded anniversary. The Queen hardly left her son's bedside for a moment. Hour after hour she sat holding his hand in an agony of anticipation, listening to his heavy, uncertain breathing. Suddenly he turned towards her, stared at her wildly, and asked: 'Who are you?' The Queen's self-possession was on the verge of dissolution, when the Prince whispered gently, 'It's Mama. It is so kind of you to come.'

The Duke of Cambridge, after anxiously following the first stages of the illness from Gloucester House, joined the family gathering at Sandringham on 9 December. The account of the fever he gave in his Diary would have provided a worthy contribution to *The Lancet*. He first heard of the Prince's illness on 23 November. 'Of course,' he wrote, 'this makes one feel very anxious.' Four days later, 'The accounts from Sandringham are very alarming. Sir W. Jenner and Dr Gull are in constant attendance; the fever is excessive, the delirium severe. 28 November. Matters very grave at Sandringham. The Prince was very ill indeed yesterday and great anxiety felt. He is very delirious and in a high state of fever. 29 November. Accounts from Sandringham very anxious. I asked leave to go, but was requested not to come at present. The Queen, I rejoice to say goes there to-day . . . 2 December. The accounts from Sandringham this morning prove that the crisis on Thursday night was a most grave one, and that great danger existed for a time, but that it is happily gone over for the moment. 4 December. Matters seem gradually to improve, but the fever, alas, continues. 8 December. The accounts this morning from Sandringham are most alarming. Last night a serious crisis seems to have set in. The fever has greatly increased, with decided congestion of one lung. Alfred [the Duke of Edinburgh] came to see me in great distress, poor boy! He is going at once to Sandringham. The Queen is also going again . . . Worse telegrams kept reaching me all day, and this afternoon one from Alice was so bad, that the end seemed at hand. I telegraphed for leave to go down myself, for I felt most miserable. I decided upon going down in the morning at all hazards. 9 December. Got a telegram from Alfred during the night, saying I might come. Sent off for a special train. Got rather better account this morning. The night was quiet and the spasm seemed to have passed away. 11 December. The awfulness of this morning, I shall never, never forget as long as I live. Between six and seven the General [Sir W. Knollys] knocked at my door to say we were sent for to the house. I rushed out of bed, dressed hurriedly, and ran to the house in intense agony. The morning was desperately cold, and the damp rose from the snow on the ground. On arrival found all assembled near the dear patient's room: a severe paroxysm of difficulty of breathing having come on after frequent attacks of a similar character during the whole of a most restless night. All looked bewildered and overcome with grief, but the doctors behaved nobly, no flinching, no loss of courage, only intense anxiety. I went into the outer lobby, where the medicines were being prepared, and nourishment mixed, and could hear the heavy breathing of the dear Prince, but was struck by the power of his dear voice, for he continually talked wanderingly, whenever the breath was sufficient to do so. After some time of intense anxiety, the paroxysm subsided and we began again to hope, but our hopes were faint indeed! However towards ten, matters seemed rather to mend, at all events to quiet down. Later, however, matters looked very bad again, as at four, violent delirium again set in. Had a long interview with Jenner and Gull, who said the case was not hopeless yet: but the anxiety was great. 13 December.

Grateful again this morning that we were allowed to pass through the night without having been called, but the night was bad, and the delirium with incessant talking continues uninterruptedly. The anxiety and grief at the house are intense, all looking forward to to-morrow with intense alarm, that being a most ominous day, the anniversary of the death of the Prince Consort. Everybody writes, everybody telegraphs, all being intent for news. The alarm and consternation and excitement in London are terrific, the loyalty displayed by the entire nation is sublime. 14 December. The ominous day has arrived and yet, praised be God, he lives, and he has slept at times during the night, with a less amount of delirium, so that again we hope. 15 December. The Prince has passed a quiet night with a great deal of sleep, all the symptoms are improved, and we begin to look with hope to the future . . . God has, in His mercy, heard all our prayers, and we have indeed cause to be grateful to Him. Am going to bed comparatively happy, after these fearful days of suspense.'

During her son's illness the Queen took entire charge of the large family gathering at Sandringham, and prevented him being smothered by solicitude. Arrivals and departures depended upon her instructions, and she guarded the Prince's door like a sentry. Ponsonby, her Private Secretary, described how he went towards the garden by a side door, when he was 'suddenly nearly carried away by a stampede of royalties,' headed by the Duke and brought up by Prince Leopold, 'going as fast as they could. We thought it was a mad bull. But they cried out: "The Queen, the Queen!" and we all dashed into the house again and waited behind the door till the road was clear.'

The Duke became obsessed with the idea that something was wrong with the drains. He conducted a tour of inspection, proclaimed Princess Louise's room uninhabitable, which in view of the congestion in the house was somewhat trying, and finally discovered a sinister smell in the library. An expert was sent for and declared he could detect nothing. The Duke grasped the man by the shoulder and led him round the room. 'My dear fellow come here—don't you smell it? Well come here, till the man at last said he did, to save himself from being pulled about the room. On this admission Jenner spoke to him seriously and the Duke violently. The man however had nothing to do with drain pipes but was only the gas man, and tried to say so once or twice, but no one would listen and he was finally dragged upstairs where the stink, they say, was suffocating. Luckily however the gas man was the right man, for it turned out after much rummaging that the smell was an escape of gas and on his doing something to his pipes the smell has entirely ceased.'[36]

The Duke's anxiety was felt from the heart for he was extremely fond of the Prince of Wales. 'I have always said their dear R.H.'s are the most *charming* couple, and the most delightful hosts it is possible to conceive, and all who know them *must* love and like them.'[37] The Prince returned the affection, and having known the Duke 'alike in boyhood and manhood as "Uncle George," their mutual relations remained for life those of an affectionate uncle and nephew. The Prince owed to his "uncle," whose profession was the army, his youthful enthusiasm for that service, and after "Uncle George" succeeded his father in the Dukedom and became Commander-in-Chief of the Army, there was much confidential intercourse between him and his "nephew" on controverted questions of military organization in regard to which the Duke was stubbornly loyal to antiquated standards . . . The genial heartiness of the Cambridge household pleasurably contrasted in the Prince's boyish eyes with the serious demeanour of the rest of Queen Victoria's English kinsfolk.'[38] This 'genial heartiness' was much frowned upon by the Prince's mother, who regarded it with intense suspicion. Writing to the Duke of Connaught in 1875, the Queen deplored her children's fondness for races, no sport, in her view, for Royalty. 'To my great grief,' she wrote, 'I hear that dear Bertie *loses* money at races! For *him* to do this is dreadful. . . . Now tho' you are the younger brother I know that he respects and looks up to you—as well he may—which alas! none of you can do, as I wish you could, to Uncle George. . . . Nothing is worse for a country than when the higher classes indulge in frivolity and vice.' She begged the Duke

of Connaught to reform his brother and to 'say you know the
terrible anxiety and grief it is to me.'[39] Prince Albert had once
accused the Cambridges of leading his eldest son astray, and the
accusation was therefore not abandoned lightly.

A great Thanksgiving Service was held at St Paul's on 27
February 1872, to celebrate the Prince's recovery. The Queen
had serious misgivings. She dreaded the fatigue 'which I think
will be too much for Bertie,' and although 'willing and very
anxious to show my warm acknowledgement of the loyalty and
sympathy shown on this occasion, I do not—I must say—like
religion to be made a vehicle for a great show. The simple
Thanksgiving, more than a month ago, was the right religious
act.'

The Duke was greatly moved by 'the loyalty and good feeling
of the people' and thought the ceremony 'the most heart-stirring
thing I ever witnessed.' For some time Queen Victoria's retirement had encouraged criticism and even republicanism, but the
country united in rejoicing over the Prince's recovery, again
showed 'itself a great and powerful monarchical nation.' 'The
morning looked fine,' wrote the Duke in his Diary describing the
Thanksgiving Ceremonies, 'and the day turned out beautiful for
the occasion, though the wind was cold. At eleven thirty drove to
Buckingham Palace with my two State Carriages and three
Equerries with an escort. There joined the Queen's procession,
which started exactly at twelve, the Speaker leading, then the
Lord Chancellor, then myself, and then the Queen's procession
following. It was a most glorious sight, the crowds enormous,
their enthusiasms and loyalty overpowering and unbounded, the
troops lining the Streets the entire way there and back. We went
by Stable Yard, Pall Mall, the Strand, Temple Bar, Fleet Street
and Ludgate Hill. The ceremony in the interior of the Cathedral
was simple but very impressive. About 14,000 people were
accommodated. The Archbishop of Canterbury preached. We
returned by the Holborn Viaduct and Holborn, Oxford Street,
the Marble Arch, Hyde Park and Constitution Hill, and were
home by three thirty. The whole thing was magnificent, and a

great national success. The Queen was delighted, and the Prince
got through it well, though he was fatigued at last. Lord Lucan
commanded the troops, Prince Edward the Infantry, and Sir
Thomas MacMahon the Cavalry. The order and regularity were
splendid.' For some time the Duke had been eager for the Queen
to emerge from seclusion. 'I only wish,' he wrote on 20 June 1867,
'the Queen would oftener consent to appear in public, as it is so
much desired by everybody and is so necessary and essential in
these times.'

While the Duke was staying at Goodwood in the Easter of 1873
he received news of the death of his steward Ramsthal, who had
been in his service since he was nine years old. 'The blow has
quite stunned me. Nobody can ever replace the dear faithful old
man, who has for forty five years shared my fortunes in life, and
has never once left me . . . May God have mercy on his dear
soul.' H.R.H. left Goodwood to attend the funeral, 'a respect due
to the memory of one who had served me so well and for whom
I entertain so strong an affection, regard and esteem.' The Queen,
who after the Prince Consort's death formed deeper friendships
with her servants than with most of her subjects, wrote an understanding letter of sympathy. 'Let me now tell you how grieved
I am at the great loss you have sustained in the death of your faithful and excellent steward and I may add *friend*. No one perhaps can
more truly appreciate your feelings than I do, who know what it
is to have an attached, devoted and faithful confidential servant.
Indeed such a loss is often more than those of one's nearest and
dearest, for a faithful servant is so identified with *all* your feelings,
wants, wishes, and habits as really to be *part* of your *existence* and
cannot be replaced . . .'[40]

The visit of the Shah of Persia in June 1873 involved the Duke
in a plague of ceremonies. The reports which proceeded His
Majesty from Berlin, the first capital of his European tour,
thoroughly alarmed the Queen and she consequently decided to
lodge her guest in Buckingham Palace while remaining herself
at Windsor. The Shah, unaccustomed to the society of European
ladies, behaved in so uninhibited a manner as to give grave

M

offence. The Persians made purchases in carriage loads, but the delight of the Berlin shopkeepers soon dwindled to dismay, when it was discovered that paying played no part in the practice of the imperial court. The apartments occupied by the Persians in the royal palace were left like a slum struck by a cyclone. Nobody, not even the Grand Vizier, ventured to tell the Shah that he must try to be punctual, that before being seated himself he should wait for the Empress to sit down, or that loud, oriental shouts at dinner were inclined to startle the company. The Shah preferred to eat most of his meals alone, sitting on a carpet, and this was perhaps fortunate, since his behaviour at public banquets was unpredictable. He liked putting his arm round his neighbour's chair, and it was his habit to chew his food for a moment and then examine it. If for any reason it displeased him he threw the remains under the table. The Shah, on reaching England, seems to have accommodated himself better to Western ways, for the Duke makes no mention of any such barbarities. '18 June. In uniform to the Station at four forty five to meet the Shah of Persia on his arrival, together with the Prince of Wales, Christian, Teck and my whole staff. Alfred and Arthur went to Dover to fetch him. The impression he produced on me was favourable. We all drove in procession to Buckingham Palace, where he lives. On leaving the Station, rain commenced and became very heavy before we arrived at the Palace. The road was lined with Troops, and crowds received him most enthusiastically. 19 June. The Shah came to pay me a visit, soon after one o'clock. His manner is dignified and good, and he understands French fairly, but without speaking it well, though he does so a little. He stayed about a quarter of an hour . . . Dined at Marlborough House, a large Full Dress Dinner for the Shah and all the Persian Princes and leading Attendants. No one could have behaved better or been more dignified than he whilst at dinner. We were only men. 24 June. Went to Datchet by Special Train with the whole of my staff at one thirty from Waterloo, arriving at two thirty. Went direct to Frogmore, where had luncheon, and rode up to the Castle at three to attend the Queen and Shah to the great Review in Windsor Park. The Shah was late in arriving, his train having been delayed . . . The Shah rode with us, the Queen and Court followed in carriages . . . The crowd on the ground was enormous and most enthusiastic . . . At the conclusion of the Review the Shah presented me with one of his own diamond swords, a magnificent gift by which I was greatly gratified and pleased.'

In November of 1873, while visiting her daughter in Mecklenburg-Strelitz, the Duchess of Cambridge had a stroke, which left her an invalid for the remaining sixteen years of her life. She was brought back to England in the following May, but, at the end of the year had another attack. The Duke, with his eye for clinical detail, wrote in his Diary on 19 December, 'While dining out a message came summoning me to Kew to bring Sir William Gull. Fortunately we were both at hand and started at ten forty five and were at Kew by eleven thirty. Found dear Mama better and recovering from an attack probably of the heart from indigestion, which seized her about nine, and for the moment took away all consciousness and rendered her rigid. Gull found the pulse and heart extremely feeble, but the momentary danger seemed past. Still it is a painfully critical state of things and the anxiety at her advanced age is distressingly great.'

The Duke's life in these years was punctuated by a sad and weary round of illness. His own gout was growing worse and there were times he was so crippled he was forced to bed. The twinges of agonizing pain to which he was liable sometimes kindled a temper which at its sunniest was scarcely sanguine. And added to all his other worries, Louisa's health, although gradually improving, still gave grounds for concern. In 1868 he bought her a little house at Horley, then in the wilds of the country, which she named 'Cambridge Lodge.' It was hoped that rural life would hasten her recovery. 'At eight o'clock went down to Horley by train to see Louisa's little cottage,' wrote the Duke on 15 June 1868. 'It was a lovely day but intensely hot. Walked to the house about a mile. It is a very nice quiet little place and will in time be very pretty. Found Louisa all the better for her stay there and much pleased to see me there. George was there also.'

Louisa now spent less time in Queen Street than in younger days, for she was often advised for her health's sake to leave London. Whenever he could, her husband would visit her. 'Please dearest,' he wrote to her on 13 August 1869, when she was staying at Buxton, 'keep my coming dark. Warn your servants not to say who I am. At these watering places people are a horrid bore and Mayors and inhabitants immediately want to get up addresses. I found this to be the case the first time I went to Scarborough and I had no peace during the whole time I was there.' Despite such excursions, Louisa still spent much of the year in Queen Street, and she generally arranged to leave London when the Duke was paying visits in England, or travelling abroad. Occasionally she met her husband's colleagues. She was present, for example, at an informal dinner given to Cardwell at Gloucester House on 18 December 1870. But she was not particularly excited by politics, and showed little desire to meet the great men of her husband's world. Her interests were centred round her family, her friends and her pets. Dogs she particularly loved. When the Duke visited Queen Street in 1869, on the anniversary of Inkerman, he found 'poor Louisa in a dreadful state of affliction at the death of her dear little dog Nelly, which I regret greatly myself. She thinks the dog was not properly treated medically after pupping.' The grief she felt at the death of this animal betrayed her compassionate heart, for she dearly loved all who surrounded her. Neither age, nor pain, nor separation, diminished for an instant her passionate devotion to her husband, whom she still loved with the same burning fervour of the early days of their marriage.

DAMMING THE DELUGE

GLADSTONE's great reforming Ministry came to an end in 1874. Its policy, according to Disraeli, had been one of 'blundering and plundering' which 'harassed every trade, worried every profession and menaced every class, institution and property in the country.' The Liberals, in part, attributed their defeat to the Licensing Act of 1872. 'We have been borne down,' said their leader, 'in a torrent of Gin and Beer.' The ensuing Conservative Government, which lasted six years, allowed the Army a period of consolidation after the avalanche of change which had swept over it. Disraeli first appointed Gathorne Hardy as Secretary for War; and when in 1878 he was raised to the peerage as Earl of Cranbrook, and became Secretary of State for India, Colonel Stanley, Lord Derby's heir, succeeded him.

Gathorne Hardy found the Duke loyal and conciliatory, although no enthusiast for new ways. 'H.R.H. is frank and friendly, and evidently expects and respects difference of opinion; he argues without any peremptoriness, and accepts without any ill-feeling an adverse decision.' The hundreds of letters the Commander-in-Chief addressed to Hardy displayed, in his opinion, 'an extraordinary knowledge of all the minutest details of the work of his office.'[1] The Radical Press echoed the Secretary for War's sentiments about the Duke's conservatism, but without qualification or restraint. An article in *The World*, a disreputable but vigorous journal, published on 19 August 1874, demanded the Commander-in-Chief's resignation, on the ground that he obstructed progress. 'During the last twenty years,' declared the article, 'war has developed from a mere trade into an abstruse science, and it is progressing with daily accelerated strides. The task of commanding the British Army has therefore enormously increased, and the Duke may well feel that it is now beyond his powers. He alone has stood still, while the whole military world was advancing. He has clung obstinately to the past, has resisted every measure of reform till it became an accomplished fact, and then has done his best secretly and insidiously to render it inoperative . . .

'We can hardly say that the Duke of Cambridge has even put himself at the head of the retrograde clique, for he is not the man to head any party; rather have the retrogradists got in front of him and pushed him backwards. . . . If minute attention to buttons and straps, and careful supervision of marching past and parade movements, are the qualifications of a great commander, not even Moltke can hold a candle to his Royal Highness . . . He seems to consider drill the be-all and end-all of a soldier's training, instead of a means by which an object is to be attained. We are by no means sure that he does not share the opinion of some fossil colonels, and looks on manoeuvres as calculated to ruin regiments. These conservative tendencies of the Duke by no means proceed from want of talent. His natural abilities are good, but he is utterly without mental culture, and knows nothing whatever of the scientific part of war. As a rule, the royal family are not given to reading, and in addition the Duke has always been surrounded by a little clique, the members of which, finding themselves very comfortable in the positions which with little merit of their own

they have secured, wish to retain those positions, and consequently have ever sought to keep down men of energy and
originality. Nothing is so obnoxious to office-holders as innovations. . . . Besides the tendency of all recent progress, all the new
regulations, has been to give merit a chance of rising; but if merit
rises, what is to become of patronage?

'. . . An officer of some standing and given to speak his mind
very plainly observed not very long ago, "The country may have
a royal duke, or it may have an army; it cannot have both." . . .
Officers who write are his aversion, and contributors to the press
are invariably kept in the background till their reputation with the
public becomes so great that they cannot be suppressed any
longer.

'. . . If, therefore, War is to be cultivated as a science, if our
military system is to be improved, if our organization and tactics
are to be based on sound principles, and to be brought into
harmony with modern conditions, the sooner his Royal Highness
resigns his command the better. We admit, however, that his
resignation would be received by the profession with varied and
mixed feelings. He has certainly made himself popular with the
men. The fact that he, a prince, should have devoted himself to
soldiering as if he had to earn his bread by it, and that he has in two
bloody actions displayed the hereditary courage of his race, has
had something to do with his popularity. He is also in appearance
and manner a soldierlike man. The lower orders like the bluff
bearing and vehement outspoken language which were the
characteristics of the Tudors . . . He always goes much into
detail—men with his description of mind always do; and he is
therefore credited with having always been engaged in studying
to promote the soldier's welfare. . . . As to the officers, there are
many who would regret his retirement. His hearty manner, his
undoubted good nature, his wonderful memory, in which are
treasured up, not only the name and face, but also the career, of
nearly every officer in the service, make the unreflecting majority
blind to his defects. Those defects are, however, serious. He is
extremely vituperative on very slight provocation, and not

seldom publicly addresses officers of rank and standing in the most humiliating language . . . The last person who speaks to him is the one by whom he is influenced . . . Finally, his chief vice—a blind Conservatism—is attractive to the majority, for in the army all old things are generally looked upon as good; and a Conservative body of officers naturally sympathize with a Conservative Commander-in-Chief.

'A large and thoughtful minority, however, appreciate the Duke's character more justly. They perceive that his energy is chiefly spent on trifles, that his activity is mainly displayed in rushing wildly about the country holding routine inspections.'

The views expressed by *The World* were, as it admitted, only those of a minority, but the minority counted Wolseley amongst its numbers. The Duke was inclined to suspect that some of the newspaper attacks upon him were directly inspired by Sir Garnet, who detested the traditional field day because he believed it detracted from the ultimate purpose of military training: preparation for actual war. 'I have just returned from one of those most tiresome field days,' he once wrote, 'in which the Duke of Cambridge delights, but which to me are hateful in the extreme. I am not good as a dissembler, and I keep my temper with difficulty when I see and hear so much that tends to rub up the wrong way every military instinct I possess.' On another occasion he told his wife, 'I hear the Duke was most annoying at Aldershot. The Field Day was abominably bad. He assembled all the junior officers when it was over and said: "Very fine horses, very well turned out; looking very well; splendid men and well drilled; but damned bad officers." '2

The Commander-in-Chief's outspokenness could only have been salutary. His constant round of tours and inspections would have achieved little if he had dispensed nothing but insincere flattery. But he was no more inclined to dissemble than was Wolseley, and it was just because he was quick to criticize that his compliments were gratifying. There were times, however, when his brusqueness provoked resentment. 'They have been comparing this inspection with the last,' wrote Colonel Henderson, a

lecturer at Sandhurst in 1894, 'when the old hero of many
banquets grunted ferociously at the pile of schemes, maps, etc.
and then darted off to revel in pork chops and other delicacies,
giving us to understand that we were very dull dogs.'

Traditional field days and parades may have disgusted military
reformers, but they provided a magnificent spectacle which
greatly assisted the work of the recruiting sergeant. Chatham was
a military station the Duke frequently visited, and the splendour
of his reviews so impressed itself on the mind of a child who
watched them that he vividly recalled the excitement of the
occasion over half a century later. 'For me, it was the army that
occupied the fore-ground of the picture,

> "The army that fights for the Queen,
> The very best army that ever was seen!"

and certainly it was an incomparably more picturesque and
colourful army than anything you imagine today. It was, moreover, conspicuously under royal patronage: for no circus, nor
even the Salvation Army, then in its youthful prime, that put
down a glorious drumfire barrage once a week under my nursery
window, could vie for entertainment with what seem to me to
have been the fairly frequent occasions on which His Royal
Highness, the Duke of Cambridge, came down in his capacity of
Commander-in-Chief, to review the Chatham Brigade. As our
house was right above the station, we could see his whole cavalcade mounting and getting under way—the expression "glittering
staff" was certainly no misnomer, with the whole street in spate
with cocked hats and scarlet and decorations; and when the grand
old warrior led it under the railway bridge, it almost seemed as if
his whiskers would have brushed the brickwork on either side.

'As one who had been habituated to play soldiers, to think
soldiers, and to daydream himself a soldier, I kept an almost
photographic impression of that spectacle, and it explained much
since to me that would have otherwise been obscure. The battlefield was a magnificent open space called the Lines, with the
ground from the South edge falling abruptly down to the valley

in which lie Rochester and the Medway . . . It was along that
edge that the enemy had taken up his position, having presumably
climbed up out of the valley, and lain down for a breather. I say
"his"—but as a matter of fact there were at least ten of him, each
man being supposed to represent a hundred. I did not suppose any
such thing. It was only fitting that the Queen's forces should
exceed these Frenchmen, as I visualized them, in quantity no less
than in quality. It was on this devoted ten, lying conspicuously on
their stomachs—for there seemed to be no question of entrench-
ing—that the whole Chatham garrison staged a long, leisurely
attack over ground suggestive of a billiard table. Undeterred by
the massacre of the Prussian Guard at St Privat under rather
similar circumstances eighteen years previously, they advanced in
three closely packed and accurately dressed scarlet lines, lying
down at frequent intervals, as much, I imagine, for the purpose of
correcting their alignment as of popping off blank. In the second
or third line a score or so of men would ever and anon spring
simultaneously to their feet to discharge an equally simultaneous
volley. I should think that under these circumstances even ten men,
counting one as one, with a sufficient number of cartridges, could
have accounted with their Martinis for a greater part of the
assailants; unless they had been conspicuously bad shots, which,
under His Highness's system of training, they most likely were,
since a straight shot was accounted as nothing in his eye compared
with a straight line. However, at long last, the spoil-sport bugles
went, just as the final charge was being prepared and the invaders
were about to be bayoneted and pitchforked, before my delighted
eyes, over the crest. Then the victors formed up intact, and with
bands thundering out the regimental tunes, marched triumphantly
past the Duke, who I think must have enjoyed this part of it most
of all. For peace-time soldiering it was the most impressive
spectacle that anyone could conceive. But when something of the
sort had been tried against a rabble of unsoldierly Boers, not so
long before, there had been a rather different tale to tell! But that
would be no bar to its being tried again, in due course, against the
selfsame enemy.

'Of course it will be said that a small child was perfectly incapable of appreciating the deep motives behind all this martial
pageantry. And that would have been true; for I had no idea at
the time of the mastering anxiety that possessed the staff and the
commanders, which was that on no account whatever should
proceedings be prolonged for a single second beyond the hour
fixed for H.R.H.'s lunch, which always consisted of chop and
tomato sauce. Any failure in this respect would be notified to all
concerned in royally unpublished terms, for the Duke had inherited from his uncles, of the Regency generation, a command of
varied and picturesque imagery far beyond the resources of
Billingsgate.'[3]

In January 1879 the Government declared war on King
Cetywayo, the Zulu leader, who threatened Britain's supremacy
in South Africa. The campaign began disastrously. Cardwell had
so weakened colonial defences that Natal had only a battalion
with which to resist a ferocious and numerous enemy. Lord
Chelmsford, who commanded the troops in South Africa, told
the Commander-in-Chief that the Zulus appeared to have no fear
whatever of death, and 'although mowed down by hundreds at a
time never faltered in their attack. Englishmen liked the foe to
come on bravely but rather injudiciously, and to be "mown down"
by guns that never jammed. They liked him to be easily surprised
and bamboozled, and then they paid the highest compliments to
his "unavailing heroism"; Mr Kipling probably compensated
him with a poem in Cockney dialect.' But if he declined 'to be
surprised and bamboozled, the public journals were apt to describe
the ensuing disaster as a "treacherous massacre." '[4] At Isandlwana,
Cetywayo captured an important base camp, full of essential
stores, equipment and ammunition, and in the process destroyed
most of the troops defending it. 'It will be a melancholy satisfaction to your Royal Highness to know,' wrote Chelmsford,
'that the imperial troops fought in the most gallant manner, and
that their courage and determination is the theme of wonder and
amazement amongst the natives who saw them fight and who
escaped to tell the tale.'[5]

The Duke pressed the Government to authorize an increase in the size of the Army. Early in the very month in which war was declared, and despite the campaign being fought at the same time in Afghanistan, reductions had been contemplated. The Conservatives were as shortsighted as the Liberals when it came to military expenditure. Confronted with reverses in Africa, reinforcements had to be despatched, and H.R.H. was authorized to promise Chelmsford two regiments of Cavalry, two field batteries, a company of Engineers, and six battalions of Infantry. Within a fortnight, the troops were collected, embarked, and had sailed: the Commander-in-Chief inspecting them before their departure.

'To Aldershot,' wrote H.R.H. in his Diary on 18 February 1879, 'to inspect the several corps for service at the Cape . . . The troops looked well, but there are a very large number of volunteers and young men, which is certainly a great disadvantage. The spirit among them, however, is excellent, so I hope they will do well. 19 February. Went by train from Fenchurch Street to Tilbury Fort to inspect the Third Batt. 60th Rifles before embarking for South Africa. They looked a strong, healthy set of young men and most orderly and regular. Passed over to Gravesend in a tug, and then saw the Draft of two hundred and fifty men from Winchester from the First Batt. and the Depot, an equally fine body of men and in excellent order.

'22 February. Went with the Duke of Connaught and my staff to Hounslow by train, and thence drove in my wagonette to the Cavalry Barracks, the snow preventing my seeing the 17th Lancers on the heath before embarkation for S. Africa. Saw Regiment on foot parade in Barrack Yard, a splendid body of men in the finest possible order and made up with excellent Drafts from 5th and 16th Lancers. 26 February. Went from Waterloo with my staff to Portsmouth, and there saw 58th Foot embark in the *Russia* . . . The Regiment looked very efficient and fit for work, and the vessel was a good one. Then on board the *Palmyra* in which the Royal Engineers embark tomorrow, also a good vessel. From thence by special train to Southampton Docks . . . There saw

94th and drafts for 57th on board the *China*, a fine vessel, but very crowded with troops. Then went on board the *England* in which Head Quarters, 17th Lancers, and General Marshall were all admirably put up and ready to sail, and then over the *Spain*, which was ready to take on board next day the left wing of King's Dragoon Guards with Generals Clifford and Newdigate. Saw the *China* and *England* sail and then returned to London.'

According to custom, the Government decided to blame the commander in the field for failures which might with more justice have been attributed to policies dictated from Whitehall. On 28 May they appointed Wolseley as Commander-in-Chief in South Africa, although by the time he reached Natal, Chelmsford had defeated Cetywayo at Ulundi. The Duke wrote to congratulate the superseded General on his victory, and generously supported him against an ungrateful Government. 'Above all, and before all, let me congratulate you and the gallant troops under your command for the glorious news which reached me by telegraph yesterday of your entire and signal success at Ulundi, ending in the complete defeat of the Zulu Army under the direct command of Cetywayo . . . Nothing, as far as can be judged by the necessary shortness of the message received, could have been better done, and happily with comparatively small loss on our side, and the moral effect thus produced will, I sincerely trust and confidently believe, put an end to the war . . . The general demonstration of joy and satisfaction felt by the public at large is all that could be wished, and it would give you intense pleasure to see it as I have been enabled to do the last two days. There is universal rejoicing from Her Majesty downward, and the feeling is as sincere as it is general . . . Let all the troops know how greatly I am gratified.' Chelmsford, in acknowledging H.R.H.'s congratulations, thanked him warmly for all his support. 'Whatever the result may be, and whatever verdict may be passed upon me as a General, I shall never forget Y.R.H.'s kindness or the generous support given to me at a moment when it was most needed.'[6]

The Duke, hearing rumours that Wolseley was to be sent out

to the Cape, was greatly disturbed. On 24 May, he discussed the prospect at St James's with his mother, and he told the Duchess and Lady Geraldine that 'he plainly saw that they are determined to send Garnet Wolseley out to the Cape!! We had a long discussion about him and the *danger* of him! and *his* being at the bottom of the whole Cardwell system!!' If Chelmsford needed to be superseded at all, H.R.H. would have preferred Lord Napier as his successor. 'Monday 26 May 1879. I forgot to mention that yesterday I saw Lord Beaconsfield on the question of Sir Garnet Wolseley being sent out as Chief Commissioner and Commander-in-Chief in South Africa, and this morning I called on Lord Salisbury and saw him on the same subject. The Cabinet decided today to send Wolseley. I should have infinitely preferred Lord Napier, but he was thought too old, which I cannot at all admit, as he is as hard a man for work as I know anywhere.' Writing to his son Adolphus on 4 June, he says, 'Wolseley's appointment was not pleasant to me though I think it was necessary to do something at once as matters at the Cape were going on badly. I admit Wolseley's intelligence but I cannot see why he should be the *only* man in the Army we have left for duties requiring energy.' It was undoubtedly hard on many officers that Parliament and the public had come to think of Wolseley as England's 'only General.' As usual, Sir Garnet took out to South Africa a carefully collected staff, chosen from the not very large circle of his supporters and admirers in the Army. Their appointments infuriated the Duke, who detested the 'Garnet Ring.' 'Went to the office,' he wrote on 29 May, 'where found to my great annoyance, that Stanley had sanctioned all Wolseley's friends, a long list of whom he had handed in, to accompany him out to the Cape. This puts me out very much . . .'

Once Wolseley arrived in South Africa he continued to offend the Duke. Lady Geraldine's Diary is full of conversations in which Sir Garnet is abused. On 3 August the Duke 'read us the telegram he had just received today from Sir Garnet Wolseley, in which he, too *impertinently* says: "Lord Chelmsford wishes to return home and *I* have given him permission to do so"!!!! For want of taste, of tact, of good feeling! so stamps the fellow for what he is a prig and a pretentious snob! No gentleman.' On 8 August H.R.H. received another 'offensive telegram,' full of 'claptrap as to all *his* reductions of expenditure! Full of attacks upon Chelmsford! In short full of self-sufficiency, arrogance, impertinence! A *cad* indeed!!' Again two days later the talk at St James's returned to 'that brute Garnet Wolseley. His insufferable pretensions! The offensiveness of his despatches, full only of himself!'

The new Commander in South Africa arrived to find the war virtually over, but after some months it flared up once more. In 1880, the Liberals were returned to power, and as at the General Election Gladstone had attacked the whole philosophy behind Disraeli's imperialism, the Boers in South Africa consequently expected the withdrawal of British forces. In December, finding this hope disappointed, they rose in revolt and won the victory of Majuba Hill. Rather than continue a war which threatened to involve all South Africa, Gladstone granted the Transvaal virtual independence. Having conceded to force what had been denied to discussion, the Government left their enemies victorious, distrustful, and resolved, if need arose, to resort again to arms.

The Duke was utterly dismayed when he heard that the Prime Minister was negotiating terms. In a letter to Adolphus written on 14 April 1881, he refers to 'this terrible peace in South Africa' which he considered 'too awfully humiliating.' 'The country is lowered in every sense of the word and our influence at home and abroad dreadfully damaged. My own idea is that we shall ere long have to fight again at the Transvaal and indeed in South Africa generally.' On 15 December 1881, the Duke presented the Minister for War with his annual review of the Army. The report concluded with a pointed rebuke for the Government. 'In submitting my usual annual report upon the state of the Army, I have this year to allude only to one war in which our troops have been engaged—that with the Boers; but this has been a most unfortunate one. During the short period of one month we suffered three defeats . . . After, on 27 February, obtaining, by a difficult night march, possession of the Majuba Hill—a decisive tactical point—we were driven headlong from it in a rout so complete and disastrous that it is almost unparalleled in the long annals of our Army. When this last victory of the Boers was won, a force had been collected in Natal from this country and from India sufficient to have crushed with certainty the insurrection and restored the tarnished prestige of our arms; but for reasons other than military an armistice, followed by a peace, was concluded with the Boers upon terms which were certainly depressing to our troops, and upon which I abstain from making any observations.'

The reverses which the British Army suffered in South Africa revived the controversy about the merits of Cardwell's system of short service. The Duke constantly complained that the reinforcements consisted of 'mere boys.' Even Wolseley admitted that many of the recruits needed a year or eighteen months' service before they became efficient soldiers and had 'done growing.' Lord Napier, the veteran of Magdala, who had probably seen more fighting than any General in the Service, was badly shaken by the news from the Cape. 'One thing appears clear,' he wrote in 1881, 'that the stubbornness of the British soldier, which used to cover all the blunders of the Commanders can no longer be counted on, and those who are playing tricks with the Army, are still in power and unconvinced . . .'[7] The first significant test of the new system in action proved that its opponents' fears were not as groundless as its advocates had alleged them to be.

Among those who volunteered for service in South Africa was the Prince Imperial, the great-nephew of the first Napoleon, and the remaining hope of the Bonapartists. He had been a Cadet at the Royal Military Academy at Woolwich, where the Duke had watched his progress with pleasure. 'Saw the Cadets,' he wrote in his Diary on 15 February 1875, 'who drilled and looked well. The Prince Imperial drilled them remarkably well when called upon. The Empress Eugénie was present throughout the day. She went with me to see the drawings, then into the Gymnasium, where the Reports were read and the Prizes given. The Prince Imperial took the seventh place in the List, a most excellent position for a Cadet eleven months younger than the greater portion

of his class, and who had to do his study in a foreign language
. . . Saw the rides, which were excellent. The Prince Imperial
took the first place, also first in fencing.' The Queen also watched
the young Prince's career with affectionate interest. She telegraphed to the Empress congratulating her 'at the success of the
dear young Prince Imperial,' and she told the Duke that she felt
sure the Academy would always be proud that the young Prince
had distinguished himself in their school, 'and above all, *behaved*
so well!'

The Prince's first request to go out to South Africa was rejected by the Government, but he persisted so vigorously that at
length they yielded. The Queen was touched by his desire 'to go
out with and serve with my brave troops.' She saw him before he
set sail for the Cape, feeling 'glad I am not his mother at the
moment.' She particularly told the Duke that 'we know he is *very*
venturesome,' and on no account should he be allowed near the
enemy. H.R.H. accordingly wrote to the High Commissioner of
South Africa, Sir Bartle Frere, telling him that the Prince Imperial was coming out merely as a 'spectator.'

On the evening of 19 June 1879, Princess Augusta and Lady
Geraldine went to the French Play, the piece being entitled *Les
Deux Mondes*. They were joined by Captain George FitzGeorge.
'In the middle of the third act the Duke came, from his Scots
Guards dinner in a very short entracte. We tried to tell him the
story! very badly! The *fourth* act had just begun when a man
came in looking for the Duke, went up to him and whispered
something on which the Duke threw a tremendous start! Aghast!
A sound of distress! Passed a bundle of telegrams the man brought
him, and went with him into the little anteroom behind our box,
where he stood reading them. My heart sank with envy, presently
he came into the box again, whispered to P.A., who exclaimed
with *horror*, "Good God!" I asked him what it was? And he
whispered to me!!! "*The Prince Imperial is killed!!*" Good God!
The horror! The pain! and dismay, poor, poor, poor, Eugénie!!!!
I read the telegram: "Killed in a reconnaissance in which he dis-
mounted from his horse, was surrounded by Zulus, and shot!"

N

Good God! It is too dreadful. The Duke went off *at once* to Lord
Sydney about breaking it to *unhappy* Eugénie! Of course P.A.
should also have left the theatre *at once*! But strange as she is! and
always for keeping a thing *secret* and a mystery, we sat *through* the
play!! It was too terrible to do and of which I, of course, did not
hear a word more and only sat in *pain*.' The Duke regarded the
news as 'overpowering in its terribleness.' The next day he wrote
in his Diary, 'The news of the Prince's death is really overwhelming and no words can describe the dismay it has caused. How it
could have happened that the Prince should have been allowed to
get into so exposed a position is quite inexplicable.'

On 21 June H.R.H. visited the Empress. 'I settled to go to
Chislehurst this morning and proceeded there at twelve o'clock.
. . . I was at once received by the poor Empress, who behaved too
beautifully and heroically in her awful sorrow and grief. She conversed with me for nearly an hour upon this sad, sad business, and
not an unkind or ungenerous word ever passed her lips. Her fate
is fearful to contemplate; all hope in life gone for ever with this
dear gallant boy. I myself feel quite broken-hearted.'

The Queen was haunted by the Prince Imperial's death. 'How
horrible. How dreadful,' she telegraphed to H.R.H. from
Balmoral, 'I am quite overwhelmed by the stunning news, and
in such sorrow for the poor dear Empress who has lost all. We
leave at one today.'[8] A letter followed the telegram, in which
grief was mingled with imperious rage. The Queen's letters, as
Lady Geraldine once observed, were inclined to be 'peremptory,
despotic as no Eastern potentate.' Surely, she asked, it was arranged that the Prince was never to leave Lord Chelmsford's
staff? How could he have been allowed in so exposed a place?
'No doubt, he, poor dear brave young man pressed to go, but he
ought *not* to have been allowed.' Just in case the Duke was not
suffering agonies of self-recrimination, she emphasized the extent
of his responsibility for the tragedy. 'I can't tell you how it
haunts me, and has upset me, and for *you* who arranged all for
his going it is most painful.' Two days later the Queen visited
Chislehurst. 'I went this afternoon and sat with the dear Empress,

and it is quite heartbreaking to see her—*so* gentle, uncomplaining and resigned, yet *so* broken-hearted. *And* one can say *nothing* to *comfort* her! I never felt anything more, and am quite miserable and overwhelmed by it! Poor dear! She asked me, did I think it *possible* it might not be true, and that it might be someone else? But I said I thought *that* was *impossible*, for his dear remains were at once recognized!'

On the same day that the Queen paid her visit to the Empress, the Duke defended the Government and the Horse Guards in the House of Lords. He read the letters of introduction which the Prince had been given for Frere and Chelmsford. 'All I can say is . . . after having read these letters, that I think, so far as the authorities at home are concerned, everybody must feel that nothing has been done by them to place the Prince in the position which, unfortunately, resulted in his death. We all deplore, deeply deplore—I am sure that everyone in this House, every man, woman, and child in this country, everyone, from the Queen on her Throne down to her humblest servant, must feel and deeply deplore—what had occurred; but certainly, as far as the authorities are concerned here, I feel that nothing has been done to produce such a catastrophe as that which we all so much lament. I have already said how deeply I sympathize with the bereaved mother, and I am sure your Lordships fully share that feeling.'

The most distressing feature of the Prince's death, as far as the Army was concerned, was not so much that he had found his way into a position of danger, although that by itself was regrettably careless of the authorities, but that some of those with him fled at the appearance of the enemy and left him to his fate. The Commander-in-Chief wrote to Chelmsford asking for a detailed investigation. 'That he should have gone to the front with so small an escort, and with a junior officer, Lieutenant Carey, alone in his company, requires explanation of the fullest kind; as also does the fact of his having been killed, poor lad, with two of his escort gallantly fighting for their lives, whilst Lieutenant Carey and the four other men who were with him returned to camp, apparently much frightened, though otherwise quite unharmed . . . At present the feeling of horror, distress, and I may say dismay, is intense, and it will require the most clear account and the most searching investigation to satisfy the world, both at home and abroad, that he was not abandoned to his fate by the officer and men who were with him . . . The condition of the poor Empress is of course lamentable in the extreme, for with this lad all her hopes are buried in the grave for ever. Had the poor dear gallant young fellow been killed in a general action, or by your side, or by the side of one of the superior officers, it would have been the will of God it should be so, and nothing further could have been said; but that he should have met the fate he did, in the manner in which thus far the telegrams describe it to us, is the point which causes so much painful comment, and which seems to all, including myself, to be so inexplicable.'[9]

The Empress behaved nobly. She begged that no one should suffer, and requested an end to all investigations. She declared that her only consolation on earth was that her son had died a soldier's death, and she wanted no recriminations. '*Mois qui ne peux plus rien désirer sur terre, je demande cela comme une dernière prière.*' She derived a sad satisfaction from the company of her son's charger, which was sent back from South Africa and was stabled at Balmoral, with a magnificent horse which had belonged to the Emperor. 'The poor Empress,' wrote the Queen, 'who is staying here with me, can't separate from them.'

Just before the Empress left for Scotland, one of her ladies in waiting wrote to the Duke, describing a dreadful episode which had taken place at Chislehurst. 'Her Majesty is much the same *very*, *very* sad, and she looks so pale and ill! She was busy last week, some boxes having arrived from South Africa. She insisted upon seeing them unpacked, and in one of these trunks was the poor little Prince's shirt, all covered with blood. The sight of it, of course, renewed her grief.'[10] The Duke did everything in his power to help the Empress. He had known her ever since his visit to Paris on his way to join his Division in the Crimea, and now in her grief he paid her constant visits and wrote her many letters. The Commander-in-Chief was still no more hardened to death

than he had been at Inkerman at the Alma, and was always deso-
lated by casualties. The numerous letters of consolation he wrote
in his lifetime were no mere token tributes: they came straight
from the heart.

The war in South Africa raised an issue on which Wolseley
and the Duke found themselves utterly opposed. In his younger
days H.R.H. had been more ready to maintain ruthless opinions
than became acceptable to him after experience of office. Writing
in 1857 to Sir Colin Campbell, commanding in India, he had told
him, 'Let me know from time to time who are your best officers,
in order that we may push them on, and also who are useless that
they may be got rid of.' 'It is essential,' he declared in another
letter, 'to weed the Army of non-effectives, especially in the
higher grades.'[11] Soon, however, he discovered that such methods
of selection were too unsettling for the Army, and he became
increasingly inclined to advocate promotion by seniority. He
admitted that in wartime there might be arguments for departing
from this principle, but he maintained in the ordinary course of
events any other method of selection would give general dissatisfaction in the Army, would involve 'serious injustice to individuals passed over,' and since the Army was 'scattered all over
the world performing a great variety of special duties,' it would be
next to impossible to compare the merits of officers who had
served in different quarters of the globe. The heart-searching and
jealousies which selection might engender, would greatly out-
weigh any alleged advantages. The proposal that promotion
should be decided by merit naturally appealed most to those
Army officers who believed themselves possessed of outstanding
qualifications. The vast majority, who had no pretensions to
superior ability and were inclined to suspect the intellectual
soldier, were perfectly content with a system which regarded
length of service as more telling than any other military accom-
plishment. The Duke's advocacy of 'seniority' was therefore
popular in the Army, and it cannot be doubted that it was a means
of promotion which maintained harmony in the higher ranks of
the service. If junior officers, on account of their supposed ability,

were to be promoted colonels over the heads of elderly majors, serious ill-feeling might ensue. Moreover what was, and who possessed, ability were matters of definition and opinion. Favouritism might easily vitiate selection. Officers inclined to a particular school of military thinking, without any conscious desire to favour those holding similar opinions, might nevertheless be tempted to imagine that those who thought as they did deserved advancement. If there was always a danger that promotion by seniority might deprive an outstanding junior officer of scope for his talents, and could even perhaps place in important commands those unqualified to hold them, there was equally the risk, if promotion was confined to merit, that the efficiency and goodwill of the Army might be corrupted and that ability would be misjudged.

Wolseley had always agitated for merit as the sole passport for preferment. The real test of an officer was not length of service but his record of achievement. 'He urged in season and out of season that merit should have precedence over seniority. He begged the Duke when there was a question of promoting an officer of doubtful value in the field: "give him orders and ribbons, but don't give him the men's lives to lose." Capacity to command troops in war, he protested, should be the one test of fitness for promotion in an army . . . The counter-argument ran that peace training often provided a very inadequate proof of capacity to lead in the field, and that a process of selection might open the door to favouritism and jobbery.'[12] Lord Roberts, who disagreed with Wolseley on most military matters, shared his views on promotion. 'I cannot forget,' he wrote in 1890, 'the lessons taught me in 1857, when, with scarcely an exception, every officer in a high position had failed.' He could not accept what the Duke told him in a letter on the subject of promotion by seniority: 'I found it always answered better than simply to select what might be a better man if by so doing I hurt the feelings and prospects of a deserving officer.'[13]

On arriving in Natal to take over command from Lord Chelmsford, Wolseley wrote to the Commander-in-Chief on 30 June 1879, on the subject of his successor should he be killed in action. 'I cannot say too much for the zeal of General Clifford. I do beg and urge upon the Government in the most earnest manner that he should be given a commission as second in command to succeed me in the event of my being shot; that is always supposing H.M.'s Government is not disposed to promote Colonel Colley to that position. He is the ablest man I know, and in the interests of the public service, if they alone are to be regarded, it would entirely be advisable that he should succeed to the command here in case of my death.' The Duke in his reply repudiated the idea that Colley could momentarily be contemplated as second in command. 'As regards the officer who would take your place in the event of anything occurring to disable you, of course this duty will devolve on Major-General Clifford, a very hard-working and able officer, in whom every confidence could be placed. I cannot at all agree in the advisability of preferring a very junior officer like Colonel Colley, however able he may be. No Army could stand these sort of preferences without entirely damping the energies of senior officers, and the balance of the advantage is very decidedly, in my opinion, in favour of the senior officer unless otherwise disqualified.'

Wolseley had all the Irishman's persistence in argument, and was not prepared to give ground, even to the Commander-in-Chief. Writing from Pretoria on 28 September he re-stated his position. 'When I wrote regarding a man to succeed me in the event of my being disposed of, I naturally assumed it would be the object of the Government that the ablest and most fitting man should succeed me. When the interests of the State are, in my opinion, concerned, I always feel it to be my duty to speak very plainly, even although I may not, when doing so, be able to do all I would, under other circumstances, do for a man like General Clifford, whom I have long known as a friend and admired as a soldier. In my humble opinion, all private interests or liking should be ignored, and all questions of professional seniority entirely put on one side when the great interests of Her Majesty's Empire are at stake. It was under the influence of these feelings that I recommended General Colley to succeed me in preference to any other officers who were senior to him in South Africa. He is *immeasurably* the ablest man here: this is a point upon which I know there are no two opinions on the part of men who know the officer I refer to, and Your Royal Highness is aware of the high opinion I entertain of General Clifford. It is but due to Her Majesty and to the State that the country should have the services of the best man to command Her Majesty's troops in the field entirely irrespective of what his present rank may be.' The Duke, however, was not convinced. 'I can assure you I take no exception to your giving me your opinions freely in your private letters, only I cannot see that the public service is benefited by our going out of our way to put some officers prominently forward on all occasions, however valuable they may be, when there are others available quite equal to perform good service also if chance be only given to them. I quite admit that the public service is the *first consideration,* and I *invariably* look to this myself. But I consider the public service is much *depressed* if certain officers are constantly brought to the front. . . . I am the first to admit that Brigadier Colley is a very able man and superior officer, and it is quite right to place every confidence in him; but there are plenty of opportunities for making his abilities of use to Her Majesty and the State, without, by so doing, injuring the feelings of others . . . No man has the public interest and service more at heart than I have, and I have nobody specially whom I wish to serve, but the *whole Army* and body of its officers in general.'[14]

When, in 1882, Wolseley was given command of the Egyptian expedition, he took advantage of his right as Commander-in-Chief in the field to correspond direct with the Secretary for War, Lord Hartington. 'There are now serving under my command,' he told him, 'some regimental Lieut.-Colonels who are entirely unfit for their positions—men who, although entrusted by regulations with the command of over eight hundred soldiers of all ranks, could not, with due regard for the lives of those soldiers and the honour and interest of the State, be allowed any independent command before an enemy . . . I hold that it is criminal to hand over in action the care of the lives of gallant soldiers to men who are deplorably ignorant of the elements of their profession. A system must be entirely and radically wrong under which officers of this stamp can obtain the position of Lieut.-Colonels in H.M.'s Army. . . . In a system of promotion by seniority neither care nor judgement need be exercised, and the fitness of an officer for his position is, in the main, left to chance. . . . An officer thus arrives at the highest position in a regiment, not in consequence of his qualifications, but simply in consequence of his place in the regimental list, frequently in the the face of known disqualifications for such a position. . . . In the Navy—the sister service of the Army—the officers to command ships are selected with the greatest care. Should not equal care be taken in choosing an officer to command a regiment or battalion?'[15]

The Duke recognized Wolseley's great ability, but regarded him as 'a desperate reformer,' who failed to look 'to the consequences in military affairs, which is a great mistake and misfortune . . . You cannot change without serious risk the military arrangements and organization which have made our power so great . . .' When Wolseley went out to the Cape in 1879, taking the usual group of friends for his staff, H.R.H. was not properly consulted, and consequently felt himself to be the victim of duplicity. He complained to Stanley that 'Sir Garnet Wolseley has made my position very uncomfortable and I can assure you I feel it most deeply. The selection of a large number of special friends is a serious blow to my position as Commander-in-Chief . . . Men have gone out *against my judgement* and this is well known to themselves and friends. Consequently they look to their patron Wolseley and no longer to me.' The Duke pointed out that Wolseley must have warned these officers to be ready to go before consulting anyone. 'This is a degree of double dealing I am not accustomed to by a General Officer in high position and which shakes my confidence in his future and my power to be of any use to him, for where there is not confidence, there is not that cordiality which is so necessary in these matters . . . I am deeply *mortified* that after twenty three years service in the past such a state of things should have arisen.'[16]

Early in 1880 there was talk of Wolseley being sent to India to succeed Sir Frederick Haines as Commander-in-Chief. The Duke resisted the suggestion, and Haines was persuaded to remain a little longer in the East. Lady Geraldine described how on 8 February H.R.H. had seen the Queen, who had written 'an admirable letter to Stanley! Quite perfect! All that he wished her to say! Told us of the presumptuous letter of Garnet Wolseley that caused it, in which he quite over-reached himself and overshot his mark! Thinking to "catch" her by speaking of the gallant *Highland* Regiment rushing to the attack with their bagpipes in the front, without naming the other Regiments at all! who had behaved quite as gallantly! and also that he wished he were in England *to help* her to carry through the views of the *Prince Consort*! In both of which he quite missed his aim! as she *only* saw his object and is extremely disgusted!! But she is anxious if he can be kept in hand, that he should be employed at the Horse Guards here where they think he can do less mischief than elsewhere! She is particularly indignant at the allusion to the Prince Consort which she says is *totally* false as he never at all had such views!!'

Wolseley soon got to hear of the opposition to his appointment, and on 20 March wrote to his wife about 'the formidable Royal party which is against me, with that silly good-meaning man the Duke of Cambridge at its head . . . It will crush me if it can, and as I am not a Party man I fear it may do so . . . I have just had a letter from that silly man Ponsonby, the Queen's Private Secretary, telling me Her Majesty is offended because I said in a letter I wrote to him, that we have never had any substantial reform in the Army since the Prince Consort died, and that were he living now, Army reform would be in a very different position from that it now occupies. This is certain, for Prince Albert was a very sensible man and not one that was likely to have taken all he was told by the Duke of Cambridge as gospel. However the Queen is a woman and can know nothing of war or of modern warfare, so she naturally leans upon her cousin of Cambridge who knows as much of modern warfare—or indeed of any warfare, as my top-boot does. She naturally adopts H.R.H.'s views, and because he hates the modern views I hold on military subjects, she thinks that I am the radical he paints me to be. I detest radicals. . . . Mr Gladstone's views are abhorrent to every instinct within me.' The Liberals 'are church wardens and parish vestry men more than Englishmen—I am a jingo of the jingoes of the highest acceptation of that title, and yet I am represented by people like the Royal George as radical!!!' Wolseley was nearly always contemptuous of those who did not agree with him, but one cannot blame him too severely for resenting being lectured on war by the Prince of Wales. 'Let him stick to his tailoring, that is his province,' was Sir Garnet's aside to his wife, 'and keep his breath for his own porridge.'

At the General Election of 1880 Gladstone had emerged from retirement, attacked Disraeli's imperial aspirations, with which H.R.H. fully sympathized, and followed a policy in South Africa which led to untold expenditure in men and money. Childers, who in Gladstone's previous Ministry had been First Lord of the Admiralty, was chosen as Secretary for War. The Duke watched the progress of the election with increasing despair. Lady Geraldine noted on 8 April, 'A little after six came the Duke very low and depressed at the dark prospects! *His* position is dreadful! And he is more to be pitied than anyone! Which brute will he get?? And have to stand by and see his Army *destroyed*! And when the sneaking dirty policy of the Brutes has drifted us into a war, then get the blame and discredit because there are neither men or materials for use! *Ungrateful* task for an ungrateful country! No wonder he is depressed.' On 11 April Lady Geraldine wrote, 'The Duke read us his letter from the Queen in which she tells him she will send for Hartington, he being the *leader* of the Opposition, and one of her *first* duties will be to see to the selection of a *safe*?? man for the War Office! She expresses her astonishment at the so entirely unexpected revolution of public opinion! But attributes it to no dislike of present policy, but to mere love of change and the notion that hard times and oppression may be helped by that!' The only spark of comfort was that H.R.H. would not have

Cardwell again at the War Office. 'One good thing he heard, that Cardwell is going, is quite weak! So, thank God! *he* at least is unfit and incapable. . . .' Cardwell's illness had begun in 1879. By 1883 he was out of his mind, and he died at Torquay in 1886. Even Wolseley, whom many accused of obsequiousness to the Liberal party, was opposed to their being returned, for although he applauded their responsiveness to military changes, he resented their indifference to imperial needs. 'If we have a change of Government,' he wrote to his wife, 'we shall have no more fighting for some time to come anywhere, for Gladstone and party would not I believe fight for the Isle of Wight if it were taken possession of by an enemy: they would find fifty reasons for concurring in the policy of masterly inactivity and some would I have no doubt go as far as to express great astonishment at it having been left so long in our possession.'[17]

Childers and the new Government soon began contemplating changes and reductions. Opening a new year in his Diary, the Duke wrote sadly in 1881, 'The year commences under deep anxiety for the future of this country and for us all who love and respect our old institutions. Under God's blessing these clouds may be dispelled, but at present nothing can be more gloomy . . . At twelve attended meeting at the War Office. It has been decided to make great changes in the Army in spite of my earnest remonstrances, but I have not succeeded in them, which I deeply deplore.' Childers, it seemed, was always 'full of new projects' many of them 'most prejudicial to the Army and extremely distasteful to myself.' 'We talked,' wrote Lady Geraldine on 29 December 1881, 'of the Duke's busy day, long War Office meeting, of Childers *busybody*! interfering in everything, wanting to change *everything*! wanting now to do away or regulate by authority the Officers Mess!! Of Garnet Wolseley supporting the Duke on the point! Of how utterly false Childers is, how he lies!' Lady Geraldine even went so far as to attribute the 'blackguard articles in the radical papers' to the Secretary for War's pen. The Duke told the Prince of Wales that Childers, far more than Wolseley, was his great enemy. Writing to the Queen in 1886, H.R.H. told her that 'Mr Childers was not "persona grata" at the Horse Guards, as you well know, and I think was more imbued with his own interests and vanity, than the good of the Army. I doubt not he meant well, but he was not a success.'[18]

The Duke, who still continued to date his correspondence from the 'Horse Guards,' was greatly disturbed to receive a letter from the Secretary for War suggesting the time had come to cease doing so. The Commander-in-Chief wrote in great agitation from Kissingen, where he was drinking the waters to alleviate gout. He declared that great issues were at stake. 'We have had so many changes of late, and the old landmarks have been so largely swept away, that it is most undesirable to make any more, and believe me that old traditions in army matters are of the *greatest value* to the Service generally, and consequently to the State.'[19]

Childers maintained, even more vigorously than Cardwell had done, that the Commander-in-Chief was the servant not master of the Secretary of State for War. Talking to Dilke he 'broke out against the Duke of Cambridge who "went chattering about the place, refused to behave as a subordinate, and wrote direct to the Queen." '[20] This implied a very exalted definition of the Minister's prerogatives, and certainly if the Duke was sometimes known to err on the side of extravagant claims, Childers was not to be outbid. It required an almost insane confidence in his own importance to suggest that the Duke might only address his cousin on military matters having first sought the Minister's permission. In a speech delivered at Pontefract on 19 January 1882, the Secretary for War harangued his audience on the need for subordinating the services entirely to Parliament. He attacked those who imagined that the Army was the Queen's. Soldiers were not 'soldiers of the Queen,' they were members of an Army of the House of Commons. The Queen could only do no wrong because her acts were those of her responsible Ministers. 'No act of discipline can be exercised, no appointment or promotion can be made, no troops can be moved, no payments can be made, without the approval, expressed or implied, of the Secretary of State.'[21]

During the two years in which Childers was at the War Office the Duke had constant occasion to write to the Queen: without permission. The Queen, so the Duke told Lady Geraldine on 16 March 1881, 'was *very* kind and gracious, very nice to him, declared staunchly she would *"never"* allow the office of Commander-in-Chief to be done away with, "she would *never stand that!"* Alas! the Queen's "nevers" and "not standing" seldom last a day!!!'

In July 1881 the Commander-in-Chief was provoked to such desperation that he sent in his resignation. It had been an exceedingly hot summer, and some men had died of sunstroke at a field day at Aldershot. Childers wrote H.R.H. a letter which the Duke regarded as a censure upon himself. Consequently on 16 July he sent a message to the Queen to say he intended resigning. 'I was greatly astonished,' wrote the Queen in her Diary, 'and said censure of George had never been implied, but only a record to be kept, that field days, should in future not be held in the middle of the day. The letter had been couched in most civil terms.' To the family circle at St James's Palace the story assumed a different significance. 'Then the Duke,' wrote Lady Geraldine on 17 July, 'gave H.R.H. [his mother] detailed accounts of his "passage of arms" with the Queen! who has been behaving very *badly* to him about those deaths from sunstroke at the Aldershot Field Day. Childers decided to write the Duke a most *offensive* letter, as he *alleged* by desire of the Queen! imputing the *blame* to him. The Duke did not really believe he had her sanction! Certainly could not accept such a letter and absolutely refused to admit that *anyone* was to blame! and sent Ellice and Whitmore to Windsor to Ponsonby, to enquire whether the letter had the Queen's sanction, and to say, if so as the Duke could not accept such a letter, he had but one course to pursue: to send in his resignation! It appears that the Queen *had* seen the letter! . . . but "did not read it, at all as the Duke did, as imputing blame to him"! Some shifty doubtful excuses, but the fact remained, the Queen *had* sanctioned a letter being written to him. On their return with this information, the Duke sat down and wrote to the Queen, sending her his resignation! "No longer enjoying her confidence and support he could no longer hold the command he for many years had had" etc.!! This he sent her. Shortly after, before she could have received this, crossing with it, he got by messenger, a most amiable letter from her!! full of apologetic excuses! that she had never understood this so, never meant it, etc., etc.!!! and begging he would think no more of it! He had to write again, thanking her, accepting the apologies, which therefore rendered his other letter and resignation nugatory, but saying that as this letter of Childers to him of course remains on record, he thought at least the Queen ought to have it nullified.'

The appointment in 1881 of Wolseley as Adjutant General led the Duke to threaten resignation for the second time in the year. The Adjutant General's office was one which necessitated constant co-operation with the Commander-in-Chief, and moreover provided its holder with dangerous opportunities for introducing changes. The Liberal Government wished to appoint Wolseley so that he would be in an effective position to resist the Duke's rearguard action against reforms, and it was in vain that H.R.H. protested that the new Adjutant General would disrupt the harmony of the Horse Guards, since that was precisely the Prime Minister's intention.

In the very year in which Wolseley's appointment was being angrily contested between the Duke and Childers, Sir Garnet aggravated the hostility of the Horse Guards by his complicity in various critical articles published in 1881, condemning traditional Army arrangements and advocating the very changes which Wolseley and his friends were known to desire.

The Duke of Cambridge had suffered too much from newspapers to regard them with favour, and as Sir Charles Phipps once told the Prince Consort, 'fear of the press' was 'inherent' in him.[22] The Duke of Wellington had always suspected officers who wrote for the papers, a practice he described as 'croaking,' and indeed he forbade officers to write for publication. Not only did he regard the habit as subversive of discipline, but he attributed to it much of the ignorant but dangerous criticism which the Army constantly encountered. 'As soon as an accident happens,'

Wellington declared, 'every man who can write, and who has a friend who can read, sits down to write his account of what he does not know, and his comments on what he does not under-stand, and these are diligently circulated and exaggerated by the idle and malicious, of whom there are plenty in all armies. The consequence is that officers and whole regiments lose their reputation and a spirit of party, which is the bane of all armies, is engendered and fomented.'

If Wolseley's opponents were inclined to blame him for attacks in the Press which although expressing his views did not actually proceed from his pen, he was in truth guilty of writing many provocative articles and of delivering speeches peppered with rash indiscretions. The newspapers, for which Sir Garnet provided an unending supply of copy, were always eager to publish his articles or those of his friends. Wolseley's set, the 'Garnet Ring,' in 1879 was given a new nickname. 'The Duke,' wrote Lady Geraldine on 13 October, 'told us of a capital new name they have got now— besides the old original "mutual admiration society"! which is so good! They call them now: "the press gang"! That is excellent.' At the first night of *The Pirates of Penzance* it did not need George Grossmith's admirable make-up to enable the audience to discover who was 'the very model of a modern Major Gen-eral.' Indeed the phrase 'All Sir Garnet' was the Victorian way of saying 'all correct.'

The Duke was naturally wounded by some of the things said about him in the newspapers, and mischief-makers were quick to allege that Wolseley was their author or inspirer. Major George FitzGeorge suggested to Wolseley that it might be advisable for him to clear up growing misunderstandings, and taking the hint, Sir Garnet sought an interview with the Com-mander-in-Chief. 'Had a long interview with Wolseley,' wrote the Duke on 26 November, 'who gave explanations and assurances that recent attacks were neither directly nor indirectly inspired by himself, nor did they come from him. Certainly these assurances were remarkably decided, and appeared frank.'

The Duke told the Queen that he had seen Wolseley. 'Saw

George C.,' she wrote on 4 December, 'who was quite quiet and thanked me for my assistance, regretting all the trouble I had had. He hoped things would go on better now, and with right, blamed Mr Childers very much, spoke of the shameful atrocious articles in *The Times*, which no one knows who they were written by. George is convinced that they were inspired by the War Office. Sir G. Wolseley he now exonerates, after having talked with him, and he hopes he will behave well . . . Mr Childers has written to me, to the effect, that Sir G. Wolseley will abstain from writing and speaking on military matters whilst he is in his present position.' Lady Geraldine was not quite as prepared as the Duke to accept Wolseley's assurances. On 29 November she wrote, 'The Duke told us how well satisfied he is, he has had his explanation from Wolseley and how great the mistake was Wolseley did not speak openly to him before! With his *marvellous* power of forgiveness and real utter forgetfulness of injury, that fine and rare quality of his, ready to *forget* all injury done to him at the first word of apology! And from his own truth and loyalty his ready belief in that of others, he is now "perfectly satisfied" that Wolseley had nothing to do with those articles! and convinced now they have honestly spoken together, he and Wolseley will get on capitally! Altogether he is much happier, quite happy now! and altogether another man from that he was last week!!' A few years later, Lady Geraldine came to the conclusion that Childers rather than Wolseley instigated the Press attacks. The Queen, she wrote on 14 December 1884, has 'fully found out how Childers *lies*! which the poor Duke had such sore reason to discover while he was at the War Office, where he always affected to be *so put out* at the abominable newspaper articles which without doubt, emanated from himself!'

Wolseley gave Colonel FitzGeorge an account of his interview with H.R.H. 'I had a satisfactory interview with His Royal Highness, and was very glad I acted upon your advice. I tried to impress upon him how impossible it would have been for me in the position which I occupied to have seen him earlier on the subject of the newspaper articles that had given him pain. In the

o

first instance it was some time before I knew that I had been put down as the author or inspirer of the articles, and when I was told it by Mr Childers I said to him frankly that I felt it insulting to me to imagine I had anything to do with them. I think it is rather hard that I should be set down as the author or inspirer of everything that appears in the Press against the administration of the Army. But let that pass; I urged as strongly as I could that in my opinion it would have been most indelicate of me to have seen the Duke about articles discussing me as Adjutant General: it would have looked as if I wished to ask for the berth, or to force myself upon His Royal Highness. I had never asked any one for it: if I had asked any one for it I should have gone straight to the Duke, although I should have felt, of course, that he would not have given it to me.'[23]

Lord Napier was disposed to blame Childers for this epidemic of Press criticism. 'Mr Childers,' he wrote from Gibraltar, 'behaves shamefully in permitting such breaches of official confidence, but the same action has characterized the proceedings of the leaders of that party.' Some of the articles had been so well informed that it was presumed that they were written with knowledge derived from official sources. 'I hope,' Napier continued, 'the Duke will not pay attention to these malignant and base attacks, but will hold his own, and if Wolseley is forced upon him, will keep him in order.' 'I was very glad,' he wrote a few months later, 'to see the St James' Gazette and the Army and Navy reply to The Times. Mr Childers must see the false ground he was getting on and that these shameful and false attacks on the Duke make H.R.H.'s position much stronger. I cannot believe that the Country wil allow a clique to worry out a Commander-in-Chief who possesses the confidence of the army in his justice and knowledge of the Service.'[24]

The efforts of the Radical Press to force the Duke to resign encouraged many Generals, and even a former War Minister, to express their confidence in H.R.H., and their hope that he would not yield to such pressure. 'Though I have felt much sympathy,' wrote Lord Cranbrook, 'with your Royal Highness under the mean and malignant attack to which you have been subjected I have hesitated to write in case I might seem to be meddling in matters which no longer concern me. I cannot however recall the frank and cordial relations with you which made my tenure of the War Office so pleasant to myself without expressing my sense of the injustice which is done to you by an anonymous press, under which personal enmity conceals itself. The fact that Your Royal Highness' position precludes you from replying makes the false insinuations the more cruel. I have reason to know the want of truth in the suggestion made that you have impeded the progress of changes which the Secretary of State had decided upon. Your opinion, as was your duty, you freely gave but never failed to act upon decisions even though averse to them. I cannot say that I am surprised, though shocked, at the subtle attempts to disparage you.'

General Steele, in command at Dublin, wrote assuring the Duke of the confidence of the army. 'I cannot resist,' he declared, 'writing a line to Your Royal Highness on the subject of those vile articles in *The Times*, evidently the production of Brackenbury dictated by Wolseley. I look with perfect dismay on the future; but I trust Your Royal Highness will not give way and entertain for one minute the idea of resigning the position of Commander-in-Chief. You may take my word that not only the older officers, but the young ones also look with dread at the prospect of the army passing into the hands of that self glorifying clique. The subject is freely discussed over here and I hear but one opinion. The intention of forcing you to resign is so obvious that I am sure Your Royal Highness will forgive me for writing so plainly and assuring you of the confidence that the large majority of the army feel towards you.'[25]

Wolseley, even after his appointment as Adjutant General, and despite holding an official position, continued to write and speak as if independent. It would be difficult to deduce from his recorded utterances that he was himself one of the foremost figures in the military hierarchy. In 1887, the year of the Queen's Jubilee, Wolseley made a number of speeches in which he arrogantly

claimed that he had reorganized the Army and rid it of inefficiency. The Duke was furious. Lady Geraldine on 24 April re-
counted a conversation in which 'we talked of the *impertinence*
of Wolseley not attending the banquet last night! because he preferred to go to a *press* dinner, to fawn upon and be fawned upon
by the press!! He had much better have let it alone, for as usual
and invariably he made a most egotistic speech, glorifying himself and offending everyone else! taking great merit to himself for
having at last succeeded in getting rid of the *theatrical* side of the
British Army!!!!! and in reducing our curiously constituted
Army to a real fighting organization!!!! Such insolence! *Always*
that insolent tone as though the Army had never done anything,
never been heard of, never existed until under, by, and through
him! Such arrogance! How marvellous a thing it is, he *never can*
make a speech without offending someone! He is no gentleman,
it is all summed up in the fact that he is a regular thorough
Irishman, that most detestable and intolerable of all God's creations.'
    The next day Lady Geraldine asked the Duke 'whether he had
brought Wolseley to book! as to the meaning of his impertinence
about his "having got rid of the theatrical side of the British
Army"? He had, and the fellow explained he meant as to uniforms! Was there ever anything so ridiculous as a cocked hat?
Fancy a cocked hat in a campaign!! to be buttoned and hooked
up to the chin!!! The Duke answered he had worn a cocked hat
all through the Crimea and had thought it a very comfortable
headdress! And as for being buttoned up, he supposed he preferred to see the dirty shirts of the men!! remarking also that
nothing can be more buttoned up and stiffer than the Prussian
Army, supposed to be *the* great military model! to which
Wolseley answered "Oh! the Prussians? Theirs is *the most*
theatrical Army in Europe!" The Duke then asked him *what*
Army then he deigned to approve? The fellow then said, in every
way the most admirable and praiseworthy and sensibly dressed
Army *he* had ever seen was the *American*!!!! After *that*, there was
no more to say! A filthy Republican rabble! Wolseley went to
the room of one of the others and affected great innocence, asking

"What did I say? I really don't know! Give me a paper that I may see! I am such a fool I always say something that is taken ill"!! A regular odious Irishman.'

On 4 May, less than a fortnight later, Wolseley again 'rejoiced us with one of his delectable speeches! at some function in the City; he told General Harman à propos of his Press Association speech, that he was so *annoyed* he had most particularly begged there might be no reporters present! on which the Duke very pertinently remarked *he* was not in the habit of begging his speeches not to be reported as himself he had no intention of saying anything he saw reason to be ashamed of!!' Later in the year Wolseley referred contemptuously to barrack-square drill as the end-all and be-all of military training. The Duke protested that the Adjutant General had no right to make such criticisms in public speeches. Sir Garnet, evading the question of his right to denounce the policy of the Commander-in-Chief, replied by saying, 'I have been always in touch with the officers who advocate progress and who attach the greatest importance to military training, that is, to the highest form of drill. These men think our military training is too much sacrificed to show parade movements, and that the soldier can be better disciplined both in body and mind by being taught the duties and evolutions he *must* practise before an enemy, than by parade movements only possible in peace.'

The Duke was not to be diverted from the issue of Wolseley's indiscretion by discussing the rights and wrongs of what he had said. 'With reference to the letter I have just received from you, and in which you say that you, in the main, agree with me, though you adhere to your views, I really don't think there can be much, if any, difference at all between us, as the more that drill is adapted daily to the details of intended movements, the more I shall be pleased . . . I am at all times most willing to attend to any suggestions or recommendations . . . to make training or equipment in any way more adapted to modern requirements. What I really do object to is that in public addresses made from time to time, very disparaging expressions occur of our old

system as compared with what you would wish to have done . . .
I am sure that you will feel with me, that the Adjutant General of
the Army when writing in public periodicals on military subjects,
carries great weight in his utterances, and that it is not desirable
that in that capacity he should express himself on controversial
matters, which are sure to elicit comment of various kinds . . . It
is undesirable for officers of the Army on full pay to express their
opinions in any other way than by the legitimate channels of
communication to the Commander-in-Chief.'[26]

The Duke opposed Wolseley's appointment to the post of
Adjutant General on two grounds. First he believed his military
views to be too revolutionary, and secondly he maintained that
Wolseley was incapable of discretion and would prove an intolerable colleague. It was for these reasons that H.R.H. refused
to recommend Wolseley to the Queen. He explained his position
in a letter to Lord Hartington, for a time the Liberal most trusted
by the Royal Family. 'Writing to Mr Childers, with whom I
have always been on the best and most cordial terms, I happened
to tell him that I could not think of Sir G. W. as the future A.G.
because whilst being on perfectly friendly terms with Wolseley,
he belonged to the new school which I did not. At this expression
Childers seems to have taken alarm and to have supposed that I
meant to imply that I wished the new A.G. to work under me, in a
direction entirely opposed to the present system. Such an idea did
not cross my mind but what I intended to convey was that whilst
Wolseley and I are on perfectly good terms as between man and
man, his views and mine on almost every subject are so divergent,
that in that special position in which he virtually is my "alter
ego," I could never feel that confidence in him, which it is
essential in the interests of the Public Service as well as to my own
comfort and even usefulness as a public officer, should exist
between the C. in C. and his right hand man the A.G. But in
saying this I did not intend to convey the idea that I wanted to
create opposition to the present order of things. I have, much
against my personal feelings, accepted them and having done so I
should fail in my duty were I not to try to carry them out, but I

must be allowed to do so through men in whom the Army and myself more particularly have real confidence, and not through the man who has never failed to take every opportunity of insulting the Army, and speaking and writing in a sense which he must have known must be distasteful to the present head of his profession, whom I consider he is bound loyally to serve and not to oppose.' The Duke continued that it would not help, as suggested by the Queen, to make Roberts Quartermaster General, 'because the Q.M.G. is entirely subordinate to the A.G. I cannot start with an A.G. *against* whom I am *guarding* myself in all directions. I must trust him for *himself*.'[27]

In his official letters the Duke exercised some restraint in his criticism of Wolseley, but in his conversations with his mother he spoke of him as a 'firebrand,' as 'underhand, untrue, false, disloyal, overbearing and bumptious to a degree! Self-opinionated and riding all rough shod.' He complained of 'the serious harm and hurt he does the Army with his theories and innovations and favouritism.'[28] Wolseley, who was only five foot seven inches, had some of the urge to assert himself of Napoleon: a comparison he would not have considered far fetched. Beside the Duke, an impressive mass of a man, he certainly looked, and possibly felt, very small. Unconsciously he cast himself in the role of David defying Goliath.

Childers told the Duke bluntly that the new system in the Army could only be made to work successfully if administered by those who looked upon it favourably, and although the Commander-in-Chief always loyally endeavoured to implement decisions to which he was opposed, it was essential to have some senior officers who looked upon reforms with enthusiasm. 'Your Royal Highness referring to Sir Garnet Wolseley, says that while personally you and he are perfect good friends, professionally you are as far as possible divergent; You, Sir, having been consistent in your Military opinions, whereas he belongs to a new school; and it is on this latter ground, and not because of any personal objection, that you would not wish to see him appointed Adjutant General. . . . Since 1869–70, new principles in military administration have been introduced and are now fully established. They have no connection with party politics, for they have been accepted as fully by the Conservative party during their six years of office from 1874 to 1880, as by Mr Cardwell who introduced them, and by myself who have completed them. . . . Now, Sir, I must remind you that to all these changes Your Royal Highness is and has been (to use the word in your letter to me) consistently opposed . . . And, Sir, you will forgive my saying that your opinions are well known to the Army, and that officers cannot but hope to find favour with you by advocating as many do, disapproval of the policy of 1869 to 1881. That Your Royal Highness, as head of the Military Department is perfectly loyal, and that you give a cordial support to the Secretary of State I should be the first to proclaim. But now that the policy which you, Sir, have consistently opposed has become the established policy of the country, I think the time has come when the Secretary of State is entitled and bound to take care that among those who have to give effect to it, the principal officers under Your Royal Highness should be identified with it in sentiment; and especially that the Adjutant General should be an officer known to the Army to be of the new, and not of the old, school. . . . It is impossible that any policy can be worked heartily and "with a will," unless a fair proportion of those who administer it look upon it favourably and even cordially.'[29]

At a meeting at the War Office on 10 October to which H.R.H. had been summoned from a tour of inspection at Plymouth, the Secretary for War attempted in vain to persuade the Duke to recommend Wolseley's appointment. 'I firmly refused to consent to such an arrangement, much to his vexation I could observe.' That deadlock had been reached soon became known. The *Court Journal* of 19 November announced: 'The most straitened relationship exists between Mr Childers and the Duke of Cambridge. The former knows absolutely less than nothing about Military administration and organization; while as every soldier will testify, the Commander-in-Chief knows not only every move but almost every individual officer . . . It is now a combat

between ignorance, as represented by Mr Childers, and knowledge, as represented by the Duke.'

An appeal to the Queen was the next inevitable move in the
struggle, and the Duke decided both in his dealings with his
cousin and with the Secretary for War, to throw the threat of
resignation into the scale. The Queen originally took the line that
the appointment was out of the question. 'Saw Sir H. Ponsonby,'
she wrote in her Diary on 16 September, 'about a letter George
had had, from Mr Childers, about the Adjutant General, which
annoys him very much. Mr Childers wants Sir G. Wolseley,
which is impossible, and which would cause George to resign.'
However, when it became evident that the Government was
determined to appoint Wolseley, and was not to be browbeaten
by missives from Balmoral, she began to advocate compromise.
As Lady Geraldine complained, 'Alas! the Queen's "nevers"
seldom last a day!'

On 17 October the Duke sent the Queen a copy of a letter he
had received the day before from Childers. 'I cannot tell you how
it has distressed me, for it places me in a most difficult position, for
either I shall be compelled to accept as Adj. General an officer in
whom I never can feel the slightest real confidence and sympathy,
or it obliges me to ask you to consider whether the time has not
come when as an honourable man, I cannot any longer continue
to hold the office I have endeavoured to fill to the best of my
ability in the interests of the Sovereign and of the Army . . .
You know that I frequently of late have accepted changes which
I have not and could not approve of. I have done so in the interests
of the Crown and of the army, as I thought my retirement might
lead to complications and difficulties of a very grave character.
But there is a limit beyond which I could go not, and that limit as
it appears to me, has by the present action been attained . . .'[30]

Lady Geraldine described in her Diary the Duke's reception of
the letter from Childers which provoked this threat of resignation.
'The Duke told us!! he has a letter from that *brute* Childers!!. . .
coolly telling him: Garnet Wolseley is to be Adjutant General!
and he has submitted the appointment to the Queen!!! It is *the*

most outrageous insolence ever perpetrated!!! And in every way *too abominable*! Nasty brute of a fellow. And what a humbugging lying brute! A *"radical"* through and through, with all that is disgusting, hateful, contemptible, despicable, dishonourable, in those of that party.'

Sir William Harcourt was staying at Balmoral when the Duke's threat of resignation arrived, and he wrote to Gladstone describing the consternation it caused. The Queen apparently had approached Harcourt hoping to obtain his advice, but he was forced to tell her that 'it was impossible for one Secretary of State to invade or intermeddle with the affairs of a department of a colleague.' Harcourt attributed the Duke's hostility to 'strong personal antipathy . . . The question as I understand it is really one of "incompatibility," which between husband and wife is often regarded as a good ground of amiable separation. It seems almost idle to hope that the Duke and Sir Garnet can live conjugally together.' Harcourt went on to say, 'I have not ventured myself to offer any suggestion, but I have endeavoured to lay before you the situation as it is. It is very like the dramatic position in *The Critic* when all the parties are at a deadlock each with his dagger at the other's throat, and how it is to be terminated is not obvious. I fear not by the formula, "In the Queen's name I bid you all drop your swords and daggers." The only thing I feel strongly is that the resignation of the Duke should if possible be averted. The Queen evidently looks to you to help her out of the scrape, of the gravity of which I think she is entirely aware . . .'[31]

The Queen, recognizing that the Government would never retract, and anxious to avoid the Duke's resignation, tried personally to persuade him to accept Wolseley as Adjutant General, arguing that H.R.H. would be in a better position to control him if he were made an official subordinate. 'The Queen has so much to do this morning,' wrote Ponsonby on her behalf, 'that Her Majesty has scarcely time to write fully to Your Royal Highness and has commanded me to do so. The Queen fears that Mr Childers thinks the success of his Army Reforms depends on the Assistance of Sir Garnet Wolseley. She believes that he fully appreciates the loyal support he has received from Your Royal Highness but that he considers Sir Garnet's aid at present almost a part of the new scheme which Your Royal Highness has undertaken to support. Her Majesty quite agrees with Your Royal Highness but thinks it would be impolitic to raise a serious controversy on this question and having given her approval to the *trial* of the new Army plan the Queen feels obliged and bound to give it every chance of success. Sir Garnet Wolseley seems just now to be a sort of half irresponsible adviser to the Secretary of State. Would it not be better that he should hold the really responsible position under Your Royal Highness? The Queen understands that this is the opinion of many distinguished officers, who while disliking the new reforms and heartily supporting Your Royal Highness' position, point out that to object to Mr Childers' wish to have Sir Garnet as Adjutant General would expose Your Royal Highness to all the attacks of those who declare that the shortcomings of the new plan are due to the attitude taken by the Commander-in-Chief. The Queen asks if Your Royal Highness would not think it preferable to send for Sir Garnet Wolseley, to tell him frankly the reasons which have made Your Royal Highness object to his appointment and then to come to an understanding with him for the harmonious conduct of the business of the office, insisting on pledges being given that no communication with the Press or Parliament should ever take place. The Queen merely mentioned this in case Your Royal Highness should find no other solution possible.'

The Commander-in-Chief received this letter while staying with the Prince of Wales at Sandringham. The Prince was strongly in favour of his 'Uncle George' resisting the Queen's attempted compromise, and doubtless the letter the Duke sent to Balmoral was influenced by his host's views. 'My dear Cousin,' he wrote, 'I received here yesterday morning a letter from Sir Henry Ponsonby, written by your direction, which has given me much pain and distress, in as much as it seems to me to modify very considerably the views you so graciously expressed to me in your last letter. From that I was under the impression that you would continue to back up my strong conviction, on public grounds, against the appointment of Sir Garnet Wolseley as Adjutant General. Sir H. Ponsonby's letter on the other hand makes me fear that I am in error in this respect and that you think it undesirable that any further opposition to the appointment should now be made. If I were in doubt as regards the importance of the step about to be taken by the Government as regards this matter, any misapprehension has been entirely cleared up by an article in this day's *Times*, which virtually, and no doubt by inspiration from high quarters, actually announces the decision come to by the Government, and that moreover in terms *most offensive* to the high office with which you have entrusted me, and which I have now filled for so many years. The Adjutant General in this article is pointed out to be the officer who is expected to give advice and carry out the orders and directions of the Secretary of State; and the Commander-in-Chief's functions are entirely ignored or set on one side. Indeed all the attributes now belonging to my office are specified and layed down in detail as belonging to the position of the Adjutant General, and it is further asserted that the Adjutant General is the Queen's Adjutant General, and that the Commander-in-Chief's position is one of much more recent date. This may be the case, but certainly not in the spirit and sense in which the relative positions of those two officers have stood towards one another as long as the present generation can remember. Such being the view now put forward in so clear and decided a manner, I hope you will permit me to put before you how *impossible* my position must become if I accept such conditions. I could not serve you, or do my duty by the Army or the Country if I am not a *free agent* in the first place, and if I am not to retain in *fact* as well as in name the powers hitherto entrusted to me. If it can be pointed out in any way that I have failed in my duty, I hope no hesitation would prevent such a statement being put forward. But suddenly to be placed in an inferior and degraded position would be unbearable to myself, and would I feel sure be unacceptable to you. I shall probably be told by the Government, represented by the Secretary of State, that he is not responsible for the article in *The Times*. This technically is most likely the case, but nobody will every persuade me that what is stated in that *Times* article is not inspired by somebody in authority, whoever that somebody may be.'

Ponsonby had said that H.R.H. had not made any 'positive charge' against Wolseley. 'I only declined,' explained the Duke, 'to do so in writing. I considered, as I still do, that the appointment rests between the Secretary of State and myself before submission to you, and *not* with Her Majesty's Government, such being a purely *Military* and *not* political appointment. To you I am only too happy to state my objections. I consider in the first place that Sir Garnet is *not* the officer I deem at present best qualified for the Post, or as having the strongest claims to it . . . In the next place I think the Army wants *rest*. Such great changes have been introduced, that time should be given to allow matters to settle down. Sir Garnet Wolseley's great object seems to be to go further and further, and to upset the little that is left of the old spirit of the officer by indiscriminate selection, by carrying education to the extremist limit, by letting men go to the Reserve after three years service, and in a variety of ways intensifying the sweeping changes that have already been effected. Thirdly I think the mode of his introduction into the office of Adjutant General would be a direct slur and imputation upon me, and on the manner in which I have performed my departmental duty as military adviser of the Secretary of State and as such a serious insult would be offered to me in my official position. Lastly Sir Garnet's close connection with the Press, and his strong expressions on Military matters in speeches and writings . . . would prove most detrimental to the interests of the Army, and would certainly turn military matters into subjects for political discussions, which in my opinion, should on all accounts be avoided when military questions are involved . . . I fear there is now no alternative left to me but to withdraw from a position which has become unbearable, certainly not by my seeking, but by the extraordinary manner in which a particular officer has been forced upon me for the post of all others which requires mutual confidence and sympathy.'[32]

Sir Francis Knollys, the Prince of Wales's Secretary, told the Duke, 'If your Royal Highness wishes to ensure real assistance from Balmoral, I venture to express an opinion that you must continue to show them a firm front and an earnest determination to resign.' When it became known that Wolseley's appointment was inevitable, the Prince himself recommended the Duke to withdraw from his command. 'Now,' he wrote, 'that it seems inevitable that Wolseley is to be Adjutant General you will have to decide as to whether after all you have said—it is compatible with your dignity to retain the position as Commander-in-Chief. Deeply as I would regret your resignation for the sake of the Queen, for all of us her children, for the Army and for the Country, it would be far better for you to do that than become a cypher and the mere tool and subordinate of Messrs Childers and Wolseley—besides what would your position be with the Army? When officers come to your levees, to your office and write to you to ask you to do this and that, what answer can you give them? Simply that you must refer the matter to Mr Childers. By your remaining you play into the hands of those who have made your position virtually untenable—by resigning you will always be a thorn in their side—but what is far more important—you will be able to benefit the Army to which you are so devoted and for whom you have worked for upwards of twenty seven years as their Commander-in-Chief, far more—when your hands are un-fettered—in your place in the House of Lords and on many other public occasions you will be able to speak your mind out—and point out the utter fallacy of this new army organization—and prove to them why you could not hold your present post any longer . . . After long and mature consideration the conclusion that I have come to is to offer this advice, in which all those who esteem and love you will I am sure concur—and if I have spoken plainly you will I am sure forgive your very affectionate nephew and cousin, Albert Edward.'[33]

When it became evident at Balmoral that somebody was

urging the Commander-in-Chief to resign, the Queen was horrified to discover it was her own son. Ponsonby, writing to the Duke on 2 December, mentioned that 'the Queen asked me who could possibly advise your Royal Highness to resign as it would be such a serious mistake to do so, and she went on to say she was sure the Prince of Wales had strongly urged you to maintain your position. Her Majesty stopped and asked me if this was not so. Of course I had to tell the Queen that I believed His Royal Highness took the very opposite view of the question. But I said nothing more as to where I derived this information.'

In the end Wolseley became Adjutant General and the Duke was prevailed upon to give up all thought of resigning. To save his face he was not required to recommend Sir Garnet to the Queen, but merely offered no objection to the appointment. The announcement, on H.R.H.'s insistence, was so worded as to emphasize the subordinate position of Wolseley to the Commander-in-Chief. Although in the years ahead there were to be many disputes between the Duke and his Adjutant General, H.R.H. soon came to appreciate Sir Garnet's ability as an administrator, and both men at least shared a common distrust of political interference in the Army.

'The Duke told us,' wrote Lady Geraldine on 16 July 1882, 'that it has turned out fortunate at this moment that he has Sir Garnet Wolseley as Adjutant General instead of Sir Charles Ellice! First he is much more hard working than him, or Horsford, and being on his mettle to make his famous *system* answer, he is determined it *shall* answer if he can make it, and works tooth and nail for that object; and above all! that he being here, no one can pretend it is not effectually worked and fails for want of being properly and fairly carried out. The Duke says of him he is decidedly clear headed and an able administrator; and that what is very amusing is that these fellows have themselves given themselves their *master* in him!!! He *wanted* the Duke to refuse all conference with the Cabinet Ministers and organize alone!! Which *unfortunately* is impossible.'

THE DUKE AND WOLSELEY

O F all Liberal measures to reform the Army, Childers was responsible for the most unpopular: the Territorial System. The idea was first proposed in 1877 by a committee under Stanley which recommended, amongst other proposals, establishing territorial regiments, combining regular soldiers with the Militia. The proposal was rejected by Disraeli, although the mere suggestion of it alarmed the Queen, who feared it would threaten regimental *esprit de corps*. The Duke told her, 'I have no hesitation in saying, that anything more distasteful to me than the recommendations of the recent Committee with reference to the Territorial Regiments I cannot conceive. The whole of my evidence before that Committee was against that one particular change.' In a speech delivered in 1878 he declared that 'the Army of England could not be localized. I have ventured to point out the variety of service for which our Army is called upon. We may look upon ourselves as an Army in a mobilized state, and if it is mobilized, you cannot make it a local Army. The Militia and

Volunteers are essential for local service, whereas the Army of England can never be local beyond its depots, for I think it a pity to attempt to imitate foreign armies because our conditions of service abroad are necessarily different from those of any other country.'[1]

Childers, however, was determined to pursue the matter and set up a committee in 1880 to examine how best to implement Stanley's proposals. A plan was suggested, but the Committee's Chairman, Sir Charles Ellice, warned the Secretary for War that 'they could not conceal from themselves that the fusing together of so many Regiments hitherto separate, and the consequent alteration of titles and abolition of numbers surrounded with associations, will inflict a shock on the feelings of officers and men of those battalions which will thus lose their cherished designations.' Undeterred by this warning, Childers decided upon making the change.

The Duke, unable to persuade the Secretary for War that the plan was disastrous, wrote first to Ponsonby and then to the Queen. 'My province,' he told Ponsonby, 'will be to carry out this plan to the best of my ability. But anything more distasteful or detrimental to the *esprit de corps*, and therefore the best interests of the service, I cannot imagine. . . . That the Army should be thoroughly disgusted by such a condition of affairs, which is now to be perpetuated by the proposed order of things, is not to be wondered at. I, alas! can only *warn*, and I do so, I fear, even at the risk of appearing obstructive, but *I am not so*, and I am only doing my duty as entrusted by the Queen with the chief command of the Army.' Hearing that Childers was going to Osborne two days after Christmas, he wrote to the Queen hoping she might 'have an opportunity of preventing the mischief that must result from Territorial Regiments, with the entire destruction of *esprit de corps*. These are no days to play tricks with the Army . . . I hope, therefore you will see Your way to making some stand upon the old Regimental system of our glorious Army. It has stood many shocks, and has done its duty nobly by the Crown and by the Country. It is worth saving. However, You are so well-informed upon all these matters, that I need not remind You of

P

them. All I can say is, that nothing can be worse than the present prospect, and the new proposals are to my mind, as regards Territorial Regiments, graver than anything that has yet been done or suggested . . . and will be most unpalatable to the Army as a whole.'[2] This plea represented H.R.H.'s second attempt to enlist the Queen's support. Earlier in the month, on 7 December, he had asked for an interview. 'Saw George C.,' wrote the Queen in her Diary, 'who was in a great and frantic state, about the proposals for the Army and the linking of battalions . . . I tried to reassure and quiet him.'

Neither the Queen nor the Duke could prevent the introduction of the Territorial System, but, as Ellice had prophesied, it was bitterly resented by the Army. Napier wrote to H.R.H. saying that he fully appreciated 'the trial that Your Royal Highness has under the present administration. The evil advice of interested soldiers misleads men at the head of affairs, whose object is to please the people with a show of economy.'[3]

In 1882 the Liberal Government found itself committed to war in Egypt, to avenge the massacre of Christians in Alexandria, and to protect the Suez Canal. When the Cabinet finally decided upon intervention it reached two characteristic decisions: to appoint Wolseley to command the expedition, and to authorize a wholly inadequate force with which to conduct the campaign. The Duke and the Adjutant General both agreed on the need to send more troops than was first envisaged, and H.R.H. persuaded Childers, for once successfully, that unless 15,000 men were despatched, it would be 'most hazardous,' and 'quite unjustifiable by all the rules of war.' He discussed on 19 August at St James's, 'the utter folly and madness of this absurd carrying on War on a Peace establishment!' He talked of 'Childers always declaring his famous organization failed because the last Government did not carry it out fully and now *he* does exactly the same, only under infinitely *worse* conditions! as they were at peace whereas now they have a great war actually on their hands of which *no one* can foretell the dimensions it will assume! Idiocy!! and all this penny wise and pound foolish only to ask a vote of credit one *half* of that they ought to have asked and to say to the Duke of Cambridge see how economical we are! At what risk? at what cost?? Of how the *next* measure of these *vile* fellows will be to do away with the red uniform!! then the last vestige of the old army is gone!! that army that conquered the world in red! the *poor* Duke! it is heart breaking work, struggling with these brutes inch by inch! fighting bravely against their destruction of *everything*!'

On 13 September, Wolseley won the battle of Tel-el-Kebir and as a result Egypt came under British control. 'The Duke,' wrote Lady Geraldine the day after the battle, 'is not only immensely pleased with the whole thing, but with Wolseley's management of it all, his disposition, and use of his troops.' Colonel George FitzGeorge, on his return from the Campaign, visited the Duchess on 5 October. 'He gave *high* praise to Wolseley! The confidence he inspires, his cheeriness and good humour, thought for others.' The Duke was delighted with Wolseley's present to him of three rifles found in Arabi's bedroom, and for a short time the Adjutant General was almost forgiven his faults and shortcomings. Moreover, not only had he sent Colonel George home with the despatches announcing the victory of Tel-el-Kebir, but he had telegraphed for Augustus FitzGeorge to join him in Egypt. H.R.H. was not to know with what reluctance Sir Garnet had acted. 'In his last letter the Duke of Cambridge said that his son Augustus was now quite well and anxious to come out; what could I do but telegraph for him? This is very unfair upon me . . . Perhaps old mother FitzGeorge would like to come also?'[4]

A great parade was held to celebrate the triumphant return of the troops from Egypt. The Duke told his mother and Lady Geraldine about the ill-feeling caused by the Queen's arrangements for the Review. 'Spoke of the Review on Saturday, and the successful efforts of the Queen to make it as unpleasant and inconvenient for everybody as possible! and to prevent anyone but herself seeing anything! long discussion as to how on earth to manage that the family should be enabled in some degree to see! the Duke and the Prince alone to be allowed to be on horseback by her carriage. Of the Princess Royal coming all the way from

Berlin for it, and seeing nothing!' The quarrels which began
some time before the parade broke out again on the day itself.
Childers was 'much affronted at not having had a place in the
cortège!! the pretension!!! Probably he thinks he ought to have
been on horseback at the door of the Queen's carriage instead of
the Duke!!! He takes it very ill.'[5] The Princess Royal cried
throughout the proceedings and the Duke of Albany was exceedingly dissatisfied with the way in which things had been
organized. He thought it a mistake that the Duke of Connaught
rode in the Queen's carriage, and the festivities of the day were
overshadowed by disagreeable dissensions.

The Campaign in Egypt led to a proposal to introduce khaki
uniform: a practical enough proposal but calculated to inspire
apoplectic opposition. At St James's the idea was deplored. There
was talk of the 'scarlet that conquered the world in the happy days
before they [the Liberal reformers] were born and the House of
Commons reigned!!! And now our troops are to wear dust colour
because red is *too dangerous* in war!!! Disgusting!'[6] At the age of
fourteen the Duke had deplored changes in uniform. He had
written to his father in 1833 telling him, 'You cannot conceive
how sorry I am that the handsome dresses of the Hussars are to be
changed.'[7] Now that he was over sixty he regarded alterations
with increased distaste.

Wolseley's views on uniform were defiantly unorthodox. As a
young soldier he had been forced to fight in the jungle 'in a
scarlet cloth jacket buttoned up to the chin, and in white buck-
skin gloves.' He nearly melted in the tropical heat and never forgot the experience. As soon as he was in a position to flout
regulations, he discarded his official uniform whenever he possibly
could, in favour of a 'sloppy, badly fitting khaki Norfolk jacket,
a dreadful garment that looked as if it had been cut out with a
knife and fork. Look at any photograph of the conqueror, taken
on his return. He is in this horrid little jacket: a wide expanse of
neck and throat is bared by the amazingly wide collar (surely of
his own design too), around which hangs his G.C.M.G. in so
slovenly a fashion as to defy every regulation governing the

wearing of such a dignified decoration. His K.C.B., stars, medals, and other decorations are spattered higgledy-piggledy and all awry over the garment, from high up on the shoulder to a crumple under the lapel near the top buttonhole, through which runs a watch-chain, festooned right and left across the breast, each end running to earth in one of the patch pockets on either side . . . The hair is just a flagrant flouting of the Queen's Regulations. How could the Duke (despite his umbrella, which he always carried with an air), the epitome of full-dress majesty, or in civilian dress the most imposing frock-coated, silk-hatted dignity—how could he with sincerity bring himself to appreciate this perky sloven who seemed to exercise devilish ingenuity in discovering means of jarring his nerves?'[8]

Eccentricities of dress might be expected in Wolseley, but it grieved the Duke when a member of the Royal Family defended khaki and described it as an 'inestimable boon.' Writing from Cairo soon after the victory at Tel-el-Kebir, the Duke of Connaught recommended the 'dust colour' uniform. 'The clothing supplied to the men—viz. red serge and blue serge trousers—was thoroughly inappropriate to this climate and the men suffered terribly from the want of a cooler and more comfortable dress. Khaki is the only sensible fighting dress for our men, and had they been dressed in it like the troops from India, it would have been an inestimable boon to all. At the present moment the clothes of the troops from England are in such a state that you would be horrified to see them, whereas the troops from India look just as clean to-day as when they disembarked. I hope you will forgive the private and unbiassed opinion of one who only has the efficiency and well-being of the Army at heart. My opinions may not be worth much, but still I know that you like hearing things, and have always allowed me to tell you what I think.'[9]

On 2 April 1883, the Commander-in-Chief made a speech at the Mansion House on the abomination of doing away with the red uniform. Lady Geraldine next day described it as 'an admirable speech,' and she referred to Lord Wolseley, who inspired so much of this restless desire for change, as 'unreliable and untrustworthy

. . . a man who will do or be anything and everything that will only push his fortunes. Perfectly courteous and outwardly civil but not to be trusted across the road!' Louisa read her husband's speech and warmly congratulated him on it. 'I was so glad love,' he wrote back on 4 April, 'you looked at my speech. I was very anxious to say what I did about the *red* uniform, about the last vestige of the old English army, Wolseley, Childers and Co. want to get rid of, but I hope they will find this more difficult than they anticipated.' Towards the end of the month H.R.H. wrote to Sir Evelyn Wood, a protégé of Wolseley's, then in command of the Egyptian contingent. Wood, like Sir Garnet, preferred whenever possible to dress as a civilian and it was this habit which drew upon him a kindly rebuke from the Duke. 'Will you forgive me,' he wrote, 'if I venture to give you a little hint about appearing always in uniform. Foreigners look to this far more than you may imagine. In England these things are not much noticed, but abroad they are, therefore as present Head of the Egyptian Contingent, I would suggest your appearing always in strict uniform and enforcing this also upon all your Europeans . . . Pardon this little suggestion.'[10]

In the summer of 1884 the Liberal Government once more found itself reluctantly involved in a campaign in Africa, this time in the Soudan. The operation was designed to rescue Gordon from Khartoum, where he was surrounded by the forces of the Mahdi. Wolseley, of course, was chosen to command the expedition. Gladstone, for as long as he dared, tried to ignore Gordon, who far from arranging the withdrawal he was instructed to undertake, in fact committed the Government to further fighting in the Soudan. Eventually public opinion compelled the Prime Minister to send troops to relieve the beleaguered town, but the decision was taken too late and preparations were inadequate.

In May 1884, the Duke complained of statesmen 'who prefer to be blind than to see what is particularly disagreeable to themselves and against their constantly repeated theories.' In the following month he wrote to Sir Donald Stewart, Commander-in-Chief in India: 'Nothing has as yet been settled as to future action in Egypt and this delay is I fear fatal to early success. This being Whitsuntide the Government have *all* been out of town . . . Valuable time is lost and as usual I fear we may again be too late.' Obviously suspecting that the Army would be blamed for the delays and indecision of the Ministry, he concluded: 'I name this to you confidentially, that you may not suppose that it is the Military Authorities who are to blame.' The next month he wrote again in despair: '. . . As usual we shall be *too* late and when action is to be taken we shall be entirely unprepared for carrying it out. I have preached and prayed on the subject till I can do so no more, and the result must be on the shoulders of the politicians.'[11]

Several months after the decision had been taken to attempt Gordon's rescue, Hartington, who, towards the end of 1882, succeeded Childers at the War Office, still apathetically resisted demands for more men. 'Even now,' wrote Lady Geraldine on 10 February 1885, 'the vile Government grudgingly *forced* to action, are doing it in the most miserably half-hearted way! Fighting and struggling against every single man to be sent out! Hartington declaring at every suggestion, that his delectable "colleagues" "will jump down his throat"! The Duke's labour immense to get the proper force sent out! Always met with: "Why so many?" "Is it necessary?" and of course not attended to, the matter referred to Wolseley, who answers, all for the greater number, and telegraphs: "The more the better, we must run no risks!" Curious alteration from his previous views!! Of Hartington's intolerable apathy and unutterable indifference! And his ignorance! resisting the Duke's *very strong* arguing to call out the Reserve "Not now"! of course! Delectable policy of "Too late"!! What's the use? What are we to do with these fellows with nothing to do for a month? Imagining they could be called out today and fit and ready tomorrow! What a man for a Minister for War!!'

Wolseley, writing from Nubia in October 1884, told the Duke, 'the more I study the question on the spot, the more certain I become that this Nile route is the only one that could ensure Khartoum being reached by a British force.' A river attack required boats. As the local craft 'leak horribly and founder at the least provocation,' Wolseley asked for vessels to be sent from England. 'What sums of money might have been saved if the Government had purchased some of those stern-paddle steamers I recommended to their notice months ago. It is always, and under our present form of Government, must, I suppose always be the same. No Ministry will expend a thousand pounds to-day to save the expenditure of £5000 which people can see will be inevitable in six or eight months' time.'[12]

The Adjutant General and the Duke were in entire agreement over the deficiencies of the Government, but they seriously differed, as usual, on the question of selection of staff. 'Wolseley,' wrote H.R.H. in his Diary on 30 August 1884, 'takes his usual entourage of Staff Officers. It is a pity he will always take the same men, but he clings to that particular idea and mode of conducting military operations. I think it is a very unfortunate thing for the *esprit de corps* of an army, which must damage it.' It was one of the Duke's favourite sayings that the British Army was too small an army to be divided into parties. 'We don't want to have any cliques or divisions in it. We cannot afford it. We want one Army, the King's Army.' The exclusiveness of Wolseley's disciples, known as the 'Garnet' or 'Ashanti' Ring, engendered the very rivalry and jealousy which the Commander-in-Chief believed to be dangerous to the good feeling of the Army as a whole.

When it became clear that Wolseley proposed to gather his old favourites about him for the expedition to the Soudan, the Duke wrote warning him that his partiality was becoming notorious. 'As to the quality of the superior or Staff Officers for purposes of war: you say very few men have the absolute requirements for active service in the field in the superior grade, so that you could tell the number off your fingers. I confess to having a better opinion of our officers in general than the view you take . . . The more fresh blood is tested on these occasions the better, and I think it a most unfortunate system to confine yourself to only a very limited number of men. You have an excellent Staff about you, I have not the least doubt; that you

should like to have a certain number of these men whom you
know intimately, and are therefore up to what you want, is most
natural, and indeed essential. But if you never go beyond this
particular batch of men, you work these and bring *nothing on*;
and this I think another serious misfortune to the interests of an
Army called upon, like ours, to serve in every part of the globe.'[13]
In further letters the Duke returned to his contention that it was
best for the Army to 'give every man a chance, and not merely
pick out the plums of the military cake.'

Wolseley for once selected his staff with rather more caution
and chose a number of officers from outside the 'Garnet Ring,'
but he continued to insist on the inefficiency of the majority of
high-ranking soldiers. 'No one can at all times be more anxious
than I am to bring out young untried men, for I know how
inefficient and ignorant of war are most of our Major Generals.
I often look over the list in that grade and shudder as I contemplate the possibility of nine out of every ten of them ever falling
by any public misfortune into any command. Why therefore
keep them on? Your Royal Highness is so soft hearted and good
natured, that many an old gentleman is kept on in the army
whom it would be better to let "die in peace" and replace him by
a young man . . . As I grow old myself, I feel this more strongly
every day. There is a dash and daring and bright energy about
youth that is worth all the caution and experience of old age. It is
those youthful qualities which tell in war, especially in these
desperate savage wars which so frequently devolve upon the
British Army.'[14]

During his voyage to Egypt in September 1884, Wolseley
wrote to the Duke requesting the formation of a Camel Corps, to
consist of forty men chosen from each of a number of picked
regiments. The Egyptian Army he dismissed as virtually useless.
'I am convinced they should never stand in the open if charged by
anyone, even by a herd of old apple-women from England.' The
majority of British troops were too young and would 'not be
able to stand the hard work.' For this reason Wolseley was
anxious to form his Camel Corps from the élite of the Guards,

Household Cavalry and Rifle Brigade. That he could not depend upon the regular battalions under his command was a damaging testimonial to the merits of Short Service of which he had been so enthusiastic an advocate. The Duke, on first reading of the proposal to form a Camel Corps from some of the best regiments in the Army, told Wolseley, 'it almost took my breath away.' The principle he believed 'unsound' and he only temporarily accepted it because there was no other way to form the sort of unit which Wolseley required. But he objected to any scheme which destroyed regimental spirit. 'After all, that is the life and soul of this Army, and every other Army.'

Wolseley, realizing that the Commander-in-Chief was troubled about the wisdom of his Camel Corps, sent him a letter designed to convert him to the project, which, incidentally, constituted yet another devastating indictment of the quality of soldier produced by Cardwell and Childers. 'It would be simple folly to take the ordinary soldier . . . and pit him against an Arab warrior. Only fancy what chance a street boy from Whitechapel or a Clod-hopper from Staffordshire, perspiring from every pore and mad from thirst, would have against the Arab, who has been bred up to fighting and whom fanaticism now gives a recklessness of death that makes him a serious enemy to the very best soldiers in the world. I should not feel myself justified in taking ordinary soldiers into action against him as long as I can get better men for the purpose . . . I may throw away my own life if I like, but I am bound by conscience, by honour to the men who trust in me and follow me, that I endeavour to save life as much as possible, even although I may run counter to the Queen's regulations and to the old peace customs of our Army in my endeavours to do so. I beg your Royal Highness to view what I do in this light.'[15]

The expedition to save Gordon failed. Time had been recklessly thrown away by Gladstone, and Wolseley reached Khartoum too late. The Government then determined to withdraw troops from the Upper Nile, contrary to the advice and wishes of the Khedive, Baring, Wolseley, Kitchener and Sir Redvers Buller. As Wolseley wrote to H.R.H. in May: 'To fly in the face of the advice given to them by everyone on the spot is a strong measure, and bespeaks great confidence in their own judgement. I am afraid, however, their action is solely influenced by party politics. The party exigencies of the moment have more weight than the interests of our Empire. This is plain speaking; but I think the time has come for all men who love their country to speak out, no matter on which side of the House they may sit, or with which they may sympathize.'[16] As a result of this withdrawal, the Mahdi overran the whole area, our native allies were barbarously massacred, the country was laid waste, and eventually a large army under Kitchener had to be despatched to recover the Soudan. The policy pursued by the Government from beginning to end was foolish to the point of madness, and the disasters which ensued were exactly those which had been predicted by the Commander-in-Chief.

Lord Hartington, as Secretary for War, very soon lost the esteem of the Royal Family. He enraged the Queen by suggesting that she had behaved unconstitutionally in telegraphing her congratulations to Wolseley on his success at the battle of Abu Klea in 1885. Hartington wrote from the War Office asking Ponsonby if it was Her Majesty's 'desire to adopt the same course on other, similar occasions.' He said that he could not help thinking that 'it would on the whole be most convenient that any message from the Queen should be sent through the Secretary of State.' The Queen justly described this proposal as 'very officious and impertinent.' She complained to her Secretary, 'The Queen has the right to telegraph congratulations and enquiries to anyone, and won't stand dictation. She won't be a machine. But the Liberals always wish to make her feel *that*, and she won't accept it.'

Wolseley, writing to his wife on his way back to England from the Soudan, prophesied that 'old George Cambridge must now be shaking in his shoes as he thinks of the returning firebrand that will be soon be on his back.' Wolseley was always a fighter and in England the Duke was the 'first enemy.' In moments of depression he admitted defeat. 'I am tired and sick of my present position . . .

The resistance of an irremovable Royal Commander-in-Chief
has beaten me.' Party changes, involving a succession of Secretaries for War, 'who neither knew Joseph nor understood his
schemes, nor had the least notion about military affairs,' added to
his difficulties.[17] 'I am tired,' he told his wife, 'having been worried
by that old obstacle to all progress I mean H.R.H. until I could
have murdered him with pleasure—it is too bad that England
should have to pay so much by loss of military efficiency for the
very doubtful honour of having this clever cunning old retrograde
as Commander-in-Chief.'[18]

Wolseley's letters display again and again this sense of frustration. Before setting out to the Soudan he described himself as
'too much worried and worked and thwarted by that mountain
of royalty H.R.H. of Cambridge . . . The Duke has to be coaxed
and flattered and terrified as one would act in dealing with some
naughty little girl or some foolish old woman. I know nothing
more wearing, because it is trying to the temper. Oh defend me
from having to deal with royalties anywhere, and yet when I say
this I cannot but feel how justly one's own servants might say the
same thing about each and all of us.' Soon after his return, he
regretted that the Commander-in-Chief never seemed to leave
London. 'What a misfortune it is that "George" has no country
house—if he had he would take holidays like all the rest of the
world instead of spending his Xmas and Easter in the society of
that rope dancer.'[19] When one of the Adjutant General's favourite
schemes was opposed by the Duke, he burst out: 'If the future of
the Army is to be decided according to the views of bow-and-
arrow generals, I despair of it.'[20]

At times the Duke forgot all his troubles with Wolseley. On
10 August 1882, the Queen wrote in her Diary: 'After luncheon
George C. came to see me. He is staying with Bertie on board
the *Osborne*. He praised Sir Garnet Wolseley very much, saying
he had behaved uncommonly well to him.' Wolseley was opposed
to Gladstone's imperial policy, he was impatient of political interference in the Army, although admittedly only when it failed to
accord with his own ideas, and he had sent George FitzGeorge

home with the Egyptian despatches. These points in his favour contributed to friendlier feelings. Later, when Louisa was dying, his sympathy touched the Duke. 'You have taken so kindly an interest,' he wrote to Wolseley, 'in my beloved one's illness that I must tell you myself that dearest Mrs FitzGeorge passed away very peacefully this morning in my presence, and surrounded by her children. I know I shall have your sympathy in this to me most severe affliction.'[21] 'The Duke read us,' wrote Lady Geraldine on 19 September 1882, 'a very nice good letter to him, from Wolseley, he gives great praise to Major George, whom he says he finds very useful indeed, always ready for work and "doing it right well" when he has it to do, and that he will make a very efficient staff officer . . . The Duke read us also a very nice letter he had from Lady Wolseley, in answer to his congratulating her on her husband's success, she says how much Wolseley values the Duke's opinion, and how much he owes him.'

Lord and Lady Wolseley exceeded the requirements of courtesy and overstepped the boundaries of truth in such flattery of the Commander-in-Chief. Lady Wolseley knew perfectly well that her husband, somewhat arrogantly it must be admitted, regarded the Duke's opinions as worthless. 'I cannot describe to you,' he once told her, 'the rubbishy nature of the Duke of Cambridge's letters to me. They are simply childish. I think it is high time he retired.' Moreover, far from believing himself indebted to H.R.H., he rightly considered that his advancement had more than once been obstructed by his influence. 'It is a curious fact,' he told his wife in a letter dated 5 August 1892, 'that I have not to thank that great German Bumble Bee for anything I have.' Wolseley's kindness to Major FitzGeorge was unashamedly calculating. 'I am sending that fellow FitzGeorge home with my despatches which ought to endear me to the Duke for ever.' His entertainingly scurrilous confidential letters provide a distasteful contrast with the flattering insincerities he employed in his attempts to humour the Commander-in-Chief. Unfortunately for Wolseley, H.R.H. was too shrewd to be deceived for long, and he saw plainly enough that he had to deal with a man 'who will do or be anything that will only push his fortunes' and who was 'unreliable and untrustworthy.'[22]

The Queen, partly forming her opinion of Wolseley from conversations with her cousin, regarded him as a self-seeking adventurer. Disraeli, who recognized the Adjutant General's ability and was anxious to improve his relations at Court, told the Queen in a letter on 24 August 1878, that it was quite true 'that Wolseley is an egoist and a braggart. So was Nelson.' In a letter to Lady Bradford, Disraeli remarked, 'Nothing can give you an idea of the jealousy, hatred, and all uncharitableness of the Horse Guards against our only soldier. The Horse Guards will ruin this country unless there is a Prime Minister who will have his way, and that cannot be counted on. You cannot get a Secretary of War to resist the Cousin of the Sovereign with whom he is placed in daily and hourly communication. I tremble when I think what may be the fate of this country if, as is not unlikely, a great struggle occurs with the Duke of Cambridge's Generals!'[23]

In 1885 Gladstone's budget was defeated owing to the Irish Members in the House voting with the Conservatives. The Liberals resigned and for some months Lord Salisbury was Prime Minister. At the end of the year he held a General Election as a result of which his political opponents won a majority of eighty six. Campbell-Bannerman became the new Secretary for War, and the Duke was so pleased to get him instead of Childers that he wrote enthusiastically to the Queen to thank her for her part in the appointment. 'I hope you will allow me to assure you how grateful I feel to you, not only on my own account but specially as regards the interests of the Army, that you insisted on Mr Campbell-Bannerman coming here as Secretary of State, in preference to Mr Childers. The former is a very nice, calm and pleasant man, well known by all here and who knows the War Office work and with whom I have no doubt I shall be able to get on very smoothly and well.'[24] Gladstone's victory was short-lived, for he split his own party by his advocacy of Home Rule for Ireland. When in the early summer of 1886 the measure was rejected, Hartington, Chamberlain and Bright all opposing it, he was forced to fight yet another election.

The excitement over the Home Rule election was immense, and the conversation at St James's centred on Gladstone's iniquity. 'Six thirty came the Duke!' wrote Lady Geraldine on 25 June, 'we spoke of the prospects of the elections.' Some people were sanguine, but the Duke was less hopeful. 'Truly his satanic Majesty helps Gladstone and he, alas! is very difficult to fight against! Of the utterly incomprehensible and marvellous aberration of the Sydneys in their *insane* love of Gladstone!! Lady Sydney having said her eyes were so inflamed and sore, but it was in a good cause; reading Gladstone's speeches!!! Of her brother, Lord Clarence, being nearly as insane: of somebody having said to him, but how is it *possible* that you, whom I believe to be an upright honest man, *can* swallow all the lies Gladstone tells? And he answered: Ah! that is because you do not understand him! He has such a wonderful mind that he can see *all* sides of a question, all around it! Now if you asked an ordinary person, is that screen in front of us gold, or silver? they would answer at once: gold! But Gladstone would never answer so! He would say: "Well! To us now it appears to be gold, but in certain lights, at certain angles, it may etc. etc. . . ." and this a sober-minded honest man considers *admirable*!! The first preliminary to being a Gladstonian is, to get rid of every *shred and particle* of commonsense and common honesty.' By 6 July Lady Geraldine and the Duchess appear to have persuaded themselves that Gladstone was 'quite mad and always had a keeper in attendance.' They discussed 'the scandal of his iniquitous family knowing this, to keep it dark, and let him thus ruin the country. . . . We could, of course, talk nothing but the election.' Eventually, to the delight of the inhabitants of St James's Palace, Lord Salisbury was returned with a secure majority, Home Rule was rejected, and the Army, at least for a few years, could expect to be left alone.

Lord Salisbury appointed W. H. Smith as Secretary for War. He had already occupied the office during the brief period of

Conservative Government the year before, and of all War Ministers he was best liked by the Duke. Smith, as a young man, had enormously expanded his father's News Agency in the Strand by securing a monopoly of Railway Bookstalls and by developing a circulating library. He entered politics in 1868 and was appointed First Lord of the Admiralty in Disraeli's Government in 1877. The Duke described him as 'a very sensible, prudent and able man and an excellent administrator.'[25] Moreover he was entirely unassuming. On 16 July 1885, Lady Geraldine wrote, 'The Duke told us Wolseley has been to Osborne to see the Queen and at his return told him she is so rejoiced and *happy* to be rid of Gladstone and his filthy lot!! She is like a school girl set free from school! Of the tact and taste Mr Smith showed this morning at the reception of the Camel Corps, remaining tranquilly among all the rest of the crowd, till the *Duke* called him up to him! as per contra to abominable Cardwell who used to *try* to take the salute!!!'

Smith was the only Secretary for War to stand up to a Chancellor of the Exchequer on the issue of reductions. Despite all the pressure that Randolph Churchill could bring to bear, he stood fast, and the Chancellor, insisting upon a cut in Army estimates, sent in his resignation. Smith, on Christmas Day 1886, wrote an account of the contest for the Commander-in-Chief. 'I am not at all surprised that Y.R.H. was startled with the news which *The Times* gave on Thursday morning. I was quite prepared for it, as the Chancellor of the Exchequer had been urging me to cut down my estimates heavily for some time, and when I had arrived at an approximation to the amount I should have to ask for, he came to me on Monday to go through the figures, and for nearly two hours he used every argument in his power to persuade me to reduce them. I could not see that it would be consistent with my duty to do so, and he left me saying he should resign his post, which intention he carried out the next morning.'[26]

Randolph Churchill's resignation was a bluff that failed. Thinking himself indispensable—a common if dangerous delusion —he imagined Lord Salisbury would insist upon the required reductions. In fact his resignation was accepted and his career ruined. The country was surprised and bewildered, and nowhere was the news more excitedly discussed than in the Cambridge family circle. On 23 December the Duke paid his daily visit to his mother. 'Our first word, of course!! was of the tremendous bombshell, the thunderclap that burst upon us this morning; Lord Randolph Churchill's resignation!!! Lord Salisbury himself they say knew it only yesterday morning, and half the Cabinet heard it only by the papers this morning!!! He resigns because he persists in refusing the estimates demanded by the War Office and Admiralty as *necessary* for the defence of the country and agreed to as such by Lord Salisbury, this being to catch a clap trap popularity by a marvellously "economical" budget!! On the one hand so self-opinionated, overbearing, masterful, so erratic, uncertain and *dangerous* as he is, he is really a good riddance! But on the other hand certainly as Leader of the House of Commons is irreplaceable, disastrous loss!! God alone knows how dangerous and hurtful he may be to us, out of office! It is perfectly infamous of him to have resigned at so critical a moment, and reveals in a most unfavourable light his self-seeking egotistic nature and total want of patriotism! It *ought* greatly to injure him with the nation! But will it? Yet! as the Duke observed, going out thus upon the question of defences, stamps and commits him for ever to the clap trap doctrine of "reduction" and peace at any price! And when eventually he resumes office, as he will, woe betide us! He will outbid Bradlaugh and Labouchère in "cutting down"!! He is a nasty fellow! without a shred of principle but that of the advancement of Lord Randolph Churchill!'

As a result of the Chancellor's resignation, and the death of the Foreign Secretary, Lord Iddesleigh, a Cabinet reshuffle took place in January 1887. Lord Salisbury took over Foreign Affairs, Smith succeeded the Prime Minister as First Lord of the Treasury, one of the rare occasions when the two offices were separated, and replaced Churchill as leader of the House of Commons. Goschen became the new Chancellor and Stanhope became Secretary for War.

'We talked,' wrote Lady Geraldine on 4 January, 'of the excessive *bore* it is for the Duke losing Mr W. H. Smith, *just* as he has got his hand in and is au fait with it all! He is himself *exceedingly* sorry to go and says he just feels now he has thoroughly mastered the whole thing and is at home, then he goes! In this *idiotic* constitution, the moment a man is *well* in the saddle and thus thoroughly understands his business, comes this stupid shuffling of the cards and immediately he is removed to another place he knows nothing about and a fresh man substituted to begin again with the ABC and learn what he has to do. A rotten system all through.'

In his long experience with War Ministers, there was no other occasion on which a Secretary of State stood his ground against his colleagues. Excuses, apologies, sometimes self-justification, was what the Duke had learned to expect. Gathorne Hardy in 1878, at a time when the Russians were at the gates of Constantinople and war in Europe threatened, unwillingly accepted reductions he knew to be dangerous. 'With a reluctant hand,' he agreed to cuts, despite his conviction that the Army was already too small. 'Such a scraping and paring,' he told H.R.H., 'as I have been going through has made me miserable but there are limits which I cannot overpass.' Two years later Stanley was excusing his surrender to the Chancellor. His argument was that the Economy was too depressed to justify even essential expenditure, and this theory he advanced at a time when Britain was the richest nation in the world. 'I assure your Royal Highness that nothing but the state of the country would lead me to assent to, and still more to propose, such reductions as are intended—but with thirty thousand people living on charity in Glasgow, and even more, I believe in Sheffield, we *cannot* ask for more taxation.'[27]

In presenting his estimates to Stanhope the Duke told him in 1888 that he wished 'to place on record, that hitherto he had been more guided in his annual demands for men by what he thought he had some chance of getting, than by what he knew to be the total military requirements of the country.' H.R.H. and Wolseley wholeheartedly agreed that party politics vitiated the problem of military expenditure. Writing in 1883, Wolseley declared, 'The interests of the Army have been subservient to the parliamentary or, more properly speaking, I should say to the party necessity of keeping its total cost down . . . The world is not in a condition that warrants us to continue in a state of complete unpreparedness for war.' The Duke told the Goldsmiths' Company in 1881: 'Army organization, and *all* army matters should *never* be a question of Party, it is a pure question of *patriotism*, how it gets dragged into Party Politics is as a question of money!' The Parties rivalled each other in their zeal for reductions. 'He wished he could persuade them when they had to vote on army matters not to think of their constituents but of this great Empire and her need of defence!'[28]

1887 was a great year of public ceremonies for the Commander-in-Chief, for it was the Golden Jubilee of the Queen's accession, and also the fiftieth anniversary of his joining the Army. As usual, long before the day of the ceremony itself, acrimonious discussions took place, and the Duchess of Cambridge, to whom gossip was a chief solace in affliction, heard from the Sub-Dean of the Chapels Royal, 'who had it from the Queen's head coachman: that the 20th June unluckily falling upon a Monday, her "most gracious" *cannot possibly* (!!!) spend a Sunday in poor London! So she comes up from Windsor to Paddington, starts *thence*!!!!! in procession, to drive to Westminster Abbey, with a *bonnet on*, as Mr Payne the coachman, deplores!! for the thanksgiving service, and then back to *Paddington* to get out at Slough to be received by the Eton boys. Thus not staying in London one night!!! . . . When she ought to come up the 19th and remain till the 29th: only ten days after all!!!'[29] In the end the Queen was prevailed upon to change her plans. As the Duke wrote in his Diary on the day itself, the great Jubilee was 'an immense success. London was in the Streets quite early in the morning, indeed during the whole previous night, and the weather was magnificent, bright sunshine with a cool breeze. I left my house, riding "Guardsman," a quarter before ten, and rode with my staff to Buckingham Palace. The several processions started thence in succession, the Queen

being the last to leave; I riding by the side of her carriage. The
streets were lined with troops the entire distance. The crowds
were quite enormous and the enthusiasm throughout the entire
route unbounded. Nothing could have been finer or more heart-
stirring. The Abbey was reached at twelve thirty where the scene
was touchingly magnificent. The return route was equally fine
and the enthusiasm overwhelming. We got back to Buckingham
Palace without any accident or mishap by two thirty, where there
was a great State Luncheon of Royalties in one room and suite
in another . . . Dined again at the Palace—another State Banquet.
The greatness of the Empire has been brought before the World
in a most marked and satisfactory manner.'

Lady Geraldine's account of the Jubilee was less restrained.
'Greatest and most *perfect* success ever known! The most splendid
and most thrilling pageant ever seen! The most touching and
magnificent display of loyalty and attachment possible to conceive. The whole thing beggars description and I cannot attempt
it, but leave it to the newspapers . . . I gave H.R.H. an account
of the marvellous sight, the wondrous success it had been! The
masses and *millions* of people, *thronging* the streets like an anthill,
and *every* window within sight, and every roof of every house,
men hanging on to the chimneys! there was never anything seen
like it! And their enthusiasm! . . . The Duke who rode on
Lifeguardsman, by the door of the Queen's carriage (and looked
so well!! all say, and I alas!! preceding them in the procession
could see nothing of him!!) told us he had never seen anything
like the enthusiasm anywhere!! It was one continuous roar of
cheering from the moment she came out of the door of her
palace till the instant she got back to it! Deafening.'

Four days after the ceremony in London a Naval Review was
held at Portsmouth, which the Duke attended in his Trinity
House uniform. He returned to London the following evening
and gave his mother a description of all that happened. 'The
Queen in the *Victoria and Albert* followed by all the official boats,
a long line! steamed through the whole line, each ironclad
manning the yards! such *few* of them as still have such things!

and cheering and firing a salute as she passed them! A quite
magnificent sight!! And such a splendid day for it!! So hot, not
a ripple, yet a most beautiful air. The illuminations at night were
quite lovely! Altogether the Duke was immensely pleased!
Quite delighted, a marvellous display of the power and greatness
of the Nation!. . . The Duke lamenting and regretting naturally
that Prince Adolphus had not taken the trouble or thought it
worthwhile to go down for it, saying it was such a fine thing and
rare occurrence, it was a *great* pity he should not have seen it,
produced a little ruffle!!! For the Grand Duchess took it up hotly
and Toko to Prince Adolphus for being so inert and wanting in
interest! saying he had better remain at home altogether; certainly
not undeserved, and in fact wholesome for him to listen to, but
painful for all of us sitting around! and distressing for the Duke.
Of the Prince of Wales having been perfectly happy in a new
uniform!!! having just got himself made *Admiral of the Fleet*!!!!
The Queen had the Empress Eugénie on board.'

With such a crowd of Royalty collected in London there was
a great deal of wrangling over precedence, a subject which
appeared of epoch-making consequence to those whose feelings
were ruffled. H.R.H. was more amused than concerned by the
outraged excitement of some of his thwarted relations. 'The
Duke,' observed Lady Geraldine on 27 June, 'who is so *rarely*
grand seigneur and above all this miserable pettiness, knowing he
is always Duke of Cambridge and can never be less whether he
sits at the top at the bottom or in the middle!! said so sensibly,
if they all come, prepared to take everything amiss and be offended
at all and everything, they had better have made up their minds
to stay away!'

The Jubilee celebrations concluded with a huge garden party,
which the Duke attended. On 30 June, he regaled his mother with
an account of Gladstone's behaviour on the occasion. 'The Duke
gave us a full account, how very pretty it was, and well done
and well managed; the Queen doing her part admirably again;
she spoke to great numbers, going about a great deal, right and
left. That brute Gladstone stood in the forefront of the circle

before her tent while she had her tea, bang opposite her, hat in hand; she said to the Duke: "Do you see Gladstone? There he has been standing hat in hand, straight opposite me this Half-hour, determined to force me to speak to him! But I am as determined *not* to speak with him!" So he continued to stand the *whole* time! But when she came out of the tent, instead of coming out in the centre, upon him, she went out at the end, and went along the line to the right, then made a circuit and took the other line to the left and most skilfully avoided him so that she neither spoke to him nor gave him her hand. But alas! the Duke heard afterwards, which is too *exasperating*, when she had so successfully and markedly avoided him, the brute contrived to get round to *inside* the house and placed himself so, that when she passed through the house to go away, at the last moment she came all suddenly *upon* him, round the corner, and was forced to give him her hand!!! Too provoking. *I* would *not* have done it even then.'

Before the celebrations of his own Military Jubilee, the Duke paid a short visit to Germany. Nearly every summer he drank the waters at Baden and Kissingen, supposedly to alleviate his gout, although the cure, if anything, appeared to aggravate his symptoms. On 16 August, while staying at Kissingen, the Duke had dinner with Bismarck; and Adolphus FitzGeorge, who accompanied his father, wrote a long account of the evening's entertainment. 'Today [15 August] Prince Bismarck the Chancellor of the Empire called on my father, he was accompanied by Baron Rottenberg, who Stevens [the Duke's A.D.C.] and I entertained in my bedroom while the Prince was with my father. They had a half hour's conversation . . . The Prince had a great reception from the people on leaving and he had already remarked to my father that at one time here the people spat in the street as he passed, by way of insult; whereas now they overwhelm him with civility. The Prince looks very much thinner and better than when I saw him at Berlin last year . . . The Prince asked us to dine tomorrow evening at six o'clock.'

On 16 August the Duke's party drove to Bismarck's lodgings. 'He occupies a fine room nicely furnished . . . We sat at a round table at one end of the room. Bismarck had two fine beasts a dog and a bitch in the room, they are his companions and constantly in the room with him. They are, as he explained, a cross made many years ago between a Danish boar hound and a grey hound and the breed was established by a Duke of Wurtemberg who found that the boar hound was too heavy to run down the deer and that the grey hound was not heavy enough to pull the deer down, hence the reason for crossing. The breed has established itself as a distinct breed and is as he says the only bastard breed in animals that has established itself permanently. The breed is called Bastard in the German equivalent. Dinner was very fair. Bismarck apologized for it saying he had to leave his cook at Berlin on the way from Varzin down with a fever. The wines were numerous including sherry and port, hock, moselle, Burgundy and beer. Bismarck drank champagne and beer. He took peas, they were very badly cooked and hard as bullets. The Doctor objected and consequently he took a second helping. In the middle of dinner he said it was the anniversary of the battle of Mars-le-Tour in which his two sons took part in the celebrated dragoon guards charge, now an historical event . . . At dinner he spoke principally to my father in German but told the above story to us in very good English. After dinner we adjourned to the far end of the room my father sitting on the sofa, Bismarck at the end of the table and we others round it. He had three large German china pipes packed full of tobacco at his side and commenced puffing away vigorously and so continued to do during the rest of the visit. He at once went into a constant flow of conversation in English entirely, explained to us the different way land property was dealt with in different parts of the Empire, criminal laws, savings banks etc. and the charming part of it was that he did not address his conversation to my father particularly but to all of us generally . . . I remarked on the facility with which he talked our language and he explained that he had learnt it as a child, but that he had not talked it except to our Ambassador at Berlin since the year 1862, but that he kept it up by reading the political articles and telegrams in *The Times*, "tho' he knew all about it beforehand, and never found anything in them new to him," and further, that he read English books occasionally. On my asking him what sort, he said "short and light or I should never get through them." My father made some remarks as to Prince William the Crown Prince's son being a little rash in his sayings and Bismarck said that he talked a great deal too much. Mr Gladstone was then pretty hotly abused all round. He [Bismarck] said he was very sick of being at work being nearly worn out like a gambler constantly playing for very high stakes. I expressed a doubt as to his being satisfied with nothing to do and he said that he delighted in being in the country watching the growth of young trees pushing their way upwards: this struck us all as being a very remarkable characteristic of the difference between his character and Gladstone's. Gladstone likes to cut down trees, destruction being his strong point, Bismarck likes to watch the growth of the trees, the growth of the Empire being his strong point, and so the conversation went on. About eight o'clock beer was handed round, we had only just had coffee and brandy, and I refused upon which he said "You must not refuse beer in Bavaria" and I consequently partook as did we all, and so the cure was temporarily thrown to the winds. At eight fifteen about, we took our leave shaking hands with the old man and I can assuredly say I never spent a pleasanter and more interesting evening; it is not everybody who has the chance of an hour's chat with the great German Chancellor and I feel pretty honoured and shall remember it so long as I live as an event in my life. I was much struck with his eyes. They are very piercing. He is tall and upright, his clothes fitted him very badly (plain clothes) hanging about his body. He probably had them made before he lost so much flesh.'

The Duke's military anniversary fell on 3 November. 'I have been overwhelmed,' he wrote in his Diary, 'with telegrams and letters of congratulation both from abroad and from home.' The Kaiser and the Emperor of Austria were among the many hundreds to send him messages. The Queen wrote a kind letter from Balmoral. 'Let me congratulate you again,' she said, 'and let me express my warm thanks for the very valuable services you have rendered to me and to our Country, of which I am deeply sensible. That you may long be spared to command my brave and gallant troops is the earnest wish of your very affectionate cousin, Victoria R.I.' The Queen created the Duke Commander-in-Chief by Letters Patent, 'which office has been in abeyance since the death of the Duke of Wellington, as I have hitherto held the office of "Commanding-in-Chief" . . . This is an honour of which I may be justly proud, and I cannot deny that I am so.'

A great banquet was held on 4 November in the Duke's honour. 'At eight thirty attended the great dinner of two hundred at the Hotel Metropole, given in my honour by the Senior United Service Club, Lord Napier of Magdala being in the Chair and the Prince of Wales on my right. All the Field-Marshals were present and a very large representative body of Officers. My health was most warmly and cordially welcomed and the whole thing passed off admirably, my speech in reply being very well received. . . . I was presented, by the united body of Officers who attended, with a very handsome gold Cigar Case, as a Memento of the event of the banquet given by them in commemoration of the occasion.'

The dinner was a spontaneous tribute of the Army, and such was the enthusiasm for it that a great number of officers had to be turned away. The Prince of Wales, Lord Napier of Magdala, Lord Wolseley, Lord Lucan, Sir Redvers Buller, and many other distinguished soldiers attended. The incident of the evening which touched him most deeply was a telegram he received shortly after the banquet began. 'To Field Marshal the Duke of Cambridge,' it ran, 'My thoughts and heart are with you. I rejoice over the recognition of your service. I send my blessing to the best son that ever lived. Your loving mother, Duchess of Cambridge.' Those who watched him receive the message feared he had received bad news for tears ran down his cheeks as he read it.

'The speeches excellent,' wrote Lady Geraldine next day, having studied all the newspapers and having heard that evening the Duke's account of the dinner. 'The Prince first rate, and as for

the Duke he excelled himself! the enthusiasm immense!!!! and
all from the heart. The gold cigar case was presented and the
Queen and the Prince together gave him a very pretty present, a
pencil about four inches long in the form of a marshal's baton,
very pretty indeed, so well modelled. . . . Sir Edward Whitmore
came, and gave us a most satisfactory full detailed account of the
whole evening! Told us he never saw such unanimity of enthusiasm! He thought they would break down the tables and smash
all the bottles and glasses, with "applause"! Declared he had not
felt so happy for years, and thought the Duke was really happy, it
was all so spontaneous and affectionate. At six thirty Lord Napier
of Magdala came; from whom we had further accounts of the
evening! After he had come in but a few minutes came the Duke!
He thanked Lord Napier again for having presided so well, and
come all the way over from France for the purpose; thanked
H.R.H. for her *charming* telegram which had greatly touched
him; as it did all those round about him to whom he showed it.'

Unfortunately there were two small clouds in an otherwise
radiant sky. His sister, the Duchess of Teck, completely ignored
the Jubilee. Lady Geraldine, who never liked Princess Mary, was
exultant with indignation. 'He has received I rejoice to say!
tokens of regard, esteem, affection and interest! except!! solely,
only, and alone *one* not!!! H.R.H. Princess Mary Adelaide!!!
Not a sign or sound from the White Lodge!!! nor from anyone
of the family!! It is too inconceivable!! and too *bad*.' Three days
later on 6 November she commented on Princess Mary's improbable excuse for overlooking the great anniversary. 'She
swore, that none, not one single member of the blessed family
ever heard one single syllable upon the subject or had a dream the
Duke had or could have completed fifty years service, far less
anything as to any celebration of it!!! A *remarkable* "fact" when
for two whole months past it has been *constantly* referred to in the
papers, which it is to be supposed *some* member of the household
sometimes reads!! And when here we have never ceased to talk
of it!!!'

Lady Geraldine was not strictly accurate when she said that

Princess Mary was the only person who forgot the Jubilee. The Duke of Clarence, the Prince of Wales's eldest son, made the same regrettable mistake. On the day of the Senior United Service Club dinner, Lady Geraldine wrote: 'Prince Eddie *here*, at Marlborough House, his own near relation, known him intimately from his birth, an officer under his command, neither comes to him, nor writes to him, nor takes the slightest notice!!!! His own uncle and Commander-in-Chief!!!! Too bad; it is no want of proper feeling, but sheer stupidity!! Alas! that fatal apathy and inertness, sleepy apathetic laziness and total want of initiative. But the White Lodge people are far more curious and incomprehensible! Unpardonable omission! Not one single one of the whole family has taken the very smallest notice!! It is too outrageous.' For Lady Geraldine no occasion was complete unless it offered an opportunity for ill-natured grumbling. Possibly the surfeit of affection she bestowed upon H.R.H., who inspired in her agonies of undeclared love, deprived her of charity towards the rest of mankind, for she rarely erred on the side of being over-indulgent, except when discussing her beloved Duke.

FAMILY AFFAIRS

GREATLY as the Duke loved his wife, she was not alone in his affections. In her last years Louisa was an invalid, and when she was out of London her husband craved for company. The Duke told Wolseley, in the summer of 1890, 'that he missed the society of some lady to whom he could be attached and in whom he could confide, and that he hated his big house at this season . . . Poor old fellow, he must have society. How I pity those who require it.'[1]

Strangely enough the lady to whom he was devoted was, like his wife, called Louisa. She was the third daughter of Sir George Wombwell of Newburgh Park, Yorkshire. In 1840 she married Henry Beauclerk, a descendant of Nell Gwynn's son, the Duke of St Albans. They had no children and appear to have separated. Mrs Beauclerk lived at Number 13, Chesham Street, Belgrave Square. They first met at a ball at Almacks in 1837, when Prince George was just eighteen, and he was introduced to her by

Adolphus FitzClarence. They began to see much of each other in 1847, the year in which H.R.H. married.

The first mention of Mrs Beauclerk in the Duke's Diary is made thirty four years after they met. Presumably she was omitted for so long a time for fear the entries might be read. On 20 November 1881, he wrote: 'I heard that L.B. was very seriously ill, which is of course a great distress to me.' Five days later he became more hopeful, 'after some very bad reports and much anxiety heard that my dear friend was better.' Mrs Beauclerk was known to the Prince of Wales, and the Duke kept him informed of her illness. 'I was sure you would take a kindly interest about Mrs Beauclerk. My anxiety on her account during the last few days has been *very great*, but I hope since the measles have come out, that her illness is fully accounted for and thank God she is today I hope really doing well.' He had been very anxious, 'but that to me is nothing if God's mercy only gets her well through her serious illness.' Three days later he wrote again with more cheerful news. 'Thank God I can give a very good account of our dear friend. She is progressing very favourably and I trust that tho' great prudence and care will be required, she is now on the road to convalescence. The relief this is to my mind I cannot describe to you. It is like awaking from a horrible dream which has been haunting me for the last five days.'[2] So agitated was the Duke by Mrs Beauclerk's illness that he himself became unwell. The Duchess of Edinburgh told Wolseley that H.R.H. had given her a full account of 'Mrs B's internal arrangements, or perhaps I should say disarrangements. She tells me the Duke is very nervous about the fat red-faced old lady to whom she says he is very much attached.'[3] It was characteristic of Wolseley that he should have described the poor lady in terms so unflattering. Lady Geraldine said, 'her figure, her whole appearance was quite marvellous! No one could have judged her more than fifty six to fifty eight.' But then in all probability this was the Duke's opinion, and his attachment to Mrs B. was such as to discourage dispassionate assessment.

Mrs Beauclerk recovered from measles, but towards the end

of 1882 she was again ill, although nobody thought her troubles
serious. Two days after Christmas the Duke at five o'clock in the
evening paid his 'usual visit to Chesham Street, where I hoped
things were better, and where I said goodbye to my dearest and
most beloved Louisa, the friend and joy of my heart and life, for
the last time, little dreaming that I should never see her again
alive.' Early in the morning of 28 December Louisa Beauclerk
died of a clot of blood—an illness which afterwards the Duke
could never hear 'mentioned without a shudder, knowing how
it brought him the destruction of all his happiness on earth.'[4]
'This dreadful day,' he wrote in his Diary, 'which has brought
on me mourning and grief was commenced by the terrible, the
crushing news, that my dearest and most beloved Louisa had
suddenly grown worse in the night and had died without much
suffering about six fifteen this morning. To me the loss is irreparable and my grief is overwhelming. The idol of my heart and
of my existence is gone from me for ever. I can now only hope
and pray that we may meet again in Heaven. God will be good
and merciful to us and will forgive us our sins . . . I did not
leave the house all the morning, but at five thirty went to see
Miss Emily Wombwell [Mrs Beauclerk's sister]. The meeting
was dreadfully awful, but she was all goodness, and kindness and
affection, and I bless her for it. I had some dinner at home and
then went to St James'. Told my dear Mother what had befallen
me and she was good and kind and affectionate and sympathetic.
I had in the morning asked my son George to tell Louisa what
had happened. He too was good and kind, and Louisa behaved
nobly, only requesting the subject might not be mentioned. The
pain and grief of all this is too awful and overwhelming and I am
entirely *crushed* by it. God help me.'
    'Most sad, sad day!' wrote Lady Geraldine after hearing the
Duke break the news to his mother, 'What sadder or bitterer than
to see a poor human heart crushed with grief! all life, worth
calling life at an end for it! a sorrow immeasurable and incon-
solable. . . . In the evening came the Duke! H.R.H. instantly
saw how upset! how stricken! and asking him what it was? he

told her! his dearly loved friend Mrs Beauclerk died this morning at six o'clock!! The blow is fearful! "as a sledge hammer" splintering his poor heart to fragments. . . . Loving and tenderly, and most touchingly he spoke of her . . . showing the marvellous depth and unbounded tenderness of his unequalled love for her through an unswerving friendship of over thirty five years! a life time. How rare, good God! how rare to find a man capable of such deep all-absorbing enduring tender love! . . . H.R.H. deeply moved by his *profound* grief!'

The Queen when she heard the news was less sympathetic. The Duke of Connaught mentioned in a letter, 'I saw Uncle George who I found terribly broken by Mrs B's death, he was quite miserable and cried dreadfully, I felt quite sorry for him.' 'I should pity your Uncle George,' came the remorseless reply, '*very* much if it were *not such a discreditable* attachment; a married woman in *society*—and the mother [Mrs FitzGeorge] of his sons alive. I believe Mrs B. had a bad influence over him and from her home many things got repeated which did Uncle George great harm.' The first the Queen heard of Mrs B. was when the Duchess of Teck in 1878 explained that her brother was unable to assist her financially, because 'he had his own family to support and a *still more* powerful influence, Mrs Beauclerk, absorbed *all* he could give.'[5]

Most people seem to have regarded Mrs B. as a delightful person. General Clifton told the Duchess of Cambridge 'What a *good* influence she had upon him and how clever a woman she was.' Lord William Paulet lamented her death greatly, 'saying what a grievous loss she is to the Duke!'[6] On the day after her death H.R.H. wrote 'Sympathy comes to me from all sides and respect and affection is shown to her dear memory. The pain, the sorrow, the reality of the affliction, increased upon me. My poor darling Angel died of a clot of blood in the vein of the left leg suddenly flying to the heart and death came upon her rapidly and without a struggle. God have mercy upon her dear soul.'

On 30 December George FitzGeorge breakfasted with his father and was 'full of kind and warm sympathy, but no real

consolation, for *she* is gone and my loss can never be repaired.'
Louisa on hearing about Mrs Beauclerk was 'most generous' and
took the announcement 'in *sorrow* and not in anger, and therefore
the subject is not referred to by me, but the position is a most
painful one.'

On New Year's Day the Duke wrote to his wife. It was not
an easy letter and he made it short.

My own Louly, My dearest Wife,

According to good old custom my *first* letter in the New Year
shall be addressed to you.

God bless you dearest and let me add from my innermost heart,
forgive me.

Ever your very own

Most affectionate and devoted husband,

George.

On 7 January, the day before the thirty-sixth anniversary of his
wedding, the Duke dined at Queen Street, 'probably it was the
best thing to do, however painful.' He described it as 'a very
unpleasant dinner to me,' but he was 'advised' to go, and 'all
were kind and good and it passed over.' Louisa was wonderfully
forgiving. 'Your kind and affectionate letter,' he wrote to her on
17 January, 'reached me this morning, and I thank you from my
heart for the generous feelings it evinces, and which I only too
gladly reciprocate. I know my darling, that you have a great,
great deal to forgive, and you have done so with a noble spirit,
which touches me more than words can express and I can only
say God bless you for it; and I will do my very utmost to soften
the sorrow I have caused. It is so painful a subject dearest that I
do not like to touch upon it, but I feel that your anxiety is to do
everything that is affectionate and good by me, however blame-
able I am.'

How much, if anything, Louisa knew about Mrs Beauclerk
before George FitzGeorge's announcement is impossible to say.
As early as 1855 she was at least aware of Mrs B.'s existence.

Writing from Frankfurt in September of that year she told her husband: 'As I was sitting at table d'hôte today a Gentleman bowed. I looked and who should it be but Mr Beauclerk . . . I think he is much altered . . . He said he had not seen you since you wrote to Mrs Beauclerk and asked them to dine with you at Brussels, two or three years ago. I was astonished to hear it.' Two years later, when the Duke was staying with the Wombwells at Newburgh Park, Louisa was evidently suspicious, for he wrote to her on 8 October saying: 'You asked me why I remained so long at G. Wombwell's. There was no reason further than that I had shooting every day, that I don't like travelling on Sunday, and waited till Monday.'

Lady Geraldine, who did not care for Mrs FitzGeorge, was enraptured by Mrs Beauclerk, and although a savagely jealous person, never appears to have resented Mrs B.'s singular position. On the contrary, she became lyrical when describing the 'romance.' 'Too touching,' she wrote on 30 December 1882, 'the proof of the *unbounded* tenderness of his immeasurable love and devotion for her . . . Certainly there never was affection so *perfect*, never such love, on the part of a *man*! Never! It is really marvellous that at his age, and at her age! his love has not only all the *adoring* devotion, but all the bright freshness, blindness, glamour, *romance* of early youth!'

The Duke's Diary was ordinarily little more than a list of engagements, but in 1883 he used it to unburden his grief. His fearful sense of loss, the memories that revived the bitterness, the shock, the agony of separation, are all recorded. 'My heart is broken,' he wrote on New Year's Day 1883, 'it can never again be what it was, for I shall never in this world see again the dear departed one, and no other human being can ever give my poor heart that happiness and that bliss, which I was permitted to enjoy for so many years in her blessed society . . . I saw Arthur Wombwell, who was kind and good to me, as all her family are thank God. I also today went to Church in Dover Street and felt so strong an impulse to take the Sacrament whilst her dear body was still on earth, that I stayed for the Communion, which certainly comforted me. I feel ashamed to confess that I had not taken it for many years, not I think since the death of my dear Father, when I took it at Cambridge House with my family. I hope God will forgive me for this and accept my sorrow at this neglect, which I now offer to Him in the spirit of devotion and love towards the spirit of the dear departed one. Later I went to the Office and at six I went with my faithful Dickins to her house, and stood by her dear coffin for the last time on Earth. It was in the Dining room and looked so solemn and still it was awful . . . I prayed . . . to the Almighty for forgiveness for that blessed spirit and for myself, in the hope that pardon would be granted to us both, and that we might be permitted, however unworthy I feel I am, to meet again in Heaven. May God hear my prayer in mercy and grace.'

2 January was the day of the funeral. The Wombwells begged him not to attend the service. 'To which,' wrote Lady Geraldine, 'as he believes it to be for her sake, he acquiesces, but in fact they did it really for his sake! dreading how he *must* inevitably break down at it, which would be so painful! Prince Teck goes to it, which gives the Duke *great* gratification.' In his own Diary the Duke wrote, 'This was the dreadful day of the funeral at Kensal Green. She expressed a wish herself, in letters she left, to be buried there and the family strictly carried out her instructions. I rejoice to think it was a bright sunny morning, the only day of sunshine we have had for a long time, and it felt to me as if Heaven by this grace had welcomed her dear soul into the region of the blessed . . . I wanted to attend the funeral, but it was thought that her memory would be more respected by my absence, and finding that the family particularly wished this, I did not go myself . . . At one forty five I drove with Tyrwhitt to Kensal Green, and by her just closed grave stood and prayed, a broken hearted man. The place was selected by Miss Emily and Arthur, and is beyond the Chapel in a nice quiet spot. I looked about me where I should purchase at once a vault for myself, for I will ensure then that I may be buried near her, which I had determined to be for years, and had indeed left a paper attached to my will to this effect,

which was my intention ever since 1849.' The Duke's desire to be interred at Kensal Green was observed by his sons and there he lies buried in a vault beside his wife, a short distance from Louisa Beauclerk.

Evening after evening he discussed his loss with his mother, and Mrs Beauclerk for a time was the chief topic of conversation, apart from an occasional criticism of Wolseley's latest outrage. The Duke described 'her loveliness, her charm, her beautiful eyes!!' He talked 'of her kindness, her generosity, never having heard her say an ill-natured word of anyone.' He told his mother, 'I positively believe, if it were humanly possible to love her more than I did then, I really loved her all these late years even more than formerly.'[7]

The Duke in his visits to St James's made pathetic attempts to appear cheerful. Three days after Mrs Beauclerk's death, Lady Geraldine deplored 'the pain of seeing him, hitherto the joy and sunshine of this house, whose dear, bright visit was the enliven-ment of H.R.H.'s day—thus bowed to the earth with grief! his very *existence* at an end.' After he had partly recovered from the first overwhelming shock, he made 'valiant, noble efforts to throw off his crushing sorrow while he is with his mother,' trying 'to be with her as usual and talk, and amuse her—while one knows how utterly brokenhearted he is.'[8]

Sad associations and anniversaries constantly revived his grief. On 20 March 1883, he visited Chesham Street for the last time before the furniture was put in store. 'At twelve o'clock went to the poor dear little house to take a last look at it, as *her* things are to be packed up and the carpets and curtains put away. The grief and sorrow I feel at seeing all *her* things, but she my *beloved one* gone for ever, was terribly painful, and yet I am glad I went once more. God have mercy on *her* dear soul.' Later in the summer when Lady Geraldine was dining at Gloucester House, the Duke went into his writing room 'and showed me the armchair and cushion in it in which she was when he last took leave of her the evening of the 27 December!!!! It has been brought to him from Chesham Street and another armchair of the same kind and "the

little table on which we used always to have our tea"!!!'⁹ For
his sixty-fourth birthday Princess Edward of Saxe-Weimar sent
H.R.H. 'a little present and some lovely roses and flowers and
these quite upset me, for they reminded me so of the dear
offerings and flowers that were sent to me on this day by my
beloved and *departed* friend. Her dear face is ever before me today
and I can think of nothing else.' Two days before Christmas the
Duke discussed with his mother how Emily Wombwell had 'now
got all Mrs Beauclerk's things arranged in her house!! Of how
he knows them all! Of her giving him yesterday an album she
had found amongst Mrs Beauclerk's things, filled with all his
speeches and everything concerning him.' As Lady Geraldine had
for many years devotedly kept just such a scrapbook, she remarked: 'curious *resemblance*!'

The Duke clung for consolation to relics of Mrs B. He derived
a sad pleasure from a starling which she had kept for fifteen years,
and every morning took it out of its cage and fed it on worms.
The very day she died his letters to her were returned, and these
he read with a melancholy fascination. On 4 February he told the
Duchess that he was 'reading over letters to Mrs B.' Some went
back to 1849. 'It strikes him so how without fail thro' *all* and *every*
of them there runs the same never changing strain of *entire
devotion* to her! when away wishing only to be back with her!
If absent for only two or three days shooting, always "the party
is pleasant enough but would that he were back with her! how
he longs for Saturday, or whichever the day, that he is to return!
how he will not fail to come to *her* on arriving." ' The resemblance
between such letters and those which he wrote his wife is striking,
and the suspicion of insincerity arises. In order to keep Mrs
FitzGeorge ignorant of her rival, duplicity was unavoidable. But
although the Duke failed to conduct his 'romance' without deceit,
there was no pretence about his devotion to his wife. It was
evidently not a situation to which either lady could be reconciled;
nor did circumstances make it easy for the Duke to be honest
without hurting feelings. The dilemma was intricate but not un-
precedented, for other husbands have made room for two in their

hearts, although few have remained so faithful—if the term may be used in such a context—to the lady of their second choice.

The first 'sad anniversary' of the loss of his 'beloved and adored friend' found the Duke longing for reunion in death. 'God knows,' he wrote, 'what I have since suffered in sorrow and anguish of mind. Real happiness in this world has quite left me and the distance of time in no sense mitigates this feeling. I miss *her* and feel *her* loss every hour, I may say, moment of the day, and *nothing* can ever replace her to me . . . Standing by *her* dear grave, I longed to be *with* her even in death!! Would that it could have been so.' Lady Dorothy Nevill, in her *Memoirs*, printed a letter she received from the Duke. At a casual glance it would seem to refer to the death of Mrs FitzGeorge, but since she died on 12 January, the mention of 'Friday next, 28th' establishes that H.R.H. was, in fact, speaking of Mrs Beauclerk. 'My Dear Lady Dorothy,—May every blessing attend you even at this *terrible period* as you call it . . . To me the time is a *most painful* one, for my thoughts are entirely absorbed by the *events* of this time last year, which you can well imagine cause very sad reflections and give me so much sorrow and grief. Friday next, 28th, was the sad day which *ended* my *happiness* in this world. I shall not fail to come and see you with pleasure after these sad days are over, and when I can make myself a little more agreeable, I hope, than I possibly could at present.'[10]

The Duke paid constant visits to Kensal Green, and continued so doing until the last year of his life. 'At one fifteen drove to Kensal Green,' he wrote on 15 January 1883, 'and once more visited the grave of my beloved one, a painful, but to me essential duty, and asked again in prayer for her forgiveness for my many shortcomings towards her and God's merciful pardon for the sins of that dear soul and for my own, which are so much, much greater.' On the second anniversary of Mrs Beauclerk's death he declared, 'the sorrow of my heart has in no respect been mitigated by time, as some said it would. After attending a service at Dover Street I went to Kensal Green and there deposited a wreath on *her dear grave*. Several others I found already there, a proof that *she* is not forgotten by others as well as myself.' In 1887, in the midst of his military jubilee, he did 'not forget *her* dear memory, in the congratulation and honours that have been accorded to me,' and visited her tomb on 5 November. At the end of the year, on 28 December, a day 'ever to be remembered with deep sorrow and grief,' he wrote in his Diary, 'It is now five years since my *beloved friend* was taken from amongst us. I went at ten to the Cemetery with Dickins to depose a beautiful wreath on *her* tomb. It looked so peaceful . . . but oh! how sad! Never shall I forget that dreadful day and a loss which is irreparable.' In 1897, when the Duke was seventy eight, fifteen years after Mrs B.'s death, he paid his annual visit to Emily Wombwell and to Kensal Green on the 'sad anniversary.' His grief was neither counterfeit nor consolable, and its intensity provides a measure of the vehemence of his love.

Despite the distractions of Chesham Street, the Duke's own family made large demands on his affection, and indeed there were moments when his devotion to his children was almost overwhelmed by aggravation at their improvidence. Louisa, so he assured her, he continued to adore 'as I did the first day we met.' 'My feelings,' he wrote on 6 September 1878, 'are unchanged. If my letters have been feeble in their expressions in this respect, believe me my darling, this can only be caused by *age* creeping over me, which may make the pen less free in its expression, though the heart is as warm as in the earlier days of our devotion.'

The Duke's Diaries contain hundreds of references to dinners in Queen Street. Generally they seem to have been family gatherings, consisting of Georgina, Mrs FitzGeorge's sister, Charles Fairbrother, Louisa's daughter, who married Captain Hamilton in 1859, and the three FitzGeorge sons. The Grand Duke and Duchess of Strelitz occasionally dined. Louisa spent part of her year either at the cottage at Horley or at various health resorts. Whenever the Duke travelled abroad, or visited some country house for a shooting party, he wrote almost daily to Louisa, but his letters throw little light on the everyday life of Queen Street.

He is at his most communicative in times of disaster. Thus on 29 June 1882, he writes: 'When I got to Queen Street found Louisa in the greatest distress her dear little dog Prince having been run over and killed by the wheel of a carriage near Bayswater Gate. It is most sad, for he was a most dear and affectionate little fellow and Louisa's constant companion, and I was myself, as was everybody, most fond of him.'

In 1886 Louisa suffered a greater affliction when her sister Georgina died. In his Diary on 15 April the Duke described his own part in this sad event. 'Rode early, then busy at home, later walked to the office. I had only just reached it, when I got a note from Louisa to say that dearest Georgina had just passed away in an attack, which had suddenly come over her. I at once went up to Queen Street, and found dearest Louisa and everybody there in great distress and I myself entered most fully into their feelings of sorrow and grief. Georgina had during the last few days been much less well, for we had been in hopes that she was gradually mending . . . She had been downstairs for some time, had even walked out into the street one day that it was mild, just in front of the house, and had several days dined with us quietly when I came there. The last day she came downstairs was on Tuesday, and I saw her downstairs for the last time on Monday, when she appeared better. On Tuesday however she felt so unwell with spasms in her chest, from which she had been suffering of late, the result no doubt of the want of power of digestion, that she went up to bed before I came to dinner. Wednesday she remained upstairs all day very unwell, had a very bad night with great pain and much vomiting, and when Louisa went up to see her today, she found her very feeble and suffering but quite herself and entering still into conversation with her, though but little. She had her beef tea and brandy for lunch, when Louisa left her, scarcely had she gone, when the nurse who had been again sent for that morning, and had only been there a couple of hours, was suddenly called to by dearest Georgina to come . . . She had hardly got her arms around her when she gave a vacant stare and poor dear she was *dead*, the doctors were immediately sent for, but all was over and no more could be done, as she was gone from us for ever. It is *too too* sad, and the suddenness of the event quite overwhelming. I stayed some time in the house and saw poor dear Georgina after she had been laid out, when her countenance was calm and placid. I then went home, later to St James's, and unfortunately had a dinner which I could not get out of, much to my distress.'

Except for Augustus, the Duke's sons caused him much anxiety. Having himself made an original marriage, his children listened to his advice on the subject with a certain scepticism. The orthodox, even old-fashioned views he was disposed to express, were so inconsistent with his own practice that they failed to impress his sons.

Although the Queen had been distant with George FitzGeorge, the Prince of Wales was more affable. In 1877 he invited George and Augustus to Sandringham, 'where,' the Duke told Adolphus, 'they are getting on swimmingly, though both have had a tumble out hunting.' The Duchess of Cambridge never set eyes on her grandsons until 1878, when 'she expressed a wish to become acquainted' with them. The meeting was a wild success, the FitzGeorges became constant visitors at St James's, thus opening new horizons of discussion. 'In the Afternoon,' wrote the Duke in his Diary on 4 January, 'took George to St James's to be introduced to my dearest mother she having affectionately expressed a wish to see all the boys. It went off very well and she expressed herself as most pleased with George.' Two days later Augustus was taken to see the Duchess 'who was much pleased with him. It is so nice of her to have done me this out of affectionate kindness.'

In January 1883, while the Duke was still overwhelmed by the shock of Mrs Beauclerk's death, Colonel George decided to retire from the Army. He had frequently threatened to do so before, much against his father's will, but now having decided to write for the newspapers and to speculate in the City, was obdurate. 'Says he cares nothing for soldiering, does not wish to be a General, knows he can never be C. in C., but "Secretary for

War I *can* be and that I *intend* to be." ' 'Too bad of him,' was
Lady Geraldine's comment, 'to annoy his father at this moment.'[11]
'George is going to have something to do with a newspaper,'
[the *Sunday Times*] wrote H.R.H. to Louisa on 15 May 1883.
'I am convinced people do not like associating with anybody
regularly connected with the Press.' He attempted to enrol
Adolphus's support against his brother. 'I hope,' he wrote to him
on 10 January, when the scheme was first made known, 'you will
help me in persuading your brother George from doing the most
foolish and imprudent thing that was ever contemplated by a
sensible and really intelligent man. He has sent in his resignation
of his commission and is thus going to throw away the excellent
position he has made for himself in the Army, with the object
of being a writer in the Press!!!! the most horrible occupation
a man can possibly take to . . . I am in utter despair.' Some years
later he told his wife, 'I must try to prevent further mischief with
this *dreadful* Newspaper and the speculative companies, which
are not occupations for a high cast Gentleman who wishes to
belong to good society to be involved in. I hope and think that
in this you agree with me.' George FitzGeorge was fascinated by
enterprising business deals, but either the dice were loaded against
him, or he had no head for figures. Neither newspapers, nor a
brewery, nor the Empire theatre, all of which lost heavily under
his ownership, ever made him the fortune he expected. On the
contrary, the Duke rescued him from a series of financial disasters.
Writing to Adolphus FitzGeorge in December 1893, he tells him
he has seen Farrer, the family solicitor, and after talking matters
over very fully, 'it breaks my heart to say it, I really believe the
best thing for George himself, and specially for his poor dear
little children is to let him go bankrupt. It is *horrible* to me but I
am afraid it is the only decision which is justified by the sad
position of affairs.'

George's marriage to Rosa Baring, which took place on 28
November 1885, did not altogether please his father, principally
because Rosa's first marriage had ended in divorce. 'Poor fellow,'
he wrote to Adolphus fifteen days before the wedding, 'I don't

think he is doing a wise thing for himself.' H.R.H. was first introduced to his son's wife on 10 April 1886. Somewhat grudgingly he described her in his Diary as 'a handsome woman certainly, with agreeable manners.' 'The Duke does not dislike her,' wrote Lady Geraldine, 'and says she is a good looking woman.' No doubt inspired from St James's, he soon managed to find ground for criticism. His daughter-in-law was 'made up, and very extravagant in her dress.' Her constant visits to Paris to buy clothes were watched with disapproval. Mrs George's Christmas present from the Duke in 1894 was a looking-glass and a handbag, and they were presented to her with accompanying jests.

Although Adolphus FitzGeorge abandoned his early extravagance, his father was dismayed by his views on marriage. While his ship was in Australia, he became engaged to a girl from Sydney: 'The most foolish and thoughtless of all possible proposals,' was how H.R.H. described the idea in a letter to his son written on 18 May 1869. 'The idea,' he continued, 'of your committing yourself to a promise of marriage to a girl who has not a sixpence and whose family are anything but nice, according to your own showing, is so preposterous that I should have thought your own good sense would have at once prevented you from so senseless a proceeding.' The Duke pulled strings at the Admiralty, Adolphus was transferred to the English Channel, and the marriage was abandoned.

In 1874 Adolphus again decided upon matrimony, and once more the Duke was opposed to the idea. He believed his son was not rich enough to marry and that a wife would prejudice his naval career. 'I adhere to my opinion,' wrote the Duke on 5 October, 'that matrimony ought not to be thought of by you for some time to come . . . I write this of myself and from nothing that was said at Horley!' The next day he wrote again to Adolphus, arguing that it would be 'most foolish and imprudent' to marry. 'It is only fair by all parties that they should clearly understand that I had not given my consent to your proposal and that I considered that it was not to your interest to marry at present and that I considered the prospect of living on

£1,200 a year a very miserable one indeed . . . You cannot say that this is a very deep or long standing affection. The young lady has moreover been brought up in much comfort and luxury.' The Duke maintained that Adolphus should go back to sea, not act rashly, and try to forget Sofia.

In two further letters, written on 11 October and 17 October, H.R.H. produced further reasons for his opposition. 'The more I think of your proposed marriage the less I like it . . . I tell you candidly I do not like the connection. It really would be extremely distasteful to me . . . I am so fond of you boys that I want you to belong to my society and not a lower sphere which this would certainly be.' A marriage such as Adolphus was contemplating would prevent him getting on in the Service, in society and in the world at large. 'Professional society such as that in which you have been living more or less all your life is very different from a civil connection of a kind that would take you entirely away from me.' H.R.H. assured his son that his advice was very sensible and should be seriously considered. 'You are now in love and don't look beyond the present time.'

'Had a long interview,' wrote the Duke in his Diary on 22 November, 'with George and Adolphus in Queen Street connected with the wish of the latter to marry, to which in his interest, I am much opposed, but upon which he is unfortunately very determined. I have now got him to promise, that he will at all events wait for two years or thereabouts.' By September of 1875 Adolphus was still anxious to marry, and Mr Holden, Sofia's father, having at first hesitated, now gave way. The Duke refused to give his consent but left the final decision to his son. 'Whenever Miss Holden becomes your wife, you may depend upon it that she will receive every consideration and good feeling as such from me.' The Duke made it clear that he would not attend the wedding. 'I am not in England' at the time arranged, 'but even if I were I don't think with my views on the subject it would be honest on my part to attend. That every blessing may attend you is my ardent hope and prayer because I have a real and sincere affection for you and your brothers, not because I think you are doing a wise or judicious thing, which to this moment I think you are not.' 'I take it for granted your brothers will support you at the wedding, but you could hardly expect your dear Mama to go all the way to Hull and back when you know that moving about is not easy for her.'[12]

Adolphus was naturally distressed that his parents refused to attend his wedding and wrote to his mother saying, 'I cannot express to you the bitter disappointment it is to me that George, dear old boy, is to be the only one of my family present at the wedding tomorrow, however in this world we must be thankful for small mercies and thank God I shall not be submitted to the degradation of having to stand unsupported. He at least will see me safe through my wedding . . . Dear Gussy has failed to come at my earnest request by telegraph, pleading that it was too late, it may have been the case. I trust it was.' Adolphus attributed Louisa's refusal to the influence of his father. He tells her that all his friends have 'pocketed their pride' and consented to come. 'I don't blame you, I believe you would have liked to have come. I believe it is all Papa's fault. God only knows why he should have been so cruel.'

The Duke wisely determined to make the best of things once the marriage was an accomplished fact. 'One thing is certain,' he told Louisa in a letter written from Paris on 13 September, 'the marriage having taken place it is better not to be on bad terms. There is no necessity for any great *intimacy* with the family at all events. You were quite *right* to decline the invitation to go to Hull for the wedding, it is just what you say, it would have given a certain amount of sanction and countenance, which it is best to avoid.' On 21 September, Adolphus's wedding day, the Duke wrote in his Diary, 'Dined with Louisa at home. She afterwards went to meet Dolly, who was alas! married today at Hull to Miss Holden, the daughter of a Solicitor there. When appointed to the *Rapid* [a ship of which he was given command] Dolly telegraphed me to give my consent to an immediate marriage before his departure. I left it to him to decide and he has consequently taken the step. May it turn out to his advantage. I regret it for his and mine . . . but must now make the best of it!' On the following day he met Sofia. 'Dolly came with his young wife to introduce her to me. She seems cheerful and lively, but I did not think her very pretty. She is short and inclined to be stout. All passed off well, as it is best now to be on friendly terms. I took leave of them, as they leave today for Southampton to embark tomorrow for the Mediterranean, where the *Rapid* is.'

The Duke's opposition to Adolphus's marriage was rather singular. Mr Holden was a rich and successful solicitor, and by Victorian standards his daughter was a thousand times more acceptable as a bride than was an actress, however remarkable she might be. As soon as he got to know Sofia the Duke relented. He told Adolphus on 19 September 1876 that he would be delighted if Sofia wrote to him from time to time. 'I have every regard and good feeling for her on your account my dear Dolly as well as her own, and therefore you need be under no sort of anxiety on that account.' He even instructed his son in the proper manner for his wife to address him. 'She should commence her letter "My Dear Duke" which is the right thing.'

In quite a short time the Duke came to regard Sofia as an ally, whose influence on his wayward son might be exerted for good. When Adolphus in 1876 wanted to give up command of the *Rapid* because he suffered so badly from sea-sickness, his father thought resignation might be mistaken for cowardice at a time when war with Russia threatened, and he discussed the matter with Sofia who entirely agreed with him. 'Really my dear fellow,' he wrote to Adolphus on 25 July, 'to read your letters one would suppose I was your bitterest enemy, whereas I am your *best* friend and there is not a wish of my heart that is not for your benefit and advancement in life. And in this sentiment I further assure you that I include Sofia, who is I know just as much interested in all that is good for you as I can be.' Sofia and the Duke between them eventually succeeded in persuading Adolphus to retain his command. H.R.H. in a letter to his daughter-in-law, written on 18 August, tells her: 'A young fellow without occupation must lead a miserable life in the long run, even though for the moment he may fancy the prospect . . . A life of idleness is a life of misery.' The letter concluded, 'I remain my dear Sofia yours very affectionately, George.' It was a tribute to her charm and to the Duke's generous nature that, within a year of a marriage he had earnestly opposed, she had become 'My dear Sofia' and he was her 'affectionate' George.

Adolphus, as a married man, almost ceased to cause his father annoyance. It is true he continued to think of leaving the Navy. 'You have known,' he wrote in 1889, 'how I always loathed and hated my profession.' The Duke told him, 'You think the Navy is made for you and not you for the Navy,' and when in 1877 Adolphus contemplated becoming Secretary of the Hull Dock Company, H.R.H. wrote him a letter on 13 June, complaining that nothing any longer surprised him, 'for I have found out, alas, that you are never disposed to take my advice . . . but I was astonished nevertheless when you tell me that you were inclined to take the Secretaryship of the Hull Dock Company. To me this seems a most outrageous idea . . . But I suppose as usual I shall be told, that you know better than I do, and if you are determined to sever yourself from all connection with the service the more fool you that is all I say. But it disgusts me beyond measure.'

Interference in the upbringing of children is a grandparent's prerogative, and, urged on by his mother, the Duke freely availed himself of his rights. In 1884 Sofia organized a charity bazaar, which the Prince and Princess of Wales consented to patronize. It was thought at St James's that Adolphus's daughter, Olga FitzGeorge, might be present. Accordingly on 15 July H.R.H. wrote to his son saying, 'I don't know if you intend Olga to be there. She is so young that for her I should say it would be better not, but of course you must do what is best. I hope if she goes you will take care that she is very quietly dressed. You know I think at times she is dressed too conspicuously, which I don't think is at all good for a child, for it turns their head. My mother has spoken to me about this once or twice, so I am anxious you should take care about this for tomorrow particularly. This is of course for *yourself only*.' When there was some idea of Olga acting in a play, her grandfather wrote, 'appearing on the stage is not desirable for this nice little girl.'

Adolphus, although more sensible about money than he had been in his early days as a young naval officer, was still disposed towards extravagant ways, and occasional rumbles of displeasure erupted from Gloucester House. In 1892 he and Sofia moved into Number 12, Eaton Square. It was, in Lady Geraldine's phrase, 'a charming house—a palazzo!! The *poor* Duke's pocket!!' The Adolphus FitzGeorges usually spent part of the winter in Monte Carlo, which the Duke after a visit in 1893, described as 'a Hell upon Earth as regards Society . . . How you and Sofia can go and stay there year after year in those stuffy and stinking Gambling Rooms I cannot conceive and I confess to you honestly it *annoys* me more than I can express, and I think it very *lowering* to a Gentleman and Lady to be sitting at the tables day after day with such *degrading company*.'[13]

Besides his visits to Chesham Street and Queen Street, hardly a day passed when the Duke was in London without him seeing his mother at St James's. His appearances were eagerly awaited by the old, stricken Duchess and her infatuated lady in waiting. Lady Geraldine resented other visitors when the Duke was there, wishing to devour every moment without distraction. 'At nine thirty the Duke came,' she wrote describing 'a cosy pleasant evening,' 'H.R.H. with her work frame! He with his little table making "Patiences"! I with my knitting. And pleasant talk.' Another evening 'was bright and lively and full of fun! Wound a ball of wool and was very gay!'[14] Once, when the Duchess of Teck left one of her sons at St James's, the Duke played with him, 'going on all fours pretending to be a big dog!'

The Duke was an excellent mimic and kept his mother in fits of laughter with his imitations. 'At eight fifteen the Duke came! and dined with Princess Frederica [of Hanover] and me. Nine fifteen up to H.R.H. He was in the highest spirits! and too amusing and funny. Gave us the most amusing representation of General Bruce in command at Edinburgh, and his *boots*!' Another time, 'he took off for H.R.H.'s amusement the way the present curate reads! Too *amusingly*! and was too funny and droll! imitating him so exactly!!' Even his near relations were not spared. 'He took off the Duke of Cumberland's voice and manner in arguing a point, so *inimitably* cleverly! so to the life! It gave the Duchess a *fit* of laughter! *too* good!'[15] This gift of mimicry proceeded from a sharp eye for detail and a capaciously retentive memory.

The Cambridge family, while rejecting most of the vices of the Regency period, retained something of its gaiety. It was for this reason that the Queen and Prince Albert regarded their circle with suspicion, and it also explains why the Prince of Wales, detesting his mother's sombre court, was attracted to 'Uncle George.' One night the Duchess 'dreamt she refused two kings, and the Duke said he was sure he could persuade Lord William Paulet to marry her!! which he did! and the marriage was arranged! Thereupon much reciprocal chaff!!' It was very 'unlike the home life of the poor dear Queen.' But conversations were not always frivolous. 'We had a very *earnest* religious talk! upon the prevalent unbelief in the World! and upon the Lord's Prayer! on which the Duke spoke so touchingly with fine and simple trust!'[16]

Often there was music in the evening. Lord Ormathwaite in his recollections of life at Court described how the old Duchess of Cambridge, although 'paralysed and a great sufferer . . . would sit in her sitting-room at St James's Palace cheerfully receiving her friends whenever well enough. She was devoted to music, and at the suggestion of the Prince and Princess of Wales, Tosti, the composer of many lovely songs, used to visit her often in the evening about six o'clock and play to her. Knowing my fondness for music, she kindly allowed me to come on these occasions and sit in the room. It was most pleasant. The Prince and Princess of Wales and many of the Royal Family used to drop in, but the Duchess was most particular that there should be no interruption of the music, and being the doyenne of the Royal Family she was allowed to have her own way. Apropos of the old Duchess being the doyenne. When she died, Queen

Victoria said: "Ah me! There is the last one gone who had the right to call me Victoria." The Duke of Cambridge used also to drop in sometimes at these little parties. The Duchess, however, discouraged her son's visits at this hour as he invariably fell asleep on his chair and interrupted the most pathetic parts of the singing

with loud snores!'[17] Although the Duke was rather prone to fall asleep in the evening, he was extremely fond of music, and often went to the opera three times a week. He did, however, draw the line at Wagner. *Götterdämmerung* he called a 'wild and improbable opera which I think horrible but dear Stephens [an A.D.C.] thinks divine.'

The Duchess always gave a family party on Christmas Eve. In 1886 the three FitzGeorges were invited to St James's. 'It was like the prettiest of bazaars! H.R.H. bore it all most beautifully!! I was quite astounded! She was far beyond my expectations! and so enjoyed the pleasure she was giving, that we could really not induce her to break up, and go to bed! though we repeatedly tried to do so, till at length the dear Duke, always kind and thoughtful, took the law into his own dear hands, and insisted on saying goodnight and *drove* all away! standing sentry till he got them out! God be praised for his dear mercy in letting us all once again spend this evening in joy together!!!' The Duke was unfailingly attentive and considerate. The Duchess described her son 'as like a sheep-dog with a flock of sheep' driving her guests away when he thought it was time for her to go to bed. 'As fast as he hunted some away on one side they came back again on the other.'

The Duchess lovingly appreciated her son's affection, and when he was out of London her conversation often turned to discussion of his thoughtfulness. On leaving for Germany in 1878, he paid his mother a farewell visit. 'After supper the Duchess talked much of him and his exquisite goodness to her, and how readily he would have even now given up his journey for her sake if she had allowed it.' On her eighty-ninth birthday Lady Geraldine 'went into her and had the pleasure of reading to her a *dear dear* note from the Duke which touched her to the heart! So kind! She spoke most lovingly of him and how *angel* good he is! Of his golden heart and *charming* nature . . . his boundless attention and goodness to her!'[18]

Both the Duchess and Lady Geraldine agreed that the Duke's readiness to forgive an injury was characteristic of his generous nature, and they contrasted the vendettas of the Prince of Wales with H.R.H.'s willingness for reconciliation. The Duchess 'spoke of how strongly marked and beautiful a trait this is in his character, and always has been! His tutors and governors always remarked it, saying however severely they punished him, he always the next time they met, bounded up to them with the same friendship and affection! And so he has been through life, I never met *anyone* who can so thoroughly and really forgive and *forget*! If annoyed and displeased he can be angry at the moment, but once having forgiven, he utterly and absolutely banishes it from his mind! So that if, some time after you by chance allude to it, you find he has *literally* forgotten it and you would really have to *recall* it to his mind. A very beautiful trait indeed! which arises from his golden heart and most charming nature.'[19]

The Duchess loved to discuss her grandchildren and their visits were always welcome. 'Colonel George came in,' wrote Lady Geraldine on 28 August 1883, 'and paid a nice visit till eleven ten. He told us he was travelling South to Carlisle and made friends with a man in the carriage with him, getting into much conversation with him, after dining together at Carlisle they exchanged cards, on reading George's name, the man said, "Ah well you have the best father in England!"!! Nice, and *wise* man!! He was a Mr North of Cumberland.' But sometimes George FitzGeorge fell out of favour. He was inclined to be argumentative, and, even worse, radical. 'Again a long argument upon the new and old military systems, upholding alas! considerable Cardwellian principles. At last the Duke broke off and spoke with H.R.H. of other things.' Lady Geraldine became 'more and more convinced Captain George is very argumentative and opinionated and terribly *modern* in ideas of "reform"!! so called! and for discarding all *former* views! and I cannot bear his *tone* with the Duke!' Despite these shortcomings, when Lord Charles Beresford in 1882 told the Duchess that George was 'a capital campaigner! always full of fun, and really an admirable caterer!' he gave her a great deal of pleasure, particularly as he concluded his eulogy by saying he thought George 'very clever, and to sum up, he has a head on his shoulders."'[20]

The Duke was fond of discussing his family problems at St James's, and the collapse of George FitzGeorge's business ventures were a sadly familiar theme of conversation. 'The Duke told us,' Lady Geraldine wrote on 19 May 1884, 'he has settled the affair of making Colonel George his A.D.C. A great worry, annoyance, and trouble it has been to him, alas! And finally of course can only be settled by the Duke having *as usual*! to pay an enormous sum for him!! He will listen to no one, least of all to the Duke! So far wiser than himself and with such true instinct for what is right and well to do and to leave undone! which Mr

George has not at all!! All the trouble he causes the Duke with these silly companies he not only gets into but *heads*!!! without capital! He is too tiresome. But the poor Duke having again largely and generously *paid* for him and advanced a *large* sum has freed him from the brewery.' When in the following year Colonel George left the Army for the *Sunday Times* Lady Geraldine described him as a 'donkey' who had he remained where he was 'might now command the Regiment!! If he had not been so obstinate and self-willed about quitting! but! he would not care to command it! Cares for nothing but idiotic newspaper scribbling!!' And then, having always been jealous of Mrs FitzGeorge, she adds, 'how preponderating must the *wretched* blood on the *other* side be!!!'[21]

Much of the conversation at St James's revolved round the Queen and there were moments when the talk was neither amiable nor loyal. The Duke sometimes complained he was ignored by Her Majesty. 'He read us the Duke of Connaught's telegram to say the Queen would "not *have time* to see him before she goes abroad"!!!! Discussion concerning this rude ungraciousness.' When he visited Windsor after Christmas in 1877 he was kept 'quite as an "outsider" they told him—the Commander-in-Chief!!—*nothing*! Neither the Queen, nor Dizzy who was there.'[22]

At St James's it was believed that the Queen was too friendly with Lord Wolseley. On 14 January 1884, they discussed 'the *strangeness* of the Queen showing such unmeasured favour to Wolseley.' 'To my mind,' Lady Geraldine observed, 'so *unloyal* of her!!' Among other signs of this excessive partiality was the invitation to Osborne of Wolseley's thirteen-year-old daughter. Wolseley himself was utterly unaware that he was a chosen favourite; on the contrary, like the Commander-in-Chief, he believed himself to be scorned and rejected. 'I am sick of Royalties,' he wrote to his wife, 'and never wish to see one of our Royal family again: I think I used to be the greatest loyalist in England, but the cruel treatment I have received from the Queen, I can never either forgive or forget.' In September 1882, he enclosed a letter to Lady Wolseley which he had just received

from the Queen, 'the only one she has ever honoured me with.
I think you will agree with me that it is as cold-blooded an
effusion as you have ever read: her only sympathies and solicitude
are for her own selfish self and her family . . . I should esteem
it a favour if the Queen would not write to me unless she can
write to me in more gracious terms than in this stilted, freezing
epistle. However let us forget this subject: I have done well for
my country and if my country's sovereign does not appreciate
my services I cannot help although I can pity her.'[23]

The Cambridges attributed some of the Queen's eccentricities
to her living too much in the society of servants and of listening
to foolish advice. 'They discussed the peculiarities of the Queen,'
wrote Lady Geraldine on 17 July 1886, 'how she sent a note to
H.R.H. saying that if the Grand Duke of Mecklenburg-Strelitz
who had just arrived from Germany, should wish to see her,
"Will you tell him that I cannot see him because I am just off to
Osborne!!!!" Too odd. Moreover! the fact of her just going to
Osborne on Tuesday!! at the very *instant* in all human probability
of a change of ministry!! H.R.H. spoke of how strange it is of
the Queen to send him such a message! Of her being so ill
surrounded!' The Prince of Wales, when his mother's *Journal*
came out, told the Duchess that he was indignant and disgusted
at the Queen publishing it. But then, he said, there was 'no one
to prevent her committing such acts.' The Duke, who did not
himself read it until some time after its publication, was informed
at St James's that it was an 'atrocious' work. 'We told him, how
besides its *offensiveness* it is so badly written! Such bad vulgar
English! So miserably futile and trivial! So dull and uninteresting.'

The Prince of Wales's hostility to the Queen's *Journal* was nothing to his indignation that his son Prince George was never
invited to shoot at Windsor until he was twenty one. 'You would
hardly believe it,' he told the Duke, 'that, I being heir to the
throne, this is the first time that my son has *ever* shot in Windsor
Park!'[24] As Prince George was amongst the best shots in England,
and had been one of a 'family party' at Sandringham which shot
six thousand head in three days, the omission was remarkable.

The conversation at St James's very often drifted back to recollections of former times. 'We talked,' wrote Lady Geraldine on 29 January 1887, 'of the extraordinary and inexplicable halucination of George IV had that he commanded the Xth Hussars at Waterloo!!! Speaking one day of it before the Duke of Wellington and referring to him for corroboration, the Duke of Wellington bowed, and said: "Your Royal Highness's memory is better than mine!" ' But despite her age, the Duchess lived very much in the present and was quite as happy to gossip about Wolseley as the Prince Regent. 'We spoke of the Dinner last night [21 May 1887] to Sir Frederick Stephenson at which the Duke was, having been very successful! Colonel George said the Duke made a capital speech which was highly appreciated! Speaking of General Stephenson's modesty he said, "We all know there are *some* generals, and it is not necessary to mention any names, but there are *some* who are very fond of always blowing their own trumpets! Now General Stephenson *never* blows his own trumpet! and as he does not you will perhaps forgive me if I blow it for him and somewhat loudly!" ' When Wolseley went up in a balloon at Chatham, Lady Geraldine, after regretting that 'the cord was not cut!' commented: 'It's so like him, that having been most *violently* and abusively opposed to the use of balloons, since he went up in it, he returned in a violent state of enthusiasm about it.'

The Duchess was always interested in foreign affairs and the doings of her numerous German relations. The death from cancer of the Kaiser Frederick III caused consternation at St James's. The Duke, on 16 June 1888, 'showed us a *charming* telegram he had received from the *poor* unhappy little Empress!!! in answer to his. "Many thanks! He was so fond of you, loved England so much, you will not forget him, I know!" ' Five days later, H.R.H. 'told us of a really admirable letter he wrote today to the young Emperor William, giving him as his uncle, good sound advice! alluding to his differences with his mother, which he was able to do as Prince William had frankly spoken with him about them! and offering "as he is very fond of her," if at any time he

could be of service between them, to do all in his powers to
smooth matters, which it would give him great happiness to
effect.'

Apart from the family, Wolseley, Cardwell and Childers,
Gladstone was the public figure most discussed at St James's.
Lady Geraldine loathed him with extravagant frenzy. The
Duchess was more temperate but was certainly no admirer of the
Liberal statesman. The Duke, while opposing his policies, sometimes expressed a reluctant respect for his character and attainments. On 2 April 1883, Lady Geraldine was told by the Duke of
his 'visit at Sandringham which he liked very much, amongst
old friends. Told us of Gladstone cutting down a tree! The
absurdity!! Previously divesting himself of hat, coat, waistcoat,
rolling up his shirt sleeves and unbuttoning his shirt front!!! The
curious sight of the Prime Minister of England at seventy-four
in this garb at this work watched by the heir apparent, the
Primate, and the Commander-in-Chief!!! Of how admirably
Gladstone read the lessons at both the morning and evening
services yesterday! worth going a distance to hear.' During the
following evening the Duke returned to the subject of the Prime
Minister, and spoke 'of his wonderful energy and earnestness, and
the extraordinary charm and fascination there certainly is about
him personally, but loathing his politics as one does and all the
harm and mischief he has done and does, yet one cannot help
being charmed with him while you came in personal contact
with him! The precise reverse of Beaconsfield. Of what a goose
Mrs Gladstone is! And how strange those four clever men, Peel,
Derby, Disraeli and Gladstone should have married four such
silly women!'

Miss Taylor, a lady in waiting called in by the Duchess to
assist the indefatigable Lady Geraldine, was of Liberal sympathies.
Once she became so indignant at hearing constant abuse of
Gladstone, that she stormed out of the drawing room of St
James's in an angry sulk. The Duke described Miss Taylor's
behaviour as 'outrageous.' Lady Geraldine considered 'she ought
to be well whipped! a thorough good thrashing is what she ought

to have.' Princess Mary was disposed to be more generous and said she considered, 'everyone has a right to their own opinion.' When Miss Taylor's father visited St James's, the Duke happened to come in, and the Duchess, to put him in the conversation, said, ' "Mr Taylor is just telling me how conservative the city is." "I know," said the Duke, with meaning, leaning across to Mr Taylor, "I know! Excellent Conservatives. *I wish everybody else were so too.*" The Duke then proceeded—on purpose!—"Oh! all the mischief is that *scoundrel* Gladstone!" so that Mr Taylor could not doubt of *His* Royal Highness's opinion of Miss Ella Taylor's outburst.'[25]

The Duke, on 20 April 1887, sent Lady Geraldine 'a most cleverly drawn envelope!! the stamp placed so as to form the head of the Queen as she kneels with it laid upon the block, Gladstone with the most wicked expression of exultant hate and fury, with his axe raised about to chop it off! So cleverly done.' The St James's circle were very angry with the Prince of Wales 'for heading the list of congratulations on Gladstone's birthday with a fulsome telegram to the brute. To *my* mind it is too disgusting and sickening! and *despicable*! He assured the Duke he had telegraphed in *his* name as well as his own—thank *God* it was only a joke.'

When the Prince of Wales failed to come up from Sandringham to the funeral of Lord Iddesleigh, Lady Geraldine was angered by 'the knowledge that had heaven in mercy delivered us from the curse of Gladstone's existence, the Prince of Wales would have run, with ten special trains and twenty extra engines, and enveloped in yards and folds of crepe, to do honour to his funeral! and curry favour with the plebs.' Gladstone's invitation to Sandringham made Lady Geraldine's 'blood boil. And I asked the Duke if he would not invite Mr Parnell and Mr Dillon to dinner tonight to meet the Prince as his most fitting companions and the most suited to his taste? It is really too disgusting. The Duke defended him, it being the exigencies of his position, but there is a way and a mode of doing things.'[26]

Towards the end of 1888 the Duchess became more seriously

ill, and on 6 April 1889, she died at the age of ninety two. The Duke, at the time, was inspecting the troops in Ireland. 'Poor dear Mama!' wrote the Duke in his Diary. 'So kind, so good, so devoted to me and oh! how much I shall miss her dear presence, but for her, dear precious darling, a happy release from prolonged sufferings.' He immediately left Dublin for London, where he arrived on the morning of 7 April. At St James's he 'found poor Lady Geraldine very calm and composed though painfully sorrowing. I at once went to my dear Mother's bedroom, and saw her dear face lying peacefully and composedly on her bed of death, a happy expression on her beloved countenance. It was a terrible moment, though for her, dearest soul, a happy release.'

The Duchess's end had come so suddenly that none of her children were with her. Apart from the nurses and Lady Geraldine, there was only one member of the Royal Family present. The Princess of Wales was at Marlborough House, and hearing that the Duchess was dying, she hastened across to St James's. 'Aunt dear, you know Alix,' she said, as she approached the bedside. But there was no response.

The funeral took place at Kew Church on 13 April, 'exactly in the same manner as that of my beloved Father, at her express will and to our complete satisfaction.' The hearse was escorted to Kew by the Life Guards, and the coffin was 'surrounded by a profusion of the most lovely flowers I ever saw collected.' The Queen was at the service where she sat between Princess Mary and Princess Augusta. It was the only funeral she ever attended, except for her son Prince Leopold's. 'The mournful ceremony was conducted in the most beautiful and solemn manner, a large number of my dear Mother's old friends being present.' After the Queen had returned to Windsor, she wrote to the Duke: 'It was a melancholy satisfaction, I assure you, for me to have been with you all three at that very impressive and touching ceremony. . . . It is a sad and solemn feeling that there is no one above us any longer, and that *we* are now *the only old ones left*.'[27]

While the Duke was still mourning his mother's loss, Louisa became seriously ill. 'I was much alarmed,' wrote the Duke on

30 July, 'by the accounts about dearest Louisa this morning.'
The doctors were 'evidently very anxious about her.' 'I therefore
gave up going down to Goodwood for the race meeting and
party, as I had intended . . . Sir Alfred Garrod went to see
Louisa at five and both he and Dr Sims found her very much less
suffering than they had expected and thought she was progressing
slowly but decidedly, they were therefore hopeful. I sat with her
later on and read to her and she seemed to like it and was much
less suffering.'

From the end of the summer of 1888 Louisa lay under sentence
of death, and despite great pain managed to disguise her suffering
from her husband. Occasionally, however, she surrendered to
outbursts of anguish which doused her gaiety and charm. The
Duke one day insisted that Sheppard, the Sub-Dean of the Chapels
Royal, should come back to Queen Street with him and be
introduced to his wife. 'Sheppard made as if he would stay in the
hall till the lady had been prepared for his visit. "What the devil
are you stopping there for?" said the Duke. "Come up with me."
They proceeded upstairs and were ushered into a room opening
into the bedroom where the patient lay. The Duke passed through
the door and told Mrs FitzGeorge that he had brought the Sub-
Dean to see her, of whose kindness to his mother he had so often
spoken, upon which, to Sheppard's consternation, he heard her say
with emphasis, "Indeed he is the last person I wish to see!" and,
on his being introduced, she turned her head away and refused to
speak. After a long pause of much embarrassment to all, Sheppard
made a courteous effort to take leave, upon which the lady
relented and said, "Mr Sheppard, you have shown me more
courtesy than I have you, and I hope you will come again,"
which he did seeing her constantly for the few months which
preceded her death.'[28]

By the beginning of 1890, Louisa was so seriously ill that the
Duke began to fear the worst. 'No improvement,' he wrote on
7 January, 'in the condition of my dearest love . . . She says
herself she feels very ill and there cannot be a doubt of the fact.
It makes me feel very, very anxious though I still *hope* for the

best but I *fear* for the worst. I went to Queen Street and then to
the office. Went back to Queen Street, dined there, and sat with
Louisa, about whom I am *very uneasy.*' On the following day he
wrote, 'Our Wedding day which we have always kept together.
. . . Louisa seemed just a shade better today, so I proposed to her
to take the Holy Communion with me tomorrow to which she
gladly assented.' On 9 January the Duke, 'After being busy at
home in the morning went at once to Queen Street to meet Mr
Sheppard. Dearest Louisa appeared stronger and better and was
able to keep her dear eyes open which she could not do the last
few days. She *rejoiced* at taking the Holy Communion with
myself, Loulings [Mrs Hamilton] and dear good faithful Rowley
[the nurse], was quite herself and most keenly attentive during the
celebration and seemed none the worse for it. To me this service
has been an immense satisfaction, and I thank God, for his great
mercy in enabling her to take it before passing away from
amongst us.' On the 10th Louisa became unconscious. 'Sims came
in the early morning to tell me, he had been sent for to Queen
Street, as dearest Louisa was in a very serious state. I at once went
there with Gussie. Her eyes were in a peculiar condition and she
had difficulty in recognizing those about her, and spoke and took
nourishment with the greatest difficulty. I think she recognized
my voice and said in a very low tone, "God bless you dear papa"
but it was very indistinct. It was evident that the end was approaching. I went home for breakfast and returned to Queen
Street. Mr Sheppard came at one, and we had prayers by her
bedside, but she was too far gone to hear them or to be able to
attend to them, the brain had evidently begun to give way. I
again returned home to write some letters and then went back to
Queen Street, she was lying in a peacefully unconscious state
though still able to hear occasionally and I think she again made
a great effort to say "Bless you dearest" but that was all. From
that time she did not speak again. We passed a most miserable day
and after being together and having a second prayer just before
dinner, remained there all night expecting the end. She lay there
quite calm and placid, breathing quiet, pulse good, extremities

still warm but peacefully unconscious. Sims came several times, but there was no change.'

Louisa was unconscious all the 11th and died early the next morning. 'My beloved wife breathed her last calmly, peacefully, softly at about four o'clock this morning. We had been expecting this painful event all through the night, but lungs and heart were so sound, that they continued to perform their functions till their strength gave way under the weakness caused by absence of all nourishment, which could no longer be taken in the unconscious state she was in. All her children as well as myself, the little nurse, dear Rowley, and the female servants were surrounding the death bed . . . May the Almighty have mercy on her dear soul and give us strength to brave up against the overwhelming loss we have sustained. After coming home, I at once wrote to Ponsonby and the Prince of Wales asking the former to announce it to the Queen, which he kindly did and I later on received a most affectionate message from Her Majesty, which I highly appreciate and which would have been such a joy to my beloved one, had she known the fact. The Prince of Wales called on me to express his sympathy and sorrow at my heavy affliction. I had some hours' rest and then went to Queen Street where dear Mr Sheppard gave us a short touching service at the death bed side. My beloved one lay lovely in death still amongst us. Her countenance was beautiful, quite young to look at, though seventy four in actual age. The sorrow of my heart has this consolation that my beloved wife is now in peace and rest after her terrible and very prolonged sufferings, and God will be merciful to her Soul. She was so good and kind and affectionate and true and generous-hearted, and my little home of fifty years with my beloved Louisa is now come to an end.'

The day after Louisa died, the Duke wrote to the Queen.

My dear Cousin,

Your most dear and gracious letter, and warm sympathy, have deeply touched me, and gives me *great consolation* in my heavy affliction. With all the greatness and importance of your position, nobody knows more about real affection than you do, my dearest cousin, who have had such painful trials to go through alas! on so many occasions. Your sympathy is a blessing to me for which I thank you from my very heart, and beg to remain,

Your most dutiful and devoted cousin,

George.[29]

On 14 January the Duke 'Returned home, breakfasted with the boys, went to Queen Street and had a last look at my beloved wife, now beautifully laid out in the shell of the coffin, so calm and placid and quite young in the face, nothing painful about it, my bracelet on her dear arm, which she always wore, and which she will take with her to the grave.'

The day of the funeral, 16 January, was warm and sunny. At eleven thirty an open hearse, smothered in a mass of magnificent wreaths, and followed by five carriages, set out from Queen Street. The Duke and his three sons were in the first carriage. In the second were Louisa Hamilton, Colonel Charles Fairbrother, Rose and Sofia. Lord Wolseley and Colonel Du Plat, Equerry to the Queen, formed part of the procession. At half past twelve the mourners reached the cemetery, where they were joined by the Duke of Teck, his wife being detained by 'influenza,' and a large number of friends. The crowd surrounding Kensal Green was so vast that barriers had to be erected and the entrance gates closed. After the coffin was lowered into the grave, it was hidden by flowers. The Duke's wreath was designed with a cross of violets in the centre, and the words 'To my Dearest Louisa' picked out in white. The vault was lined with ivy and laurels, and was covered by a great marquee. 'The last sad day has come,' wrote the Duke, 'and is painful in the extreme. Went at eleven to Queen Street and at eleven thirty the mournful procession moved from the dear little house. I followed the hearse with my three sons . . . All along the route the sympathy and good feeling evinced was very marked. Arrived at Kensal Green Chapel exactly at twelve thirty. Dear Mr Sheppard read the burial service quite beautifully.

All our friends attended in large number, and there was a great
crowd outside all very respectful and sympathetic. She is buried
behind the chapel in a piece of ground I bought for myself some
years ago where I purpose to be laid myself by her dear side.
Nothing could be more solemn and appropriate.'

After the service, the family drove back to Queen Street.
There the Will was read which was 'most just and generous to
all her children. Horley goes to Charles, the Queen Street home
is settled on Augustus with all the furniture in it on the payment
of £800, her jewels are divided amongst her children . . . I am
executor with Bateson.'

The Duke remained in England until the end of the month,
when he left for Cannes. The day after the funeral he spent a
painful afternoon looking over his wife's possessions in Queen
Street, 'My sons all most affectionate and good to me.' On 19
January he went with Augustus FitzGeorge to the grave 'looking
so nice and peaceful, but oh! how sad. Also went to the grave of
my dearest friend.' Finally, a week after the funeral, he went 'to
Queen Street to take affectionate leave of the dear old house,
including the poor dear room in which she died, where I have
spent so many happy years of my life with my beloved wife. It
overwhelmed me with grief and sorrow.' At Cannes, away from
all associations connected with Louisa, he nevertheless longed for
her 'indescribably' and especially missed 'hearing from or writing
to her daily, as has always been our habit since we first met.'
The very first thing he did on his return to England was to visit
Kensal Green. 'Very busy all morning,' he wrote on 19 March,
'many people looking in upon me. I had before gone to the
cemetery to visit my beloved wife's tomb. It was a sad, sad, visit
and yet I was relieved in making it. George went with me. The
wreaths were still being crowded on the grave, a painful spectacle, then also looked at the other poor grave nearby, which
looked peaceful and well looked after.' He had only returned
from Cannes reluctantly, hating 'the idea of going home where
I shall feel my isolation more than ever, for I really have lost
with dear Mama the *Home* and the daily life connected with it

absolutely and entirely and there is nothing to me that can replace it on my return.'

The Duke, who never forgot anniversaries, lived over again the miseries of Louisa's death in January 1891. 'My thoughts,' he wrote, 'were entirely absorbed with the sad recollections of last year, for this was the night that my beloved Wife Louisa passed away from amongst us. Oh! how I deplore her loss, to me so great and irreparable. No words can express the intense sorrow that oppresses and depresses my heart.' Writing to Adolphus on 13 January he tells him, 'I daily, hourly I may say, miss her dear presence from amongst us. She was so good and true to me, such a real friend, always giving the best and soundest advice, and so thoroughly unselfish, and having only mine and all of your good at heart. In short my dear Dolly I feel thoroughly miserable and can only hope and pray *she* is now in a better world, where ere very long, I may be permitted to join her again.' In 1892, on 31 October, Louisa's birthday, he wrote in his Diary, 'How many happy days I have spent with her this anniversary in former days!! Now how all is changed and how isolated one feels. It is very sad and I felt all day greatly depressed.'

From everything that the Duke did, said and wrote, it is evident that he was devoted to Louisa, and it appears that his passion for Mrs Beauclerk in no way diminished his affection for his wife. Mrs FitzGeorge's position—as the *Daily Telegraph* obituary expressed it—'was one scarcely without difficulty or disadvantage. But so considerable was her natural grace and dignity, so marked her tact and intelligence, her experience and judgement, that she easily surmounted any of the inconveniences that may have lain in her path.' The fact that Louisa could not inhabit the Duke's official world, enabled him to live two lives, and to escape from the official flunkery of Gloucester House, literally by the back door, into the cosy family establishment in Queen Street.

Lady Geraldine, no doubt expressing the view of the Duchess, and, certainly in this instance, of the Queen, deplored the marriage and detested Louisa. Her opinions, of course, were poisoned by almost hysterical jealousy and her views on marriage were narrowly aristocratic. Moreover her references to Louisa amount to little more than sinister hints, mysterious allusions and criticism of her manners, which neither the evidence of Mrs FitzGeorge's letters nor of her husband's correspondence and Diaries in any way supports. On 2 December 1906, Lady Geraldine noted that she was reading Sheppard's *Life* of the Duke. 'The Chapter on my Duchess's death is deeply touching and beautiful! but the following Chapter!!! turned all to gall.' It was devoted to Mrs FitzGeorge.

In 1884, the conversation at St James's turned to the circumstances of the marriage of the Grand Duke of Hesse. 'The Duke spoke strongly on "when a man, through some unfortunate accident, makes a great mistake he must abide by it!" Yes! upon that alas! *He* has honourably acted all his life, and cruelly suffered for it, poor true and good heart.' Two years later Lady Geraldine recorded a remark Lord William Paulet made to the Duchess. 'We spoke much of the Duke! which is always pleasant to do! for he has such a just appreciation of his work! Such a properly high opinion of him, such a deep feeling and regret for the never sufficiently to be lamented sacrifice of his existence.'[30]

Sofia seems to have shared Lady Geraldine's opinions of her mother-in-law. On 9 March 1904, shortly before the Duke's death, Lady Geraldine visited Kew Cottage, where 'Mrs Dolly' was staying. They had a long discussion about the Duke's health and then the conversation turned to the old days. 'So much, so much she told me! and so much which corroborated all that I have thought and believed . . . One very curious thing she told me, that all of the three sons were christened at the Chapel Royal Savoy!!! too strange! One detestable thing she told me of '47!!! [the year of the Duke's marriage] Oh! but the pain of it all! It would even poison the paper destroying it utterly! leaving nothing! Nothing! Nothing!!! And, O God! the price paid!!!' Soon after the Duke's funeral, Lady Geraldine deplored his being buried in that 'hateful mausoleum.' On 30 March 1904 she wrote, 'Oh! how I detest his being at Kensal Green! and what *pain* the whole thing is.' Sofia again told 'me many things about *her* that entirely corroborated much I have seen and heard from others, and my own intimate convictions . . . This made me more than ever miserable and still yet more embitters the bitter thought of where he lies!' Later, Mrs Dolly, talking of her brother-in-law Augustus's 'disastrously offensive manner,' said, 'He is so *exactly* like his mother. *Exactly* her voice, manner, tone, and character!'

Lady Geraldine's views were more often than not expressed with extravagant vigour, but they were recorded after all in a private journal with no thought of publication. She was neither obliged nor accustomed to weigh her words, and her likes were as passionate as her dislikes were vehement. Her hopeless infatuation for the Duke, her unthinking acceptance of social conventions, and her distracted jealousy, all encouraged her to blackguard Mrs FitzGeorge. Her ill-defined accusations contain, at worst, therefore, only a grain of truth. That the Duke's married life was happy is proved by his utter dejection when Louisa died. Nor while she lived had he ever expressed even one fleeting moment of regret. In taking her for his wife he had wittingly defied convention. It had been no hasty decision: indeed, strictly speaking, it had been reached too late. Lady Geraldine's attempt to represent it as a rash and precipitate indiscretion, while plausible enough as a theory, is without substance in fact, and her malicious prattle in no way detracts from one of the great romances of the nineteenth century.

T

COMMANDER-IN-CHIEF

W HEN the Duke heard that W. H. Smith was to leave the War Office he was very despondent. 'Thinks all and everything is going to the dogs! Most depressing and despairing reports this evening [7 January 1887]. Edward Stanhope is to go to the War Office, the Duke knows nothing at all of him for or against, hopes he may do! But we spoke of the unutterable harm to the Service of the State, of the inane and idiotic practice of this *eternal* shuffling of the cards and the moment a man gets to know and thoroughly understand and be capable of his work, whisk! he is moved off to something fresh of which he knows nothing! Now not only no Government lasts twelve months but the self-same Government never can have its Ministers at their same posts for six or four months!! They have had *four* Secretarys of State at the War Office within a year!!!!'

Although Stanhope was a Tory, the Duke quickly grew to distrust him, and thought him in some ways worse than Cardwell or Childers. Smith was deeply regretted. 'We spoke,' wrote Lady

Geraldine on 15 April 1888, 'of how admirably well Mr W. H. Smith had led the Commons for the year past! Of the *very* high regard and esteem, the very *high* opinion of him, the Duke has! "He is such a *gentleman*! such a man of his word! you can so entirely trust him." He has such solidity and stirling worth.'

After working for a few months with the new Secretary for War, the Duke decided that he was 'an odious prig' and 'far away the worst War Minister he has yet had to endure, knows *nothing on earth* of the subject, yet believes himself so mightily clever he will not ask or take advice from *anyone*, and acts entirely off his own bat, then when shown what a mistake he has made "Ah well! *it is done*!" '[1]

Stanhope did not improve on further acquaintance. He was so 'impertinent' to the Duke that he was once more driven to threats of resignation. Describing an interview he had with the War Minister on 16 January 1889, H.R.H. told Lady Geraldine, 'he had had a most unpleasant meeting at the War Office today! That little *beast* Stanhope more nasty than ever! No War Minister he has yet had *ever* assumed the insolence of tone towards him personally of this *beastly* little whippersnapper who might be his son. Nasty filthy little prig! Childers and even Cardwell were always, at least outwardly, civil courteous and deferential to him personally! To schoolmaster him as a chidden schoolboy was reserved for the Conservative Government to do!! He told him plainly today if it goes on it is quite impossible for him to stay.'

Mrs Mitford, another of the Duchess's occasional ladies in waiting, was lectured by the Commander-in-Chief on the short-comings of the Secretary for State. Lady Geraldine thought it 'imprudent' to talk so freely before such a 'dangerous gossip.' Indeed H.R.H. was liable to let his indignation outrun his dis-cretion and was not always careful in his choice of an audience. Mischief-makers were only too ready to repeat what he said: such reports being sometimes invented, often distorted, and invariably embellished. On this occasion he 'spoke with Mrs Mitford of that shining light Edward Stanhope, to show her how wretched a creature he, alas! is; as he proved to her by too many instances, what a regular little pettifogging lawyer he is, and so overbearing and opinionated, worse than that so unreliable and not truthful! telling one man the Duke has agreed to so and so, or even that the Duke *wishes* so and so, when the Duke has unmistakably and repeatedly urged on him the exact reverse! and while pretending to hold the military authorities responsible, representing them to the public as being so, he *does* all off his own ultra-civilian bat, without consulting them at all; tomorrow he is to bring in, in the House of Commons a bill concerning the national defences, and he has never consulted the Duke upon a word of it!!! Or even shown it to him!! nor to the Adjutant General! and then, he quibbles so *beside* the truth! Before the Estimates were made out, he said to the Duke and the rest of the military authorities, "You must not ask for more men, because the Chancellor of the Exchequer *will not give them*." In the face of this of course the military authorities did not ask for them; thereupon, without mentioning a word of these preliminaries, or any details of how or why, in the House of Commons he shields himself from attack by the all-round assertion: "They were never asked for"!! So disingenuous! It is indeed a miserable task to have to work with such a Minister!'[2]

Wolseley's assessment of Stanhope was much the same as the Commander-in-Chief's. He described him as 'nothing more than a little party politician dressed up as a Statesman . . . I have striven hard to help him to make up for his absolute ignorance upon every point large and small of his work, but to no purpose. He is a prig pure and simple . . . I long for a rest or power; at present I have neither and have to serve a ridiculous Commander-in-Chief who knows nothing of War and a real first class prig (i.e. Stanhope) who only cares for party politics.' The Adjutant General opposed Stanhope so vigorously that the War Minister sent him as Commander-in-Chief to Ireland to get him out of the way. 'Little Stanhope nearly ruined me,' wrote Wolseley, in retrospect, 'and I often think I ought to have stood up and fought the little cunning, jealous and suspicious sparrow, without any mercy. I think I could have killed him but I had pity on him for

I despised him. You ought never to lose a chance to kill an enemy or a man as hostile as he was to me whenever you can. He was an underhand little reptile that I scotched only when I should have killed him.' In a letter to Sir Henry Ponsonby, Wolseley described Stanhope as 'this smallest of minded men whom it has ever been my fortune in life to meet and to do business with.'[3]

Lord Wolseley, on 23 April 1888, made one of his famous speeches, widely reported by the Press and the Duke, although he thought that the Adjutant General had no business to be so outspoken, could not but sympathize with the sentiments expressed. 'We spoke of Wolseley having made a very trenchant speech last night, a *tremendous* onslaught on *all* governments, of whom he says they sacrifice everything to Party! Everything done or left undone, to suit Party needs and interest. Most *strictly* and accurately true! but the Duke considers he has no business to be so outspoken, being an official, and therefore bound to greater reticence. Though *I* still cannot but feel it is well the truth should sometimes be spoken!! The fact is Wolseley is very angry at a great deal that is doing at present, very sore, and utterly disgusted with Mr Stanhope whom he thinks (and small blame to him for it!) a conceited ass!'

In May 1888 the *Daily Telegraph* published a sensational article headed 'England in danger—no guns, no men.' It referred to the 'deplorable neglect of Parliament and the mischievous system adopted by successive ministries in deliberately hiding the truth from the people.' It maintained that the Army was too small, its equipment obsolete, and its barrack accommodation inadequate. The paper claimed that these charges proceeded from the 'highest military authority.' The Duke when he read the article 'was much put out . . . I requested Harman to go to try to find Mr Lawson and ask him what it meant, as I knew nothing of such a statement or announcement . . . Harman returned saying that the "highest military authority" referred to was not myself.' That evening H.R.H. answered a question put to him in the House of Lords about his responsibility for what had been said. He told their Lordships that nobody could have been more astonished than he

was himself when he noticed 'this extraordinary sensational article
. . . I can only say that I have reason to believe that "the highest
military authority" which I admit that, up to this moment, I
believed I was, is intended for somebody else.'

Sir Henry Ponsonby, in explaining the episode to the Queen,
attributed the confusion which had arisen to the *Daily Telegraph*
basing its article on a speech made by the Commander-in-Chief.
A short time before, the Under-Secretary for War, addressing
the citizens of Guildford, had told them that the responsibility for
providing an efficient army rested with the military authorities.
This was too much for the Duke, whose demands for recruits
had been rejected, and who was indignantly fighting to prevent
excessive reductions. Both H.R.H. and Wolseley replied by
publicly declaring that the Army was too small, and that it was
iniquitous to hold them responsible, when try as they would, the
Secretary for State refused them money and men. As Ponsonby
declared with surprised satisfaction: 'His Royal Highness and
Lord Wolseley are entirely agreed on the subject.' Although the
Government were angry, 'Lord Wolseley's friends are strong in
his favour, and maintain that the Duke of Cambridge and he have
done a real service in creating an excitement about the Army.'[4]

If the Commander-in-Chief retained any illusions about
Stanhope or Conservative Governments, they were dispelled by
the appointment in June 1888 of a Royal Commission to report
on War Office organization under the chairmanship of Lord
Hartington, who had recently left the Liberal party over the issue
of Home Rule. It reported in 1890 that the complete responsibility of the Secretary of State to Parliament and the country for
all Army matters must be accepted as definitely established.
Amongst its recommendations, 'almost buried by diplomatic
tribute and complimentary verbiage,' was the proposal to abolish
the post of Commander-in-Chief, and to remodel the War
Office on the lines of the Board of Admiralty. A chief of staff,
corresponding to the First Naval Lord, was to be the senior
military official. The Duke regarded the whole report as 'deplorable.' Before he had time to do more than thumb through its

contents, he was in a flurry of indignation and excitement. Stanhope was subjected to a heavy fusillade from the Horse Guards, and the Queen, at Windsor, was overwhelmed with letters, telegrams and visits. She did, however, reassure her agitated cousin by insisting that she was fully determined to retain the post of Commander-in-Chief unimpaired. When Ponsonby submitted one of the Duke's letters to her, expressing alarm at the Hartington Report, she endorsed the memorandum: 'This cannot be allowed for one moment, and Sir Henry should take steps to prevent this being even discussed. V.R.I.'[5]

During the next few days Ponsonby received a bewildering array of additional instructions. He was told to tell Smith—who had been a member of the Commission—and Stanhope, how shocked the Queen was 'at the nature of the Army Commission report so far as the Horse Guards are concerned: and would you tell them both she entirely disapproves of the idea of a Board such as that at the Admiralty, and cannot listen to it for a moment.' Next he was told that the Queen proposed to write to the Prime Minister, Lord Salisbury, and inform him that she had 'talked fully over the subject of this truly abominable report,' that she quite agreed with the Duke that its recommendations were 'reckless' and 'incredibly thoughtless,' and moreover that she was 'beyond measure shocked' that they 'should have emanated from a Conservative Government.' Writing to her Private Secretary she told him, 'The Queen wishes a satisfactory arrangement, but the C.-in-C.'s position must not be lessened or weakened. One of the greatest prerogatives of the Sovereign is the *direct communication*, with an immovable and non-political officer of high rank, *about the Army*.'[6]

The Commander-in-Chief underestimated the Queen's vigilance, for she was ever sensitive to the remotest threat to prerogative, and did not require his prompting to appreciate the damage which would be done to the monarchy if the Hartington Report were accepted. But whether she needed the Duke's advice or not, it was none the less proffered unsparingly. To emphasize the gravity of the situation H.R.H. again talked of resignation, a threat so frequently employed that its effectiveness was diminishing. He warned Ponsonby that as 'Mr Stanhope leans to the side of the Commission,' its recommendations would be accepted 'unless the Queen is *very, very firm* and *decided.*' Ponsonby reassured the Duke: 'I think Her Majesty will consent to no great change which is opposed by Your Royal Highness, and Lord Salisbury apparently does not approve of any alteration in the position of the Commander-in-Chief.'[7]

The Duke never discovered that, at the time of the publication of the Hartington Report, there was an even more sinister threat to his position than the proposal to abolish his office. Ponsonby wrote at the Queen's command a letter to the Prince of Wales, understandably described as 'strictly confidential,' since 'it would obviously lead to serious difficulties if the Duke of Cambridge were to hear of it.'[8] The plan which was to be kept from the Commander-in-Chief, was proposed by Lord Wolseley. In a number of letters to Ponsonby he discussed the Commission's suggestions. To abolish the office of Commander-in-Chief he regarded as a 'step backwards.' 'We sorely want a doctor I admit, but Brackenbury and Co. have sent us an executioner.'[9] His solution was to persuade the Duke of Cambridge to resign, and to replace him by Prince Arthur, Duke of Connaught. The Queen thought the plan decidedly attractive although she foresaw difficulties.

The Cabinet considered the proposal but finally rejected it. What induced them to do so, Wolseley could never discover. Stanhope merely informed him the reasons were 'political.' 'What I conceive to be at the bottom of the matter,' Wolseley told Ponsonby, 'is that they have made up their minds to do away with the office of Commander-in-Chief . . . It is hard that a man should be held to be disqualified for high military command because he is the Queen's son. Behind all this matter is the Duke of Cambridge. Hartington, and all the Secretaries of State here in my time, have suffered so much at his hands, have had all needful reforms in the Army so blocked by him that one and all were determined never to have another Prince here who might prove equally immovable and irremovable. I am so fond of the Duke of Cambridge that I hate even thinking of this, but I am sure it is true, and I think everyone who has been long here knows this as well as I do.' Ponsonby replied by pointing out possible objections to the appointment of the Duke of Connaught and stressing the difficulty of overcoming opposition. 'Before I for ever relinquish the subject,' came the answer, 'I wish to fire one more shot in what I believe to be the interests of the Duke of Connaught and of the Army. If what I say is high treason I hope I may be forgiven. I may as well be hanged as high as Haman as on an ordinary gallows. In writing this note I wish above all things in the interest of the Army and therefore of the State to adopt some line of conduct that will secure us in the future as in the past a Commander-in-Chief.

'To secure to any future Commander-in-Chief the powers which the Duke of Cambridge inherited from the Duke of Wellington, I am well aware the Duke of Cambridge has himself rendered impossible.

'No Government of any shade of politics would ever or could ever again allow anyone to be able to prevent nearly all reform in our military organization as the Duke of Cambridge has done for years past; as you know that his action has more than once produced between the Queen and her Cabinet a strained condition of things that was to be deprecated on every ground.

'In our endeavours to retain the post of Commander-in-Chief in the Army, this fact must be recognized, for I am sure it was in the minds of many who sat upon Lord Hartington's Commission. If we succeed in retaining the post at all, we must be prepared to see it shorn of much of its present importance. I know privately that it is Mr Stanhope's wish to retain the Duke of Cambridge as Commander-in-Chief for another two years longer. He will then be seventy-three years of age. The idea is then to get rid of him and have no successor to his office, but instead to have a Chief of the Staff to the Secretary of State for War. In other words, some political creature of his own.

'The Duke of Cambridge says many times every week that he

will at once resign and consults me and Harman as to the propriety of doing so. Between ourselves, I don't think he has the
least intention of ever doing this until he receives a hint from the
Queen that he should do so.

'Now I come to my proposition: Why should not Lord Salisbury allow the Duke of Connaught to succeed him at once? If
necessary make the tenure of that office seven, or even five years.
. . . My own selfish object in bringing this forward is, that under
the Duke of Connaught the Army would be brought up to date
in all matters of military instruction, organization, and tactical
efficiency. Personally, I like the Duke of Cambridge so much that
I hate saying this, but it is well known to all the rising officers in
the Army that, as long as he continues to be Commander-in-
Chief, this much wished for condition of things is impossible, is
not to be thought of. It is not the Duke of Cambridge's fault: he
was educated in a bad military school and cannot forget the lessons
it taught him, nor can he take in and learn those which modern
war has taught all foreign nations.

'I hope it may not be thought that it is from any ill-feeling
towards the Duke of Cambridge I write this. In my heart I
entertain strong feelings of personal attachment to him. No one
can know him, and see him daily as I have done for years, and
not admire his amiable qualities. But in the interests of the Army
I would like to see him replaced by the Duke of Connaught *at
once*. . . . As a punishment for my treason don't send me an
ultimatum of "resignation or of compulsory removal." I give my
views for what they are worth. They may be foolish, they are
certainly honest.'[10]

Not only did the Cabinet reject Wolseley's plan, but the
Queen in the end decided that it was impracticable, and that she
could not 'seem to advance the interests of her own son.' On 7
August she wrote in her Diary: 'Saw Sir H. Ponsonby later,
about a remarkable letter from Lord Wolseley, strongly urging
that George C. should be got to resign, Arthur to be appointed
his successor. This I consider an impossibility, though it might in
some ways be a good thing. Arthur is of the same opinion.' But

she entirely agreed with Wolseley that her son was handicapped by being royal. 'It is too shameful keeping him out of all important places on account of his birth.' Moreover she suspected that 'the Government think most foolishly Arthur would be as retrograde and old-fashioned as the dear Duke of Cambridge, whereas he is the very reverse.'[11] In the end the proposals of the Hartington Committee were set aside, the claims of the Duke of Connaught were rejected, and the Commander-in-Chief remained in unchallenged possession at the Horse Guards.

One criticism which was levelled against H.R.H. during the discussions on the Commission's report was that he could hardly be performing his duties satisfactorily when his health apparently required him to spend long periods abroad. The Queen was well aware of what was said and did little to encourage these trips overseas. 'Tho' I granted you the desired leave,' she wrote on 29 December 1891, 'I must impress you with the necessity of it not exceeding on any account four weeks, as I am sure that your frequent and lengthened absences are not good and enable those who are inimical to the office of Commander-in-Chief to argue that if he is so often away it shows that we can do without him.'[12] Admittedly H.R.H. was an indefatigable correspondent, but there were times when his presence at the Horse Guards was much to be desired. The Tranby Croft scandal was such an occasion.

In September 1891 the Prince of Wales stayed at Tranby Croft for the Doncaster races. His host, Arthur Wilson, was a rich shipowner from Hull. Amongst the guests was Sir William Gordon-Cumming, Colonel of the Scots Guards. Sir William was accused of cheating at baccarat, and was induced to sign a paper promising never to touch cards again. He maintained his innocence throughout, but agreed to the arrangement to avoid a scandal involving the Heir to the Throne. His fellow guests, for their part, undertook 'to preserve silence' about the accusation which had been made, and there the matter should have ended. Subsequently the story leaked out and Sir William brought a slander action against Mrs Wilson and other members of the house party. The case, which lasted seven days, came before Lord

Chief Justice Coleridge on 1 June 1891, and the Prince of Wales reluctantly appeared as a witness for the defence. The Press, suffering from one of its more acute fits of morality, attacked him unmercifully for indulging in such wickedness, and published to the world the horrifying news that the counters which had been employed were stamped with the Prince's monogram. The Queen's eldest son, it seemed, was so depraved a gambler that night after night he risked losing money to his friends, if not his immortal soul to the devil. A verdict for the defendants was returned, but the public behaved as if the Prince had been on trial.

The Queen contemplated the proceedings with profound distaste. She instructed the Duke of Cambridge, on his return from his visit to Egypt, to lecture her son on the evils of gambling—a task one might have thought the National Press had rendered superfluous. The Duke, on arrival at Sandringham, lost his nerve, if, as Wolseley once unkindly observed, one can lose what one has never possessed.[13] He tried to persuade Sir Francis Knollys to deliver the Queen's message, and on Sir Francis declining to do so, it failed to reach its destination.[14] H.R.H. told his son Adolphus, the 'scandal is painfully disgusting and anything more unfortunately managed from beginning to end I cannot imagine.'

When the charges made against Sir William became public, Lord Coventry, one of the guests at Tranby Croft, brought the case to the attention of Sir Redvers Buller, who in 1890 had succeeded Lord Wolseley as Adjutant General. He wrote to Buller, rather than the Commander-in-Chief, because the latter was in Egypt. 'We feel it incumbent upon us,' he declared, 'to place the facts officially before you that a full enquiry may forthwith be instituted into so grave and serious an accusation against a gentleman holding Her Majesty's Commission.'[15] Sir Redvers thereupon investigated the affair and reported his findings to the Queen and the Duke.

In a letter written to Ponsonby on 13 February, the Adjutant General gave a lucid summary of all that had occurred. He argued that if Sir William were required to resign from his regiment, or if a court martial were immediately held, such proceedings would prejudice the civil trial then pending. Buller, after consulting the Judge Advocate General, decided it would be unjust to institute a military enquiry before the action for slander had been decided in court. In writing to the Duke, he mentioned two features of the affair which he regarded as unsatisfactory. He maintained that no hostess should ever have permitted one of her guests to be watched, almost trapped, as Sir William had been. Hearing of the suspicions that had arisen, she should have contrived to avoid any further games of baccarat. A conjurer could be procured, or some wretched guest conscripted to sing, recite, or play the piano. Perhaps if all other contrivances failed, they might, as a last desperate resort, even fall back on conversation. The second irregularity, as Buller saw it, was that all having sworn to preserve secrecy, the story should later have come out.[16]

The Commander-in-Chief was opposed to the idea of delaying military proceedings until the civil trial was over. 'Impress upon the Secretary of State,' he telegraphed to Buller, 'I consider honour of Army requires immediate action on military part. How can an officer accused of cheating be allowed to wear Queen's uniform?' The Prince of Wales, who, in truth, had had much to endure, was in no mood for temperate measures. He felt even more strongly than his Uncle George that an immediate court martial should be held. A court martial, if it found Sir William guilty, would dispose of the civil action, and would moreover avoid publicity for the Prince.

Lord Wolseley, writing to his wife on 12 February, said he was 'very much amused' by a letter he had received telling him that the Prince of Wales was 'furious with the way in which Buller had disposed of the Cummings scandal—postponing all military action until the civil trials come off in November next.' The Prince was indeed angry and agitated for a court martial. Writing to H.R.H. he declared, 'It is enough to make the great Duke of Wellington rise from his tomb and point his finger of scorn at the Horse Guards—over which he presided so long and with such honour! Not only the officers but even the men are affected by the Adjutant General's decision. The conduct of the A.G. is inexplicable but he cannot have the interests of the Army at heart, acting in the way he has. I always knew he was a born soldier—and equally imagined he was a gentleman, but from henceforth I can never look upon him in the latter category!'[17] If the Prince was to be credited, Buller's sense of fair play, a quality which many have considered to be amongst the foremost attributes of a gentleman, deprived him of the right to be so regarded. With a fine disdain for the traditions of English justice, the Heir to the Throne took Sir William's guilt for granted, and the idea of a trial, or of weighing evidence, seemed to him a waste of time. Cumming's version of the affair, so he told the Duke, 'was false from beginning to end.' He had 'not a leg to stand on, and his protestations of innocence are useless. His conduct throughout has been simply scandalous.'[18]

Sir Francis Knollys, writing on his master's behalf, protested against the Adjutant General's postponement of military action, which sanctioned 'a man of whose guilt no impartial person can for one moment entertain the slightest doubt, to remain from February to November in Her Majesty's service because his Solicitor, in order to gain time, says the case will be prejudiced by the authorities allowing a court of enquiry to be held . . . and after nine or ten months all the details of this lamentable affair will be again brought forward and discussed to the great edification of the Republicans and Socialists.' However, Knollys continued, the Prince is glad 'to hear that the Guards Club are going to take the matter up.' 'Everybody wished Your Royal Highness had been here, in which case an immediate enquiry would have been held.' As it is, the slander trial 'when it comes off will be a great calamity to the Royal Family, to Society and the Army.'[19]

The Prince of Wales was not alone in begging the Commander-in-Chief to use 'his influence to insist upon this fellow being tried by the military authorities as would be done in every civilized country in the world.' The Duke of Fife wrote protesting against 'this most unfortunate and extraordinary decision.' He declared that 'the action of the Adjutant General had filled everybody with amazement' and that, to preserve the honour of the Army, measures must, at once, be taken.[20] But Buller had already committed the Duke, who supported the decision, although disapproving of it. The affair was not only unfortunate for the Prince and the Army, but had given inadvertently undue prominence to H.R.H.'s absence abroad. Knollys, writing to Ponsonby, observed, 'The Duke of Cambridge is playing the part of Antony, with Cleopatra up the Nile, in Egypt,'[21] and he vigorously complained about the Commander-in-Chief being absent from his post for nearly three months.

The lady whom Knollys dubbed 'Cleopatra' was Mrs Vyner. Bob Vyner was a rich Yorkshire squire, who in 1865 married Eleanor, daughter of the Reverend Slingsby Duncomb Shafto. She became an intimate friend of the Prince of Wales, cultivated the Tecks, and numbered the Duke of Cambridge amongst her most ardent admirers. 'After talking to your mother,' Frank Harris once told Lady Alwynne Compton, 'one feels a sort of intimate sympathy with her, almost as though it were love.' 'The curious part of it is,' replied Lady Alwynne, 'that she is in love with you for the time being, she's extraordinarily sympathetic.'[22]

After the Duke fell a hopeless victim to Mrs Vyner's charm, Lady Geraldine regarded her with venomous malice. 'Great God in heaven!' she wrote on 11 December 1891. 'What *can* he see in her? What can he? What *can* attract him? Of all the *absolutely uninteresting unattractive* women I have ever seen she is far away the most entirely so, she has not an *attraction* of any kind, she is really very *plain*, singularly undistinguished, not the *ghost* of a figure, fat, podgy, shapeless yet at the same time arms like a knitting needle! A *most* silly way of going into fits of giggles into her pocket handkerchief about nothing at all, a provoking way of talking, not an attraction in the world. And O God, O God, most clearly and decidedly to me, has not a spark of real feeling for him!! I am as sure of it as anything on earth!' Lady Geraldine, contrasting her own dedicated devotion to the Duke with Mrs Vyner's flighty affection, described it as bearing the same relation 'as a farthing rushlight to the great sun.' It was Lady Geraldine's conviction that the Duke's association with Mrs Vyner had ruined his character, and she deplored the influence of the '*hateful* Vyner lot.' 'Have been reading the old, old journals,' wrote Lady Geraldine on 13 November 1893, 'it is all like a strange trance and dream to me, for he is now a totally, entirely, absolutely, *utterly different man*, in *all* and every way and *everything*!!! from what he was then! When I read of and remember him *then*, as he was! and see and hear him now, it is positively as though it were two altogether different persons! Inconceivable!!'

The Duke first became acquainted with the Vyners at Homburg in August 1888. 'That fatal time!! that *ended* all life for me,' was how Lady Geraldine described it in 1894 as she was reading through her Diaries. 'Reached another volume,' she noted on 2 June, 'of the dear past!! which volume I see goes as far as July 1888! just before the end of my life!! As in a month from then it was *destroyed* by the vile hateful *Diablesse*.' In February of 1889 the Duke stayed a fortnight at Cannes, and enjoyed himself so much that he spent part of the winter there for the rest of his life. He always put up at the Hôtel Prince de Galles, where he occupied the same 'charming apartments.' It was conveniently close to the Château St Anne, the Vyners' 'quite beautiful' villa, with its 'delightful and beautifully kept garden, quite perfection.' Bob Vyner rented the shooting on the island of St Marguerite, and many 'charming excursions' took place across the bay. The Vyners entertained nearly all distinguished English visitors to Cannes. The Prince of Wales paid many visits to the Château, and even Mr and Mrs Gladstone were invited. 'He made himself most agreeable,' wrote H.R.H. on 17 February, 'and is looking very well.' That Mrs Vyner fraternized with the arch-traitor did not help endear the 'Diablesse' to some of the Duke's friends. When the visit ended on 28 February, H.R.H. wrote in his Diary, 'Alas! My stay here is come to an end to my great sorrow for I have *delighted* in it, and only long and hope to be able to come again in future years.'

After Louisa's death in 1890, the Duke saw even more of the Vyners and their circle. Writing in his Diary on 30 December he commented: 'The last day of rather an eventful year, of much sorrow, though latterly also of much comfort.' In 1891 he went to Egypt to join the Vyners there. On his way out Mrs Elizabeth Butler entertained him. 'We had the Duke of Cambridge to luncheon. He arrived yesterday on board the *Surprise* from Malta, and Will, of course, received him officially, but not royally, as he is travelling incog., and he came here to tea. To-day we had a large party to meet him, and a very genial luncheon it was, not to say rollicking. The day was exquisite, and out of the open windows the sea sparkled, blue and calm. H.R.H. seemed to me rather feeble, but in the best of humours; a wonderful old man to come to Egypt for the first time at seventy two, braving this burning sun and with such a high colour to begin with! One felt as though one was talking to George III to hear that "What, what, what? Who, who, who? Why, why, why?" Col. Lane, one of his suite, said he had never seen him in better spirits. I was gratified at his praise of our cook—very loud praise, literally, as he is not only rather deaf himself, but speaks to people as though they also were a "little hard of hearing." "Very good cook, my dear" (to me). "Very good cook, Butler" (across the table to Will). "Very good cook, eh, Sykes?" (very loud to Christopher Sykes, further off). "You are a *gourmet*, you know better about these things than I do, eh?" C.S.: "I ought to have learned something about it at Gloucester House, sir!" H.R.H. (to me): "Your health, my dear." "Butler, your very good health!" Aside to me: "What's the Consul's name?" I: "Sir Charles Cookson." "Sir Charles, your health!" When I hand the salt to H.R.H. he stops my hand: "I wouldn't quarrel with her for the world, Butler." And so the feast goes on, our august guest plying me with questions about the relationship and antecedents of everyone at the table; about the manners and customs of the populace of Alexandria; the state of commerce; the climate. I answer to the best of my ability with the most unsatisfactory information. He started at four for Cairo, leaving a most kindly impression on my memory. The last of the old Georgian type! "Your mutton was good, my dear; not at all *goaty*," were his valedictory words.'23

U

Mrs Vyner, although sometimes callous about the pathetic attentions of her elderly admirer, did provide him with that companionship for which he ever hungered, and which, in younger days, had been supplied by Mrs Beauclerk, by the Duchess of Cambridge, and by Mrs FitzGeorge. When he left Cannes for England on 1 March 1894, he did so 'with a very heavy heart, as regards those of the dear "Château."' Whether Bob Vyner was equally sorry to see him depart remains a matter for conjecture.

Lady Geraldine, after leaving St James's, took a small house in Upper Brook Street. Whenever he was in London the Duke visited her constantly, and she was often invited to Gloucester House. Mrs Hamilton, on 15 December 1893, even invited her to Queen Street, to meet H.R.H. 'At eight o'clock in a hansom to Queen Street!!! to meet the Duke!! What turmoil of strange thoughts and feelings at going in for the first time into *that* house! Curious that I should have lived to know and frequent *both* houses.' The conversation at Brook Street was often of life in the old days, and whenever it turned to the present, Lady Geraldine's obsession with Mrs Vyner somehow nearly always won the upper hand. 'We talked of the new play which came out last night at the Haymarket, *A Woman of No Importance* by Oscar Wilde! Of what an *animal* he is! The Duke saw him last year at Homburg where he bored him to death, because the *beastly Diablesse* chose to think it smart to be by way of being "amused" by him!!'[24]

On Christmas Eve 1893, when the Duke called at Upper Brook Street with his present, a quarrel arose which made H.R.H. purple with rage and left Lady Geraldine sobbing and broken hearted, 'Sore wounded at every point, all round, everywhere, and deeply grieving in my soul for the way he is now entirely giving up ever being at the Horse Guards, neglecting his duty! *he*!!!! who *lived* for duty, and before this pernicious foul *vile influence* was the most conscientious man that breathed and the hardest worker! Grieving for this sad inconceivable change and all it entails and how it plays into the hands of those who *want*

to get rid of him and invites the attacks of such curs as Labouchère
. . . I foolishly asked what was to become of the Horse Guards
for the three months absence?' The discussion became angry, and
Lady Geraldine accused H.R.H. of sacrificing everything for Mrs
Vyner. Her repressed passion and jealousy erupted and a tearful
scene ensued. Lord Roberts, himself to become Commander-in-
Chief in succession to Wolseley, said that 'for some time before
the old Duke was retired, he practically did nothing—the ordinary
routine of the office was carried by Gipps.'[25] So the accusations
Lady Geraldine blurted out in the heat of argument were more
than half-truths, and that, of course, was what made them unacceptable, that was why her front door banged so violently, and
that accounted for a scowling old gentleman seen storming down
Upper Brook Street in the season of goodwill.

Amongst Lady Geraldine's menagerie of aversions, the Duchess
of Teck held a prominent place. Her 'beslobbering and beslavering
the vile Diablesse' was 'absolutely sickening,' particularly as she
had been 'infamous' and 'past all language abominable to and
about poor unfortunate Mrs Beauclerk!!! and relentlessly perse-
cuted her!' The Duke occasionally joined Lady Geraldine in her
censures. He was vexed when Princess Mary misrepresented the
financial help he had given her in discussions with the Queen.
Everything about his sister was vast and generous: the way she
looked, the way she ran into debt, the way she forgave and forgot
animosities. When Wolseley succeeded H.R.H. as Commander-
in-Chief she saw no reason to make that the grounds for a ven-
detta, although to ask her brother to invite Wolseley to dinner
was perhaps imposing something of a strain on his geniality. 'He
has observed for himself, I rejoice to say, what *riles* my whole
being, the sickening way Princess Mary is kowtowing all she can
to odious Wolseley and making all the fuss imaginable of him
and is *profoundly* disgusted with her!! as well he may be! He told
me of her rascally bad taste, when he was consulting her as to
whom he should invite to meet her last night, suggesting he
should invite the Wolseleys! But he frankly told her his opinion
of it and of her suggesting it!! Tonight he has a big dinner of

twenty for all the Horse Guards staff and to which he has had to ask Wolseley—not pleasant! but of course in his present position at the Horse Guards not to be avoided, that is quite one thing, to ask him with his wife for last night, a footing he has never yet been on, is a very different thing!!'[26]

As Wolseley grew older he grew very little more tolerant or modest. He was convinced that most soldiers were bigoted traditionalists, and that he, and a select few officers, alone appreciated the revolution taking place in warfare. 'I have just been to an Alma Day parade,' he wrote on 20 September 1887. 'It is a fine thing to keep alive the memory of those old battles, if we really remember how and why they were won. They are damnably mischievous if we think because they were won we must always win again. Half the Army is still living, not on the memory of the Crimea, for which God be praised, but of the Peninsula.'[27] The Duke, in his eyes, was the embodiment of the old school. 'When that Royal personage is present,' he said of a field day at Aldershot, 'the whole thing is merely skittles he believes is like War. It is sad to think that the English people who pay so much for this little army, can only have a plaything kept up to amuse Royal princes who know as much of war as I do of Theology.'[28]

Wolseley, who saw H.R.H. at close quarters, was aware of how old he was becoming. 'Poor man,' he said in 1894, 'he looks bundled up like an old clothes bundle.' But pity him as he might, the Duke's infirmities led Wolseley to the irresistible conclusion that he was unfit for office and should, if necessary, be ignored, circumvented, or removed. Wolseley's practice of ignoring his chief naturally led to resentment. 'Quite between ourselves,' the Prince of Wales told Ponsonby in 1888, 'there is no doubt that Wolseley gets hold of Stanhope behind the Duke's back to work his own schemes. . . . W. is doubtless a very able man and if we were engaged in another war would command our army in the field, but he is false to the backbone, and can never be trusted. He is I know thoroughly disloyal to the Duke and much more so than he has any idea of. However there he is, in a position of great power and there he intends to remain.'[29]

In his last year of office the Duke was seventy six, and there were times when life became almost too much for him. On returning to Gloucester House from Cannes in the year Louisa died, he wrote in his Diary on 23 March, 'I got back all right and am well enough but oh! so *sad* and so worried. I dislike my life and all the worries connected with it and shall be glad when I am out of all these troubles, which seem to grow worse and worse every day I live.' Such moments of depression and despair were exceptional; but he had reached an age when most of his friends were gone, and hardly a day passed without him deploring the deaths of those that remained. 'I came home,' he wrote on New Year's Day, 1894, 'to begin the year in my room alone, thinking of the past and of many dear kind friends and relations many of whom have passed away for ever, but are dear to my memory.' All around him the old order was changing. At 'dear old Rumpenheim,' the summer residence near Frankfurt where he and his German relations congregated every year, the installation of central heating appeared to him desecration. That it was superfluous, Lady Geraldine knew to her dismay. In the tropical heat of August, she once complained, the arrangements are 'as though we were living in the North Pole in December!'

The Cambridges were so long lived a family that Queen Mary used to refer proudly to the 'Cambridge constitution.' The Duke, despite his gout, his failing hearing, and the partial loss of the sight of one eye, was remarkably vigorous for his years. 'My seventy-fifth birthday,' he recorded in his Diary, 'a good old age, but happily I can still do a great deal, as proved today, when I was over seven hours in the saddle.' Lady Geraldine, on 13 July 1894, was told by the Duke 'of the intolerable number of dinner engagements he has! night after night! how much too much it is. Of *alas*!! how seedy he has been!! Poor dear heart! Actually stayed in bed all Tuesday—what that tells to one who *knows* him! He whom nothing on earth can induce to stay in bed *half* a day when most imperatively necessary with some serious bronchitis or most severe gout!! But was so utterly *done*, he simply felt he could not get up! said he would stay in bed the morning and then stayed on and on and finally did not get up till dinner time, shows how he had been over-taxing himself and how *much* too much he has been doing. It is fabulous! Literally no man of *forty* does any one day what he does the whole of every day, day after day, week after week, month after month! It *is* too much. I am so thankful he did at last for once take a bed day!'

The Duke was a very large man, and his visits to Baden and Kissingen entailed dieting as well as drinking the waters, and seeing Mrs Vyner. 'I am delighted, and feel as light as a *feather*!' was his comment on discovering he had reduced his weight to a little under sixteen stone. Lady Paget, who met him at Kissingen, described him as 'very stout heavy and gouty. How he can stand the bumping about on fiery horses over bad roads in this torrid heat I do not know. Every night a rayless copper sun sets in a sky of brass and the leaves hang scorched and motionless on the dusty trees. The Duke is like Princess Mary, very English, he has a great deal of common sense, but lacks energy to enforce it. He swears, but he is kind. He generally hangs or leans upon the person nearest him. I found his weight prodigious in some of our morning rambles. After dinner, and even at dinner, he gets very sleepy, and his head drops on the shoulder of the lady nearest him.'[30]

The Duke continued shooting until a year or two before his death. At the age of seventy four he killed over two hundred head himself one December day at Sandringham. The total bag was 3,564, shot by ten guns. Owing to the failing sight of his right eye he shot with a gun having a crooked stock. H.R.H., as Ranger of the Royal Parks, would often shoot the ducks on the Serpentine early in the morning, but Labouchère objected to the exercise of such rights, particularly in Richmond Park, and suggested that some arrangement should be made 'with that eminent warrior the Duke of Cambridge, so that H.R.H. may disport himself elsewhere than in a park intended for the recreation of the public.'[31]

While shooting at Sandringham he saw a certain amount of the Prince of Wales's sons: the Duke of Clarence, Prince Eddie, and Prince George, the Duke of York. H.R.H. was fond of them both, and did what he could to assist the Duke of Clarence's military career. But although he thought Prince Eddie 'charming,' and 'as nice a youth as could be,' his 'unaffected' simplicity, and 'lamentable ignorance' were serious drawbacks to getting on in the world. The Duke was inclined to blame Dalton, the Prince's tutor, for having taught him nothing. 'He [Prince Eddie] sat one night next the Duke when the talk turned on the Crimean War: *he knew nothing about it*!!!! Knew *nothing* of the Battle of the Alma!!! It is past all conceiving! One other sad failing he has from the Prince, he is an inveterate and incurable dawdler, never ready, never there!'

After returning from a visit to Aldershot during his mother's lifetime, the Duke told her of his successful inspection, and spoke of Prince Eddie's incurable apathy. 'He cannot learn his drill, so that he is not *yet* in the ranks! The Duke wanted to try him in some most elementary movement, the Colonel begged him not to attempt it as the Prince had not an *idea* how to do it! The Duke of course not wishing to expose him, let it alone!' After two more years at Aldershot the Prince had made better progress than expected, but he had still a distressing amount to learn. 'We talked of how right alas! our judgement of stupid Dalton was, who taught Prince Eddie *absolutely nothing*!! Major Miles the instructor he has been under at Aldershot is quite *astounded* at his utter ignorance. . . . It is clearly Dalton's fault, for it is not that he is unteachable, as Major Miles, having found him thus ignorant, is equally astonished how much he has got on with him and thinks, under the circumstances his papers are infinitely better than he dared to expect. He has his father's dislike for a book and never looks into one, but learns all orally, and retains what he thus learns.'[32]

When, towards the end of 1891, the Duke received the news that his niece, Princess May, was engaged to the Duke of Clarence, his pleasure at the excellence of the match was not unqualified. Then, early in the New Year, while H.R.H. was at Cannes, he received a telegram on 11 January, from his sister Mary, announcing that 'Dear Eddy had been attacked at Sandringham by influenza in a very serious form.' Two days later the Prince contracted pneumonia. 'We are all dreadfully staggered by the suddenness of this serious account, which we so little anticipated.' The following morning, on return from a stroll, 'several telegrams awaited me. I guessed the worst: poor dear Eddy had passed away. He died this morning at nine fifteen. It is a fearful catastrophe, so sudden, so unexpected and in the very prime of life and in apparent health when I last saw him this day week. It is really overwhelming. One can hardly realize the painfully sad event which has so suddenly come upon us and the results which may arise out of it.'

The Duke was very fond of Princess May. He praised her 'immensely! as "charming"! and a very sensible woman.' He was therefore delighted when she afterwards became engaged to Prince George, of whom he had an equally high opinion, although he was opposed to the wedding being arranged so soon after Prince Eddie's death. During one of his visits to Upper Brook Street he told Lady Geraldine about a function at Richmond, 'Where the Duke of York opened the new foot-bridge and automatic lock, and described to me the curious and interesting construction of the latter; of how well the Duke of York does, his *remarkably* good manner, and speaks well with a very good clear distinct voice and enunciation; but how much he, the Duke, regrets the Duke of York told him the other day he "can't bear London, and *going out* and *hates* society," which he thinks a very great pity, and misfortune in his position.' And again, in another conversation, 'the Duke said he had seen the Duke of York in the morning just returned from Aberdeen; praised him immensely, has a very great liking for and excellent opinion of him, declares he has a "charming nature"! If so, certainly he gets it from his angel mother! The Duke is extremely fond of him and rates him very high.'[33]

The wedding took place on 6 July 1893. 'The streets were crowded last night and London almost impassable. My house was full of my friends and others having been asked by me to come to my house and see the Procession pass. Left for Buckingham Palace in State with Augusta and thence we all proceeded in four distinct processions. Volunteers lined Constitution Hill, the troops the streets. The crowds were enormous. The ceremony was well conducted and everything passed off admirably, we returned from St James's in a similar procession to Buckingham Palace, where there was a State luncheon given by the Queen. Stayed to see the Duke and Duchess of York leave for Sandringham. The streets were lined with troops all the way to Liverpool St. Station, and their reception admirable. Dined in the evening at Marlborough House, a party of forty eight, all Royalties. We all went to a stand looking over the wall in Pall Mall to see the crowds pass for the illuminations which were general and the crush in the streets marvellous. Weather lovely.' There was one disagreeable episode at the celebration at Buckingham Palace. The Queen, on seeing Mr Gladstone, who for the last time was again her Prime Minister, avoided shaking hands with him and gave him 'only a very stiff bow.' Undeterred by his frosty reception he passed behind her and sat down in her tent unasked. 'The Queen indignant said to P.A. [Princess Augusta] "Does he perhaps think this is a public tent!!"'[34]

Gladstone's victory in the 1892 election brought Campbell-Bannerman back once more to the War Office. Before his appointment was announced, the Duke was terrified that some extreme radical would be wished upon him. When the news became known that Dilke had won a seat, it was feared that the Prime Minister, 'lying canting hypocrite that he is,' might even 'give him the *War Office*!!!! Of how his first act will be to get rid of the Duke and abolish the "Commander-in-Chief"!!!! *brutes*!—He wishes, if one can possibly speak of wishing, in such a choice!—he might get Campbell-Bannerman back again, who at least is personally decent to deal with.' 'Mr Campbell-Bannerman,' the Duke had told the Queen in 1886, 'is a very nice, calm and pleasant man, well known to all here [Horse Guards], and who knows the War Office work, and with whom I have no doubt I shall be able to get on very smoothly.'[35]

The fear that the new Liberal Government would attack the
Commander-in-Chief was soon proved to be justified. Gladstone,
who retired in 1894, left it to his successor, Rosebery, to strike the
fatal blow. Finally the Duke was forced to resign, but not without
an immense struggle. In April 1895, H.R.H. made a speech
emphatically declaring that he had not the slightest intention of
retiring. When the Prince of Wales hinted to his uncle that
resignation might become necessary, and that the Queen could
not indefinitely resist her Ministers' advice, the Commander-in-
Chief told him that he wished at least to remain at his post until
1896, when he would have completed forty years in office. He
was fortified in this resolution by the support of Colonel Augustus
FitzGeorge, who now lived with him at Gloucester House and
helped manage his affairs. Bigge, Ponsonby's assistant and, in
June 1895, successor, wrote to Knollys: 'The Prince of Wales has
heard on the very best authority that *Augustus* FitzGeorge is at
the bottom of the Duke's line of conduct. The Duke does exactly
what this son tells him, and if they want the matter to be settled
they must "square" him.'[36]

On 7 May the Queen had a long interview with the Duke, in
which he told her that his anxiety was to do what was in the best
interests of the Crown, and to prevent his office ever becoming
'parliamentary.' 'What he *wishes*,' the Queen wrote in her Diary,
'is not to be kicked out by these violent radicals, who have made
such *attacks* on him. I assured him that would not be. He was ready
to resign, but could not allow himself to be turned out, and his
last words were: "I place myself in your hands." ' A few days
later H.R.H. went to Windsor and the Queen was surprised to
find him 'firmly resolved not to resign although H.M. pointed
out that resignation would be advisable on every ground. H.R.H.
repeated previous arguments as to yielding to popular clamour,
his capacity for work etc. . . . To go now would be to
show "the white feather" . . . The Queen told Colonel Bigge
she could not have said more to H.R.H. without being
rude.'[37] The Duke was in too great perplexity to be consistent,
and he was buffeted round the four points of the compass

by contradictory advice: most of it admittedly of his own seeking.

Lady Geraldine was at first inclined to think that he ought to resign at once, 'and retire with dignity, and not wait to be kicked out by those yelping curs.' But she agreed with what the Duke told Campbell-Bannerman about the need for a Royal Prince at the head of the Army. They stand quite 'aloof from politics and keep quite out of intrigues of *all* sorts (that is! *he* certainly has!!) whereas suppose you had Lord Roberts as the head of the Army, *every man* of Wolseley's following would be tabooed and kept down, and if Wolseley was at the head, ditto ditto would be the case with all Robert's following! And so all the way through.' The Duke of Richmond, however, 'most strongly and positively advised and urged him not to resign,' and Lady Geraldine, anxious that H.R.H. should 'not play into the Queen and Prince's hands,' seems to have come to the view that it would be best to 'leave it to them, if they can behave so infamously, after all his long services, "to kick him out like a dog!".'[38]

The Queen discussed the problem with Rosebery on 9 May, and although she told him 'I did not agree with the whole affair, and the haste exhibited,' she could not but see the force of the Prime Minister's argument that 'there was a feeling abroad that George was too old, though he was extremely popular; and that it was not only a few Radicals, but also the opposition, which would not support the Government in defending George's position.' If other officers, it was asked, had to retire at sixty seven, how could it be right for H.R.H. to remain in office at seventy six? On 16 May the Queen saw the Secretary for War after luncheon, 'who was very kind and sensible. He believed that, if George C. were to resign about November, there would be a great demonstration in his favour, and that things would be so arranged that he would leave regretted by the whole nation. Should he, however, cling to office it might lead to regrettable unpleasantness. Mr C.-Bannerman spoke with great kindness and affection of George, saying that he felt a filial affection for him. . . . Saw George C., which was a trying and painful interview.

He was quite calm, but would not see the reason for resigning, so that our interview led to nothing, which is very despairing.'

Campbell-Bannerman, who acted throughout these melancholy proceedings with tact and consideration, saw H.R.H. the day after his visit to Windsor. Although the Duke resisted the idea of resigning, it appeared that he was willing to 'place himself in the Queen's hands.' The distinction involved showed, in the War Minister's phrase, 'a refinement worthy of the Schoolmen,' but he believed it advisable to humour the Duke. Campbell-Bannerman, describing the interview to Bigge, said that the Duke was 'as always most kindly and extremely frank. He gave an explanation of his position which for the first time made me clearly understand the distinction he draws between the resignation of his office, and placing himself in the Queen's hands. By resignation he thinks it would be implied that he took some blame to himself, that he admitted the argument of age, that he confessed failure, that he gave way to vulgar attacks. If he was not conscious of failure, why should he resign? On the other hand, if he places himself in H.M.'s hands, what he means is that he is ready to do whatever, on the advice of her Ministers, she desires. And by way of illustrating what he meant, he recited to me the letter which H.M. would probably write to him. Her Majesty, he thought, would say, "Since I saw you, I have considered the matter, and I find that my Ministers are of opinion that an altered organization should be given to the administration of the Army: that this alteration involves a considerable change in the duties of your office and cannot be carried out while you hold it, and therefore I think it best that you should," etc. etc. I really think there is force in the distinction H.R.H. draws: he will not resign, but if the Queen asks him to do so, he will give up his office.'[39]

The Prince of Wales misguidedly attempted to ease the situation. He was 'sorry that the Queen should have to go through such an ordeal with the Duke,' and he decided to do what he could on his own to impress upon his uncle that he should retire. His method of broaching so delicate a subject was clumsy and injudicious. While driving to Kempton Park races with the

Duke, 'à deux in his carriage, suddenly says to him "Oh! *by the by* (!!!!!!!!!) I have a message for you from the Queen reflecting upon it all round and weighing it, she is convinced that the only plan is for you to resign"!!! proceeding to explain that the sooner the better! certainly before the end of the year. And kindly suggesting "You might go to India!!! to make a break! *as you would miss it at first*." '[40] 'It is such disgusting, filthy ingratitude,' wrote Lady Geraldine on 19 May, 'after all he has endured and swallowed and fought and struggled for all but forty years for the Queen's sake, who has never manfully and honestly supported him! The whole thing is intrigue, it is perfectly clear, between the Prince, and Lord Rosebery, two beastly opportunists! Lord Rosebery thinking to avoid difficulties for his government is ready to throw the Duke as a sop to the radical wolves.'

The Duke, on 19 May, 'had a lengthened conversation with Campbell-Bannerman on a wish expressed that I should, before the end of this year, retire from my command of the Army with a view to great changes being made at the War Office. This decision has filled me with the very deepest sorrow as I still feel quite equal to the performance of my duties, and never anticipated such a decision being come to without my willing consent, but I must submit as best I can to the inevitable, but I own that I am disgusted with this, to my mind, most unjustifiable proceeding, though Mr C.-B. was most amiable in all he said.' On the same day he received a letter from the Queen saying that she had reluctantly decided upon his resignation. The city of refuge, to which in the last resort he had ever turned for succour, had pulled up the drawbridge and refused him admittance. 'My dear George,' ran the letter, 'since seeing you on Thursday I have given much anxious thought to the question of your tenure of the office of Commander-in-Chief. I quite appreciate the reasons which make you reluctant to resign the Office which you have so long held with the greatest advantage to the Army, and with my most entire confidence and approbation. I have, however, come to the conclusion, on the advice of my Ministers, that considerable changes in the distribution of duties among the Headquarters of my Army are desirable. These alterations cannot be effected without reconstituting the particular duties assigned to the Commander-in-Chief, and therefore, though with much pain, I have arrived at the decision that, for your own sake as well as in the public interest, it is inexpedient that you should much longer retain that position, from which I think you should be relieved at the close of your Autumn duties. This necessary change will be as painful to me as it is to you, but I am sure it is best so. Believe me, always your very affectionate Cousin and Friend, Victoria R. & I.'[41]

'My dear Cousin,' replied the Duke the following day, 'It was with great pain and deep sorrow that I read the letter you sent me yesterday, for, although I was fully aware that a change was contemplated which would result in my being called upon to relinquish my high position as head of your Majesty's Army, it certainly did not occur to me that the change had been so far prepared that it would be necessary for you to come to an immediate decision. To me therefore it has come like a surprise in this respect, but of course I accept the inevitable, though I deeply regret it, not alone or even chiefly on personal grounds, but for the interests of the Crown and Army, so seriously involved in any changes in the direction indicated. I have now only to express the hope, that after a service to your Majesty of fifty eight years, thirty nine of which as your Commander-in-Chief, my feelings may be spared every mortification that may be avoidable in making so great an alteration in my future position; and feeling assured that I have done my utmost to perform my duties absolutely for the interests of the Crown, the Country, and the Army, I remain, my dear cousin, Your most dutiful cousin, George.'[42]

The Duke, by remaining deaf to hints, had forced the Queen to be blunt, even brutal, but, as he saw it, she had surrendered to her Ministers and betrayed him in the process. Sir Redvers Buller, the Adjutant General, 'thought the Duke had been clumsily dealt with. H.R.H. said he came to Windsor, saw the Queen, who apparently quite understood he would not resign, returned satisfied and then two days later got a letter which he thought was not

a kind one, virtually giving him the "sack" as H.R.H. termed it.'
The Duke was 'bitterly hurt with the Queen,' and regarded
himself as the victim of a 'court intrigue.' Unaccustomed to
keeping his indignation to himself, he complained of his ill-treatment to Princess Edward of Saxe-Weimar. As a result, Lady
Geraldine was deeply annoyed and disturbed 'to hear the *dreadful*
indiscretion of Princess Edward *repeating* everything the Duke has
told her and been saying to her all this week at Kew! and to note,
what I alas, know too well, the dire effects of *his* indiscretion in
speaking so *terribly* openly and fully to *everybody*, to and before
every sort and kind of person! It is too disastrous.'[43] Sir Arthur
Bigge was told early in June by Sir Reginald Gipps that 'he never
remembered any important subject having been kept so secret,'
and as Sir Arthur, very wisely, was anxious 'that the outside world
should not know that H.R.H. is holding out,' Princess Edward's
chatter was especially unfortunate.

Although the Commander-in-Chief had no choice but to
resign, he determined to fight a strenuous rearguard over the
exact date of his retirement. Lord Rosebery nearly cracked under
the strain of battle. He sent Bigge a telegram in cypher saying:
'The Duke, I am afraid, gets worse and worse.' The Prime
Minister had a long-standing engagement to dine at Gloucester
House, and 'having had a somewhat painful correspondence with
the Duke of Cambridge,' and the evening of the dinner coming
only the day after Campbell-Bannerman was to announce the
resignation, he was 'most anxious to get off this engagement.
Would it be possible for Lord Rosebery to be commanded to
Windsor that night?'[44]

Wherever the Duke went he made no attempt to disguise his
sorrow, and scarcely bothered to pretend that he had consented
to retire. At the Staff College, on his last annual visit, 'standing
with his back to the anteroom fire, in full regalia, in the familiar
attitude, hands clasped behind his back, the head thrust slightly
forward, shoulders a little rounded, he closed his usual address,
summing up the merits and imperfections of the outgoing class,
with the words, "Gentlemen, I have been told that I am now a

fifth wheel to the coach, and that it is time that I made way for
a man who is younger and more closely in touch with the military
requirements of the present day." His voice broke as he made the
announcement, and he gruffly continued in soldierly fashion, in
spite of obvious emotion, to explain the high principles of loyalty,
honour, and affection for the Army which had inspired him in
his life's work. There was not one there, however imbued as he
might be with the new doctrine, who did not share the sadness
with which the old Duke, their real friend, told of his imminent
severance from the command of the Army he loved so well.'
Even more distressing was the Duke's farewell to his Staff on 31
October. 'My last day at the office. It is also dearest Louisa's
[Mrs FitzGeorge's] birthday, once so happy, now a sad anniversary.
I drove early to Kensal Green, where I found everything as it
should be, but very sad. On my return had luncheon at home,
Mildmay with us. I then drove to the old Horse Guards . . .
From there went to the Pall Mall office and at four thirty took
leave of all the officers of my own department . . . where a very
large number attended. I made them a farewell address which I
believe was good though extremely painful and distressing to
me. In the evening I had a dinner at home, a farewell to all my
Horse Guards staff . . . It is a sad moment to me and I feel it
intensely, the general feeling of regret at my departure and
sympathy with me as well as appreciation of my long service
being my only consolation.' Sir Henry Wilson, in his Diary,
described the last leave-taking at the Horse Guards. 'At four
o'clock all the H.Q. Staff assembled in the Military Secretary's
room, and the old Duke of Cambridge came in and bid us goodbye. The poor old man broke down.'[45]

   The Duke's resignation was announced on 21 June, and the day
after, Lady Geraldine saw him at Gloucester House. 'We went
downstairs for a little refreshment. I was able to say one quarter
of a word to him of my regret and grief, when he came, kind and
dear, to ask if I would not have some tea. He touched his head
and with a *laugh*!! said "kicked out!!" More sad than words can
express!!' To the end of his life H.R.H. maintained that he had

been ill treated. On 12 February 1904, a month before he died, 'he spoke of the way beastly Rosebery's Government *kicked him out* after forty years' service and how abominably badly they behaved to him!' Writing to his friend Lady Dorothy Nevill, thanking her for a kind note of sympathy, he made it quite clear that his retirement had not been voluntary. 'I never resigned nor even contemplated resignation,' he informed her, 'but when told that these proposed changes were to be carried out, I had no choice left but that of not offering any resistance in my person and thus it has, alas! come about. It simply amounts to my being most summarily *turned* out, and at the shortest notice without my retirement being awarded to me!! *Strong order this I think!!!* after thirty nine years in my present high position. It is *very* sad, but my friends are *most kind*.'⁴⁶ On 27 September he made a speech at Edinburgh in which he told his audience that 'he believed that he could have gone on much longer at his post, but it had been thought advisable that others should follow him. He only hoped that his successors would have at the end of their career as much sentiment respecting their office as he experienced at that moment. . . . In conclusion his Royal Highness, who had spoken with considerable emotion, declared that he would withdraw from public life with the conviction that he had endeavoured always to do his duty.'

It was a splendid tribute to Campbell-Bannerman that it never seems to have occurred to the Duke to blame him for what had happened. Bigge complimented the Secretary for War on acting 'throughout these painful negotiations . . . with the greatest tact and kindliness of heart.'⁴⁷ The Queen invested him at Windsor with a G.C.B. 'It is specially meant,' he told a friend, 'as a mark of her approval of my conduct of the negotiations about the poor old Duke of Cambridge. She has repeatedly told me that no one except myself could have managed it. That is a little strong, but she is very effusive about it.' The negotiations left him 'quite worn out. I carried the Queen with me throughout and most of her family. She was in fact most interested and anxious. The difficulty was the poor old dear himself, and I am thankful to say

x

he is still most friendly and grateful to me for the way I have managed the whole business, and we have never been other than friends. Such a result I am very proud of, and I can now rest on my laurels.'[48]

If Campbell-Bannerman escaped censure, the Duke was not disposed to be so charitable towards the Queen, the Prince of Wales and Lord Rosebery. 'A little before seven came the Duke!' wrote Lady Geraldine on 24 June. 'He had tea. Much depressed and disgusted with the whole thing!. . . We discussed the whole miserable affair. *All* had behaved so badly! and treated him so shamefully! Rosebery a regular cur! The worst of all the Queen! who bowls him over altogether! Utterly selfish, without a particle of consideration for him! who has so long and so gallantly fought her battles for her. She and the Prince only excel each other in opportunism! and are besides too stupid in their short-sightedness, ever more and more submitting to become nothing but the most contemptible of figureheads!'

Lady Geraldine was passionately indignant at the way Queen Victoria treated the Duke, allowing him to be 'sent away like a footman in disgrace.' 'Happily dear heart! the universal expressions of appreciation and regret of most of the press, his many friends, and the Army are "very flattering" and soothing to him.' 'It does make my blood boil,' she wrote on 16 July, 'how abominably she behaves to him! She [the Queen] is such a coward, for when she was likely to see him at last Saturday's review, she had it conveyed to him not to allude to her to the subject, she did not wish to discuss it.' A week later she complained, 'It is too *abominable*, too *infamous* of the Queen! rouses all my fiercest bitterest indignation against her!! The other day when she had him to dine and sleep at Windsor *she never* made the *most distant allusion* to his losing the command, by a single word!!!'

On the evening of 21 June, Campbell-Bannerman announced the news of the Duke's impending retirement, and later that very same night the Government was defeated in the House of Commons. The Conservatives moved a surprise vote of censure against the Secretary for War, on the Army's reserves of cordite.

It was carried by a majority of seven, Rosebery at once resigned and Lord Salisbury returned to power. For a moment the Duke thought that he might after all retain his post, but Lord Lansdowne, the new War Minister, soon disappointed such hopes. One consequence of the change of Government was that Wolseley was appointed to succeed H.R.H. rather than Sir Redvers Buller, the Liberals' candidate for the office. 'It sets my brain on fire,' wrote Lady Geraldine, 'the way they behave. Lord Lansdowne!!! whom I have so erroneously believed to be a *gentleman*! The insolence of him, when the Duke was discussing with him the question of some fitting title to be given him to preserve *some* connection with the Army and give him status, (which *probably*, if they were *men* and not sneaks, *ought* to be Honorary Commander-in-Chief for life, of course, and spontaneously conferred, without query!!!). He had the insolence to answer: "Yes! but then it must be clearly understood *that* you do not interfere in Army matters, there must be no interference with the Army!" God!! How my blood boils to write it!! The insolence of the word "interfere"! Beastly little whippersnapper. In no one thing has he shown a spark of good feeling!'⁴⁹

The Duke himself, when Lansdowne was appointed Secretary for War, described him, on 1 July, after their first official interview, as 'very nice as he is always and a great gentleman.' Evidently he did not altogether share Lady Geraldine's vehement emotions, but he did regard his retirement as 'a terrible blow and I think most ungenerous and unfair, particularly as to the manner in which it was brought about.' The Conservative Government, which he had hoped might reverse Rosebery's decision, very soon made it clear that it would 'do nothing to mitigate the painful position I am placed in, which greatly distresses me.'⁵⁰

Wolseley, who had long plotted and preached the Duke's retirement, and who was now himself to become Commander-in-Chief, with greatly reduced powers, felt a certain chivalrous sympathy for his vanquished enemy. He wrote him a generous letter on his resignation. 'I know,' he told his wife, 'the old gentleman likes and dislikes me by turns, just as I do him. But he

is down on his luck.'[51] The Duke was consoled by the condo-
lences he received and the affection and regrets displayed. 'Was
alone in my room,' he wrote on the first day of 1896, 'thinking
of all my dear friends in various parts of the world. Thus closed
a year of sad reminiscences, as with it has closed my active service,
very unexpectedly to myself, though very flattering to me from
the great feeling of sympathy and regret expressed to me in all
manners and ways by the whole Army and by the Nation at
large.' Writing to General Harrison in November 1895 he told
him how comforted he was by the regard the Army had shown
him. 'It is very gratifying to me,' he declared, 'to know and feel
that the whole Army regrets my departure from the Chief
Command of a noble service of which I have always felt proud,
and which I believe to be in as efficient a condition as it is possible
that it could have been made during the period I have had to
control it. I withdraw with the deepest sorrow and regret, and
the feelings of my heart and all my interest in life will continue
with and for the Army till the end of my days.'[52]

The Queen, despite scepticism felt in certain quarters, was
anxious to do whatever she could to mitigate her cousin's sorrow.
She appointed him her first personal Aide-de-Camp, she promised
to continue to consult him on Army affairs, and to support him
in his struggle with the Government over his retiring pension. It
is true that H.R.H. in the end received no sort of a grant, that
he was seldom referred to on military matters, and that the duties
of first personal Aide-de-Camp, as defined in the letter appointing
him to the position, were, on Wolseley's insistence, transferred to
the new Commander-in-Chief. But the Queen was sincere in her
gratitude and in her desire to be considerate. 'It is with great and
much pain,' she told H.R.H., 'that I see you leave the high,
important and responsible office which you have held so worthily
for nearly forty years. Accept also my sincerest thanks for the
great services you have rendered to the Country, to the Army
and myself, which will ever be most gratefully remembered.
Believe me that I feel deeply for you in this severance of a *tie*
which existed so long between you and the Army. It is not,

however, a *real* severance, for you are a Field Marshal and Colonel of many Regiments. I need not either say that I shall be glad to have your opinion on affairs of importance connected with the Army. I shall gladly support anything which the Government may feel able to propose for you. With renewed expressions of my affection and friendship. Believe me always, Your very affectionate Cousin and Friend.' The Princess of Wales, always considerate and full of good feeling, sent him a telegram saying, 'My thoughts are much with you, dear Uncle George, through all this most trying time. I share your sorrow from my heart; it is very hard for you, and will be regretted by all. Best love from here. Alix.'

Of all the hundreds of letters he received, he was particularly touched by one from Florence Nightingale. As a sharp critic of military affairs, she could easily have remained silent. She wrote out of no sense of formal politeness, but from personal knowledge and appreciation. 'Will you allow me to offer to Y.R.H., at the close of nearly forty years work for the Army, something more than the sympathy of silence on your retirement? My excuse for intrusion at such a time as this, is the honour of having been allowed to work with the Army and for it in days gone by. It has endowed my life with interests, occupations, and friendships that have enabled me to follow and to understand more fully than would have been otherwise possible the advance made since then in the health, comfort, and general well-being of our soldiers. Very few now living can know how much of that advance is owing to the patient personal efforts of Y.R.H., which date back to the times when by far the most serious dangers to the soldiers in peace or war were bad food, insufficient accommodation for man and horse, and an absolute neglect of sanitary measures . . . It requires one who, to some extent at least, has been an official, to realize that nothing less than many years of minute attention to matters of detail, each of which brought its own special contribution to the soldier's welfare, could have made his position and profession what it is to-day. To transform the fashions of a profession is harder than to succeed in a hundred campaigns, for it requires an enthusiasm for the drudgery of detail of which the public have no knowledge, and for which, therefore, they give no thanks. But rewarded work has never been so good as thankless work, and if known work has been the admiration of the world, it is the unknown work that is its salvation.'[53]

The early weeks of the Duke's retirement were so filled with farewell dinners that he had scarcely time to brood over the events of the past months. The enthusiasm shown was exhilarating. '*All* say, everywhere, that *never* was cheering heard like the cheers that greet him, at all times! They told also, of the Mansion House dinner last night, Lord James of Hereford said in his life he had never heard such a noise as the Duke's name was received with! Again and again renewed, a perfect *storm* of cheers! adding "I know *I* broke two plates with my fork, in trying to add to the noise"! The Duke spoke of how gratifying to him the unanimity of good feeling shown him is! With tears in his dear eyes! saying "I am going through in my life what occurs to most after their death!" Only it is not many "who come so well off! but it is really as though I were dead, and shown what is said of me after it!" '[54]

END OF AN ERA

AFTER fifty eight years as a serving officer, the Duke clung to every opportunity to preserve his associations with the Army. As first personal Aide-de-Camp to the Queen, he had, in her own words, 'the right of attending me on all military occasions, and of holding the Parade on my birthday.' The appointment had been made to enable H.R.H. to keep up his connection with the Army, 'who are deeply attached to you.'[1] The pleasure he derived from being in uniform again, and taking a parade, touchingly evinced his passionate fondness for the world of soldiering. As the old gentlemen at Henley Regatta pathetically renew their youth by sporting Edwardian blazers and Leander caps perched on their grey heads, so the retired Commander-in-Chief momentarily revived the glory of former days, as mounted on a specially exercised charger, he took the salute, dressed in his Field Marshal's uniform. But despite the Queen's promise that the Duke should take the Birthday Parade, Wolseley insisted on doing so himself. 'Would not any man who had a spark of decent feeling,' commented Lady Geraldine, 'say to his predecessor who so shortly ago was his superior officer and had been for a *lifetime*, it were a *pleasure* to see him for an hour in his old position!' The Duke and Duchess of York were hotly indignant when they heard that Uncle George was being elbowed out by Wolseley and declared it was too outrageous to be allowed.[2]

As had been predicted, the Queen capitulated, and her first A.D.C., who by her own suggestion was entitled to the salute on her birthday, was invited as a mere spectator to watch Wolseley take the parade. Lady Geraldine was almost choked by her 'unutterable wrath and boiling indignation.' Wolseley was described as a 'sneak,' 'snob,' and a 'dirty dog devoid of one single feeling of a gentleman.' When the Queen went 'back from her word,' and 'positively allows and agrees that the mongrel shall take the salute . . . there are no words to express the outrage it is.' Lady Geraldine having exhausted the vocabulary of obloquy, and finding 'no words' to express her rancour, must have been provoked to such tongue-tied silence by a singular transgression. The Diarist, however, did not remain deprived of invective for long. 'When instead of standing by him as she should have done,' the account continues, the Queen 'so *shamefully* threw the Duke over and forced him to resign, she herself wrote to him by way of a sop, *such* a sop!! that she made him her first A.D.C.!! and that at her Birthday Parade he should *always take the salute*, a perfectly spontaneous suggestion of her own, unsought, unasked, and now because this beastly snob has the vulgar insolence to announce he does not choose it shall be, she throws her prerogative to the winds, does away with the faint *myth* of it being *her* Army, succumbs and kowtows and *dares* not say she will have it! In this which is purely a compliment, a mere civil acknowledgement that her cousin for forty years faithfully administered "*her*" Army. It is too sickening, and makes me so angry it makes me quite ill! I have no words and no language for it, and cannot write about it, it is such a burning shame.'[3]

The Duke, with considerable foresight, had bought properties in the Coombe and Kingston districts, at a time when they were entirely rural. Their values greatly increased as London spread which made him a rich man. But although not without resources of his own, H.R.H. believed that, after so many years of service, he was entitled to a pension. The Queen declared the idea was 'preposterous,' Campbell-Bannerman opposed it, and eventually the Cabinet decided it was out of the question. Lord Lansdowne, while negotiations were still in progress, suggested that antici-pated opposition might be disarmed if as a 'small concession' H.R.H. were to give permission, as Ranger of the Royal Parks, for the troops to drill in Hyde Park on the grass in front of Knightsbridge Barracks, and for the volunteers to hold field days in Richmond Park. While the Duke was wintering at Cannes in 1896, the familiar telegrams, letters and memoranda sped back and forth. The Queen, Bigge, the Prince of Wales, Lord Salisbury, Lord Lansdowne, all agreed that the Duke's request for a pension could not be met, and in the end he abandoned the idea himself, but not without an added sense of ingratitude and injustice. He told Lady Geraldine, on 1 April 1896, that he had decided it would be 'impossible to submit himself to the ordeal of an annual allowance voted yearly in each successive estimates with yearly insult and insolence from the curs of the House of Commons!! But it diminishes his income by £4,500 per annum.' Within a year, he had been turned out of office, he had been refused a pension, he had not even been permitted the privilege of taking the salute on Horse Guards Parade. After over half a century of holding the Queen's commission he had hoped for more than abrupt dismissal. But England has seldom lavished gratitude on its public servants, and they may consider themselves fortunate if after a lifetime of service they are permitted to languish in destitute obscurity.

It took the Duke a considerable time to accustom himself to the leisure of retirement. His inner resources were few. He read very little and he was becoming too infirm to spend an entire day shooting. He craved companionship, but had outlived most of his friends. The pleasures that remained to him were the company of his sons and grandchildren, Mrs Vyner and her circle, winters at Cannes, summers in Germany, and long conversations about the past, his family and the Army.

In the last years of his life he was able to give more time to the numerous charities he had always supported. While still a young man it had been discovered that he was a persuasive speaker and generous with his help, and consequently he had been appointed a governor of several schools and hospitals. Even in the days of his Commanding-in-Chief, he had never believed in remote patronage, and had regularly attended board meetings at Christ's Hospital, Wellington College, Service associations, and a dozen other institutions from the Royal Soldiers' Daughters' Home to the Victoria Hospital, Kingston-on-Thames. In all of these he took a deep personal interest and to all gave more than his name and a donation. But however ingeniously he devised occupations, they were at best inadequate substitutes for the work and routine which a lifetime of habit had made part of his existence. He particularly missed receiving official despatches, and felt like a 'fish out of water,' getting only scraps of news, instead of full information.

The Queen's Diamond Jubilee celebrations in 1897 crowded London with envoys, princes, and foreign relations. The round of parades and reviews and commemoration days which filled the end of June delighted the Duke. His imperial pride swelled at the sight of troops from Canada, Africa and India, and the ceremonies of Jubilee Day itself, 22 June, he described as the 'most glorious and notable,' he ever attended. 'The effect will, I think, be prodigious for good throughout the world, and especially for this Empire.' The morning was a glorious one, 'not too bright, but mild air . . . I was up early, and all my guests arrived in good time. About a hundred or more were in my rooms. I drove to the Royal Mews at nine forty five where I mounted my Chestnut Horse "Rifleman" which carried me most admirably all through the day. The procession started punctually at eleven fifteen. I rode on the left hand of the Queen's carriage. All the arrangements including the "turn out" were perfect, the behaviour of the people magnificent, the decorations lovely.' That evening H.R.H.

attended a state banquet at the Palace and a reception afterwards. He was seventy eight at the time, but expressed surprise when he finally returned to Gloucester House to find that he was more than ready for sleep.

Four days later, dressed in his Trinity House uniform, he joined the royal train to Portsmouth for the great Naval Review. 'Embarked at the Dockyard with the Prince [of Wales] and Princess and all the Royalties and special Ambassadors in the Royal Yacht *Victoria and Albert*. We were thirty one. The day cleared up beautifully, and the afternoon was perfect for this special occasion. Steamed out to Spithead, where the grand fleet of one hundred and sixty six vessels was anchored in four long lines, each extending a mile. It was a grand and noble sight of wealth and strength and very heart-stirring. We steamed up and down the lines and anchored in the very centre abreast the flag-ship . . . whilst the foreign Admirals and their Flag Captains, as well as our own, came on board to be received by the Prince of Wales. We then proceeded back into harbour . . . I stayed at Government House . . . After dinner had a magnificent sight of the Fleet, brilliantly illuminated with electric light—a truly heart-stirring sight and a sign of the development of the Empire over the Seas. The Prince and Princess steamed out in the Royal Yacht, and as they left the Lines to return to harbour, the entire Fleet fired a simultaneous salute of twenty one guns, which produced a grand effect.' The next evening the Duke gave a dinner at Gloucester House, 'in plain clothes' to the Prince of Wales and 'all the Royal Princes and special Ambassadors for the Jubilee.' The food was excellent—the Duke's chef was one of the best in London—the plate looked 'charming' and the band of the Grenadiers melodiously punctuated the conversation. On 1 July, yet another 'perfect day,' H.R.H. joined the Prince of Wales's train for the Review at Aldershot. On arrival at Farnborough he rode over to the encampment with the Duke of York. Augustus FitzGeorge was put in charge of the Grand Duchess and Princess Mary, for whom the Duke had sent down carriages for the occasion. 'The luncheon was very well done, the Royalties at a

large table, and the suites and others in a tent to the number of
eighty. The Prince and we all then rode quietly to the Parade
Ground . . . which was green and fresh to look at and the road
well watered, so we had no dust. The Queen arrived at four
thirty. The crowd on the ground and in the stands erected was
very great . . . The Duke of Connaught commanded, and made
all the arrangements, which were quite perfect and not a hitch or
accident took place. The Queen was much pleased, and well she
might be! I never saw a finer parade at Aldershot.'

The Duchess of Teck's visit to the Jubilee Review was one of
her last public appearances. Earlier in the year she had been taken
seriously ill in the night and had been saved by immediate
surgery, but her recovery was only temporary, and at three a.m.
on the morning of 27 October, after a second emergency operation, her heart failed. The Duke at the time was staying at
Sandringham, and on receiving 'a most painful and unexpected
telegram from poor Teck, announcing to me the afflicting news
of the sudden death of my dear sister Mary,' he, and the Prince
of Wales, started at once for London; the Duke of York joined
them at Cambridge. After luncheon they set out for White
Lodge, Richmond, where Nelson dipping his finger in port had
drawn on the tablecloth the plan of the battle of Trafalgar, and
where for many years past the Teck family had lived and entertained beyond their means. On arrival at White Lodge H.R.H.
found the place thronged with agitated relations. 'Saw dearest
Mary on her deathbed. She reminded me so very much of the
countenance of my dearest Mother. Heard all the details of Mary's
last moments. The operation had been successfully performed.
She came to, and spoke a few words, then fell into a comatose
state, the heart having given way from the shock to the system,
and she expired very quietly at three o'clock in the morning . . .
Am overwhelmed with letters and telegrams of condolence . . .
from all parts at home and abroad.'

The funeral was held on 3 November at St George's Chapel,
Windsor. 'We were in plain clothes, but there was a dignity and
real devotion about it, which was most impressive and gratifying

and the hymns and singing of the choir were perfect.' At a Memorial Service held at White Lodge on 31 October, the Duke had been unable to hear the prayers and psalms, which distressed him very much, so the service at Windsor, sad though it was, consoled him at least by being audible. Even before his wife's death, Prince Teck's mind had been failing, he had been given to fits of unaccountable laughter and his conversation had become incoherent. The Duke for a time visited his brother-in-law after his sister's death, but found him 'daily growing worse' and 'much more confused in his mind and very difficult to understand.' When Teck died in 1900 it was a relief to his family, for his mind had gone, and for two years he had been kept completely secluded at White Lodge, surrounded by attendants and not even seeing his children.

The last years of the Duke's life were constantly saddened by deaths. Even Gladstone's end he regretted. 'Mr Gladstone died this morning,' he wrote on 29 May 1898, 'calmly and peacefully, a great man less in the world, after a most remarkable career. Personally he was always very amiable to me, though a dangerous politician with a most remarkable intellect.' On 16 December the same year, Christopher Sykes, the Prince of Wales's long-suffering companion and a close friend of the Duke, succumbed after a brief illness. 'I am deeply grieved,' wrote H.R.H., 'though not surprised. He was always a most loyal friend to me and I shall greatly miss him, poor dear fellow.' On 15 March 1901, Charles Fairbrother died, the Duke previously had deplored that he saw so little of him, 'but he seems to prefer a solitary life.' Then, while at Cannes, a telegram came to say that 'Charles died last night at eleven thirty. Poor fellow, a happy release of a very unhappy man, as he would have no friends and specially avoided all the members of his family. He never came near my house since Christmas year, which is too sad.' But accustomed as he grew to such losses, there was one departed friend he never forgot. 'Deposited a wreath on poor Mrs Beauclerk's grave as tomorrow was the day of her death twenty years ago. How time flies, I could hardly believe it, also visited my dear Louisa's grave.'

The outbreak of the Boer War in 1899, which H.R.H. followed with professional interest, gave him a new lease of life. He even went to Waterloo station to see Sir Redvers Buller off to the front, and he eagerly inspected regiments going out to South Africa. The French at Cannes were pro-Boer, and this so incensed H.R.H. that he wintered instead at Monte Carlo, which he hated, and where he missed his friends of the Château. His last visit to the Queen, on 4 December 1900, was taken up with discussing the war. 'I found her fairly well, though much distressed . . . at the state of military affairs generally.'

In the New Year, on 19 January, the Duke set out for Monte Carlo. Before leaving, he had read depressing accounts of the Queen's health in the newspapers, but the Duchess of York advised him to start as intended. At Paris the reports were so gloomy that he decided to return to England. 'On reaching Charing Cross at seven forty-five, heard that the dear Queen had passed away quietly and calmly surrounded by her children and grandchildren . . . It is a fearful blow and great catastrophe not only for England but for the world at large.' The Duke shared in the universal feeling that it was almost impossible to conceive of England without the Queen. 'Parliaments,' as Gladstone had once observed, 'and Ministers pass, but she abides in lifelong duty, and she is to them as the oak in the forest is to the annual harvest in the field.'

The next day, at two o'clock, the Duke was summoned to St James's to attend a Privy Council. He was received by the Prince of Wales 'most graciously and kindly and with great dignity and affection.' The Prince 'accepted the Throne under the title of Edward VII in an extremely well expressed address.' That evening he 'dined with the Duke of York to meet the King.' The Queen's funeral was held on 2 February. 'Fortunately the day was dry, though cold and dreary. I drove to Victoria Station with Prince Edward and Dolly, now in waiting, and there joined all the Kings and Royalties, whence I rode with the King and Emperor behind the hearse. The Royal train with the Queen's body arrived at eleven, and then we all started. I drove in the fourth carriage with Edward Weimar and Lord Wolseley. The crowds were very enormous, but their demeanour magnificent, solemn and silent. Got to Paddington at one, and left for Windsor by train at a few minutes afterwards. At Windsor Station there was a sad delay by the Artillery horse in the shaft of the gun carriage kicking violently. Fortunately no injury resulted; the horses were taken out, and the Guard of Honour of Bluejackets put in their place and dragged the remains up to St George's Chapel. We walked through the town, following in procession, and I managed to get through it, leaning on Dolly's arm. The Church was crowded, the Archbishop of Canterbury and the Bishop of Winchester officiating; the service was choral. We then walked back to the castle where lunch was served to us in the usual dining room . . . After that I returned to London by seven o'clock, being dead beat, and I just crawled into bed.'

H.R.H., who was very much broken by the Queen's death, discussed it with the Duke of Grafton, whom he met after the Service at Windsor. ' "I shall go soon myself," he groaned, and to cheer him up the Duke of Grafton said he was nearly as old himself, upon which the old Duke said almost cheerfully, "Ah! We will both go together." '[4] H.R.H. was so fatigued by the funeral that the following day he 'rested and slept alternately,' a procedure he followed after Edward VII's coronation in August, the last great ceremony he ever attended. Apart from the Grand Duchess, he was the only surviving member of the Royal Family who could recall Queen Victoria's coronation, and his advice on precedent was anxiously sought.

In August 1903 the Duke paid a visit to Germany, but his strength was gradually failing, and he was forced more and more to withdraw from public life. 'I keep on going,' he said, 'for I notice that when men give up their ordinary pursuits and do nothing they generally die very soon.' On 6 October he abandoned his Diary: 'Age tells so much now upon me that I have no alternative. I give it up with reluctance and great regret.' Early in 1904 his final illness began. There was no fight left in him. At the beginning of the year the office of Commander-in-Chief

had been abolished. Nearly all his friends were dead. His sister
Augusta, his sons, Lady Geraldine, the King, Queen Alexandra,
the Wales's, and Mrs Vyner, were all that were left of his
once crowded world. He no longer had anything to live for, and
so 'prayed God to take him, he is so *weary* of waiting.' 'He
[Augustus FitzGeorge] tells me,' wrote Lady Geraldine on 8
March, 'the Duke speaks mostly of old, old far away days; of his
early days, not wandering, quite all there, but thinking, asking,
nothing or very little of the present, full of recollections of the
Past!' On 17 March, only a few days before his eighty-fifth
birthday, he passed peacefully away in the presence of Mrs
Hamilton and his three sons.

'With profound regret,' said *The Times* the following morning,
'we have to announce that His Royal Highness the Duke of
Cambridge died at Gloucester House, Piccadilly, yesterday
morning shortly after half-past-ten o'clock. Soon after two
o'clock in the morning His Royal Highness was seized with
another attack of haemorrhage of the stomach and became restless,
and about daybreak there was a recurrence of the haemorrhage.
At nine o'clock a messenger was despatched to His Royal
Highness's domestic chaplain, the Reverend Doctor Sheppard,
Sub-Dean of the Chapels Royal, who arrived promptly at
Gloucester House and read prayers at the bedside. The bulletin
issued at nine o'clock clearly indicated that the end was approaching. It was as follows: "The Duke of Cambridge passed a restless
night. There has been a recurrence of haemorrhage this morning.
His Royal Highness is now in a condition of profound exhaus-
tion." From this time onwards, the Duke, greatly weakened by
loss of blood, became rapidly worse, and the end was so painless
and peaceful that those at the bedside hardly realized the actual
passing.'

The newspapers were smothered in obituaries, portraying a
man moving in a royal world of aldermen, red carpets, brass
bands, silver trowels and illuminated addresses; a world of
grandeur, decorations, epaulettes, orders, Field Marshals' batons
and resounding titles. But although the Duke had wrung many

a mayor by the hand, and although his own sister was the Grand Duchess of Mecklenburg-Strelitz, there was a world elsewhere: the world of Chesham Street, of Queen Street, of Horley and of Kensal Green. The newspapers thought of the Duke of Cambridge as the first grandson to be born to George III and the last to die. Hardly anyone living recalled H.R.H. as a young man: the youthful Commander-in-Chief, the scourge of Sir George Brown, the handsome husband of an enchanting bride. He was remembered as a crippled old gentleman shuffling down Piccadilly, leaning heavily on his son's arm. But even this faded image of an active man commanded affection and respect.

In the House of Commons, the Prime Minister, Mr Balfour, spoke of the Duke's services to England, both in the field and in the office of Commander-in-Chief. 'Although I suppose it would be too much to hope,' he said, 'that at any time of our political history questions connected with the War Office should be outside the pale of controversy, there is one thing in which every man will agree—namely, that the Duke of Cambridge devoted to this great office his whole time, his whole energy, his whole strength, and that he was intimately and profoundly acquainted with every question that affected the British Army, and that throughout his whole career he possessed the confidence of both officers and men.' Campbell-Bannerman, speaking for the Opposition, described the Duke as 'the true friend of all his friends,' whose 'personal charm drew to him everyone with whom he came in contact.' 'The Duke of Cambridge,' he declared, 'was devoted with an intensity of devotion beyond description to the Army of which he was Commander-in-Chief for many years.'

At his own desire the Duke was buried at Kensal Green, but the King ordered that the first part of the service should be held in Westminster Abbey. Princess Augusta, writing to her niece the Princess of Wales, regretted that 'he will not be laid to rest in the family vault at Windsor, and is to be taken to a strange resting place, so far away from us all!'[5] The day before the funeral fixed for 22 March, a short service was held at Gloucester House. The Duke's body rested in a polished oak coffin exactly like that chosen

Y

for Queen Victoria. Above it was placed the crossed batons of a Field Marshal, surmounted with a coronet of a Prince of the Blood Royal. Edward VII, Queen Alexandra, the Prince and Princess of Wales, the Teck boys (the eldest of whom in 1917 was created Marquess of Cambridge), Mrs Hamilton, the FitzGeorges, Lady Geraldine and the Duke's servants, assembled in the state dining room for prayers.

The day of the funeral was bright, with a hint of spring—a detail which in any other circumstance the Duke himself would have noted in his Diary. The south transept of the Abbey, reserved for military mourners, was a mass of scarlet and glinting light. The coffin was wrapped in the Union Jack with the Royal Standard draped over it. Rear Admiral Adolphus FitzGeorge and Colonel Augustus FitzGeorge, upon whom the very next day the King conferred the K.C.V.O., although they had been relegated to the ninth carriage in the procession to the Abbey, were permitted to stand by their father's remains. Colonel George FitzGeorge sat in a private pew with his son. He had recently suffered from a stroke and was unable to appear in uniform. The Abbey was packed with representatives of Emperors and Kings, with Ministers, Members of both Houses, and a vast company of officers. Amongst the pall-bearers were Lord Wolseley, Lord Roberts, Sir Evelyn Wood, Sir Redvers Buller and Sir John French. There were representatives present of Trinity House, the Royal Parks, several hospitals, charities, and a variety of institutions with which the Duke had been associated. While the congregation assembled, a march was played which Purcell had composed for the funeral of Queen Mary and which had been used at his own burial service.

As the mourners left the Abbey the Guards' Massed Bands struck up the Dead March in *Saul* and the sound of guns fired from St James's Park heralded the funeral procession. The five-mile-long route was lined with dense masses of people who stood in the brilliant sunshine in absolute silence. As the coffin passed the soldiers lining the road presented arms, afterwards resting on reversed arms until the cortège had passed. Princess May described it as 'the most impressive and beautiful sight . . . I have ever seen, too upsetting for words, and I cried floods all the time . . . Aunt Alix [the Queen] was so feeling and dear to me . . . she feels Uncle's death very much indeed.' In the procession, Lord Roberts and Lord Wolseley were put into the same carriage. For years they had not spoken to each other. About the only thing they had in common was that they were both successors of the Duke as Commander-in-Chief.[6] Finally at Kensal Green there was another short service and a hymn was sung by the choir of the Chapels Royal. As the coffin of the Duke was placed in the vault beside that of Mrs FitzGeorge, three volleys were fired by men of the Grenadier Guards and a bugler sounded the 'Last Post.'

Had the Duke of Cambridge been born the son of a country squire instead of a grandson of George III, he would have been fortunate to figure in some regimental history; but being a Prince of the Blood, he had 'greatness thrust upon him.' As Commander-in-Chief he performed the duties of his office to the complete satisfaction of the Army: except for a handful of progressive officers who were exasperated by his obstruction of reform. His rough and forthright manner, his affection for those under his command, his enviable grasp for the details of his profession, his endless industry, his constant defence of regimental traditions, and his repeated struggles to prevent reductions, won him the regard of both officers and men. The frustration of successive Secretaries for War was a measure of the success he achieved in defending the soldier's interests. No other Commander-in-Chief ever held office so long, or was so loved by the rank and file. For all Wolseley's brilliance and for all his achievements, he never even momentarily challenged the Duke in the Army's affection.

The Duke's conservatism has been represented as destructive of all improvement, whereas many of the reforms he resisted were ignorantly conceived, opposed by some of the shrewdest officers in the Army, and were often inspired by political, not military, necessity. Although as Commander-in-Chief he may have grown excessively sceptical of the merits of changes enthusiastically

advocated by successive Secretaries of State, it need not be
assumed that every proposal described as a 'reform' by its expo-
nents was invariably a change for the better. Indeed improvements
whose merits are not in dispute, may be ill timed and ill devised.
General Harman in 1888 told Ponsonby: 'The Duke is the best
friend the Army has, and knows its requirements better than any
living man, and were it not for what many are pleased to call
"his obstruction" to the reforms that are so constantly being
advanced, the Service instead of being the popular profession it
ow is would soon become quite the reverse.'[7]

The Duke's reluctance to countenance alterations, which he
maintained unsettled the Army, involved him in repeated colli-
sions both with War Ministers, and with a group of officers led
by Wolseley. From the clash of their opposing views emerged a
number of moderate and necessary changes. 'Providence, with a
curiously perpetual regard for England, seems to have sent her
this diametrically opposed pair [H.R.H. and Wolseley]: one to
save her from being caught unawares entangled in the cobwebs
of antiquity, and the other to temper the remorseless blast of
revolution to the healthy breeze of evolution.'[8]

The Duke's opponents, although relatively few in numbers,
were energetic publicists. H.R.H. had frequent occasion to
deplore their subversive speeches and controversial newspaper
articles. They made a great noise, and because they attacked
established things, were able to accuse those who dissented from
their views of bigotry. They distorted intricate issues so that they
appeared simple, and they did scant justice to their opponents'
views. They represented themselves as fearless and enlightened
reformers, while they portrayed the Horse Guards officials as
uncritical retrogrades. They painted the conflict as a struggle
between new and old, between modern methods based on the
lessons of contemporary war, and outdated traditions deriving
from Napoleonic times. It was a battle between Wolseley, 'the
very model of a modern Major General,' and an old-fashioned
Crimean soldier, who had forgotten nothing and learnt nothing.
Such were the simple terms to which the argument was reduced.

Subsequent writers, attracted by the loud and compelling clamour of Wolseley and his disciples, have overlooked his opponents' views. Cardwell and Childers have been accepted at their own exalted estimates, and although some reluctance has been shown to swallow all that Wolseley said about himself by way of congratulation, his opinions about the Duke of Cambridge have been handed from history book to history book as if they were holy lore which it would be blasphemy to dispute.

The Duke's conservatism was more an attitude of mind than a political creed. As Commander-in-Chief he officially strove to avoid commitment to party, but his sympathy for Tory imperialism was widely known. Once, while listening to a debate in the House of Commons he so far forgot himself as to cheer Disraeli for denouncing Liberal reforms. When Gladstone was Prime Minister, H.R.H. would audibly criticize Government measures in a stage whisper to some neighbouring peer in the House of Lords, or would sit 'in the centre of the front gallery of the House of Commons, whence he could observe the Treasury bench and look down upon the Premier with a face that did not speak unbounded trust. Who knows? Perhaps the Liberal leader in his view was a dangerous person who ought, if he had his deserts, to be dragged off and summarily tried by a drum-head court-martial . . . At the dinner to Lord Roberts at the Mansion House in 1893 for instance, when Home Rule was the absorbing topic of political discussion, he spoke of the *United* Kingdom with such a marked stress on the first of those two words that the City Tories cheered vociferously.'[9]

At one of his last functions as Commander-in-Chief he addressed his military colleagues as follows: 'Gentlemen, there have been great changes in my time—great changes. But I can say this. Every change has been made at the right time, and the right time is when you cannot help it.' At a luncheon at the Mansion House he told his audience 'Everybody nowadays is asking for change; they want to change this and they want to change that; in fact, they want to change everything. I don't see any good in changing everything. We have done very well as we are, and I don't see that any change is needed. I'm quite satisfied with things as they are.'[10]

The Duke's satisfaction with 'things as they are' made him insensitive to hallowed abuses. 'He seems to have believed, quite honestly, that the Army as he had found it, created by such a master of war as the Duke of Wellington, must be the best for all time, and he had not realized the changes which had since taken place in the armies of Europe.' Sir William Robertson has told how H.R.H. once took the chair at a lecture given to officers of the Aldershot garrison on the subject of foreign cavalry, 'when he proved to be a veritable Balaam in commending the lecturer to the audience. "Why should we want to know anything about foreign cavalry?" he asked. "We have better cavalry of our own. I fear, gentlemen, that the Army is in danger of becoming a mere debating society." '[11]

Writing in his Diary on 5 November 1881, the anniversary of Inkerman Day, the Duke remarks: 'What glorious recollections are connected with that memorable day and how things have changed since then, too sad and I prefer the *past* to the present.' Breakfasting with Sir Almeric Fitzroy some time after Queen Victoria's death, the Duke was 'very outspoken, as ever, and regretted the indifference to old-time usages,' which marked Edwardian times. When the Duchess of Cambridge died he kept the house and grounds of Kew Cottage exactly as they were in her lifetime. Not a picture was changed or a stick of furniture moved. Indeed when it was realized that the piano in the library had been placed out of position, Mrs Mold, the housekeeper, had it immediately turned round 'and put as it was when Princess Mary used to play to Prince Teck.' Kew Cottage, at least, was a province where no busybody could meddle with the past.

Some of the Duke's resistance to innovations in the Army proceeded from his conviction that change should be gradual. He was quite capable of appreciating the need for 'modifications to bring matters about to modern requirements,' but he believed it was 'far more advantageous' to introduce reforms 'slowly and gradually . . . and to give time for reflection on trial.' 'The

Army,' he told Wolseley in 1890, 'has of late years had more changes than enough, and wants absolute *rest* from constant surprises . . . I am afraid you don't believe in *sentiment*, but I do so *strongly*, especially in military matters . . . I am old-fashioned, you will say; but I don't think I can be accused of having sacrificed any real efficiency to old-fashioned notions of the past.'[12] The Duke's military experience led him to conclude that the spirit of an army depended upon tradition, regimental pride and trust between officers and men. As the woodman's axe in a matter of hours can destroy the growth of centuries, so rash reforms could overnight annihilate the morale of the Queen's Army. Rational reforms, however efficient in themselves, if they diminished the soldier's will to fight, if they deprived him of a sense of patriotism and history, or made him careless of the honour of his regiment, were a liability rather than an asset.

Sometimes the Duke's resistance to change hardened into unthinking habit, and encouraged him to condemn what he had not troubled to understand. During the manœuvres of 1871 H.R.H. had remarked that 'outpost duties of Infantry still require much study.' Accepting the hint, Hamley, the Commandant of the Staff College, examined the subject and evolved a new system. In the autumn of 1876, 'He applied for an opportunity of testing his new methods by putting them into practice with troops from Aldershot . . . The Duke signified a desire to be present . . . The day was a vile one, the troops hazy as to what was required of them, and their officers little inclined to enthusiasm over the experiment . . . The Duke, accompanied by Airey, who was on the eve of relinquishing the appointment of Adjutant General, rode round the outpost line. He had been puzzled at the preliminary explanation he received, and mystification grew as he listened to the answers to questions he put to regimental officers he encountered. One thing was sufficiently clear to him: that here was a complete reversal of the existing system. He turned to Airey and exclaimed, "If this is right, Airey, what we have been doing all our lives is wrong!" Airey assented. The Duke called for the assembly of all officers. Hamley and his students were there, the General Officer Commanding-in-Chief, Aldershot Command, and his staff, hanging on the words of the Army's Chief. Without inviting the umpires' comments the Duke gave his criticism. He roundly condemned the new system, and mercilessly lashed Hamley with vigorous destructive sarcasm in front of all. Nor would he listen then or later to any submission by Hamley to the effect that the experiment, as staged, was an unfair one, on unsuitable ground, by troops who had no opportunity of grasping the parts they were playing before an audience who had taken no trouble to discover what they were to see, nor to read his pamphlet on the subject.'[13]

Although Hamley's schemes did not commend themselves to the Commander-in-Chief, he often expressed interest in novelties. When Colonel Burnaby crossed the Channel by balloon in 1882, he was sent to report himself to the Duke on his return from what had been an unauthorized expedition. Instead of a stinging rebuke, the Colonel found himself subjected to a cross-examination about flying. H.R.H. 'was much interested in the enterprise, and admired Burnaby's pluck, and said he would like to go up in a balloon himself with Burnaby, only he feared "there would be such a hullabaloo." '[14]

The Duke was fascinated by the invention of the phonograph, and a recording he made on one of the earliest machines is still in existence. He was the first member of the royal family 'to make a practical trial of the motorcar in the early stage of its legal existence.' While staying with Sir Berkeley Digby Sheffield in January 1897 at Normanby Park in Lincolnshire, one of the guests took H.R.H. a drive in his Bollée car, despite the fact that snow lay thick on the ground. 'After the mechanism had been thoroughly explained his Royal Highness took his seat as a passenger and made a prolonged tour in the park. The going was heavy on account of the snow, and some slight ascents were slowly negotiated, but the Bollée acquitted herself most satisfactorily. At the end of the trip the Duke not only expressed his delight with the novel sport, but mounting into the chauffeur's seat, he made some little runs on his own account, to test his powers of steering and controlling motorcars.'[15] When Edward VII took the Duke a drive on 25 August 1901, H.R.H. observed: 'We went most steadily and safely and without dust, but I cannot say I like the mode of conveyance and prefer carriages *with* horses.'

At no time was the Duke unaware that his critics thought him reactionary and obstructive. When discussing his career with Colonel Verner, appointed to write his official military biography, he concluded an interview by saying: 'You can let them know that I am not quite such a damned old fool as some of them say.' In a speech delivered at Edinburgh in 1895, just before he gave up office, he said that he had sometimes been 'twitted' with the statement that age had made him very loath to carry out changes. 'A man could not pass through life as long as he had without having seen some very remarkable changes in every sphere, and as science advanced and intelligence increased, change must find its way into every condition of life and into every profession. Therefore to say that he had objected to changes was simply ridiculous. He should not be in the position which he had held for thirty nine years if such had been the case, but he had always felt that changes must be effected with much prudence and consideration. If they made changes for change's sake, he thought they were doing a most dangerous thing indeed. If, on the other hand, they made changes for the sake of improving and advancing, not only would they be beneficial in themselves, but they were essential in order to keep pace with the world at large. Therefore he could not understand how anyone in his position could put his face against changes which must come. He had never hindered these changes, but had accepted them and supported them, and led them to a great extent.'[16]

Many of the Secretaries for War with whom the Duke worked paid tribute to the loyal way in which he carried out decisions once they had been reached. While he was Commander-in-Chief the Army was utterly transformed from top to bottom, and not always in accordance with his ideas. 'Only when those transformations can be viewed from some distance of time in their true perspective,' wrote Fortescue in his great *History of the British*

Army, 'can justice be done to the unfailing loyalty and tact with which the Duke discharged his most difficult and trying duties.'[17]

Even the Commander-in-Chief's most ferocious critics could hardly pretend that he did not possess an extraordinary knowledge of military affairs. Gathorne Hardy, when he went to the War Office, was greatly impressed by the Duke's familiarity with 'all the minutest details of the work of his high office.' H.R.H.'s grasp of his duties was assisted by an enviable memory. Once Princess Augusta was looking in her room for 'John Gilpin,' 'on which the Duke set forth and recited to us the whole poem straight off!! I should think it is a hundred years since he heard, or thought of it!!' 'The Duke's mastery of the working of the whole complex machinery of the Army was phenomenal,' wrote Lord Redesdale. 'Still more extraordinary was his knowledge of its officers. This was due to the fact that during the whole time of his tenure of office no promotion to any rank above that of captain was made without his personal investigation and sanction. In this way, being gifted with a singularly retentive memory, he had an intimate acquaintance with the careers and capabilities of all the senior officers.'[18]

Randolph Churchill in 1887 presided over a Committee of Enquiry into Army Finance. One of the Committee members was a Lancashire M.P. called Jennings, who boasted that he would expose the Duke's incompetence by ruthless cross-examination, and was amazed to find himself come off worst in the encounter. Jennings pressed the Commander-in-Chief to tell him how many guns and how much ammunition the Army had available in an emergency. ' "I cannot tell you," said the Duke. "I fear I must insist on an answer," said Jennings, and appealed to the Chairman for support, which he received. "If you don't know your duty, sir, I know mine," said the Duke, "and that is not to tender our official secrets to the whole of Europe, as you propose. I won't answer." Jennings, after his illustrious opponent had left the chair, said to me admiringly: "That old man knows as much about his business as the very best storekeeper does about his shop." '[19]

The high opinion which Jennings formed of the Commander-in-Chief was shared by many whose expert knowledge entitled them to speak with more authority. General Dillon, an experienced and able officer, delighted the Duchess of Cambridge by his appreciation of her son. 'General Dillon came,' wrote Lady Geraldine on 5 September 1880. 'He began speaking of the Duke and it did one's heart *good* to hear in what terms!! The immensely high opinions of him, of his nobility and greatness of character, his worth, his high qualities, abilities and merits! Most touching and gratifying to hear his honest and most genuine admiration for him! He told us that one day he was speaking with Sir Charles Yorke of the Duke's *marvellous* knowledge of the Army and every individual in it and Sir Charles enlarging on his great qualities, said: "With his extraordinary powers of memory, his quickness of perception, his wonderful precision of judgement, he does not at all realize how *great* he is!" As Dillon said, impossible to condense a character more correctly and accurately! He talked of his excellent speeches, how well expressed and never missing a point, bringing everything in! And said what a misfortune they had not all been cut out and collected. He spoke of his great and extraordinary industry, the *amount* of work he does! That at the office everything is in his own handwriting, how he reads and signs everything! Every promotion, every nomination his own doing, *his* own decision; how his own first thought, *his* judgement always proves the best, "He could buy and sell us all!" How able and clear and concise his writings are, always hitting the point! He told us he had just read such a *clever, able, admirable* paper from him upon Kandahar and all the Afghanistan question! which is to go to the Queen and the Cabinet and Lord Ripon, quite admirable and again his taste and tact and judgement in such a paper as he had to write to Wolseley at the Cape, in fact a reprimand! but so *ably* and judiciously done and with such good feeling, that he, Wolseley, could not but feel it as such, yet it was *impossible* he *could* take exception to it, or resent it! He told us how all the Army felt *no one* but he could hold his position! And how he Dillon was talking with someone the other day of how remarkable it is in the length of time he has been in that prominent responsible position how *little* that is ill natured or nasty has ever been said against him, how the ill disposed have been unable to find anything to fasten upon! Of his excellence and kindliness of heart and consideration for others! Of his *great* and perfect honesty, that can evince no suspicion; his *total* absence of vanity!'

Nearly all attacks on the Duke may be traced to Wolseley and his 'Press gang.' 'The dear old Bumble-bee,' he told his wife in 1890, 'is to me now thank God as far removed as the dodo is from the thoughts of a modern ornithologist—what a huge mass of humbug he is and what a swindle upon the public. Drawing a very large sum annually from the State and remaining on to injure our Army still further as much as he can. It would have paid the nation, hand over hand to have given him an extra £20,000 a year twenty years ago to leave the Army. Had he done so, we should now have had an Army.'[20]

It is not always easy to know what Wolseley really thought or believed. His letters to his wife were intended principally to amuse her, and in order to be entertaining he exaggerated, as Irishmen will. The Duke only too often exasperated him and frustrated his plans. Consequently it relieved him to say behind the old man's back what he could not say to his face. In Wolseley's autobiography, intended for the world, and written when the flames of controversy had turned to ashes, he described the Duke of Cambridge as 'a very clever Prince, who knew the Army thoroughly, and was looked up to and most justly liked by all ranks in it. Educated to believe in the Army as he found it, because it had been made by the Great Duke of Wellington, he honestly and firmly believed that what had been created by such a master of war must be the best for all time. He had not, apparently, fully taken in the great changes which the system of universal military service had produced in European armies. He refused to believe in an Army Reserve, and honestly looked upon our endeavour to create one here as not only a mad folly, but as a crime against the State. No more loyal and devoted Englishman ever wore a red coat, but nothing would or could convince him that an Army Reserve in this country would be forthcoming when wanted. Recent experience, however, has proved how absolutely wrong the old school of officers were upon this point, and no man more than His Royal Highness has ever been thoroughly converted to modern ideas on this point. I have mentioned this about a Royal Personage under whom I was long privileged to work, because I liked him more and more the better I knew him. Indeed no one who served for so many years on his staff could fail to love his amiable qualities, or to admire his manliness of feeling. His honesty of purpose, loyalty to the Army, devotion to duty, sincere patriotism and deep and real attachment to his Queen and country pervaded all he did. I rejoice to have this opportunity for thus expressing my feelings regarding so great a Personage, because in the course of our long intimacy I had often to differ materially from his views upon Army matters and to propose changes in which, at the time, he did not always concur.'[21]

Wolseley, despite many notable conflicts with the Duke, was chivalrous to him in his old age, and used to visit him until the end. 'Lord Wolseley came at twelve,' wrote the Duke on 8 July 1903, 'and we had a long talk together over most of the events of the present day, which was most interesting to me. He is always most agreeable.' After the Duke's death, Sir Adolphus FitzGeorge wrote to Wolseley consulting him on the advisability of presenting his father's papers to the Royal United Service Institution. Wolseley replied that the idea was an admirable one. He continued his letter by saying that although he often differed from the Duke's views upon Army matters, 'I always had a great respect for His opinions. They were invariably honest and straightforward, and coming from a Soldier of very long experience in our Army, they always deserved—and met with from me—the most serious consideration. At all times and upon all occasions, even when we differed most, I never for a moment forgot that He was a member of our Royal Family, and I have reason to know that he fully recognized that fact. He was usually outspoken in His views upon men and measures, but He never "hit below the belt." He was a very good friend and a strong hater. Unfortunately for Him, He often had about Him flatterers who were bad counsellors and who led Him astray, that is, according to my poor judgement. His weak point was—I thought—listening to them, and I was, perhaps, too much behind the scenes to remain silent when, as I thought, they misled Him. Had He been left to exercise his own judgement, he would, I felt, have avoided much of the trouble he had with some of the Secretaries of State for War whom He was called upon to deal with. This was my opinion, because He certainly was a man of great ability.'[22]

One of the most frequent duties of the Commander-in-Chief was making speeches. As the Duke supported many charities, and as he was the obvious person to propose the toast of the Army on almost any occasion, he was overwhelmed with requests and invitations. 'He was a capital after-dinner speaker,' wrote Lord Redesdale. 'His downright, honest periods, given out with that sonorous and beautiful voice for which the descendants of George the Third are famous, went straight home to the hearts of his audience.' 'As a speaker of a certain kind,' said a soldier who had often heard him, 'the Duke was certainly second to none in the Kingdom. H.R.H. came down to inspect the regiment at Aldershot before it sailed for India somewhere in the Nineties. I was present on the occasion as a guest of the regiment. At the end of the inspection, the Duke formed the regiment up in quarter-column and made a speech which lasted some ten minutes. At the end of that time I will not say that there was not a dry eye in the regiment, but I will certainly say that a number of the N.C.O.'s and men were very visibly affected. It was a very wonderful speech, manly and vigorous, but at the same time intensely pathetic. The Duke was at that time an old man, and the speech was in the nature of a lasting farewell to a regiment which he loved.'[23]

The Army's affection for the Duke was partly inspired by the trouble he always took over individuals. Every soldier, no matter what his rank, knew he could go to the Duke 'and that he would spare neither time nor trouble to redress any genuine injustice.'

Sir Harry Johnston described H.R.H. as 'one of the kindest and most considerate persons I ever encountered: far more patient and painstaking as a listener and a setter-right than his colleague Lord Wolseley—infinitely more so than a Kitchener or a Buller.' It was one of the principal reasons why the Duke 'won something that Wolseley with his faultless efficiency, never won; the deep, universal affection of his Army.' The Duke's papers abound with letters in which he concerned himself with the plight of individuals. An officer's widow, Mrs Harriet Middleton, whose husband died on service in India, sent the Duke a copy of the last letter she received from him. 'I feel,' he told his wife, 'that my work here has in many ways affected my health, but I have worked honestly for the good of my regiment and country and for my dear and good master the Duke of Cambridge. He will I know assist you with the darling boys and you may go to him with perfect confidence that he will treat you kindly for my sake. Tell him what I say and I should like him to know how grateful I am to him for all his many favours and personal kindness to me.'[24] What form the Duke's help took is not related, but a letter of gratitude shows that the appeal was not unavailing.

The position of the Commander-in-Chief was in some ways patriarchal. He knew almost every officer by sight and name, and he felt particularly responsible for Army Cadets. His frequent visits to Woolwich and Sandhurst made him familiar with the rising generation of soldiers. When necessity demanded, H.R.H. upbraided the young gentlemen for a variety of shortcomings. 'The Duke goes to Woolwich,' wrote Lady Geraldine on 23 July 1886. 'He was not pleased! The report of the Cadets, as to conduct was *excellent*, but as to their studies very bad indeed! so that he had to pitch into them tremendously, he did not wish to do so before the reporters, for it to go forth to the whole world, so he made them a speech in public, pro bono publico! and then sent them all into another room and there in private pitched into them finely!!'

The Duke's immense correspondence with Generals all over the globe reveals the detailed interest and knowledge he showed in their campaigns, in their personal welfare and in the troops under their command. Lord Napier, to mention a single example, never forgot the 'generous support' H.R.H. afforded him in Abyssinia in 1868. Often the Commander-in-Chief would sit up late into the night, writing letters full of advice and encouragement and news from England, to catch the Indian Mail. He was no remote figurehead, supreme and unapproachable, but a genial ever-present Chief, easily moved to wrath, but with a heart full of compassion. Lady Jephson relates that her brother 'was once walking behind two soldiers when the Duke drove past. "There goes *dear* old Garge," said one, "long life to him!".'[25]

Those who knew the Duke intimately, officers immediately under him in the Horse Guards or his A.D.C.'s, found him a thoughtful and delightful companion. Airey, just before retiring from being Adjutant General, told the Duchess of Cambridge that 'in all the fifteen years I have been connected with H.R.H. *never once* have I had an angry, impatient fretful word from him!' Edmond Mildmay, an A.D.C. since Crimean days, declared that the Duke was 'without exception the most *charming* travelling companion anyone ever travelled with!! Always cheery, bright, taking everything well, facilitating everything, so that Edmond always feels the Duke is travelling with him, not he with the Duke!'[26]

Outside the War Office, in the middle of the road, stands a statue of the Duke of Cambridge, looking down Whitehall towards the Cenotaph. It was Edward VII who suggested that the memorial should take the form of a 'big man on a big horse.' Lady Geraldine, who visited the sculptor, Captain Jones, in his studio, thought his work 'a very fine and noble thing.' At the present time not many people notice it, as they hurry by, and those inquisitive enough to give it a second glance, wonder who on earth the Duke of Cambridge was, and what he did to earn so prominent a position. The answer is simple. He devoted his entire life to the service of his Queen and country—ideals which in Victorian days required neither apology nor justification—and for almost forty years, in an age of revolutionary change, preserved, despite repeated assaults, those customs and traditions which are the life and soul of an army. He preferred sentiment to calculation and men to measures; and he knew from the roots of his being, what many of his adversaries never fully appreciated: that British soldiers were not figures in a ledger, but creatures of flesh and blood, 'mortal men,' who needed to be cajoled, humoured, and, in supreme moments, inspired. No army could have sustained those feats of endurance and courage, which became almost commonplaces of Victorian achievement, unless possessed by a living sense of past glories and triumphs. We owe it to the Duke of Cambridge that, despite the reorganization of every regiment in the Kingdom, old customs endured, old traditions flourished and old loyalties survived. That this was so, was no mere indulgence of the reactionary whim of a royal retrograde: it was the salvation of the Queen's Army.

THE DUKE OF CAMBRIDGE'S CONTEMPORARIES 1856–1895

PRIME MINISTERS		SECRETARIES OF STATE FOR WAR		ADJUTANTS GENERAL
1856	Palmerston		Panmure	Sir G. Wetherall
1858	Derby	1858	General Peel	1860 Sir J. Y. Scarlett
1859	Palmerston	1859	Sidney Herbert	1865 Lord William
1865	Russell	1861	Sir G. Lewis	Paulet
1866	Derby	1863	Earl de Grey	1870 Sir R. Airey
1868	Disraeli		(Marquis of	1876 Sir C. Ellice
1868	Gladstone		Ripon)	1882 Sir G. Wolseley
1874	Beaconsfield	1866	Hartington	1882 Sir R. Taylor
1880	Gladstone	1866	General Peel	1882 Lord Wolseley
1885	Salisbury	1867	Sir J. Pakington	1885 Sir A. Alison
1886	Gladstone	1868	Cardwell	1885 Viscount Wolseley
1886	Salisbury	1874	Gathorne Hardy	1890 Sir R. Buller
1892	Gladstone		(Earl of	
1894	Rosebery		Cranbrook)	
1895	Salisbury	1878	Col. Stanley	
			(Earl of Derby)	
		1880	Childers	
		1882	Hartington	
		1885	W. H. Smith	
		1886	Campbell- Bannerman	
		1886	W. H. Smith	
		1887	Stanhope	
		1892	Campbell- Bannerman	
		1895	Lansdowne	

NOTE ON SECRETARY OF STATE-AT-WAR

Originally the Secretary-at-War was Military Secretary to the Commander-in-Chief, but in 1704 the civilian Head of the War Department assumed the title. The post was absorbed in 1854 in that of Secretary for War, and was formally abolished in 1863. The Secretary for War was a Secretary of State with wider powers and responsibilities than those exercised by the Secretary-at-War.

NOTE ON SOURCES

There are two main manuscript sources for the life of H.R.H. the Duke of Cambridge. The first is the Royal Archives at Windsor Castle, and the second the papers in the possession of the FitzGeorge family. In addition to these, there are papers in the political collections of the British Museum, the Public Record Office, and in the library of the Royal United Service Institution.

The material in the Royal Archives falls into five categories. First there are the Duke's own papers, as yet uncatalogued, kept in the Diary Room. Secondly there are the Papers of the Cambridge family, including Queen Mary's Papers. Thirdly there are a miscellany of Royal Manuscripts (e.g. the Queen's Diary, the Queen's letters, the Duke of Connaught's papers, etc.). Fourthly there is a huge section devoted to Army affairs, and finally there is Lady Geraldine Somerset's Diary.

The FitzGeorge collection consists mainly of letters of H.R.H. and Mrs FitzGeorge, letters of the FitzGeorge sons to and from their parents, letters to H.R.H. from the Queen, and the Duke's Diaries. Some of these, which were available to the official biographers soon after H.R.H.'s death, have since been lost.

The principal printed sources are Sheppard's *Memoir* and Verner's *Military Life of H.R.H. the Duke of Cambridge*: both in two volumes.

A large number of other manuscripts and books have been consulted. Reference to the 'Notes on Chapters' will give further details of some of the material on which this biography is based.

NOTES ON CHAPTERS

The following notes are designed to give the sources of information upon which the Chapters are based. I have used the abbreviation R.A. for the Royal Archives at Windsor. I have not given references in the text (i) to the source of extracts which the text itself reveals. For example, a dated Diary entry has been left to speak for itself. Where the name of an author is omitted it may be presumed to be the Duke. The 'Note on Sources' indicates where letters, Diaries, etc. may be consulted. (ii) To letters, etc. in the FitzGeorge Collection, which is uncatalogued and not generally available. Reference is only made to the FitzGeorge Collection where the text omits information, such as the date of a letter or who it is from. (iii) To brief quotations from reasonably obvious or unimportant sources.

It is not to be presumed that an extract for which a Manuscript source is given has therefore never appeared in print. I have read both in Manuscript, in Manuscript copies, in published collections, and in books quoting such collections, extracts, for example, from Queen Victoria's letters or Cardwell's papers. References made in these notes to such extracts have been ascribed indiscriminately to the original document, to published collected papers or to secondary sources. The inconsistency involved seemed preferable to the overwhelming labour of eliminating it.

NOTES ON CHAPTER I

1. *The Complete Peerage.* Edited by the Hon. Vicery Gibbs. St Catherine Press. 1912. Vol. II. pp. 496–7.
2. *A Short Memoir of his late Royal Highness Adolphus Duke of Cambridge.* Lieut.-General Sir James Reynett. A pamphlet. 1858. p. 28.
3. *Queen Adelaide.* Mark Hopkirk. John Murray. 1946. p. 10.
4. *H.R.H. George Duke of Cambridge.* Sheppard. Longmans. 1906. Vol. I. p. 5.
5. *The Journal of Mrs Arbuthnot.* Edited by Francis Bamford and the Duke of Wellington. Macmillan & Co. Ltd. 1950. Vol. II. pp. 252–3.

6. *The Life and Letters of The Fourth Earl of Clarendon*. Sir H. Maxwell. Edward Arnold. 1913. Vol. I. p. 48.
7. *Correspondence of Sarah Spencer Lady Lyttelton 1787–1870*. Edited by the Hon. Mrs Hugh Wyndham. John Murray. 1912. p. 294.
8. *Gossip of the Century*. Byrne. Ward and Downey. 1892. Vol. I. pp. 67–9.
9. *A Memoir of Her Royal Highness Princess Mary Adelaide Duchess of Teck*. C. Kinloch Cooke. John Murray. 1900. Vol. I. p. 24.
10. *Memories*. Lord Redesdale. Hutchinson. 1915. Vol. II. p. 703.
11. Ella Taylor's Reminiscences. R.A. Addl. Mss. A/8. 390.
12. *A Memoir of Her Royal Highness Princess Mary Adelaide Duchess of Teck*. C. Kinloch Cooke. John Murray. 1900. Vol. I. pp. 26–7.
13. Lady Geraldine Somerset's Diary. 11 November 1886. R.A.
14. *H.R.H. George Duke of Cambridge*. Sheppard. Longmans. 1906. Vol. I. pp. 9–10.
15. *Letters of Dorothea Princess Lieven*. Edited by Lionel G. Robinson. Longmans. 1902. p. 373.
16. Diary of Queen Adelaide. R.A. Georgian Addl. Mss. 21/7.
17. *Bygone Years. Recollections*. Leveson Gower. Murray. 1905. p. 4.
18. *Lord James of Hereford*. Lord Askwith. Bevin. 1930. p. 213.
19. Diary of Queen Adelaide. Preface. R.A. Georgian Addl. Mss. 21/7.
20. Lady Geraldine Somerset's Diary. 25 December 1886. R.A.
21. *Glimpses of King William IV and Queen Adelaide*. Cecil White. Brimley Johnson. 1902. pp. 33–4.
22. *H.R.H. George Duke of Cambridge*. Sheppard. Longmans. 1906. Vol. I. p. 26.
23. *H.R.H. George Duke of Cambridge*. Sheppard. Longmans. 1906. Vol. I. pp. 39–40.
24. The Queen's Diary. 16 May 1838. R.A.
25. *H.R.H. George Duke of Cambridge*. Sheppard. Longmans. 1906. Vol. I. pp. 56–7.
26. *Military Life of H.R.H. The Duke of Cambridge*. Verner. Murray. 1905. Vol. I. pp. 23–4.
27. Prince Albert to his Father. 6 March 1838. R.A. Addl. Mss. A/14.
28. *Henry Ponsonby, His Life and Letters*. Arthur Ponsonby. Macmillan. 1953. p. 92.
29. *Under Five Reigns*. Lady Dorothy Nevill. Methuen & Co. Ltd. 1910. p. 262. *Dramatic Reminiscences*. G. Vandenhoff. Thomas W. Cooper & Co. 1860. p. 90. *The World*. 22 January 1890.
30. *Memoirs*. Sir Almeric Fitzroy. Hutchinson & Co. 1925. pp. 299–300.
31. Duke of Cambridge to the Queen. 21 April 1889. R.A. L.2.111.
32. Duke of Cambridge to Adolphus FitzGeorge. 11 September and 29 October 1869. FitzGeorge Papers.

33. Queen to Duke of Connaught. 11 October 1882. R.A. Addl. Mss. A/15. 3785.
34. *Famous Morganatic Marriages*. Kingston. Stanley Paul. 1919. p. 157.
35. Duke of Cambridge to the Queen. 13 January 1890. R.A. Z.72.22.
36. *Famous Morganatic Marriages*. Kingston. Stanley Paul. 1919. p. 160.

NOTES ON CHAPTER II

1. *The Greville Memoirs*. Edited by Strachey and Fulford. Macmillan. 1938. Vol. 5. pp. 49–50, 77–9.
2. Lady Geraldine Somerset's Diary. 7 April 1884. R.A.
3. *Military Life of H.R.H. The Duke of Cambridge*. Verner. Murray. 1905. Vol. 1. p. 26.
4. *H.R.H. George Duke of Cambridge*. Sheppard. Longmans. 1906. Vol. 1. p. 85.
5. *H.R.H. George Duke of Cambridge*. Sheppard. Longmans. 1906. Vol. 1. p. 88.
6. Duke of Cambridge to W. F. Forster. 5 January and June 1848. Duke's Papers. R.A.
7. Duke of Cambridge to W. F. Forster. 21 December 1849. Duke's Papers. R.A.
8. *The Letters of Queen Victoria*. Edited by G. E. Buckle. Murray. 1926. Second series. Vol. II. p. 151.
9. *H.R.H. George Duke of Cambridge*. Sheppard. Longmans. 1906. Vol. 1. pp. 88–9.
10. Memorandum, April 1849. Dublin. FitzGeorge Papers.
11. *H.R.H. George Duke of Cambridge*. Sheppard. Longmans. 1906. Vol. 1. p. 94.
12. *A Memoir of Her Royal Highness Princess Mary Adelaide Duchess of Teck*. C. Kinloch Cooke. Murray. 1900. Vol. 1. p. 116.
13. Memorandum of Prince Albert. R.A. L.23.19.
14. The Queen to Lord John Russell. 1850. R.A. L.23, 20 and 21.
15. Prince Albert to Duke of Saxe-Coburg. R.A. Add. A/14.96.
16. Memorandum of Prince Albert. 1850. R.A. L.23.32.
17. FitzGeorge Papers.
18. *A Memoir of Her Royal Highness Princess Mary Adelaide Duchess of Teck*. C. Kinloch Cooke. Murray. 1900. Vol. 1. pp. 131–2.
19. The Queen to Duke of Cambridge. 18 November 1852. FitzGeorge Papers.
20. Memorandum of Prince Albert. September 1852. R.A. E2.L4.
21. *The War Office Past and Present*. Wheeler. Methuen. 1914. pp. 135–6.

22. Mrs FitzGeorge to Duke of Cambridge. December. Undated. Duke of Cambridge to Mrs FitzGeorge. 6 October 1850 and 29 January 1851. FitzGeorge Papers.
23. Mrs FitzGeorge to Duke of Cambridge. Undated. Duke of Cambridge to Mrs FitzGeorge. 26 June 1848. FitzGeorge Papers.
24. *A History of the British Army.* J. W. Fortescue. Macmillan. 1899–1930. Vol. XIII. p. 534.
25. *The War Office.* Hampden Gordon. Putnam. 1935. p. 35.
26. *The Military Forces of the Crown.* Clode. Murray. 1869. Vol. 1. p. 263.
27. *Story of a Soldier's Life.* Wolseley. Constable. 1903. Vol. 1. p. 53.
28. *Parliament and the Army.* Lieut.-Colonel Omond. Cambridge University Press. 1933. p. 82.
29. *The Staff and the Staff College.* Godwin-Austen. Constable. 1927. p. 86.
30. Lord Wolseley to the Duke of Cambridge. 11 December 1884. Duke's Papers. R.A.
31. *The Destruction of Lord Raglan.* Hibbert. Longmans. 1961. p. 8.

NOTES ON CHAPTER III

1. *H.R.H. George Duke of Cambridge.* Sheppard. Longmans. 1906. Vol. I. p. 121.
2. *Military Life of H.R.H. The Duke of Cambridge.* Verner. Murray. 1905. Vol. I. p. 66.
3. Colonel Seymour to Colonel Phipps. Scutari. 27 May 1854. R.A. F.1.11.
4. Prince Edward of Saxe-Weimar to the Queen. 8 July 1854. R.A. F.1.17.
5. *Seventy-one Years of a Guardsman's Life.* General Sir George Higginson. Smith, Elder and Co. 1916. p. 129.
6. Mrs FitzGeorge to the Duke of Cambridge. 11 September 1854. FitzGeorge Papers.
7. *This for Remembrance.* Lord Coleridge. Fisher Unwin. 1925. p. 89.
8. Mrs FitzGeorge to the Duke of Cambridge. 20 September, 5 June and 30 June 1854. FitzGeorge Papers.
9. Duke of Cambridge to Mrs FitzGeorge. 28 June, 18 June 1854. FitzGeorge Papers.
10. Mrs FitzGeorge to the Duke of Cambridge. 16 October, 1 and 14 June, 6 July 1854. FitzGeorge Papers.
11. Lord Wolseley to the Duke of Cambridge. 9 November 1894. Duke's Papers. R.A.
12. Mrs FitzGeorge to the Duke of Cambridge. 1 June, 24 May 1854. Duke of Cambridge to Mrs FitzGeorge. 18 June 1854. FitzGeorge Papers.
13. *The Destruction of Lord Raglan.* Hibbert. Longmans. 1961. p. 181.
14. Captain Gordon. 6 December 1854. R.A. F.1.35.

15. Duke of Newcastle to Lord Raglan. 27 November 1854. Public Record Office. W.O. 6/70. p. 50.
16. *The Three Sergeants*. Morris. Quoted Verner Vol. I. p. 83.
17. Prince of Wales. Memorandum. 1856. R.A. T.1.110.
18. *The Correspondence of Priscilla, Countess of Westmorland*. Edited by Lady Weigall. Murray. 1909. p. 247.
19. *Richard Cobden. The International Man*. J. A. Hobson. Fisher Unwin. 1918. p. 115.
20. Duke of Cambridge to Duchess of Cambridge. 18 November. R.A. Addl. Mss. 8/8. 208.
21. Duke of Cambridge to Mrs FitzGeorge. 14 and 22 November 1854. FitzGeorge Papers.
22. Prince Edward of Saxe-Weimar to the Queen. 28 November 1854. R.A. G.20.29.
23. Duke of Cambridge to Mrs FitzGeorge. 29 November 1854. FitzGeorge Papers.
24. Queen to Duke of Cambridge. 15 December 1854. R.A. G.20.128.
25. *The Life of Florence Nightingale*. Sir E. Cook. Macmillan. 1914. Vol. I. pp. 384–5.
26. Lord W. Paulet to the Duke of Cambridge. 26 March 1855. Duke's Papers. R.A.
27. Duke of Cambridge to Duchess of Cambridge. 8 November 1854, 1 January 1855, 30 November 1854, 18 December 1854, 7 January 1855, 22 January 1855. R.A. G.18.119. Addl. Mss. A/8, 175, 172, 194, 176, 180.
28. The Queen to Lord Raglan. 1 January 1855. R.A. G.21.65.
29. The Queen to the Duke of Cambridge. 19 January 1855. R.A. G.22.59.
30. The Queen to Lord Raglan. 18 February 1855. R.A. G.24.73.
31. The Duke of Cambridge to the Queen. 24 November 1854. R.A. G.20.31.
32. *The Invasion of the Crimea*. Kinglake. Blackwood. 1863–1887. Vol. III. pp. 132–3.
33. Lord Wolseley to his Wife. 10 November 1884, 12 August 1887, 26 September 1884. Library of Royal United Service Institution.
34. Colonel Gordon to General Grey. 7 November 1854. Lord James Murray to Sir George Couper. 16 December 1854. Colonel Phipps to the Queen. Undated. R.A. G.18.112, G.20.129, F1.85.
35. *Louis Napoleon and the Recovery of France*. Simpson. Longmans. 1923. p. 270. Footnote 3.
36. Duke of Cambridge to Lord Hardinge. 4 February 1856. Duke's Papers. R.A.
37. *The Panmure Papers*. Edited by Sir G. Douglas. Hodder and Stoughton. 1908. Vol. I. p. 112.

38. *The Panmure Papers*. Edited by Sir G. Douglas. Hodder and Stoughton. 1908. Vol. I. pp. 282, 227–8, 379, 380.
39. *A History of the British Army*. Fortescue. 1899–1930. Vol. XIII. p. 140.
40. Sir G. Cornewall Lewis to Duke of Cambridge. 28 January 1863. Duke's Papers. R.A.
41. Sir George Brown to Duke of Cambridge. 4 February 1864. Duke's Papers. R.A.
42. The Duke of Cambridge to De Lacy Evans. 4 February 1864. Duke's Papers. R.A.
43. De Lacy Evans to the Duke of Cambridge. 7 February 1864. Duke's Papers. R.A.
44. Lord Clyde to the Duke of Cambridge. 11 February 1864. Duke's Papers. R.A.
45. Sir George Brown to the Duke of Cambridge. 11 February 1864. Duke's Papers. R.A.
46. *The Panmure Papers*. Edited by Sir G. Douglas. Hodder and Stoughton. 1908. Vol. I. p. 152.
47. *The Destruction of Lord Raglan*. Hibbert. Longmans. 1961. pp. 232–3.

NOTES ON CHAPTER IV

1. *The Letters of Queen Victoria*. Ed. Benson and Esher. Murray. 1907. First Series. Vol. III. pp. 252–3.
2. *H.R.H. George Duke of Cambridge*. Sheppard. Longmans. 1906. Vol. I. pp. 177–8, 179.
3. Mrs FitzGeorge to the Duke of Cambridge. 28 September 1856. FitzGeorge Papers.
4. *The Panmure Papers*. Ed. Sir G. Douglas. Hodder and Stoughton. 1908. Vol. I. pp. 86, 126.
5. *The Life of H.R.H. The Prince Consort*. Sir T. Martin. Smith, Elder and Co. 1874–1880. Vol. II. p. 255.
6. *The Life of Lord Roberts*. James. Hollis and Carter. 1954. p. 224.
7. *A History of the British Army*. Fortescue. Macmillan. 1899–1930. Vol. XIII. p. 539.
8. Duke of Cambridge to Sir Hope Grant. 3 December 1859. Duke's Papers. R.A.
9. *Military Life of H.R.H. The Duke of Cambridge*. Verner. Murray. 1905. Vol. I. p. 170.
10. Duke of Cambridge to Sir Colin Campbell. 10 December 1857. Duke's Papers. R.A.
11. *Military Life of H.R.H. The Duke of Cambridge*. Verner. Murray. 1905. Vol. I. pp. 215, 271.

12. The Duke of Cambridge to Lord Mansfield. 27 November 1865. Duke's Papers. R.A.

13. Queen to Lord Palmerston. 19 July 1857. Lord Palmerston to the Queen. 18 July 1857. R.A. E.9.81 and 80.

14. *The Monarchy in Politics*. Farrer. Fisher and Unwin. 1917. pp. 288–93.

15. *Military Life of H.R.H. The Duke of Cambridge*. Verner. Murray. 1905. Vol. I. p. 269.

16. Sir George Lewis to Duke of Cambridge. 8 October 1861. Duke of Cambridge to Sir George Lewis. 8 October 1861. Duke's Papers. R.A.

17. *The Life of Lord Wolseley*. Sir F. Maurice and Sir G. Arthur. Heinemann. 1924. p. 236.

18. *The Staff and the Staff College*. Godwin-Austen. Constable. 1927. pp. 225, 155.

19. *Stray Recollections*. Sir C. Callwell. Arnold. 1923. Vol. I. p. 289.

20. *The Staff and the Staff College*. Godwin-Austen. Constable. 1927. pp. 117–18.

21. *The Panmure Papers*. Ed. Sir G. Douglas. Hodder and Stoughton. 1908. Vol. I. pp. 283, 288.

22. *The Staff and the Staff College*. Godwin-Austen. Constable. 1927. p. 74.

23. *Stray Recollections*. Sir C. Callwell. Arnold. 1923. Vol. I. pp. 287–8.

24. *Records and Reactions*. Earl of Midleton. Murray. 1939. pp. 81–2.

25. *Notes of a Nomad*. Lady Jephson. Hutchinson. 1918. pp. 177–8.

26. *Sixty Years of a Soldier's Life*. Sir A. Turner. Methuen. 1912. pp. 30–1.

27. Duke of Cambridge to Sir Colin Campbell. 25 May 1858. 26 December 1857. Duke's Papers. R.A.

28. Duchess of Gloucester to Princess Mary Adelaide. 28 November 1851. R.A. Addl. Mss. A/8. L.342.

29. *A Memoir of Her Royal Highness Princess Mary Adelaide Duchess of Teck*. C. Kinloch Cooke. Murray. 1900. Vol. I. p. 89.

30. *H.R.H. George Duke of Cambridge*. Sheppard. Longmans. 1906. Vol. I. pp. 221–2.

31. The Queen to the King of the Belgians. 23 July 1863. R.A. Addl. Mss. Y.110.4.

32. *H.R.H. George Duke of Cambridge*. Sheppard. Longmans. 1906. Vol. I. p. 226.

33. Queen to King Leopold of the Belgians. Windsor, 9 June 1863. R.A. Addl. Mss. Y.109.34.

34. Duke of Cambridge to Lord de Grey. 8 March 1864. Duke's Papers. R.A.

35. *Military Life of H.R.H. The Duke of Cambridge*. Verner. Murray. 1905. Vol. I. pp. 297–8.

36. Duke of Cambridge to Sir Donald Rose. 5 April 1883. Duke's Papers. R.A.

37. *The War Office Past and Present*. Wheeler. Methuen. 1914. p. 169.

38. Duke of Cambridge to Queen. 31 December 1860. R.A. E.12.109.
39. Duke of Cambridge to Mrs FitzGeorge. 4 August 1858. Duke's Diary. 5 May 1866. FitzGeorge Papers.
40. Duke of Cambridge to Adolphus FitzGeorge. 29 October 1868. FitzGeorge Papers.
41. Duke of Cambridge to Adolphus FitzGeorge. 31 October, 17 October 1865. FitzGeorge Papers.
42. Duke of Cambridge to Adolphus FitzGeorge. 18 May, 3 December 1866, 27 March 1867. FitzGeorge Papers.
43. Duke of Cambridge to Mrs FitzGeorge. 1 October 1857. FitzGeorge Papers.
44. Duke of Cambridge to Mrs FitzGeorge. 31 August 1856. FitzGeorge Papers.
45. Duke's Diary. 3 April 1867. FitzGeorge Papers.
46. Duke of Cambridge to Mrs FitzGeorge. 2 August 1867. FitzGeorge Papers.

NOTES ON CHAPTER V

1. The Duke of Cambridge to Sir W. Mansfield. 10 December 1868. Duke's Papers. R.A.
2. *Lord Cardwell at the War Office*. Sir R. Biddulph. Murray. 1904. Appendix 1. pp. 249–54.
3. *Military Life of H.R.H. The Duke of Cambridge*. Verner. Murray. 1905. Vol. I. pp. 409, 416.
4. *Lord Haliburton*. Atlay. Smith, Elder & Co. 1909. p. 16.
5. Duke of Cambridge to General Forster. 31 August 1871. Duke's Papers. R.A.
6. *Military Life of H.R.H. The Duke of Cambridge*. Verner. Murray. 1905. Vol. I. p. 401. *The Reign of Queen Victoria*. Hector Bolitho. Collins. 1949. p. 268.
7. Lord Airey to the Duke of Cambridge. 20 August 1870. Duke's Papers. R.A.
8. Duke of Cambridge to Cardwell. 29 July 1870. 28 December 1869. Public Record Office. GD. 48. 3/14 and 12.
9. *Military Life of H.R.H. The Duke of Cambridge*. Verner. Murray. 1905. Vol. I. pp. 392, 399.
10. *The Life of Lord Wolseley*. Sir F. Maurice and Sir G. Arthur. Heinemann. 1924. p. xx.
11. Lord Lansdowne to Sir F. Knollys. 8 June 1897. R.A. T.10.63.
12. Queen's Diary. 2 August, 24 February 1871. R.A.
13. *Concerning Queen Victoria and Her Son*. Sir G. Arthur. Robert Hale. 1953. p. 153.

14. Lord A. Loftus to Duke of Cambridge. 21 July, 23 July, 30 July 1870. Duke's Papers. R.A.

15. *Queen Mary*. James Pope-Hennessy. Allen and Unwin. 1959. p. 101.

16. *Life of Lord Kitchener*. Sir G. Arthur. Macmillan. 1920. Vol. I. pp. 10–11.

17. *Letters of Field-Marshal Lord Napier of Magdala*. Ed. Lt. Col. Napier. Simpkin Marshall. 1936. pp. 28–9.

18. *From Wellington to Wavel*. Sir G. Arthur. Hutchinson. 1942. p. 72.

19. *The Life of Lord Roberts*. James. Hollis and Carter. 1954. pp. 170–1.

20. *Hansard*. 21 February 1871.

21. *Letters of Queen Victoria*. Ed. G. E. Buckle. Murray. 1928. Second Series. Vol. II. pp. 162–3.

22. *Money or Merit*. de Fonblanque. Charles J. Skeet. 1857. p. 12.

23. *Punch*. 5 August 1871.

24. *A Letter on Army Reform*. M. J. Higgins. Varty. 1855. pp. 3–4, 8.

25. *Lord Cardwell at the War Office*. Sir R. Biddulph. Murray. 1904. pp. 76, 78, 116.

26. 'Edward' T. Cardwell: Peelite. *Transactions of the American Philosophical Society*. New Series. Vol. 49. Part 2. 1959. p. 81. *Lord Cardwell at the War Office*. Sir R. Biddulph. Murray. 1904. pp. 116–17.

27. *Military Life of H.R.H. The Duke of Cambridge*. Verner. Murray. 1905. Vol. II. pp. 6–7.

28. *A Personal History of the Horse Guards*. Stocqueler. Hurst and Blackett. 1873. pp. 153–4.

29. *Military Forces of the Crown*. Clode. Murray. 1869. Vol. II. p. 86.

30. *Parliament and the Army*. Omond. Cambridge University Press. 1933. pp. 120–1. *Panmure Papers*. Ed. Sir G. Douglas. Hodder and Stoughton. 1908. Vol. II. p. 492.

31. Cardwell to Duke of Cambridge. 3 June 1871. Duke of Cambridge to Cardwell. 3 June 1871. Public Record Office. GD. 48. 4/15.

32. Duke of Cambridge to the Queen. 6 and 12 July 1871. Duke's Papers. R.A.

33. Queen to Gladstone (copy). 8 July 1871. Duke's Papers. R.A.

34. *The Letters of Queen Victoria*. Ed. G. E. Buckle. Murray. 1928. Second Series. Vol. II. p. 143.

35. *A Personal History of the Horse Guards*. Stocqueler. Hurst and Blackett. 1873. p. 285.

36. *Henry Ponsonby. His Life from His Letters*. A. Ponsonby. Macmillan. 1943. pp. 99–100.

37. *Under Five Reigns*. Lady Dorothy Nevill. Methuen. 1910. pp. 204–5.

38. *King Edward VII*. Sir S. Lee. Macmillan. 1925. Vol. I. pp. 13–14.

39. Queen to Duke of Connaught. 25 July 1875. R.A. Z.207.3.

40. Queen to Duke of Cambridge. 17 April 1873. FitzGeorge Papers.

NOTES ON CHAPTER VI

1. *Gathorne Hardy, First Earl of Cranbrook. A Memoir.* Ed. A. E. Gathorne Hardy. Longmans. 1910. Vol. I. p. 343.
2. *The Life of Lord Wolseley.* Sir F. Maurice and Sir G. Arthur. Heinemann. 1924. pp. 254, 284. Wolseley to Lady Wolseley. 7 July 1886. Royal United Service Institution.
3. *Before the Lamps Went Out.* Wingfield-Stratford. Hodder and Stoughton. 1945. pp. 21–3.
4. *From Wellington to Wavell.* Sir G. Arthur. Hutchinson. 1942. p. 74.
5. *Military Life of H.R.H. The Duke of Cambridge.* Verner. Murray. 1906. Vol. II. pp. 148–9.
6. *Military Life of H.R.H. The Duke of Cambridge.* Verner. Murray. 1906. Vol. II. pp. 159–60, 160–1.
7. *Letters of Field-Marshal Lord Napier.* Ed. H. D. Napier. Jarrold and Sons. 1936. p. 101.
8. Queen to Duke of Cambridge. 20 July 1879. Duke's Papers. R.A.
9. *Military Life of H.R.H. The Duke of Cambridge.* Verner. Murray. 1906. Vol. II. pp. 156–7.
10. Christine V de Aros to Duke of Cambridge. 11 August 1879. Duke's Papers. R.A.
11. Duke of Cambridge to Sir C. Campbell. 10 October, 24 November 1857. Duke's Papers. R.A.
12. *The Life of Lord Wolseley.* Sir F. Maurice and Sir G. Arthur. Heinemann. 1924. p. 236.
13. *Life of Lord Roberts.* James. Hollis and Carter. 1954. p. 212.
14. *Military Life of H.R.H. The Duke of Cambridge.* Verner. Murray. 1906. Vol. II. pp. 159, 165, 170–1, 172–3.
15. *The Life of Lord Wolseley.* Sir F. Maurice and Sir G. Arthur. Heinemann. 1924. p. 213.
16. Duke of Cambridge to Sir E. Johnson. 17 April 1879. Duke of Cambridge to Colonel Stanley. 31 May 1879. Duke's Papers. R.A.
17. Lord Wolseley to Lady Wolseley. 11 April 1880. Royal United Service Institution.
18. Duke of Cambridge to the Queen. February 1886. R.A. C.37.285.
19. *The Life and Correspondence of the Right Hon. Hugh C. E. Childers.* Lieut.-Colonel Spencer Childers. Murray. 1901. Vol. II. p. 53.
20. *The Life of Sir Charles Dilke.* Gwyn and Tuckwell. Murray. 1917. Vol. I. p. 472.
21. *The Life and Correspondence of the Right Hon. Hugh C. E. Childers.* Lieut.-Colonel Spencer Childers. Murray. 1901. Vol. II. p. 57.
22. Sir C. Phipps to Prince Consort. 5 June 1858. R.A. E.10.82.

23. *The Life of Lord Wolseley.* Sir F. Maurice and Sir G. Arthur. Heinemann. 1924. p. 140.
24. *Letters of Field-Marshal Lord Napier of Magdala.* Ed. Lieut.-Col. Napier. Jarrold & Sons. 1936. pp. 111, 114.
25. Lord Cranbrook to Duke of Cambridge. 24 November 1881. General Steele to Duke of Cambridge. 13 November 1881. Duke's Papers. R.A.
26. *The Life of Lord Wolseley.* Sir F. Maurice and Sir G. Arthur. Heinemann. 1924. pp. 231–2.
27. Duke of Cambridge to Lord Hartington. 28 September 1881. Duke's Papers. R.A.
28. Lady Geraldine Somerset's Diary. 8 August 1855. R.A.
29. Right Hon. Hugh Childers to Duke of Cambridge. 13 September 1881. Duke's Papers. R.A.
30. Duke of Cambridge to the Queen. 17 October 1881. Duke's Papers. R.A.
31. *The Life of Sir William Harcourt.* Constable. 1923. Vol. I. p. 416.
32. Sir H. Ponsonby to Duke of Cambridge. 7 November 1881. Duke of Cambridge to Queen. 10 November 1881. FitzGeorge Papers.
33. Prince of Wales to Duke of Cambridge. 28 November 1881. FitzGeorge Papers.

NOTES ON CHAPTER VII

1. *Military Life of H.R.H. The Duke of Cambridge.* Verner. Murray. 1905. Vol. II. pp. 202, 204–5.
2. Duke of Cambridge to Ponsonby. 21 December 1880. Duke of Cambridge to the Queen. 27 December 1880. Duke's Papers. R.A.
3. *Letters of Field-Marshal Lord Napier of Magdala.* Ed. Lt.-Colonel Napier. Jarrold and Sons. 1936. p. 95.
4. Lord Wolseley to Lady Wolseley. 3 September 1882. Royal United Service Institution.
5. Lady Geraldine Somerset's Diary. 16 November 1882. R.A.
6. Lady Geraldine Somerset's Diary. 14 March 1882. R.A.
7. Prince George to Duke of Cambridge. 19 August 1833. R.A. Addl. Mss. A/8. 501.
8. *The Staff and the Staff College.* Godwin-Austen. Constable. 1927. p. 184.
9. *Military Life of H.R.H. the Duke of Cambridge.* Verner. Murray. 1905. Vol. II. p. 251.
10. Duke of Cambridge to Sir E. Wood. 27 April 1883. Duke's Papers. R.A.
11. Duke of Cambridge to Sir Donald Stewart. 30 May, 6 June, 4 July 1884. Duke's Papers. R.A.
12. *Military Life of H.R.H. The Duke of Cambridge.* Verner. Murray. 1905. Vol. II. p. 270.
13. *The Staff and the Staff College.* Godwin-Austen. Constable. 1927. p. 207.

14. Lord Wolseley to Duke of Cambridge. 4 April 1885. Duke's Papers. R.A.
15. Lord Wolseley to Duke of Cambridge. 23 October 1884. Duke's Papers. R.A.
16. *Military Life of H.R.H. The Duke of Cambridge.* Verner. Murray. 1905. Vol. II. p. 299.
17. *The Life of Lord Wolseley.* Sir F. Maurice and Sir G. Arthur. Heinemann. 1924. p. 252.
18. Lord Wolseley to Lady Wolseley. 1 February 1887. Royal United Service Institution.
19. Lord Wolseley to Lady Wolseley. 20 September 1884. 1 February 1887. Royal United Service Institution.
20. *Records and Reactions.* Earl of Midleton. Murray. 1939. p. 82.
21. *The Life of Lord Wolseley.* Sir F. Maurice and Sir G. Arthur. Heinemann. 1924. p. 253.
22. Lord Wolseley to Lady Wolseley. 8 December 1855. 21 September 1882. Royal United Service Institution. Lady Geraldine Somerset's Diary. 3 April 1883. R.A.
23. *The Letters of Disraeli to Lady Bradford and Lady Chesterfield.* Ed. Marquis of Zetland. Ernest Benn. 1929. Vol. II. p. 254.
24. *The Life of the Right Hon. Sir Henry Campbell-Bannerman.* J. A. Spender. Hodder and Stoughton. 1923. Vol. I. p. 99.
25. Duke's Diary. 8 January 1887. FitzGeorge Papers.
26. *Military Life of H.R.H. The Duke of Cambridge.* Verner. Murray. 1905. Vol. II. pp. 335-6.
27. Gathorne Hardy to Duke of Cambridge. 6 February 1877. Colonel Stanley to Duke of Cambridge. 2 February 1879. Duke's Papers. R.A.
28. *Military Life of H.R.H. The Duke of Cambridge.* Verner. Murray. 1905. Vol. II. p. 313. Lady Geraldine Somerset's Diary. 16 February 1881. R.A.
29. Lady Geraldine Somerset's Diary. 22 January 1887. R.A.

NOTES ON CHAPTER VIII

1. Lord Wolseley to Lady Wolseley. 31 August 1890. Royal United Service Institution.
2. Duke of Cambridge to Prince of Wales. 26 and 29 November 1881. R.A. Addl. Mss. A/5. 28 and 29.
3. Lord Wolseley to Lady Wolseley. 9 April 1882 [misdated]. Royal United Service Institution.
4. Lady Geraldine Somerset's Diary. 14 February 1884. R.A.
5. Duke of Connaught to the Queen. 11 January 1883. Queen to Duke of Connaught. 13 January 1883. R.A. Addl. Mss. A/15. 3886, 3891. Queen to Sir T. Biddulph. R.A. Addl. Mss. A/22. 306.

6. Lady Geraldine Somerset's Diary. 15 January 1883. 25 May 1884. R.A.
7. Lady Geraldine Somerset's Diary. 3, 7 January 1883. R.A.
8. Lady Geraldine Somerset's Diary. 14 January 1883. R.A.
9. Lady Geraldine Somerset's Diary. 10 August 1883. R.A.
10. *Under Five Reigns.* Lady Dorothy Nevill. Methuen. 1910. p. 263.
11. Lady Geraldine Somerset's Diary. 11 January, 10 January 1883. R.A.
12. Duke of Cambridge to Adolphus FitzGeorge. 16, 19 September 1875. FitzGeorge Papers.
13. Duke of Cambridge to Adolphus FitzGeorge. 13 March 1893. FitzGeorge Papers.
14. Lady Geraldine Somerset's Diary. 17 November 1880. 16 December 1879. R.A.
15. Lady Geraldine Somerset's Diary. 21 October 1879. 15 July 1883. 8 December 1878. R.A.
16. Lady Geraldine Somerset's Diary. 30 January 1883. 7 April 1878. R.A.
17. *When I was at Court.* Lord Ormathwaite. Hutchinson and Co. 1937. pp. 54–5.
18. Lady Geraldine Somerset's Diary. 8 August 1878. 25 July 1886. R.A.
19. Lady Geraldine Somerset's Diary. 14 March 1886. R.A.
20. Lady Geraldine Somerset's Diary. 28 December 1879. 18 February 1879. 26 September 1882. R.A.
21. Lady Geraldine Somerset's Diary. 25 September 1885. R.A.
22. Lady Geraldine Somerset's Diary. 11 March 1882. 28 December 1877. R.A.
23. Lord Wolseley to Lady Wolseley. 31 July 1880. 28 September 1882. Royal United Service Institution.
24. Lady Geraldine Somerset's Diary. 15, 26 January, 12 February 1884. R.A.
25. Lady Geraldine Somerset's Diary. 30 January 1882. R.A.
26. Lady Geraldine Somerset's Diary. 18, 28 January 1887. R.A.
27. *H.R.H. George Duke of Cambridge.* Sheppard. Longmans. 1906. Vol. II. p. 200.
28. *Memoirs.* Sir A. Fitzroy. Hutchinson. 1925. p. 300.
29. Duke of Cambridge to the Queen. 18 January 1890. R.A. Z.72.22.
30. Lady Geraldine Somerset's Diary. 14 May 1884. 19 August 1886. R.A.

NOTES ON CHAPTER IX

1. Lady Geraldine Somerset's Diary. 14 October 1887. R.A.
2. Lady Geraldine Somerset's Diary. 2 May 1888. R.A.
3. Lord Wolseley to Lady Wolseley. 9 April 1888. 25 June 1895. Royal United Service Institution. Lord Wolseley to Sir H. Ponsonby. 5 May 1890. R.A. W.12.66.

ibassies of Other Days and Further Recollections. Lady Paget. Hutchinson.
23. Vol. II. p. 413.

abby. Hesketh Pearson. Hamish Hamilton. 1936. p. 250.

Lady Geraldine Somerset's Diary. 19 January, 5 November 1885. 30
January 1887. R.A.

Lady Geraldine Somerset's Diary. 20 April 1895. 21 May, 27 July 1894.
R.A.

. Lady Geraldine Somerset's Diary. 7 July 1893. R.A.

. Lady Geraldine Somerset's Diary. 17 July 1892. R.A. Duke of Cambridge
   to the Queen. February 1886. R.A. C.37.285.

6. Memoranda. Sir A. Bigge. R.A. E.41.28 and 47. Sir F. Knollys to Sir A.
   Bigge. 1 June 1895. R.A. E.41.71.

37. Memorandum. Sir A. Bigge. 16 May 1895. R.A. E.41.49.

38. Lady Geraldine Somerset's Diary. 7 May, 18 May 1895. R.A.

39. *The Life of the Right Hon. Sir H. Campbell-Bannerman.* J. A. Spender.
    Hodder and Stoughton. 1923. Vol. I. pp. 149–50.

40. Sir F. Knollys to Sir A. Bigge. 12 May 1895. R.A. E.41.26. Lady Geraldine
    Somerset's Diary. 18 May 1895. R.A.

41. *Military Life of H.R.H. The Duke of Cambridge.* Verner. Murray. 1905.
    Vol. II. pp. 395–6.

42. *The Letters of Queen Victoria.* Ed. G. E. Buckle. Murray. 1926. Third
    Series. Vol. II. p. 513.

43. Memorandum of Sir A. Bigge. R.A. E.41.129. Lady Geraldine Somerset's
    Diary. 10 June 1895.

44. Lord Rosebery to Sir A. Bigge. 19 June 1895. R.A. E.41.104.

45. *The Staff and the Staff College.* Godwin-Austen. Constable. 1927. p. 222.
    Field-Marshal Sir Henry Wilson. Sir C. E. Callwell. Cassell. 1927. Vol. I.
    p. 19.

46. *The Life and Letters of Lady Dorothy Nevill.* R. Nevill. Methuen. 1919.
    p. 136.

47. Memorandum. Sir A. Bigge. 20 May 1895. R.A. E.41.57.

48. *The Life of the Rt. Hon. Sir Henry Campbell-Bannerman.* J. A. Spender.
    Hodder and Stoughton. 1923. Vol. I. p. 157.

49. Lady Geraldine Somerset's Diary. 20 October 1895. R.A.

50. Duke's Diary. 20 June, 16 August 1895. FitzGeorge Papers.

51. Lord Wolseley to Lady Wolseley. 23 August 1895. Royal United Service
    Institution.

52. *Recollections of a Life in the British Army.* Sir R. Harrison. Smith Elder &
    Co. 1908. pp. 326–7.

53. *Military Life of H.R.H. The Duke of Cambridge.* Verner. Murray. 1905.
    Vol. II. pp. 404–5, 403, 402–3.

54. Lady Geraldine Somerset's Diary. 10 November 1895. R.A.

4. *The Letters of Queen Victoria.* Ed. G. E.
   Series. Vol. I. p. 411.
5. Queen to Sir H. Ponsonby. March 1890. R
6. F. Edwards to Sir H. Ponsonby. 19 March
   to Sir H. Ponsonby. 20 March 1890. R.A
   Queen Victoria. Ed. G. E. Buckle. Murray. 1
   p. 599.
7. Duke of Cambridge to Sir H. Ponsonby. 3 Apr.
   Sir H. Ponsonby to Duke of Cambridge. 5 April
8. Sir H. Ponsonby to Prince of Wales. 12 August 189
9. Lord Wolseley to Sir H. Ponsonby. 10 April 1890.
10. *The Letters of Queen Victoria.* Ed. G. E. Buckle. M
    Series. Vol. I. pp. 625, 627–9.
11. *The Letters of Queen Victoria.* Ed. G. E. Buckle. Murr
    Series. Vol. I. p. 630.
12. Queen to Duke of Cambridge. 29 December 1891. R.A. Z.
13. Lord Wolseley to Lady Wolseley. 19 August 1890. Royal U
    Institution.
14. *Henry Ponsonby. Queen Victoria's Private Secretary.* Ed. A.
    Macmillan. 1942. p. 108.
15. Lord Coventry to Sir Redvers Buller. 4 February 1891. Fit
    Papers.
16. Sir Redvers Buller to the Queen. Sir Redvers Buller to the Du
    Cambridge. 13 February 1891. FitzGeorge Papers.
17. Prince of Wales to Duke of Cambridge. 13 February 1891. FitzGeo
    Papers.
18. Memorandum of Prince of Wales. Undated. [1891]. FitzGeorge Papers.
19. Sir F. Knollys to Duke of Cambridge. 13 February 1891. FitzGeorge
    Papers.
20. Duke of Fife to Duke of Cambridge. 13 June 1891. FitzGeorge Papers.
21. Sir F. Knollys to Sir H. Ponsonby. 15 February 1891. R.A.Y.182.11.
22. *Life and Adventures.* Frank Harris. Richards Press. 1947. p. 455.
23. *An Autobiography.* Elizabeth Butler. Constable. 1922. pp. 218–19.
24. Lady Geraldine Somerset's Diary. 15 December 1893. R.A.
25. *The Life of Lord Roberts.* David James. Hollis and Carter. 1954. p. 381.
26. Lady Geraldine Somerset's Diary. 18 May 1893. 30 December 1895.
    R.A.
27. *The Life of Lord Wolseley.* Sir F. Maurice and Sir G. Arthur. Heinemann.
    1924. p. 225.
28. Lord Wolseley to Lady Wolseley. 25 August 1889. Royal United Service
    Institution.
29. Prince of Wales to Sir H. Ponsonby. R.A. W.10.88.

358

30. En
    19
31. L
32.
33.
34
3

AA

NOTES ON CHAPTER X

1. *Military Life of H.R.H. The Duke of Cambridge.* Verner. Murray. 1905. Vol. II. p. 399.
2. Lady Geraldine Somerset's Diary. 2 May, 15 February 1896. R.A.
3. Lady Geraldine Somerset's Diary. 8 May 1896. R.A.
4. *Memoirs.* Sir Almeric Fitzroy. Hutchinson. 1925. Vol. I. p. 45.
5. *Queen Mary.* J. Pope-Hennessy. Allen and Unwin. 1959. p. 388.
6. *Queen Mary.* J. Pope-Hennessy. Allen and Unwin. 1959. p. 388. *A Picture of Life.* Mersey. Murray. 1941. p. 208.
7. *Henry Ponsonby. His Life from His Letters.* A. Ponsonby. Macmillan. 1943. p. 93.
8. *The Staff and the Staff College.* Godwin-Austen. Constable. 1927. p. 226.
9. *Fifty Years of Fleet Street.* Sir J. Robinson. Macmillan. 1904. pp. 299–300.
10. *The Life of Lord Wolseley.* Sir F. Maurice and Sir G. Arthur. Heinemann. 1924. p. 234. *Victorians, Edwardians and Georgians.* J. Boon. Hutchinson. 1928. p. 233.
11. *From Private to Field Marshal.* Sir W. Robertson. Constable. 1921. p. 17.
12. *Military Life of H.R.H. The Duke of Cambridge.* Verner. Murray. 1905. Vol. II. p. 363.
13. *The Staff and the Staff College.* Godwin-Austen. Constable. 1927. pp. 179–80.
14. *Memoirs Discreet and Indiscreet.* Herbert Jenkins. 1917. p. 55.
15. *Motoring Annual and Motorist's Year Book.* 1903.
16. *The Times.* 27 September 1895.
17. *A History of the British Army.* J. W. Fortescue. Macmillan. 1899–1930. Vol. XIII. p. 557.
18. *Gathorne Hardy, First Earl of Cranbrook.* A. Gathorne Hardy. Longmans. 1910. Vol. I. p. 343. Lady Geraldine Somerset's Diary. 19 April 1885. R.A. *Memories.* Lord Redesdale. Hutchinson. 1915. Vol. II. p. 700.
19. *Records and Reactions.* Lord Midleton. Murray. 1939. pp. 82–3.
20. Lord Wolseley to Lady Wolseley. 9 October 1890. Royal United Service Institution.
21. *The Story of a Soldier's Life.* Wolseley. Constable. 1903. Vol. II. pp. 234–5.
22. Lord Wolseley to Sir A. FitzGeorge. December 1906. FitzGeorge Papers.
23. *Memories.* Lord Redesdale. Hutchinson. 1915. p. 700. *Forty Years On.* Lord E. Hamilton. Hodder and Stoughton. 1922. p. 185.
24. *The Story of My Life.* Sir H. Johnston. Chatto and Windus. 1923. p. 153. Mrs Middleton to the Duke of Cambridge. 29 April 1875. Duke's Papers. R.A.
25. *Notes of a Nomad.* Lady Jephson. Hutchinson. 1918. p. 177.
26. Lady Geraldine Somerset's Diary. 5 August 1876. 31 October 1884. R.A.

SELECT BIBLIOGRAPHY

ARTHUR, Sir George. *From Wellington to Wavell*. Hutchinson & Co. 1942.
BAMFORD (Ed.). *The Journal of Mrs Arbuthnot*. Macmillan. 1950.
BIDDULPH, General Sir Robert. *Lord Cardwell at the War Office*. Murray. 1904.
BOND. 'The Retirement of the Duke of Cambridge.' *Journal of the Royal United Service Institution*. No. 624. 1961.
BUCKLE, G. E. (Ed.). *The Letters of Queen Victoria*. Murray. 1926.
CHILDERS, Lieut.-Colonel Spencer. *The Life and Correspondence of the Rt. Hon. Hugh C. E. Childers*. Murray. 1901.
CLODE. *The Military Forces of the Crown; Their Administration and Government*. Murray. 1869.
DOUGLAS, Sir George (Ed.). *The Panmure Papers*. Hodder and Stoughton. 1908.
DUFF. *The Life Story of H.R.H. The Duke of Cambridge*. Stanley Paul. 1938.
ERICKSON. 'Edward T. Cardwell: Peelite.' *Transactions of the American Philosophical Society*. Vol. 49, part 2. American Philosophical Society. 1959.
FARRER. *The Monarchy in Politics*. Fisher and Unwin. 1917.
FORTESCUE. *A History of the British Army*. 13 Volumes. Macmillan. 1899–1930.
GATHORNE HARDY, A. E. (Ed.). *Gathorne Hardy, First Earl of Cranbrook—a Memoir*. Longmans. 1910.
GODWIN-AUSTEN. *The Staff and the Staff College*. Constable. 1927.
HAMPDEN GORDON. *The War Office*. Putnam. 1935.
HIBBERT. *The Destruction of Lord Raglan*. Longmans. 1961.
JAMES, David. *The Life of Lord Roberts*. Hollis and Carter. 1954.
KINGLAKE. *The Invasion of the Crimea*. 8 Volumes. Blackwood. 1863–1887.
KINGSTON. *Famous Morganatic Marriages*. Stanley Paul. 1919.
KINLOCH COOKE. *A Memoir of Her Royal Highness Princess Mary Adelaide Duchess of Teck*. Murray. 2 Volumes. 1900.
LEE, Sir Sidney. *King Edward VII—A Biography*. Macmillan. 2 Volumes. 1925.
MARTIN, Sir T. *The Life of H.R.H. The Prince Consort*. Smith, Elder and Co. 5 Volumes. 1874–1880.
MAURICE, Sir F. and ARTHUR, Sir G. *The Life of Lord Wolseley*. Heinemann. 1924.
MAXWELL, Sir H. *The Life and Letters of the Fourth Earl of Clarendon*. Arnold. 2 Volumes. 1913.
NAPIER (Ed.). *Letters of Field-Marshal Lord Napier of Magdala*. Simpkin Marshall. 1936.
OMOND. *Parliament and the Army*. Cambridge University Press. 1933.
PONSONBY, A. *Henry Ponsonby, Queen Victoria's Private Secretary, His Life from His Letters*. Macmillan. 1943.
POPE-HENNESSY. *Queen Mary*. Allen and Unwin. 1959.
ROBERTSON, Sir William. *From Private to Field-Marshal*. Constable. 1921.

SANDARS. *The Life and Times of Queen Adelaide.* Stanley Paul. 1915.

SHEPPARD. *H.R.H. George Duke of Cambridge.* Longmans. 2 Volumes. 1906.

SPENDER, J. A. *The Life of the Right Hon. Sir Henry Campbell-Bannerman.* Hodder and Stoughton. 2 Volumes. 1923.

STOCQUELER. *A Personal History of the Horse Guards from 1750 to 1872.* Hurst and Blackett. 1873.

STRACHEY and FULFORD (Ed.). *The Greville Memoirs.* Macmillan. 1938.

VERNER. *Military Life of H.R.H. The Duke of Cambridge.* Murray. 2 Volumes. 1905.

WHEELER. *The War Office Past and Present.* Methuen. 1914.

WOLSELEY, Field-Marshal Viscount. *The Story of a Soldier's Life.* Constable. 1903.

WYNDHAM (Ed.). *Correspondence of Sarah Spencer Lady Lyttelton 1787–1870.* Murray. 1912.

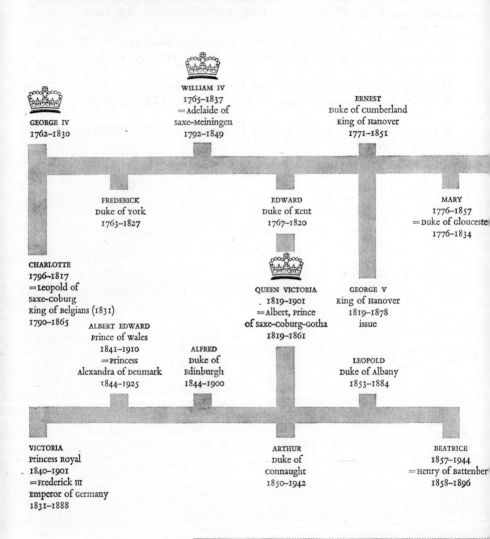

GEORGE IV
1762–1830

WILLIAM IV
1765–1837
=Adelaide of
Saxe-Meiningen
1792–1849

ERNEST
Duke of Cumberland
King of Hanover
1771–1851

FREDERICK
Duke of York
1763–1827

EDWARD
Duke of Kent
1767–1820

MARY
1776–1857
=Duke of Gloucester
1776–1834

CHARLOTTE
1796–1817
=Leopold of
Saxe-Coburg
King of Belgians (1831)
1790–1865

QUEEN VICTORIA
1819–1901
=Albert, Prince
of Saxe-Coburg-Gotha
1819–1861

GEORGE V
King of Hanover
1819–1878
issue

ALBERT EDWARD
Prince of Wales
1841–1910
=Princess
Alexandra of Denmark
1844–1925

ALFRED
Duke of
Edinburgh
1844–1900

LEOPOLD
Duke of Albany
1853–1884

VICTORIA
Princess Royal
1840–1901
=Frederick III
Emperor of Germany
1831–1888

ARTHUR
Duke of
Connaught
1850–1942

BEATRICE
1857–1944
=Henry of Battenberg
1858–1896

GEORGE
FITZGEORGE
1843–1907
=Rosa Baring
(1885)

ADOLPHUS
FITZGEORGE
1846–1922
=Sofia Holden
(1875)

GEORGE II
1683–1760

FREDERICK
prince of wales
1707–1751

GEORGE III
1738–1820

MARY
1723–1772
=frederick II
of Hesse Cassel
1747–1837

A Simplified family tree
of the
DUKE OF CAMBRIDGE'S
relations.

Except for Augustus Fitz-
George and Francis Teck,
who never married, all
the Princess Royal's gen-
eration had issue.

GEORGE
Duke of cambridge

ADOLPHUS = AUGUSTA
Duke of cambridge   1799–1889
1774–1850

GEORGE
Duke of cambridge
1819–1904
=Louisa Fairbrother
1816–1890

AUGUSTA
1822–1916
=Frederick, Grand
Duke of Mecklenburg-strelitz
1819–1904

MARY ADELAIDE
1833–1897
=Duke of Teck
1837–1900

QUEEN MARY
1867–1953

FRANCIS
1870–1910

AUGUSTUS
FITZGEORGE
1847–1928

ADOLPHUS
FREDERICK V
1848–1914

ADOLPHUS
2nd Duke of Teck
1st Marquess of
cambridge
1868–1927

EARL OF
ATHLONE
1874–1957

INDEX

AA*

9/st-

GEORGE IV
1762–1830

WILLIAM IV
1765–1837
= Adelaide of
Saxe-Meiningen
1792–1849

ERNEST
Duke of Cumberland
King of Hanover
1771–1851

FREDERICK
Duke of York
1763–1827

EDWARD
Duke of Kent
1767–1820

MARY
1776–1857
= Duke of Glouceste
1776–1834

CHARLOTTE
1796–1817
= Leopold of
Saxe-Coburg
King of Belgians (1831)
1790–1865

ALBERT EDWARD
Prince of Wales
1841–1910
= Princess
Alexandra of Denmark
1844–1925

QUEEN VICTORIA
1819–1901
= Albert, Prince
of Saxe-Coburg-Gotha
1819–1861

ALFRED
Duke of
Edinburgh
1844–1900

GEORGE V
King of Hanover
1819–1878
issue

LEOPOLD
Duke of Albany
1853–1884

VICTORIA
Princess Royal
1840–1901
= Frederick III
Emperor of Germany
1831–1888

ARTHUR
Duke of
Connaught
1850–1942

BEATRICE
1857–1944
= Henry of Battenber
1858–1896

GEORGE
FITZGEORGE

ADOLPHUS
FITZGEORGE